Sunday Mornings at Oyster Bay

Joseph O Arata

j oluf pukkelsen publishing

j oluf pukkelsen publishing

ISBN-13: 978-0692681060
ISBN-10: 069268106X

for my wife and daughter

花桜

早春に咲く

桃色は

小さい足の

指の花びら

Pont Neuf, Paris, Sunday, June 28, 2015

My wife and daughter are waving their arms to catch my attention. They are standing on the sidewalk of the *Pont Neuf.* Its name means New Bridge but it's the oldest bridge in Paris. Arbitrary words. A bridge of stone, built from the money of the rich and drunkards, taxes on casks of wine, a communal place, for the wealthy and poor alike, a story place, a picture place, over there is the Eiffel Tower and that way we see Our Lady of Paris, *Notre-Dame de Paris,* but this bridge is not a palace, not a cathedral, *ceci tuera cela'... this will kill that...* I am standing and searching through the books at the *bouquinistes de Paris,* the bookstalls; my wife and daughter, they are the *piétonne,* I am the *flâneur.* My wife and daughter are tired from walking all day. It's hot and humid. But the sun is going down... they sit on one of the stone curved bastions inside the bridge. I walk over to them and we cross the bridge together. We stop by the Bronze King. We are in the middle of the bridge, on a piece of land*, Île de la Cité...* the Seine runs this way and that way, a river between two bookshelves. That way at the beginning of the bridge, whence we came, is the author, and this way that we are going, is the sign... we stand at the point of relational transcendence, in a golden sunset...

Book One

Erosion Backwords 2015-1992

Sunrise – Hurrah Away

O say hey ho America, here we go, all adrift to go, let's go… in the beginning he was reared by a perfect mommy, can you see by dawn it's early, lift the hairy blind, let light into the lair, peekaboo, pee pee, it's me. Who am I? Sanctus, Sanctus, Sanctus. *Skal vi, andemo via, ikimasho, allons-y. De tre bukkene bruse*, please don't eat me, left alone in the dark, under the Brooklyn Bridge, *troll kalla mik*, to wrestle with the undefined demo(n)tic of my words; what is my name? Signumommy, it's your blushing boy. He's crowning, cock crowing, frowning, crying, sun rising, Stephen deedless, wordless. In the beginning is the relation. Eh Joe you are fifty-nine years old now, holy wit. *Fy faen*! The phantoms are running away. Once upon a time in the dark woods of Europe there lived three little piggy perceptions, who lived in three little houses, made of sticks, straw, and bricks, and that contained everything, including three blind mice… see… *inductio, intuitus, deduction;* eyes of the modern world, the world of falling objects, the new subject "in the beginning," middle, ending. Past, present, future. One, two, three; *en, to, tre; uno, due, tre; ichi, ni, san; un, deux, trois.* Chance, law, habit. All or nothing. Is that the place to be? Where is this place and where does the path begin? In the *phantasia? Phantasiari?* Who am I not? *Genius malignus.* Why is there something? Why is there not nothing? Holy, Holy, Holy. The ordinal in the infinite. The *ord* in the ordinary, in the common vernacular across the sea, I see… says the blind man, *jeg ser, jeg ser,* have I come to the wrong place? Norsemen cometh! See how they run. A smack in the face. *Philargyria. Avaritia.* Desire. The birth of the subject and object. Tollege is not college. O great round wonder, roll on. I hear hip hip hurrah, that's okay, hooray, blunderbuss, old thunder guts, covetousness, blood and lustiness in his four eyes, cast upward to the celestial crown. Shining cities of beastly teeth. But what's this I see? The filth of the floor, wife of the blacksmith, hammering words, one of the roughs, common toughs, wild Cyclops of a crew, the vision is one, voiceless in Tatarus, eyeless in Eros I onward go, we don't ask its name, we just take it! It's loose-fish. Take the land, spacious and void, not the words. An alias pun. We have our words. We have all we need… guns and a bibel. I'll eat my heart out. I like action. What are these people up to? The limit is beyond the land, the sky, and the sea. No measure make, all treasures take, distribution should *not* undo excess, and each man *not* have enough, have less, but jealous, greedy, sullen envy, has bred the red, but he can't hate you, despise you, big fat bully baby in the mirror you, money you, smothering you, exceptional you, false object you, not all of you, not every broken dark, wretched part of you, for how other could he touch your disunited states of otherness enduring, receding, and melting behind all of your sparkling emanations, accidents, and habits, and not carry something of you along with him, oh daddy doo-doo, he writes poo-poo, kaka, kakanai, tell me a story, *jishin, kamanari, kaji, oyaji* scratch my back. I can't see them. I can't write it if I can't see it, ah *jigokuhen, skriket*, write me as I am, screen of hell, scream of nature, do you prefer that? Without this reflection that bounces from you, the world is my representation of my anxiety, you got to believe under father's roof, hurrah for Kazzazamazov! It's a pip pip. Plopped into the infinite sea, little me, a horseshoe crab, driftwood, hold my small hand, eternity in my eyes, revealed to the rest of the world. Alone, alone, all, all alone. Pip is an Other, *Ding an sich*, ding-dong-ding… *sonnez les matines!* Hush. Don't say a word… wolf rises in the heart. If it works, use it! *Pika-pika*… boom-boom. Remove the mask, no ought from is, there's nought beyond, and here they come, white and blank, with their guns and bible, and tomorrow is Monday, and it's October, and I must get dressed and go to work. Janitors carry the keys to the city. Porters haul the objects of history. Let's play. America's game, snap, go, fling. So let's go, hop on, climb in, here we go, all aboard, hurrah away, play ball, first pitch, round the bases, first, second, third, the hurrah game, hurrah the speeding ball, heave-ho! It heaps me! Westward ho! Eastward ho! And we moved. October, home, and work again. Major jazz notes, bop bebop, doo-wop, minor blues chords, boogie-woogie, bang it, oh hey ho bang thy tambourine, oh man, rig it, dig it, stig it, quig it, three rock chords, that's what a white man calls fun, hey ho, scat scat rats. Save my sweat. Oh drat you god rot! Oh yeah, oh Lord, hey ho! Strike through; strike three, and what else could it be, but after all is said and done, then that you still somehow produced Herman Melville, Louis Armstrong, and the 1969 New York Mets? Yes… but in exchange for what? And though he grants that you might take out a contingent credit for them, he also grants that you take out an absolute and determined death credit for your prisons, violence, guns, bombs and your stinking greed and for the dishonest, dissolute Anglo-American-Dutch cowboy named Roy

Lee Dunn, of the native southern meridian, who robbed him of a hundred bucks in 1980 just two days after Ronald Reagan was elected President; and for the American Jews named Amberstein and Fraudsky and Mushman, of the New York above-the-law firm, *Judge, Shrink & Shrink*, who sent him away from home before reaching the age of leaving home, who stared at him in silence like he was nothing, and who spoke of his father to his face to humiliate his father in his presence; and for the American Italians named Porco and Stronzo, who betrayed him with lies of fabricated freedom, and who bestowed an ugly psykhotic Amerikan kan-do hustler neurosis on him; but for all that, there was the Mexican-American named Umberto who took him in when he was down and out in Los Angeles, and there was the Scotsman O'Donnell, "*as aye*," who bestowed the poet's laurels on him when he was lost and going nowhere and walking in place for too many Sunday mornings at Oyster Bay, a frozen flâneur, and there was the Brooklyn kid named Tommy with whom he explored the streets of New York City, and there was the Londoner named Leonardo who helped him find his way in that good old city, and there was her, in Paris, and her, in Tokyo, and her, in Vienna. He always felt that he lived in a foreign land, and therefore he had to go to a foreign land to find something not foreign... does he offend you? Well, you have offended him. Amerika. Kafka imagined you. Armies of the cockroach night fell down the kitchen walls. Skyscrapers exploded and Lady Liberty held high a sword. He walks in place... the world goes on. No... but no credit for your Grand Canyon, Niagara Falls and your mighty Mississippi River, so-named, they were here already. These words have no origins and we have no destiny. The endless paths are always just a path, from word to word, from book to book. Erosion reveals the limited possible spaces between the lines. The bottom is up, the beginning is the end. The path of philosophy drops its cherry blossoms on his head and feet. If he stops walking on the paths the spaces will fill him with nothingness. To experience, to walk, to write, is to push back against these walls and its world of emptiness. There are some who leap... but all will fall. As we know, there is no America without the world and there is no world without America. When America was born, the world was born. O foreigner! O stranger! Up there... the clouds passing... now he could have written that America somehow produced Jack Kerouac, Bob Dylan, and Willie Mays; or Henry Miller, the Ramones, and Muhammad Ali, but he didn't, and yet he just did... and he could have named other

7

names but he has to stop somewhere. A preamble to a ramble. *Ikke sant?* Like here. Eh no? In understanding this experience, this voyage, know that the beginning is the place that the ending begins…

Invitation to a Voyage

Is this a philosophical text or literary text? Is this theory or fiction? Let's look, shall we? Why is he here? He's a pure object. He's not a physical part of the environment. He is objective in that he is present to me… but who is this me? I am writing these words. I am a subject that stands here, walking in place you might say, as myself drawn out in difference against all that is the universe. That's a big word. So it has very little meaning, or too much. Nevertheless, here I am. A substance, a subject, an essence, an accident, under the weight of the world, existence, being, non-being, nothing, brought to bear, to bear this bareness, upon which the accidents of one's life is brought low, to its experience, and you, reader, and him, who is named Stephen in this text, are there, are objective, present to my awareness, but perhaps you are "real" and Stephen is not "real." It takes time to figure this out. There is a relation between Stephen and me. I will try to capture it now. I have to eat and sleep and perform other bodily functions. I don't have much time. But while he is here, I must make the most of his presence. What is the story of this young man who discovered in himself a propensity to ask, let us call them, metaphysical questions? Stephen is sixteen, seventeen years old, and he is removed from the academic environment that would have purposed his interest in asking these questions, within the traditional Western canon developed for that purpose, but would he have still asked these questions if he had taken or mis-taken that path? We can never know. Erosion reveals fossils. So thusly removed, not actually removed, because he was never there to be removed, so in the sense of never being placed on the path properly speaking… so he's exempt from this path, this objective determinant; he was born into the subject that was socially birthed, what sets him apart, with no academic, scholastic education, to guide him; he is a subject without an object, walking in place, with a certain attitude toward life, the world, society? What path was this inevitable path? Think about it. Stephen was shy, introverted, aloof, with no direction, rudderless, faint hopes, feelings of meaninglessness, of futility, of absurdity, lost… but with a literary and philosophical bent, where did that come from? So of course for him, nothing exists before the nineteenth century. There was no one before the Romantics, who fled the monasteries and the academies, fled from Galileo, from most of modern philosophy too... except the self as divine subject, as individual against the given, into an idealized Nature, or later, forsaking the woods, into the new cities... the cities that became the new "realism," God-empty, Hugo, Zola, snatched from the medieval scholars, the God-full, because for them, the "real" was out there, Nature, but fallen, corrupt, the new ideal was inside the mind, representation, of itself to itself, Descartes, Locke, Hume, Kant, the transcendental subject, sensorial non-subject, and nature, by the mind measured, weighed, with instruments extending the mind into the farthest reaches of the galaxies... so philosophy moved into its own subject-object, being-nothing... but Stephen stems from the Romantic mindset, that which turned away from "mere" physical nature and the academy, to Ideal Nature, or to the Unreal City, but here and now, a subject subjecting itself to bare life, the existential, how to live? Otherwise, why ask why is life worth living or an idea worth dying for? If life is absurd, why not suicide? Murder? Stephen had no interest in Greek, Latin, medieval, scholastic, how could he, outside of the learned path? He was on his own, but not really... there were signs everywhere, and he followed the ones that led to Kierkegaard, Dostoyevsky, Nietzsche, Sartre, Camus, the literary/philosophical, so over the years book to book, reading to reading, thrown back on his own subjectivity, like an art no longer representative of its time, no patrons, university, courts, from Baudelaire to *dérive,* the city, the monster creeping through the library, the library of where books are found, out there, anywhere. Stephen was a freak, on whatever dark path he took, where he found a book, in his time in the 1970s, in literary modernism/post-modernism, living in that slash, walking in place, going nowhere, getting nowhere, about to break, all these signs and relations pointing nowhere, but to each other, endlessly, all bogged down in his room, like in his mind, a vast vat of representation, crushing his mind within its own subjectivity, cluttered, piled up and in chaos... how to arrange these objects to make order out of the given? In the beginning was the thing. So we are now beginning our journey back in time, but really above time, above nature/culture, back and forth, through mistakes and lies and I will not again return to this moment here and now, but you reader, you are here and now and so farewell and bon voyage.

Walking in Place

Not to follow in his father's footsteps would be like walking in place. Going nowhere. Not to follow in this society's preordained path would be like walking in place. Going nowhere. He can't stay here and there's nowhere to go. Was there ever a choice? Or was it hard indifferent fate? A highly charged brain baffled by an artificial dilemma? Or was it just a causal slippage of a roll of the dice? We live within some absurd mixture of chance, will and fate, in combinations inseparable and indissoluble. But how can you go nowhere? We are baffled until tomorrow, and tomorrow we are baffled again. He is walking. He is dreaming of walking, just walking. In mountains. In forests. In cities. He is invisible. He has no hands to grasp… to touch, he enters a strange and alien world. The ground beneath him is eroding. The house is decomposing like the body. Is he leaving this place to march with armies, or sit in an office high above staring down to the streets? When he was a youth he saw great outer spaces and stars. He found inner space on the threshold of a space that pointed in many directions, to an experienced place. He could not follow the promised path that a community advocated for him and recommended for him, a blinkered and inevitable step upon the shadow arrival of his father's binary footsteps of large black working shoes, but a notch, a toe length longer and more along the way toward the calling of American manhood in the middle class confinement of Plato's transparent screens. Newton's third law… and the slave must receive the logos in order to be ordered to act. Is writing this book an act of liberation? And why would he have to prove it?

He could not walk in his father's footsteps. Anxiety, fear and trembling kept him trapped in, while boredom and desire pushed him out. So he walked in place, year after year. Stephen walks in place. The world goes on. Stephen walks in place. The world goes on. Spatial suppression, temporal quagmire. And as he walked in place he read and read and read and read as one who should not read. He bumped his head against the door and walked in place and read and read and read as one who should not read… a dismounted Quixote, who walks much and reads much, knows much and sees much… but why bother to walk? to read? to see? to know?

These books in Stephen's room are not only about walking at night down a deserted city street, or riding horses in the Wild West, or taking to ships to encounter the great white whale, or hopping freight trains just to go somewhere, or riding in cars from East Coast to West Coast, or flying in

airplanes to exotic destinations, or blasting off in rockets to the moon…
but it's the same path that Bashō walked to the interior of the deep and
unknowable north country of Japan, with just his two legs… walking
towards something or somewhere else… or the same streets of Paris that
Baudelaire or Henry Miller walked, towards something or somewhere
else… or the same ship that Melville set out on… like the fabled ship in
the violent storm at sea heading towards its manifest destined Westward
Course to the New World, with the foolish man crawling toward the East,
backward upon the deck of the ship because he thought that he was testing
the limits of his freedom… like going from Oyster Bay to Manhattan in
1975 and pretending that you came here from nowhere, free to write the
limits of somewhere. Stephen had to travel somewhere and that was all
there was to it. It was about the time spent somewhere far enough away
from the originary events, to make one's origins disappear, as if never to
have belonged here in the first place, but to belong somewhere else, a
denial of something in you that is not you, but still not enough of you,
where did this not enough come from? This rupture? This going off the
rails, this walking in place until you walk right out of your skin? Walking in
place like a wind-up toy, building momentum, then breaking through the
door… the self flees to the other, and the other flees to self, a relational
visibility here and gone, and a translational distortion through which
meaning arises. It's the sadness of objects, *mono no aware*, and Stephen
writes and writes and writes as one who should not write, because when
the writer sees society in himself, and no society wants to be seen by a
writer who sees society in himself, the writer flees, to flee there, because
who among us is without fault? And just as Herman Melville had been
frozen out as a public voice and driven into cold silence and metrical
poetry and a secure job as a customs inspector in New York City at
approximately the same time that Arthur Rimbaud had been frozen out
from poetry and Paris and driven into silence and the coffee trade business
in the subtropical highland sun of Harar in Africa, so there are only their
spectral remnants that remain for Stephen, in the afterword of silenced
voices, and they died in the same year, 1891, just two months apart, in far
away places… in buried ashes of the blankness of somewhere else…
revealed as words raining down from bookshelves, eroding experience in
time, eroding old buried shallow surfaces and disclosing a new surface
made of old objects and faded documents. Like the night that withdraws

revealing the break of day. Why does Stephen always ask this question that does not answer: Why do I feel excluded from being a writer and a reader if I can read and write? It is not a question with a reverse question mark turned inward on itself, and it's not that he can just turn his back on himself. The answer that is not an answer is that he feels excluded from being a writer and a reader because he is excluded. Left alone in the dark. But is he himself just excluding himself? And yet this voice that was force-fed with ordinary words is now competent enough to refuse the oath and the orders given in that very same language, and then go silent in words withheld. Do you really believe that this is all just a fiction? This room. This self. This little girl in the white dress. She appears in an old newsreel from the time of the Spanish Civil War, and she is running from the shooting guns, and she finally finds shelter with others against the wall of a building, and she sits down, and she notices a dark spot on her white dress, and she gently tries to brush the spot away, and watching this film Stephen knows that she must be dead now, but there she is, an image, a fiction, and she looks so concerned, so worried about her white dress, at that moment, there is a consciousness there, and Stephen feels for her because somehow she is still there, for Stephen has brought her back to life, and yet they are all dead now, and we are all dead, or how else could we live inside this fiction? Who is the phantom that keeps these words alive. Is it you reader?

The first steps. The steps on the side of the rocks of Norway. His uncle shouting, "Hoy! Hoy!" The steps of a pilgrimage. The inward steps. The blind steps. As he walks the sidewalk he walks into the past. There is no future. The future is an illusion. He walks on the crumbled dry dog shit, the sticky candy gum of the child, the cigarette butts of yesterday; he walks on the sidewalk with the foot print that was made in soft cement and the date scratched by a finger. Beneath cement the dirt, the weeds pushing through cracks, always eroding. He walks on the past as it exposes itself as the past before itself. No going forward. No foreword. No beginning. Our life erodes beneath our feet revealing what's already been there. Walking the path from the I-It to the I-You is fraught with anxieties. One may have one's own path but the path is always on the land cultivated, overgrown, and over-determined. There are ghosts there unlike the ghosts on the path through these books. Why is that word here, any word? Because he extracted it from a book that he was reading, like a tooth extracted from a mouth that makes no sounds, a silent word, in fact, every word in this book has been extracted from books, every article, preposition, noun, verb, adverb… all twenty-six letters, and shuffled around in experience and imagination. The only path that he has to take is to the kitchen and toilet. *Angya*… to go by foot… a pilgrimage to the phantoms. Hide behind the *sudare*. Draw the blinds. Walking in place he goes nowhere, not even a straight line, but like a jammed typewriter, all the keys stuck and letter on letter in a smudge of ink; the story in this book goes nowhere, the story of his life goes nowhere. Walking in place above the world. Walking in place all over the world. Not standing in place… just to collapse. Not marching in place… into a burning wall of power. But walking in place he was going somewhere in search of the not enough, in books, in signs, pointing, to some other place. Walt Whitman singing the democratic universal logos of the walking world that produced the American chorus is not particular to its oligarchic occasions, but a voice produced within the world that informed it. And now he is tired of walking in place. What happens if he stops? If he lay down would he be able to get up again? If he stopped would he be able to start again? And yet… why bother at all?

Apologia #1 - Europe, The Porters, The Hinge

Why bother to write? We do not ask: Why write? But: Why *bother* to write? Sartre asks: Why write? It's a problem for philosophers, sociologists, psychologists. As Aristotle asked: Why do objects fall to earth? To find their natural place in the world. As Galileo also asked, perplexed, as an empirical scientist. Why do objects fall to earth? But he did not ask why do objects *bother* to fall? Why do objects take the time out of their busy day to bother to fall? Why do objects have good or bad intentions to fall? Like the brick that fell from a building in Brooklyn and killed an innocent girl walking to school? It insinuates intention, will… oh my god, an author! Why write? We know who writes. Man writes. Man the object writes. Why fall? The rock as object falls. Why bother? The existential empirical author bothers. Does this bother you, reader? One can theorize about Ahab and Moby Dick forever… but in the end the one thing that is clear is that Ahab intended to destroy that goddam whale. One could go on and on throwing harpoons here and there, left and right, toward hell or heaven, signs of this and that… but be that as it may, Ahab was intent on destroying that Moby Dick. Did Melville intend it? It doesn't matter… and though one cannot send to sea a fictional Ahab in a book from 1851 to seek a real whale in the ocean of 2015, or send a sea captain from 2015 to seek a whale named Moby Dick in a book from 1851... unless they can jump off the page, and they can't, all are signs and objects and things and stuff... but some are real and some are fiction... some are false and some are true... and fiction is not always false... and real is not always true... and an image in a mirror is a trick, an illusion, step away, walk away, and make of it what you will, for what would there be to make of it, if there was nothing of it to be made? So make do... but you can't just go on forever making do without making doo doo... you have to stop to take a shit, and know it's not bullshit.

Stephen is in his room. It is Sunday, November 10, 1974. They carry the things of this world. They come from Greece. They come from Alexandria. They come from Jerusalem. Stephen closed his eyes. The room was very hot. Do I exist? Who am I? Well, that's a deaf and dumb question. Stephen knows exactly who he is... because it's those origins, that identity, the original imprint, of who he is, that he is trying to dispel, toward which he is directing his questions. The real question is: Who am I to write? We do not ask, who am I? We ask, who am I to write? To write for, to write to, to write of, to write toward the object, the work as object. Who came first, the reader or the writer? Who's on second? The reader? Who? Narrative combined with these objects are the so-called real world. The narrative is born of experience. The object, the *petite madeleine* dipped in tea, closes the gap. The porters carry the things of the world. The things that have been lost, and retrieved, revived, recalled, returned, renewed, removed, recollected, remembered... but here am I... Stephen is in the present, in this room, his consciousness is dealing with his immediate experience of this messy moment in time... but his mind reaches backward into the past, pulling at the objects that the porters have left at the door, and pushing against the door that blocks his way, and Stephen's problem is how to pick up these objects and present them, to offer, to give, as a present of presence, but the objects slip through his fingers, slip through his mind, slip through his words. In order to offer he must hold the objects tightly, securely, he must re-present his present of lost time...

John Locke wrote these words on a blank sheet of paper: from Experience. Oh those sensible, external Objects. Out there. And upon these sensations the operations of the mind perform their fluid dance. But whence these operators? Innate structure? Words? Logic? Tales of separation. The state of nature. The state of innocence. Then the fall. A mind at the end of its tether. Those damn smart alecks and smart asses. Return to the senses! Out out damn Descartes and abstractions! But Hume says, wait an ungodly minute. These impressions, these sensations, or some strange truth of the divine, have no place here, because nothing can be drawn from such, except pretty pictures. This is your idea? But what sensation gave root to this idea? Ask yourself. Skepticism unresolved. So the question is now, not why write, or why bother to write, but what are the causes in experience of this writing? How is Stephen to answer this question? The writing itself answers the question of the origins? But the writing itself is not his immediate and direct experience in the present, it's his representation of his memory in history presented in the present. And Hume's objects are bouncing off each other in space. We grab at them by habit. Associations in experience. And now the Germans march in. Again. Kant writes that knowledge begins with experience. Objects touch our senses. And the porters carry in the final object. We begin with experience, but our knowledge does not all arise from experience. And the janitor unlocks the doors of the subject. The transcendental subject. But, of course, Stephen doesn't think that he has transcended anything; he's stuck in his room, walking in place. His immediate experience is of the absurd, the existential. He doesn't give a fart about concepts with or without intuitions. C'mon History, isn't it time to end this ongoing battle. Give us the final war. End human experience. Give us money and God and innocence again. Create a new and final world. A final Word, Logos. Creation done and over with. Then annihilation, the icing on the cake of history. Stephen does not desire to constitute his world anymore. He's tired. A consciousness wearies the truth, like proofs. Therefore, why bother to write? There is nothing left to say. Husserl writes: Return to the things themselves. Heidegger writes: Return to being-in-the-world... writing is always a return. And then Germany invades France, again. The torch is passed on... Sartre, Merleau-Ponty, Foucault, Derrida... but in Stephen's room, the room of a writer, the flame has gone out. There is nothing outside the room. But in the room there are some objects, ironically collected and recollected from places outside the room. This is a problem. How did those objects get in here? Why did these objects get in here? How does Stephen get out of here? Is this a locked-room mystery at the end of the tether of theory? Narrate your escape. He is looking... seeing... trying...

15

A Japanese Ghost Story

So we pause now to consider the future dead, with a Japanese ghost story in a sinister and eerie future at the end of a world that should be excluded from being the world. On a Sunday morning in the north country of Japan an old woman and an old man are lying on futons on the tatami floor and looking out through the empty space of the open sliding shoji doors. She is looking at the cherry tree, its petals falling... where is my Sakura? Never, never, never... forever. The cherry tree is almost bare. He is looking at a chestnut tree. The bark is black. In the morning the trees are still there. This reminded the old man of a time in his youth, alone and frightened, that he walked down the long dark hallway of his grandmother's house, and behind some dusty curtains he stepped into the two cold and moldy front rooms, the room to his left is where his father was born, the room he entered is where his grandmother, aunt and uncle would sit in chairs by the windows and look down at all the comings and goings on South Street. There is a photograph of him and his older sister in a frame on top of an oval table. He is sitting on her lap. She is around six years old and he is around a year old. He looks at the photograph. That's me, he thinks. He picks the frame up from the table and opens the back. In the back he removes some cardboard that is placed behind the photograph. There is a white piece of paper. He has a pencil and he writes the month, day, year and the exact time to the minute on the paper: May 20, 1965 7:32 p.m. There are ten previous dates and times written above the one that he has just written, dating back to January 1964. He puts the paper back in the frame and covers it with the cardboard, and he puts the frame back onto the oval table. He will return sometime in the future and replicate this simple procedure. Just to make sure it's still there. That everything is as it should be. That nothing is lost. That nothing much changes. That the world is both real and a fiction. That life is not a deception. That he exists. This is his postcard to the finite future. If the automobile had only existed in Descartes' time, perhaps we could have been spared three hundred years of subject-object metaphysical perplexities and bewilderments. How could he not trust his senses, his experience, and trust also the senses of the others, driving down the Long Island Expressway? *Je vois... Je vois...* says the blind man. Beep-beep. No exit. But Descartes drives fast. He drives a 1965 Mustang, and he doesn't see the small boy run out into the street. The car hits the boy. Accidents happen, Descartes says, but nevertheless I am sorry that I hit you with this godamn ghost of a machine, I think. To return to our ghost story in Japan: She, the old woman, never lived in her memories. She never thought much about the subject-object dichotomy. In spring the cherry tree, in summer the cuckoo, in autumn the moon, and in winter the cold and snow. It's 6 p.m. and the old man said: the chestnut tree is blocking my view of the mountain. The old woman said: it's not in the way. Can you not see parts of the mountain between the leaves of the tree, wholly other and partly hidden? *Mieru... mieru...* did you not notice the ghost sitting under the chestnut tree? The ghosts are arriving. There is nothing of the tree in the word tree. But is there something of the ghost in the word ghost? See the roundness at the top of the tree. Tree at the center of the world. Is the potential tree in the nut? The potential subject in the seed? Not if it is not of a world? Does this world contain ghosts as objects? This dream of language. Outside, the leaves fall from the tree. He rakes the leaves that fall from the tree. He rakes the *objects* that fall from the *object*. He does *something* to the leaves that do *something* from the tree. He does *something* to the *objects* that do *something* from the *object*. *Subject something object.* Leaves from trees rake. *Object* from *object* does *something*. Language has become the alchemy of the banal. Analogy of the lack. He rakes the stones in the garden... she watches the leaves fall... silently... nothing more to say... ecstasy of life... but how can a vision of horror be put in words? These feeble words? Something to say... about the horror of life. Let me see if I can describe hell in words... give me an image... not a metaphor! a ghost? No, his mothet told him never to fear ghosts, only fear the living. So, a real image... out there... in the world, flesh, consciousness, a fire... the young girl woke in the night and saw the chestnut tree outside the window and screamed and died, or a person burning in a fire... burning alive in a fire... a real person burning alive in a fire... the bright burning light... the black rain... struggling toward a miserable death... shame, humiliation... the water... the earthquake... the ghosts of Tohoku... is that my daughter? Oh God... No!... no dignity... forgive me... the horror... these words... I'm at a loss... am I mad? So the pure and ghostly object is known, present to my awareness, dependent on mind, but the thing is not known, independent of mind, and of my beliefs, opinions, desires, feelings, thoughts, but once I try to think of a thing that is unknown it becomes known so I can't think of a thing without creating an object that is known, real or not, like Stephen... am I mistaken?

Apologia #2 – The Author, The Door Broken from the Hinge

Descartes and Kant were sharing an umbrella one cold gray rainy day in Paris on the rue Bordet, walking toward the rue de la Montagne-Sainte-Geneviève. Descartes was frightened by the strong winds and the crowds. It was a bad dream. He could barely walk; it was as if he were walking in place, standing still, and so he entered a church. Kant refused to enter. A Monsieur M. has something to give you. What? It's a watermelon! Back out on the sidewalk they came to a crossroad. The rain pelted down. Descartes carried the large watermelon in his arms. It was too heavy. It smashed on the ground and splattered into sections. Look! The seeds! The seeds of wisdom! The seeds of science! Kant looked at the clock. It's time, he said. He picked up a piece of watermelon and began eating it. It's sweet. He then spit out the seeds. Ah Fichte! No seeds! Let's walk this way instead. Stop! You are book stabbers! Walking toward the fountain, they saw some phantoms coming closer. The phantoms were walking from the four streets towards the intersection, looking for cover from the rain. Nietzsche and Heidegger were coming from the north. There were clear signs that Saussure and Peirce were coming from another direction, but on different sides of the street. Michel de Montaigne with his Raymond, and Blaise Pascal with his Mistress, coming up the other street. Husserl with Sartre, tapping his feet to a jazz beat, on the road, outside, in the world, with all these others, baby, dig it, out in the crowd, the in crowd. They were moving toward the intersection. There was Derrida and his saucy crew, outside, in the text. There was Foucault. And from the opposite street there walked Vattimo, Agamben, Eco, Ferraris, and even a Maserati... why walk when you can drive an Italian sport's car? They were talking about hermeneutics, semiotics, structuralism, interpretation, weak thought, negative realism, new realism, ontology, epistemology, metaphysics, theory, community, consensus, history, experience, common sense, nothing outside text, nothing social outside text, and they were walking toward the intersection, but they were not getting any closer to Descartes or Kant than before... were they even moving? Are my eyes deceiving me? How long must I wait? I want to leave. I want to tell the story... why can't I leave? Am I trapped? I pretend that I am. I feign that I am. I play that I am...oh but this pain in my left side, and this numbness... do I need this body? Do do understand, Kant? Stop walking! Stand still! Sensation without content is empty! Just use your imagination, Descartes! The forced image of shit!

Nonsense! Where's the janitor? The porter? This book that I am writing is not like a note that I leave on the refrigerator door in the early morning for my wife, that says, "I will be home tonight at 8." There is a clear intention on the author's part, and the even more clear intention of the text, the author states it with "authority," in the presence of these words, a message, an act, that he will be home tonight at 8, and a connection is formed, a communication, because this is the real author, not the person who is writing this book, who could be anyone, but in this case, something is the case, because I woke early this morning, I wrote a note, I stuck it on the refrigerator door, and then she wakes, sees the note, the note wasn't there yesterday, or was it? Did she not notice it? But she believes that her eyes, her memory, did not deceive her, no, it wasn't there yesterday. She's pretty sure, never 100%, but sure enough. She interprets the note as a sign of the fact that I will be home tonight at 8. End of story. There isn't really any story. But if I had written this note: I will be home... or had I written this note: I will be home tonight at 8 barring any unforeseen circumstances. What a cliché! But the former is not enough and the latter is too much. Of course I would not write those words; would I write it to be funny? Ironical? It would induce worrisome thoughts, it would make the mind wander... but it could be the beginning of a narrative, and now we may have a story, at last. It's not that the common sense note or a complex novel is equal to the intensity of the poem that I write over and over again on pieces of paper and then rip up each page into small pieces and toss them out the window of my garret on the rue Guisarde because I have doubts about the poem and my ability to write... why bother? Now, in theory, someone could come along, (a street-cleaner, who does not read them and disposes of them?) walking on the pavement, who picks up some of the pieces of paper, and thinks that this is certainly a sign of some poor poet distraught over his work, suffering from self-doubt, who tore up these pages and flung them out the window, up there, look up there, from the top window, because look here, see the words... no sense, put them together, perhaps this way, a poem, quite indecipherable. Well, that might very well be the correct interpretation, but, obviously, at this point, it doesn't matter to the so-called author, or the reader, because he picked up just several scraps of the paper and has now thrown them back on the ground and has continued walking down the street... or, the pieces of paper could have been thrown out the window of my high-rise apartment in Manhattan, and someone could, in theory, come along and say, look, there must have been a ticker-tape parade here recently, look at all these pieces of paper, and this could generate another interpretation that, of course, you can see how lazy these city workers are, don't do their job properly, and we now have another narrative, with political connotations. Or if I just put the intact poem in a bottle and walk down to the pier, and stare out to sea, like Ishmael, and think, maybe I'll throw the bottle into the water, or throw myself into the river, the bottle and poem addressed to the phantoms of the future, at the border, same as this book that I am writing is addressed to the phantoms at the border, the phantom reader, a border at the edge of the woods, but it's not my woods and I am forbidden to enter. It's not my woods, it's the woods of the readers, and though I see my *doppelgänger* coming out on the path, I the author, can not enter. There is a sign. Authors Forbidden. So we could go on and on, but that note to my wife is at home, there is an at-homeness there, in her interpretation of the words stating the following proposition: I will be home tonight at 8... there is the fact of the matter. It could be false, it could prove to be false, but that was not my intention. I could be delayed for hundreds of reasons. An accident, the train derailed, drinks with a friend... but that's when the narrative begins, not in my note... but if not, if I am home at 8, or approximately at 8, then this big white object has handed her a singular meaning, a common gesture, a communal vehicle of obligation, a sacrament, which is my note, like a grace note, because the refrigerator is God. Here it comes, big and white, with guns and a bible, and tomorrow back to work. As for my note, the author is the author, but for this book that I am writing, I am not the author... I just bring it to fruition... inversely and perversely, against nature... it's like labor pains before the impregnation, which is almost too easy, it's pleasurable, it's an aesthetic pleasure of the imagination, but the labor comes first... sex comes after... it's against natural law. Why do I indulge in this pseudo-philosophical discourse? Am I not searching for a narrative? If the state can hold the arm, the state can hold the tongue! Walking in place, I can't get the narrative started. There is a fog in the streets. There is a fog in the woods. Movement... Zeno proved that I could never leave this room. That I could walk in place forever. Nothing moves. I will never get out of here. But Zeno admitted that he had to move his tongue to make his point. These words are moving like a narrative across the page... and yet...

3-11-2011

There is a photograph of Stephen and his wife in her childhood home in Tohoku. It's 1996. The two of them are sitting on the tatami floor. Stephen is holding their baby. He has written a poem for her. He is writing it with a brush of black ink. The room has a *kamidana*, a small shrine to remember the departed. The incense is burning. It's summer. It's hot. The sliding doors are open. The house is on a small mountain. It has a burnt-rust colored tiled roof. It has a foundation built on blocks. It has beautifully painted *fusama*, sliding panels. That photograph has become a kind of impossibly real fiction. The object is gone. The house was destroyed in the earthquake. A degree of difference both paradoxical and sublime.

Apologia #3 - America, The Janitors, The Door Keeper

Who was this Jesus that a dead man should chase Erik Thorvaldssen from his own land and his own son follow this dead man? Forget Norway then. Preach to the weak and say that they have power (but it's not true) and then let many follow his might to their doom. It is written that in the beginning there were the Greeks and the Jews. The Logos/Tanakh. Greekjew. Jewgreek. Goycee Games. *Kan du leke med ord?* The Hebraic-Hellenic. Do you really believe that Augustine of Hippo heard a child's voice say *take up and read* and opened exactly to Romans 13:13-14? Forsake the flesh. Time? Don't ask. Flesh? Please ask. You are a writer, would you tell me that it's not contrived? A necessary fiction? Like the self? From these origins have sprung Western Civilization. The radical priests and the righteous prophets. The smart alecks and the smart asses. What follows is an American Genealogy of the Law of Rule in a Prophetic and Poetic Voice. Speaking in Tongues-in-Cheek. Here is a dialectic that cannot be synthesized. Here is a dialogic that will not be resolved.

This story follows two lines of metaphor that begin by running in a non-Euclidean parallel until they reach a pole at a terminal point from which they break apart and once again go their separate ways, but only after having caused massive destruction. Let us begin:

In the beginning was The Day of Doom. Michael Wigglesworth, the bestselling author, who waits with joy to see his Day of Doom. The Puritan Prophets of Doom. A City on the Hill. By 1980 the City on the Hill was a Shining City, the threat of radioactive nuclear war, fallout, black rain… shines like the Japanese fishermen in the trawler in the Pacific Ocean.

Then came Bacon, Locke and Newton, as refined by Thomas Jefferson. The Prophets of the Day of Property. Property precedes Government. Creative production reduced to the political. Ascending Capitalism. The Day of Doom is a poem of Judgment, the Declaration of Independence is a poem of Happiness, an Empire of Liberty, and in the years toward the end of the 18th century, 1798-1800, an alliance of Nationalists disguised as Federalists and Anti-Federalists, who are determined to protect their rights and property, and protect themselves from their own government, from the People, who John Adams, a monarchist, calls "a motley rabble of saucy boys, negroes, and molattoes, Irish teagues, and outlandish jack tarrs..." who in turn ask why are we not protected from private tyranny, from the company, from the employer, from the externalities of the other? This merged, fused into an American False Aporia: Adams/Jefferson. Checks and Balances. A false pretense that private power is freedom. Accumulate, accumulate. A liberal political nexus of conversation and consensus. The Alien and Sedition Act/Liberty. Under the Sedition Act it is a crime to "write, print, utter, or publish... any false, scandalous and malicious writing or writings against the government of the United States." Don't speak or write unless you are a True Believer! Adams and Jefferson in positions of government enforce this law. This was a relatively calm period for those involved, except for the rhetoric which was awfully vehement at times, especially in the "free" press. The quotes around the word "free" stand for "sometimes yes" and "sometimes not so much." And before we get lost in a recursive argument that spins out of control... Workers, Slaves and Native-Americans were not much involved. The destruction did not reach the level that it did in France during the French Revolution and the Reign of Terror that followed from it. This is before a doctrinaire Socialism or a scattered Anarchism poisoned the air. After these consensual points of political life split apart there then appeared two prophets in the American 19th century. They were born in the same year and died a year apart. They wrote in the style of the Biblical narrative, the Homeric epic, the Shakespearean O-rag. It was realism and symbolism like hot iron pounded on the anvil and shaped into fluttering words with wings. The first prophet is Herman Melville and his Book is *Moby-Dick*. The Pequod is the National Ship of State. The ship is named for the Pequot, who were an indigenous tribe decimated by the English colonists and small-pox. Their Day of Doom occurred at Mystic: *A fiery Oven... Thus did the Lord judge among the*

Our Subject (is not a subject?)

So Stephen, how did you get from a cracked blacktop basketball court in a small-town schoolyard of an elementary school named after President Theodore Roosevelt on a Sunday morning at Oyster Bay, New York, United States of America, in the month of October in the year 1969 to... twenty years later in 1989 and you are sitting on a bench waiting for a train? You are alone and it is late at night. You have no family ties to this place, no responsibilities to specific persons, no commitments, you are in a faraway land where you are called an outsider, the street signs are in a different language, and you speak a different language from the people here, and you are reading a book in your language that was translated from the language that the people read here. A book about a journey to the unknown land to the north of this country where you are now... a journey enacted exactly three hundred years ago, in 1689... and sitting here you think the most unbelievable of all thoughts, that you are happy... thinking about that journey recorded in this book and translated into the English language makes you happy... you have little money, no resources, it's like you've seen a phantom, that you are chasing this phantom, and you think that at this moment in time you would not want to be any other place in the world except for here where you are right now. You are the phantom. You are nothing... the voices of the dead are everywhere; they cry out in pain and they cry out in ecstasy. You are not hiding and you are not lost. You have no origins back there and no future ahead... you are a neon bulb in a city of millions of bulbs but your bulb is the brightest... until it pops... and the light goes out of the eye... in the blink of an eye all happiness is extinguished... and that's why you have come to this place. To sit in darkness. And that was 1689... and now in 1989 the Emperor of Japan has died, the Berlin Wall is being torn down, and it's also 200 years since 1789 and the French Revolution...

You were asked by a Japanese friend to build a mailbox for him. You thought it a rather peculiar idea, but you gave it a go. It turned out a mess. You really botched it. You cut out geometrical shapes, triangles, squares, rectangles, circles... your friend was a mathematician, and you attached these shapes to the sides of the rectangular box that you had made and painted the mailbox in various bright colors. Imagine the look on the mailman's face. You showed your friend the finished product and you both agreed to call the object a mailbox. You were a little ashamed that you had made such a muddle of it. It lacked craftsmanship. It lacked technique. Your friend, Iwata-san, looked at it rather intently and then he suddenly exclaimed: It's a Kandinsky mailbox! Its imperfections make it art!

Years later, after you had returned to America, you mailed a postcard to your friend. You tried to visualize the postcard inside the Kandinsky mailbox like the sound of one hand clapping. Thousands of miles from there you was here, clapping with the other hand. Somehow the clapping hands met across time and space. The postcard was a print of Kandinsky's *Composition X*, from 1939, created when the world was on the brink of world war. The painting reminded you of Japan for some reason. Maybe because of the colors and figures and the fish-like shape that looked like a *Koi* banner strung across a street in a remote Japanese village.

Stephen was sitting at the train station in the outer reaches of Tokyo. He was reading Matsuo Bashō's *Oku no Hosomichi*. A travel journal that Bashō wrote in the spring of 1689. A famous text that combines prose and poetry. Bashō travels to the mysterious and hidden deep north. He stops at various places where the poets of old have left traces of their immersion in life and literature. Bashō isolates the appearances of these phantoms by bringing them to the foreground and rubbing them against the currents of time. In June 1944 the Japanese writer Osamu Dazai traveled from Tokyo to his birthplace in the deep north, a remote hilly and swampy tip of the Tohoku Region, beyond the limits of Bashō's journey. Dazai writes a travelogue in which he combines both personal anecdotes and geographical and topographical facts and figures. He often muses on Bashō. And then the modern, cynical and anti-capitalist touch of a fallen decadent aristocrat inserts itself wearily into the text. Dazai writes that Bashō must have been a good businessman, taking his celebrated journey to the deep north just for his personal ambitious desire of expanding the Bashō school of poetics far and wide. It's an unconventional grumble. The obliteration of the subject-object, the iteration of the will to the persona. The inaccessible solitude of being. The ironic "I" in a state of love and revolution. Dazai killed himself. He and his mistress drowned together in the Tamagawa Canal. It was a Sunday. The sun set that day and the next day just like any other day. He was not excluded from being a writer. He was qualified to be a writer. He was disqualified to be a human. He said so himself.

Writing is what Stephen resolves to do subsequent to his obligation to be, proceeding from here in world-weariness, how he copes, how he labors, how he chooses his next step in walking in place. What kind of labor? He who ploughs. He who was a ploughman on the hillsides of Liguria. He who was a ploughman in the rice paddies of Tohoku. At the end of each line he turned around and ploughed back again. Loose-words toppled over the furrows. Barren seeds that will not sprout again. There is a fence he cannot vault. Back and forth. A hopeless Sisyphus. The misfit, the introvert, the outsider, the self-outcast, are you not tired of reading about this myth? The American illusion of Emersonian self-reliance, of Whitmanesque democratic freedom en-masse, the subjective, the subject, Descartes, Kant, Rousseau vs. Hobbes, state of nature, before the fact, after the fact, the fact that I am, and I think, therefore what the fuck should I do? After the flood, after the erosion, after the maelstrom, after the volcano... Being, Time, Nothingness, such big concepts meant nothing to him at the time, such obscure concepts escaped time in the boredom of his room, not Hegel, not Marx, no absolute systems of blind certainty. The meaning of knowledge? The meaning of being? No where to go and I can't stay here... that was it... the boredom as centrifugal force throwing him outward but never reaching beyond the limit of these words, these walls. Is it infinite on the other side? The anxiety as centripetal force throwing him inward but never reaching the center... is there a void on the inside? An emptiness? A romantic and jaded gloss: Little Boy Empty found a hole in the bottom of his soul. He knew he had to fill it in to cure the pain he felt within; but when he looked around to his regret he found that he had dug another hole in the bottom of his soul. Endless excavation. No theorist can declare the author dead. The author doesn't sign his name as a mathematical formula, or as an engineering feat or as a logical proposition. The theorist is charged with attempted murder. Perhaps the "death of the author" was really a suicide! A visitation from the shabby devil in the white night. Dostoyevsky's Ivan saying "Who doesn't desire his father's death?" So the self-punishment is directed at the stronger object, the mother... so the withdrawn misfit who does not kill himself ends up in Greenwich Village or Paris or London or Tokyo or a tower of rock on the solitary coast at the end of the world... and so the outward rebel who murders the old woman ends up in jail or with a bullet in his head... but accidents happen. And no one knows... which will it be? If he were to kill himself, who would be here to write this shit? If you were to kill him, who would be here to write this shit? And if he were to kill you, who would be here to read this shit? That is actually the most important part of this relationship. O Dear Reader. You, again. Damn you. Reader. But again, who would be here? You... and again? Who? You! And again, who? You! Thou! And I, also as reader. I and Thou. One and Many.

Okay. Let's put our words on the paper. He should prefer not to... What? What? What? Not to do what you are told to do, not to do what you are ordered to do? Do you have the right to be so lazy? So well read? Very well then. Seek the words... turn these words upside down, turn your world upside down, find the will, not the brick wall, not the closed door. Bartleby, are there not enough words in the world to describe your world in impossible mimesis because words are not of this world? There's the corner, Bartleby, put on your dunce cap, you are a disgraceful spectacle, a trapped rat cowering in the corner of the prison wall; it's your world, interpret it as you will, *du må bare gjøre som du vil...* stand up and reveal your true self. Tell the truth. I am Bartleby. I am Bartleby. I am Bartleby. Will the real Bartleby please stand up? Ah, it's only Fiction. Ah, but it's Literal. *Dans tous les sens...* What is your real name and what do you do, sir? My name is Herman Melville and I am a writer. Ah, but it's a Fact. Ah, it's only Lyrical. *Dans tous les sens...*

He'd rather get his hands dirty in the archive, on the printing press, with black ink, than sit up high on a throne of theory. He is a writer without an identity, and he displaces no one but himself, and he prefers to read, and let the emphasis be put on the word *read*, that he prefers to read Camus to Sartre (although *What is Literature?* is an absolutely funny text; Simone Weil to Simone de Beauvoir (although shacking up with naïve Algren in Chicago? Nice career move... ooh la la), Bakunin to Marx (although he had a plausible critique); Dostoyevsky to Tolstoy (although Stephen read Tolstoy and Dostoyevsky when he was eighteen and again at fifty... he hasn't changed his mind with age), Kerouac to Bellow (although it's a hard fact that Chicago is still a somber city and somberly American in its bellowing), Henry Miller to Steinbeck (although Stephen loved *The Red Pony* in seventh grade) Melville to Whitman (although contradiction and multitudes have its advantages); Joyce to Woolf (although she was good on rooms); Dos Passos to Dos Passos (although... it's your guess); Jeffers to Frost (although I'd prefer not to... ice or fire?), Hamsun to Kipling (although, *just so* how did the British get its Empire?), Céline to Gide (although Isabelle has clues... and those Jews leading those goy boys into the dark alley to show them how to sodomize each other in order to bring the Caucasian race into a state of servility, stooped to be conquerd by the dark and yellow races... isn't satire fun?), Kierkegaard to Hegel (although perhaps the emphasis should not be on the word read... it's the door to the madhouse), Nietzsche to Kant (although sometimes Stephen would prefer happily and with no effort to constitute the world rather than have with enormous effort to create with these words this damn book), Rudolf Rocker to Ayn Rand (although *The Virtue of Selfishness* is a most enjoyable psychotic romp), Foucault to Barthes (although as authors they might negate each other and where would that leave Stephen?)... so shun him, shoo him away like a dirty little fly, and Charles William Mouche, let's not forget him... Stephen appears to prefer his intellectuals libertarian-left and his writers weirdly to the right... with a few notable exceptions... is he right or is he right? He is left speechless. But he had those good old American heroes growing up. Why did you reject and abandon them and take up with those dirty foreigners and these disreputable Americans? And yet there were the astronauts of the Mercury, Gemini, and Apollo programs. John Glenn was your first hero, let's just say. You had a friend in your fourth grade class whose father worked for Grumman. He brought in a piece of tinfoil-like substance, aluminized Kapton foil, which was to be used on the outside of the Apollo Lunar Module, the LM-5, Eagle. That was for his science project. Your science project was called *Space Stations and Satellites*. In your fourth grade class that year, 1966, your teacher was obsessed and passionate about the space program, stars and astronomy. Of course she was influenced by the dominant culture, and encouraged to promote the idea that we, America, will land a man on the moon before the decade is out, and therefore win the race to the moon, and achieve an important victory in the Cold War, besting those Russians.

You had pictures that your mother clipped from newspapers that you kept in a scrapbook. She kept all the *New York Daily News* front-page headlines. The assassinations of John F. Kennedy, Bobby Kennedy, Martin Luther King, the deaths of Douglas MacArthur and Winston Churchill, the landing on the moon... and you kept all the headlines and stories about the 1969 New York Mets. And that was your father's influence, baseball, the New York Mets, and your hero was Tom Seaver. You watched or listened to every game that he pitched, hung on every strike, ball and hit. You knew all the statistics that mattered then. HR RBI AVG W L ERA

And then there was the high school library. It was there that you hid out when cutting classes. They knew you were there and they let you stay there, without bothering you anymore, because something was up. What was up? You hid out in the aisle at the back of the library by the big window. It was there that you were accosted by the creepy and prematurely big-breasted Mindy Funklestein, making some lewd sexual comments to you, and you coughed and blushed and wanted to jump out the window. But it was here that you made your own discovery. The books of Jules Verne. You read *20,000 Leagues Under the Sea*, and the library became your *Nautilus*, and you were Captain Nemo.

Then in 1969 it all came together. Man landed on the moon and the Mets won the World Series. But you started coming apart. You had to appear in family court before a judge for the second time. Two strikes and you're out. They make their own rules. This is not baseball. This is the law. This is *their* law. No more free trips to the icebox for a glass of milk anytime you want it anymore, said the Judge. So you were sent away to a home for children in upstate New York.

When you returned home you were disoriented and lost at sea. Your time had eroded. The *Nautilus* had been sucked into the maelstrom. You were afloat like Ishmael. You were a drunken boat. And in the 1970s you spiraled downward and downward into a maelstrom of swirling anxiety and disarrangement of the senses. Walking in place, compulsively. By the end of that decade the last rains and winds of time had eroded your youth, and it was the either/or of the serious/frivolous questions that Albert Camus asked in those two books that you read over and over... suicide or murder?

Erosion just revealed new irregular surfaces. You washed up on a foreign shore. You survived. The inexplicable and contingent paths that uncannily connected the text-in-progress of the self to the text of the thing-in-itself and thereby disclosed the discursive as a subject that both annihilates itself and transcends itself in space and time. You saved yourself by leaving the country of your birth and by living in books and yanking out the roots of presence under the bench that you sat on that Sunday morning at Highgate Wood, or the bench at that Tokyo train station. You began chasing phantoms around the world. That's what she said. In Vienna in 1988, she said, "You are just chasing phantoms." But when you stood before the house or in the room where an author had lived, or stood over the grave where an author was buried, you knew in spite of post-modern jargon about the death of the author, that you were paying homage to these dead men and women and the books that they wrote because that's what kept you alive when you were in the lower depths and no person living could have pulled you out. One man and a dead man's book, yo ho ho and a bottle of rum. It took a volcano on a South Sea island. It took the concurrent paths of the prevailing trade winds. From walking in place to getting away, and getting away from *all that* is not just seeking out some place of isolation and seclusion. How could you define *all that*? That's why you call it *all that*. You can't define all or nothing, you can't define Being, only those broken parts that you seized just after midnight, that you carried with you, through the dark alleys, the black robes dragging on the dirty streets, Herman Melville and Louis Armstrong and the 1969 Mets, the shadows of memory and desire, that fall into the world like a waterfall of words falls into a forest with a path never found. There is no path to find.

Thoreau at Walden, Miller in Paris, Kerouac and Cassady riding in an automobile, Rimbaud leaving Charleville, then leaving France for Africa... Baudelaire on the boulevards, Hamsun in Chicago, Céline in Detroit, Stephen in London, Paris, Norway, Japan... they escaped from something to become something that they were not at the beginning... or something that they were in the beginning but had to escape to discover it... but they can't escape their ashes and traces, their documental life, their history, their object-hood, even the poet Robinson Jeffers' Inhumanist is not hiding from society or civilization. He is not a fugitive. He is isolating himself from mankind but he is not hiding himself. He is not hiding from himself. He is forgotten by society. Society is not looking for him, not searching for him. All documents about him have been destroyed or left to rot in an old file cabinet. He is not hiding from something because he has now become nothing. Erased. Stephen, are you hiding from yourself?

Stephen at ten years old is hiding. He is trying to hide. From whom and what? He suffers from an obscure fear and anxiety about something... of something unknown or repressed. This fear and anxiety is doubled and deepened by the fear and anxiety of being found. Stephen has locked himself in the bathroom. He sits on the toilet crying. His mother is on the other side of the door pleading with him to come out. She found him. She has not lost him yet, as he will lose her to a doubled and deepened death, the memory death of Alzheimer's and physical decay of dying. Even his friend with whom he walks to school has now arrived and is trying to coax

Stephen out of the bathroom. Humiliation is added to the bitter admixture. The school shrink Mr. Porco who is acting as the truant officer for some concealed reason has now arrived in his little green MGB convertible. He is aggressively pulling on the bathroom door handle, but at the same time he is trying to use enticing words to work their false charm on Stephen. And worst of all, Stephen is told that his father is on his way. The school called him at his job at the other elementary school in town where he works as a janitor. His father will be very angry and also humiliated. Why do they have to think about me? Stephen wonders. Why should it matter?

Stephen looks, stares, gazes at the doorknob in front of him. Anxiety bloats things. Stephen thinks: O lucky object. Do you not feel my anxiety and fear? Do you not experience my anxiety and fear? Why can't I be an inanimate object like this doorknob, round, white, and cold to the touch of my hand? Why do you make me feel sad? There is nobody looking for you. Nobody is thinking about you. No one else is conscious of you. There is only me at this moment. I make you live. I am the reason that you exist. I make you appear to me. I am an object of a different kind. They will not notice you now as I notice you now. They will grab you from the other side of the door, pull you from the other side, and rattle you but your nerves of steel don't rattle like my nerves of flesh rattle. They will not notice you now until they break you and then dad will curse you in this knowledge of you. Dad will replace you. You will be tossed into the trash and taken away to a landfill where you will rust and rot until you are no more, until you are no thing. Can I not be cursed and discarded? Cursed and replaced? I am broken. What do they want with me? To put me back together? Do they believe that they can save me? Do they believe that they can save society by saving me? It's the law? I'm lost... and this is how it all begins... unhand me you bastards!

Stephen places his hand on the doorknob. He gives up... he gives in. No escape. It is finished. For now. But it is not over. Far from it. Is he coming out of his shell? The doorknob now feels warm and not cold. Did the contact of his warm hand with the doorknob pass this pleasure of heat on? Are you not the same doorknob now? Stephen grabs, turns, and pulls. You *are* the same. And they who are on the other side of the door *are* the same. "Do not touch me," he says, as he steps forth from the toilet. They can never deplete and diminish him. Stephen withdraws into himself... for now... he walks in place... he pierces the darkness. Life is exhausting. No return. If language is sacred to the oath then silence is the absence of the curse. He abstains.

The sixties was the decade you ascended through childhood. The symbolic significance of the decade began, if you had a literary bent, with Hemingway's suicide in 1961 by shotgun, and ended with Kerouac's death in 1969 by drinking himself to death, another kind of suicide. But that's an adult and too clever literary reflection. What do you remember? He remembers a crayon drawing of a rocket and the moon. That was in kindergarten in 1962. The drawing was pinned to the bulletin board outside the classroom. He was proud. He remembers president John F. Kennedy's announcement about going to the moon that ended with landing on the moon. He remembers Kennedy's assassination and walking home from school that day, passing the ghostly windows of Raynham Hall. He remembers a new National League baseball team that began in 1962 and that ended in 1969 with victory in the World Series. He remembers wanting to play the trumpet like Louis Armstrong and Herb Albert. The school gave him the alto horn instead. Can you do something, dad? What are you going to do? Stephen hated it. He gave up the alto horn after two lessons.

The Word "I"

He has his life, doesn't he? This so-called "I" who dares to write? Who calls to him? Raise your hand when I call your name. America calls to you. To begin with the end in sight. I am just and almost beginning this book and ending this sentence with the same word, and that word is "I". The "I" that I am and the "I" that is the word that is just a word. No more quotation marks! I am removing the quotation marks. None of this has any importance. These goose eyes. These hooks. Little Willy. I can eat and I can sleep and I can shit and say not the word "I" nor what "I" or society claims to see in me nor say not the "I" and just eat and just sleep and just shit and just speak eat shit sleep. The entire world is inside the toilet of words. Swallowed up in the belly. And the mountain is nothing like the mountain. Splitting infinity into word and object. Say it in the language of the people: *je suis… je pense… donc je suis…* but what do the people know? Modernity split the first atom. Split the *cogito* into the *I am….* split the atom into a bomb. Dante writes: *El cominciò: Figliuol, segui i miei passi…* I cannot follow your steps. Dazai writes: *taberu… nemui…* eat… sleep… who needs a subject? The ground of being is slipping... I pee on the I... the schizoid I... the self-identity of a first-person pronoun. I cover the I with shit... that's my prescription for you my dear twin patient... just like Doktor Destouches. I am that I am. I am not that I am. Neurosis speaks. Blah blah blah. Psychosis is silent. Should I stop here? *Hold kjeften*! Enough!

It is the same word and it is not the same word. See, there are two of them. Like two Moby Dicks that is one Moby Dick. The monomaniacal "I" that is the peg-leg that attempts to remain intact. And the voyaging "I" that takes the reader aboard the ship and its inevitable destiny of doom. It is practically the same word on Monday, the same word on Tuesday, the same word on Wednesday, and so forth... and that's so very convenient. So Pragmatic. So business as usual. If you make an atom bomb you will use your atom bomb. We have the bomb. Why do we need philosophers or poets anymore? We make demands of science, and then technology and profit find a way. Not *The Way*, after all, we are post-modern people. There is no *The Way*. If you begin with the I you will end with the I. There must be a literal sense of the word, or how could metaphor and paraphrase be possible? It conventionally agrees to present a referral, a designation, and a representation of itself to itself. Step into the mirror. A relation that relates a self to some other kind of self that is not itself. The speaker and the spoken of. It darkens the text in a dark room of black candles. It separates time. It slices space. It gets you through the communicative days, the consensual days, the social and dutiful working days. But is it in a different place? It's in the same place in the text, barring external censorship or internal lesion. No, Fido! Don't forget to save your document!

But is it in a different place on Monday, a different place on Tuesday, and a different place on Wednesday, and so forth... is it in the beginning as it is at the end? Or *was* it in the beginning as it was at the end? *Ab initio*. Is it in another time? Or another place? Or *will* be... in the future tense is there some sense of an open-ended sentence? Words without end. *In medias res*. Amen. And where did this *is* come from? And where did this *it* come from? And where did this *you* come from? And who is the other I? That finger-pointing letter pointing back at me. And who is this *me*? And what is the difference among these sacrificial pronouns? And what does it desire? Is the other Other an impostor? Which Other? Who is the real one? Who is the original one? Or are they just endless commentaries from the textual and sexual case histories of an overzealous rat trapped in a maze? Is the rat aware of a freedom beyond the walls? Is Bartleby? The rodent philosophers sniffing through the old unglued documents in the fragmented archives and sweeping away the shattered dust to find that it has no voice? Did I just clear my throat? No voice to tell you what to do.

There are two, perhaps more, perhaps there are many more of these creepy one-legged creatures running around in our local language mind, confusing us, echoing piercingly against the wall, ringing like tinnitus, it's all in your head, and causing self-doubt. And they have had many protean names over the years, crawling out of their black holes, looking for something to attach themselves to, the parasites, to a metaphor, something like *being*, something like *is*, like *am*, it is, one is, he is, she is, you are, we are, they are. Says Pip. But he's gone. Far gone. What came first the "I" or the "Am?" The bulwark of context. It's understood. Most of all, the protean I. So-called pronouns. So-called proper names. My history of proper names. Shall I spell it out for you? The unspoken spoken. They don't get along very well, with *is*, with *being*, with the wonderful copulation with copula, in a tricky predictive and predicative relationship, along with something called action. At a distance? But what is distance? Distance is spirit. The distance between a self and some other kind of self is spirit. But which Other are we speaking about? Are we speaking now? Then to whom am I speaking? Am I not writing? Am I not speaking to myself? Am I not silently speaking to my writing, as it were? Is my writing a guilty reflection of the interrogation of the self? Is there anyone home? Hume thought not. I want to convey my past experience, and something else, but what? I am not quite certain what this what is. But I am sitting here writing, and that is what I am experiencing now. But now the *now* is already gone, peg-leg is back, as my words move in this direction and look backward from here. Where? Slow down. I am experiencing vertigo. Seasickness. I am experiencing the experience of writing. I am experiencing the experience of thinking, I think, he says doubtfully. Ideas pop into my head. Images pop into my head. Words pop into my head. I pause. I think. I hesitate. I erase. I write. I am getting nowhere. I'm stuck here. I am stuck in a singular time and a singular space. I encounter distractions and de-simulacrums, abruptions and abortions, in the perceived suspension and deferral of my meaning. I could write down today's date, the exact time, for this exact moment at least, inscribe it, record it, as they say, for posterity. And where did this *they* come from? When did we get so plural? But nothing lasts, and I have to get somewhere… but there's nowhere to go and I can't stay here. It was on a Sunday morning that I decided to try my luck at becoming a writer. That was over forty years ago. Now look at where I am… what I am… I am a sick man. So I will speak about myself. I have lost all my self-respect. What else? I have to know, to get inside the shoes of the other, but it's my other, my banishment, my uncanny, un-localized and unmapped place. Forget the here and now. It has no structure. It's built on a fleeting whim. I need an edifice. I need an artifice. I need rigor and precision. I need a meticulous routine. I need an exact formula to synthesize these words upon a scaffolding built above the world. A transcendence. Can I just speak and stutter rhetorically, repeatedly, that here is the story of the subject? The self. This is the inexhaustible I. This is the little puny penis of a vertical mark. This is the missing leg and crippled legs of Captain Ahab and Rimbaud and Uncle Stevie. *Je suis intact. Jeg husker alt.* I am master of all that I survey in the endless horizon of the unreachable thing-in-itself. The scaffolding is collapsing! The ship is sinking! O helmsman! The poop deck falls in on itself. The shit fell on me. The natural obscurity of things, wrote Baudelaire. The ungraspable phantom of life, wrote Melville. A helpless crying infant in the basket on the water. I feel that I am at the center of the universe. Another duplicitous *I am*. I hope you like italic. This is not italic. I am wearing my bowler hat today. Do I not appear distinguished? Theodore Roosevelt wore his cowboy hat in his own wild west of the mind, but the real outlaws and cowboys wore derby hats. Without my authoritative appearance what else do I have on offer? Do I just sit around analyzing concepts? Look out the windows of my university office and mull over analytic concepts and constructive concepts? Hey, Tiberius, fetch me a new carburetor for my chariot you perverted asshole! Hey, Doctor Tut, did that old fart and hunchback Rameses II die from an abscessed tooth and arthritis or did he in the ordinary way of speaking just drop dead? The workingman and slave want to know. Nobody was talking to you so just move on. Nothing to see here. You'll hear our commanding voice in due time. But look at my hat! Get out of here you little tramp! What treachery of my words and images! Flowers and fade to black. No resolution. This is not the flow of words in time. I am not on the endless road or riding the straight tracks of the train. It's not a reaching back to pull everything forward. Walking in place is simply a metaphor for reading, with an underwritten urge to go somewhere else; life is elsewhere… walking the streets of a city is simply a metaphor for writing, a sojourn down a newly discovered street or a walk down the same street, until the street, its buildings, its pedestrians, are changed, torn down, or have moved away... But how can a center exist, be located, be defined, if there is no edge out there? Who decides upon my circumscription? My circumcision? Thanks mom and dad? My confession of being? I am outside the edge. It's sharp. A razor's edge at the tip of words. I just said that *I am*. I just wrote that I am. I am outside the edge. I think therefore I am. I am therefore I think. To be is to be perceived. The world is my representation. I place a rock on the grass. My father drives us home. I see the rock in my mind. Am I floating? I can see myself floating. I am myself and I can see myself. But it's not in a mirror that I see my reflection. It's not a reflection. I am not myself today, as they say. I imagine myself going to retrieve the rock. I believe it's out there. It is there. It is still there. Am I so gullible, so naïve? An ant walks over it. I follow the road in my mind, like a ghost, a phantom. I arrive at the rock. I pick it up. I bring it home. There are now two rocks. There is the rock that I left out there and the rock that I brought home. But the rock that I brought home is not just a representation, not just a signification, not just a concept, not just a flick of a neuron. Is the rock that I brought home the same as the rock that I imagined in the beginning? They are the same but not the same? The rock is out there in the night, on the grass, by the school, where I placed it. It is in its place. It found its place because I found it a place? Or did I have help? Is that what Aristotle meant when he said that things fall to their natural place? It's not surprising. Or must it be surprising? Chesterton on Thursday said that you take the tube from here to Victoria because you know that Victoria is the next stop. And that's surprising! If it were Baker Street instead of Victoria, well, then all is lost... Anarchy!

I am in bed looking out the window at the tops of the trees. I am in my room in the house on the hill in Oyster Bay. That other rock is with me here too, many years later. Is it just an image on the wall of the cave? Is that what Plato meant when he said that there is an ideal form? Is that what our present philosophers mean when they say that philosophy is dead and history is dead and the author is dead? It's useless. In other words it's not practical. It's not real. It is make-believe. Fiction. I have carried these rocks for a long time. My sack of rocks is getting heavy. They are sinking fast to the bottom of the dark sea. Almost lost forever. Not retrievable. But not in a reductive sense. They have never found their place, their substance, nor their form. Not that I can tell. My sack of rocks has been getting heavier and heavier over the years, because I have over time placed rocks all over the world. I moved them with my hands. I moved them with my mind. I disturbed the universe. So too did Galileo. But these words have disturbed nothing. I placed a rock in England, on the top of Primrose Hill; and in Paris, on a ledge of the Eiffel Tower, by a faded Marlboro cigarette box; and in Norway, on the rock foundation, it's all that remains, of the house that my mother was born in; and in Japan, by the statue of Bashō, on the path to Chusonji... I am now attempting to retrieve all the rocks in my mind. Little pebbles, little fragments. They are out there and they are here with me now. The same rocks. Here and there. And they are spinning like atoms and eroding in time, in mind. A paradox, a contradiction, an aporia... so be it. Forty years of rock collecting. Out there they are like feathers upon the earth. In here they are like talus, scree, tumbling and rumbling fragments of forgetting; I am no Sisyphus, no Prometheus, no Odysseus, and I am standing by the shore, drifting away, waving adieu. I await the muted call and grab the proffered word from the night sky. I see the lighthouse beaming through the fog. *Hun som husker alt, husker ingenting.* How can I tell the story from the storyteller? This narrative of forty years of reading and forgetting, remembering and forgetting, and remembering and forgetting again, is no more than a long stinking breath of parody and paraphrase. It begins as an implied singular signature and commences as an implied impersonal pronoun. The self to itself and the marking of extraterritorial metaphor. To have the authorities, in the person of a school psychologist and a truant officer, looking for me, coming for me, for my discernible documented self, at my home, hiding somewhere my invisible self. Who am I to hold their interest? Who am I to hold their attention? Why should they care in this careless way? These authorities hound me, therefore I am. To be detached from my identity, from home and town and friends, to be sent away, by a black-robed judge named Amberstein. To see my name, written by the Other, the imposter aunt, on my clothes, my initials in black marker written on my underwear, **SKC**, and on my stuff, on my personal belongings... therefore I am. Do I desire to be? Do I desire to have the desire to be? I was misgiven this life, this name, this place, this time, and this language. Not as a gift but as a marriage of self to self that is the poison unto death... *jeg gift*... but the only truly gifted thing is death.

We were born into this shit, right Bucko? What else is there to say? In the absence of presence is the desire for self-presence. But is it the same self on Monday, the same self on Tuesday, the same self on Wednesday, and so forth? Ask poor Hamlet in the dark corner of the castle, feigning his madness. Ask Descartes in the heated room of his self-revelations.

And the subject for today is an object lesson. I am a biological fact of being, flesh and blood, cast into the world and subjected to otherness, subjected to place, subjected to time, subjected to consciousness, subjected to parents, subjected to siblings, subjected to family, subjected to self, subjected to language, subjected to society, subjected to institutions, subjected to culture, subjected to violence, subjected to religion, subjected to science, subjected to conscience, subjected to love, subjected to hate, subjected to desire, subjected to money, subjected to hope, subjected to will, subjected to happiness, subjected to disease, subjected to despair, subjected to death, and so on...

Subjected to King, subjected to Rule, subjected to Law, subjected to State, subjected to Nation, subjected to Capital, subjected to Police, subjected to War, subjected to X, and so on...

Subjected to act, subjected to eat, subjected to cry, subjected to crawl, subjected to walk, subjected to run, subjected to play, subjected to grow, subjected to learn, subjected to remember, subjected to forget, subjected to fornicate, subjected to urinate, subjected to defecate, and so on...

Subjected to the self becoming in Otherness other than itself... becoming an object, becoming a name, becoming a text, becoming a job, becoming a soldier, becoming a bartender, becoming a janitor... who cleans toilets, mops up piss and shit, and so on... becoming a mother, becoming a nurse's aide, who cleans up piss and shit, and so on... becoming a printer's devil... becoming a writer who writes a book he names *Sunday Mornings at Oyster Bay*... and so on... but forty-years of scattered writing do not make a book until the words find their closure, their resting place, their bounded-ness, their abandonment, their totality in an object named in the name of the book. The named book that is opened and all is open-ended, a sealed box once opened releasing a contagion into the world... never to be resealed again? Do I dare release this biological contagion into the world? Cast it into the world? Cast in the mold of my hidden self? Waxing moon... parody... pastiche... paraphrase... this "impassable path" that was at one time the path to meaning and meaningfulness, the path to presence and sacrament, to Being in the World and in the Word. In the beginning man stamped his feet on nature, trod on its wild grasses, chopped at its vines, for to be a path in the beginning is to be a path that was passable. It's tautological. It was intended by man as a passage from here to there... is there no path anymore? The path? But what kind of objects fell in the way of The Path. Galileo? Copernicus? Newton? Darwin? The measurable? The formulaic? The mathematizable? The weighed? Does *The Origins of the Species* weigh more than *Moby-Dick*? Which is weightier? Nietzsche, Freud, Marx? Were they but the fallen trees across the path? Just a fallen tree? A few fallen trees? Would that make the path impassable? Certainly surmountable, but by what? But why bother? Many paths taken and not taken? Faith... will... or was there a great rift, a great fissure that split the earth in two and made greater an un-crossable void? A gap. Mind and extension. Object to object. This great contradiction... this paradox... a contradiction developed in time, because the path to be a path had to be passable... an inconsistency developed in history, in diachronic steps. The text is out there... and once the so-called author is no more, dead, his body i.e. his text, his pickings for the vultures of commentary, critical theory and hermeneutic onslaught... survives until the last utterance... like an object survives until its last utterances? When is that demarcation line present to us? To read the name as writ in water on paper digitally produced in the brave new world... we are immortal... while the ashes and bones of that body are scattered to the wind... how could words be sacramental in the author's absence? Only his absence and the last sign, the written word or the dying voice that says, all right... all right... all right... his last words to me, to anyone... words scribbled across the world like sutures on a skull, masked by a flesh full of scars. The presence in silence is homesick for meaning again. Not lines nor curves, only tattered edges, in dregs of waste that rats define with scampering legs across the electrical lines. These words wade to the waste, leeched by a lack of nerve. Language is the distraction we dare to avoid within the void that we give to each other in subtraction from the other other who would beseech us beyond speech to be quiet... and not go on with lies and shit. Holes of black and blanks of white fill the night with emptiness. Hark! Hark! The herald announced, serious as death. To put words in The Word, to put paths in The Path, is to name a thing with the breath of time still warm on the neck. Ha! Ha! said the clown, comical as all heck. World-ward in a whirlwind words fell like arrows. Deflected in the mirror of memory, they never struck; laughing beneath the leaves is the mischievous Puck.

The beginning and the end. The beginning is the most difficult. I always find myself returning there. I can't escape from there. The ending you can just walk away from... which is also difficult... but how not to walk back to the beginning when there really is no beginning? It's an endless loop, as Vico and Joyce demonstrated. No path that way. And yet it returns. The repressed. This winding path... this impassable path... there are many beginnings. There are many words. Orpheus brought back the universal beetle in the humus mouth of a bow-bent Jesus. The illegitimate arrow's intrusion in innocent air, and from his green stalk sleep over the mad bat of my blooming Eurydice, to the cave where her tears of night crash silently in darkness, in nothingness. What is stranger to the poet, the world or these words, or both?

With Apologies to Kierkegaard (more of the word "I")

The premise of this book is simple, once discovered. The subject, the I, the A is B but B is not A, the possessive, obsessive personal fiction, as in *I am living at,* or *my mother died,* or *I am a sick man,* or *I first met Roy not long after,* or *I would go to bed early,* or *if I remember well,* or *one's-self I sing,* or *I hadn't said a word,* or *mine has been a life of shame,* or *I was walking around starving,* or *I have dreamed of the wind-blown clouds and a life of wandering,* or *I found myself within a dark forest,* or *I believe that no materials exist for a full and satisfactory biography of this man,* or *Reader, I myself am the subject of my book,* or *The man I shall portray will be myself,* or *I can't be bothered, I just can't be bothered,* or *I am beginning this book,* or *America, I can't hate you...* and so on... or something of that nature, the self (which is unlike itself or my sisters or strangers) who writes (which is unlike Socrates or Jesus or my mother or father, of which no writing exists; well, there are a few letters) must discover after numerous experiential attempts at writing, and living, in fact forty fifty sixty years give or take, what is worth retaining of what is remembered of what is forgotten, and how much of it is worth containing in a book formed with cracked pieces of dead (de)composed sieved words of decaying matter and the slippages of meaning across and over time (which is unlike the imposed phantoms and the sewage of meaninglessness across and over time). And who decides its worth or worthlessness? The Author? The Other? The self must include the Other, the foreign (which is unlike itself, and so let's begin

45

with the mother). This making of self (which is unlike itself, and so let's end with the father) who embodied otherness at birth is reborn as otherness at death. This is the death of the father. The self who embodied and burdened itself on the mother and father. This self adds a self-signification, always unique, and mindfully oblique, rarely original, never wholly unlike itself, based on the experience of the self in its process of becoming spirit. Spirit is unlike itself. It is becoming. It is memory, that which the self imparts to itself, and which over time is reflected back to the self in broken parts, the forced and violent damage of encounters in the far away night. This yields inevitable repetition of itself as a self. An ellipsis. The other offers paraphrase and parody. The self and the other unite across time. The point at which all known paths are traversed is the final aporia. This is the reluctant closure. A binding. A tale of separation. The anxiety of exposure. The signed specimen that signifies process and atrophy, deterioration and death. These markers and this ellipsis… are like stepping-stones. They can be located anywhere. On some shelf as far away and as long ago as memory survives. Paris, Norway, Japan, Vienna, London, New York, Chicago; it doesn't matter. Time does not matter. When you look down from the mountain do you see your past? No, you see the valley and the river and the fields… there may be many markers or there may be just one marker. This is one marker. In your hands I commend my spirit… my letter? Which one really killeth? This book facing toward a subtraction and addition of its art, its style, toward being and nothing, toward God and man. The destination is never revealed. It's a moving target. Being awake, being alive, being born are momentary arrows in nature. Traces of vibrating bows. Their downward fall is inevitable. But listen to the sound of the bow. The innocence of the lack of knowledge of possible being. A place, a name, otherness. Sleep, death, not being born are the gifts of grace in the impossible epilogue of experience. An archive of memory and an idiosyncrasy of reading. A collection of broken selves masquerading as one intact self. Philosophical Questions that will not be answered in this book, that have no place in this book, but must be asked anyway… because I am a neurotic compulsive? So… and yet… even if… both-and… is this literature or theory or, God forbid, therapy?

Note to Author
You need to write something here to fill up this blank and empty space at the bottom of the page. This is not a footnote. Okay, I wrote that. Isn't this fun?

Who is this I that I write of?
Who is this I that I write for?
Is this I of the world?
Is this I for the world?
Is this I in the world?
What in the world is the world?

What is this thing called I?
Is it a thing, an object?
Is it a subject?
Is it either/or?
What is it about this I?
What is it about this I that escapes me?
Can this I escape from the prison of my mind?
What crime did this I commit?
Is this a mystery story?
Where is this I hiding?
Where in the world is this I?
Where in the world am I?

Did this I just run away from me?
Who is this I that I as writer write of?
Why do I write?
Why do I write what I write?
Why do I write "I"?
Ergo who am I?
Ergo what am I?
Ergo what sort of person am I?
Am I the existential and psychological I?
Am I the here and now I?
Am I the trapped in self-consciousness I?
Am I the grammatical and first-person pronoun I?
Am I the I to whom the world appears?
Am I a thing in itself?
Am I an other?
Am I myself?
I don't feel myself today.

Am I the fictional and projected I?
Am I the cogito?
Am I the intuitions are blind without concepts I?
Am I the no facts, only interpretations I?
Am I the nothing outside text I?
Am I the ordinary and positive I?
Am I the speechless and silent I?

Am I the stuck inside of mobile text I
With the writer's blues again?

Am I the death of the author I?
Am I therefore a ghost? A phantom?
Am I chasing phantoms?
Am I the amnesiac's I?
Am I an I prior to self-reflection?
Am I just a literary device because science cannot live with subjectivity?
Am I nothing?
Am I Being?
To be or not to be?

Am I thinking?
Am I doubting?
Can I doubt that I am?
Can I doubt that I am if I am thinking?
Can I think that I am if I am doubting?
Am I am?
Here I am!
I can... I can...
Am I running?
Am I remembering?
See I
See I run
See I run around this paper jungle
The bee stings me
The *to be* stings me
The lines of snakes beneath my feet strike at me

Am I the I of anxiety and *angst*?
Am I the I of fear and trembling?
See I jump
See I leap
Is this a leap of faith?
I jump off this paper
With these black burning letters
Falling into a white ice emptiness,
The squid squirts black ink in my eyes
See I run away
Can I leave my I behind?
Is there another I to run away with me?
Can I merge an I with an I?
Therefore I and I and I?
Like peg-leg Ahab
With two natural legs... three natural legs?
Is this I natural or artificial?
Is this I biological or chemical?
Am I superfluous?
Am I an infinite regression?
Am I finite and contingent?

I can stumble and fall...
I will follow lemmings and penguins...
And the white whale of doom,
See... I am falling
Or am I diving?
Therefore am I choosing?
Choosing this or that...?
Can I intend to fall as I intend to dive?
Oh goody good intentions...
Can I be free freely?
Oh see
Can you see I?
I here. I there.
I nowhere. I everywhere.
Here now. There now.

But still I?
No here. No there.
But still I?
Don't look back I.
Edge of the paper I.
No exit I.
Hell is I.
I take a bow.
I exit.
What is man? Asked I.
Who am I? Asked I.
Am I not God?
Am I not Plato?
Am I not St Augustine?
Am I not the man in the street?
Am I the Everyman I?
Am I every I ever written?
Or spoken?
I write that I write.
Logos. Presence. Voice.
In the beginning…
Why am I something rather than nothing?

I write a short biography of my mother's life,
I read it to her.
She has Alzheimer's.
She says, it's not about me.
I say, yes, it's about you.
She says, you are wrong.
I say, but it's your story.
She says, it's not about me. I don't know her. Or you…
Then she says: but I still love you!
And hugs me.
But then who is this I that still loves me?
Not her memory of me?
Not her herself?
Self is spirit.

But what is spirit?
What is self?
A transcendental I?
A banal and verbal I?
Who is this I that I write of?
What is its meaning?
No meaning in the past.
No meaning in the future.
Only meaning in the here and now
Can give meaning to man?
Not before the fact.
Not after the fact.
Into this state of nature
Is born a baby placed in a basket
On a river,
A drunken basket
Nature
Red and raw
Tooth and claw
Who calls from the riverbank?
I know that voice.
Voice of the other.
You? Society? Culture? Civilization?
What can I know?
Experience
Things
Words
Documents
They have their lives
Don't they?

The rest is... a sign, a symbol, a metaphor, a word... a fiction... a book. I take a book out from the library. You take a book out from the library. We both take out *Madame Bovary*. Did we take out the same book? When do I cease being I? When do you cease being you? When does this object cease being this book? When does this book cease being this object? If I tear out the first page of *Madame Bovary* and replace it with the first page of

Sentimental Education, is it still *Madame Bovary?* If I rip out the first half of the pages of *Madame Bovary,* replace them with blanks, and write my own story on the blank pages, is it still *Madame Bovary?* It's an object but is it still a pure object? Is it a particular book? I can go back in time to touch the hand that wrote Madame Bovary but I can't go back in time to make love to Madame Bovary. If every possible copy of *Madame Bovary* disappears off the face of the earth, physical and digital, in whatever possible form, and if professors and experts are invited from the four corners of the earth to "rewrite" *Madame Bovary* from scratch, from memory, in French, English, Japanese, etc., are these books still Madame Bovary? And which book would be the original? Would it be the English, the French, the Japanese, or some other version? If I am in the library and fall asleep at a desk and nobody knows that I am there until midnight when a Cro-Magnon comes through a time portal and frightens me and I throw a book at him and he takes the book with him through the time portal back to his cave, is that book still a book? Is it then only an object to him? Less than fiction? If the Cro-Magnons are sitting around a fire and passing the book around and curiously looking at it but then one disgruntled Cro-Magnon throws it in the fire and it burns, are the Cro-Magnons guilty of book burning? Are Cro-Magnons fascists? If the next night hundreds of Cro-Magnons come through the time portal, and take thousands of books with them, and pile them up in the cave as kindling, are they guilty of a crime? Are they guilty of repressing the right to free speech? Or in the future when all our books would be good for burning for any cold-blooded species that survives the apocalypse and is able to make fire in a land of fire, would there be any relevance to the question of the legality or the philosophical questions of freedom of speech, of expression, of press? Such questions will not be asked simply because no one will be there to ask them. Glue food for cockroaches. All our fictions would be destroyed too. Or rather our fictions could not be destroyed because they never existed in the first place. And yet did not our fictions have effects? The transcendental ego scratches against the backs of our brains like hungry mice in between the walls. When the Cro-Magnons met the Neanderthals on the landscapes of France and Spain, did the Cro-Magnons kill the Neanderthals with weapons or did they kill them with words? If Gustave Flaubert is invited to a masked costume party and comes dressed as Madame Bovary, is he really Madame Bovary? Flaubert is Madame Bovary but Madame Bovary is not

Flaubert? Respect the tale, text, not the author. The author is the text but the text is not the author. The sunset is not just grammar, but perception and knowledge... or, the author is the text but the text is not the author. This most sublime and profound paradox. I am that other but that other is not me. There is that spot in the middle of the bridge that transcends us.

I take a book out from the library.

Document 67-2256

No. 3652   Expires Dec. 3, 1967
Name: Stephen Cazzaza
Address: 101 Summit Street, Oyster Bay
Present this card each time you borrow a book
You are responsible for books borrowed on this card
Oyster Bay Public Library Identification Card

The letter I (and its namesakes) has no support. It has no round bottom like C and G that can roll back and forth like Japanese Daruma dolls. Do these writers build the structure of their books on the word I? This insecure I? It would be so easy to push it over... so easy to topple it... like the myth of Gustave Courbet pulling down the great "I" of the Vendôme Column. You desire not to desire? You desire real democracy? Collapse the I. You'll have to cut off more than its foreskin to achieve that! Look at the quotation marks around the I... that's no help! *Mai oui...* but Courbet didn't have the problem of the tottering I... he had the *Je*, a buddy system; if the J topples over it can lean on the e. Or Knut Hamsun, he had the *Jeg*, a stronger buddy system yet! Or Osamu Dazai in Japan, with the I-Novel. The *Watashi*... in this form:私 so sturdy, so intricate and complex, so powerful and sometimes more powerful in its absence! The *Watashi* has many protean forms and subtle implications. *Boku... watakushi... ore...* oh the tragic sufferers. *Fich! Ich!* Enough with the I! Out! Out! Damn word!

Sundays are the longest chapters... and today is Sunday. The J is my Kafka K...but now it's my S... and this is how you finally and foolishly choose to begin this book at this late and empty hour, even though some parts of it were begun forty years ago and some forty minutes ago... but what is time after all when confined inside the creative process? Time sneaks by... and you leave behind somewhere all the false beginnings and fancy facades of folly below yo ho ho and beyond that and now you decide if you actually do decide to impose the black badge of finality if there can be finality upon this irony, this ambiguity, this absurdity, this monstrosity, this deformity, this still birth, these irrational steps downward to the cellar and tripping and falling and stumbling and tumbling over the threshold into the dark and deep beneath you... below (see below) and keep going, falling... why? Because you are falling into the beginning that cannot be the beginning... it is nothing at all... all in all is nothing at all... subject in subject is a paradox, the pre-beginning, the prologue is epilogue, which is the impossible aporia that tautologically erases itself as it writes itself, and writes itself as it erases itself... the word before the word is no word at all... the thought after no thought is no thought at all... the J is my K... unknown, unknowable, anonymous, alien, trapped, this sickness, this nausea, this castle, this trial, this stranger, this underground, the J is so misshapen, a mishap, a misfortune... like the K... just a twist here and torsion there and like little Johan writhen and tortured and all meaning dissolving... these are hints and hindrances and hindsight... but I transcribe to the other, I bestow and bequeath my J... which is *Je* or the *Jeg* or the I... or the *Watashi*, but not itself to the other (but how could that get in here?) Do these verbalizations of play end when you come to the end of your language? Like you come to the end of your tether... the end of your rope, the knots, the burns on the skin, oh and now I see I think... you had already begun many years ago and maybe only yesterday...

In the beginning I was falling from the sky and I was crying as I was falling and I was calling for help as I was crying as I was falling from the sky... and on the land I saw a man and the man was crying too... and I was wondering why he was crying when I was falling out of the sky of blue.

In the beginning I was drowning in the river and I was crying as I was drowning and I was calling for help as I was crying as I was drowning in the river... and on the land I saw a man and the man was crying too... and I was wondering why he was crying when I was the one drowning in a sea of blue.

In the beginning I was dying as I was lying in bed and I was crying as I was dying and I was calling for help as I was dying as I was crying as I was lying in bed... and in my room I saw a man and the man was crying too... and I was wondering why he was crying when I was dying in a bed of blue... in the beginning...

"I got to go..." I said.

"Go where?" said my mother.

"Bathroom," added my father.

Several moments pass...

"Oh, I got to go."

"So go... you don't have to announce it, do you? Do you want me to go for you?" said my father.

"No..." I said. "No one else can shit for me..."

...or die for me, I said, departing, walking down the stairs, as the French say... but in French.

I stepped out into the hallway. The other students were veering passed me from the classroom door. I froze. My mind expanded like a balloon. I was about to explode. My mind went blank. Is this a dream? Can I wake myself up? Suddenly the halls were empty and I found myself standing on the landing between the third and fourth floors. I could not remember what my next class was... could not remember the room, the floor... anxiety crushed my consciousness and flattened my memory... fear of what? I could not say... I was stuck between floors... I sat down on the stairs and waited... the bell rang... I walked into the hallway with the crowd and went down the stairs and out the backdoor...

You know, as much as I have read in my unguided way, I'm not some autodidact who reads every book in the library from A to Z... and yet I always return to the roots of my awakening... the existential drift... I'm still that sixteen-year-old in his room with his head against the wall in tears of anxiety and loneliness... walking in place, who found the only words that spoke to him were the existential, the dreadful practice of every day... that lonely confused kid who felt the weight of his self-consciousness like a rock, a crucible, on the mind... who felt despair, who never could see the big picture, who never could read into the great systems of social order... the utopian dreams...to hell with systems! Who read instead the books that rubbed against the grain of society, writers who were solitarily confined in walking in unknown places, and whose words defied and defiled the white paper, whose words defined the edges, where the ink spills like blood, Kierkegaard, Dostoyevsky, Baudelaire, Rimbaud, Hamsun, Céline, Miller, Cendrars, Kerouac... and if I name names, I name myself...

To receive a name from whom names were given... for the name is freely given and the name is given from the named... we didn't ask the name, we just gave it, and to be subject to a name from whom names were subjected is for the name to be handed down and the name is handed down from the named... and being so named he is known out there in the world... but there is no out there in the world from in here in the mind when the mind is a self-target for the arrows of anxiety... and yet they are coming here to reveal him... but there is nothing here and it is everything... they are coming here to reveal him to himself as he himself conceals himself to himself... none of these words are philosophically technical... or rigorously terminological... just a forgotten remembered memory of a moment out of disjointed time... in the sense of an elaboration of an emotional memory becoming a flux of faint mental images hardened by the elaboration and sedimentation of language... so there is a young boy of thirteen... a boy thrown into the bushes... internally driven by external forces... he takes a walk down a path, a kind of secret path... in the back yard and along the side of the other back yards... at the back of the back yards, to a place well enshrouded by bushes and leaves... but there is only one path to here and it's a straight path that terminates in empirical hidden-ness... he encounters a high fence and he is frightened of heights so he will not escape anymore on this day... a plunked-down object in the world... of no escape... of no exit... his name is on their lips... his identity is known... he knows that they know him by name... he knows that they are thinking of him... and they must also know that he is thinking of them... therefore they must know his fear... his fear of them, if they are capable of empathy... if they are not psychotic... which may be the case... power and institutions... he is conscious of himself being conscious of them... like a stalking animal is conscious of its body and simultaneously conscious of its prey... but the boy is a subjective prey so he is self-conscious in a way that the animal is not... he is not self-conscious in the way that he is self-conscious in the presence of others... he is self-conscious in the way that he is conscious of death and nothingness... death and nothing are the boy's prey... why for one so young you might ask?... they are there in his alone-ness, in his separateness... they hang over him like his anxiety... like a sword... a beheadedness of being... a questioning of here and now... a stuck-ness in the now, yielding a tentative self-presence in the here... why the fuck do they care? The rule enforcer has withdrawn... the behavior en-shaper has ascended... his reappearance is inevitable... the minder of minds removes the body... but I am alone... this amounts to my aloneness and accounts for my aloneness as a subject for this world... subjected to its horror... subjected to its pain... to night... to nothing... to time... to being... as subjected to this specific path... being led down the path... the opening unto the light of the world... the path you must take... and the path you take to escape... and the paths you take, that you impossibly choose to take... the path of a future and undetermined freedom as an embodiment of being... a subject about to move... to turn... to incarnate this event... to see... that I do not belong here as I am... but walking in place and falling I am becoming myself in fear and trembling... it appears to me as something strange and fortuitous but it feels to me like some strange impossible destiny. Rimbaud was right. I am an other. I am other than I am to become myself again. The elevation of the other and the decentering of the subject, the dis-identification of the self, of self-presence, to become a stranger to oneself, not to pass judgment, not to categorize, not to compartmentalize, not to partition, not to part the part, not to reduce the irreducible... but then paradoxically to barricade the mind against the orders of the other, the voice of the parents, the priests, the teachers, the generals, the police, the judges, to swear against the swearing in, to abstain, and partake of the same again... and protect itself from the other. Janus, at the exact hour of midnight, looks down, looks up, tastes wine, tastes bread, the moment that presence in absence appears...

There is a crime scene here. Who killed the subject? Who killed the author? The subtext is the self-text. A moving shadow disrupting the surface. Gasping for air. The dark night passes like a dream. I speak again at break of day. I write. I can't. I will. My *I* is an affliction of the will. The light blinds. I am writing these words. What more do you want of me? I feel these words in my throat. Am I gagging? Am I eating my words? Is this a gag? None of this matters. You have to get through all this to go on. The tongue wags. The jaw drops. Ancient man rises in the dust. Do I need this physical wall to speak through this hot prison skull? Do I need a limit? A measure?

Our world is not bereft of plenitude. The things of our world are not hidden in a chamber of white ice and blankness. Nor in the heated room of Descartes' mind. Close my eyes. Close my mouth. Close my ears. Touch nothing. Smell nothing. Can I doubt that I am thinking? Am I deceived? By whom? By words? By the self? Loss of self? Unknown self? History? By the unconscious? By false consciousness? Inside is more scary than the outside? They are before our eyes. The world is not just pieces of unseen molecules spinning. Not just atomized specks called particles or waves or strings, but you can't swim in those waves or tie those strings in a knot or play marbles with those particles? But maybe you can. What else are words for? And what else? Is there anything else? Is it just a whale spouting water of no consequence? Is it just a hairy creature grunting words of no consequence? Is it just someone named Hamlet speaking words words words of no consequence. To himself. In his mind. But yet we hear him. Why? Why not these words? But it's also a void of plenty. Contradiction. The ambiguities. A filled nothingness or a fulfilled emptiness...

In the beginning was the thing. In sensation was this thing brought into awareness. This object perceived, but sensation is not perception nor understanding. If it were, there would be no way out of this circle of representation, of thought, of arbitrary words. It's the canteen, gun, and helmet that my father carried with him when he trudged up the hills of Italy in World War Two and when he marched into a city still called Rome but that was no longer the Rome of a dead ancient empire. My Norwegian uncle used to tease me by saying that my father helped to hang Mussolini from a lamp-post. But my father really only dreamed of playing first base for the New York Giants, who are also no more, but that dream died long ago and nothing seemed ever to take its place. My father is also no more. My father used to tell me about the game that he went to at the Polo Grounds in 1933. He went with his Uncle Harry and his older brother. It was a doubleheader on a Sunday. My father always told me that in the first game the Giants beat the St. Louis Cardinals 1-0 and the game lasted 18 innings. The Giants pitcher Carl Hubbell pitched the entire 18 innings and the Cardinals pitcher Dizzy Dean also pitched the entire game. The game is inscribed in many books of baseball statistics and was also engraved in my father's memory. But did his memory deceive him?

My father and I were at a Mets game at Shea Stadium in 1969. Willie McCovey hit a home run. The event of that home run is also inscribed in a book. But that the home run was a line drive off the narrow right field scoreboard, and that my father told me that it was the hardest ball that he ever saw hit, that not even Bill Terry or Mel Ott or Willie Mays or Bobby Thompson (though Thompson's playoff home run in 1956 took on a life of its own) ever hit one that hard, and his words to me and that memory are not inscribed in that book, his words and the moment of that event on that day are only recorded in my memory and my perspective from my seat. And when I die it dies with me. Except that I've inscribed it here. In words. In this book. No more. But I still talk about it. There was another game that we saw at Shea Stadium in 1969, and I don't remember much of the game, but I do remember some drunk guy who sat in front of us. He stood up most of the game holding a plastic glass of beer in his hand. He wobbled around as he shouted and gestured toward the field. The Mets had a second baseman named Ken Boswell. The drunk enjoyed saying his name. He dragged it out and slurred the name: Baaarzz-Well... Baaarzz-Well... and he kept saying it over and over throughout the game. The only reason that I mention this episode is that my father and I for the next thirty years or so would reiterate this nonsensical and absurd verbal memory of the drunk. It would spring up from our memories spontaneously, as if we had some proleptic notion simultaneously and we both would blurt out: *Baaarzz-Well... Baaarz-Well.* The word had to be uttered precisely for the full effect, with a drunken sounding *Baaarz* and a lilting suddenly sharper pitched *Well*, that only the two of us knew, like some private language, from a private memory. Life of Father and Son.

Would you like to be accused of a murder that you know you didn't commit but that you still might have doubts about it because you know that you sleepwalk or have hallucinations or are protecting someone or have had psychic trauma in your life. And then have the judge, not a family court judge, not Judge Amberstein, but Judge Nietzsche, who begins the proceedings by declaring that the prosecution and the defense should disregard the facts of the case because we know at least since Descartes, Hegel and Kant, that there are only subjective interpretations. Nevertheless, be practical. Well, under these circumstances it might be normal to panic, because you are quite certain that you know the facts, but will the jurors be convinced by your testimony? Then again you might surmise that the jurors under these proscribed rules could only establish reasonable doubt. But would they? Is this what they call a dilemma?

The defense attorney is a pro bono defender of the people, a certain Mr. Kafka. But it really should be my brother on trial! Not me! He was reading Dostoyevsky's *Crime and Punishment*. He killed an old woman by stabbing her one time in the back. He then ran across the street. I was on the other side of the street and he was running toward me. A car hit him. He died. So I ran to him and picked up the bloodstained knife. I was accused of the crime. The prosecution's lawyer spoke first, "Well, here are our interpretation of the facts." But the judge pounded his gavel and said that there are no facts. "Ok, then here is my interpretation of the events of the crime." Is there a pattern of events in our science of experience? Is there an authentic search for the patterns in one's life? Are these events without meaning because they are just arbitrary or arbitrarily just? Well, if you can't be just... be arbitrary, said the Judge, and his act without intention is just a mechanical stab at ontology? An absurd human fidelity to the human race or an instinctive human fidelity to life? He still has his life... he has his life, doesn't he? You doubt your memory or the documents in your hand? Is there nothing to justify this? Only record and represent. These are men who act with authority and have the institutional authority to act. In the name of the law. He wanted to live, just live... not a great act, not a speech-act... he stuttered... but he understood his orders and the false charges against him.

Billy Budd is hanged at dawn. Guilty of fomenting an insurrection and mutiny in a time of war. A report of the event is logged in a book. Institutional force is inscribed in documents. Force knows that it just has to act and it's too late. Fate and history. Time will tell. But it's always been too late. Force rules all... and then false documents justify actions. But why bother to justify? To rationalize? To explain the inexplicable? What can you do? They are not just *above* the law; they *are* the law. The presence of the voice in a spatial assignment is politically authoritarian. The theft of words in a temporal disjointment is politically aesthetic. Oh, your honor Nietzsche, how did the Nazis interpret you? I am not on trial! I agree.

Someone on the war ship had to scribble some words, scribble down his experience of the event, the spectacle, a poem. Somewhere in some archive, somewhere in oblivion, there is a document that subverts the law, some dirty and heretical printed matter, that subverts the official version pronounced as the final word on the matter. Is there a final word? Is it too late to speak? No voice from silence. I am illiterate. I stutter. I strike out. The mask reveals another mask. The erosion reveals just more surface. Why do these philosophers want to silence the voice of the subject? We haven't all had our chance to speak and be heard, or write and be read, yet. Emerson had the words of the day. Seize the words of the night! The letter can kill. The spirit can kill. The facts can kill. The interpretation can kill.

Minner som min mor fortalte mig

"...Jesus lever, Jesus lever, og kan ei forandre seg; far og mor, ja hjem og fremtid – alt, ja alt Han er for meg..."

"ja, ja, det er slutten...lille Tulle..."

Her grandpa whom she called Papa put the *sangboken*, the songbook, gently down on the table. Little Tulle smiled at him. She was so restless. Now she had permission to go outside and play. It was a bright Sunday morning. The sun glaring low across the fjord, shadowing and shimmering on the gray and silver water of Lundevågen, and brilliantly bouncing over the red rooftops of the hilly and harbor town of Farsund, on the other side of the fjord, flashing back on the small white house out of whose door little Tulle runs out of and into the sloping field, her house shining under the rocky bulk of a small mountain dotted with several other similar small white wooden dwellings, and grazing cows, the sunlight falling softly on her yellow-reddish hair, as she picks petals from a wildflower, the North Sea winds swirling the grass and bundled stacks of hay... and she speaks softly... counting... ein... to... tre... fer... fem...

The Countdown

10-9-8-7-6-5-4-3-2-1

...fire... he pulled the trigger... blast off...

The missile ascended in its parabolic flight, reached its vertex, focused on its target, its arc feeling the force of gravity and the missile pulling downward towards its destination. The missile landed at the feet of PFC Joe Cazzaza.

"Hit the dirt!" shouted voices. It was mud. Italian mud. Best glue in the world. The mortars impacted the earth. The base of the hill was right in front of him. The foxhole was too far behind. He ran up the hill as fast as he could. Smoke engulfed him. A hot bit of shrapnel cut across his back. He kept going. Company B trudged up the hill to engage the enemy. Tossing grenades into the darkness. Guns flashing. Why do those damn kraut guns never flash in the darkness like our guns? His platoon went up the brow of the slope, up the northeast slope of Hill 131. The mortars and machine-guns were held ready. Company B drew some machine-gun fire, but it soon stopped. The enemy had abandoned their positions on the hilltop, and with no more German assaults, Joe Cazzaza advanced straight up the hill. At the crest the squad struck a minefield, which was surrounded by concertina wire. A German soldier was draped dead on the wire, collapsed over his machine gun. Several mines exploded. Five men were killed and seven wounded. Joe's best buddy stumbled toward him and fell at his feet. Santa Maria Infante would soon be taken. The small village in the hills was completely destroyed. It was just a pile of rubble. Mud and rubble.

Stephen ran over to retrieve the plastic white missile with the rubber-nosed tip. His father bent down from his chair, picked it up, and handed it to Stephen. His father said nothing. Stephen ran back to his new Christmas toy: the X-500 Missile Defense Base and Rocket Launcher. He pushed the missile back into its spring-loaded launcher and counted down from 10 again... fire! He shouted... he pulled the trigger... blastoff! He shouted... pssshaah. The toy missile hit his father on the arm this time. His father puffed his pipe. He didn't flinch. Stephen picked up the missile from the floor and noticed his toy car. He grabbed the car and pushed it along the floor. Vroom vroom. Beep-beep. He pushed the toy car until it bumped into his father's big black working shoe. Stephen pushed the car over his father's shoe, up his leg, up his arm, over his back, down his chest, over his stomach, down his leg, over his shoe and back onto the floor. He pretended to drive the car on the secret road. He returned to his toy and prepared to launch another rocket into space.

Four years later, in 1966, Stephen advanced from his fourth grade class to the school finals in the Science Fair with his project *Space Stations and Satellites*. He covered a small rubber ball with crate paper and taped black squares around the ball. He hung it in a box and strung a piece of yarn from the back of the box, upon which he had drawn a picture of the earth, to the ball. This was Telstar, the communication satellite. He also got a round rubber black tube that he suspended from a wire attached to a wooden stand that his father had built. On the side of the tube Stephen attached some white paper upon which he had drawn what he assumed was the insides of a space station. And finally he had poster boards, which his father bought in the paper store, with depictions of the Mercury and Gemini capsules and the Atlas booster rocket. It was college material the school principal told Stephen's father. Joe Cazzaza just kind of uncomfortably and silently smiled. Stephen was very shy and his speech that he had to make to accompany his displays was not well prepared. He did not advance to the next level.

Stephen remembers clearly the principal of his elementary school saying to him and his father that Stephen was college material. His father had this dumbfounded expression on his face. He was in school in the thirties. He didn't have much of a chance and then the war called him away anyhow. But in the sixties the nation was in a race with the Soviet Union and we had to educate those children who hadn't had the chance before. Of course all that is changing now. Since the 1970s. We have been given the opportunity to work more, and receive less.

Stephen and a few other boys took an audio-visual class with the principal, in his office! They would wheel in the 16mm projector and learn how to thread the film. Stephen on several occasions had to set up the projector and the screen in the gym. The *Red Balloon* and *An Occurrence at Owl Creek Bridge* were two films the students watched on rainy days when they couldn't go outside for recess. Narrative wonder!

Document 5.4.1

Future Scientists of America
Of the National Science Teachers Association
Presents to
Stephen Cazzaza
Of the Theodore Roosevelt Elementary School
This Certificate of
ACHIEVEMENT IN SCIENCE
Awarded this 10th day of June, 1966

In the same school year that the Science Fair was held, his teacher asked her students to write a poem. Stephen thought about the great white booster rocket. The flames and smoke. They had taken a field trip to Hayden Planetarium. They had taken a field trip to Jones Beach to peer through the telescope at the night sky. The teacher had chosen only four children for the trip. One was Stephen. The teacher drove the children herself. Stephen was proud.

He also imagined a solitary white lighthouse. He was choosing between spacebound or earthbound. Isolation. His mother told him stories about her childhood in Norway during the war. Oh I could write a book about my life, his mother said. But what does that mean? You had a life, didn't you?

Stephen wrote this poem when he was ten years old:
The lighthouse is a lonely place to be.
The beacon is a guiding light
For all the ships that sail at night.
The lighthouse is a lonely place to be.
It is being, I suppose, just like me.

The Downfall

Thinking back now, some fifty years later, Stephen doesn't recall being that lonely at that time, or feeling that lonely at that time, though subsequently he became conscious that he was indeed like a lighthouse on some desolate rocky coastline, the waves crashing at his feet, the beacon dim in the fog, and turning and turning around in this world, flashing into darkness, a pained and despairing point of light. I suppose he wrote that he was lonely because that's what he thought a poem had to be about... loneliness, sadness, and metaphors. The urging of being unto some inanimate otherness; he was *like* a lighthouse; or even more disturbing: he *is* a lighthouse. This was strange and sacramental language and it was filled with fear and loathing. I don't think he wrote another poem until he tossed off the mantle of childish reveries and was visited by that other intruder into our self-ridden minds, knowledge of death, of good and evil, our awareness of its mighty sting, the end of being, the passing into mystery, the loss of time and our beleaguered habitation of space. O dem bones, dem bones. Youth is a land of magic. Vultures and chopsticks gracefully lifting the fragments of transposed memory, the order of things turned backward and forward in an instant; a moment in time held in deferment, a meeting in space... Oh it is so fucking hard waking early on a gloomy sad Sunday morning and writing this kind of shit... such an effort to get up after the day breaks and all is blank here... mom has Alzheimer's. Dad died over ten years ago now. And me? I've become just a goddamn cynic and nihilist.

Still it goes... I am back... it has only been a month. Or is all this contrived? Stephen remembers his uncle typed up his poem on a 1930s Barr-Morse typewriter with the round white keys and black letters. His uncle, who had contracted polio in 1917, and walked with crutches all his life, was the only member of his family to attend college, Rider College, for a brief spell. He had a nervous breakdown at college and had to be taken home by some college buddies. He spent some time in Pilgrim State.

When his brother Joe, Stephen's father, was off in North Africa and Italy in 1944, Stevie had another breakdown and returned to Pilgrim State.

Document 9.4.8

State of New York
Department of Mental Hygiene
Pilgrim State Hospital

I.   In consideration of the placement on convalescent status or a period of one year from Pilgrim State Hospital of West Brentwood, New York, Stephen Cazzaza a patient in said hospital, by the director, I Fiorenza Cazzaza of 105 South Street, Oyster Bay, New York, Mother of said patient, having been made fully acquainted with his mental condition do hereby agree with the Director to maintain, provide and care for said patient, and I do expressly state that I have the means wherewith to do so.

II.   I do further assume all responsibility for his acts and welfare while on placement of convalescent status.

III.   I also agree to defray all necessary expenses if it is necessary to return him to the hospital.

IV.   I also further agree to have him brought to the mental clinic Pilgrim State Hospital Mental Clinic, West Brentwood, New York, once a month during hours listed below with some member of the family with whom he resides.

V.   I further agree to notify the hospital in writing of the mental condition of the patient at times specified or requested.

VI.   I agree to promptly notify the hospital should the patient die during convalescent status.

Inscribed this 10th day of June 1944

After the war Uncle Stevie took a correspondence course in "watch and jewelry repair," and he worked for a while in Smith's Jewelers, which was located on the other side of South Street, directly across from Uncle Stevie's home, with its front rooms and windows, a section of the brick artifice that occupied the west side of South Street, the Cazzaza Building as it would come to be known for many years and even to this day when all the Cazzazas have gone away. From the windows in the front rooms his mother and sister could watch him cross the street and go to work in the morning, and the same when he came back home after work. He came out of the alley beneath their front rooms and returned into the alley on his way home. Stevie worked in the jewelers for a few years but then withdrew from the world and remained in his room where he lived in partial isolation along with his mother and sister who dwelled in the old brick structure for the next forty years as the family had dwelled there for the previous thirty years. Uncle Stevie every now and then made his way down the stairs and through the alley to buy the newspapers in the paper store.

Uncle Stevie is my namesake. My name is Stephen. Please don't mistake me for the name of that person on the cover of this book. The Author, he says with a spiteful smirk. He was shot and is fighting (perhaps not fighting) for his life in a hospital in New York City. Did I mention that yet? Or was I shot? I get so mixed up. After forty years of this crap I have lost track. I was thinking of my Uncle Stevie... an image in my mind, if that is what it is... a movement, a thought, and I realized that I am the only person in the universe who is thinking of this singular person who once lived and had his name inscribed in signatures and documents, from birth through school to work to death... in the multiple ways that a society will take down names and numbers... names and numbers that fade with time, and I remember his funeral and the hearse driving past the "Cazzaza building" on South Street as was the custom for all the funerals of Cazzazas, and in the church service which was attended by just the closest family members, no more than ten or twelve, and that as we walked up the aisle leaving the church my father noticed a woman by herself sitting in a pew in the back of the church and he spoke with her briefly and I heard her say that she went to school with my uncle, and that was it... and now as I am writing and thinking this, that nobody is left of my uncle's sisters and brothers... that he lived with his sister in the building on South Street and that I... I alone like Ishmael, like Elijah, like Professor Pierre Aronnax, live to tell his brief story which no one can know... that I alone am thinking of him, only in my mind, and that he is one of millions upon millions of people who lived on this earth and will be forgotten... even every baby born now today and the oldest of the living will one day be forgotten... completely. And our knowledge is only the knowledge of knowledge that is given to us in vain, in the absurd hope of hope. Captain Nemo bows before the pictures of his wife and children. Captain Ahab sees his wife and child in Starbuck's eyes. For a moment they turn away from the horror. The horror. Enough. Enough. This feeling, this mood, as I near sleep and think of him, this vague and ambiguous image and memory, that I am so alone in this thought, that I am as alone as I can be with this thought, that I have to let go of this thought, this image, whatever it is, that I have to let it go that I might survive… there is no escape from civilization. Gaze from the window to the streets of the city. O my intended, he uttered your name at the last breath… the big white lie.

So what follows is what I suppose is a book- fiction? a novel? And it is supposed to be about something or other, if I am not mistaken. It should have its intentionality, about something, for something, for whatever reasons; that something is the case; just like my ten-year-old self thought about what a poem was supposed to be about (just *like* my ten-year-old self? Am I just a metaphor, a simile, a symbol of my previous self, some marks on paper?) a kind of uttered falsehood elevated to the intensity level of immaculate delivery of an un-payable debt… to whom do I owe this debt? Damn I'm doing my level best. To let it become or not to let it become? Bring it to light or leave it forever in darkness? Not even darkness. Darker than darkness. Before the darkness. To withhold this gift or to offer this gift? A gift of death? How did Dr. Destouches offer his creation to the world? How did Doktor Frankenstein introduce his creature to the world? He abandoned it. Am I a freak of nature? Should I abandon this monstrosity? The creature and I have a lot in common. We both discovered a satchel of books. We are both autodidacts. We both just (dis)figured it out as we went merrily and brightly along the way. We both have a funny way of walking in place… well, at least Boris Karloff's interpretation of the monster. What did the bitch in heat, the wolf, howl at Modernism's apex? It's just a book written by a self-taught workingman. Yes, Virginia, there is a Molly. The classic movie monsters. Frankenstein's monster, the werewolf, and Dracula. Boris Karloff, Lon Chaney Jr., and Bela Lugosi. Oh how my mother loved the movies, and the *film noir*, my mother liked the anti-hero Richard Widmark, as long as he was a decent man in real life, she read in some magazine that he was, and she loved the classic horror flicks. My parents saw Bela Lugosi on a stage in Glen Cove one Halloween night in 1950… a spook show. He rose from his coffin and addressed the audience. "Good eeee-vening." Then they watched some terrible B movie... well, mother and father, here is my terrible B book.

Or I should prefer not to... prefer not to what? Prefer not to dance? Prefer not to sing? Prefer not to run? Prefer not to jump? Prefer not to stand? Prefer not to walk? Prefer not to live? Prefer not to die? Prefer not to write this book? Eh Bartleby? Even that strangely sympathetic capitalist treats you as if you were a human being. Do you remember the German Romantic poets? Prefer not to... not to be... the pre-verb, the Ur-verb, being and nothingness. Sleep is good, said the creature. Death is better, said the creature. Never to be born is the best, said the creature... *nie geboren sein*... and never to be created, said the creature in the high Gothic night. And this object? This book? Was it created? Was it born? Ah, once we lived as the gods so what more do we need? The Romantic yearning for life against death. Heine. Holderlin. Hegel. Heidegger. Herder. Was that other final H born of that urging of passion and soil and blood? *Sturm und Drang*. Should we include the S? Schelling? Schlegel? Schiller? My God, how incredibly Superficial. Can I un-birth the thing that has grown inside of me for so long? Abandon it? Ah Birth! Ah Bartleby! Ah Creation! Ah Creature! There it is... the monster, the book, if it could talk it would say to me that you are my creator but I am your master! I bow before thee O master. Lead on. But Bartleby and Baudelaire lead to what end of night? "When just a child," stated Baudelaire, "I felt two contradictory sentiments in my heart, the horror of life and the ecstasy of life."

I am such a lazy and nervous person, therefore, now, just for fun, because it's getting rather morose in here, for those of you who have chosen to continue down this much trodden and beaten road too much taken (don't believe the lies about rugged individuality and Frostian Yankee know-how and Thoreauvian disobedience and Emersonian self-reliance and Whitmanesque universality, and Jeffersonian democracy, because they were booted overboard by Herman Melville long ago, booted overboard a crew of false idols of an artificial paradise, who didn't work hard enough at keeping the natural forces of evil at bay, all hail Ahab!) and here's a little game, a lack of confidence trick. You can try to figure out which sentences at the head of paragraphs were once upon a time meant to be the first lines of this book. Intended to be? "In the beginning" is not the beginning, as wise Kierkegaard once wrote. It is a fable. Yes, like waves receding from the shore... boats against the current, beat on beat on beat on... borne back... you've read that somewhere before... nothing new under the sun... on a Sunday morning... and tomorrow... tomorrow... tomorrow... Monday and Tuesday and Wednesday and Thursday and Friday, creeps the middle days of laborious pace, the days of labor and the nights of sleep, pilfering segments of time that belong to power, occupying confidential space that is owned by the other, following repetitive points and directives that lead nowhere, no escaping to the sea, to the road, to the sky... all points on the grid are business points, heavy traffic in all directions, horizontally to end up at the foot of the ladder, vertically to end down at the bottom of the ditch, the perch, the crossroads, the engineer's flight... the third man of the enlightened world... the architect, the technocrat, the fall of the house of usury and the fall of the tower of greed, art and science and work... to begin up and begin down... here to there... there to here... here to here... there to there... no where to go and I can't stay here, to roll on the grass, down the hill, toward the end, toward the cliff... to come to the edge as the whirlwind is twisting and rising... to raise your arms and shout to the blood red horizon in the East... behold the man... the downfall is coming... the bombs are falling... Friday night the author dies... Saturday we travel through our trials and travails... harrowing hell...

It is a beautiful Sunday morning in spring. Judgment Day. You are all guilty. Original Sin. Father didn't care one way or the other. No advice for me. No semblance of emotion from him. He stood in the middle of the bridge. He did not say to me that I should go in that direction. There was no map. I am the map. No terrain. I am geography. Behold the body of the man. And Sunday night we join together to mourn the modern, to moan, to groan, because the night leads to the light, to the day, to the dollar, to work... and to bad faith and bad blood... as Rimbaud exclaimed: Here they come, white and blank, with their guns and a bible, and tomorrow is Monday, and it's October, and I must get dressed and go to work. Here is my other work... my theft of time... all is blank and white here, in the unborn... the journey to the end of birth, the subject before the act, before the word, before the interpretation, the arbitrary sign...

It's time to put an end to philosophy. Why continue to let my "literary" words be abused like this? Why let them fall into the clutches of philosophy? Charles Sanders Peirce worried that his precise philosophical and logical words would "fall into literary clutches," *pace* deconstruction.

Acceptance Speech of Stephen K. Cazzaza
Evening of May 30, 20--

Henry Ruggles J. Thurston Howell III Literary Award.
Awarded for fiction by an American writer.
Awarded to *Sunday Mornings at Oyster Bay* by Stephen K. Cazzaza

The Speech:

Good evening

As my father used to say: Let's just get it over with. My father wasn't talking about an ironic and odious smile of the W. C. Fields manner; he was talking about life, or rather life-lived. Give me the untroubled life, the unengaged life, the quiet life, the undisturbed life, the non-confrontational life, and what's wrong with that? Stay in your room; tend your garden. So said Pascal and Voltaire. I'm ashamed to admit it. What is a writer in his eyes? Never wanted to embarrass the old man. But he couldn't do that either. He couldn't be that alone, within his own mind, the misery of the isolated mind, or within another's mind, a thought, a book, or a green thumb; though he certainly had calloused hands. He planted tulip bulbs upside down. There was a need for money and there was a war to be fought. Let's just get it over with. He applied those words to almost any situation in his life that involved an unfamiliar social activity, that involved meeting new people, that involved anything out of the normal routines of daily life, and sometimes did involve the normal routines of daily life, like cutting grass and home maintenance, like shitting and showering and shopping and paying bills with what little money he had, because the American Dream required it, producing, exchanging, spending, consuming, upkeep, keeping up with the Joneses, no, it's about getting ahead of the Joneses... right? We are all just temporarily not millionaires, someone said; and he just wanted to get it over with; and that was all my mother had, buying stuff, besides her kids. She'd kill for us. She'd go to jail for us. And she was satisfied with us because at least we didn't end up in jail or as drug addicts? But could she be so sure of even that? The illusions of America infect any mind that inhabits that space and time of supreme denial, no matter whence or when it saw the light of day. American exceptionalism! How can you not love that? How could I've written anything if I loved them? That much. As you say to a child with your arms wide open. It was the Post-World War Two world. And as my mother said, when dividing up her memories, there was *"før krigen, under krigen og etter krigen."* There was before the war, during the war and after the war. But there is a bigger question to ask: Why bother at all? Camus asked it. My father was a child of the Depression; that was certainly something that needed to get over with. He was an Army conscript of the Second World War, North Africa and Italy; that was certainly something that needed to get over with. And then a family man with responsibilities in the America of the 1950s and 1960s; was that something that he needed to get over with? I don't know. He was a bartender for twelve years and every long night spent with drunks and the bullshit that they speak was something that he needed to get over with; he was a janitor for the next twenty years and every long day and every long night of work cleaning toilets and mopping up floors was something that he needed to get over with.

He was exactly what America wanted and was everything America despised. A sucker. Never give a sucker an even break. And if that is a contradiction then it is a contradiction deep-rooted in the American soil and its bloody desire for oil and power, a slick black sign of the generative dynamo of exuberant energy that stalks the edge of the cage, expanding and enveloping and leaving the husks of men in the ditch on the side of the road. In other words, more clearly, the American system, and its institutions. He was not a go-getter, not a hustler; he was not part of that "all-devouring word, business," as Whitman saw it in one of his rare phlegmatic moods and then promptly retracted his words by proclaiming great things and advancement for the embryonic nation; it's all right Walt, you contain multitudes and contradictions...

My father was happiest when after work he headed straight to the bar and had a few drinks with the regulars, or when he smoked a cigar or puffed on his pipe and watched the TV, the Lawrence Welk Show, Mitch Miller and his Gang, or a Mets game; the Mets game he gave up on long before he finished his cigar. And retired life was much of the same, drinking, eating and watching TV and, well, enough of that. He died from prostate cancer at eighty; my mother is eighty-six; she has Alzheimer's disease; her memories are no longer divided by major events or small events, rather divided by a terrible wall, and there's nothing on the other side; there's no more I want to say on the matter. I just want to get this over with. Despair, depression... is truth on the other side? Who really knows what's normal? Like Whitman in his great poem *The Sleepers,* we hover... everything and everyone is an exception. We contain multitudes. As for me, there's no despair, there's no depression... just a deep cloying sadness of things, of objects, of finitude, of impermanence, of passing... as the Japanese say, *mono no aware...*

I'll just indulge myself with one brief anecdote to finish. And try to explain why I bothered to show up here for this at all. Years ago my wife and I were browsing in a used bookstore. One of the books she picked up was a journal kept by the French film director Jean Cocteau while he was making the movie *Beauty and the Beast.* I came across a line that I've always remembered. It has to do with awards. I can't remember the exact words so I'll paraphrase: Cocteau quotes his friend Erik Satie, who said to Cocteau, that the point of an award is not to refuse it, the point of an award is not to deserve it in the first place. Jean-Paul Sartre refused his Noble Prize for literature. He failed, according to Jean Cocteau and Erik Satie, unless he actually believed that he deserved it

I never believed that my book, this book, would be considered for any type of award. I believed that my book was outside the mainstream, part of a tradition of revolt, dissent, dissolution and decadence and more in the lineage of Charles Baudelaire, Arthur Rimbaud, Herman Melville, Knut Hamsun, Marcel Proust, James Joyce, Louis-Ferdinand Céline, Robinson Jeffers, John Cowper Powys, Henry Miller, Osamu Dazai, and Jack Kerouac... seekers, searchers, wanderers, modernity, the age of the transitory and the uncertain, that great confrontation with capitalism... but I guess I was wrong. So you have given this award to a book that is a failure. And not to be ungracious and refuse the award because I didn't do a good enough job of not deserving it in the first place, I thank you for it, in the best ironic sense of the post-modern. And now all this is over with. It's time to begin again, like poor old Finnegan... hod carrier of history, and return to the things of this world.

Thank you

...bang... pop... crash... boom...

Sundown and Gunned Down

A man walked up the aisle against the east wall. He pulled a gun out from his jacket, aimed, and fired. Someone shouted: Oh my God they shot the author! They killed the author!

Author Shot at Award Ceremony
By Sigmund Simon Argorilla

The author Stephen Cazzaza is in critical condition at New York Hospital after being shot twice by an unknown assailant at the Albert Hotel last Friday evening as he was leaving the stage during a literary award ceremony. The shooter is in police custody. His identity has not been released... stay tuned... more to come...

He Was Leaving...

The town that Stephen lived in was a small town but it wasn't very far away in distance or for that matter in cultural remoteness from a big town, a really big town, New York City.

The television broadcast stations, CBS, NBC, ABC, channels 2, 4, 7, respectively, on your dial, were concentrated in New York City and brought the local news, sports, weather and entertainment out to the small town because the small town was easily within the reception area of the broadcast stations and accessible by means of a television antenna brandishing various lengths of elements mounted on a pole attached to the roof and pointed in the general direction of the source of the analog signal, which would be roughly west and more or less south, and then strategically rearranged after strong winds and rain and whatnot to reduce static, white noise and ghosting, whereby you followed several blurred fuzzy baseballs instead of one true white baseball flying determinately through the air, as depicted on channel 9 WOR, on the black and white screen of the 12-inch General Electric television that Stephen watches along with his father, as when Willie McCovey smashes a screaming line drive coming across the sky and over the right field wall at Shea Stadium and the Mets lose again and poor Bob Murphy has to give you the unhappy recap, unless of course Tom Seaver is pitching and then the Mets have a more than slim chance to win despite a wretched contingent of feeble hitters... but he doesn't pitch here anymore. It was an August day, a Sunday, in the late summer of 1977 and Tom Seaver was playing for the Cincinnati Reds because, according to a Daily News journalist, he was virtually a Commie Red anyway and as an agitator had to be ousted from the rest of the obedient flock. He had been exiled to Ohio back in June in what was in journalistic hyperbole called the "Midnight Massacre," and he returned to New York to pitch against the Mets and his former teammate and southpaw hurler Jerry Koosman on that ambivalent gloomy Sunday in August before a throng of over 46,000 spectators, which included Stephen and his father. The Reds won 5-1. Seaver pitched a complete game and struck out eleven. The Mets finished the season with 98 losses. Shea Stadium had become Grant's Tomb, named in dishonor of M. Donald Grant, a Wall Street stockbroker and the chairman of the board of the New York Metropolitan Baseball Club, Inc., of the former and never realized Continental League, and at present falsely posturing as the National League's New York Mets, a team once amazing and miraculous and lovable and believable, but now consigned to the abysmal basement, last place, the very lowest level of baseball hell.

And it was a hellish and turbulent summer in New York, make no mistake, because of harsh and forbidding conditions, but it was also an exciting, rousing, and thought-provoking time. There was a financial crisis, another downward turn in capitalism's fun roller-coaster ride. There was a rancorous mayoral contest. The lights went out all over the place. Shea Stadium went dark in the bottom of the sixth inning, which was symbolically appropriate; it reflected and echoed the pessimism and despair of Met fans. It was not the resounding echo of cheering and joy that had descended from the upper reaches of Shea Stadium when Stephen attended games with his father back in the sixties and the tumultuous roar of the crowd settled upon him like an avalanche of exhilaration. He never heard anything like it before or since.

And the Bronx was burning. There was looting and rioting. The Yankees were winning, drat, albeit their clubhouse was conflict-ridden. New York had been a Met town from 1964 until at least the mid-seventies, before the evildoer Steinbrenner's reign. Stephen had friends who were Yankee fans; but one day he said that a broken-down Mickey Mantle swung like a rusted gate, and fists were flying.

And Elvis had only just died. And crazy aunt Teresa and crippled uncle Stevie died. The Ramones were alive, strumming, and thrumming at CBGB. The .44 caliber killer, Son of Sam, was recently apprehended in Yonkers and brought into police custody. There had been rumors that he was out here on Long Island. There were endless speculation and gossip among Stephen's three sisters and their friends. Don't go out at night! Don't sit in your car! And before year's end both Groucho Marx and Charlie Chaplin would be dead. It was not a funny year, but out of economic degradation comes a better and more vibrant culture, Nietzsche said, and laughs could still be had if you wanted such a thing, by watching two uptight Manhattanites and their Jewasp sexual angst being played out in the movie Annie Hall. People were lining up around the blocks to see that one.

Stephen grew up watching movies with his mom and dad. Either in the movie theater on Audrey Avenue where this little old guy named Pete collected the ticket stubs, or on the television. The other independent UHF television stations in New York, in addition to WOR 9, were WNEW 5, and WPIX 11. It became a yearly tradition to watch certain movies at certain seasonal times of the year. And channels 5, 9 11, respectively, on your dial, provided a warehouse of black and white speckled and dotted films. At Christmas Stephen and his family all sat down to watch *A Christmas Carol*, the definitive version with Alastair Sim. At Thanksgiving for some reason *King Kong* and *Mighty Joe Young* were aired and attentively watched, along with Laurel and Hardy in *March of the Wooden Soldiers*. Halloween brought Vincent Price in *House on Haunted Hill.* They'll come for me next and then they'll come for you. The Fourth of July was always enjoyed along with multi-talented Jimmy Cagney in *Yankee Doodle Dandy*.

But now Stephen was twenty-one. A dropout. No fun. No future. No certain plans. Working as a landscaper on one of the huge estates of the North Shore Long Island wealthy. They were still here. No, it was not a funny year. Then on a Sunday morning in September he boarded a train of the Long Island Railroad, at Oyster Bay, the last station on the line, and departed for New York City. He was leaving Combray. He was leaving Charleville. He was leaving Orero. She was leaving Lundevågen. He was leaving Lowell. He was leaving Brooklyn. He was leaving Edo. He was leaving... he was leaving... *Si tu peux rester, reste; Pars, s'il le faut.* But I can't stay here and there's nowhere to go... but everywhere?

Invocation #1
Starting from a strange community on a slender fish-shaped island, in the tilting presence of this continent, this country, this state, this city, this town, this hamlet, this humdrum, from the Fifth-month grass and muck

under his youthful feet, over the big lawns and beach sands and paved tar roads and concrete, through the ash-heap in the valley of abstract Moloch, to the business of all-eyes are on us pragmatic Mammon, the filth of the floor in Mahagonny, the fleeting glimpse of the pristine lilac shore, the celestial beauty, the crowning wonder, all of a sudden the dark forest, the alley between the bar and the paper store, the maelstrom, the descent, from the mountains to the sea, katabasis, the door, the madness, the murder, the loomings of violence; hark! America, we have all we need, guns and a bibel, protect us from them Injuns and slaves, in the native blood-red soil of slaughter and endless black ribbons hung from plantation trees, cottonmouths in the south, schooners across the prairies, the worker's toil, the man-made canal, the main street banal, hammer and nails, blood on the rails, the towers of cement and steel, the rivers, the roads, the mountains and fields, from ocean to ocean white with foaming at the mouth, the carcass of the buffalo and the mighty hunted whales; America, we have all we need, drawing-room coffee spoons, long harpoons, tall tales, tall sails, guns and a bible, and a bright light to guide us over the land where we live anew, new world of happiness and century of doom, over hill, over dale, over the seven seas, Company B in Italy, Army squad leader, sergeant Joe Cazzaza, Naples and Vesuvius, and to the north, grandfather pray for little Tulle, carrying hay on her back, to bring to the cows, thumbing her nose at a Nazi soldier, the maelstrom, future fated bride and groom, hated tide of immigrants, laborer's pride, this land was ours, beep-beep boom, the last ride, the forsaken neighbor, desolate and void, restless and paranoid, the lone pilgrim, the cross and crossroads, the enterprising hustler, the go-getter greed, the material progress, that's what makes America great, boys, and a piece of brick to scrawl this obscenity upon the white steps of your mansions, the hollow last green gasp of desire; Stephen climbing the pile of oyster shells down by the docks, looking out to the bay, the city of gold on the blackened hill; America, we have all we need, money, missiles, bombs, pills, prisons, guns and a bible, and when the brown boot comes down upon the nape, escape, crash of the dollar sign on Main Street, the horror, the war and shit, exterminate the swine whore who bore it, the class wage war automobile, the ghoulish hired hands grasping at the grinding wheel, flight, exile, silence, in the presence of other continents and other cities, above and below the invisible tropics, from jagged coasts of shallow commodities, to hunger and mysteries and wild cod off a North Sea coastal town, Farsund, Orero, London, Vienna, the last story told at the end of night in a blue room in Paris, a slashed wrist, the blank beast, the journey of the sun and moon on the narrow road to the East, and in the beginning once upon my words on paper, hast eaten the flesh, hast seen the white

Invocation #2

lines flashing by on the road. Merging traffic. Merging into character. To Chicago, mundane city, prosaic city, practical people, REAL city, most American of all cities, here we come, I'm driving a silver van, my daughter says I'm the man in the silver van, my wife says my name, Stephen, is that my name? A year ago in May my father died, almost a year ago in September the Trade Centers came crashing down on the world, and here we are driving on the road, among the moving, hauling, traveling, ever faster and faster, cattle, hogs, lumber, grain, on the canals, trucks and trains, Route 66, the Mother Road, the Dust Bowl, but in Illinois it was "slab all the way." Bland houses in corn maze patterns, suburban trimmed grass, where does the city end and nature begin? This is the prairie land, heart of the Midwest, gate to the western skies, the wide Mississippi, the tall grass, the fearful open, where they first gathered by the rivers, fur traders and French priests when the Europeans came, then Easterners came, settlers moved west, a sea of grass, space was destroyed by the railroads and the great Reaper McCormick, out of the eastern forests and down from the skyscrapers to encounter the great wide open, space annihilated by time, prehistoric ancestors climbed out of the trees and entered the grass lands of the world, the grass lands of the American Midwest, the Ilanos of Venezuela, the Pampas of Argentina, the Campos of Brazil, the Steppes of Central Asia, the Savannas of Africa, the grass of the baseball field and the lawns of suburbia, fires on the prairie, Chicago burnt in 1871, winds from the prairie blew, this landscape looked upon by native romantics, the tall grass by the railroad tracks, but who saw the workers? The chinks, the micks, the guineas, who sees you, a worker, Bucky Hely, who sees you?

Journeying toward the threshold of the heartland, the oracular snake of the Mississippi rising up in the mist to strike at me, heartless exile of the riverboats twain splitting in descending Western courses and spitting into the cardinal winds, bending the alphabetic rice stalks, driverless, rudderless, wheels rolling here and there, wherever rivers and roads go, the only direction left is down, right as rain, dismal, abysmal, search, anabasis, fall of common graces, common places, common faces, the broad flat and open expanses of light, the prairie madness, the settlers on their prairie schooners, the tales of separation, the long silences of the endless grassland, the hands working the land, the broken wooden blades of the plows, a place to work, to grow, to spread the Word of God, to spread the seeds, to spread the ink, to spread the sky over the isolation like a vast smothering blanket of grief. Entering the real city. Oh my slouching and drooping heavy shoulders. I remember the sadness of the janitor sweeping left and right, mopping up and down. The drowning sound of the toilet draining, swirling around and around and one good eye staring into it. The trolly conductor wearing a black armband on his sleeve. The hinge that creaks in the night. Here I am in America sitting in another chair, no longer reading the newspaper, just another place in the sad burning world, another restless spotless along the weary way, where the day crosses the paths of time at the last intersection of life, slowing modes of transportation, car I drive, train I ride, walk like Walt, walk the line, walk like a man, this place as well as another to begin this story at the end of the dreary day, because when the dream fades over the hills beyond the foreign cities and the exotic lands where once my heart opened, and wines flowed, in the end you go where the work is... right, Jack? Hit the hay, Henry, and all your talk is of yesterday and tomorrow, and all your sweat and tears are in the heavy nightmare-moulded clay of today... hey hey Arthur, run away, run away, bound away, but I rise at five in darkness like a farmer named Knut, I sleep at eight... I wake at one to pee, I dream of the sea, Herman... all the livelong day... strumming on the old banjo... and singing... *senro wa tsuzuku yo doko made mo...* on the old shamisen and that poor man...

Invocation #3

Bartleby is a non-self, perhaps an anti-self, just an awkward body with slightly moveable parts, an absurd self-conscious subject not in search of a barely glimpsed or discernible self... and therefore not to find an alleged genuine and authentic self... and therefore only already anxiously there, so in effect not positing an essential self, an a priori nature, an essence prior to existence, prior to history, prior to self-making, prior to primordial Being... the non-question of the absence of the meaning of Being... or, on the other hand, nothing to overcome, nothing to be transformed, nothing to be made from scratch. Who moves these parts? Slip of tongue. Foot in mouth. Hand to mouth. Head over heels in nothing. Head spinning in nothing. Then what about the question of the meaning of being? Who questions? After all, what is this self that is to be discovered? It's actually the question of the meaning of self... what is the self capable of... doing... in life? But Bartleby, like the rest of us, may not want to know what he is capable of doing... So Bartleby does not refuse, does not rebel, does not protest... Bartleby just prefers not to... do... anything... Bartleby who copies that which has been written by the Other, Bartleby who reads that which has been addressed to the Other... the unknown proposition of the Other, and where is Bartleby between these two conceptual horizons of oblivion? The dead spirit and the dead letter... Dead words and dead people... law and no law, passive nihilism, everything is permitted... speaking in an emptiness, subject in and subject of, subject for and object in the so-called world... to act and to be acted upon... to leap or to fall... no where to go and can't stay here... boredom and anxiety, down into the maelstrom, spewed out of the volcano... the fear of erosion, the trembling of the earthquake... the horseshoe crab and the driftwood... the non-changing self and the drunken self... the adaptive dialectic of power, weak or strong... man-made and natural disasters... transformations of repetition without resolution... in other words, a book. In other words, a prison of self. In other words, the Word, which is silence. The peace of Bartleby curled up in the corner against the cold brick wall.

We have asked the question of who writes. We ask the question of who does not write. Answer: Get a real job you lousy bum.

Introduction to a Conversation during the Plague.

Verba volant, scripta manent

Bucky Hely found himself driving east for no apparent reason. There was a reason of course. It just wasn't apparent. And any direction was not the reason. Bucky has been estranged and living apart from his wife and two sons for over a month. The boys are full grown men now. They will be fine. One boy is in Madison and the other in Champaign. It cost a hell of a lot to get them through college, but Bucky knew it was the right thing to do, even if it will keep him in debt through his impossible retirement. But Bucky might not be fine. He lost his job. Then bad things got worse. There were marital arguments, depression, and alcohol. Julia told him to leave the house and he has not been seen or heard from since. She assumed he went to stay with his parents, as usual, which he did, but for only a few days. So his wife and his parents did not report him as a missing person... until they finally spoke with each other on the telephone and realized that he had not contacted anyone for over a month. The police were notified at this point.

East. He's been this way before. That was a long time ago, just out of high school; his father had sent him off to West Point in 1975. Sent him packing, as Bucky recalls it, and that lasted a little over a year. Then he returned home to St Paul, Minnesota. His father was troubled, disappointed and very upset. A year later Bucky was traveling back east again, to Fordham University in Manhattan. Coach Lombardi went there. It was a good Catholic school. The St Paul, Minnesota kid going east, just like F. Scott Fitzgerald before him, or the Great character that arose from the common Gatz. Bucky never spoke a word about that to his father. But that was the dream, to go to New York City and write. He returned home after an unproductive year at Fordham. However, he liked New York City. He found that the city suited him. Therefore there was a third attempt. This time he would depart on his own terms. He went to New York again, not as student, nor to become an Army officer, but on this stint to do what he wanted to do, write, either books, or maybe song lyrics, like F. Scott Fitzgerald, or like that other Minnesota lad, Bob Dylan.

It was 1978. Three years had been wasted, according to his father. Bucky was officially the black sheep of the family. Bucky was the youngest of six offspring in an upper middle-class Irish Catholic family. His siblings had successful careers, a dentist, two lawyers, a professor, and a Navy pilot. They had distinguished themselves in life. They had respectability. They had made something of their lives. What did Bucky have? He had his life, didn't he? Do what you will, just do as you will, was his father's final words on the matter.

After five years in New York City, after too many all-nights, too many drugs, too much booze, no success as a writer of stories or songs, *The New Yorker* never even replied, the elitist fucks, Bucky went back home to St. Paul again. This time he brought a girl back with him to meet his family. They were soon married. Bucky declined his parent's wish to hold a big wedding ceremony. It was a small civil service. Then Bucky and Julia moved to Chicago. He had to get away from his family. He had to start over.

Bucky found work in a printing company. This made sense to him. He would be around paper and ink. He started as a press jogger, a lowly position that paid the minimum, but after a few years he was more involved in running the web presses. It was a union job. Pretty good pay. Lots of overtime. It was a company that printed various newspapers in different languages for the many ethnic groups in the Chicagoland area. Newspapers printed in English, Spanish, Korean, Chinese, Japanese, Russian, Polish, Romanian, Bulgarian, Hebrew, Danish, German, even Ethiopian; newspapers for colleges, high schools, communists, socialists, anti-abortionists, gays, unions, you name it, and so on...

Bucky never talked to anyone at his job about his upbringing; West Point, Fordham, and his dream of becoming a writer, or about his time in New York City. He knew better. They wouldn't have believed it; they wouldn't have been interested, and they would have wondered why he was there slopping ink if that was the case. He was quiet, downcast, and when he did talk with his fellow workers, he would say things like: there's gotta be a better way; we can get fired at any time, the bosses don't care; and the workers looked at him with dumbfounded and astonished expressions of indifference.

Then Bucky met Stephen at work. Stephen moved to Chicago in 2002 with his wife and daughter. Stephen started working at the printing company in 2003. Bucky started working there way back in 1984. They were the same age. They found some common ground after the usual aloof time of mutual distrust found in the workplace. They had similar interests, discussed only to each other in private moments of isolation from the other workers. And then, in the year 2009, after Bucky had been working nearly twenty-five years at The Randolph and Haines Publishing Company, the bottom fell out. The economy plummeted in December of 2008. The company was going under. It had been going under even before the collapse. It had started out publishing a daily local newspaper in the 1950s, had editors, copywriters, the whole lot, but when the newspaper folded it continued as a printing company, even though the name never changed from publishing to printing. It had been a standardly organized company, developed on long-established business procedures. It was a traditional company for a big city like Chicago. The pressmen were unionized. The company had a president, a board of directors, and shareholders; the biggest shareholder was a wealthy woman whose husband had been run over and killed by an automobile in London, while attending the Gold Cup horse race at Ascot, cheering on the American bred Drum Taps, thus leaving her the great responsibility of overseeing his vast holdings. She was a Beltway Liberal Socialite who donated freely and excessively to Bill Clinton's presidential campaigns, supported a myriad of liberal causes in the confines of Washington D.C., but in the last several years profits were plummeting for The Randolph and Haines Publishing Company, and therefore the company was sold. The new buyers then promptly merged Rudolph and Haines, an old type web-press company, with a sheet-fed press company that went by the name of Dodd Printing Company. Dodd Printing was owned by a man whose family has been in the printing business since 1910. It began with a small print-shop in Chicago, started by Reuben Staples Sechard Dodd, formerly of Sligo, Ireland. Reuben produced a large Irish-German clan, twelve children, wealthy and feuding, and ruthless. The present owner was Rudolph Ben Dodd, grandson of Reuben, and son of David Joyce Dodd.

Rudolph was a "the market is always right" capitalist. Each ensuing generation of the family Dodd proved more progressively greedy, anti-union, and anti-government, not the other way around, as some may be inclined to believe. Rudolph, the latest incarnation of much vaunted American ingenuity and gluttony, owns a house in Wisconsin by the shores of Lake Geneva, owns a sprawling leaf-enshrouded house in a wealthy northern suburb of Chicago, and owns a 1920's Art Deco house in Key Largo, Florida, which he inherited from his father, who in turn had inherited it from his father. Rudolph ruthlessly low-balled his siblings, most of whom he feuded with, except two of his brothers whom he set up with cozy cubicles in his present company, because his mother said that he had to. He also owns his own yacht and flies his own airplane.

One week after the merger was complete, the ax fell sharply. Every day a worker was let go, sometimes two or three a day until a skeleton crew was assembled that would produce just enough to keep the company afloat. The usual comments were heard as the poor bastards were hurried out the door. "I put forty-five years into this company and all I get is... it's just wrong, just wrong... whatta am I gonna do now, I have a family... there goes the health insurance..."

Work harder, smarter, and faster was Dodd's diktat to the remaining workers. And if they did not work faster, he'd go back to the floor and turn the machines on to a higher speed. Avoid overtime. It's like… I mean… it's like… a slew of analogies spat forth from his mouth as his head ticked in a violent twitching manner. Often a slew of profanities emanated from his office, a corner cubicle cluttered with piles of papers and printed material, these epithets were not directed at the person that he was yelling at, but through that person toward some non-present object of his pent-up bile. "Goddamn kike shyster lawyers, that commie nigger Obama. You want money you'll have to crawl up my ass to get it."

Bucky had belonged to the union in the old company. During the merger the union membership was dissolved. The contract stunk anyway. There was no strike clause. There were meetings and meetings at the old company but Rudolph Ben Dodd was not about to allow the union into his open shop. Bucky was not the most militant and disruptive union activist, but he was at odds with a fellow pressman named Danny, who Bucky called a rat and a fink and a brown nose and a piece of shit, to his face. Danny led the charge, co-opted the pressmen, the joggers, the paper throwers, as if the Mexicans even had a choice, if they wanted to keep their jobs, and as a result, Danny was not one of the pressmen that was let go. Bucky was. So Stephen invited Bucky out for a drink the day he was laid off. Stephen said let's go to the bar, goddammit, and have a drink and a conversation, you know a little therapeutic unburdening, leave this goddamn work place, this plague on our lives, let's withdraw from this workplace psychosis that we inhabit like rats… let's retreat to the bar and talk up the devil, the demonic, and see whatever is to follow from that and our pretensions and presumptions of being humans… or non-humans… alienated, you know Bucky, all that Marxist stuff… and see what we can do about all that is to follow from here on out… and understand all that is to follow from here on out… right through the center, rip it up… there's no beginning, Bucky, so just start whenever… talk… you are a subject with a voice. Speak. It is said that history has no subject. Balderdash. A subject can hold a stick of dynamite. History can hold nothing. History is an empty receptacle until it is filled with garbage. We are born into that garbage.

They went to the local gin mill and talked about their memories of New York City in the 1970s and other not disagreeable subjects. Both had dreams of becoming a writer. Bucky ended up working here for the past twenty-five years and then was booted out the revolving door without even a few kind words.

Do It like Herman Do It

…but listen Bucky, I want to talk to you about something. How'd you end up in Chicago? It's long and complicated… just chance… I got all the time in the world. Bucky and Stephen stood at the bar until the stool got bored. They took their beers to a table in the back. Bucky did most of the talking at the start of their conversation. Oh man, at least I can collect unemployment, I hope. I did get laid off. Poor Paul, remember, he was the prepress manager, boy did they screw him over. He did the job as well as he could under the circumstances. He discovered that they had decided to replace him as prepress manager. He had no knowledge of this until his wife totally by chance discovered a post for his position at a job search website. Naturally he was stunned and humiliated. He told me about it. The company had never sat him down and stated to him that they were unsatisfied with his job performance. The company never informed him that he was to be replaced. Paul never was anything but a dedicated and work-producing manager and was always direct and honest. In fact he went above and beyond in performing his duties, even to the extent that he had to resolve issues dealing with computer hardware and server and IT issues that he was not qualified to deal with, and really wasn't his job, and he told me that he stated this when the company hired him. And the IT guy, what's his name? He knew squat. But he was an ass-kisser. I guess Paul was underpaid, you know, that's why they took him on. And yet he did the best he could under the circumstances and was able to fix problems that occurred on numerous occasions. It must have caused all kinds of frustration, anxiety and stress, because of the many obstacles that he had to surmount just to get the jobs done. The shit we have had to put up with here. The company "forgot" to pay our life insurance. And didn't tell us for six months! And no one had work reviews like we were told we would get every six months, or raises, but none in 10 years! And cost of living increases… do you know what Dodd says? He says it's not his problem… what does he have to do with the cost of living… why do we even have to talk about this? It should never come to this! And so Paul resigned. We all felt bad for him, but he had to do it. And then they asked him to stay on. Imagine that? They knew he was a good worker. It's like firing the manager of a baseball team and then telling him oh you can stay on as bench coach. And you know the bastards fought his unemployment the whole way. What a fucked up system. He had to go through one decision after another.

He was married with kids too. He got the unemployment to begin with. They paid him for six months and then the company appealed it. What the fuck! Then it went to a law judge who decided in his favor, and then the company appealed it again, and it went before a Board of Review, and they said he resigned for personal reasons! You are goddman right it was for personal reasons! They wanted to replace Paul. They humiliated him. And now he has to pay back six months of unemployment. What a fucking joke! He could take it to Circuit Court, but I think he wants to leave it all behind... forget it! The rich man wins again! The fucking Nazi bastard wins. Good job America. It must be tough to deal with that shit. He paid his taxes to the great corrupt bankrupt state of Illinois and they just fuck him over. A real hardship to pay all his unemployment back. Man, the pricks that run this company. Just a few pennies in unemployment tax... they get what they want. Why do we have to talk about this? Do we really have to talk about it? Who wants to hear it? I don't want to hear it. You don't want to hear it. The reader certainly does not want to read it. This everyday bullshit. This bullshit of the daily grind. Why put this shit in a book? Just because it's the everyday life of most of the world? Artists are above that, right? Work... and that creep Danny passed a letter around, at the old company, before the merger. That's when I knew something was up. Here, I still have it, in my wallet. Read it. He unfolded the ink-stained paper and handed it to Stephen.

Document 10.6.6

My fellow pressmen, after an unenthusiastic union meeting held in October of 2009, I distributed a petition asking union members if they would like to be represented by the union. The results were that the majority of members no longer saw a benefit of union representation. Some members chose not to sign the petition either way. At that same meeting in October it was stated by Jimmy Giaboni, our union rep, that "if youse guys do not wish to have a union, that is okay by me." Therefore, I have taken this issue upon myself because, quite simply, I strongly feel that the new owners are much more "employee friendly" and individually we can do much better standing alone than with a union. No disrespect to the union, but here are some important points to consider when making your decision.

    1. Dues for the most part benefit the union (not the members).

2. Over half of union employees are paid over the union scale by the company not the union.

3. Full time non-union employees are never forced to give up any of their 40 hours because of slow days.

4. Non-union employees are also receiving annual raises and the same benefits.

5. Many printers are non-union and workers have similar pay and benefits, and don't have to pay dues.

6. Union protects poor workers, and limits the company's ability to reward good workers.

7. Good print craftsman are hard to find and can negotiate as good or better compensation with employers based on experience, skill, and performance.

8. Increases in the last 5-year contract had raises that were below the cost of living increases.

Sincerely, Danny Czwelewski

Can you believe that pollack rat? I love that line about how individually we can do much better standing alone than with a union. That's so fucking post-Reagan. I don't think he even wrote it. He had some help. There's been no raises at all since we moved. This is so fucked up. He stood alone all right. Now he's the pressroom manager. He's just a brownnoser. He talks with Dodd like he's a buddy of his. Dodd just humors him, just another expendable production idiot to him. But he is the right kind of employee for Dodd. I can't believe I've been breaking my ass for over twenty-five years for this. It's over. There's nothing left. My wife will not be happy. We've been having troubles lately anyway. This will just make it worse, much worse. At least the two boys are out of college. I'm fifty-five. I doubt I can find work, and with this economy. The government isn't going to bail me out of this mess. It's not 1933... there are no great social movements, no socialists, no communists, no anarchists, not many unions left... and Obama sure ain't no FDR... Wall Street is waiting for the Invisible Hand and the Magic of the Market Place to rise up and save them. Cunning bastards. Where did it go wrong? I mean... I was kinda happy with the boys growing up. That was good for the most part. It had its ups and downs of course but over all... but when I think back... like you... what you told me... but I never... at least you travelled. You lived in different countries. I still didn't publish a book. But you tried. Maybe not enough. Yeah, but you got married, have a daughter... she'll be in college soon. You started late. You gave it a shot. True. Married at thirty-seven. My daughter was born two years after. But you went to New York and tried too. Yeah, that was after West Point and Fordham. My big failures. Then I went on my own, for myself. My father didn't get it. Funny we were in New York at the same time. I was there from 1977 until 1983... best years of my life in a way, of course, no wife, no kids, no family, so what the hell, right? But... lucky I got out alive... if I stayed I'd be dead, long ago. And you grew up there. Bucky's eyes were already glazing over from the booze. He got suddenly quiet. The booze made Stephen more talkative. I was fed up with it. I wanted to hit the road. See the world. Write. I had a friend in New York back in the 70s. His name was Tommy. He was older than I was. By about four or five years maybe. He was in Vietnam. I wasn't old enough for that. But I worried about it when I was around fourteen and fifteen, thought if the war kept going on then I would have to go, but there was already talk of ending it. When I was eighteen I had to register, in 74, but after that the draft was ended. I think I would have fled to Norway or something. I asked Tommy about it. He said he thought it was the *right thing to do*, that's all he felt at the time. As opposed to that hippie stuff that he saw as *the thing to do* at the time. He was more about the right thing than the happening thing I guess. Though he wasn't in any way a conservative type. He could be very reckless and adventurous. Very spontaneous. He wasn't really political. He enjoyed listening to Gore Vidal when he was on television back then; he used to look forward to his appearance on the David Susskind Show when Vidal gave his *State of the Union* talk. Tommy was no Socialist. But he admired Vidal's caustic wit. He also stayed up most of the night watching late night TV, old movies, the Tom Snyder show, he liked him too. Snyder always had great and odd guests, Joey the Hitman or Henry Miller. Tommy went to see Disney's *Pinocchio* by himself one time and sat in the front row with a bunch of children, eating popcorn. I don't know what the mothers of those kids were thinking. But he was harmless. He was scared shitless when he saw *The Exorcist,* you know, because he believed in the devil. Even though afterward he said the movie was just funny and stupid. We saw *Caligula*, the unexpurgated version, in a theatre in Brooklyn. That was also funny and stupid. It was probably after those movies that he went to see *Pinocchio*, just to cleanse his soul. We saw *Annie*

Hall. He didn't care for Woody Allen. *King Kong,* on top on the Trade Centers... Jessica Lange had the best legs; I took him to see Dylan's *Renaldo and Clara* at the Waverly in the Village. It was like four hours long but he actually liked it. *Apocalypse Now,* that disturbed him. He kept talking about one scene where the Vietcong are running through an open field. He said that they weren't that stupid. So that was another movie that was funny and stupid. We saw the *The Last Waltz* at the Ziegfeld in Manhattan. This movie should be played LOUD. He liked Dylan. But he wasn't really into music. He liked opera, *Madame Butterfly.* He liked Top Forty stuff too. He used to sing silly top 40 shit like "Which Way You Goin' Billy?" We had fun listening to sixties music, like "Eve of Destruction." He liked to sing that but he didn't really take it seriously. He didn't really *know* music. He didn't really fit in with the times. He thought it was just nonsense really, was very cynical. I remember after a CBGB show, we went to a bar, a real dive, and got drunk. There was some guy who started talking to us about William Burroughs. He was trying to find him. He had to talk with him. It was important but he couldn't tell us. There was something called the Nova Convention at the time. It was held at an old theater on Second Avenue or near there. I asked Tommy if he wanted to go and he came along. We were drunk. I think Burroughs read from his books. I remember Frank Zappa was there. And this guy in the bar was telling us all about it. And Tommy and I started goofing on him. We told him we saw Burroughs in CBGB just now and told him all kinds of paranoid stuff that I took from Burroughs's books. Because I had read them. So I knew. The guy I think was delusional. I kept saying to him: Do it like Herman do it. Do it like Herman do it. But New York in the seventies was a very edgy place with a twisted gestalt of nervous crazy energy. Tommy liked to stare down people on the subway. See who would break first. It was really nutty. I always wanted just to blend in, observe. Tommy lived a rather precarious existence. Almost a bum's life. He lived in a dump of an apartment in Brooklyn. Worked part time jobs, was directionless. But didn't blame the war or the country. He was a lapsed Catholic. Two of his uncles were priests here in Chicago. I remember he told me and that he used to have long all night phone conversations with them about various religious matters. And his sister was a nun. He actually went to a seminary to study to be a priest for a while. Then the war. After he got out of Vietnam he went to Hunter College, studied to be a lawyer. Dropped out. I haven't heard from him in over thirty years. Last I heard from someone who knew him was that he was living at the YMCA and was in pretty bad shape. I said goodbye to him on a sidewalk in Brooklyn because I was leaving for California, hitting the road, you know, and I tried to entice him to come with, he almost relented, but in the end he couldn't leave New York he said. That was in 1980. That was it. Never saw him again. But back in the 70s he was great to hang out with. He kinda did whatever I wanted to do and then I followed him around to do it. We'd go into the Village and SoHo, to the bars, clubs, art galleries, book stores, movies, Times Square, and though he wasn't that interested in a lot of that stuff that I wanted to do at the time, he seemed to enjoy it. Hard to explain. But I would set the agenda and he would lead the way. I was shy and introverted. He was very out-going. We went to CBGB a couple of times. But I wasn't into the music scene. I was a writer. That's how I saw myself. One time he smashed a fire extinguisher through a window inside the Chelsea Hotel, on impulse, it was scary sometimes, and another time he peed on a hooker as she walked into his apartment after he picked her up and she ran off screaming. Nothing happened. And he gave her twenty bucks already. I used to ask him why he did those things. He didn't know. Just an impulse. Man is evil, he said. That's what he said. I remember when I first met him, and we were both reading Dostoyevsky at the same time. I think he was reading *Crime and Punishment* and I was reading *Brothers Karamazov*. But he also read all kinds of paranoid conspiracy stuff, books about the CIA, Kennedy's assassination, John Birch stuff, end of the world crap, like that Hal Lindsay book, I forgot the name, aliens, Padre Pio, the stigmata, he starting watching that Armstrong on TV, all crazy stuff, all these yellow torn paperbacks piled up in the corner of his apartment, mixed in with empty beer cans and booze bottles and empty Chinese food containers. Fucking roaches everywhere. He found it interesting that I wanted to be a writer. He used to call me a passive nihilist. One time we were in a restaurant, some cheap joint in Times Square, maybe Tad's Steakhouse, you know, grab a tray, shout your order to the cook, steak, gravy, potatoes and garlic bread, and we were talking and suddenly he yelled out really loud: You are such a fucking crazy anarchist bastard! Really loud. Then a few moments later he did it again. And again. I don't think anyone blinked an eye. They just ignored us. Now the swat team and the FBI would converge on the place in minutes. He liked to walk around Times Square. I think he felt like some fallen Holy Man in the pits of a degenerate hell, and he liked it. He would stop and talk with anyone. Any wack job on the street. Some incoherent babble. We were walking down the street and some black pimp was playing catch with one of his hookers, a really attractive blond. They were bouncing a tennis ball to each other on the sidewalk. I tried to cross the street because I knew Tommy was going to do or say something. Of course he walked right between them and grabbed the tennis ball when she threw it. The black pimp looked at him with dagger eyes. But Tommy just tossed it to him and laughed. And we walked on. I used to give him stuff to read. Henry Miller, Sartre, Camus, Rimbaud, Baudelaire, a lot of French stuff, Ginsberg's *Howl* and *Kaddish*, he liked confessional writing, broken down souls, didn't like formal and clever stuff, didn't care for TS Eliot. He especially liked Gregory Corso's poem about marriage, it was his favorite of the ones that I gave him to read. We read it to each other. It was so funny to read it out loud. How do two would be writers end up working at a printing company? Bucky? You listening? Stephen looked in Bucky's eyes and saw his own reflection. No. Can't be. I'm not like that. Conversational Narcissus. Like what's his name? This is an unburdening. I haven't been able to have this conversation for twenty years. Not since Europe. Not since Asia. Back then. The same printing company at that. It's not like we are Whitman or Twain or all the others back then who set type in some small print shop. Didn't Lincoln say that the print shop was the poor boy's college? We are saps. Wage slaves. Trapped to profit, capital and health insurance. You know, capitalist production makes a man forget he has a dick, and capitalist consumption makes him remember that he does have a dick. That's the great contradiction of this world. I was always on the left, I think. I had a kind of media liberal view when I was young in the sixties. Kennedy was great. You know, the Camelot legend. I remember the somber quiet of the town that day he was shot, walking home from second grade, passing Raynham Hall, an old revolutionary war spy house. We believed, you know, us kids, that a ghost inhabited the house, and sometimes you could see her walking past one of the second floor windows. Our boys in Vietnam were fighting the good fight. Johnny Unitas with his high tops and crew cut was better than Joe Namath with his long hair and fu manchu mustache and white shoes. The hairs versus the squares. We trusted Walter Cronkite. We loved old Hollywood movies. I watched them with my mother and father all the time. They knew all the names of the actors, even the obscure character actors. And sport's movies, Ronald Reagan as Grover Cleveland Alexander, yes, that movie exists and I loved it as a kid. The movies about Lou Gehrig, Babe Ruth, Jackie Robinson, Dizzy Dean and Jim Thorpe, and those corny movies with Joe E. Brown, and *Rhubarb* with the cat that owns the Brooklyn Loons. That's all I watched when I played hooky and stayed home, the *Million Dollar Movie*. Now I can't stand to see a movie, a Hollywood biopic, just rings so false to me now. And then by the mid-seventies I was getting the *Socialist Workers* newspaper. I also got the *Village Voice*. I can't even remember why I got them or how this change in me took place. *Stereo Review* to get the music reviews. *Rolling Stone*. I had subscriptions to them. I wanted to go live in Greenwich Village. Listening to some punk and some roots rock music. I was all over the place back then. Political and then not political. One day I was reading Camus, Sartre, Nietzsche, Kierkegaard, Dostoyevsky, existentialism, the next day it was poetry, Rimbaud, Baudelaire, then Céline, Hamsun, Henry Miller, and Kerouac, and then Robert Graves, Robinson Jeffers, nature, science, hey I won a science project in fourth grade, *Space Stations and Satellites*, you know Telstar, we were the space age kids thanks to Sputnik, and then I lost interest in poetry, and then I noticed that the writers who influenced me the most were apolitical or even right wing... and then I turned toward anarchism, libertarian socialism, Rocker, and when I went to Europe, things changed again... I was more politicized, more outside my skin so to speak, social democracy, at least you get something, healthcare, cheaper higher education, and I looked back toward this country from afar, and didn't like what I saw... but basically my views are the same... except now I am more cynical and bitter. I was a working class kid. I wasn't allowed to be a theoretical socialist even if I wanted to do that. I have working class prejudices. I wasn't going to end up behind the ivy walls of an institution. I am an autodidact. The only downfall of not having had a formal education is that I'm not sure how to pronounce certain words, like autodidact, a priori, aporia, does it rhyme with gloria? I was born into a house with parents and siblings, in my case, that spoke English and we lived in a particular part of the United States and lived within a certain strata of the industrial capitalist system. In fact I didn't just hear English as a child. My mother was Norwegian and spoke to me in broken English and Norwegian. When I started school and the teacher told me to count to three, I would say, one, two, tree. I would say, I trew the ball. I would say, first, second, tird. I couldn't pronounce the word *the*, I said duh, so the school authorities in these matters declared that I had a speech impediment and had to take special speech classes. It was the fast and easy way to diagnose a kid's brain... do you know the biblical story of the word shibboleth? If I couldn't pronounce the *th* then something must be wrong with me. So shoot me! I just picked up my mother's pronunciation... Socialism without liberty is an order imposed from above. Liberty without socialism is a disorder imposed from below. Democracy without style is repressive. Bucky raised his head from the table. Had he actually been listening to Stephen? Bucky said: But you came back to America. Why? My wife. We got married. Legal reasons. My daughter was born. I had to become a responsible citizen. My expatriate life was over. I had to enter the work force. I had to survive by those conventions of this society, its rules and laws... and the application of them; there is nothing heroic about being a working stiff... nothing romantic... you end up doing what the corporate state wants... you know, at least, even in the fifties, as complacent as it was, but at least there were unions and pensions... and cheap higher education, my God what I will have to pay for my daughter to attend a college! But it was already being dismantled, the New Deal... there's that saying attributed to Jay Gould... he said that he could hire half the working class to kill the other half... that's true... but he doesn't have to hire them... the system does it by itself... every morning I get in that damn car and I drive in that murderous rush to insanity... of course I hate them now... a theoretical socialist behind his ivy wall can talk about the heroic working class, the lower middle class... but if you move among them, you end up hating them because you hate the system so much... and ultimately you despise yourself, you despise what you have become. And I hate cars. On the road bullshit. A car hit me when I was seven. Some rich kid was driving his brand new car and bam... right in front of the firehouse on Main Street! I was running across the street chasing my friends... maybe he couldn't have helped it. The stupid violence of things. I had a slight concussion. I remember seeing my uncle's blurry face looking down at me. Some say the car was speeding. I was in the hospital for a few days. All I remember is that my father finished off the hospital food that I didn't want to eat, and the nurse walking pass my bed and saying, "This one goes home today." But we didn't sue his family or whatever. Didn't do it in those days. My father would never want that trouble. My father was just there. He never said much. My father took me to Mets games. That was the one thing he managed to do. He was an old New York Giant fan as a kid. He saw a few games at the Polo Grounds in the 1930s. We would drive out to Walt Whitman shopping center in Huntington. Yeah really, a shopping center named after Walt Whitman! There was a Macy's store there that had a booth that sold Met's tickets. There was a big black and white photograph of Shea Stadium on the wall behind the booth. They just had a certain allotment of tickets because this was before computers and buying tickets online. I still have some of the yellow tickets in their little envelope. I loved going to Shea Stadium. I know in later years visiting teams and sport's reporters put the place down. But it was great at the time. Shea was like some young chick of the swinging sixties. She even hung out with the Beatles and prayed with the Pope. She wore bright clothes, mini-skirts with Pop Art patterns. And then in the year of Woodstock and man walking on the moon, Shea spread her flashy orange and blue feathers and flew over the meadows, and chased the dark bird of Baltimore away, a miracle to behold. Then a few years later a big bully came to town offering a red rose. But Shea saw the deception and threw herself on the gears of the big red machine and stopped it in its tracks. A little guy beat up this bully. Middle age was tough for Shea. Her favorite man was cast off to that red machine and she went into rehab. She returned one night in October of 1986. She dolled herself up and strutted her stuff and distracted a guy name Bill. Poor Bill. But then a slut from Brooklyn with her Brooklyn makeup and her Brooklyn accent came back to town. Shea was jealous and she just turned off her charm. Then one day she was gone. A new corporate female who broke through the glass ceiling replaced her... I'm just talking. Gloomy Sunday talk. Oh, it's Friday? Bucky mumbled: What? How did you get mixed up with printing? That was back in the mid-eighties. Some friends in London had an Apple computer. I thought maybe I could do a literary zine or something like that. Publish expats in Europe. Of course it didn't work out. I'm an introvert. Not pushy. My father was the same way. He had a saying: Let's just get it over with. I guess I'm the same. I'm too anxious. An introvert. A worrywart. My mother was the same way. But my wife says that if worrying made things better she would worry more than anyone, but it doesn't make anything better. Of course she's right... but... I look for things to turn out bad, so I'll be mentally prepared. So far nothing has turned out that bad. In terms of death and suffering and horror. Just the usual pain and sickness and decay, so far. Knock on wood, right? Well, I just happened to know someone who got me this job. Just random. As I told you before, I started out as a jogger, the mailroom, did different stuff. Bucky's eyes watered and he finished the beer and ordered another shot of whiskey. Only been doing it for thirteen years now. Since I was forty-two. Of course to support my wife and daughter. I am responsible that way. I wonder sometimes how so many writers… whatever, painters, like Gauguin, Verlaine, just took off, left their families. Was it really so different back then? What? They were French? Funny. What did you do before that to survive? I'd like to say I lived off my wits. But really I lived off people I suppose. I wanted to be a writer. Not become part of the rat race. A wage slave. Yet here I am. I'll drink to that. Wage slavery. Capitalism…. Printing. Paper. It's a dead end. I mean look at what we print. Some high school newspapers, park districts, financial forms, and yellow page directories for places no one has ever heard of… because it's some place in the boonies that the internet hasn't reached yet… after we went digital and computer to plate, all the film strippers and camera work, shooting boards and stuff, all were laid off. Soon offset will be a relic. It's all gonna be digital. Press a button and right to the press. Bucky nodded and said: That Danny is a fink. What a shit. He is the worse pressman there is. But he got himself to be pressroom manager. He can't even set ink. Do you remember old Rusty? That guy was colorblind but now he was a pressman! And he was the best ink setter I ever saw. He could just look at the tints on the different plates and get it right. He got let go too. He was here longer than I was. You have to see it. Capitalism sees. That's all it has… it's both near-sighted and far-sighted. It sees short-term profits and long-term interest. It can't be anything else but what it is. Capitalism is elsewhere. It makes you a subject for the eyes of capitalism and makes you an object in the eyes of capitalism. There's no contradictions within its own self-perpetuating system. Capitalism is like post-modernism. It's a meta-language. Everything gets resolved and reduced to the bottom line. Which is a physics that doesn't exist. That's its ontology. Its *raison d'etre*. It doesn't know. It doesn't think. It doesn't exist. It has no presence. It has no voice. We are spending most of our waking hours at work or driving back and forth to work. Driving is a risk. The workplace is a risk. This country is heralded as a great democracy. But when you and I enter that building, when we go through those doors, we know there is no democracy, we are not among equals, we have to deal with people that we don't like, people that are put in a position to be disliked, all frustrated, hating their jobs, but we do that wonderful thing, we put money in a pot, we buy lottery tickets, another risk, we put money into 401K plans, we tie it all to the Stock Market, another risk... we get down on our knees and thank god for the great creator, the great job creator, whose money we are stealing, oh but you say you want to get a job at one of those trendy new companies, online companies, where you can take naps in the middle of the day, and you can think outside the box! What are we god damn five-year olds that we have to take naps! And that box you are outside of is really just a tiny box within a very big box called capitalism, which you cannot think outside of, which is almost impossible to get outside of... and survive. I've said enough. Let's get another drink. If I ever get published... I want a real book. Paper... ah to hell with books. I'm past my prime. Out to pasture. Over the hill. I missed the boat. Could have been the Titanic. It was for Kerouac. Sad, said Bucky, and his head dropped down on the table once again. You know my father had a bar. Not like this one. He had a bar with his brother, my uncle Frank. It was back on Long Island in a town called Northport. Bucky droned from his mouth plastered to his arm: Didn't Kerouac live in Northport? Yeah, that's right. I was gonna say. And I often wondered if he came into my father's bar. My father had the bar from 1950 until 1962. That's what he always told me. Then he got a job as a janitor in the school district in Oyster Bay, where we lived. That was in 1962. But I remember, even though I was only around five or six that he had a few part time jobs after the bar and before the school job, which he kept until he retired, twenty years later in 1983. I remember he worked as a furniture mover for a store in Huntington, and as an usher in a new movie theater... but not for long, so I think he was out of the bar by 1961 or so. And Kerouac, who you mentioned, moved to Northport in 1958, I believe around then. And all his biographers say, and I've read several, is that he drank in the local bars. It's always been a kind of mystery to me. You see my father and his brother sold the bar business to a guy and his mother who worked as cooks for them. They made sandwiches and whatnot. And their cook is always mentioned as the guy whose bar Kerouac went to and drank, which he probably did, but later. My father's bar was called Frank and Joe's Commercial Restaurant, ha ha, believe it or not, but it was just a dive, a bum bar, my father told me himself that there were always fights and shit like that. And he was tired of it, breaking up fights, cleaning up vomit, mopping up, and so they sold it to their cook, who renamed the bar after himself… whatever that was, I don't remember. There were other bars on the street, Main Street, also bum bars, the street had old trolley tracks running down the middle, but hadn't been used in years. I have some pictures of the bar, my father wearing his white apron and standing behind the counter. I remember that he burned me with his cigarette one time, by accident, and I was crying, I guess that's why I remember it, I couldn't have been more than three or four years old. And I remember the arcade bowling game with the shiny disk you slid and the pins made a cranking noise as they bent back and up and all the lights flashing. A lot of the customers were scow workers and guys off the boats, but it also had its regulars and I can remember their names for some reason, they had these odd nicknames and such, Crack, Whip, Old Beane, Wookie, Toots... and the building was owned by my aunt and her husband, and they were first cousins, she had a baby who died at birth, she was this scary Italian type with short cropped hair, and she used to keep the bums in line and throw them out, she was tough... but she loved opera... and her husband was the one who owned a lot of property and had a construction and brick company that built a lot of the buildings in town. He was very quiet and secretive. I remember when we went to see my aunt she would be nervous that her husband would come home from work and see us there. She would give us stuff that she collected from somewhere, clothes and household junk, it was all stored in the garages in the backyard of the stores and apartments, and it smelled of cat piss, but my father never refused, because he always had to borrow some money from her, twenty or forty bucks to hold us over to the next paycheck, and that was an excuse to show up and see what stuff she wanted to give us... and we would go through the stuff and my mother would make yuck sounds and the stuff made everyone itch, yet we would still find a few things worth keeping, like finding a pearl in a pile of stinking oyster shells, and the rest went into a Salvation Army container or Goodwill or something like that, and for Christmas we would drive over to Northport to get a box full of wrapped presents, sometimes really nice stuff, a wallet with five bucks inside or socks and stuff like that, this was later after my father was out of the bar, and I used to drive with him, I remember him telling me the names of the towns as we drove, for some reason it was a big deal to him that I learned the names of these towns as we drove on this road, it was called route 25A, from Oyster Bay to Northport, we drove though Cold Spring Harbor, Centerport, Huntington... but we always had to leave fast before my aunt's husband came home. We rarely were invited inside her place. When we did go in, we didn't get passed the kitchen that was through the back door. It was pretty crummy. Cats were sleeping on the kitchen table. Cluttered. Smelly. And they had money too but never took a trip, a vacation. My father worked for his construction company when the war was over. But there was some kind of feud between my father's family and his family going way back, maybe, maybe back to Italy. They were peasants I'm sure from a village called Orero, I think, in the mountains behind Genoa. Their families came over from Italy together and my grandfather and my aunt's husband's father worked together to build up these two properties in Oyster Bay and Northport. But something happened... I think it had something to do with my grandfather's will and money. I'm not sure. It's something I've tried to figure out from old pictures and documents that were left in my father's home in Oyster Bay. His mother lived there until she died in 1969 and my aunt and uncle lived there until they sold the property to some Italians and Jews, who converted the place into offices and businesses, blocked off the alley, and killed the local community... the building took up a whole swath of South Street, right downtown, and my grandfather had a fruit and vegetable store and in the back of the store and upstairs is where they lived. He bought more property to the north and rented out apartments and shops... I'm not sure what kind... I remember when I was young there was a bar, a paper store, a meat market, a small grocery store, and an alley right in the middle, which led to the backyard, macadamized, you know flattened compacted pebbles, with a laneway that led out. I have old pictures from the twenties. Just barrels and a concrete workshop and shacks and chicken coops and grape vines for making wine. My father didn't remember his father though, because his father died when my father was around seven or eight. There was some crazy story about how he was shot by police at a family picnic because someone had killed a rich guy in the village, in front of my grandfather's fruit and vegetable store, but nobody ever spoke about it and I was afraid to ask. My father and his brothers didn't want to take over their father's store, they really didn't want to keep the property, it was a burden, my father ended up having to tar the flat roofs and fix things. They never raised the rents in fifty years, and one of my uncles worked for the meat market in the store that supposedly they owned. They really were peasants and couldn't adapt to American money-making ways... I really shouldn't be so hard on them, but I never understood how they just sold this place for nothing to some money-grubbing types of Italians and Jews, and had never managed to have a store there and whatever... oh well who cares now... they had a subservient streak in them, and they weren't like these others, and maybe that should be looked on as a good thing. I don't know. Whatever their father had, as an immigrant in America, never rubbed off on them. But they were mostly kids of the Depression and their father died in 1927 or so... and they had to be raised by their mother. And one of my uncles had polio and an aunt had spinal meningitis, her left side was partially paralyzed. They were the ones who lived with their mother in the building on South Street. They never married. I used to go sleep over there when I was a kid. Or when I pretended to run away I would go there. I slept on the floor between my grandmother in a bed by the wall, and she was bedridden from diabetes and almost blind, though she lived until she was 87, and my aunt who slept on the couch, or fell asleep in a chair, watching TV all night. And in the morning my uncle walked over me with his crutches to get to the kitchen to make his breakfast. He made the same breakfast every morning, black coffee, burnt toast, fried eggs and burnt bacon. Did you ever ask your father if he remembered Kerouac? Yeah, I did. I said did you ever have a guy in your bar named Jack Kerouac, and he said that he never heard of him. I didn't think he would know his name. But they were about the same age. My father was born in 1921 and Kerouac in 1922. But somehow they seem like a different generation. My father was in the army in World War Two, in North Africa and Italy, a sergeant, a squad leader... the generation of Victorian values and the manhood view of Theodore Roosevelt still prevailed. Kerouac seems like a different generation. But it was Kerouac and his friends who tried to break away from that worldview. I can't imagine my father being anything like Kerouac and his crowd. My father drank whiskey and beer but he never did drugs and never travelled and never looked for kicks in the American night, and never read many books... though there is a funny story about the time he went with some crowd from the bar in Oyster Bay to a Giants football game in New Jersey, and that they got him to take a few drags of some marijuana while on the bus ride. It was actually a notorious game in Giants lore, the game where Joe Pisarcik handed off the ball to Larry Csonka, but the ball was fumbled and Herman Edwards of the Eagles picked it up and ran into the end zone and the Giants lost. He should of just took a knee. My father said the stadium just went silent. He hadn't been to a game since the 50s and that was the last game he went to. By now Bucky was silent and nodding off. Whiskey and beer. But he revived and slurred into speech: My parents still live in St Paul. They have lived in the same house for almost sixty years. They both grew up just a few blocks from there, on the same street. It's a neighborhood called St Anthony's Park. There were six kids in my family and we all grew up in that house. It's a big old Victorian house on a small hill. They'll never leave. My father was an editor of a newspaper and my mother was a high school English teacher. Both retired. Still involved in the community. Liberal Democrats. Love Obama. Makes the country even greater in their eyes. No questions asked. They are both the same age, eighty-six, still going strong, I guess, I don't talk to them as much as my other siblings. My oldest brother is sixty-three, the dentist. I have two sisters and three bothers. I'm the youngest. I don't talk to them much either. They are all "successful." Two lawyers, a dentist, a college professor, and a Navy pilot, a Blue Angel! Real big shots. Me? This is me. Dirty ink on my hands, drunk in a bar, and as of today, no fucking job. A wife who can't stand me. Two grown sons, both out of college and gainfully employed. Hey, I paid for their college with this job. American Dream, right? But we don't speak too often. The marriage was all right when the boys were small, but I think she resented me for taking her away from her family in Connecticut, though we met in New York, where she was working. She thought she was coming to St Paul to meet my parents and stay for a short while, get married and fly off to somewhere and I would become a famous writer... oh shit, who cares anymore. What about your parents, Stephen? My father died in 2001. He missed the last two Giants Super Bowl wins. He died of Prostate cancer. I think he died prematurely from a MRSA staph infection. His doctor, the oncologist, denied that he got it in the hospital. He must have got it in the community she said. After his PSA blood levels went up the urologist sent him to her, and my father went through a barrage of tests and drugs, had his testicles removed, and it was straight down hill from there. I think if they left him alone, just gave him morphine or something he would have lived longer. When he was in the hospital the damn urologist used to come in and sign a sheet of paper to say that he was there, and get paid for it, but he never even came into my father's room to see how he was doing and say hello. It's all such a huge capitalist bureaucratic scam, the healthcare system in this country, but you know that, we talked about it before. And the oncologist used to see him in a radioactive suit with this huge headgear, something out of a 1950's cold war B movie. God, living and dying in this country, no dignity, no common graces, no common places, and no common faces... just common money and common profit, but not for the common people. There are plenty of guns and bibles for the common people. There is a fanfare for the wealthy man. This was all predictable. This guy calling himself a social democrat, nothing new, we had presidents, we had FDR, the New Deal, we had LBJ, the Great Society, but FDR got the "Good War" and LBJ got the "Bad War" in the 60s, after the "Good War, the New Deal," the corporate right went to work dismantling it, and after the 60s the Neoliberal elites and their "Crisis of Democracy," as a threat to global capitalism and the New World Order, so from the 70s until now the old Republican establishment and the Neo-Liberals conspired to freeze the vast masses and destroy the working class, the poor, the middle classes, they succeeded, by the 80s with their idol Reagan, but they needed to grab the electorate, some ideology to dupe them, they pulled in the religious, the tea party, the poorer whites, it's like the 30s when big business got frightened of the left and thought Hitler was the answer, so here we are, fear and hate, Thatcher-Reagan, Neo-Liberalism, Trilateral Commission and Carter, nothing conspiratorial about it, just the wealthy protecting their wealth, owning the means of production, now we have the Democrats like a relic of Tammany Hall and a Henry Fordism with Mussolini bombast, the nativists, the war on terror replacing the cold war, the poorer whites voting against their own interests, now in England they brought back the labor, after Clinton's acolyte Blair, party of Kinnock and Benn... but here we have our own guy, and now these Tea Party nuts, the moderate Republicans wanted them and they got them, to get a majority, but they can't control them, looks like Germany in the 1930s, the big capitalists there wanted the Nazi Party to crush the left, but they crushed everyone. You know I felt more free back then, maybe just youth, but it really was, in a way, you know, back in the 60s and 70s, I don't mean it like some right-wing nutters say, you know, take back our country bullshit, but of course the institutions were always racist, still are, damn, look at where we work, I've heard all kind of shit here, and Dodd, I was told by Jimmy, the handyman, the guy is always doing tasks for Dodd, favors, like driving the company truck to Indiana to pick up a good deal on new tires for his Mercedes, or taking his belt to be fixed, really, his fucking belt, he's so cheap, and he gives Jimmy coupons for his favors, and the coupons are expired, he collects them in a box from all these free magazines he subscribes to, and they pile up like all the shit in his office, but Jimmy told me that when he went to his house, because he does favors there too, for his wife and shit, like raking and cutting branches and snow shoveling, he gives him nothing extra, just his regular hourly rate, but that he showed him, Dodd showed Jimmy this private locked room that was filled with all kinds of Nazi World War Two memorabilia, really, old Nazi flags and stuff like that... I guess Dodd thought Jimmy was one of his guys, so yeah the places that I've worked at over the years, sure, they are capitalist and racist, and the big institutions in this country have always been that way, it's part of the system, but I still believe there was a time in the 60s and 70s when there was a social space, a public space, that was more open and free, it's not like that today, the police are ready, they know what to do to quell protests, Chicago 1968 won't happen that way again, but back then, outside of the system there was still a place, I don't remember this kind of fear back then, I went to see a concert, you know, in the 70s, no one cared what we drank or smoked, there was a concert at Hofstra in the 70s, Jeff Beck and the Mahavishnu Orchestra, man, I couldn't see the stage because of the smoke from grass, no one checked you at the entrance, even the 50s man, I know it was conformist and the black listing, but at least working class people had stronger unions, and better pensions, and social security was solvent... before it was raided to fight the Vietnam war, and there was still that outside social space, the Beats, the underground jazz.. yeah I know women and gays are better today.. but hell they vote for Republicans too, they got money, some of them, there are still class differences, really, but the class struggle has been suppressed in the mainstream media... yeah personal freedom, everyone got the vaccine of the the phony 1950s, so after that just do your thing, tune in, turn on, drop out, personal choice, but what did we get? We got Reagan, Bushes, Clinton, Obama... oh fuck, who cares anymore... my mother lives in Iowa with my sister. She's eighty-three and has Alzheimer. The really sad thing is that she used to tell me these stories about her life growing up in Norway, ever since I was small, every detail she could remember, being raised by her grandparents, the war, and now it's all gone. She remembers some names, vaguely, who they were, but can't put it together, like a puzzle piece by itself. When she talks it's like listening to her dreams made conscious. She stayed with us recently and it was such an ordeal. Physically, she's in good shape, but she'll get dizzy and pass out sometimes, almost like a seizure. Her personality is intact, though, she was always feisty and spunky. But it's as if she's not there, like lost floating shadows evaporating and fading into white. Why are you doing all the talking? I'm the one whose life is fucked up. And what's the name of this book you have been writing? It's called *Sunday Mornings at Oyster Bay*. And I'm doing all the talking because it's my book. I can't believe I just said that. Wrote that. Why do I feel the need to intrude? But it's not exactly a novel! How's that title sound to you? It sounds like a memoir of some aristocrat. Is it about Theodore Roosevelt? Poor Bucky, the captive listener. What? I'm a little drunk. I have a follow up... *Saturday Nights at a Quiet Café*. It was in 1969 that Stephen discovered the truth. The truth about himself. Is there a narrative in here? I feel like something just changed. It was an eventful year for Stephen and the country. America landed a man on the moon. The Mets won the World Series and in doing so burned off 90% of their allotted Karma, and burned off 9% more in 1986 when Mookie hit the ground ball to first base and it went right through the legs of... well, you don't care about his teams, and in May his grandmother died. Stephen was a habitual truant. There was this small crew-cut creep of a shrink at his high school, a short guinea who drove around in a shitty little green MG. He would pick Stephen up for school... anyway... he eventually was happy to get rid of Stephen. Ha! He thought Stephen was a bad influence on his friends. What a joke. If he only knew where Stephen's friends ended up. Anyway Stephen's Uncle Frank comes knocking on their front door and tells Stephen's mother that his mother has died, Stephen's grandmother, and Stephen was standing in the middle of the staircase listening, trying to overhear their conversation, and he heard his uncle sniffling, and then Stephen said to his mother after his uncle left, because Stephen was home playing hooky again, that now he had an excuse not to be in school. What a lousy self-serving insensitive crappy thing to say, right? Bucky? You know, to justify his absence from school by finding relief from his anxiety in his grandmother's death. By the fall of that year Stephen was starting eight grade, and he had turned thirteen, but he was still refusing to go to school. He was absent so much that the State of New York saw fit to drag him to family court and have him stand before a judge, black robed and flag and all, and with the fat truant officer there, not the shrink, the fat truant officer who was about to retire, poor guy, he had a small office under the stairwell that had once been a broom closet and the students could hear him snoring loudly during school hours when they walked down the halls, but he spoke up to the judge much to Stephen's surprise and got the judge to just put him on probation and sign an oath more or less that he would obey certain rules and shit and promise that he would attend school regularly, and have psychiatric counseling, and Stephen remembers his father driving home that day. Stephen was sitting in the back seat looking out the window, and thinking to himself that there is no future, that it's futile to live this life, its meaninglessness, its absurdity, my God you know he was only thirteen! But he knew he wasn't going to keep his promise. Stephen told himself that he would but deep down, whatever that means, he knew he would not… and that's the other truth that he learned about himself, he couldn't trust himself… which self? Stephen would pray at night to wake up to a new world, free from what he saw as persecution, why do they torment him? Why do they care? Why do they have to know that he exists? No wonder he took to reading the existentialist writers… but morning came and he had to go to school… but he couldn't. Something would happen and because of his shyness, his introversion, his anxiety, these are just shadow terms, whatever it was, he just couldn't. And you know he had friends. He played baseball and football with his friends on the weekend and after school… but… as he got older he couldn't deal with school… whatever the fear was it was stronger than the threat of going back to court and being sent away. So he found myself before the judge again, not the same one, but some Jew bitch, she was a horror, and no truant officer or anyone to speak up for him… no little shitty school psychiatrist, just standing there alone with his father nodding and nothing to say, as usual… and she said that there won't be any more free trips to the ice box for a glass of milk anytime you want it anymore… what an awful thing to say but it really drove the point home. Stephen was doomed. He was to be sent to some children's home in upstate New York. So these probation officers came to his house one morning by surprise and took him shopping to buy all this clothes at some crappy two-bit clothes store and filled up a whole big box of stuff. What the hell was that about? Then the two probation officers and the school shrink drove him upstate to this children's home. It was in Auburn. The fucker had a red corvette and that's all they talked about the whole trip and how you had to flash the peace sign to another Corvette driver when you passed them on the road, the V stands for vet right, as in Cor-vette, not for peace, what assholes. So they spent the night there and Stephen stayed overnight at the home and slept in a room with another kid, his name was Peter and he told Stephen he was a bed wetter, and the aunt, that's what they had to call the house parents, as they were called, aunt and uncle, though that didn't make them parents of course, the idiots, well Stephen couldn't call them that because no they were not his real uncle and aunt but after a while he gave in and called them that... and the aunt came to his bedside and asked him what his religion was, so Stephen told her he was a Methodist, he hadn't been to church or Sunday school for several years but whatever, and so the probation officers and the shrink drove him home the next day. Stephen remembers the shrink telling him oh I think we should try it, and if you don't like it you can write me a letter and you can get out. What a fucking lie! Little was Stephen aware of the whole dastardly plot. Stephen wrote to him and his parents but there was no way he would get out. Unless he ran away but then things would be worse, then they had him, probably for life, and he was a very practical kid. Stephen never saw the shrink again until a day in 1979, ten years later, when he... oh fuck who cares... but by that time he had already planned and attempted to kill himself so why not kill the fucking shrink. Stephen thinks he's had too much to drink. Hey Bucky, you awake? Man, if you want to have distrust implanted into you at an early age. But on top of that the whole thing was a legal scam. Stephen's father had to pay for the clothes and his time at this home. Nobody even told him. What a scam between the state and the private sector, what goddam capitalist swine... a swindle... and dig this, the cops came to his workplace, an elementary school, where he worked as a janitor, and locked him up for a night for not paying. Stephen was still at the children's home. He didn't know until later... so the goons started docking his father's paycheck every two weeks, a janitor's pay. And so he stopped paying the mortgage on the house. He never told Stephen's mother that he stopped paying. The house where Stephen spent his youth in the 1960s, the house that held all his youthful memories of that wonderful time notwithstanding what happened in the end. The house up on the hill, on Summit Street... so they came to the house and started painting the walls and got paint over all their stuff, Stephen's mother told him about it later and she was crying while they were doing this and of course his father never stood up to them and then one night a rat ran across the living room floor. His father let the place go, it was derelict, the ceiling was caving in, in a bedroom where Stephen use to throw a rubber ball against the wall and pretend he was playing in a baseball game. Stephen can still smell the musty mildew smell of that room but he still remembers those years as the happiest time of his youth, at least until he finally slipped out of America and lived in Europe and Asia. Stephen didn't really want to come back here, but... anyway, as he was saying, when he was released from the children's home he returned to the apartments that his father's family owned and that they always returned to live much to his mother's regret... that building on South Street... and Stephen was back in high school but the friends that he once had before he was sent upstate looked at him suspiciously, like what happened to him, so he was kind of ostracized, and he was only fifteen and by sixteen he just quit. He just quit it all. He did get some of his old friends back, and he remembers calling them by their wrong names, because he would displace the names of the kids he knew in the children's home upstate and misname his old friends from Oyster Bay... it was embarrassing, and they had grown taller and suddenly they were better than he was in basketball and football because he didn't progress with them but had to play sports with these misfit kids in the home upstate and he was much better than they were to his surprise, he thought they would be better because many were from the city and the first time they went to play basketball he watched them dribble and shoot and realized that they were awful and that he was better. When he got back home he would wake up in the morning and think he was still upstate in the children's home, and wake up in sweats, and then the great relief when he realized he wasn't there anymore but he was back home... don't know how he made it through the seventies... he will tell you how he made it. Stephen discovered books and writers, and music, and New York City, just a short ride on the train. He discovered books and New York City! But for many years he used to wake up still thinking he was in Auburn. After he returned home in 1971, after almost two years in Auburn, he often woke and thought he was still there... not exactly a nightmare. In some ways it was worse because based on a reality that he had already experienced. He awoke in fear and sweat... and finally the great relief when he realized that he was not there anymore. It's been at least forty years or more since he woke in fear of that. Until early this morning... it brought all of it back... all of it.... and more... not quite tea and *petitie madeleine*... that's the dream of a bourgeois... see, Bucky, we are not supposed to be having this conversation, this dialogue, not now; I wrote something, back in my days and nights of youthful dreams and useless labor, about the person I should have been, the person I was meant to be, was destined to become, as opposed to the other person I was at the time, a would-be writer traveling around Europe and Asia, a writer, not a wage-earner, oh I did do some odd jobs to make a buck here and there, some painting and wall-papering, like my old man, he told the draft board he worked in construction and house painting, including a little window work... that's what the draft board guy wrote on his papers, did some window work, I find that so funny, I mean why even say it... so sometimes it's hard to feel sympathy for the working class, stuck in factories and wage labor... when I really wanted to escape from all that, so why should I preach to them about worker's rights and shit when I didn't want it, and mind you, I wasn't educated, I wasn't an intellectual looking down on my poor, who was I to come up with theories and ideas and practices to change their lives... tell them to think the unthinkable and speak the unspeakable... I had been there, and now I am here again... I worked on an estate as a landscaper, at a shipyard, at an electric company, I drove a fish delivery truck... sure, make your life better, you have the weekend and the eight hour day, and steal some time from them, and if you have the energy use the night for song and dance and drink until you pass out... but this conversation we are having is something the person, the self, whatever that was, that I was, that I should have been, can't be having now... and now that I have become for now that person that I was always meant to be, a working stiff with responsibilities, and I accept them, I can do no other thing, so just like my father, and yet we are having this conversation that we are still not supposed to be having... and yet, I can't escape this vicious circle, these tales of separation, this disillusionment, but how do I know that nothing can be done, it makes no sense, it's not sensible, my parents were not meant to read, and it's more than that, those who should not read give birth to those who should not write, and those who should not speak, or speak up... my friend Tommy always said that he understood greed. It's part of nature. A natural desire of man. The desire and the desired. The subject and the object. Where does the desire go? And if we remove the object, that obscure object, it's still no good not to have the object there if we still have the innate desire! If its nature it's useful. Desire money, growth, investment, commerce, wages, greed at the beginning and greed at the end. What is taken is taken back. Slave-master. Lord-serf. Employer-employee. But now we are free to choose? That's what he said. Not the other Deadly Sins but greed he understood. Greed is the basic foundation of all substantiation of moral law. Why do we have laws and rules for controlling behavior? Is it because we are by nature greedy and corrupt? Then why bother? Or does greed outclass cooperation? Or does environment ultimately decide the course of nature's way? Or is it that society creates greed as a value, a virtue, and then we create laws? Why would we create a society of greed only to create laws to control it? Who created this society? The powerful? The Constitution is a document of greed. To possess and keep their property. Is property theft? So they created a society of greed for themselves and a society of law for the others! Not everyone can have it all. If science is going to dispel fear and anxiety it also has to dispel greed and need. Capitalism is cancer. A mixed economy is Keysianism, which is like chemotherapy. Stalinism and Hitlerism are the Black Plague. Libertarian-Socialism is more of a miracle cure. Marxism became a plague. So avoid the plague like in the Decameron. I am one of the people. Their subjective feelings stewed in the cauldron of birth and class. I hate them as I hate myself. So find a cause. I don't believe in the people. A man of the left or a man of the people? The man of the left doesn't care for the people. The man of the people doesn't care for the ideals of the left. Do I still believe in the cause? We are what we are for whatever reasons. Power. Knowledge. Nature. Nurture. Hint of despotism in saying the cause surpasses the stupid masses. So better stand clear. Dictators don't care. What's above the neck in that round thing with a hole from which sounds are uttered. They just put the boot on the neck and that's that. The problem with ideology, a belief system, is why don't all those dumb fuckers agree with me. Money, like God, is an absolutist faith. So here we are, ranting and drunk, but really we are silent and absent. Do it like Herman do it. Bucky stared at me and said something like why are you doing all the talking when I just lost my fucking job... do it like Herman do it... that's what I say to myself when I'm writing. I whisper to myself: Do it like Herman do it. Do it like Herman do it.

Directions and Misdirections

Around Christmas time, driving east, Bucky suddenly turned the car around. He had seen the sign for Route 66 in Illinois. He picked up the old Route 66 off an interchange of Hwy 55. Go West, young man... no, and he wasn't that young. He drove until he found a westbound highway that took him to Iowa. When he saw the signs for Hwy 61 he thought about heading South, Memphis, New Orleans, down the Mississippi, past Mark Twain's boyhood home. He had another idea. He had driven past Ronald Reagan's birthplace, boyhood home, and he saw signs for John Wayne's home, Hebert Hoover's home... Buffalo Bill Museum... ah the Midwest!

He then headed north. He stopped at a hardware store and bought a garden hose, duct tape, and a dozen aerosol spray paint canisters. He bought three 5-gallon tanks and filled them with gasoline. The back of the white Nissan pickup truck was filled with newspapers that he had collected from his job. English, Spanish, Korean, Chinese, Japanese, Russian, Polish, Romanian, Hebrew, Danish, German... a babel of meaningless newsprint, in the beginning was the word, made flesh, newspapers strapped and bound with plastic wraps, and he drove on, looping around in search of directions in time, not lost, not wasted, not forgotten, and he didn't feel as if he even occupied space anymore. His mind was all. He was like a harpoon line strapped around the white whale... driven off course... monomaniacal.

He hasn't eaten in 24 hours, and hasn't slept in 48 hours. Should he stop and see his mother and father? His sisters and brothers? His boys? Hell, they are already grown... no... he went farther north into Minnesota, to the woods where they went camping as kids. He drove deep off road into the woods, pulled over and stopped, and without hesitation he placed the bible on his lap and the gun on top of the bible. He took out the old Ronsen lighter that his father had bequeathed to him because they had a custom of smoking cigars together, clicked it and held its tiny flame out the window in his left hand, picked up the gun with his right, put the barrel in his mouth. He tossed the lighter into the back of the truck, and then pulled the trigger. An explosion of flames and he was gone. Three months later two hikers found his charred remains under a thin blanket of thawing March snow, a mantle of smooth pure white...

death... Detective Abe Desurd Jr. could not believe his eyes. In all his years on the force both here in Chicago and back in New York where he started following his old man's footsteps, he had never seen anything like this. In the bedroom he saw the body of a beautiful woman. The naked and dead body of a beautiful woman, sprawled on the large luxury bed, mattress soaked in blood. And in the bathroom the naked corpse of an elderly gentleman, in his 70s perhaps, on the tiled floor, arms draped over the toilet. There was blood, shit, vomit, and piss, everywhere. Detective Desurd turned to his partner, one little Jimmy Frisaro, who said, "Fuckin'-A, chief, what a mess."

"Sure is, b-b-b-buddy, lots of mopping up." Desurd got down on his haunches and poked his finger around in the excrement and other human excretions. They didn't call him Abe "The Turd" Desurd for nothing. He was a hands on kind of guy. "Call in B-b-b-big Ed," he said to Jimmy. Goddamn speech impediment. His father had it, and his uncle too.

Big Ed "The Janitor" Stoolwitzski was the top honcho in forensics. There ain't nothing that once was inside a human body that found its way to the outside of a human body that Big Ed hadn't seen with naked eyes or enhanced eyes through a microscope. Snot, sperm, ear wax, dead skin, saliva, Big Ed knew everything about anything post-mortem, about anything that came from emptying, ejaculating, evacuating, relieving, sneezing, spitting, bleeding... well you get the picture.

"Hey, Abe, I heard they found that missing person. Hely. Dumb mick set himself on fire in the woods in Minnesota."

Stephen had heard about it at work. That was back in March. Poor Bucky. And who was the murdered woman? Who was the beautiful corpse? That was just another news story. And a twenty-year-old shot dead in a drive-by shooting... right in front of where they live.

The Building on South Street in the Town

Stephen thought about calling his mother. It was a Sunday afternoon. It was the Fourth of July. It was the year 2010. He made himself a glass of chocolate milk and sat down on the couch in front of the television. His daughter sat in a chair across from him. As he tasted the chocolate milk he had a strange recollection of a Sunday morning at Oyster Bay, making himself a chocolate drink of Sealtest milk and Bosco, in the house of his crippled Aunt Luisa, his crippled Uncle Stevie, and his crippled grandmother. He had slept over, as he liked to do... at their house... and when he ran away from home, as he often did, this is where he would go, and his parents knew. They had no phone in this building on South Street... it was 1965... he was nine. The interior of the building has been altered noticeably since the 1920s, when the family ran a fruit and vegetable store that occupied the ground floor and its sizable front windows that faced to South Street. An alleyway was adjacent to the store. In the backyard there were five broken concrete steps ascending up to the back door. Once inside the small foyer, the kitchen was entered to the left by passing under an archway. The kitchen was in the back of the fruit and vegetable store. To the right was another arched entrance, leading into a storage area. Directly in front were stairs. At the top of the stairs was a long hallway flanked by doors. At the end of the hallway were two rooms. There were two doors on the left side of the hallway. These were bedrooms. On the right side of the hallway was a bathroom with a big tub with iron claws. The bathroom was followed by a storage room, which was followed by a small workshop with a skylight. At the end of the hall was a sitting room. In the back of the sitting room, in the corner, there was a door behind which was another storage room, a lengthy murky room that reached to the wall of the workshop. Next to the sitting room was another bedroom. This was Giuseppe and Fiorenza's bedroom. It was in this room that Fiorenza gave birth to four of her five children, the most recent and final child being Joe Cazzaza, Stephen's father; it later became Joe's bedroom, after his father died.

At the top of the flight of steps and to the left was a living room that wrapped around the staircase. There was a window with no glass that looked down upon the twenty steps of the stairway, a wooden banister on the right side. You could see who was coming up. A narrow room lined with windows looked out upon the backyard. In the center there was a door that opened to a wooden porch that was attached to the building and held up by two wooden poles. The porch was above the concrete stairs in the back of the building. All the rooms had tin ceilings with embossed ovals and fleur-de-lis designs.

The upstairs interior had slightly changed by the time Stephen was sleeping over in the mid-sixties. The space downstairs was no longer a kitchen and the fruit and vegetable store had been divided into two shops. The space by the alley became a bar for most of the years after the fruit and vegetable store had been closed, starting soon after 1933 when prohibition ended. The other half saw many different kinds of stores come and go. The family moved upstairs. The archways in the vestibule were boarded up. Stephen walked up the stairs, looked down the hallway, and at the top of the stairs turned left into the living room. The hallway was dark and foreboding. The rooms at the end of the hall were now designated as the "front rooms." There was a curtain that hung at the end of the hallway. Stephen was scared to go down there by himself, especially at night. The rooms were mostly abandoned and old furniture stood collecting dust.

Immediately upon entering the living room there was a large brown gas heater that had been installed in the fifties, with an aluminum tube rising into the ceiling, the only heater in the building. Behind the heater was a door that was blocked by the heater. This was the bedroom of Uncle Stevie. He walked with the help of crutches. He was a victim of polio in his youth. There was also a bed in the living room. Grandma slept here. She was bedridden. She was almost blind from cataracts and was also a diabetic. Aunt Luisa gave her insulin injections. Her water pan was under the bed. Aunt Luisa tested her urine with Glucose strips. Grandma's small black purse was hidden under her many piled pillows.

There was a table by the side of the bed that held her food tray, and a brush and mirror with which she daily combed her long thick gray hair. She rarely used the wheelchair with the lattice strapped backing anymore, except for infrequent excursions down the long hallway to sit in a window of the front room overlooking South Street to watch the Memorial Day Parade or other special occasions.

Aunt Luisa customarily sat in a chair in front of a large upright Philco radio at the head of Grandma's bed. The radio was no longer used. It didn't work. But the dial lit up orange when it was turned on. At the foot of the bed, on top of an old large broken television, was another television, a small GE black and white television. Across from Grandma's bed was a sofa; above it were four framed paintings of cats. Aunt Luisa sometimes slept on this couch, but normally she just fell asleep in the chair, watching the small GE TV. She never slept in her bedroom. Stephen has never even seen the inside of her bedroom and has only caught an occasional glimpse of Uncle Stevie's bedroom, which was fascinating for Stephen because his room contained his jewelry and watch repair equipment. The other rooms were locked or the doors eternally closed and Stephen had seldom seen the interior of these rooms. It made everything more secretive and impenetrable to him. He dreamed about the contents of these rooms.

Stephen slept on the floor between Grandma's bed and the couch. The long room facing the backyard had been converted into a kitchen long ago. In the morning Uncle Stevie stepped over Stephen with his poking crutches. Uncle Stevie made his breakfast, burnt toast and bacon, and a sunny side up egg cooked in the bacon's grease, and downed with black coffee made in the glass pot percolating on the stove. Smoke filled the air. Aunt Luisa opened the door leading out to the porch. The wood of the porch was rotting. The front end tilted downward. Stephen would warily walk out there feeling the wood sloping down toward the backyard. Across the yard stood the old cement workshop that conjured up dreams of ghosts in Stephen's head. Aunt Luisa hung her clothes out to dry on a clothesline on the side of the porch. All the clotheslines in the backyard were attached to pulleys fastened to a single electric pole that stood above the artesian well at its base, clothes hanging and dripping upon the cars and delivery trucks below. Sometimes the top of a larger truck would come in contact with a line of heavy drooping clothes, smearing the clothes with dirt. When discovered curses would fly in many tongues.

This was the first building that Giuseppe Cazzaza had purchased in town. On the other side of the alleyway to the north was a building that Giuseppe purchased in 1914. It was a section of the same building as Giuseppe's and constructed at the same time. The front of the entire building on South Street showed thirteen windows, all part of one indistinguishable structure, with the alley in the middle. Four of the windows comprised the two "front rooms" and the other nine windows on the other half comprised the windows in two apartments in the front. There were also two apartments in back. The odd number thirteenth window was at the end of a long hallway with four doors, entrances to the four apartments, two at the front and two at the back. Italian, German, Polish, Irish, Jewish, and Norwegian residents have occupied the four apartments over the years. That portion of the building had a long solid cement porch in the back with a wooden stairway unreliably secured to the side of the building above the rear of the alleyway. The alleyway was covered by one of the front apartments in the other side of the building until it terminated about halfway through the building and then the alley opened above to an unblocked view upward just before encountering the bottom of the wood stairway that hugged the side of the building. Under the stairway were several rusting mailboxes.

In front of the long cement porch, separated by an iron balustrade, was the top of the roof of an additional extension that was added later. The roof was covered with black tar paper and slanted. The extension was built to extend the stores and consisted of storage for the paper store and the backroom of the meat market where butchers in bloodstained aprons did much chopping and cutting of beef and pork and lamb. Stephen's Uncle Frank was one of the butchers.

Giuseppe also built his own building, and a two-story concrete workshop, both completed in 1919. The building was perpendicular to the other buildings. It was built of solid concrete walls and floors. It was built right up to the back of the meat market. The building had five large garage doors. In the middle was the stairs up to the second floor. There was a door to an apartment on each side of the top landing of the stairs. The garage near the meat market contained a large freezer. All the buildings had flat tar roofs and the roofs were always leaking. The workshop was on the other side of the yard, directly across from the tilted wooden porch. Stephen only remembers a dusty large room upstairs with broken out windows and old workbenches. There were concrete stairs at the end of the building and at the bottom of the stairs were the remnants of an old grapevine, once Giuseppe's produce for making wine. They still grew there, year after year, inviting aggressive bees that also swarmed around the metal meat barrels containing white fat. The workshop was left to deteriorate with the rest of the structures. There was no money for maintenance and nobody cared. The rents were never raised. Joe Cazzaza had to tar the roofs. There was no one else to do it. Stephen helped his dad when he was old enough, but he didn't like climbing up ladders to get on the roof. But from the roof he got a view of the whole town. He could see the large oil tanks down by the docks. There was a carved nub of ambiguous land situated between the dredged boat-docking channel of the Sagamore Yacht Club and the muddy inlet by the large colorful oil tanks of the Commander Oil Company. This area was called the docks. The docks were a dangerous place. For ten-year-old Stephen it was both a dangerous place and a place of adventure. Theodore Roosevelt Memorial Park occupied the land to the west on the other side of the boat berths. And to the east there was a patch of high reeds with beaten-down narrow paths that was good for playing games of tracking and hiding. There was a wall topped by a narrow foot-wide ledge on the side of the oil company. The water came up at least two feet against the wall at high tide. Stephen and his friends walked sideways along the wall and imagined that they were escaping prisoners of war, their backs brushing up against the brick building behind them and the dirty water down below in front. When the tide was low in the inlet it revealed a slick and shiny exposed black surface swirling with rainbow pools of water and oil, and was filled with holes from which tiny fiddler crabs emerged, sometimes helped from their hideaway by Stephen digging down a few inches beside the hole and lifting the mud upward, the fiddler crabs scuttling out. There was an old rowboat tied to a rusty metal loop in the wall. There were old derelict oil tanker trucks dating back to the thirties parked in a field. Stephen pretended to drive them. Inside the cab it smelled of old musty leather. The newer Chevrolet Commander trucks had a full sized plastic replica of a German shepherd on top of the roof. At the end of the road there was a gray wooden building with a conveyor belt along which oyster shells rumbled and tumbled into a high pile. Stephen climbed to the top of the shells and looked out to the bay and breathed in the briny air. There was also the old guy named Joe who lived in a shack by the docks and sold white boxes of bloodworms wriggling in kelp and used as bait for fishing. A dollar a box. Stephen and his friends fished from the dock at the entrance to the boat basin. They caught flounder. Sometimes they caught eel and bergalls and smashed them dead on the dock and threw them back. If they cast out far enough they might get lucky and catch a porgy or a blue. There was also a Joe the Iceman and a Joe the Oilman and a Joe the Barber. Or maybe they were the same guy. They were all of Italian descent.

Stephen and a few of his friends went fishing off the docks, boys around ten years old, unruly, adventurous, Huck Finns. That day, in the distance, they watched fists of dark clouds gather and heard thunder claps. They saw lightning, like fingers, splay, display, and play in the sky. A gray phantom moved across the bay, heading towards them, the wind slapping the waves. They ran to the top of a twenty foot high pile of discarded oyster shells to watch the storm approach, and when it hit, a sudden downpour soaked them. They ran for cover in the old shack with its conveyor belts stuck out from windows. After the cloudburst, sun poured down. They returned to town and joyously ran and jumped through gutters filled with racing wild water backed-up from the over-flowing sewers, carrying their fishing poles.

On their way back from the docks Stephen and his friends drank the cool water pouring from a spigot into a concrete sink that was located in front of an old building that once housed the Sagamore Water Company. At one time a well at the Battery section at the end of South Street gathered the water that was then bottled and delivered locally by wagon or sent on barges to New York City. There were many natural springs that ran through town. One spring that was tapped skirted the edge of the Cazzaza's backyard where a concrete basin with a tin and wood cover caught the flow and emptied it through a spout. At one time a water tower collected the water. The tower is long gone. This creek ran down the side of White Street, where Stephen watched it flow under the shaded trees, one of his favorite spots in town. There were several artesian wells in town. Many were accessible and public. People would line up at the wells to fill bottles and jugs. There was a well up the cove, where Stephen and his friends, on their hikes to see the Roosevelt Bird Sanctuary or Sagamore Hill, stopped to drink the fine cool water, both on their way there and on their return to town.

The Bar in the Other Town

Stephen phoned his mother. It was a Sunday afternoon. It was the Fourth of July. It was the year 2010. Stephen's mother said: I am going home to Lundevågen. It's by the water. Where the water turns to ice. I see my grandfather on the side of the hill. Coming down *Haukneeben.* How do you spell that Mom? It's not down on any map. "Tulle, Tulle," he calls to me. And prays for me among the cows. Papa? Papa? Tulle, coming down the hill with her friend Nelly, walking toward the fjord, became aware of the two dark figures coming up the path. She and her friend scramble behind some bushes and a large rock. The two Nazi soldiers continue walking on the path and stop near the rock. They talk in German. They light cigarettes. They then continue walking up the path. Tulle and Nelly wait until the soldiers cannot be seen from the path. Then the two girls walk back to the path. They turn around and make faces and wiggle their fingers in front of their noses, a gesture of disrespect toward the soldiers. Tulle and Nelly walk down the path until they reach the water. They look across the water. They see the town of Farsund. They see the church steeple high on a hill. They see the white houses along the water's edge. They see the red boathouses. They see the birds darting swiftly through the air skimming over the water. They see the waves undulate. These events that hang in memory like icicles. See the boat is coming! Papa is coming on the boat! See Nelly, my papa! He followed me here. Across the ocean. To watch over me. I came on a big ship. I was disappointed when I first saw New York City. The buildings were not as tall as I imagined them to be. And now I am going home. I can't remember. Joe will pick me up. At the Baker mansion. Who are you? These memories that melt away with the heat of disease. Lost shadows of memory going white... neon in the window. It glared off the smudged glass, it said BEER ON TAP, and glimmered into the darkness within. Jack and Bobby left through the back door of the bar. "Careful you don't bump your heads!" said Joe. They bent down and walked out of the slanted extension to the building, a passage to the back yard, a dark passage lined with empty beer bottles and wooden soda crates and cardboard liquor boxes. They walked out on the macadam surface into a space not occupied by cars and delivery trucks. "Here, toss it." Jack threw the baseball to Bobby. They played catch without gloves. "Got any mitts around, Joe?" A little boy stood by Joe, a small hand clutching his father's pants. Stephen looked up at his father with a certain yearning expression on his face that said, "Can I play too?" Jack and Bobby beckoned the boy to come over. Joe gave his son a slight knee shove and Stephen walked over toward Bobby. "Here you go, catch." Stephen dropped the ball and picked it up and tossed it at Jack.

Jack was in his late thirties, dark, brooding. He wasn't a regular in the bar and when he did stop in for a shot he didn't stay too long. Joe didn't remember ever seeing him before and Bobby had just got into a conversation with him because Bobby was carrying a baseball. The baseball was intended for Stephen. Bobby was a minor league ball player, a promising shortstop in the Philadelphia Phillies system. He's already been tagged with the "good glove, no hit" label. It would stick with him the rest of his career. Bobby was twenty-one, thin and tall. He and Joe have become good buddies lately. They talk a lot of baseball. Joe slides beers to Bobby and the conversation ensues. Joe and his brother Frank own the business and their sister Toots and her husband own the property.

Jack is a writer who recently has received some notoriety in the press. Not all of it favorable. But Joe and Bobby don't know Jack from squat.

Joe and Frank's Commercial Restaurant was actually a dive bar. Joe occasionally used the cocktail shaker but mainly served beer and shots and sandwiches. There were tables in the back for the more adventurous. A bowling arcade machine stood against the wall opposite the bar.

Bobby's usual was a few beers and Jack's a few shots. Joe wore his full white apron. Bobby handed the baseball to Stephen and said, "It's for you, kid. Keep it." Stephen looked around. He turned toward his dad, and then toward Jack and then Bobby. They were all enticing him to throw the ball their way. Stephen turned in the other direction and threw the ball to nobody. Then he laughed.

Jack walked out of the alley to Main Street and toward another bar across the street. Joe would never remember seeing him again. When they got back into the bar, Joe lifted Stephen up and sat him down on the bar countertop. Stephen held the baseball in two hands. His father wouldn't let him wander around with him behind the bar anymore, ever since the time he accidentally burned Stephen with his cigarette. A straight row of aspiring vagrants and derelicts, male and female, slumped and slouched on stools, gravitating toward the dark burnished hickory, nursing their drinks and taking long lonesome drags on their cigarettes.

Stephen ended the conversation with his mother. Said love you, said bye. She said that he made her day. She always said that. He took another sip of chocolate milk and closed his eyes.

Chocolate Milk and Bad Words

After the bar Stephen's father worked as a janitor at an elementary school. There were two elementary schools in the town. Stephen attended Theodore Roosevelt Elementary School; his father worked at the other school, fortunately. He worked the day shift for two weeks, then the night shift for two weeks. Stephen went with him on Friday nights. He shot baskets in the gym while his father swept the floors, emptied the trash, and cleaned the toilets. Stephen was a shy and sensitive boy. He was the completely not-all-American anxietized boy. A gym teacher yelled at him once, a fat female gym teacher, and tears welled up in his eyes. It didn't take much to upset him. At Roosevelt school he was quiet and shy, especially in groups, especially around girls. He lived with his three sisters and mother. Girls. Roosevelt school represented authority, anxiety and apprehension and a lack of freedom. In contrast, the school where his father work represented freedom, or lack of anxiety and apprehension. At night just the two of them in the entire school and his father busy making the rounds. Stephen would feel rebellious and transgressive. He went into the teacher's desks, the teacher's lounge, and the supply room to steal pencils and paperclips. Then one time his father was waxing the floors. The floor waxer bumped against the wall and left a mark. His father cursed. He had heard his father curse before, many times, and Stephen was becoming an adept at the foulest of language himself. But this time his father said a curse that Stephen had never heard him say before. It embarrassed him. He felt strangely upset. He hid in the hall. Didn't want to meet his father's eyes in his anger. He knew the word. He knew what it referred to. But for some reason Stephen was surprised when his father spewed out, "Dirty cunt."

Stephen had heard his father curse many times. There was no reason to be surprised. On school mornings his mother would yell to him, "Stephen, wake up, time for school." Is that my name? I heard that name again. "Stephen, get up for school." There's a joke about Socrates, who repeated the Delphic maxim, *Know Thyself*, and it goes something like this: The father is angry. "Little bastard! Little son of a bitch! Little fucking nut!"

You see, I have other names. Know thyself? I know that I know nothing. I am *little*. That is consistent. The father slams the front door. He is off to work. The telephone rings. It's the school. "Stephen is not in school." They also know who this Stephen is... the other is coercing itself back into myself.

It was a Sunday Afternoon in Chicago

It was a Sunday afternoon in Chicago and it was the Fourth of July and it sounded like firecrackers... pop... pop... pop... pop... and it woke him up. The chocolate milk. These working-class memories. These working-class words like dirty cunt. Not bourgeois words like *le dimanche matin a Combray*... Oh gloomy Sunday. Why go on? Waking early Sunday morning... *le dimanche, ja'i eu de la peine a me reveiller*... the day breaks, it is blank here, for reasons...

That chocolate drink that he drank at his grandmother's place with the crippled aunt and crippled uncle... and now again... a reverie on the couch... waking and sleeping, *je le vois d'ici par les beaux dimanches*... dreaming, desirous, remembrance... croissants, chocolate crêpes on the Boulevard de Montparnasse, red wine, a baguette, *merci, pauvre, fais ce que voudras, du må bare gjøre som du vil*, Torhild... red currents, *rips, rips, rips*, pan, a loaf of bread, *det var en overraskelse, o takk jesus, oh min stakkar Oscar, anpan*, *anko, itadakimasu,* bagels on Brick Lane, *fichs,* a Sunday afternoon after the deluge… A Sunday afternoon in Vienna, locks opening and closing on the Thames… just another little inconvenience in our miserable little lives… he reached into the water and pulled out a horseshoe crab by its tail… he drifted like driftwood into a fog of sleep… there also was a gun dropped near the basketball court by Theodore Roosevelt Elementary School, and a black Bible in a red box that had been stabbed with a fisherman's knife from Norway, and a red Chevy Nova, 350 HP, speeding down the New Jersey Turnpike and the Belt Parkway, and a red Ford Torino station wagon driven to California and as he remembers it… or he read it in a book somewhere… I am living at the Hotel des Bain… a jangle and a discord… it's not down on any map… it was not long after his father died… who never gave him any advice anyway… *det var i den Tid, jeg gik omkring og sulted… den sommeren 1984 i en liten Norsk kystby…* sun and moon are eternal travelers… Ichinoseki… golden Chusunji… the severed heads of the Fujiwara clan… Father died today or was it nine years ago… *Jeg ved ikke.* Pause. *Pause. La voyage c'est la recherché de ce rien du tout, de ce petit vertige pour couillons…* the dog barked… shoosh Camden… his daughter stood in the door… and it woke him up… *Klang von Jugend…* the siren wails… and it woke him up… ambulance going to the hospital across the street… Chicago Fire Department… Emergency Medical Services… No. 56… chasing them as a kid back in Com bay… he means Oyster Bay… he wanted to be a fireman like his uncle and grandfather…

It was a Sunday afternoon and it was the Fourth of July and it sounded like firecrackers… pop… pop… pop… pop… …but then they heard a thud and a thump and the building slightly shook. Stephen and his daughter got up and went to the window. A car had crashed through the fire hydrant and collided with a tree.

…on the couch… waking and sleeping… the airplane landed at Kennedy Airport in New York City on a cold evening in January. It was 1993 and he was returning home after living an expatriate life for nearly a decade in Europe and Asia. The country had a new president – not that he cared – and he wasn't even sure why he decided to return. But here they were, starting a new life in the new world. The taxi drove toward Bay Ridge along the bumpy Belt Parkway as lights flickered and glared and reminded him of those occasions as a boy he lay in the back seat his father driving home from Brooklyn late at night with the parkway yellow lights flickering through the windows of whichever of many used cars that his dad happened to own at the time, the Chevy Bel Air, the Impala, the Ford, the Dodge; he liked Dodges for some obscure reason, perhaps because his first new car was a Dodge... just like the trombone he wanted his son to play, because he liked Tommy Dorsey, but his son liked Herb Alpert and the Tijuana Brass and Louis Armstrong, and wanted to play the trumpet... and now it's 2010 and his dad died nine years ago... oh memory... oh memory... oh yeah...

The Town and the Alley

Stephen is standing on a sidewalk in front of a dark alleyway and a two-story brick building in the middle of a town. The alleyway is between a bar and a paper store. He doesn't quite recognize the place. Yet it is familiar. He knows from experience that it is not anywhere in New York City, not Brooklyn, nor the Village, that it is not an island off the coast of Norway, not a piney moonlit forest of coastal North Carolina, not a car-strewn yard in Pacoima, California, not an East End flat in Bethnal Green, London, not the Hotel des Bains on the Rue Delambre in Paris, not the apartment of a ballerina in Vienna, not a paper and tatami room in Kawasaki-Daishi, Japan, not an airless room in Kowloon, Hong Kong, not a windy cold street of Chicago and a dead kid in a car; he is certain of all that, but he knows it's a small town, and he knows it's an American town. But it seems long ago. Seems far away. The Rima sculpture in Hyde Park. W. H. Hudson. Obscure writer... it's not that... what is it?

The covered alleyway is on his left; a telephone pole is behind him at the edge of the curb, with a sewer grate, and then the street. Across the street is a Queen Anne style building from the 1880s, a drug store.

There is a tree to the north about three store fronts away down the sidewalk, and a tree to the south about two store fronts away, the branches and leaves sprawl upward toward the windows of the second-story of the building. There are thirteen windows in a row. He looks up to see if anyone is in one of the windows, looking down at him. He backs up a few steps to get a better angle, and leans back on a green and brown-paneled station wagon with orange license plates parked behind him and near the telephone pole. It all seems very familiar. A bell rings from the clock tower on top of the building at the street corner. To the right of the alley is a bar. He is looking through the window of the bar. It's a single large window positioned to the right of the bar's main door, which is set back slightly into the entrance way with a small step up to the chipped tiled platform. The window is surrounded by a dark brown stained wood frame, a red neon sign in the window proclaims "Beer on Tap." A chalk board hangs between the door and the window, with the daily lunch specials scrawled in yellow. A brown and white double-striped canopy with "Old Homestead" printed across the front flap is unfurled and flutters in the breeze and hangs a third of the way across the sidewalk.

The bricks that constitute the section of the building that comprises the bar are painted a dark brown. The alleyway adjacent to the bar is also painted a dark brown on its front and abutments, but is painted a dark mustard-yellow on the inside. The alleyway's entrance is arched with vertical bricks and above that is a decorative series of protruding arched brick-ends, the top of the alleyway's arch being around ten feet high. The second-floor of the building is whitewashed. There are thirteen two-paned windows, under each a lintel sticks out, painted dark brown on the facing edge. The sidewalk where he stands is cracked and patched with cement. If it were later in the day he would probably see his father through the bar window at the far end of the counter, standing with a couple of bar-buddies, two old-timers, chatting over a "just got home from work" beer.

On the other side of the alley is the paper-store. It must be very early in the morning because there are stacks of newspapers tied up with twine and piled up on the black and white tile entrance, glass display windows angled-outward on each side and around to the front. *New York Times, Daily News,* and *Newsday.* The twine of the *Daily News* stack has been cut and several newspapers pulled out, and nickels and dimes left on the top of the stack. He walks over and looks down at the *Daily News,* his dad's customary paper, and checks the date: June 17, 1977. He flips the paper over to see the sport's section. Tom Seaver was traded! Fuck no!

The alleyway is dark. Halfway through the alleyway is the side-door to the bar; the door his dad uses after he parks in the backyard with the other cars and the delivery trucks, or parks up the lane if he can't find an open spot in the yard. Stephen and his friends like to knock hard on the bar's side-door and run away. The door opens and someone yells. The strains from the jukebox is accompanied by a rousing sing-a-long by the patrons... My My My Delilah, Why Why Why Delilah... Tom Jones... What? Haven't these fuckers ever heard of the Ramones!

Just pass the side door of the bar the alleyway opens to sunlight where the buildings separate. Here the alley juts out to the left about a foot and a half, a result of the makeshift way his grandfather tore-down and built up and added on to these structures. This creates a corner in the middle of the alley right outside the bar door, where drunks exiting take their one more piss for the road home. Or wherever they go. The alley exudes the odor of stale beer, stale air, urine, cigar smoke, and hot tar from the roof in summer. A narrow rectangular window with an iron grill at the base of the brick wall next to the bar's side door is used for the lowering and rolling of beer kegs into the cellar, hauled on dollies from beer trucks parked in the busy backyard. Stale beer and cigar smoke, that familiar odor that reminds him of his dad.

But this corner in the alley has seen more than piss. It is stained with sweat, spit, vomit, semen, blood… a result of fucking, raping, fighting, and a few stabbings.

He runs out of the alleyway and stands on the same spot as before. He turns around and it is not the same. He is looking at a marsh, and in the middle of the marsh, maybe it's a swamp, a steady stream is flowing northward, narrowing as it empties into the bay and material experience. He enters a time vortex in the dark alleyway. A massive ice sheet drags rock sand gravel from the land, leaving it piled up at a southern limit. The pressure from the ice's weight grinds the rocks to dust. Milky melt water flows from the ice in rivulets. Rock sand gravel are washed out and tumble along in the swiftest rivers, eventually spreading out as outwash plains at the foot of the moraine. The immensity of the ice sheet dwarfs the pebbles that represent stability in the present day aggregate landform, one of these pebbles is called Long Island, a neatly deposited moraine in southeastern New York State, extending east-northeast from Manhattan Island. It is 118 miles long and varying from 12 to 20 miles in width.

The climate changes. The glacier begins melting. A marginal film of soil gathers on top of the edge of the ice sheet. Trapped dust and debris are released by a great thaw. More dust is scattered over the ice sheet from the uncovered countryside. Dust rising. Small and larger plants, spruce trees spring up. This primeval forest falls as the ice formation beneath it gives way. Streams and rivers run over rocky beds. Water brakes loose and inundates the velum earth and vellum word in the generation of vegetative and verbal life. Water runs through conduits and burrows of ice. It gushes and spurts forth in fountains and artesian wells.

Harsh piercing winds rush down from snow-lashed uplands in elevations to the north. The landscape is barren. Acheronian dust and water secrete the ice, sand and sill. A whirlwind of rain falls in torrents. Fog shrouds and dampens the newly emerging plants. Lakes are formed when forests fall into covert ice gaps. Plants colonize the rim of the sea. A marsh is precariously enrooted at the limbo lip of the ocean's mystic voice. Seabirds conjoin on the sheltered shores, trekking their way northward in search of nestable tundra. Seeds encased in mud on the seabird's feet desquamate when the mud dries and becomes new settlers on the spartan frontier. At mid-tide range a tall grainy grass grows. At high-water level a fine and loose grass grows. A blush of sea lavender effloresces among the grasses. On sandy banks by the alluvion brink a chubby small plant with stems swells with water. These are the pioneers of a new world, stalking the horizon. Soft-shell clams, quahog larvae, raccoons, minks, annelids, insects and birds. Small ponds surrounded by cattail and sedges. Cedar swamps. Seawater. Storms. Salt. Osprey perch on rotting cedars. The dowitcher, the lone sandpiper, the yellowlegs. Widgeon grass-eating ducks upend in pools swarming with fish captured in high tides. Bacteria and algae inhabit the isolated pools. Bald eagles make nests in the tallest pines. Marsh hawks nest on hills. White-footed mice scamper through the clustered stems. Sharp-tailed sparrows and short-eared owls interweave over the marsh. A black-crowned night heron nests in a tree on a small island. The island is moving. And unto the marsh comes Aliaspun... his feet drag on the floor of the jail house... and he walks right through the brick wall... Walt Whitman waits for him...

Aliaspun and Whitman, arm in arm, walk up South Street and stand on the spot and then enter the dark alleyway. In the backyard they take a drink of water from the artesian well.

Beyond the marsh looking east there is a hill suddenly looming in the near distance. There is a wide open area to the south and more marsh to the north about a hundred feet away. There is a dirt trail, built by the Matinecock tribe, of which Aliaspun is a member, and the town fathers are building a highway to run into the trail. It is the year 1653 and the settlers have promised to pay the sachem Sagamore in trinkets to purchase what they call the Town Splot, this spot where Stephen stands. They later rename the highway Main Street and the old trail they name South Street. And in 1668 they name Caleb the official "Ordinary Keeper," to establish a pub, and become the town's first innkeeper.

The founders have allowed for six acre lots to fill the town spot, with names like Wright, Weeks, Smith, Townsend, goode olde Anglo-Saxon names... English, Dutch, English, English, English, English, Dutch, English, for two hundred and fifty years until the world is turned upside down and emptied of its detritus, when Giuseppe Stefano Cazzaza from a small village called Orero, in Liguria, Italy, moves into the town and settles there and purchases that land, those buildings, where Stephen stands on South Street, and there he sees his Grandfather...

It is in 1916... it's the Fourth of July parade. There is a film crew from the Vitagraph Studios here to capture the day; ex-president Theodore Roosevelt will be attending. Roosevelt was involved with Vitagraph Studios in making a propaganda film supporting America's intervention in the war. It was called *The Battle Cry of Peace.* In other words: War is Peace. The Germans are destroying New York! But the proud and fearless men of America are cleaning their rifles and preparing for battle.

Stephen's grandfather, Giuseppe Cazzaza, is standing in the street, before the parade begins, posing for a photograph in front of a parade float, a paper liberty bell wrapped in red white and blue bunting. He wears a suit and tie, a vest, a derby hat tipped down slightly over his forehead.

Later, Giuseppe and his wife Fiorenza are standing in front of their fruit and vegetable store. Young Stevie Roosevelt Cazzaza is standing with his tiny crutches, his brother Frankie Lincoln Cazzaza is standing next to him. In the window the fruits and vegetables are covered with brown paper to shield them from the sunlight. There is a wooden cover extending over the sidewalk, held up by metal poles. The boys are squinting in the sunlight. Frankie shielding his eyes. A large poster in the window says:

FOR VICTORY BUY MORE BONDS FOURTH LIBERTY LOAN

There are adverts under the store window in molded frames. The bricks of the alley and building are unpainted. They are red. Like the fire trucks.... in the parade... Stephen runs out of the alley...

He is standing on the spot in front of the alleyway again. His grandfather's fruit and vegetable store is on his right. But there are no fruits or vegetables in the windows. It's dark inside. The advertising displays are torn and peeling from the windows.

The newspapers are piled in front of the paper-store, as usual. He walks over and checks the date on the *Daily News*: October 8, 1933. There are separate piles for the *Daily Mirror, the Sun,* and *New York Times....* *The Daily News* was the first tabloid in America. One of the headlines: Giants Beat Washington Win Series 4-1.

He walks through the alleyway. In the backyard he sees three boys sitting on the running board of an old black Studebaker. The smaller younger boy sits between two older boys, about twelve years of age. The two older boys hold baseball gloves in their hands, two brown flat mitts. There is a large concrete shack behind the Studebaker.

Document 1.2.7

A partial list of automobile ownership in Oyster Bay in 1920

1963	**Giuseppe Cazzaza**	**South Street**	**Studebaker**
4148	Louis De B. Moore		Del Belle
4159	George Bullock		Renault
5306	Arthur H. Saunders		Cole
5813	Victor Commock		Loxier
8084	Louis C. Tiffany		Crane
9446	J. Bennett		Packard
12316	**Giuseppe Cazzaza**		**REO**
13252	C. Bayles		Regal
13255	E. V. Valkenburg		Chalmers
17276	L. Hepburn		Cadillac

In the center of the building at the top carved in cement: **CAZZAZA 1919**. The stairs at the end of the shack lead up to a workshop. The rooms under the workshop are filled with an assorted collection of scrap metal, old lumber, bricks, concrete blocks, coal, cut logs, shovels, old tools, wheel barrows, rags... the yard has a macadam surface, and there are wooden crumbling lean-tos and small tool sheds, many barrels, and scattered bricks... and up the laneway there are chicken coops but no chickens, grapevines unpruned, a water storage tank on a telephone pole reached by metal stairs, and under it an artesian well, water gathering in a concrete container and pouring from a conduit into a sunken cement sink with a drain...

The three boys, the one boy is Stephen's father, went this summer to the Polo Grounds with Uncle Harry and a friend's father. Stephen's dad's father never had an interest in baseball or football. If he wanted to go... he died in 1927. The car took them down Northern Boulevard. They saw a doubleheader at the Polo Grounds. The St Louis Cardinals vs. the Giants. They saw Carl Hubbell pitch against Dizzy Dean. His father told Stephen about the game. Hubbell defeated Dean in 18 innings, 1-0. His father's favorite player was the Giant's Bill Terry. His dad wanted to play first base like Terry. Dad is tall for his age, will be bigger than his older brothers. The boys run to play catch in a field by the laneway. The backyard with its large dark green doors under the concrete buildings. Cross slats on the doors, small windows at top, behind one door is the old REO truck that belonged to papa, broken down, never used again after he died. His truck for trips to the city to bring home produce. If it isn't a REO it isn't a "Speed Wagon." Giuseppe paid $1500 in 1919 for the truck.

Stephen's dad followed the baseball games on the radio and newspapers. When he was about the same age as his father was in 1933, thirteen, in 1969, Stephen watched the New York Mets on the small 12-inch GE Black and White television, and cut out clippings from the *Daily News* and taped them in a scrapbook. *Kranepool, the Big Stick, wearing number seven, giving it a lotta oomph, kicking up sand, rounding second trying to stretch a double into a triple, in the first game of a double-header, is out at third base, in a cloud of dust, in the eight inning of yesterday's game, between the New York Mets and the Chicago Cubs...* who writes these captions of postmodern indeterminacy?

Stephen walks passed Raynham Hall, built circa 1740, this colonial and half saltbox house was the home of Robert Townsend, who served as George Washington's chief spy. Culper Jr. was his code name. He worked for the American spy corps that Washington established to gather information on British troop movements. Robert Townsend was instrumental in aiding the disclosure of Benedict Arnold's plot to surrender West Point to the British. Stephen stood on the sidewalk and gazed over the white picket fence. There were two large links of chain in the garden. Above the links was a sign: These links are part of the chain which was used to span the Hudson River to prevent the British Fleet from reaching West Point. The chain was forged March 1778 by the Sterling Iron Works owned by Peter Townsend of Orange County.

From the sidewalk Stephen looked into the windows of Raynham Hall. A story among his classmates is that a female ghost dressed in white can be seen walking pass the window. Stephen didn't want to look for too long. He got an eerie feeling. He has to walk pass this house to and from school. Stephen crossed South Street and stood at the entrance to the alley.

The Spot. Three dimensions of space. And Time. But it's just in your head. Only if you were reading these marks on paper on a train, on an elevator, really space... but in the mind? He had a dream that his father was proud of him. Stephen walks over to the paper-store and looks at the newspapers piled up. The *Daily News* headline. It's 1993 and he's just returned to America. He looks through the bar's window and sees himself and his father. The two of them are having a beer, sitting on stools at the counter; this is the bar that his father frequented when they lived in this town, his after-work bar, and this is many years after his father gave up his own bar. The bar he had with his brother Frankie in Northport from 1950 to 1962.

A few of his old drinking buddies are here. They want to know what Stephen has been up to. They remember him as a quiet kid who quietly got into mischief. Ten years of traveling. London. Paris. Japan. He is shy and reticent. Not talkative. He never liked to come in here. As a boy he had his coke and left, while his dad downed his beers and chasers. They ask his father, and his father says that he's a writer and has written a few books.

Earth shattering silence... how can I convey the stupefying brain implosion of this revelation? It is utterly impossible that he spoke those words. This was far worse than obscenity, far worse than dirty cunt.

How is it possible for him to say this? Did Stephen not protect his father from this secret knowledge? Which of them must now die from shame? Which of them must now become the killer in this story? But there is no shame, guilt, nor responsibility... because there is no free will. Stephen is a freak accident. Peasants begat peasants, not poets. Stephen is exempt from this calling... did he not realize that he had played all the roles? He was confused with his self-identity. Was he son, father, husband, and brother? How many roles did Stephen play? How many others? Could he be a writer? Is that a role? Is that an identity that is authentic? Was he searching for a self, an authentic self? Why could he not tell his father that he was a writer? Through the veil of illusion that is Stephen's mind. It's all in your head. Numerous scenarios of desire. Existential anxiety... this is what his reading has taught him, perhaps. Fiction and theory, so on a cold winter night in 1979 he walks into the alley and puts the gun up to his temple.

It was a Sunday afternoon and it was the Fourth of July and it sounded like firecrackers... pop... pop... pop... pop... but then they heard a thud and a thump and the building slightly shook. Stephen and his daughter got up and went to the window. A car had crashed through the fire hydrant and collided with a tree. In the middle of the street stood a cop with full tribal tattoos on his arms and his gun drawn and pointed at the car. He motioned for another cop to check down the side street.

He didn't shoot himself. Because... things didn't happen that way. But things could have happened that way? In this world or in an alternative world? Or fiction? This existential contingency at the border of being?

Men Die in Bathrooms

In the beginning, there was nothing to be said; there were no words, only the Word; nothing happened yet; and then birth, life, experience, and death. Such stuff. Such deeds. The Big Bang in the beginning... not bullshit "In the beginning." He learned that from Kierkegaard. And then he was there to say it. And in the end, what more needs to be said, women die in bedrooms, men die in bathrooms. Or childbirth and wars...

He saw his mother night after night bring a man to her bed, turn off the light, let the stranger slip out the back door, pull up the blanket, curl-up and bleed. Blood. Just like all the miscarriages. He saw his father night after night creep along the wall in darkness, find the light-switch, stand up to pee, sit down to shit, and bend over to vomit. Blood, shit, piss and vomit. Just like moping up the filth of the floor, of all the bums, after he closed up the bar in Northport. Then at 2 a.m. the drive home on 25A. The father names the towns for Stephen to remember... Cove Neck... Cold Spring Harbor... Huntington... Northport... St Patrick's Cemetery where up on a hill Giuseppe Cazzaza was interred, alone, awaiting his family to join him.

That was his mother with her romance novel and his father with his newspaper. The romantic agony and the sports section scores.

Perhaps the 44-year-old housewife and mother of four hides a dirty book under her mattress. Perhaps the 50-year-old husband and father goes to the local gin mill after work and flirts with the female bartender. Imagine that! They never had girl bartenders in his day. But at what point do they step out of the bedroom and bathroom and enter the vast landscape of history? Never. Working-class people... never. She washing the asses of the elderly; he mopping the puke of the drunks. And their son was never meant to do this. This writing stuff. Freak of nature. Freak of freedom, of free will, of chance...

Yet before it ends, something had to be said; it had to begin at some place, at some time. There had to be some kind of history. A story. But how to tell this story? Let's begin. It's a far away place and a time long ago.

Let's say... that... perhaps his mother grew up in Norway, and was a young girl of fourteen when the Nazis invaded, and perhaps she lost her virginity to a Russian soldier, an ex-prisoner, after the war; or perhaps, let's say, better yet, that she had had an affair with a German officer, who kept her as his mistress, and with whom she had an illegitimate child, a misshapen dwarf and brute, who, after the war, was persecuted and tormented by the locals of a small coastal fishing town. Until he had enough humiliation and plotted his revenge.

Let's say... that... perhaps his father was a soldier in World War Two, a conscript, and he caught the clap from a prostitute, who also stole his money, in Naples, back in February of 1944, and one night, drunk as a skunk, he went back and strangled her to death in some narrow dark alley-way, and perhaps he also later bravely led his squadron up the titted hills on goat paths to reach Santa Maria Infante and took a bullet in the back.

Perhaps his mother and father did have these primary experiences some seasons long ago and far away, and have never come close to such lived life again, for he did not choose to go to war and she did not choose for a war to come to her; and perhaps they grew old together, despite all, and she cared for him when he was dying of cancer, and she watched helplessly as he stumbled down the hallway to the bathroom, and when he didn't come out for an hour while puking blood and trying to shit out solid black bricks, called to him, are you all right, Babe?

Long ago they were a young married couple, just after the war, on the threshold of the complacent 1950s, and wanted to settle down to suburban bliss, because he had just survived a war and had no desire to live like Ernest Hemingway or Henry Miller or Jack Kerouac, whoever they were, and she had lived through the same war but in a different country and could now live vicariously through Hollywood starlets up on that big screen, and live to buy into the American Dream. She had the excitement of the movies and shopping and he had the social anti-social life of the bar.

His father did not choose to go to war, or ship out to sea, or head out to unexplored territories, or hit the road, or take flight to a foreign city to find freedom, creative freedom. He had no desire to evade the domestic snares, the civic duties that bind, and the social and personal responsibilities that cripple. He headed straight to the middle way, crushed between the rich and the poor. It was Rome and home, and his hometown and his home teams were good enough for him. It's the long dark hallway that leads to the bathroom but that was fine with him too. And now it's 2 a.m. and all the bums are gone from the bar, and there's Joe, mopping up. And as for her, it was America and the dream of happiness thereof....

He never saw his father read a book in his life, though his father probably saw a thousand Hollywood movies. He was a child of the depression, a World War II soldier, a working-class boy, a construction worker, a bartender, and a janitor. It was a lifetime of mopping up.

His father and uncle Frank had a bar in Northport in the 1950s, and he likes to imagine that his father served him a drink on occasion, it is possible, you know... his father had no idea who he was... when at 3 a.m. his father steps outside to Main Street, fed up with the boozing, screaming broads and brawling, fed up with the stale beer, swearing, shouting, sweating, shit, and sits on the curb, feet in the gutter, and the stranger sits next to his father. Did they have the conversation that he never had with his father? About becoming a writer? About being a writer? His father met three famous writers in his life and he didn't even know who they were. Not that it matters. As if he spoke with Pound in Italy... where they hung niggers for rape, and perhaps could have hanged his father for rape and murder... but... his father doesn't understand him, talking about Buddha and jazz and the American night. Or did they just, probably, talk baseball. Good working-class men. Baseball, that's what they talked about.... not books and being a writer!

There was a regular in the bar, who played Minor League baseball; he later played in the Major Leagues, a good glove, no hit shortstop for the Phillies; in the bar, that year, he was only 4 or so, he gave him a baseball. That baseball meant a lot to him. A decade later in 1969, he is playing catch with the same baseball in a parking lot, and the ball flicks off his glove. He chases it and watches it go down the drain. On his knees he stares into that dark hole for minutes. He goes to games with his dad and one day maybe meet the shortstop. Almost met him in 1976 at Cooperstown... but the bus was pulling out and he waved from the bus window... go fishing camping take him out to a ball game...

The Mets won the World Series that year; and man landed on the moon! Has he not mentioned that already? In 1970 Stephen caught a foul ball during the old timers game... and in 1972 he and his father were at Shea Stadium; Willie Mays was playing in his first game with the Mets. Sudden Sam McDowell was on the mound for the Giants and he walked the first three batters and then Rusty Staub hit a Grand Slam. The Giants scored four runs to tie the game by the fifth inning when Willie Mays stepped up to the plate in the drizzling rain and smacked a line drive home run into the bullpen in left field. Mets won the game 5-4. Stephen remembers driving home with his dad that day on 25A in the light rain like falling ashes from the ash heaps... like words that one day he would discover...

His father liked to tell him about the game that he went to at the Polo Grounds in 1933, when he was twelve. A double-header. The great Carl "King" Hubbell pitched 18 innings and the Giants beat Dizzy Dean and the Cardinals, score 1-0. We asked why bother to write? Why bother to remember?

Chicago 2010

As Stephen slowly drifted away from his erstwhile dream of a writer's life, as the years accumulated like the books on the shelves, and then on the floor, and then in boxes, and then discarded, deserted, and his own papers and manuscripts, neglected, resurrected, neglected, resurrected, the weight of dust and doubt and disease and debilitation and degeneration gathering in the maelstrom, a body of wreckage, broken and torn, about to go plunging under forever, sucked into the final unawakening, standing at the brink of the white hole of the un-nameable and the threshold of forgetfulness's ingress, when even the spectral words that mindfully adhere together in their limited and constrained path, like a string of dim lights that barely illuminates the obscurity behind each unturned page, as time approaches and departs on the solid ground of embodied space, and that holds all things together like a bright salmon flashing in a wild river rushing to the sea, are forever cast out, subsumed by the greater whole, indistinct particles twinkling in the waves, until the last page is reached, the end that is un-ended, and whatever words that yet have meaning are well met by the blank stare of existence in itself... he saw himself in the mirror one cold morning and he shattered into fragmented shards and slivers... the old youthful dream was dead but the new ancient dream survived, the new dream of despairing hope, of persistent myth, of absurd selfhood... of in the beginning... of initiation, of ceremony, of ritual, because each dawning day is the last inconceivable denial of annihilation.

Shall I Go On?

So where and when should we start? Have we not already started? Should we start in the alley on South Street in 1979? Or should we begin on a cold January evening in Brooklyn at the corner of 54th Street and 8th Avenue in the year 1993? And should we end it on a Sunday afternoon in Chicago? That is, should we end it today? October 21, 2010. Should we end what today? These are rhetorical questions. There is no need for you to answer. Don't bud in. We need more time. We need a hundred years, at least.

1. He would have killed himself by now, at fifty-five, had he not been such a simple sort...

2. The only reason he hasn't killed himself... yet, at fifty-five, is because he's such a simple sort...

Dilemma, which to choose? Is this a choice that Stephen must make? Jean-Paul Sartre in the mid 1950s when he was extolling the virtues of the Soviet state and its workers working to build the Communist Paradise and therefore they had no need to visit any other paradise, like a horrible bourgeois as Gauguin or Rimbaud, was just frenetically writing it all down, engagé, for the cause, and not revising or rereading, like a disgusting bourgeois like Flaubert or Proust... and yet, in America, at the same time, Jack Kerouac was also getting it all down frenetically, without revising, spontaneous bop prosody, but Jack was no voice of the Communist state, far from it, yet, the irony, both of them pumping away, puking words, on Amphetamines and Corydrane, both phenomenologists, as it were. There is an interesting paradox to this, and that is what we shall pursue in these pages. We need to begin in the year 1892... 1893... descend the western course, hover over the dead... O sleepers awake!

Stephen was conceived of northern and southern European peasant stock, crucified upon the economic cross of the American working-class, resurrected into the mysterious revelations of self-hood, and transfigured into an improbable freak of society and nature, as so many before, poet, writer... we need to end in the year 1992.

America, there goes hypocrisy, invisible as bacteria to the naked eye. Guns and a bibel... Full stop. Pause. The beginning and the end. It's not that the beginning and the end are natural objects in the world that can be analyzed... it's just the tricky part, the spooky part, the unknown part, and then comes the easy part, the stuff in the middle. Maybe not so easy... there's lots of work to be done yet. And yet? That's just the last of it, the tail end of it, or should that be the tale end of it? Actually it all begins long before that, up by the face, the mouth, when some fool of an early human blabbered in his brain something there like a word, and never stopped feeding on that pale bit of bacteria... here's a sample of that culture: let's call it the filth of the floor, and then proceed through the door on the right, to the basement, the cellar, yes we go that way, follow the line of immovable type, it doesn't cost much, maybe your soul? How would that be possible? Faust is dead. Gutenberg is dead. Somewhere there will be something like a beginning and an ending... and in between a hundred years will pass like scurrying black cockroaches across the table and floor when you turn the light on in the kitchen... whooo! Look at em go! No way you can slow the little filthy bastards. Tommy inadvertently brought them out from Brooklyn; his place off 69th Street, out to South Street, in his bag, or from his clothes, maybe even while he was wearing them.

Stephen used to drive with his father to his job when his father worked the night shift, to the elementary school, to mop the floors and clean the toilets... driving through the new development, where the Jew kids ran out in the street and caught his eye and stood there without getting out of the way... little Jew bastards he'd say... after he finished his work Stephen and his dad would shoot hoops in the gym, play 21...

And his only son, who would one day be alone in the office of a man whom Stephen knew had wronged him. The school shrink. The bastard son of a bitch of a guinea had a crew cut back then, driving around in a little shitty green MG, but now longish grey hair and beard. Stephen had the gun in his jacket pocket. The gun he had picked up in the schoolyard by the basketball courts after Ronnie shot Keith. The nightmare of holding the gun to his head in the alley one night at midnight but not pulling the trigger. He could see the fear in the bastard's eyes. He could've shot the fucker dead then and there. Stephen told him that he didn't care if he went to jail. The bastard said to him… that *you are already in jail.* Wrong thing to say asshole and Stephen pulled the gun out of his pocket. Did he become the killer? This would be the worse shame of all the shame that his father has had to endure because of him… you fuckin' nut. That night that he was in the alleyway with the gun, but… he ran out to the parking lot in front of Food Town supermarket, and dropped the gun down the sewer drain, the same drain where he had lost a baseball ten years ago. And before the guinea shrink, there was the kike shrink, she was talking with him and mentioned his father. She asked him if he was ashamed of his father, just a janitor. The fucking kike bitch, oh how he wanted to rip her fucking Jew nose from her fat ugly face. Enter the dark alley. The dark dread of honesty. There is no celestial crown at the end of this alley… just the filth of the floor. Rake the muck! Should I go on? Well, if you don't like it, you can get the fuck out of here. Leave. Go. There's the door. Shut it. Unfortunately, I'll still be here a while longer… it's only been forty years already… what's a few more years…

Chicago 2008

Everything grew wild in the backyard of his childhood. The lilac, the forsythia, the rosebush… but never trimmed and pruned. The dandelions, the grass trodden down… mostly dirt. The pine, maple, spruce, and oak trees. His father took no interest in their upkeep. The backyard, that's where he would go… to get away, run away, escape, hide, move, play; play hooky, play stickball, build a tree house, build a fort, dig a ditch, excavate under the porch, a hideout for his friends, in his backyard. It's funny though, that when he grew up— over forty years later he still has dreams about landscaping the backyard. He unfailingly dreamed that he cultivated the backyard, cut the grass, pruned the roses, trimmed the hedges, planted a vegetable garden and some flowers… something his dad would never do. His dad put in tulip bulbs upside down, some part time weekend work that he did for some Nazi butcher. Stephen had adult dreams of a place, a proving ground, a small landscape, and a childhood memory that became a dream of a virtual landscape of the mind.

Well, the scroll rolled into Chicago on a cool October day. He took his wife and daughter along with him; they got in the car and drove downtown. And there it was: the famous literary artifact, Jack Kerouac's scroll of *On the*

Road, rolled out under the glass of a long road of a table. It was yellow, taped, patched, X'd-out, with handwritten corrections, chewed by dog, admired by beat man, as prophesied, holy object, relic of the past, a museum piece. After fifteen minutes or so, they walked out of the terra cotta building, part of a college, and into the cold windy air of the Loop.

Jack came to Chicago alone on a bus in 1947 and stayed at the Y, dug the Loop, heard the Jazz, the sound of the American night. Walking to the car Stephen thinks of Sal Paradise and Dean Moriarty, he even thinks of old Jack Kerouac and Neal Cassidy, both dead... unlike Sal and Dean... he thinks of Sal and Dean rolling into Chicago in 1949 at 110 miles per hour in a Cadillac limo, which they parked in an alley, and went off by foot to explore the weird town, old brown, glowing red, the great roar of Chicago. It was in Chicago that Kerouac saw America as a vast backyard that contained all his friends, east to New York and west to San Francisco, all doing something frantic and rushing-about, going, running, escaping, hiding, moving, playing, digging, and driving (driving, something that Stephen couldn't do yet in the backyard of his childhood) to get away, run away, escape, hide, move, play, play hooky, play stickball, build a tree house, build a fort, digging a ditch, excavate under the porch, an underground hideout for his friends, in his backyard. Then Kerouac returned to New York, rolled some architect's tracing paper into a typewriter, and in three weeks built a fort over mythic America that echoes an endless note from a cool and crooked horn that sounded like a cavalry charge into unknown terrain. He taped it all together and rolled it up like a holy scroll of old, like a sketch of a new and secret landscape.

When they got home from seeing the scroll Stephen took down from the shelf an old, beat-up, tattered, battered, Penguin paperback of *On the Road* that he had got in London back in the 1980s. He had taken this copy with him through Europe, Norway, Paris, and far off the road to Japan... this paperback, it's the one that mattered to him, this "physical copy" that accompanied him through time and space, and yet somehow is the same (not same) book that others also read, somewhere in time and space, dear reader. And why not for the hell of it he got his old white Olympiette typewriter from 1974 out of the closet and he rolled in some tracing paper that he got in Japan years ago... and he typed... he hears the metal strike the ribbon and platen, it still works! He sees the letters appear on the paper as if from nowhere, the next best view to being there, and when he gets to the bottom of the page, he pulls the paper out and he finds the link... the link is in the ink! He hears his daughter in her room using her computer to "type" one of her stories, which, at 13, she is too embarrassed to show him. She types on the same (not same) letters, keys, that Jack typed on... she types fast, non-stop, the words appearing on the screen in the simulacrum (hateful word) of the new digital realm. Inkless, paperless, boundless... it's where the scroll goes, where the scroll goes, it's where the unknowable angel knows, where the unknowable angel knows, if the stone can still roll, if the stone can still roll, knows if his father will ever find through toil and toll to ghostly come here again in pain and prune the rose in the backyard of his mind, which is the biological redemption of the brain. The tracing paper that he used to type on came from the Miyazawa Kenji Museum in Hanamaki, Japan. Miyazaki wrote: I have linked the pieces of paper with ink, among the rice stalks and miscanthus... but now also among the lilac, forsythia and roses. Did you know that Eddie Poe made a scroll? Was Poe also trying to get it all down, before it was too late? But Poe had no great social cause. Poe had death.

Chicago 2005

And he was a teenage philosopher (A Course in French Culture for American Autodidacts). In his room with his books and music, what did his father think and never said a thing... Stephen stayed quiet to protect his father, but who would protect the son from his own anger, this anxiety, and these killer instincts. They first removed the barricade of the Enlightenment, mocked the empty skull of Descartes, "read" our minds on the matter, but it was their story that they wrote there, and no one read that book before: Progress. We then set out to save the world, swore loyalty oaths to God and state, proclaimed allegiance to flags thumb-tacked to maps, claimed property rights on colonized lands and language, the potatoes of Stendhal, the coffee of Balzac, but extensive recursion leads to ambiguity, complexity and memory loss: the Human Condition. Crazed armies of rats placed in a world-weary maze; and Proust invented the pattern of time: Modernity. We now face the uncertain face of reality, a long Greek chorus of clichés: literary, poetic, philosophical, stuff about beauty, consciousness and free will, theories of everything and theories for anything. Non-theories, anti-theories, anti-rationalism and anti-science. The removed mask, the scarred surface of the earth, the revealed silence, the erased word, the bottomless text, the blah blah blah of words words words, the absent presence, the signified nothing. But worse than this litany of ancient unanswered questions and enigmas are the lies and deceptions of public officials, the concentration of state and executive power, the erosion of civil liberties, locke stock and barrel hook line and sinker. We have read all the books and lived all the lies, the sad fishy flesh of Mallarmé the oceanic existence and essence of Sartre the filet of Foucault the slice and dice of Derrida. Perhaps as the ring of truth shifts through time it sometimes aligns with the rings of the perceptual, intentional and conceptual, but you doubt it, kind of. America, unaligned, misaligned, maligned, your rings like black holes and bullet holes, wounds, a blood bath. And the earth is bestirred and barricades broken, a great earth-remover plowing an ocean of boulevards through a city of medieval French streets. No hidden hand held up high to halt the storm-troopers revealing the chaos of capitalism and class; no lover's embrace on wide tree-lined pavements, no bright cafes, no Baudelaire, no Rimbaud, no wealthy patrons to look into the eyes of the poor and offer a handout, or call the cops. This then is no nouveau Napoleonic Paris, this is New Orleans, old-like city of the New Order, and where have they all been scattered? The rats from the social experiments in the maze? Scattered to the urban gutters and garbage and rural refuse of the wealthy nations, scavenging to the next block over where the shopping street meets the merchant's quarters and beyond to the green lawns of suburbia where nature never ends. There are soldiers and mercenaries in the streets with guns, just returned from Iraq, and dark spies, secret agents, CIA, NSA, FBI. That does not bode well for civil liberties... and the next time we meet by the barricades, the poor will not call the government nor the police for help, nor expect it; the rich patron will not bother to call the *maître de* to remove the poor man and his ragged family from his sight; nor the state bother to offer alms; the next time we meet, we meet at the barricades, in the street. *Bains de Sang.* Here comes his dad again to clean up, to mop up, the blood, vomit, piss and shit... the eternal return of dad, the eternal return of this goddamn mess.

Chicago 2003

An academic nostalgia for apple pie for alpha male America for articles and prepositions in the iambic ice cream cinema of a simple narration... good guys and bad guys... cheaters at poker and guns drawn first... the walk down at high noon... three shots fired... these three dots... when you write shit like this, smile... the parting ways of theory and history a literary bedtime story... once upon a time there were punctuation and rhyme heading down that old dusty road of good intentions to apocalypse over there over there the ellipsis at the end of the red and black line... signifying here now next to nothing... so beware so beware... juggernaut by the rivers of Babylon where Adam and Eve lay down and fucked-up in the Garden of Eden the absurd human race into being... and nothingness... and fell for an apple pie and ice cream from that tempting twinkle-eyed serpent Lucifer himself appearing directly from an off-off Broadway production of A Season in Hell performed on the rubble of the fallen towers of mamona and Moloch starring the fallen-angel child-poet Arthur Rimbaud sleeping homeless by the dime stores and bus stations on a bench with Jack Kerouac eating apple pie and ice cream and Bobby Zimmerman is there too with his Okie cap harmonica and guitar singing Which Side are You On Boys? Are you with Albert Camus the last living man on the atomic beach or Jean-Paul Sartre dressed like Hamlet smoking tobacco waiting to be shot in a cemetery? And everyone listening to Kafka crooning like Bing Crosby on the road to Morocco... and little Arthur calling for the burning of libraries and museums taking a last fart on poetry and then to arms dealing in Arab lands...hashish and hallucinations giant insects and pulsating pricks and fell for a few French postmodern philosophers sucking on an American lollipop culture with Lolita from a Motel 6... an ancient scribe holds in his hand a stylus trimmed from a reed cut from the marshes of the Euphrates River where writing was born and writes on the soft moist clay tablet that the walls are crumbling down...the fires the plunder pillage and looting and the barbarians are within our walls... and in London Paris Tangiers the writer pounding the typewriter... a personal history... a nation's history... world history... people's history... is this what they meant by the end of history?... silence... a banned book a burned book year one oh get off your butts and get real jobs little Arthur, Bobby and Jack... march this way up Highway 61 and down Route 66 for the eight-hour workday in Chicago 1886... ride the rail from Charleville to Paris for the Paris Commune of 1871 a budding journalist... walking out of Paris a poet disillusioned all the way home by foot... days of rage spent in a provincial town while the workers are being slaughtered in Paris... after that it was All or Nothing a book for All and None Nietzsche mad on the ridge at twilight the tightrope walker between Art and Politics so how can you be a worker now?... you're on strike... against work... when all else fails, there's debauchery, decadence, and the derangement of the senses... my senses have been stripped fade into my own parade passing by in celebration of myself... eyewitness and not activist... as I am another... as I am my own witness... passive nihilist ticker tape parade in New York City... for heroes like Lindbergh John Glenn and the Miracle Mets... waving flags... and standing on Broadway in the white rain of confetti... Wall Street and the New York Times roared for the heroes of the first Gulf War... the burden on the bent shoulders in the city of big shoulders, now the vultures are stealthily circling, and the poet sits waiting, is he a vulture too? An assassin? The poet sits over blank paper, pen in hand, waiting...waiting for the bombs and missiles to drop, there is no time to think said Dylan before he boarded the slow train, the mystery train, south bound with Elvis to the enigma of Jesus, to the cotton mouth lethal injections of Texas, Jesus on the jookbox, Bible belting out a song just to watch her die... come on in my kitchen it's gonna rain hard outside, so why is she waiting? And why can't he write a word? He can't prevent it... not the poet... he'd give his arm to prevent the suffering, not a thread of hair to help either side win... would he have marched off to Spain in 1937? Robinson Jeffers wouldn't lift a finger then, for either side... but he wouldn't shake Hitler's hand like Knut Hamsun either... and the bombast of Ezra Pound and the silence of T. S. Eliot... political art? The art of politics? He wants to write a topical poem, contemporaneous with the moment history is made, news in the making, but it's only the moment of the news, delayed, relayed through the satellite in the sputniked sky, to a logo-ed, virtual talking head, a smiling face flashing white teeth like a neon sign, advertising news of the Deed/Word into the world, at the lambent altar of the television screen, the Word speaks from the Burning Bush, the preordained script, the fundamental lie, in the beginning was the Deed, said Goethe, but he didn't have to watch endless reruns...the poet remembers the vultures circling the Carolina blue skies for days over the recently developed land cleared of ain't worth nuttin pine trees and the dilapidated farmhouse and the barn... all pulled down... all laid waste, wetlands filled, no more peanuts, cotton, watermelons, and the illiterate farmer dead, look away, look away, I'm bound away... and now Yankees and retired soldiers, their dogs, guns, fishing poles and wives, occupy the Dixieland with modular homes and seeping septic tanks... damn environmentalists... people gotta live somewhere a young Marine from Camp Lejeune was arrested for murder, he had killed his wife... so he made a deal... told the cops where the body was hidden, told them where he dumped the body four months ago... (at the end of the dirt road that passed by our house)... the vultures were circling for days the body was found on the edge of the developer's land, thank goodness not on my land, imagine the paper work... the sheriff and the SBI put up the yellow ribbon CRIME SCENE DO NOT CROSS the skeletal remains were found matted to the earth, the skin of the hand had slipped off like a glove, the fingers were sliced off, the Marine was trying to take away her fingerprints... her identity... you remember the FBI man on the TV a few years back saying that Kosovo was the world's largest crime scene, sometimes it seems the whole world is a crime scene, tie a yellow ribbon around the whole damn world, the military jets storm overhead, don't complain about the noise, it's the sound of freedom, tie a yellow ribbon to the tail of the jet and circumnavigate the globe, draw the lie in the sand, DO NOT CROSS   CRIME SCENE sometimes it seems the whole damn world is a crime scene... last year we moved to Chicago, source of old Route 66... American Dream road, see the USA in your Chevrolet, Lincoln County Road ... perhaps no more road going... dat's fer da birds... the time has come to build that bookcase, with wood from Dante's dark woods, to construct (or deconstruct) a classic bookcase, avant-garde bookcase, all that is the case bookcase, a library in a suitcase, fundamental floor to abstract ceiling, surrealist corner to existentialist corner, shelves for your paper bohemians to collect bourgeois dust, we have met in obscure places and traveled around the world, and now the time has come to take them out of their crates and boxes, and grow old, yellow, sly and foxed together... comity and domesticity, settle like dust, he supposes the books will have to be domesticated too! Domesticate the wild child Rimbaud, the mad Céline, the lewd Henry Miller, the brawlers and boozers, Hemingway and Bukowski, all the wandering Jews, calm the Calibans and tame the shrews, heap them on the shelves like bodies at an Indian pyre, a pile of ashes, a homebody like Proust may be happy at last, and aloof Jeffers too, grudgingly dragged around the world, some itching to go, some to stay, but together at last... and some will just have to be discarded, donated to the rehabilitation center down the street, discarded books for discarded people... the stiff zombie walkers in the cold, perhaps a book would do them good, said Jung perhaps a job, said Freud perhaps will just have to wait for evolution, said Darwin perhaps, said Einstein, perhaps Chicago, built of iron freight trains, wheat, lumber, hog butcher for the world, wrote Sandburg... the hogs hoisted, wheeled around, stuck and disassembled... everything is used... waste is criminal... we use everything, everything but the squeal... only the squeal is left, said meatpacking king Armour... twenty pigs slaughtered every minute, but we don't do numbers, Henry Ford saw the pigs disassembled and marveled, and took from it the idea for an assembly line for cars, reverse engineering, machines are assembled... dreams are disassembled... two cars in every garage, every man a king, sticks of dynamite in every bottom draw of a desk in the anarchist press room, Ford's factory a laboratory concocting biological warfare, cars, technology, information... weapons of mass production... and millions dead and disabled, superhighways to spread the disease, and here is my brain, Herr Doktor... sliced and diced, a pitiful little gray thing... the cause of all this trouble, you say, it boggles the mind... the mind?... that's some spooky shit said Descartes, let's slash off the brain print... remove this false identity, only the squeal is left... of priests and nuns and peasants... disappeared, well, there you go again said Ronald Reagan... and here we go again... Bush, Cheney, Rumsfeld, back in the saddle again... watch the wheel turn, grab the knife, stick the pig... the horrible blood letting, but it will all appear so clean, so sanitized on CNN, so clean and sanitized on the computer's monitor in the Pentagon's dark dungeon of doom's day buttons... nothing left but the squeals, collateral damage... but the dead have no voice... the living left wounded less of a voice, only a senseless squeal remains... and the killers have no conscience, let's trim the hogs, hoss, feast on the bloody balls of these swine, you swine, the vultures circling, smelling the potential blood, the oil...the poet sits waiting for a word... waiting for the bombs and missiles to fall... waiting for the news? Waiting for the Deed to happen...it happened... this is a work in progress, this will always be a work in progress, this that can't stop saying what it wants to say because time keeps hovering over the back of his head casting shadows on the page beneath his eyes like a black hawk helicopter firing missiles... spitting blood... spilling guts, brains and limbs lodging in the black hole of his brain, a child screaming terrified in this putrid dark recess of his mind, a listless body, no illumination... mind/brain, it's all the same, a huge, horrible, frightened bird whose wings drag upon the earth... an 18th century Frenchman said that if the state can control the arm, it can control the tongue... materialism presupposes it, assures it, assumes it, for every action there is an equal smack in the face... for no damn good reason... can democracy deter random smacks when state power tends toward fascism? What barrier? If mind/body falls toward each other, into the slash that can't even slice cheese, philosophically, does not the rest fall? Power/privilege state/church civilian/military and if some Tarkovskian zone of the mind, a small segment, is so preoccupied with death and destruction and tragedy like the world with this malignancy, this cancer that grows across the scarred face of reality... so be it... pick and choose... what is waste? What is useful? Surrender to time and space and history, give up the ghost... it is finished, said Jesus of Nazareth, that's all folks, said Porky Pig of Looney Tunes, The End, as the novelists used to write on the last page before they discovered that in the beginning does not mean in the beginning, that the Deed is privileged, that the Road Runner said beep-beep to the beats and their Grandpa Kierkegaard on the road, hapless coyote, dynamite's the thing? And known by the company you keep the Danish philosopher walked away from God and walked into the devil's arms, because sometimes when you are so right, you're wrong, bombs away... peeing off the side of a moving truck on Route 66... wow, how great is that... but maybe that's the point, a great wow of the mundane, a Campbell soup can, a faux solidarity with the workingman... is that all there is to it? That everything lives in time, green nasty mean time, and the child without arms, blown to pieces, in time, the authentic and the artificial, the earth revolves around the sun, in time... Anno Domini... 2003... another prosthesis for God, another war begun...in time... oh lord this piece of shit word-accumulation like a culture-vulture of capital, Das Kapital on Madison Avenue, useless production, can he eat paper? Shelter under a pencil? Offered to this mess of a world like a soldier offering an artificial arm to that child, here kid... humanitarian aid... a poem, just words, words, words... like those wedges carved in clay in Mesopotamia, in an unknown town, by the river Euphrates, 5000 years ago, see how worthless it all is... how fragile, out the door and up in smoke... many forgotten volumes of lore, it's as if he is reading a novel 38,000 feet in the air, inside an airplane bound for Tokyo, and at any moment disintegrating in flames, reduced to ashes... to atoms... shooting through the sky with the last images in his mind from a goddamn novel, Leo Tolstoy or Louis L'Amour, no distinction, no difference, just images born of words, quoth the raven "nevermore"... memory is images burned into mind, oh thing of evil, ravens like letters flying off the page into eternal darkness, leaving a fading shadow fragment... unlifted...the shadow of a plane over the rice fields approaching Hiroshima, time hovering over his head... on a mission from God... a crusade... a great yawl of his insatiable jaws clenched and gnawing on slivers of flesh hanging from the corners of his mouth, arms extended like ghosts from the Maruki murals, like the wax figures he saw in the museum in Hiroshima, the image of the body burnt into earth, never lifted nevermore, and a deep husky old voice finally says you blew it folks... you had your chance and you blew it, what a wonderful world... it's old Louis Armstrong in Chicago, 1926... man, you cats done give me the Heebie Jeebies scat scat scat, now let me blow! A new punctuation, a new popular rhyme, and a new voice thar she blows! Moby-Dick, Huck Finn and Walt Whitman at the gate, blowing away old Europe's dark edifice, blowing away Washington Irving's White Christmas (or is that Irving Berlin's?) blowing away his bio of Columbus and the flat earth myth, blowing away Rudy Vallee and his megaphoney white smoothness, paving the way for the husky singers, the gravel road rawness of Woody Guthrie, Mississippi John Hurt, Dylan, and out of the American grain a memory blown out like an empty egg shell, the great amnesia that covers the pastures of plenty (for some) like a fog creeping over the Mississippi River by Davenport, Iowa, where Kerouac ate that apple pie and ice cream in the American night, after he passed through the transient bop loop of Charley Parker to Miles Davis, and from where Bix blew toward Chicago... and Kerouac hitched out of Chi on a dynamite truck with a red flag...sweet irony... and he stands on the shore of Lake Michigan and his mind drifts back to 1886... 1887... because you read it in a book somewhere that they hanged four of them for their ideas, their speech, for the Word, not their actions, not the Deed... oh control thy tongue, hold thy tongue, wag thy tongue, it was when they first asked: are you a Socialist, Communist, Anarchist? Long before House Un-American Activities Committee, the actual transcript: Q Are you now, or have you ever been, a member of any Socialistic Organization? A No his wife's immigration papers asked are you or have you ever been an anarchist, or a member of or affiliated with any Communist or other totalitarian party, including any subdivision or affiliate? But eventually they cleaned the blood off the streets by the Haymarket, they mopped up this great most American of cities by 1893, in time to celebrate Columbus and his arrival in America, the World's Colombian Exposition, the embodiment of Progress and Reason, year 401, Henry Adams said that Chicago asked in 1893 for the first time the question whether the American people knew where they were driving... Chicago was the first expression of American thought as a unity... hey, where are you driving, America? To work? Well, the workers cleaned her up, the dirty work... washed the blood off Desplaines Street, and erected a beautiful unreal White City (they called the real city the Black City...) the first virtual city, a plan for Utopia, and five years later we brought Utopia to Cuba, the Philippines, the birth of Empire... the undeclared Empire, the hire-a-thug Empire, Pax Americana... American thought as a unity... looking backward... from the Idealist Wilson to the romantic Theodore Roosevelt who sent the Great White Fleet on a tour of the world... hey, they are still on tour... look... Operation Iraqi Freedom Tour 2003, tickets available through all major broadcast networks, Fox and CNN. Mayor Carter Harrison in his inaugural speech of 1893, promoting Chicago for the Colombian Exposition, said Chicago... laves her beautiful limbs daily in Lake Michigan and comes out clean and pure every morning... not long after he was shot down in cold blood on his doorstep. More mopping up and more mopping up to come... just wait till Rumsfeld's favorite guy Al Capone gets here... and now he stands here on the shore of Lake Michigan and looking East he thinks of that French lady in the harbor of New York City... he once stood inside her head and felt the private mental reality of freedom... (seems you can't go into her head anymore!) And he sees that she laves her beautiful limbs daily in New York Harbor and comes out soiled and bloody every morning... what's harder to clean, a man or an institution? Oh nostalgia the inherent goodness of apple pie and ice cream, of baseball and his dad's old army tattoo... he never considered removing the black smear on his forearm that was once a red white and blue tattoo of eagle and flag... child of the depression, World War II soldier, working class boy, construction worker bartender janitor a lifetime of mopping up somebody else's vomit and shit and all the filth of the floor. Get your mops out, readers, here we go... we've only just begun, like the song says, the one they played at his sister's wedding, at all those weddings that ended in acrimony and filth...

The Boy on the Shore

He did not die. That was another lie. He only wanted to escape. He wanted a perfect silence. He wanted exile. He did not die. After all, it was not he. It was another. The train went on without him. His sister cried from the window. The rain fell. The train continued on to Paris. He rose from his hospital bed, a disembodied voice, an elongated spirit. He walked down to the harbor. He bought his ticket to the New World. His name was Jean; yes, that was his name now. He boarded the ship in the port of Marseille. He saw his future in the ocean's horizon. He was the future. He was modernity. Absolutely. He was off to see the New World. He stood on the deck, propped up against the railing. A child, walking with his mother, stared at the strange man, standing there with his one leg. Jean spat overboard. The mother grabbed the child's hand tighter and pulled him away. He arrived the first day of the New Year 1892. The golden door of liberty and hope opened for the first time, far from the Europe of fear and trembling. The old bearded poet met him at Ellis Island. The old bearded poet who was dying, who rose from his sickbed in Camden to journey back home once more. The old bearded poet showed the still young man, clean-shaven, the sites and sounds of his city. The great metropolis, the Manahatta. The Village. They journeyed to Brooklyn, the beautiful hills, on the ferry, and out to the island, Paumanok, and to the beach at Oyster Bay, where they sat on the sands and watched the waves and the drunken boats. A young boy came to the shore. Have you seen Isabelle?

In words beginning... the boy stood on the shore. Is that you, Stephen? You still have doubt? You still see yourself as a freak, an aberration, a monster in the library? You must leave your father and mother behind. The voyage is about to begin. The only reason to go is to get away.

In books beginning with beginnings, in books ending with endings, words are contained, taboo, whole and transcendent. The boy stood at the overlapping edge of water and sand. In books beginning with endings, in books ending with beginnings, words are boundless, unlawful, plural and immanent. The boy stood on the shore. You got your feet wet. How can the beginning be undone? How can the ending be begun? Negation and affirmation are infinite. You are erased from the word and words are the eraser. In modern scholastic terminology, you are deleted from the datum, and the algorithmic code is the deleter. You byte the circuit. You are regulated to the semantic funhouse, where you recite nonsense verses, senile babbler of solipsisms; soliloquizer in the ashes and dust of the epilogue. To paraphrase Mallarmé: "My spirit is sad, alas, and I have told all the stories."

The boy stood on the shore. Shall you erase the boy from the shore? Shall you delete him? Disassimilate him? Disassemble him? Deauthorize him? Unspeak him? Abort him? That would put an end to this, right now, right here... *pause*... à la Céline...

What of the driftwood and the horseshoe crab? Didn't I tell you about them? They are there too. Must I erase them too? What declension unto level baseness shall undermine them? What flat nonsense from flexure shall underwrite them? The stasis of a horizontal line of letters across the face of the page is the desire of Narcissus for himself. You follow this line and imbrue your hands and scald your feet. But you descend like Orpheus on spiraling stairs, enthralled by encounters in the darkness of foreign city streets. Narcissus sings into his own ears. Shall you turn back? This is your last warning. After how many steps ascending shall the light from the basement door catch a glimpse of Eurydice's face? How heavy she is! To hear the cries of withholding and unoffering for fear of the cries of refusal and rejection is to see her skull without its flesh when the light reveals it. Could you go on with that knowledge? Hell is the bottom of a shelf. The box in the attic. The crumpled paper in the wastebasket. The flames of the manuscript. She is indeed heavy to bear. Shall creation miscarry? Trip on the top step. Must you carry the dead back down? You are standing on the threshold of the door. The boy is standing on the shore. You feel vertigo. You feel a semiotic twinge of futility, nausea, and absurdity... modern ailments. Shall you open the door? If we open it will you open it? If we push will you push? Can we trust you? Can you trust us? The waves beckon the boy away. The wind picks up. Dark clouds gather in the distance. The mirrored sea is breaking open a thousand entrances to the labyrinth. Odysseus is on the sea again.

The boy stood on the shore. It's October 12, 1964, or perhaps it's 1892. The boy is eight years old. He is silent. The boy told the two poets of a secret tree house that he and his friends had discovered. It was up the cove, where the rich dwell. So they followed the boy. It is up the hill, there's an iron gate. A white mansion on the hill. I've seen it with my own eyes, my friends and me were curious to see the land beyond the woods. They stood at the bottom step of the mansion. The boy picked up a piece of brick and scrawled an obscene word on the white step. They did not erase the word. They laughed. The old poet... these two, the words encompassing all, all into the self; and the other, a private and obscure tongue, a self drunk and lost.... and a self extolled and celebrated. And they walked back into the town...

The Town and the Bully

The village of Oyster Bay is located on the north shore of Long Island, about thirty miles from New York City. Oyster Bay Harbor is approximately two miles square. It is parted through the center by a peninsular called Center Island, which used to be an island, originally called Hog Island. There is a large house on one of the points, usually referred to as the Widdlesworth mansion. In 1949, Torhild, a bright beautiful Norwegian girl, almost two years off the boat, worked as a maid in the mansion, at that time the domicile of another wealthy family, the Smiths, the Widdlesworths having all died out, as you shall see: Anglo-Saxon Race Suicide, with the sole exception of one Charles William Barbour Mouche, the famous French writer.

The harbor's throat enters Long Island Sound just above Cove Neck, between Plum Point on Center Island and Cooper's Bluff on Cove Neck, not far from Sagamore Hill, the home and summer White House of Theodore Roosevelt. The harbor is be-girded by wooded hills that ascend impetuously to modest heights of over one hundred feet. These hills are crowned with ponds, gullies and streams flowing northward to the harbor. In geological terms the topography is characteristic of that encountered at the drop-off end of a continental ice sheet.

The land north of the Long Island Railroad comprises Theodore Roosevelt Memorial Park and the beach by the harbor. This area was a salt marsh in the 17th century where local Native Americans hunted and fished. And before it was a park it was a dump with shacks.

Sand and small stones and shells. The gentle movements of a cool October day made captive the mood. The beach was empty. Masts of sailboats were swaying like white sticks, marking time with the waves like a metronome. Boats were bobbing and bowing, their ropes jerking at the fixed moorings. A long erratic brush stroke of slate-gray was smeared just above the horizon, beneath which a blaze of orange embers flared from the sunken furnace beneath the olive-dark pencil line of the far shore.

At one end of the beach there were large rocks piled in a line commencing at a point halfway up the beach and submerging and terminating about twenty feet out in the water. The small beach is angled in a diagonal direction from the ebbing and briny water's brim to the far top-end of the beach where the canting sands crescendo at the granite-block seawall. At low tide various trash and settled flotsam are exposed among the flora and patches of sea-grass shaped like a map of England, at least for now, in the future the shape may differ; perhaps like a map of Norway or Japan. The stone and shell-dappled yellow sands stretch out from the sun-bleached wall to the water's brink where the sand transforms into a subconscious rim of black viscous sand that extends to the bulging protrusion of the wall and advances its slimy imprint upon the uncovered base where an occasional water rat can be seen scurrying along and quickly darting into a dark crack. The seawall, which is about three feet high on the land side and varies from three to ten feet in depth on the water side, fronts the bay and backs the park from the beach to the small fishing pier which projects out at an angle into the bay, the pier is no more than twenty-five feet in length, the end of which meets the end of another small pier reaching out symmetrically from the opposite side and hardly a dime's throw away, leaving only enough space between them for boats to enter the small craft harbor, where sailboats and speedboats are docked. The two piers stand like half-closed rusted gates of a lock to an abandoned canal.

On the landside, skirting the wall, is a path filled with little round pinkish and grayish pebbles. There is a flagpole that stands within a grassy knoll of pansies and marigolds by a white anchor. The formation of the wall zigzags out into the water in a series of angles and then curves smoothly around 180 degrees before the shape of the wall breaks acutely again into three sideway steps back and forth to the corner near the flagpole, and then proceeds straight on until it ends at the fishing pier and its white fence carved with initials and dates and gull droppings. The short squat wall is made of large square and rectangular blocks, the tops of which have been rendered over in broken places like patchwork.

South of the harbor and east of the beach is a large square sun-lit field bounded by eight feet wide paths. At the north end of the field the path abuts the sea wall, at the border of the field five park benches are set lengthways confronting the bay; on the east end a chain-link fence surrounds the deeply trenched small craft harbor; on the west end a smaller field with several oval tiered flower beds, here the path is lined with large old oak trees; and on the south end beyond the path a green wooden pavilion where the American Legion and Fire Department and other such organizations hold their annual cookouts and fund-raisers, events which bring out the town's freeloaders and drunks. There is also a brick building with restroom facilities. There once stood a marble facility that was torn down. The park's boundary concludes just beyond the pavilion where a fence separates the park from the railroad tracks. The original turn-of-the-century ticket window and waiting room of the train station are still in operation.

Located in the park is an area shaded by oak trees. Twelve diversely formed edifices of rock, including two long low walls of cemented stones, surrounded by trees and planted firmly in the earth, are ceremoniously positioned in a rambling roundabout manner in the field. Embedded in one of the large upright rocks is a brown metal plaque that reads:

ROOSEVELT MEMORIAL OAK
To the sacred memory of
THEODORE ROOSEVELT
THE GREAT AMERICAN
PRESIDENT of the United States
1901-1909
Planted Palm Sunday 1919 A.D.

The grass is wet and the ground saturated. An early morning rain had soaked the soft earth and filled the shallow pools of an artesian well to excess, the water running over the brim. The gray-blue stone fountain is compiled of a four feet long narrow wall flanked at both ends by a headless eagle, each eagle stationed with its wings stretched upward and pinned back, talons clutching a wider base which steps down and juts out at each end. The heads of the eagles have been broken off. In the center at the top of the five feet high wall a short oxidized copper pipe pours water from opposing ends, issuing forth in a moderate flow down the sides of the wall, tarnishing it a green bell-shaped discoloration. The water falls into semi-circular receptacles about a foot high, at the front-top of each a half-rounded gullet has been cut to let the water slowly trickle down into a long one inch deep and eight inch wide conduit adjoined on each side by a three foot wide flat stone surface, level with the grass, which some running water trickles over. The troughs descend in successive layers before the water drains off into shallow pools. A twig floated through the conduit, tumbling over like a tiny log and evading the obstructions of clogged autumn scented leaves. When the twig snagged, it slowly broke itself loose and rushed onward in the channeled momentum of the water. The twig ultimately toppled into the pool. The series of dedicatory stones were erected in honor of Theodore Roosevelt. Once, nearby, there stood the statue of Captain Roger Bethell, until it was removed. But the other rocks remain. There is a thick rectangular stone slab of granite fixed upon a supporting foundation of fist-sized cemented stones. This slab was a front step to a summerhouse of the Roosevelt family where Teddy went when he was a small boy. It is the focal point of the memorial landmark, being situated in the center. Slightly to the left of this stone slab, ten feet away, is a gray rock resting on a substratum of cement. Next to that rock, proceeding clockwise is another similar but large rock. There is a blank impression in the cement because the bronze plaque has been removed. Straight in front of the stone slab in the center, parallel with it, is a stonewall. The wall is a foot thick mass of small round cobblestones with five distinct alcoves on the inner side of the wall, horizontally aligned across the front, spaced a short distance apart. Roosevelt memorabilia is lodged in cement in each square niche, each article representing some aspect of his career. A rock from Cuba, an empty shell from a navy gun, a bronze book referring to his autobiography, a rock from the Panama canal, a brick, and more rocks from origins unknown because the plaques providing the information are gone, stolen no doubt. At the end of the wall are three more large rocks, the center one bearing the inscription cited above. Continuing clockwise next comes another even longer cobblestone wall with seven alcoves, each with its entrenched rock. This wall is at a right angle to the other wall; the stone slab in the center is perpendicular to this longer wall. Behind the stone slab in the center are three more large rocks, and there is another rock to the immediate left of the stone slab, thus forming a circuit of twelve stone structures with the stone slab in the center like a sacrificial altar. The Druid of Empire haunts his Stonehenge. A light rain is falling and a black coffin is washed ashore. Four men carry the black coffin from the shore to the rock enclosure and place the coffin on the stone slab.

Colonel Mayhem: Is all our company here?

Colonel Mischief: All are present and unaccounted for.

Colonel Bully: What is the play? And name the players, manly by manly, according to the script.

Colonel Mischief: A most lamentable comedy called Empire.

Colonel Bully: A splendid capital piece of work.

Colonel Mishap: Role-call! Colonel Bully?

Colonel Bully: Here. Tyrant or lover?

Colonel Mishap: Lover.

Colonel Bully: But my humor is for a tyrant. Let me play the tyrant. Let me play all the parts. Let me play the woman. I'll speak in a monstrous and squeally voice. Let me play the lion; I'll roar! Roar as gently as a dove. Let me play the ass too! The people will be delighted. They will say: Let him roar! Let him roar again!

Colonel Mischief: Yet there are things in this comedy that will never please the ladies. First, the sword must never be drawn, which the ladies cannot abide.

Colonel Mishap: I believe we must leave the killing out.

Colonel Bully: Not a whit. We must not shrink from hard contests. Bolder and stronger peoples will pass us by, and will win for themselves the domination of the world. We must always be prepared. We are not the clay; we are the shapers. War makes the mold and war breaks the mold. Violence makes the world's values. Remember, gentlemen, there is a crack in our Liberty Bell. Our faith shines through that crack. I see ships, gentlemen, ships and more ships... I see airplanes, rockets, missiles, and bombs to make the mold and break the mold. We are the greatest industrial nation in the world. The ladies will sit on the piazzas. We must build large piazzas to accommodate the ladies. My house has a large and spacious piazza with a delightful view of Oyster Bay Harbor. We must build larger and larger; everything must be bigger and bigger...

Colonel Mishap: Even the mistakes?

Colonel Bully: ...and... nothing can contain the American spirit. The ladies can watch and listen from a safe distance. It will be a splendid show. The greatest show on earth. But it will cost. The people must get their money's worth. It pays to advertise. I have a device; a subterfuge, a cunning ruse... write me a prologue and let the prologue seem to say that we will do no harm with our swords, that our intentions are good, that we are righteous, and that the peoples of the world shall be lifted up...

Colonel Mishap: Will not the ladies be afeared of the lion too?

Colonel Bully: Another prologue will tell that he is not a lion, yet make it certain that he is neither a mouse.

Colonel Mishap: Nay, you must name his name! I am no such thing as a lion. I am a man as other men are. Let him name his name and tell the people plainly that he is a...

Colonel Bully: An ass!

Colonel Mayhem: Whether they will or no, Americans must begin to look outward. The sea! The ships!

Colonel Mischief: The sky! The airplane! Space! Rockets! Discoveries!

Colonel Mishap: Missiles! Bombs! We shall become masters of nature and masters of mankind. When they see with their own eyes, the people will believe. The man is like a lion. We are all things to all people. The world shall have faith is us.

Colonel Bully: The good faith of the United States is a mighty valuable asset and must not be impaired.

Colonel Mischief: O Colonel Bully thy asset is impaired! The revealer is revealed! We are devalued. Debunked. We have become death...

Colonel Bully: Traitor! Foolish translator! Cut out his tongue!

Colonel Mischief: From a bestiary to bestiality...

Colonel Bully: I have revealed the River of Doubt. The hunter must know his prey. The great white hunter must kill if he is to hang his trophies on the wall. Every house must have a large piazza for the ladies and a large drawing room for elephant tusks and bear and lion skins, where men can meet and trade and wager on the future of the world.

Colonel Mischief: O the complexity of the making of the weapons of death and the simplicity of breaking the mold! The simplicity of the morality and intellect of dropping the bombs... lions and asses... from a bestiary to bestiality.

Colonel Bully: There is nothing simple in defense. In the defensive strategies and maneuverings of great minds. It is the eternal flame of freedom that we are defending.

Colonel Mischief: What said Macbeth: From this instant there's nothing serious in mortality; all is but toys, renown and grace are dead.

Colonel Bully: Traitor, you are deferred and referred.

Colonel Mischief: You are revealed.

Colonel Bully: Open the black coffin. At the oak we meet; and there we may rehearse most obscenely and courageously. I wish to preach, not the doctrine of ignoble ease, but the doctrine of the strenuous life. Take pains; pull your weight... open the coffin, I say.

Enter Faeries: Phoenix, Sidewinder, Sparrow, Stinger, and Trident...

Colonel Bully: When the soldiers, I mean players, are all dead, there need none to be blamed. After the act, just act, it will be too late, iron fate, not above the law, we are the law, therefore... open the coffin, I say!

Faeries open the coffin. Enter the Bomb.

Colonel Bully: We are all gathered here in is His name. When I give the word, fire! However reluctantly, we may be forced to the exercise of an international police power. In flagrant cases of wrongdoing or impotence. But we are not impotent. When I give the word... however reluctantly... fire! Words in flame. Cities in flame. Jungles in flame. The word made flesh. *Has Comido Carne de Gente?* Now, then, be the prophet and the fulfiller one. And the bombs are falling... from this instant there's nothing...

Colonel Bully: Let me have my toys... uh guns, gentlemen. If I can't have my warships, I still have my big stick!

The Colonels form a circle. They chant: We gots guns, dey gots guns, all god's chillun got guns!

Got guns and a bibel and a hoe...

Whitman and Rimbaud are hiding in the bushes and roaring with laughter. Stephen sees several ships approaching in the mist of the bay... a sailor jumps into the water and swims to shore. Rising from the water he casts a weary eye on Whitman and Rimbaud. Where's Toby? Are these the Marquesas Isles? Call me Herman.

No, this is the Long Isle!

Ships! Ships!

"There are fine oysters here, whence our nation has given it the name Oyster Bay." So wrote Captain David Petersen de Vries in his "Voyages from Holland to America A.D. 1632 to 1644." He anchored in the harbor on June 4, aboard a West Indian Company yacht assigned to the New Netherland Director-General at New Amsterdam.

"Oyster Bay so called from the great abundance of fine and delicate oysters which are found there has on its borders fine maize lands formerly cultivated by the Indians some of which they still work. They could be had for a trifle. This land is situated on such a beautiful bay and rivers that it could at little cost be converted into good farms fit for the plough. There are here and there also some fine hay valleys. Martin Gerritson's Bay or Martinnehouck is much deeper and wider than Oyster bay and runs westward in and divides into three rivers, two of which are navigable: the smaller stream runs up in front of the Indian village of Matinnehouck where they have their plantations. This tribe is not strong and consists of about thirty families. In or about this bay there were formerly great numbers of Indian plantations, which now lie waste and vacant."

The ownership of the land in Oyster Bay was a point of contention between the Dutch and the English. Oyster Bay formed a dividing line between the Dutch province of New Netherland and English settlers from New England. What proved to be a temporary agreement was drawn up on September 19, 1650 between the Dutch and the English at Hartford. Peter Stuyvesant and Commissioners from New England decreed that the boundary should be run from "the Westernmost part of the oyster bay soe and in a straight line to the Sea."

The dispute over location was not settled until King Charles II bestowed upon his brother James, Duke of York, an enormous tract of land in North America in 1664, which included Long Island. The Duke promptly dispatched a fleet to capture New Netherland, and Oyster Bay was no longer "betwixt the English and the Duch."

The tides coursed into the harbor, into the small cove, the rest moved westerly, following the hollow around Moses Point, then in a south-easterly direction, meeting the main current traveling toward the other side of Center Island and into West Harbor. This creates choppy waters at Moses Point, where the sloop called *Desire* beats and bumps against the small rough waves. It is coming from the end of its journey from Plymouth, Massachusetts, carrying the families and belongings of the first settlers at Oyster Bay.

"I, being at the first settlement of Oyster Bay which was in the year 1653, Peter Wright, William Leverich, and Samuel Mayo, they being the first three purchasers, as by the grand deed from the Indian sachem..."

Have you thrown in your lot with the Puritans in Plymouth? Why have you come? What do you seek? Religious freedom? There is but one minister among you; most are farmers. Is it better land for grazing and planting? Was their truly more cause to fear wealth than poverty in that soil? Black loam brings little labor. But glacial moraine mirrored your emptiness. Your unfulfillment is our legacy; the world jangles over the pits of hell for fear of your pride and death. If only your *Mayflower* had landed in sunnier climes? But your heart was ice and your mind fire. The bridge to

God was melting, so you turned to fire, and consumed the silence with your emptiness and loneliness.

The sloop *Desire* sailed into West harbor and entered local history… it's so dark dark dark amid the bombs bursting in dawn's early light. Strike the iron when hot! The woman in the callicoe gown standing in the kitchen by the large chimney; she is the wife of the blacksmith, and he is standing under the chestnut tree striking the iron. Half-blind New World eyes. Vengeful Samson between the gateposts, to the east and west. Stone clashed with bronze, bronze clashed with iron. *Eisen und Blut* in Europe for a thousand years, from the stark fjords of Norway to the bloody Mediterranean Sea. A long legacy of violence. Sacred smoke blew over the guns of the iron people. Profane smoke blew out from the barrels of the conquerors. The world had never seen such violence. The world had never seen such wonders. Patience Wright, the blacksmith's wife writes a letter to friends back in jolly ole England, sitting in her salt-box house with thatched-roof; she ends her letter prophetically, Cassandra-like, consoling her soul about her harsh new world life. "Dear friends, sory we are that there should be occasion of writing at all unto you… we have all we need… guns and a bibel."

There was another ship: 76 feet long from stem to stern, with an oak keel cutting the waters and 16 pairs of pine oars rapping the waves. A 35-foot pine mast was festooned with a big billowy square sail waving against a burnished and blue sky. Why have you come? What was your need? What do you seek? Was it the pressures of geography? Economics? A hunger for land? Fame? Wealth? Profit? Material goods? Trade? Piracy? And conquest? What do you trade? Furs, slaves, grains, fish, timber, salt, glass, hides, wine, cattle, horses, glue, falcons, bears, walrus ivory, silks, woolens, amber, hazel nuts, honey, seal oil, malt, soapstone dishes, weapons, ornaments, basalt millstones, silver, guns, bibles…

The broad-waisted open boat called a knorr sailed toward the blood-soaked and broad open land. The knorr has sailed from the southern tip of Greenland to places named by Leif Eiriksson: Helluland, grassless and barren; Markland, white sands and forests; and finally Vinland, where the sun sleeps close to the water over Labrador, and the low dark hills across the Strait of Belle Isle appear like twenty Viking ships. On the north side of Newfoundland the grassy fields of L'Anse Aux Meadows, where blueberries make the maroon wine. Vinland of grass? Vinland of wine? Still

500 years before Columbus... How far did you come? St. Lawrence Estuary? Baie de Chaleur? New Brunswick? Nova Scotia? New England? Minnesota? Long Island Sound? Bay Ridge, Brooklyn? Oyster Bay, langt eilan? And another ship... Torhild Andersen stood on the deck of the ship. What was her need? The ship, a transatlantic steamer, the *SS Stavangerfjord*, entered the harbor; on the passenger list is the name Froken Torhild Andersen, from Lundevågen, Farsund, Norway. It is July 1947. She has come to America to meet her mother for the first time. Unfortunately, she never had a chance to meet her father. This is a short column in the Bay Ridge Norwegian newspaper.

Document 1.3.2

Erik Andersen, 47 år gammel, fra Oslo, blev kl. 2 natt til 12. oktober overfalt og rovet på 57. st., naer 6, ave., Brooklyn.

Some men came out of a car and knocked him over the head. They stole 5 dollars from him and fled in the car. He went to the hospital and was pronounced fine and released. A few days later he was found dead in Sunset Park.

Take note of the day: October 12, Columbus Day. Among the dead that day is an immigrant from Norway, Torhild's father, murdered in Brooklyn. Beautiful Isle of Somewhere! Land of the true, where we live anew...

Three more ships entered the harbor. The *Nina, Pinta,* and *Santa Maria.* But not from the port of Genoa, not carrying rice, wine, silk, olive oil, soap, marble... carrying Greed and Glory and the Word of God. *Vi saluto, o Maria, pienza di grazie, il Signore e con Voi; e benedetta il frutto delle vostre viscere, Gesu.*

Columbus Day! Christopher Columbus, born on one of the narrow, winding and sloping streets of Genoa, Italy; and on another street in a nearby mountain valley outside Genoa, in the village of Orero, in the year 1870, Giuseppe Cazzaza was born. Why did you come, Giuseppe?

On another ship... in 1893, on the *SS Fulda...*

Giovanni Cazzaza and Lucia Vespucci were married in Orero, Italy, on May 5, 1841. They had four sons and a daughter: Giacomo was the oldest; then came Giovanni, Giuseppe, Maurizio and Gina. In 1889 Gina married Giancarlo Bacigalupo. Giancarlo was a foreman in a slate quarry, a family business, his father was the previous foreman, and they had done well, but lately times were hard. In 1893, Giovanni, Giuseppe, Maurizio, Gina and

Giancarlo left Italy for America, never to return. The oldest brother Giacomo decided to remain in Italy. He had married Sophia Giacosa in 1890. In 1892 a son was born whom they named Cardeo. In Manhattan, Giuseppe, Giovanni and Maurizio lived on Mercer Street, in the same building as Giancarlo and Gina. Working together, Giuseppe and Giancarlo saved enough money to move out of the city by 1904. Giuseppe found the small village of Oyster Bay to his liking, and moved there, in 1904, taking along his wife Fiorenza and their two-year-old girl Silvia; and because Fiorenza's two sisters, Leonora and Teresa, didn't want to part from each other, they came too. They would be useful in the shop that Giuseppe dreamed of opening.

Giancarlo found a place in the village of Northport. He and Gina and their two sons, Johnny, who was ten, and Anthony, who was eight at the time, in 1904, settled in Northport, about 12 miles from Oyster Bay. Giuseppe Cazzaza and Giancarlo Bacigalupo built up the two properties, so similar in style, made of solid two feet thick concrete and brick walls. Giancarlo opened his fruit and vegetable store the same year as Giuseppe opened his store. Johnny Bacigalupo worked hard to please his father; Anthony not so much. Later Giancarlo started a cement and block company, and Johnny eventually took it over, turning it into a major building company that built half the homes on Main Street in Northport. And Giovanni, he went to Sayville… but his story is rather vague. They say he lived in a shack in the woods and howled at the moon.

Hills

Why like Sisyphus to push this rock of a book to the top of that hill only to watch it roll back down, again and again. They charged up the hill. The squad leader Sgt. Joe Cazzaza called out the names of his men. There was Blair of Iowa, Homer of South Carolina, Blaine of Michigan, Leo of Illinois, Jack of San Francisco, Hank of Wisconsin, Rocco of Brooklyn… these men called to serve and had little choice but to act honorably; the poet who is the soldier now, the artist who is the soldier now, look at the books they carried with them… these recruits of the 88th…If this should ever end and if we are not dead and gone when the day turns dark or the night turns light and if we are still part of this life that may yet be lost on the side of this hill, this rock, this bush, this tree, this foxhole grave, this burnt edifice of old Italia, this saint and that, then Rome and home, buddies, Rome and home... from Gruber to the Brenner... over hill, over dale, we will hit the dusty trail, and those caissons go rolling along. Rome and home and memory recaptured, the 1933 New York Giants. There was Bill Terry of Georgia, Mel Ott of Louisiana, Carl Hubbell of Missouri... The doubleheader at the Polo Grounds, the Giants versus the Cardinals, a great and lasting memory for 12-year-old Joe Cazzaza, Hubbell defeated Dizzy Dean... that's the way he remembered it sixty years later, that's how he told it to his son, when the dead numbers of the numbered dead accumulated past the years of the great ending V Day... and he told his son about the 1934 NY Giants sneaker's game...

They charged up the hill. The body summoned by the heart's desire. A man cannot shrink from his destiny, from the battle, from the action, the pure act, cannot shirk one's duty, this great chance to be alive, a bright and crowded hour of time. His men followed behind the fearless and empowered death master, there was James of Harvard, William of Yale, Henry of the Indian Territories, Colonel Bob the Oilman... eager to volunteer... to act purely, a glorified deed... to volunteer... to serve. And then one soldier was felled by a bullet to the head, his sword plummeted into the dirt, the bursting sounds and booms, explosions, and dirt pluming up from the blood and sweat ground, a chunk of meat missing from his head, a chunk of meat, like an aborted fetus, and yet the Colonel charged up the hill. They crawled ever upward toward the celestial crown.

Tommy of Brooklyn called out to the other men... there was Jimmy of Vermont, Leroy of Alabama, and James of Mississippi... a bullet ripped the flesh wide open, the shrapnel tearing the flesh off the bones, and he felt the warm blood running down his arms and legs and he touched the blood with his own hands, here, feel it, you've been wounded Corporal, the V. C. cut you to the quick, man, and you're dead, we're all dead, you got fifty bullet holes in you and you're dead, we're in hell, boys, you can smell the fire, they just tossed us in a helicopter with the empty supply cases dropping right on top of us, hands and feet sticking out everywhere, flying with that angel of mercy out of hell, the whirlybird sputtering up dirt... oh the whirlybird crew, the whirlybird crew...

The children climbed over the split-rail fence and charged up the hill. There was a large white mansion cresting on the high edge of the vast hilly lawn.

The boy from Iowa, Blair, hit the ground... is he a man now? Now that the blood is pouring from his nostrils and mouth... the bullets flying, damn German guns, the Lugar, so sharp and clean... not like our lousy guns throwing off sparks in the darkness... a bullet scrapes along Sgt. Joe Cazzaza's back or maybe it was some shrapnel, hot and blistering, down he goes... and Stephen and his father watching the greatest drama ever made for television, *Combat!* and war movies on 1960's television... because he never played cowboys and indians, because it was a transitional time from playing World War Two soldiers to playing astronauts going to the moon... Stephen and his friends advanced on the hill. They reached the top of the hill. Stephen looked down. At the bottom he saw the dead. The dead Apache... the buffalo carcasses... and farther up the hill the Union and Confederate dead, and then the Spanish dead, the Philipinos, the Moro, slaughtered in the ditches, the Germans, the Japanese, the Vietnamese in the ditches... and the boy stood on the top of the hill with his three friends. He held the stick in his hand, the play sword, the play rifle... G.I. Joe... G.I. Joe... fighting man from head to toe... and he looked down into the smoke billowing up and saw Sgt. Joe Cazzaza appear out of it, a specter, a phantom, with his gun and canteen and jacket and Beretta torn from a dead Italian's hand... and the boy reached out his hand to his father, and helped pull the squad leader out of the death and smoke, first to the top of the hill, the glory, the story that he later told his wife and his son, I was first to the top of the hill, and Stephen's friends called to him, come along now, and they ran over toward the field with the big white mansion looming with prestige, then down the road, and the gatekeeper came out and grabbed Jimmy by the arm and twisted it back, and then a big black limousine drove pass them, and Jimmy broke loose and ran towards his friends, keep off, this is private property yelled the gatekeeper, who was the head groundskeeper, and the boys ran toward the woods, passing the courtyard in back of the mansion house, where Stephen saw his Uncle Frank step out from a Van Heffer meat truck with packages in his arms to deliver, as Anthony did many years ago, and a boy scrawls with a piece of brick on the walkway, Fuck the Rich... and they run into the woods, find a bridle path covered with the horseshit of the wealthy, and see a tree house... and brawny sailors carried their boat up the hills of Farsund.

Aliaspun on hillside... Stephen's father never gave him any advice about anything. Joe's nephew finds the gun, the Beretta, that Joe had brought back with him from the war, in the bottom draw of Joe's closet, and still loaded with bullets he holds it up and points it and pulls the trigger...

Maurizio and Rocky climbed over the fence and went up the hill toward the sound of a female voice singing... *Ave Maria*...

It Was a Sunday Afternoon in Chicago – Reprise

It was a Sunday afternoon in Chicago and it was the Fourth of July and it sounded like firecrackers... pop... pop... pop... pop... but then they heard a thud and a thump and the building slightly shook. They got up and went to the window. A car had crashed through the fire hydrant and collided with a tree. In the middle of the street stood a cop with a full tribal tattoo on his arm and his gun drawn and pointed at the car. He motioned for another cop to check down the alleyway.

When on the Fourth of July the firecrackers, the flags, the parades, the music, the food, the firecrackers... pop, pop, pop, pop... that many more or less but who remembers exactly everything and what else to expect this day, or any other, and pretending to be shot, jerking back in the black chair, daughter smiling, oh you're back, and hearing a thud and crash, and now surprised and look at each other, she on couch, him in chair, in front of television, playing... and going to the window, looking down from the second floor of the building, seeing the car crashed into the tree, the fire hydrant run over, water shooting up, and slouched over the steering wheel a body blood soaking through t-shirt, and a cop with tattooed arm, gun drawn, in the middle of the street, pointing to the other cop to go that way... are really gunshots... pop, pop, pop, pop... an ambulance, the body dragged out, pants sliding off...

A year later and a woman with several prancing kids placed a cross and balloons and a sheet of paper on the site where a new tree had been planted by the city.

The sign said:

Becker O. Brown 1989-2010

Rest in Peace

We got all we need guns and a bible... thank you Jesus.
Oh takk Jesus... takk Jesus...

Is that enough? Am I ready? Shall I go on? Give me a sign... sign, everywhere a sign...

The Best View in Town

Joe Cazzaza had the best view, sitting in front of the television, or down at the movies... all up there on the big screen, American movies. And that television right in your own house, right in your own living room. That was the best view, the best view of America. His only view. He loved those old Hollywood actors, Spencer Tracy, Jimmy Cagney, Mario Lanza, and the music of Tommy Dorsey and his trombone. Stephen was amazed how his parents knew all the names of the actors from the 30s and 40s and 50s. Together they watched a movie on channel WOR 9 or WPIX 11 and his mother would name all of them, even the character actors; how had she learned so much since she came from Norway? And his father had the right to love them. He was a kid during the Depression; and his father, an Italian named Giuseppe from the mountains behind Genoa, who died when Joe was six years old, died in the year 1927, just before the Great Depression, and the family had to struggle on without him, his brothers and sisters, all older than he; so he was the baby, he was the Babe, also a high school baseball nickname, and then he was sent to war, to fight Hitler, and he came home with a few medals, three Bronze Stars, and he married the pretty Norwegian girl, and he lived in the greatest country in the history of the world, and he had the best view; a light flashed on the big screen, and he had the best view; he turned on that little black and white General Electric television, and he had the best view in town, the best view of America, watching *The Honeymooners*, *I Love Lucy*, the Giants and Colts championship game of 1958, Mitch Miller and the Gang, sing along, let me call you sweetheart, he sang to her, Lawrence Welk, the Amazin' Mets...

His father came home from the war. The late 40s, 50s, still in the New Deal era, which saved capitalism from itself for the sake of the working class and middle class, perhaps... in some ways... there were still pensions, unions, self-respect, underneath the conformity of a more growing corporate world... like Theodore Roosevelt and his Square Deal saved capitalism from misguided socialists and evil anarchists... but the Cold War starts up and it inaugurates an era of fear, false security, missiles, missile gaps and my country, 'tis of thee... and the rebels against, small in number, the Beats, jazz hipsters, nonconformists, etc., growing up absurd, against daddy's conservative mores, but if not inclined the working class was not bad off, and Truman tried national health like European Social Democracy, but here there was the fear of the Russians.... Oh if Henry Wallace had still been VP... all those concessions to the rich but then 60s youth dropped out and in slipped the 70s, and neo-liberalism, Chicago School, and Capitalism once again saved itself from itself, but this time exclusively for the rich and corporate, and by the 80s the country was run by fear, greed, guns and a bibel... and a bad actor named Reagan... an olde American tale... 1653... Patience Wright... "Oh sorry that I have the occasion to write to you at all... we have all we need... fear of the Other, fear of God, and we are a practical people, we have all we need, horse-carts and iron traizes, ox chaines and iron kittels, brass cittels, scillets, gridirons, putter plates, potts, funnels, cubards, tubs, feather beds, pillows, ruges, curtings, grinding stones, peck aves, collers, sadels, bridels, skinners, saltsellers, peuter potts, sausars, porrengers, cupes, trayes, wheeles, heckells, breeches, cotes, looking glasses, guns and a bibel..."

The April air. It is unstable, stale and indifferent, a suppositional spring condensed into formal memory, a vague destructive tendency, a trend, a story, driven by the scent of lilacs; lilacs dangling like lanterns in the darkness over wild backyards of his youth. His hand. He put his hand over the mouth, the mouth of nature and society, obstructing their breath... oxygen. Until he gasped, flapped, writhed like a transparent fish in a strange net of neurons, red lights and rank beer and piss stains on the alley wall, bartender janitor father, what are you doing here?

On his knees and screamed please please please, as Stephen said to his sister after talking her out of a dark closet where she was hiding, naked, on a cold December night, please please please he begged her and led her down the stairs to be sent away to a Mental Institution somewhere out on Long Island, caw caw caw, like he was sent away in 1970, by a school shrink and a judge in a black robe with the American flag draped behind her head, telling him, a thirteen-year-old boy: There won't be any free trips to the ice box anytime you want a glass of milk anymore... sarcastic authoritarian bitch! Fuck her, fuck him, fuck them all to hell!

"They wouldn't do that to him, would they?" Torhild asked her husband. "Sure they would..." he answered, just as he answered her when she said the same thing in 1965, "They wouldn't do that to her, would they?"

He remembers his father's goddamn cursing hammer and how he hid his head like a rusted nail, his aggressive words and kicks pounded on him whenever either would fail or not fail at anything that mattered, or didn't matter and what did any of it matter? How he'd scream and scream in temper's rage, between himself, mother and father in a family cage, I will not, he'd say, ya little bastard, he'd say, don't call him that, my mother would say, his Mother was that way, his dad could curse like a starving lion, fucking shit son of a bitch, and the chairs went flying, and he'd slammed the door as he left the house, but later he'd come back calmly crawling like a mouse, and mom would apologize, hugging each of her kids with tears in her eyes, and dad nothing would say, dad was that way, and mommy told him to say his prayers, and daddy told him about the three little bears, now I lay me down to sleep, once upon a time, once upon a time…

I pray the Lord my soul to take. God bless Mommy, Daddy, Sylvia, Susan, Simone, and Tante Tobine and everybody in the whole world.

But who is Tante Tobine? She was his mother's aunt who lived far away in a mysterious place called Norway. And that is all that grabbed his attention. Not Death, not Prayer, not the Lord, not my Soul to take, but the mystery of memory and time and the words… of Tante Tobine in faraway and long ago mysterious Norway!

O kind April air. Magical youthful presence: they saw the Mets' opening day at Shea. A wild pitch whizzed by the great Johnny Bench. The winning run scored. Stephen saw the lilacs and forsythias and breathed the scent of flowers at his grandmother's funeral. He saw a man collapse on the bottom stairs and die; they worked to revive him; his friends shouted at him: Breathe in, Henry, Breathe in! He saw the misfit boys rub bodies together underwater in Auburn's YMCA pool; he saw his friend Tommy on the RR train to Greenwich Village and he refused to come with him on the road to California because he believed New York was the center of the universe; his rat infested hovel on 5th Avenue in Brooklyn?

Stephen saw the rock foundation of the house in which his mother was born in Norway; he saw the cherry blossoms in Kyoto, he saw the old Polish artist, the Jewish lover, the French amour, the best friend in a London mist of memory; he called out their names, and they called back: Breathe in! Breathe in! The kind April air… youthful presence, from New York to San Francisco, years going by like white lines on the road, Jack and Neil in a green automobile, girls in the alley, boys at the bus stop, girls in the valley, boys in the bar, girls on the hood top, and the boys in the car… crucified upon puritan America's cross: the intersection of the road and the railroad track. O cruel April air… breathe in, breathe in. Breathe in, breathe in. Pain of birth, breath of birth, pain of death, breath of death, claw of cancer, exposed like Prometheus, your liver to devour, or explode, like Jack's liver, breathe in, Allen, breathe in. They called his father Babe (now dying of prostrate cancer). Memory, Babe, share all with your sons, fathers, breathe in Dad, breathe in, the door is open, and he'll hold it open for him.

Stephen opened the door of the car and helped his father get out... back from the hospital, tests and drugs, but who wants to watch an old man dying of cancer, or the New York Mets, even playing in the World Series, even in the new millennium, even in the year 2000, playing against the evil Yankees. Or the following year, dying in the bed, 2001, the game on the TV... Mets are on, Dad... playing Giants, oh who wants to watch he says... remember Bill Terry?... remember the game at the Polo Grounds that you went to see, Carl Hubbell beat Dizzy Dean in 18 innings 1-0? Hey dad, Baaarz-Well! Baaarz-Well! Oh I gotta go.... he made it... didn't shit his pants... hey look what life has done to me...mama mia... bite my ear, didn't shit his pants like the time the bees stung him, working on some rich Jew's estate, ambulance came, but the doctor came first, imagine! The doctor and his nurse, running over the mound of grass to the poolside, and saved his life, and think of things, connect things, like those childhood dot to dot puzzles that make a picture, a simple math problem, linear narrative, think of things, objects, not words, the baseball on the shelf that Stephen caught at the Mets game 30 years ago, a thing, think of it, not words, you can see it in your mind, think of things, the WW II medals in the glass case that Stephen had made for him over 40 years ago, hangs on the wall, think of things that conjure heroic deeds, in the beginning was the deed, things that define him, his father, dying of cancer, and think of the past, memories and consciousness, and these words, what else is there? Things... smudged eyeglasses, cigar butts in the ash tray, old watches, coins, old driver's licenses, old bills, think of things that connect to the past, to memory, connect those dots, reveal the big picture, the whole story, think of things and deeds that define a life, varied experience, language that defines a life, falters at defining life, like he faltered at language, speaking, talking, except for a few baseball stories, a few war stories, all that he had, and then the son was taller, but the father was always heavier, and his hands were bigger and calloused, and he never hugged him, and now his once large depression child hands, construction worker hands, army sergeant hands, bartender and janitor hands, couldn't hold a baby in his hands for fear of dropping her, hang at the end of his thin arms and gaunt wrists, the arm with the tattoo from the war, the eagle and flag, just a black smear now, and for the first time he weighs more than his father, and he dissipates into the son's consciousness, his memory, and he grows into his body, and he never dreamed, he said, conscious or unconscious, and he understands now why he had to protect him from himself, from his father's death when he was six, the depression childhood, the war, the hands that never held a book, but he saw thousands of Hollywood movies… connect things.

He has died… he had become a toothpick of cancer, the old eagle and furled flag tattoo of red white and blue on his forearm, the tattoo he got at some sleazy joint in Time's Square before he went into the Army, had shriveled up to a black smear and suddenly like an unspoken language he was not there, but there… a word, just text, all the way down to nothing… is that it? All the way down into the maelstrom of memory. They had very little to say to each other. Baseball. Football. Stephen regrets sometimes that he won't be able to take his father to a game at Wrigley Field, see those odious Cubs, not the 1969 Cubs, no Leo the Lip, like his father took him as a young boy to Shea Stadium. Stephen has a memory of one game that really stands out, a home run that Willie McCovey hit against the narrow scoreboard in right field, bam, zoom, it went so fast that it was still rising when it hit the scoreboard… that scoreboard is no longer there, the memory of that event barely a toothpick. His father said that he never saw a ball hit that hard. No, not even by Bill Terry or Mel Ott or a young Willie Mays. Though his father told him that Dizzy Dean once said that Bill Terry hit the ball so hard one time it went through Dean's legs and was caught by the centerfielder. That's rocket hard! As for memory… that game he talked about seeing as a twelve year old, the double-header at the Polo Grounds, well the facts were, oh but fuck the facts for now… we are a fiction. We ain't real, right? Only interpretation. But even interpretation has its limits, right?

Let's have a death scene instead. Water. The dying person always asks for water. His next to last words were: Water please. *Mizu kudasi*, as the Japanese momentary survivors of the greatest crime of the 20th century said… *mizu kudasai*… and naked burnt bodies falling into the rivers… and I heard another word in Japanese. It was *daijobu*. It means all right. What could possibly be *daijobu?* I am writing in English but my hand fights against me... I can't write anymore... I'm done... and when I finally did write again, I kept writing the same word over and over. *Daijobu... daijobu... daijobu... daijobu...* James Joyce wouldn't say it. You did... but you're not a genius. Stephen said the great conflicted lie, I love you, you were a good father; he said I will take care of Grandma, you can let go now, the Hospice people said to say that, you don't have to fight no more, and not speaking for two weeks he said softly, "All right." He said *All Right*, like his favorite, Tommy Dorsey and his Orchestra... *Well hello Joe what do you know... well all right dig dig dig well alright tonight is the night well all right...* like Elvis, *that's all right, mama, anyway you do,* like Dylan, *don't think twice, it's all right... it's all right, ma, I'm only bleeding. ... All right* said Jack to Neil, *it's all right there old buddy... it's all right now... its all right honey... say it's all right... whoa... have a good time... baby it's all right now... don't you know it's gonna be all right... and I say it's all right... everything gonna be all right tonight...*

He died the next morning. May 19, 2001. Time of death: 2:45 a.m. Stephen kissed his father's cold clammy forehead and touched his war tattoo. Then he went into the kitchen with his mom, as the others, the strangers, removed the body from the house.

Stephen's father saved virtually nothing. His mother saved everything. Birthday cards, Christmas cards, and letters. She even saved the clothes that seven-year-old Stephen had worn when a car hit him. She kept his corduroy trousers and shirt neatly folded in the drawer of one of the many closets that her husband had built for her at every location to which they moved. And they moved often.

Besides some clothes and shoes and his old janitor uniform there were just two old White Owl cigar boxes in his father's room. Joe Cazzaza returned from the war with a Beretta gun, a canteen, an ammo belt, a folding shovel, a jacket, and some medals. As a boy Stephen played with the belt, helmet, canteen and shovel and those things disappeared over the years. The jacket and medals were somehow spared from Stephen's playful big soldier war games with his friends.

Stephen looked through the cigar boxes. Is this all that he wanted to save? There were his Honorable Discharge papers. There were driver's licenses and vehicle registrations. The oldest was from 1947. Plate number NU8694, a 1947 Dodge 4-door sedan, model D-24. In 1958 he owned a 2-door, 6-cylinder 1957 Chevrolet, model 2102. They were both new cars. But then by 1960 until his death all the cars are used cars. In 1960 a used

Dodge, and in 1971 a used 1963 Chevrolet Impala, and in 1976 a used 1962 Chevrolet, and in 1983 a used 1980 Pontiac and in 1985 a used 1982 Ford wagon, and in 1992 a used 1988 Nissan.

Stephen also found a few bills. A Long Island Lighting Company bill from 1959 for gas and electric that amounted to $25.03. An Oyster Bay Lumber Company bill from 1960 that amounted to $15.55. An Oyster Bay Meat Market bill from 1976 that amounted to $4.80, for a London broil steak, and a Saunder's Drug Store bill from 1961 that amounted to $29.07, with a hand written note at the bottom that requested a payment. There were more bills and there were tax forms from as far back as 1947, filled out in pencil, probably practice copies. There were wartime letters from his family. There were letters from his wife when she was in Norway. There were a few watches. There were a few coins. There was a United States War Ration Book with numbered stamps that belonged to his mother. There were three unused stamps, numbers 19, 20 and 22. There was a business card from the bar in Northport. It had a picture of the inside of the bar on one side and on the other side:

Document 13-48455

Tel. 1633 NPT

NORTHPORT RESTAURANT

84 Main Street

Northport, L. I. New York

THE FINEST IN FOODS – LIQUORS

W. C. Harmann, Prop.

The name at the bottom is scratched out and Stephen's father wrote in pencil underneath it: Joe and Frank Cazzaza.

And then Stephen was sitting and sobbing, reading the letters that his mother wrote to his father. There were four letters from the summer of 1951. They were married in 1949 and their first daughter was born in February 1951. Torhild took the baby girl to Norway that summer. They crossed the ocean on an ocean liner. Torhild had packed everything into the big trunk that had belonged to Joe's father, the trunk that Giuseppe had brought from Italy in 1893. It was in good shape and had a secret compartment. But nobody had discovered the secret compartment in the top back of the trunk, nor what it contained.

Document 51-457

Lundevågen den 11/9 1951

Min egen elskede Babe…

Vi igjen skrive et brev til dig. Vinter nu så på brev fra dig. Men kaskje jeg vil få idag. Vi få bare posten her 4 ganger i uken. It is Thursday morning. The time is only 8 clock. But am goen to the town today and I want to writ you a letter so I can mail it. I hope the time go fast now. Sylvia and I is fine. She is calling papa all day. Sometime she call mama but it is much papa. Hope you are ok to. I had party for Sylvia yesterday. I had som girls and the mothers. I tok som pictures of em, and am goen to send em to you later. You have nice daughter. She looks mor like you every day. Poor me som have to live all my life with you to people. I am goen to gett a boy like me. Everybody tease me and say that now you see you pretty daughter you don't want to look of me no. But if you don't poor you. I love you so much and wish I was with you again. I love you. I love you. I love you always always. It is nice wather today. I hope it is not to cold now I am goen to live Norway. I hope I am not getten seasick again. It be hard to go with Sylvia now she is getten so big. My grandmother and aunt dont like to let me go. I feel sorry for my aunt som have to stand home. It is longsom here in the winter. I wont like to stand here this winter and go skiing but I kun not stand away from you so long time monkey. I be happy to be with you again. I miss you loving and kiss. I am sa lonlig for you. I hope you like the pictures of send you. The nose is a little short. It is nice the one of Sylvia. I look bad the one of me, dont let anyone see me. I hope you are not angry a me you now I am a little devil somtime. But it is all because I love you so much stinky. I don't understand why you want to marry me. I hope you are not sorry you marry me. I was so happy to se my grandma and Norge again. But I am afraid to giv you to much worrys. I sleep wit you picture but I trow it most away an the floor because it dont help me. I was so nasty to you sometime. But I am goen to be so good to you now. I be back with you again. You can be the boss. I love you. I miss you hug and kissing and wish many night you hvere here. I am goen to tie you with a rope in the bed so I can have you with me all the time. I have to close now. I goen to writ again soon. Send my regard to you family. I am goen to throw you out of my bed now to I get home. I am the boss you now. I love you kiss and stromboli. I love you so much and miss you and never goen to liv you any mo. I love you always dear sweetheart, stinky, monkey, spekketi boy, stromboli boy, ginni boy, my boy always, always all my life, you can not love any but me and I am goen to squeexe you to break and can breathe any mo.

I love you always you wife always Torhild xxxxxxxxxx

Rimbaud died in 1891. Melville died in 1891. Whitman died in 1892. They stand on the sands of the shore at Oyster Bay. The phantoms are coming. Arthur takes an envelope from his pocket. A letter. It's a letter from his sister. He reads it to Walter and Herman.

My Dear Arthur
I am your sister and you are my brother. You are yourself. You are not another self. You may be in despair but it is an immediate and unreflective despair. Why desire to be another self? If your despair seems to emerge from your self-consciousness, it is because you cannot will to be yourself, or just a self, or an other self. You are a peasant, a poet, and a good businessman. But you are still just our poor Arthur. It is like the old story of the peasant boy who went to Paris to be a poet. The peasant poet was wined and dined and showered with accolades. He published a small book of poems. His friends celebrated with him. They bought him new clothes and took him out drinking. The peasant poet was so happy and drunk he thought to walk all the way to his provincial home to show his dear sister what he had achieved in Paris. But he was so drunk he collapsed on the road. A wagon came along the road and the driver seeing the peasant poet lying in the road shouted out for him to move or he will ride over his legs. The peasant poet raised his head and looked at his legs and the book of poems and said to the driver to go on ahead for those are not my fancy clothes and not my book. For how could those things belong to him? He's just a peasant. He should know his place. The sickness of life leads to death. If you displace God you will displace yourself. Do not be bored. Avoid the abyss. Stay away from decadence. You will not die... come home, Oh Dear Author... I mean Arthur...

Your dear sister Isabelle

Kierkegaard tells a variation of the story of the peasant in his book *The Sickness unto Death*. Stephen cannot play the part of the writer. This book is the fancy clothes of the peasant. It is an illusion. A fiction. A tall tale. The writer's new clothes. And yet Stephen's crushed legs are the proof of its existence. Here is another proof of his existence: birth. A birth certificate… documents are narrative… the author is born… *mais oui*, the author is dead so how can he be born again?

Document 56-0223

NEW YORK STATE DEPARTMENT OF HEALTH
OFFICE OF VITAL STATISTICS
ALBANY
CERTIFICATE OF BIRTH REGISTRATION
This is to certify that a birth certificate has been filed for

Stephen Knut Cazzaza

Born on **MAY 22, 1956** at **GLEN COVE**

Son of **Joseph John Cazzaza**
(name of father)
Torhild Andersen
(maiden name of mother)

Date Filed May 28, 1956 **LOCAL REGISTRAR**

9-11-2001

There is a photograph of Stephen and his wife atop the World Trade Center building. It's 1993. That photograph has become a kind of impossibly real fiction. The object is gone. And the two of them appear suspended in air. The man who took the photograph worked in that building and died on that day. A degree of difference both paradoxical and sublime.

We have arrived at the year 1992. Now we must pause. Stephen is in Paris. He is sitting at a café table and reading a book. And at the end of this book (not the book that Stephen is reading, but this book that Stephen is writing and perhaps you dear reader are reading) we shall return to this spot here once again, and go ahead that way… the way whence we have come… and onward towards the unending… so listen Isabelle, I want to read you something… and yes I know about you and John… but now is not the time nor the place…

But first, a hundred years ago…

Book Two
Malstrøm Inwords 1892-1969

Italy 1892

They ran up the hill. Their faces covered with sweat and the fine dust of shattered slate rock, what the locals call the "sleeping bread." The blood of the others was beginning to cake and crack on their workman's clothes. When Francesco realized that he was still carrying several wires and blasting caps in his shaking hand, he tossed them into the woods. The two men followed the path to a high ridge. At the top of the hill they turned around and saw the large black cloud of smoke rising up from the valley. The surrounding mountains were marked with the steel hand of slate quarrying. They looked at each other and ran down the other side of the hill and entered a terraced olive grove, olives small and deep red, and walked their way through the village of Cicagna and to their homes in Orero.

The two men were in their early twenties, both of them short and stocky. They wore their white shirts with the sleeves rolled up, covered with a vest, and peaked caps atop their heads of dark brown hair. They had mustaches.

The sound of the explosion was heard all the way to the sea. The echo reverberated through the Fontanabuona Valley on that summer day in 1892, from Genova to Chiavari to the Sistri Lavante and Lerici and the Gulf of La Spezia where Shelley drowned and his body washed up on the beach at Viareggio… from the Gulf of Paradise to the Gulf of Tigullio.

The two men who set off the dynamite that killed Giacomo Bacigalupo were never caught. They were never even taken under suspicion by the local police. Francesco was on a boat out of Genova within weeks of the explosion. He was heading for foreign lands, over sea, over mountains. He was now *i senza patria*, without country, but he believed in that old Italian adage *tutto u mondo, u l'e paize*, all the world is a village. Francesco went to France.

The other man saw his friend off from the dock in Genova, and stayed behind with his family, until it was decided that they too should leave, but his family decided to go to America.

Norway 1892

On a quiet Saturday morning in the middle of May in the year 1892 a mob comprised of local merchants, artisans, ship-builders, fishermen, farmers, soldiers, sailors, merchant mariners, peasants, poets and journalists, gathered by the front door of a common-looking house located on a narrow road near the harbor of a small Norwegian south coastal town. The mob was neither armed nor dangerous; there were no anarchists nor revolutionaries, no May Day stragglers reveling drunkenly toward Utopia.

In a few days the 17th of May Parade will be held... yet the gathering constituted a mob by vice of the fiction that they were unwelcome and seemingly had nothing better to do with their time than to wait to gawk at the old man who lived in the small house and would soon, God willing, appear to them as he has appeared to them in five year intervals for as long as anyone could remember.

They have been waiting all morning, perhaps one hundred people, which is approximately the same number of people who gathered five years ago, ten years ago, fifteen years ago, twenty years ago; and which is slightly more people than twenty-five years ago, and certainly substantially more people than fifty years ago, when there were perhaps just a few people.

It all began some seventy to eighty years ago. Back then there was no one waiting for the old man to appear from the front door of the small white house by the harbor of a small Norwegian town.

The door opened. The old man came out from the front door, now as then; he was young then; he's 103 years old now. He was born in 1789, in the same house. The old man appeared. By God he's still alive! The old man barely acknowledged the mob, the sheep, as he called them, even though he expected them to be there, as usual. He carried a wooden ladder strapped across his back, and a pail and paintbrush. No one in the crowd would dare tell him not to do what he was about to do, and has been doing every five years for so many years... and perhaps only God could persuade him not to do it, yet once again, at his extremely advanced age. Of course what he is doing, he is doing for God... not man. He ignored the people.

The first time Leif painted the church steeple was in 1814. He was twenty-five.

Leif walked into the town square, now as then, and took a look at the four Linden trees, and proceeded up the hill.

The mob followed. Leif entered the white church at the top of the hill, near the graveyard. The crowd's eyes rose upward. Several moments later a small door opened at the bottom of the steeple and Leif pushed the ladder through and then stepped out on the ledge, placing the pail of white paint and the brush down on the gutter. He placed the ladder against the steeple (how many different steeples over the years?) and climbed up. The crowd was apprehensive. Like the first modern man ascending to a new century, lost in the white sky, in nothingness.

Then it happened. It had to happen, eventually. That's the nature of time and space. It's what the mob came for, naturally. You can't say that they were exceedingly surprised, even though still saddened and dismayed. Leif slipped on a rung and toppled downward, landing on the top step of the entrance to the church. His ladder and brush also falling… thumps…

The crowded surged inward.

A twenty-two-year-old named Oscar picked up the ladder and brush, and without anyone saying a word to him, or he a word to anyone else, Oscar swung the ladder over his back and entered the church. After several moments passed, he appeared through the small door in the base of the steeple. And now Oscar, simply because he just so happened to be there and acted in this absurd manner, was from that moment onward unofficially, and without much endorsement nor encouragement, ordained the new painter of the steeple. Oh what a stupid impulse! What a fool! Oscar scolded himself.

It was not long after Oscar painted the steeple that he went away. No one knew where. His mother and father were vague. Perhaps he went to Oslo to study… but five years later (in 1897) he returned. A few days before the 17th of May parade he was painting the steeple. It was his solemn duty. Then he was gone again. Once again the rumors. He was in Berlin, Paris, London, studying painting, seeking his fame and fortune. He was back in 1902 to paint the steeple again. Then gone… perhaps to darkest Africa? Perhaps devoured by cannibals? But he was back in 1907, and then returned again in 1912, and off again… but this time he returned early and did not go away. The Great War was underway. Norway was neutral.

One Sunday in May, in 1917, after not painting the steeple before the parade, he appeared in church. Filled with a congregation and the pastor reciting from the bible a passage…. Oscar walked in and down the aisle, carrying his ladder. No one spoke to him. He silently walked to the back of the church and went through the narrow passageway that leads to the narrow staircase. He went up to the steeple. The bell rang and the church emptied. No one went home. They waited outside, but Oscar did not appear. Oscar sat down inside the steeple. Oscar placed a stick of dynamite at his feet, lit the fuse, closed his eyes tight and blew himself up.

The church was repaired and a new copper steeple erected. Aanen took over the responsibility of painting the church steeple.

New York City 1893

Giuseppe opened the door of the green REO truck. He was in a green field at the edge of a forest with the top of a fire tower visible above the trees. People were singing and playing games; children running. He poured a glass of homemade and illegal red wine. He felt happy. He saw his brother Maurizio coming through the woods, followed by a small hunchback man. He heard his daughter singing. One spring day in 1927 the father had taken his family on a picnic to Schiff's field on the outskirts of town. (Or was it really a gathering of anarchists, as some people believe to this day?) The father heard the roar of engines. Police cars and paddy wagons and Harley 74 motorcycles. There was no more singing. The music ceased to be heard. The accordion was squelched; the violin shrieked in a different way than it usually did when Luigi played it; the children screamed. There was loud metallic hammering. A frenetic whirling around. There was blood on the father's hand. He couldn't believe it. The taste of cheese and red wine still fresh in his mouth. He was dying. Lying there in the grass and dying. Grass tickled his nose. He looked up and the last thing that he saw through blurry eyes was his young son Joe.

"Papa? Papa?"

Another voice said, "Giuseppe?"

Another voice said, "Jesus, Mary, and Joseph."

Another voice said, "Mama mia."

A voice said, "Papa." Those were the last words that he heard as his consciousness ran out of his mind like rats abandoning a sinking ship. Life was over. Liberty was over. His happiness had come to an end. The course of human events ran through his mind...

...Giuseppe Stefano Cazzaza stood on the deck of the transatlantic steamer *Fulda* sailing into New York Harbor and looked up at the futuristic sunset gates of a sky lined with running rust on steel gray. There was nothing there. Oh the sky was there all right, but the bridge wasn't there, not in the year 1893, and Giuseppe not for a mind's moment imagined that there would ever be a bridge there, directly up above him, from where he now stands on the ship, a bridge that would be named after one of his fellow countrymen of long ago, the Italian explorer Giovanni da Verrazano, who had led a French expedition along the Eastern Seaboard from the Carolinas up to Nova Scotia in 1524, along the way textbookly becoming the first European to set eyes upon the many pristine wonders of what would one day be named Staten Island and Brooklyn, when sailing into New York Bay (and to Giuseppe's eyes it all remains a pristine wonder), a bridge that would be 4260 feet long, that would one day connect Staten Island and Brooklyn, a bridge of minimalist magnificence; no, Giuseppe never imagined such a thing. Giuseppe only imagined some vague "better life" waiting for him and his family. His family, the ones who came along, consisted of his brother Maurizio, with his letter from Francesco in his breast pocket, who was an aspiring sculptor who treasured the work of the Florentine sculptor Donatello; his brother Giovanni, who was "howling mad," and his sister Gina and her husband Giancarlo Bacigalupo, all former residents of Liguria, Italy, the alleged birthplace of that other noted explorer, Christopher Columbus.

The Manhattan skyline came into view, and then that speck over there turned out to be the Statue of Liberty, recently unveiled in 1886 by President Grover Cleveland, and designed by Auguste Bartholdi, the French sculptor who modeled Lady Liberty's face on his mother's own severe and righteous visage, and whose work Maurizio did not particularly treasure, being unfamiliar.

"The tomb of Washington!" "The tomb of Lincoln!" "The tomb of Napoleon!" Voices of storied pomp rippled over the huddled masses on the deck where hay mattresses were being passed overhead and flung into the water.

"No! No! No!" Giuseppe spoke up and corrected his fellow compatriots, the steerage passengers who have now crowded on deck, standing behind him and pointing to the Statue of Liberty and waving to the land of the free. "No," said Giuseppe, "It is the tomb of Columbus!" Said with the pride of a Genoese.

175

The mammoth towers of the Brooklyn Bridge, which were for a long time (what is time at the beginning ocean's end of so much manifest space but European corruption, wars, endless wars, blood, history, to be left behind in the ruins and ashes of the Old World?) the tallest shapes in New York, appeared up the East River like a dream to Giuseppe, because like in a dream the disembodied image seemed untouchable, ungraspable, unencompassable, and yet it brought sweat to the brow, chills to the spine, the heart racing towards the finish line. "Shapes of the sleepers of bridges, vast frameworks, girders, arches," wrote the Brooklyn poet Walt Whitman, who had lived out his last days of the Republic in Camden, New Jersey, who died last year, who accepted everything, who longed for poets whom nature accepts absolutely, singing the strong light work of engineers, our modern wonders, seeing the horizons rising to the skies, the sea inlaid with eloquent gentle wires, Whitman dead, he who shaped a book about democracy, and Giuseppe Cazzaza another Lazarus to be reborn, who shall witness the Empire taking shape, and accept one of the men who helped shape it, Theodore Roosevelt, even shake hands with him no less. But who didn't shake hands with Teddy Roosevelt? Roosevelt shook more hands than any other president; at a single reception it is reported that he shook over 8,000 hands! And the way he handled babies, leoninely mauling them; he would never kissed them... it was said by the naturalist John Burroughs that Roosevelt killed mosquitoes like lions, and lions like mosquitoes. He shook hands and held babies with as much vigor. He wasn't about to mollycoddle anyone, to use a term Roosevelt coined himself. Giuseppe would one day witness such vigor himself when he shakes Roosevelt's hand, and then Roosevelt ambles up to Giuseppe's seven-month-old baby and picks him up and breathes American life into the boy.

Giuseppe, standing on the dock of the ship breathing the same living air as the good gray poet had inhaled; Giuseppe, who has never heard the name of Walt Whitman, but who reveres the name of that other potent light of democracy, Thomas Jefferson, while the blood-red skies darken and coagulate and harden over Manhattan Island, closing over a day that existed somewhere in time. Beautiful Isle of Somewhere! Land of the true, where we live anew...

The gargantuan monolithic modernity of Manhattan was born in the ramparts of the Brooklyn Bridge. Architecture was the big cigar-puffing puffed face of the gold pocket-watch Gilded Age capitalists made public, forests razed to the ground, cathedrals raised to the dollar, driven expansion and nerve-jangled suspension, reaching to the other side, climbing to the top. Giuseppe felt as if he were standing on the top of the New World; a feeling that wouldn't persist once he disembarked into the dark lower depths of the Lower East Side of Manhattan, into the slums of Mulberry Bend and Baxter Street, the squalor of the tenements clustered and congested, around the back alleyways and stable lanes, the acrid decay of tubercular air, the ash-barrels, heaps of garbage, the dirt and filth and daily death of infants, the rent collector trampling through the maze of narrow passages like a rat biting, not kissing, a baby in his mother's arms.

Giuseppe took a deep breath of the golden timeless air, the New World yearning-to-breathe-free-air. He held a pamphlet in his hand, written in English, and sent to him when he was still back in Genoa, by his friend in America who had immigrated here several years earlier, and who now worked at an orange grove in Florida. Before coming to America, Giuseppe was considering which of several destinations would be the most desirable. He and Maurizio had heated arguments about leaving, staying, and where to go. Argentina and Brazil were two possibilities. In fact, before the turn of the century, more Italians had gone to Argentina and Brazil than had come to America. The climate and language were a dim and distant reminder of home; and dagoes weren't very welcomed in America. There was an incident in New Orleans in 1890 that nearly induced Giuseppe to consider going elsewhere than America. Eleven Italians were lynched by a mob after the murder of the superintendent of police, who had been waging a war on Italian gangs. The police combed the Italian neighborhoods and rounded up hundreds of suspected gang members; they were arrested and nine were put on trial and subsequently acquitted by a jury. The public was outraged by the verdict and the newspapers called for "justice." A mob broke into the prison and lynched eleven men. The Italian government insisted that the lynch mob be brought to justice. But the United States government refused to act. There was talk of war. Theodore Roosevelt, at a dinner with "various Dago diplomats," commented on the lynchings, "Personally, I think it rather a good thing."

Giuseppe and his brother Maurizio read the story in a newspaper from Genoa. Maurizio said that he would never go to such a place. Maurizio and his friend Francesco had other ideas that they discussed long into the night. But Giuseppe professed his undying faith in America; justice will be done, he boldly asserted. In early 1892 the American government offered an indemnity to the families of the lynched victims. Giuseppe felt justified because an injustice had been recognized and rectified and who knows if these damn Sicilian gangs weren't guilty anyway. But the murderers weren't punished. And this, among other things, caused Maurizio to read more and more anarchist literature, unbeknownst to Giuseppe, and Giuseppe read the slogans of the pamphlet.

The pamphlet contained earlier Anglo-Saxon "colonist's" as opposed to immigrant-rush, nuggets of American wisdom (though Franklin D. Roosevelt once addressed a collective colony of Daughters of the American Revolution as "fellow immigrants" much to their dismay), contained extracts from the "Mayflower" Compact, Declaration of Independence, Bill of Rights, Lincoln's Gettysburg Address, Washington's Farewell Address, Webster's reply to Hayne (an odd one that has since dropped out from the canon), Star-Spangled Banner, extracts from poems by Longfellow and Lowell and Emerson, and other such rich gems of the Republic. Giuseppe has been reading the pamphlet though hardly understanding every line, even now his lips are moving under his wide whisk-broom sweep of a reddish mustache as he intones the daunting consonants, words that may or may not be of any use when confronting the immigration officers with their big black stamp of WOP (without papers), confronting the immigration officers in the huge rotunda of Castle Garden located near the Battery at the point of Manhattan, the point of entry for emigrants since 1855, when it became the official Emigrant Landing Depot, and which previously had been a fort built for the War of 1812 to defend against British attack from the sea, and then a reception hall where fireworks displays were held for the likes of President Andrew Jackson and the Marquis de La Fayette, and then a concert hall where Jenny "the Swedish nightingale" Lind sang for a packed house of New York elite.

Giuseppe had read about Castle Garden in an Italian book that quoted the New York Times in an 1874 article which stated that Castle Garden had become so famous in Europe that few emigrants could be entreated to sail anywhere else. They "come to Castle Garden where they will be safe, and if out of money, they can remain until it is sent to them." Sent by whom? By the government perhaps? That's crazy. What a great country thought Giuseppe. He assumed that these conditions still prevailed. Maybe even an opera singer from the Metropolitan Opera will be there to greet us and sing for us while we wait in line, perhaps? And maybe they shoot off some of those fireworks when we arrive? Just think of it, Maurizio! But Maurizio didn't think about it very much. Giuseppe was thinking about it all the time. The book was one of the reasons Giuseppe's inclinations were swayed toward America, along with an invitation from his friend in Florida, but Giuseppe didn't want to be a farmer; he wanted to be a city man; a man of stone, not of the field; nevertheless, that remained a backup plan in the land of opportunity. In the years of the last decade of the 19th century Giuseppe also felt confirmed in his decision to relocate to America instead of Argentina or Brazil, because those countries became embroiled in social turmoil. Brazil was catapulted into civil war in 1893-94 and a cholera epidemic in 1895 struck the Italian enclave of Espirito Santo. In Argentina an anarchist movement had risen up to lead the way in nineteen major strikes in Buenos Aires in 1895, and sixteen in 1896. Giuseppe felt relieved that he had made the right choice, though Maurizio had his doubts and would have preferred to have gone to Argentina with the anarchists but he never said a word about it to Giuseppe, and after ten years in Manhattan Giuseppe was already making plans to get out of the city. It appeared to be a happily-ever-after story of an immigrant family, a multi-generational epic evolving along the branches of the tribal tree where the apes cling, afraid to enter the grasslands; a legacy to be passed on to future generations, and be enriched upon; to be made rich upon; if the future generations played their cards right, that is. After all it was a gambler's paradise. Risk it all or nothing.

Castle Garden would be used as an emigration depot for the last time in 1891. It had earned a reputation as a place that protected immigrants, whereas Ellis Island, the new reception venue that opened on 1 January 1892, became known as "Heartbreak Island," a "cross between Devil's Island and Alcatraz," whose sole reason for existing was to keep out the wretched refuse of the teeming shores of southern Europe, and the list grew rapidly in following years to include idiots, paupers, lunatics, criminals, moral turpitudists, those with loathsome diseases, illiterates, polygamists, the feeble-minded, morons, prostitutes, and anarchists, especially anarchists, just to mention a few of the un-elect.

Giuseppe placed his battered suitcase on the deck; a suitcase and a trunk, that's all they took with them, and he reached into his jacket pocket and felt for his papers. He was reassured. It was like sailing into a dream. Giuseppe and Maurizio leaned on the railing and took deep breaths. But when someone standing next to Giuseppe tried to steal his suitcase, Maurizio quickly stuck a knife up to the thief's back. The thief quickly dropped the suitcase and Maurizio pushed him away. *Sicilian bastardo!* Maurizio had no delusions about dreams. Maurizio smiled at Giuseppe, who was unaware that anything had happened. He was lost in a reverie of the New World. Giuseppe picked up the suitcase again. He held the pamphlet open with his left hand; he held the suitcase in his right hand, his large, and yellow, hard-callused mason's hands. The pamphlet waved in the breeze just like the emblematic drawing of the American flag at the top of the page seemed to be waving o'er the land of the free, o'er the sketched-map of the country, the forty-three states, the capitals, the mountains, the rivers, from sea to shining sea, and Giuseppe has been learning all the names by heart, trying to memorize them: Albany, New York; Boston, Massachusetts; Hartford, Connecticut; Blue Ridge Mountains, Adirondacks, Smokey Mountains, Rocky Mountains; Mississippi River, Columbia River, Colorado River; and all the names of the presidents in order, Washington, Adams, Jefferson, above all Jefferson, Giuseppe's favorite, right up to the present day president, Benjamin Harrison. And Giuseppe begins reading aloud the opening lines of Jefferson's Declaration of Independence: VENINA-DACORSAVA-YUMANA-VENTAS.

Thomas Jefferson was Giuseppe's first American hero; that is, until he moved to a small town on Long Island where Theodore Roosevelt made his home. Giuseppe's previous heroes included Columbus and Garibaldi. In Genoa he had very little contact with the opera heroes or soccer heroes of his region. There wasn't much of it to speak of. The Genoa Cricket and Athletic Club would not be founded until 1893, by a group of Englishmen. By then Giuseppe was gone and well out of it and would never return to Genoa. The English gentlemen fielded a football team but they didn't't let any Italians play with their ball until four years later. In 1898 Genoa won the first Italian football championship and Giuseppe read about that event in an Italian newspaper published in New York. By now, he could have cared less. In 1898 Theodore Roosevelt was charging up San Juan Hill in the Spanish-American War. That was news! As for opera, the Metropolitan was the bastion of New York's highborn, popping their champagne corks during a performance, occupying the 122 boxes, while a mainly serious

Germanic crowd occupied the regular seats. When Caruso arrived in 1903, Giuseppe became more interested, and then Arturo Toscanini arrived in 1908, along with a new manager, Giulio Gatti-Casazza, who was no relation to Giuseppe, even though their names were spelled the same; or, rather, had been. Giuseppe's name had been spelled that way too, but because the immigration people spelled his name as they did, Cazzaza, and surely it was a sign of a new beginning in the New World, so Giuseppe never bothered to write it any other way again. Not that Giuseppe would have to do much writing. But Giuseppe did read everything about opera that he could find. His first child, Silvia, would become an opera devotee; she would even study to be a singer with the renowned teacher Luigi Bollo. She promised that one day she would take her papa to the Metropolitan.

Giuseppe lights a cigar that he holds in his strong mason's hand. Builder of cathedrals, shaper of stone, when in the course of a line of masonry... O America, wrote Whitman, because you build for mankind I build for you. Bricks of a skyscraper and leaves of grass. Giuseppe puffs golden smoke into the golden air beside the golden door. Ah Genoese, thy dream! Thy dream!

Maurizio and Giuseppe marched down the plank, carrying the trunk between them, followed by their family members. Maurizio held no expectations about a "better life," about the "pursuit of happiness" that Giuseppe goes on and on about. But then Maurizio was very unlike Giuseppe. Those who knew him back in Orero called Maurizio cold and even ruthless. Maurizio felt a strange foreboding of doom, of disaster, of impending tragedies. What is this pursuit of happiness? But he consoled himself with the thought that New York wasn't such a bad place for a sculptor, why just look at the stone, the cement, the Statue of Liberty herself, the iron and steel, the shapes of things to come, the hardness of the city. Though couched in a soft oracular haze, the sharp edges and brutal bombast were exceptionally ugly, but that was okay (to use one English slang word that Maurizio knows), because he's a sculptor of ugliness; he likes ugly things, like Donatello's "Job" and his Mary Magdalene. A pumpkinhead and a hag. Maurizio felt certain that there would be lots of ugly things to sculpt here in New York, America. It was never the United States, it was always America. *Le Merica*. His art would redeem his rootlessness.

In Giuseppe's opinion it was Thomas Jefferson who had produced America's first great and serious literary masterpiece, The Declaration of Independence. He was not unique in his judgment. Someday, he boasted, he will travel to Washington D.C. and see the actual parchment in all its glory. Anyone can see it, for free, this is democracy! Giuseppe never made it to the Metropolitan Opera House, and he also never made it to Washington D.C.

Thomas Jefferson was the author of democracy, according to Giuseppe, and he was never lax in telling his brother that this was so. Life, liberty, and the pursuit of happiness.

It wouldn't be long before Giuseppe was on his way, leaving behind the Mulberry Bends for the quaint little Mulberry Streets of a small town, but no ordinary small town, mind you; Theodore Roosevelt lived there! Or near there. But for every Mulberry Street there was a Mulberry Bend, and there had even been a Mulberry Row, on the immortal champion of democracy's plantation in Virginia, where Jefferson's slaves had lived in shacks. And before Jefferson's elitist declaration of freedom for white landowners there was the people's literature: the first bestseller in America was a poem titled "The Day of Doom," written by the Right Reverend Michael Wigglesworth, published in 1662. It enlightens the new natives of the Day of Judgment and the sentencing to Hell of sinners and infants who died before baptism. O fear and trembling. The pursuit of happiness and the pursuit of doom... together, that's what made America great, boys... that's what makes America great! Pika-pika boom-boom beep-beep.

And every great American hero became Giuseppe's hero; but Jefferson, Lincoln, and Theodore Roosevelt stood head and shoulders above the rest, just as they would when enshrined in stone on Mount Rushmore. In fact, Giuseppe had anticipated the stone monument by years when he had asked Maurizio to sculpt small busts of the three presidents and stuck them together over the mantelpiece. It was inspired. They vaguely resembled their namesakes, and Maurizio had done his best to subvert their images, adding a satirical touch. It's the best I can do: Maurizio lied to his brother. Giuseppe would name two of his three sons after Lincoln and Roosevelt; his third and youngest son he considered naming Jefferson, but changed his mind when he discovered a new American hero... himself. He named his youngest son the anglicized Joseph John Cazzaza.

New York City 1895

Two figures casting long shadows walked along the street under the glimmer of gaslight on a balmy night in June 1895. It was past midnight. They tread softly and they spoke softly, one of them carried a policeman's nightstick, a big stick, 26 inches of solid oak. He was not a policeman, rather the recently sworn in president of the Board of Commissioners of the New York City Police Department. His name was Theodore Roosevelt. He wore a black evening coat, collar turned up, and had his hat pulled down to his bespectacled eyes; a great white set of teeth flashed and illuminated the pavement and the deserted street. His journalist and photographer sidekick, Jacob Riis, an immigrant Dane who had revealed how the other half lives in a sequence of books, accompanied Theodore Roosevelt. They had been stealthily inspecting the Lower East Side streets of the city, having set out from Police Headquarters at 300 Mulberry Street, prowling for a loitering and lazy patrolman or the higher ranked roundsman on his beat, and were now returning to headquarters just a few hours before dawn's early light. They had dined at an all night eatery in the Bowery, on steak, salad and beer.

Earlier that very afternoon the indefatigable Roosevelt and his crony Riis with others in tow had scrutinized and examined the murky Sixth and Fourteenth Wards, paying particular attention to the area consisting of Mott Street, Baxter Street, Baird Street and Mulberry Street. Roosevelt, Riis, and two health inspectors, peeked into alleys and doorways. Roosevelt recited his observations and the health inspectors offered comments and took notes.

"On this street, Mr. Commissioner, there are a great number of Italians, followed in number by some Hebrews, and the rest are made of Chinese, mixed nationalities, and a few colored people."

"Mixed... did you say... what kind of mix?" queried the Commissioner.

"Mixed nationality whites... Irish, German... "

"But not mixed with the coloreds and the chink?"

Well, Mr. Commissioner... there may be some."

"Have you read Max Nordau's book, E*ntartung... Degeneration.* Have you not read Brooks Adams's *Laws of Civilization and Decay?*"

"No sir, I have not."

"Read them, I implore you, they are about the decadence and weariness of our present civilization. The French are foremost holding in contempt all tradition and morality and custom… we cannot let the stench of Europe infiltrate America! That's why you and I are here… to lift these people up… have you not seen what I have seen? Are you blind, man? The jealous, greedy, sullen envy will make anarchists of them all! This is what bred the Commune! The dangerous classes, the Jew banker, the savage Indians, Negroes, chinks, the lower sorts, the Irish and now these dagoes… the white race will not endure. There must be action, not ennui from our best men, but duty, loyalty, purity, and character. Well then… let us proceed."

"This tenement… this is number 29, Baxter…" spoke the inspector.

"Look, Riis, that sign, **Please No Slamb Door.**"

"Well, Theodore, though the spelling is not correct… this does show some kind of consideration for the others."

"Indeed. Take note of this, inspectors… as I speak please record my words… as we entered the house, made of wood, we discovered three persons assorting old rags and paper in the yard and children playing in the rubbish. Pools of dirty water. Inside… follow me… we entered a dark room, with low ceilings, insufficient air space, terrible dampness in rooms, old cigar stumps… this house is unfit for human habitation! Let's depart at once…"

The committee, led by the feisty and determined Roosevelt, walked down the street and stopped in front of another tenement house.

"This is number 55," said one of the inspectors.

"Let us enter," ordered Roosevelt. "This building is cracked and dilapidated. The floor is decayed. There is water leakage from a water closet perhaps. Old paper, rags and rope on the floor…"

A man stepped out from one of the doors. "Gentlemen, what is your mission here?"

Roosevelt taken aback, blurted "Mission? Our mission? We are here to remedy this squalor. Who is the owner of this house?"

"Why I am…"

"These conditions are degrading! Will you not attempt to make a decent habitation?"

"Well, evidently my premises do not suit ye fine gentlemen… but of course it makes no difference does it not? Because I for certain think your time is very short here anyhow…"

"Our time is indeed long enough to see these insufferable conditions… it is a fit dwelling place for only a rat," said Roosevelt.

"Rats need a place too…"

Roosevelt inhaled and forcefully exhaled. He turned around and stormed out. The committee marched off down the street, following behind the quick stepping Roosevelt. They stopped in front of a window.

"Number… is there a number? Ah, here it is… Baxter, number 42…" said one of the inspectors. "This is a restaurant."

Roosevelt spied into the window. His face pressed against the glass. "There are three men, sitting at a table, eating, they are bullated and bleary eyed. These are sickening conditions for a restaurant."

Roosevelt had seen enough that day. The committee walked back toward Mulberry Street. They stopped one last time in front of number 41 Mulberry Street. A decently dressed and bright and lovely Italian woman with a small child in her arms, stood in front of the door.

She spoke, "Are you get us a park I wish to God you will. We need it here."

"What is the child's name?" asked Roosevelt.

"He name is Emilio. Emilio Baldazzi."

"Remember, your child is an American now! He shall learn the English language. There is room for but one language. English."

Roosevelt nodded and walked up Mulberry Street until the committee reached Police Headquarters.

The horror that was Mulberry Bend would be transformed into a park, Mulberry Bend Park, and renamed in 1911 as Columbus Park.

Regeneration of the lost white soul was the plight of the ruling race. Moral transformation of the bothersome lesser breeds was its mandate. In his younger and more vulnerable years, as a member of the New York state assembly, Roosevelt was scoffed and mocked as a dude, a Jane-Dandy, our own Oscar Wilde, with a high pitched voice that whined incessantly. He was defensive and scrappy. He picked fights. He believed in fighting words. He was willing to box the ears off of any opponent. Sock him and he will stay plastered. The Anglo-Saxon race was committing race suicide. The rise of Industrial Capitalist Civilization had allowed ambitious and misguided men to pursue material happiness, turn away from a virtuous civic life, the physical type of the Eastern states has degenerated, decreasing fertility of the New York and New England stock, lack of virility, and those with the money touch, and shirk the social responsibilities of their class. The urban centers were filling up with degenerates of all kinds, low life immigrants, bringing with them those perverted socialistic ideas, the worst being the anarchist, and the poets of a debauched sort, imported from decadent France, types like Flaubert, Baudelaire, with their sexual depravity and their drugs. Roosevelt preferred that Frenchman Arthur de Gobineau's *Essai sur l'inégalité des races humaines*. Roosevelt did not hate. It was biology. It was natural history. It was science.

The primitive in man's heart must rise like the wolf, to combat the spineless ways of the modern world; it requires a controlled form of blood hysteria, when the blood mounts to the eyes. The little boy weakling impelled the big manly wolf-like beast in the heart to go west and conquer his shortcomings. Of course the cowboys were equally good at living a life that demanded crude forms of dissipation, but this was of a manly sort of indulgence and part and parcel of the perfect freedom of the West. Roosevelt hunted and galloped on horseback over these rolling, limitless prairies, with his rifle in hand. He was a man with the bark on. Roosevelt ran away to the Wild West to let the wolf rise. The weaklings died because they couldn't hold their own in the rough warfare of these surroundings. Roosevelt would make a man out of himself and the place to do it is the Wild West. Get away from the weak and nervous Easterners. We need national expansion to reverse the decline. We need to breed the good stock. Cast off effeminate behavior, consumerism, selfishness, unhealthy modernism, liberated women in urban settings, extend the close of the frontier, Anglo-Saxon self-reliance, self-control, self-sufficiency, self-mastery, sing the self, and there are no Slavs or Huns or Jews in the West, no Norwegian farmers, no French flâneurs, no Italian fruit dealers, no Chinee opium dens, no Jap tea ceremony. No these cowboys are the brave white medieval knights, the Vikings rounding the coasts, the great explorers, the great conquerors, invaders, inventors, adventurers, pirates, animal tamers, civilization builders, but do not provoke us oh my darling! For we will cut you down, and we will do it cleanly.

Roosevelt and Riis headed out from the all night restaurant. Roosevelt was in good humor and held forth on various subjects while rapidly rambling by foot with Jacob Riis to Police Headquarters in the early hours before dawn. The worshipful Riis nodded and concurred with each of Roosevelt's forceful declarations. "The different nationalities are in the habit of parading on certain days… a senseless and objectionable custom… white slave traffic… the men should be whipped… get to them through their skins… these men, and women are worse than murderers… no toleration of any tenderloin or red light district… that Crane's novel… about prostitution, the cause is not only because of an economic hardship, but lack of strong character, we must build character… our realist novelists… oh but they somehow lack… morals… like Tolstoy they don't pass judgment on their character's behavior, don't admonish them, no moral instruction… Howells was sympathetic to the Haymarket anarchists… I would have hung the bastards myself… and I am suspicious of Twain, and Crane, and his filthy life and book, Wharton and James, effete, the money people, but no action, no action… get action."

A group of street urchins hastened past them. They were running away from a young boy that they had waylaid, robbed and beaten. Roosevelt overheard them speaking as they ran by… "Dat mug scrapped like a damn dago. He was dead easy. Hully gee."

One bumped into Roosevelt. "Hey chump, youse runned plump inta me."

"Steady boy!" said Roosevelt.

"Oh, gee, go teh hell," said the boy.

"Little street Arabs, do you have homes?" said Teddy.

"Git off da urt," said the boy and ran off with the others.

Earlier in the evening on Mulberry Street Roosevelt and Riis had encountered two dark figures walking toward them on the pavement. The two men, immigrants from Italy, had arrived on the transatlantic steamer *Fulda* in 1893. On the ship's manifest, Giuseppe Cazzaza was listed as a common laborer, and Maurizio Cazzaza as a stonemason. They were brothers. They had come to America with another brother, and their sister and brother-in-law. Giuseppe is twenty-five years old, and Maurizio is twenty-two.

Roosevelt saw them approaching and became cautious: "Jake, are they native born roughs or of the low foreign element, not straight New York, or Irish? Rascality… like those gamins that fled by us…"

Giuseppe was pushing an empty fruit cart. They were setting out early as usual to collect fruits and vegetables for their stall on Delancey Street. Maurizio works with his brother, but sometimes he strays from his duties and wanders off during the day, much to Giuseppe's consternation.

Maurizio has been up to Union Square and has heard among others Emma Goldman speak about labor strikes. Giuseppe wasn't aware that his brother was involved in such "dangerous matters." He would be upset, no doubt, if he knew that his brother had such disloyal and underhanded ideas in his head. There are secrets that remained preserved in the spectral shadows of even the most clannish families. Both men were surprisingly well dressed. Not as dapper as the foppish Roosevelt of course, but for recent immigrants, fairly smartly attired. Roosevelt halted in front of the two men and stood with a swagger, glaring intently at them, teeth clenched. "Gentleman, what is your mission at this late hour?"

"We go work. Get produce," said Giuseppe, whose English language skills were marginally superior to Maurizio's.

Walking by, Roosevelt heard Maurizio quote by heart, *"Nel mezzo del ... di nostra vita mi... per una selva oscura, che la ... via..."*

Broken and fading words... Roosevelt recognized it at once as being the beginning of Dante's *Commedia...* midway on my life's journey I found myself in a dark wood... Roosevelt was flabbergasted and followed the men, but they had already disappeared around the corner. To think that he heard it on Mulberry Street.

Giuseppe and Maurizio walked pass a storefront with monkeys in the window. Maurizio stopped and stared and laughed at the monkeys.

Giuseppe said, "Let's go. *Andemo via.*"

Yes. Let's go. But Maurizio did not move.

The brothers didn't have a ring-tailed monkey and a hand organ. They have never been to an animal store to buy a monkey from a German importer. Their acquaintance Salvatore bought a monkey. He entertains with his monkey in Washington Square Park, not far from 235 Mercer Street, where Fiorenza Maggio lives with her family. Giuseppe saw her at church three Sundays ago, at St. Anthony, over on Thompson Street. Giuseppe and Salvatore are both pursuing her, vying for her affections. Stupida Salvatore, who spent at least $100, all his savings, to invest in a hand organ and a ring-tailed monkey, just to impress Fiorenza. But Salvatore wasn't going to be like the other unmarried men who got hired out to work on railroads and aqueducts by the padrones and ended up in the South working in sulfite mines under armed guard. He was enamored of the dream. The American Dream. The rags to riches dream. But my family is not rag pickers. *Sicilian bastardo,* intoned Maurizio to himself. The

Cazzaza brothers were born in the vicinity of Orero, near the port of Genoa, the Cicagna Valley in the province of Liguria, in the north of Italy. Sicilians were a whole other tribe.

Antonio Maggio thinks little of the silly Salvatore and his monkey, named Mateo. Antonio is Fiorenzo's handlebar-mustachioed father, a dark-eyed man of overbearing melancholy. Just look at the family photographs taken at the studio at 61 Bond Street. No one smiles. Luigia, Antonia's wife, looks terribly mortified, and the children look just plain sad. Antonio is a watchmaker, a skill that he learned back in Turin, Italy, from his father. Giuseppe knows that Antonio prefers him to Salvatore. Marriage is being discussed, but Giuseppe and Fiorenza are not speaking about it to each other. Things will work out. But it's not in their hands. Fiorenza has two brothers and three sisters. Louis, the older boy, was born in Italy. Henry is the youngest, was born in America. And Fiorenza was born in America. It was in St. Anthony's that Fiorenza was baptized in 1882.

Document 0.1.9

Certificate of Baptism
Church of St Anthony
Franciscan Friars

151 Thompson Street

New York, N.Y.

This is to Certify

That Fiorenza Victoria Adela Luise Maggio

Child of Antonio Maggio

And Luise Maggio

Born on the 7 day of May 1882

Baptized

On the 11 day of June 1882

According to the Rite of the Roman Catholic Church

By the Rev. Camillus

Sponsors John-Baptist Maggio

Victoria Maggio

As appears from the Baptismal Register of this Church

Book 1882 page 53

Fiorenza's father Antonio made a declaration of intention to become an American citizen, five years ago.

Document 1.1.2
United States of America

Be it remembered, that on the 18th day of February in the year of our Lord one thousand eight hundred and ninety personally appeared Antonio Maggio in the Superior Court of the City of New York and made his declaration of intention to become a Citizen of the United States of America, in the words following, to wit:

I, Antonio Maggio do declare on oath, that it is bona fide my Intention to become a Citizen of the United States of America, and to renounce forever all allegiance and fidelity to any foreign Prince, Potentate, State or Sovereignty whatever, and particularly to the King of Italy of whom I am a subject.

Sworn this 18th day of February 1890

Antonio Maggio   X   his mark

Residence, 235 Mercer Street

Thomas Boese, clerk

Last summer Giuseppe Cazzaza with the financial help of his childhood friend and brother-in-law, Giancarlo Bacigalupo, invested in a pushcart, and has just recently rented a large stall on Delancey Street, also with the help of Giancarlo. Giuseppe fancies himself a businessman. One day he'll follow the others out to Astoria, Corona, Long Island City, and then beyond. His family had worked in the slate quarrying business back in the old country; in fact, Giancarlo's father was a foreman in a slate company, but times were hard and Italians dreamed of America. Though many also dreamed of Brazil and Argentina. Maurizio fancies himself an artist, a sculptor, and secretly holds to anarchist ideals. Giuseppe was somewhat tolerant of his brother's artistic inclinations, but anarchist! Maurizio didn't want his brother to know about that part of him, not yet anyway. Some crazed anarchist's bastards in Italy had murdered Giancarlo's father.

Maurizio received a letter from Francesco, the crazed anarchist bastard. He was writing to tell Maurizio that Paris has become a very dangerous place now for anarchists. There has been a crackdown on anarchists groups.

There were the executions of the self-proclaimed anarchists Ravachol, Vaillant, Emile Henry and Caserio, who stabbed and killed the French President Sadi Carnot. The anarchists were being rounded up and their newspapers shut down. Francesco will be escaping to London with a few of his friends. He will write again when he gets to London.

Maurizio had to be very careful that his brother would not find these letters from Francesco. This is a translation from the Italian of Francesco's letter to Maurizio.

Document 17-385

Belleville, Paris, France   27 June 1895

Maurizio, my dear comrade,

I now finally have the time to write to you. I hope you will receive my letter in New York now that you have left Orero and gone with your family to America as your family was discussing before the incident. The ship that you waved goodbye to me in Genova was going to France. I lived in a French city by the sea, called Marseille, as I told you in my first letter to you before you left Orero. I met some of our brothers there. I lived there for three months and then we travelled to Paris. I now live in an area called Belleville. Here there are many hungry people. There are many places to go for drinks. But we must live a measured life. We cannot have shaking hands holding the… truth. But I am learning a trade. I am a typographer. Ha! Can you believe it? But I enjoy this work. It is a craft. I copy words that I do not understand. I am also learning bookbinding. I met a man who I am told is a very intelligent man. His name is Rocker. He is the same age as me. He is a German but his ideas are like mine. I am learning much from him. We speak with each other in a strange silent language. We speak a fragment of Italian, a fragment of English, a fragment of French… but mostly we speak with our eyes and our hands! Waving our hands about madly. We understand each other perfectly. I am learning some French and English. *Fermez ça!* Shut up! I say chotta-aapa! Do you know these words? Monsieur Rocker is also a typographer. We met at the printing shop. He lives with a man named Rappaport, also a typographer. I am lucky to get this work and to meet these men. So we have in common making words appear on paper and making revolution appear in the world! That is our abundant hope. I live with two brothers from home. They are friends with Malatesta. I want to meet the great Malatesta one day. Have you read Proudhon yet? He was a typographer too! A Frenchman. He is our papa. He says property is theft! I hope you can find books in America. There is in my plans the idea of going to London. It has become dangerous here in Paris for our brothers. There have been bombings by individualists! Malatesta says that propaganda by the deed, you know the meaning of this? That it is an act of hate, and hate will not make a better world... but I see these poor people of Paris and think, how can one not hate?

You must write to this address from your new land... and tell me of the life there... I will write to you from London when I arrive...

Your comrade Francesco

Giuseppe didn't know anything about Theodore Roosevelt either, who certainly was not an anarchist. Roosevelt preferred the anarchists hanged or shot by his wild boys of the west. And that's exactly what happened to the Haymarket anarchists in Chicago. They were hanged. William Dean Howells called it "judicial murder."

But within ten years Giuseppe would know and come to admire Theodore Roosevelt. Giuseppe will live in Roosevelt's little town on Long Island. He will shake his hand, but not on this night.

Tonight, Theodore Roosevelt dreamed of the many voices he had heard in the dark streets, the alleys, and the tenements. Chinese, German, Yiddish, Russian, Polish, Italian... even the voice of Dante... the real life voices of the swarming millions... Roosevelt wanted to have fun meeting every class of people in New York City... and woke in the night, in a cold sweat, in the mist of the babelic babble of the American dream, and let out a scream.

His wife, Edith, and his children gathered around him, staring at him in fear, holding their various pets, dog, snake, rodent...

Roosevelt clamored in a delirium of fever: "...Oh the inferno! The inferno! Degenerates! In the beginning was the word! It was English! The word was English. The English-speaking people... Anglo-Saxon superiority! Oh in Xanadu did Kubla Khan... from far ancestral voices prophesying war... war! Honor! Duty! Oh you degenerate fiends... fiends! The wolf... the wolf rises in my heart..."

New York City 1896

On a hot and windless day, June 6, 1896, two Norwegian fishermen set out in an 18 foot rowboat from the Battery Park at the base of Manhattan, attempting to row across the north Atlantic Ocean without sail, steam, or rudder. The rowboat, Fox, was named in honor of Richard Kyle Fox, publisher and editor of the National Police Gazette. The Gazette was America's leading illustrated newspaper of the shocking and sensational, centering on crime, scandal, gossip, sex, murder, bridge jumpers, and sports, principally boxing. They used pink paper and advertised dubious patent medicines to cure, among other infirmities, venereal disease. Fox broke new ground by using illustrations in a popular newspaper. Joseph Pulitzer's newspaper and this year Hearst arrived in New York to take over the World.

One day the two Norwegians showed up at the offices of the Gazette at Franklin Square and made a desperate appeal to Fox for sponsorship. Fox liked the two square heads. They were the right kind of people. He hated all other new comers. Fox was an immigrant from Ireland. He knew the right kind of people when he saw them. Immigrants like himself, just a mick off the boat from Belfast. This could be another great story. What's more American than poor immigrant boys clawing their way tooth and nail to wealth and respectability by good old free enterprise. The essence of the American Dream. The Europeans may have come for gold and silver, but look what they got in return: tobacco, potatoes, corn, Coca-Cola, chocolate, sunflowers, chewing gum and peanuts. These boys were not those dirty Southern and Eastern Europeans. Not guineas, kikes. They were of the right stock. Doubtless to say, Fox was a bigot. He chiefly hated the Chinese, the chink. He backed the two Norwegians and their crazy enterprise and adventure.

The rowboat was docked to a flotation device not far from Castle Garden, no longer the main depot for arriving immigrants. The rowboat was stocked with provisions bought at Rafferty's Canned Goods and Fancy Groceries over on Front Street. There was an assortment of oars in the rowboat: long and short, made of ash and spruce. The boat departed at 5 p.m. as the tide flowed outward to the sea. A small crowd gathered in the park to see them off. The crazy risk takers. They'll never make it. I wonder if Theodore Roosevelt would have approved? He despised Hearst and Pulitzer... their yellow journalism. Yet these two hardy men exemplified the strenuous life, did they not? Well, I wonder. Soon Hearst would promote Teddy's little war with Spain.

They rowed out of the harbor and looked up at the futuristic sunset gates of a sky lined with running rust on steel gray. There was nothing there. Oh the sky was there all right, but the bridge wasn't there, not in the year 1896, and Frank and George not for a moment imagined that there would ever be a bridge there, directly up above them, from where they rowed, a bridge that would be named after the Italian explorer Giovanni da Verrazano.

George and Frank were at liberty to pursue their doom, descend into Davy Jones locker, or ascend to their happiness, the American Dream, the act of desperation. They arrived at the Scilly Islands off the British coast in 55 days. A record. They continued on to La Havre in France and rowed up the Seine to Paris. They planned a big tour of the major European cities. They would display their boat and lecture. But the people did not come out to see them. After two weeks in Paris and two months in England, they went to Norway. In the small coastal town of Farsund a crowd of locals greeted them enthusiastically. Their names were George Harbo and Frank Samuelsen. George and Frank were immigrants to the USA. Frank came in 1893, the year of the Panic, the same year as Giuseppe and Maurizio Cazzaza. Brawny sailors carried their boat up the hills of Farsund. This was Frank's hometown. And the writer Hamsun was there... and one man, Aanen, from Lunde, who lived across the fjord, was in the crowd. He was the man who painted the steeple after Oscar blew himself up.

Years later, Aanen's granddaughter, Torhild, worked in a nursing home in Farsund, in 1942-1943, during the German occupation. Frank was a resident in the nursing home. Torhild remembers Frank as a well-mannered, quiet gentleman who was able to take care of himself. She also remembers him briefly mentioning his great disappointment. And that he told her that he had received a medal from the King of Norway. She also remembers him being chased about by an old woman. Fame and fortune, the American Dream, that George and Frank sought... probably wouldn't have suited Frank.

Maurizio Cazzaza walked in the park. It was a pleasant and warm day in September. A Saturday. The hellish and hot days of August had been unbearable. Many had died from the heat. Bodies were pulled from the tenements and alleys daily. Workers succumbed on the streets. "Wild" dogs were shot on site. The city and its officialdom did little to alleviate the suffering. Laissez-faire capitalism ruled the day. Don't disturb the markets. Family, church, charities... let them help. That populist and demagogue, the boy orator from Nebraska, William Jennings Bryant, had come to town stomping for the presidency. The eastern elites, the moneyed interests, Wall Street financiers, the newspapers, the local Republicans, even Tammany avoided him, had a field day denigrating the silverite. Bryant was called a lunatic, an anarchist, and a madman. There were articles written by "alienists" proclaiming that Bryant was of unsound mind. A Mattoid! A speech and rally at Madison Square Garden was a debacle. Thousands walked out. By the time Bryant left the city Wall Street breathed a sigh of relief. They ran him out of town. The only exception was Hearst's paper *The World*... why? To sell more papers to the plebs of course.

Maurizio Cazzaza sat down on a park bench by a fountain. It's been three years since Maurizio and his brother Giuseppe descended from that ship and into the economic upheaval of 1893. Giuseppe and his best friend from youth, Giancarlo Bacigalupo, who were inseparable back in Orero, had big American dreams. Giancarlo, whose father had been a somewhat well-to-do foreman at a slate quarry in the mountains beyond Genoa, had befriended the poorer Giuseppe when they were kids, and when Giancarlo's father was murdered by some deranged anarchists, and his mother died not long after, then Giancarlo decided to go to America, and persuaded Giuseppe to come, with his family, to seek their fortune. Giancarlo had inherited some property and money, enough to get started, and was able to find better accommodations than most when he settled in Manhattan. He found a building on Wooster Street and rented two apartments, avoiding the worst of the slums by just several blocks. Giancarlo and Giuseppe were ambitious.

Not Maurizio. He liked to stroll. He liked this park. He preferred this park to Washington Square, which was nearer to his home, a park for which Italians had collected money to erect a statue of General Giuseppe Garibaldi (the Sword of Italian Unification) in Washington Square Park, dedicated in 1888. Giuseppe and Giancarlo contributed. Maurizio's attitude was bah!

This park was grander. This was City Hall Park. Maurizio sat on a bench by a fountain near the City Hall building. French Revival. He marveled at Printing House Square across the way. The gold-domed World building, the squat Sun building, the Tribune building, once the tallest in the world, with a clock in its steeple, then the majestic Times building, with its tall arched windows. Ever since Maurizio found a job at a small print shop newspapers have fascinated him. City Hall Park had wide walkways, lined with benches and trees. The classical City Hall building was in the center of the park, surrounded by Printers Row and municipal buildings. A dozen or so wide stairs led up to the white columns of City Hall's entrance. Topped by a round tower and a figure with uplifted arm. Maurizio sat and stared in amazement, astonished by the commotion around him, the center of New York's political and news world, with Wall Street not far off, the center of its financial world, and beyond the Printer Row buildings the East River and the towers of the Brooklyn Bridge, whose promenade Maurizio loved to walk, while EL trains roared by.

Maurizio sat on the bench. A few newspaper reporters were walking by Maurizio's bench. One was a baseball reporter and the other his correspondent, who attended a game at the Polo Grounds, and had rushed down the 3rd Avenue El to meet the reporter by the bench. They were engaged in a lively conversation. Maurizio overheard bits of their strange dialogue, understanding nothing. "It's awful... a near riot... I thought they would attack Freedman... seventh place... managed by an actor... ruin of the game... but what a game... what a game... Giants 10... Baltimore 1... oh boy that Meekin is a wow... and George Davis... and the Hoosier Thunderbolt... what a fastball... almost killed someone... he won't sign him..." The reporters ran over to their newspaper offices across from the park at Broadway. There was a huge bulletin board. The reporters looked at the chalk writing and smiled. **RIOT AT THE POLO GROUNDS.**

Maurizio sat and observed. There were some well-dressed men and unruly kids and fine-tailored ladies, and a few men dressed in rags. "Bums! Hobos!" The children yelled at them and pointed at them.

The printshop where Maurizio worked was just a few blocks away from here. Maurizio, the aspiring sculptor, the makeshift radical and socialist, had attended a rally in Union Square on May Day, and cavorted among an assorted group of anarchists, socialists, labor and union delegates, ragtag bohemian hanger-ons, some striking, some protesting, some there to hear the Italian anarchist Pietro Gorii, who sang, accompanying himself on a mandolin, his song, *Inno del primo maggio... verde maggio de genere umano...*

that's why Maurizio was there, and while he was there he met an older American, Jimmy Delcambre, who was able to speak to Maurizio in broken Italian and some bits of English. He was a master typesetter and he invited Maurizio to the printshop. Maurizio ended up employed, a damn wage slave. But how else survive? Giuseppe will be proud of him.

The printshop was located at Broadway and Fulton, next to the newspaper offices in the *Mail and Express* Building. Taller buildings surrounded the small printshop. There stood several ornate buildings the tallest of which was the *Mail and Express* building, whose narrow chateau-like façade was decorated in a mishmash of rococo trimmings in the manner of the popular Beaux Arts movement, with an extended mansard tower and an overelaborate spire that was topped by a flowing banner on a pole with the words **Mail & Express** printed in thick san-serif letters. In the basement the enormous presses rumbled and shook the foundation. The printshop where Maurizio worked was in the basement of the building next door to the *Mail and Express*. David Dryhard, a retiring gent who had inherited the shop from his father, kept an askew eye on the shop floor.

David, being the only offspring of Daisy and Charles Dryhard, had taken over the shop when his father died at the young age of forty-three. David's father started the business in 1824 with just one press, a Columbia press, all metal, and American built.

When Maurizio started working at the shop, Jimmy showed him the old presses that stood quietly in the dark corners of the pressroom. There was the old Columbia, but also a Stanhope and some small wooden screw presses.

David Dryhard was a bachelor who spent most of his time sitting in his office reading newspapers, the *Sun, Times, Journal,* and puffed on a big cigar and cackled and laughed. He pretty much let the employees run the shop. He was very careless about what got printed on his presses and some of the employees brought in a good portion of the jobs. So on any given day anything from a flyer, a poster, political leaflets, a wedding invitation, a circular, or an indecent book printed on yellow paper, could be running on the presses.

Jimmy introduced Maurizio to the oldest employee, Kid Murphy, a fifty-year-old journeyman. The Kid was once a legendary "Swift," one of the rare few who could set type at incredible speeds. The Kid competed in tournaments and fairs and dime stores all along the East Coast and

Midwest. "Swift" competitions were all the rage in the 1880s, but with the advent of the Linotype the "Swifts" converted back to plain old typesetters.

"You know," said Jimmy, "The Kid and me both worked at a case at the *Tribune* for twenty years, that was Greeley's paper, then Reid came in, and Reid brought in Mergenthaler and his Linotype machine... you probably never heard of them, well to make a long story short, some of us were out of work. Reid thought if we couldn't find work again it was our fault, some kind of moral defect... that's what he said when we were cast off, bantlings to the rocks below, damn him, but now there are so many big newspapers, the *World*, the *Journal*, the *Sun*, *Times*, *Post*... you know Hearst just ransacked the staff writers at the *World*, and they sell their newspapers at 2 cents and now 1 cent... but I'm happy here... work at my own pace... have a drink at noon break... I'm not going back to the big newspapers... right, Kid? You old mick. They were all Irish back then, even now, the typesetters. But Kid was fast. He could be bungling and a little inaccurate when he raced, and I was slower, but I was accurate, and I never raced. I took pride in my craft. We didn't like these guys performing and showing off. It made the bosses think that we were going slow on purpose and could go faster like the "Swifts." Work faster and faster. But we wanted quality... design... a good page... the capitalists wanted profits. Work harder and faster and smarter was their mantra. The bosses thought we were there just to take their money. I was a member of the Local 6. We condemned the type racing. We wanted to control our pace. Anyway, the Lino ended all that. But even yet they are racing with the Linotype. I heard some mick named Reilly at the *Tribune* was racing the machine against handset compositors... it's like racing a horse against a turtle. Makes no sense."

Jimmy started to cough hard. "I'm okay. You know I have outlived the best of them. And the Kid has too. The ventilation was so bad in most printshops that I worked, what with vapors of gas and kerosene... gaslight or that electrical light, it strained the eyes and lungs, but I'm forty-six, and most of us don't make it beyond forty. I know many who have succumbed. It's the conditions. That's why it's good here. That's why I'm still among the living. This place is rare. We run the place and just smile at old man Dryhard. You'll get by."

Maurizio walked home from City Hall Park. Tomorrow is a big day. Jimmy asked him if he would like to come to a protest march starting out from Union Square. Maurizio didn't hesitate. Of course he will come. But he has to be careful. It's Sunday and Giuseppe goes to church.

On Sunday, after Giuseppe and his sister Gina and his brother-in-law Giancarlo, with their 2-year-old son, Johnny, left for church, Maurizio started out to Union Square. He walked up Broadway. When he reached 10th Street he could see the trees in Union Square beyond the length of the street with a trolley slowing advancing on its tracks, and a few horse-drawn carriages stopping at the curbs unloading their wares. He stopped briefly in front of some offices for services providing shorthand and type. He wondered what shorthand meant. Above the office there was a projecting sign that read Lofts for Rent. Another sign read David Marks and Sons Fine Clothing. He passed the majestic Broadway Central Hotel and the smaller New York Hotel. He passed lamp-posts and a large round clock on its post. He could see at the top of Broadway, George Washington's equestrian statue, surrounded by bushes and a low iron fence.

When he reached Union Square there were already many groups of people gathered in different places in the park. Young boys were selling newspapers. Men and women were handing out leaflets. Some carried signs. Maurizio met up with Jimmy and his group. They are anarchists. Maurizio didn't know that Jimmy was an anarchist. Maurizio told Jimmy, "Me too."

After many speeches and loud shouts and hand clapping, the different groups formed together and started out from Union Square. Maurizio marched with Jimmy's group. There were several Italians in the group. They marched down toward the Cooper Union, where some of the groups dispersed in different directions, but Maurizio stayed with Jimmy's group and they marched on down Nassau Street toward City Hall Park. Several policemen have appeared and are following the marchers. They were near Wall Street and its *cordon sanitaire*. They marched down Williams Street. They stopped in front of Delmonico's Restaurant, with its ship-like prow. The police started to advance on them. They were in the financial district. "Is this a restricted area?" Jimmy's not sure, but the cops were sure.

Theodore Roosevelt, Jacob Riis, Lincoln Steffens and a cop named Schmittenberg were having lunch at Delmonico's. Roosevelt was holding forth on police matters and partaking of a New York Strip Steak with crisp golden onion rings, anticipating the famous Baked Alaska for dessert.

Mark Twain, Stephen Crane and William Dean Howells lunched a year ago at Delmonico's. This year Twain wasn't available. He was off making much-needed money on one of those horrendous speaking tours. Poor Twain, his beloved eldest daughter Suzy had recently died from meningitis. Twain had remained in England, when his wife and daughter sailed home. Howells shook his head as he conveyed the story to Crane. Howells had lost his adored daughter Winifred in 1889. He couldn't bring himself to write to Twain in England. It would awaken thoughts of his own poor daughter, and yet he wrote to him, that the universe is all a crazy blunder, and Twain replied, bittter bitter bitter. So Crane and Howells met. They were unaware that Roosevelt and his entourage were dining in the next room.

Stephen Crane, who wrote about the seedy side, the wild side, the lower East Side, the Bowery, the wild west, about thugs, hoodlums, hooligans, prostitutes, peddlers, beggars, strays, was no more political than say, Henry James, who wrote about the upper echelons, the swells, the wealthy, the elite, snobbish, gay, the American Girl, Europe. Crane had guided Howells around the same ethnic streets that Roosevelt had surveyed.

When the march of protesters past by the window of Delmonico's, and a commotion erupted outside on the sidewalks of New York, because a cop had just bashed in the brains of Maurizio Cazzaza, it wasn't William Dean Howells, the theoretical socialist, the Tolstoyan pacifist, but Crane, the apolitical man of action, who burst forth from his seat and went outside to witness and perhaps join in on the melee. Did he take this action to perhaps raise a voice against an injustice? Or perhaps just to enter the fray, because his sense of individual moral outrage was more immediate and visceral than the others? Or did he do it just for the experience, something to write about? His sense was more alive than the theoretical socialist and practical aristocrat Howells, who favored Indian extermination, oh these moral ambiguities, but Howells also supported the Haymarket anarchists when few took up their cause... middle class whimpering, not to say that there was not great moral courage involved for Howells, or Twain when he spoke out about the Philippines. And yet...

Schittenberg followed Crane out the door, followed by Roosevelt, bursting from his seat in the restaurant to the sidewalk with his keen sense of indignation in tow... use violence to quell the mob... hang those anarchists bastards... Roosevelt with Riis and Steffens and several cops...

breaking up the marchers… afterward Crane wondered how Mark Twain, the carbuncled libertarian soon-to-be anti-imperialist, would have conducted himself during the skirmish.

Roosevelt, who was first considered for the sanitation department, to mop up the streets of New York City, but really wanted to mop up the police and the city's slack morals… if I may interject, leave the mopping up to men like Joe Cazzaza…

Roosevelt arrived on the scene and screamed in a beaten Maurizio's bloody face, "You low anarchist scum… you damn dago… you should be whipped or strung up…. get to you through your skin, boy, through your skiiiin." Roosevelt's teeth grinding right close to Maurizio's face. Saliva dripping and spit spraying. To Maurizio this man was clearly insane.

Then Roosevelt spied Crane and grabbed him by the collar. "You." Roosevelt knew Crane and had admired his book *The Red Badge of Courage*. They had lunched together recently, Roosevelt had brought Riis along, to talk about the dire social problems in the city. Roosevelt was more concerned that Crane, whom Hearst had asked to write a series of articles about the Tenderloin district for the *New York Journal*, may write about the conduct of his police department and their methods of regulating crowd restrictions at Madison Square Garden, where William Jennings Bryan, whom Roosevelt reviled as a populist mob-leading demagogue, had made his acceptance speech for the Democratic Party's nomination for President. The articles appeared in a New Jersey newspaper and Crane used his initials for the byline. Roosevelt and Crane's inconsequential relationship deteriorated even more when Roosevelt was informed that Crane would testify in court on the behalf of an alleged prostitute. Crane reported that he had been interviewing two chorus girls on Broadway. And that afterward another girl had joined them, and that later when he accompanied one of the chorus girls to a nearby trolley car, the other girls were arrested by a plainclothes policeman. The chorus girl screamed out, "That's my husband!" Crane, flummoxed, concurred, and the policeman grudgingly released her. But he could not help the other girl. Crane protested her innocence. The officer called her a "common prostitute." This infuriated the priggish Roosevelt.

"Baseball, you played baseball, Crane, right? Not a manly sport. For mollycoddled men. You think you can throw a ball by me, Crane? Let's try it. Hasten forth to the park!"

While they marched over to a small vacant lot Roosevelt called out to Crane. "See here Crane, I want to speak with you about Madge..." Roosevelt was referring to Crane's novel *Maggie, A Girl of the Streets*. "... the ending is too ambiguous. There should have been a moral lesson..."

Schmittenberg the cop confiscated a tattered brown baseball and a bat from several kids who were playing in the vacant lot. The cop handed Crane the ball and sneered at him. Crane held the ball in his hand. Roosevelt kept waving his hand at Crane, indicating that he should move back a bit. "A fair and manly distance, Crane, back, back, back, good... there! Get action!"

Crane reared back and flung the ball right at Roosevelt's head. He flinched but avoided the ball. Crane threw another pitch. The ball sailed passed Roosevelt's maladroit and graceless swing of the bat and smashed against a brick wall. Roosevelt glared at Crane. Roosevelt threw the bat to the ground. He turned and walked away. Crane stood there. Then Crane blurted out, "There is no joy in Teddy Land, the mighty Roosevelt has struck out!" And Crane began singing a popular tune of the day as he walked towards Howells. "Casey would dance with the strawberry blonde and the band played on..."

William Dean Howells watched in vast amusement. And now Roosevelt spotted Howells. "You, Howells, you admire Tolstoy? He is a pacifist, full of mushiness, too sentimental, too soft, can't stand the sight of blood."

Howells replied, "Tolstoy is the greatest writer. He gives me the heart to hope that the world may be made over in the image of Him who died for it."

"You defended the Chicago anarchists. They got exactly what they deserved. You have socialistic ideals, Howells... dangerous, ominous, worse than these populists. You belong to the governing class, Howells, show some manliness. Tolstoy's *The Kreutzer Sonata* is a filthy and repulsive book. He has a diseased mind. It is not wholesome. He is insane. The United States Post Office rightly prohibited its printing in newspapers, because it is an obscenity. What's become of you Howells? You once upon a time had written a satisfactory review of my book, *The Winning of the West*. We know that the wolf, the savage, lurks in our hearts. That men who are leaders must keep the passions and evil impulses at bay, but that there are times when a man must rise to the occasion, and the wolf follows the heart's desire. War is cleansing. We must not turn away from blood and slaughter, we must look it in the eye. The extermination of the red savages of the plains... hideous demons... you wrote that, Howells, because you know that it was ultimately beneficial to the race, the white race, and that it was inevitable."

Howells was speechless. That was twenty years ago. It was an exhibition in Philadelphia. The Centennial Exposition. There was much celebration. The New World. The advancement and great achievements of the Nordic race, the Anglo-Saxons, our civilization. There were some photographs. I've never been west of the Mississippi.

A few weeks later a mail bomb was detected in a package addressed to Roosevelt.

1898

Two years later and Maurizio is still working at the print shop. The life of a sculptor, the life of an artist, was not going to be easy in America.

One day a certain "circular" was being run on one of the presses. A print run of about 10,000. An extremely large run for this shop. Maurizio was informed that this was a silly... in fact it was a circular for a green goods scam operator, a rather poor exemplar of the practice, for no "respectable" green goods operator would print his circular at such a disreputable print shop, a lowly print shop whose usual output consisted of anarchist literature and seedy pornography. How would that stand up in court? Such lousy character witnesses! Jimmy explained to Maurizio that the green goods circular was about a scam. It's just a get rich on a dupe scheme. Jimmy tried to explain the green goods scam to Maurizio.

"Here's what they do," said Jimmy. "These circulars are mailed out, see. The operators of the scam mailed them out, all over the country. The circular says that certain engraved plates of U.S. currency have come into their possession. They say they were discarded and lost. They somehow found them. They put a few notes of real money in the envelope, and say that these notes were printed from the engraving. But the money is real, see. Not counterfeit. That's the green goods, the money. They tell the guy that he can buy the counterfeit money from them, cheaper, see, you know, for ten bucks you get a hundred bucks, for a hundred you get a thousand, right, doesn't cost them anything because supposedly they are printing the money, just paper and ink. So if he agrees they tell the guy to show up in New York and stay at a particular hotel. There he meets a so-called steerer, yeah, and they exchange a secret word, and then he *steers* him to a room, where some operators are waiting with a bag of money. They show the guy the goods. It's real money. But it's supposed to be fake. Then somehow the guy is distracted and they switch bags. They hurry the guy out of the room, you know, maybe the cops are coming, and the guy is put on a train, and when he gets home he opens the bag and its filled with pieces of blank cut paper. And of course what can he do? He can't go to the authorities and tell them he was buying counterfeit money. But it's not done much anymore. The Lexow and Roosevelt and Comstock cracked down... if they knew what we printed!"

Maurizio understood enough to say, "America... everybody to be rich... I laugh..."

"I laugh too," said Jimmy." "Let's go. Get some bread, cheese and wine and go to the park."

When Theodore Roosevelt was done with the cop business he turned his ever-active mind toward that other cop business, war. He had his first taste of the supreme glory of war and Empire in 1898. Henry Adams titled him "the Dutch-American Napoleon." Roosevelt loved the navy. He had written its history in the War of 1812. President McKinley offered him the position of Assistant Secretary of the Navy. Get out of that sordid police business. He accepted and was appointed in 1897. On February 25, 1898 he happened to be acting secretary and sent out a cable to Admiral Dewey. "Order the squadron... to Hong Kong. Keep full of coal. In the event of declaration of war Spain, your duty will be to see that the Spanish squadron does not leave the Asiatic coast, and then offensive operations in the Philippine Islands..."

"The very devil seemed to possess him yesterday afternoon," wrote Secretary of the Navy John D. Long. He was never permitted to be acting secretary again. War came. Bully! Americans and Filipinos fought side by side against the "common enemy." Dewey destroyed the Spanish Fleet on the 1st of May. Independence for the Filipino! The citizens of the Philippine Islands can now set up a government of their own devising and preference. After Spain was vanquished, obliterated, her sovereignty and ownership of the archipelago at end, American ingenuity contrived of a staggeringly civilized and honorable deed: Buy the land from Spain. What Roosevelt wanted was an Empire, to be a World Power. We needed the

Pacific, forget those patriots fighting for independence, America stands for Progress, Christendom and Civilization, what matters that in the "last ten months three thousand two hundred and twenty-seven Filipinos have been killed and 694 wounded." Let them cry blackmail! Indian giver! They're not Christians anyway. What are they? Catholics? Exactly. McKinley got down on his knees to pray. So America instigated, in John Hay's splendid phrase, a "splendid little war." And we have never quit. We tour the world in search of "peace with honor." We tour the world with our "loot-basket and butcher knife," wrote Mark Twain. We tour the world with missionary zeal; we serve both Mammon and God because we have devised it that Mammon and God serve each other. We are the American Presence. We are the fat American tourists reading newspapers on the park benches of the world's cities.

Roosevelt, implicating himself in the splendid little war, said, "I have done as much as anyone to bring on this war, because I believed it must come, and the sooner the better..." And Roosevelt, a man of many words, speaks to a throng of admirers at Oyster Bay, who have gathered on this day to hail the returned conquering hero. "The men were being shot down like sheep. I recollect giving an order to an orderly. He rose and saluted, then fell dead across my knees. I saw Captain Buck O'Neill walking up and down in front of his men. One of them said, 'Lie down, Captain; you'll be hit.' He laughed and said, 'The Spanish bullet has not been made that can kill me.' The next minute he fell dead, a bullet hole through the head. He was a man of absolute courage..." There was no sense of irony in any of this. He saw only the heroic, the glory, and the honor.

Roosevelt resigned as Assistant Secretary of the Navy in 1898. He wanted to get into the fracas himself. He organized the First US Volunteer Calvary Regiment, known as the "Rough Riders," for service in the Spanish-American War. The Rough Riders landed in Cuba in June. Colonel Roosevelt addressed his fellow citizens at Oyster Bay, on returning from Cuba. "We moved up to Santiago, and camped on a hillside with a ridge in front of us. At dawn our artillery got on that ridge and opened fire. That was fine music to us, but pretty soon the Spaniards began to reply, and instead of dislodging our artillery they shot over it, and the shrapnel came at us. Of course, they didn't mean to hit us, because they couldn't see us, but that was like the Spaniards. We went through the jungle in a hurry, forded the river and were then halted for an hour under heavy fire. I see in the newspapers that there has been some talk as to whether we took San Juan Hill or not. We didn't stop to ask the name of the hill, we just took it."

Among the audience that day were two brothers, Italian immigrants, Giuseppe Cazzaza, who would soon become an American citizen, and Maurizio Cazzaza, who would not, and was something of an anarchist, so they say. Giuseppe had come by train from the city to Oyster Bay to see the great hero.

In 1889 a final extension added four miles of track from Locust Valley to Oyster Bay, the additional rails were needed to create a connection to New England. A large pier was built to enable the loading of passenger cars onto a ferry. The ferry lasted only a few years. The extra four miles also helped Theodore Roosevelt take the train from town to city when he became president.

The Cazzaza brothers would return several years later and settle in the town for good. The refuse was pouring in. The purity of native Americanism engrained in the money and privilege of the English and Dutch was being polluted by the influx of detritus from the Mediterranean and Mitteleuropa, Roman Catholics and Jews, and the People of Oyster Bay hated every last one of them; though Theodore Roosevelt counseled tolerance to his fellow village dwellers. Someone has to take out the trash.

It was on that hot sunny day in late summer of 1898 that Giuseppe and Maurizio first came to Oyster Bay. They came for two reasons: first, because Fiorenza wanted some sheet music and located in Oyster Bay was Groebl Brothers   Piano and Organs   Sheet Music 10c a Copy   Largest Music Store Outside of New York   South Street   Oyster Bay... and the second reason, really the first, was that Colonel Theodore Roosevelt had triumphantly returned from Cuba with his Rough Riders, and Giuseppe had followed the story in the New York Journal, from the sinking of the *Maine* in February, to Dewey's victory in May, to Teddy's romp up San Juan Hill in July. And now Theodore Roosevelt was going to make a speech to a small crowd gathered in Oyster Bay, and Giuseppe was bound and determined to attend; he desperately wanted to see and hear the great man; somehow it would make more real the fact of America as a land of freedom in Giuseppe's mind. As for Maurizio, he seemed indifferent.

After Roosevelt's speech, Giuseppe was elated; he decided then and there that he had to become an American citizen as soon as possible. The puffed and proud Giuseppe was also determined to master the English language; but that wouldn't be as easy as mastering a feeling for patriotism. On their way to the railroad station, after the speech, Giuseppe and Maurizio stopped for a bite to eat at Downing's Restaurant & Oyster Saloon South Street Delicious Soda Nuts of All Kinds.

On the way back to the train station Maurizio sang the song that he and Giuseppe would sing six years later, in 1904, when they returned to Oyster Bay, looking to settle there and then send for the family to join them, walking into town with only their knapsacks filled with clothes and a few bottles of red wine, a song about *per un sol piato di macheroni.*

And Giancarlo went to Northport and Giovanni went to Sayville... the race was on... middle class America called... to make it big in America... and only six months after that day in 1904 when they had come to Oyster Bay for good, Giuseppe purchased some property on South Street and sent for his wife and child and two sisters-in-law to come out from the city and join him. And only two years after that day in 1904, he built the building that housed his fruit and vegetable store. And in 1914 Giuseppe bought more property, adjacent to his building:

Document 4.3.6

Arthur Weekes hereby agrees to sell to Giuseppe Cazzaza who hereby agrees to purchase that certain lot of land together with the building thereon situated on South Street in the village of Oyster Bay, Nassau County, New York, adjoining the property of said Giuseppe Cazzaza on the north and continuing a frontage of forty-four feet and six inches and in depth on the southerly side one hundred and forty-five feet on the northerly side of one hundred and thirty-eight feet and a breath of forty-four feet and six inches in the rear be said several dimensions more or less for the price of fifteen thousand dollars payable as follows five thousand dollars on the execution of this contract the receipt whereof is hereby acknowledged seven thousand dollars executing and delivering a purchase money bond and mortgage for that amount with interest of 5% to run five years from date said mortgage and the balance three thousand dollars in cash on the delivery of the deed which is on September 1st 1914 at eight o'clock am at the place of business of said purchaser in witness whereof the parties to this contract have hereunto set their hands and seals this 25th day of August 1914 in presence of Elia Preggo Arthur Weekes Giuseppe Cazzaza Jake the Cop Aliaspun

Just another document from the lost details of American history called macaroni and all written down in scribbled script on a piece of paper torn from an account book on the counter between the apples and oranges. Jake the Cop was the only cop in Oyster Bay at the time. He actually wrote Jake the Cop on the contract; his real name was Jake Clancy O'Toole. He was helping to explain the words of the contract to Giuseppe; Giuseppe hasn't mastered the legalese of English yet. Jake didn't even wear a uniform, just some flat fireman's hat given to him by Giuseppe and converted into a cop hat by means of a badge pinned in front. Jake the Cop was one of Giuseppe's best friends. In later Prohibition years Jake kept a hushed mouth about all the wine that Giuseppe was making in the garage, all the bootlegging in Hoffman's, all the gambling and whoring in Belsen and White's. And Jake didn't even require some graft. This wasn't New York City, this wasn't Tammany Hall, this was a quaint little village, and practically rural, but later when a real authorized police station was established, the corruption and the graft began. Jake was actually a constable. He was paid for each arrest that he made. The arrests were usually of vagrants and drunks. The jail had only one cell in the basement. But Jake managed to find at least one drunk or vagrant per night and collected his fee. I guess he was an honest cop.

But Jake the Cop didn't get along with Giuseppe's brother at all. He had it in for Maurizio. But nothing bothered Maurizio, least of all some crummy flatfoot. Jake the Cop kept a peeping Pinkerton eye on Maurizio. It was Jake the Cop who would every once in a while climb to the roof and see what was going on with all those rocks and sculptures. Jake was suspicious of the none-too-sociable Maurizio. Why, the dumb guinea, a word Jake never used around Giuseppe, but would liberally use to refer to Maurizio, why, the dumb guinea never even said hello or good morning! Oh yeah, one more thing, how did Aliaspun's name, a character from a Roger Bethell novel, get on this old yellow document that I have copied? It sure is curious, isn't it, Jake? I think you'd better take a look and see what's up. And here is one more document. It seems that Giuseppe finally did become an American citizen, on a day in July in the year 1900.

Document 2.5.1

Be It Remembered, that at a District Court of the United States of America, held in and for the Southern District of New York, on the eleventh day of July in the year of our Lord one thousand nine hundred, Giuseppe Stefano Cazzaza at present of the City of New York, having appeared in said Court and applied to be admitted a Citizen of the United States, pursuant to the directions of the Acts of Congress of the United States of America, entitled: "An Act to establish an uniform rule of Naturalization, etc.," passed 14th of April, 1802, and to the directions of the Acts of said Congress, subsequently passed on that subject; and having thereupon produced to the Court such evidence, and made such declaration and renunciation as are by said Acts required, it was Thereupon Ordered by the said Court that he be admitted, and he was accordingly admitted to be a Citizen of the United States of America. In Testimony Whereof, the seal of the said Court is hereunto affixed this 11th day of July, in the year of our Lord one thousand nine hundred, and of our Independence the one hundred and twenty-fifth.

Welcome to the 20th Century

Be It Remembered. The American Century. A bright and better day!

1901

Theodore Roosevelt had been in Washington just long enough to be given the oath of office as vice-president. Roosevelt made his inaugural speech in the Senate chamber, promising greatness for America and mankind; stating in so many words that so goes America, so goes mankind. Then he returned to Sagamore Hill where a meeting with Captain Roger Bethell had been arranged. One of many arranged meetings for that day, but this one was decidedly different.

Captain Bethell had first met Roosevelt at Harvard. Roosevelt was class of '80. Bethell was '82. Bethell was graduated with high honors, a summa cum laude degree. Roosevelt was called Teddy then, a name he later eschewed. Teddy was of slight build and wore muttonchop whiskers; weighed no more than 135 pounds. He was prudish, priggish, sententious and, as always, self-righteous, and he modeled his ideal American on that, his own, self-image. He was a chivalrous and direct-thinking impulsive spirit, from the days of the crusades. Literature, like life, was based on the same moral philosophy. Longfellow was his poet. Tolstoy was disapproved of, because his characters acted in immoral ways, and the author never rectified or censured their actions. Tolstoy thought the same about

Shakespeare! So you can imagine how deep Roosevelt's self-righteousness ran. The act was the thing for Roosevelt. And reform. And that's when things got messy.

It was rumored that Roosevelt and Bethell had had a falling out. This arranged meeting was to determine if Captain Roger Bethell had lost his mind and was no longer fit to serve. It all started, reputedly... when...

Captain Bethell (at the time a Lieutenant Commander) was on board the U.S.S Charleston when Assistant Secretary of the Navy Theodore Roosevelt ordered the U.S. Pacific fleet to the Philippine Islands. On May 1, 1898, Commodore George Dewey, on board his flagship Olympia, entered Manila Bay and destroyed the Spanish Fleet. Theodore Roosevelt sent a vague personal message congratulating his old Harvard friend Captain Bethell, whom Roosevelt got a commission to serve in the navy to fight in the Spanish-American War because Roger Bethell, a foppish aristocrat like his friend Teddy, came to admire the ideas of Admiral Mahan; Bethell also showed an interest in the works of Richard Henry Dana and Henry Adams and John la Farge and Lafacadio Hearn and Ernest Fenollosa; like many around Boston and Harvard at the time Bethell was especially keen on the Orient and wanted to make the journey to China and Japan. Oriental art was in fashion among Bostonians. But Roger Bethell wanted more than just to collect trinkets; he was searching for something, was it Nirvana? But before Nirvana and Zen Buddhism and bonsai came his way, Bethell was still a man of action.

But the battle was a dud and Hearst couldn't or didn't want to play up Bethell, a friend of Roosevelt, who might in the future support Roosevelt if he ever ran for higher office. Hearst was to play up Roosevelt and the Rough Riders in Cuba, not at the time knowing that he had created a legend that Roosevelt would ride to the White House. Bethell would be no hero, thus spoke Hearst, and that was the final edition.

On June 19, the U.S.S. Charleston under the command of Captain Henry Glass sailed into Apra Harbor and fired a single cannon shot at the island of Guam. It was not the first American ship to sail into the harbor; hundreds of whale ships had passed this way in the 1840s. But the American Presence was not so formidable then. The Spanish commander on Guam apologized in a message to the U.S. Navy ship for not having any ammunition to fire as a return salute.

A war! What war? Nobody told the Spanish commander anything about a war. The commander surrendered Guam to the American Navy the next day. Captain Bethell was one of the first officers to go ashore. Without the given authority, the Spanish commander offered to sell him the island for $1,000,000; after all, the Philippines were bought for $20,100,000, including the cost of damages to Spanish property. And what was the damage to Spanish property on Guam? One cannon ball that had sputtered up some dust! Big deal! Bethell imagined big deals all right. Tourist promotions to Japanese; promoters and speculators controlling what was left to them by the military that would control the rest. Captain Bethell was a man of vision, an expansionist, an imperialist, weaned on Admiral Mahan and Theodore Roosevelt, gun-ho on history as the victor conceives it to be for the glory of the Nation, the Empire, in a hail of bellowing cannon balls. But one cannon ball? That was not worthy of history.

But then the great "madness" came.

Call me Ashpail, keeper of the burnt dreams of dominion over the animals of the sea and sky. Reptiles with wings clawing the dollars out of the jungles. But suddenly Captain Bethell was staring out to sea. He saw something move. A whale. A white whale. It rose from the sea and plunged back in, great fins flapping like wings. Captain Bethell saw that they actually were wings. The great white beast soared into the sky. See'st thou that sight, oh Bethell! Shudder, shudder! See'st thou the numbers of the beasts. Beast 29 Beast 52 flashing across the sky. Moby the missile. What could it mean? Not too late is it, even now, the third day, to desist. See! The Beast seeks thee not. It is thou, that madly seekest the Beast. The American Presence. Take the land. Sell it to the highest bidder. Is this the end of all my bursting prayers? All my life-long fidelities? The Beast turns to meet us. My God, stand by me now! The white whale fell from the sky. When it entered the water there was a splash like none Captain Bethell had ever seen on the seven seas. A great mushroom splash, he thought to himself. The American Presence in the world, everywhere. Thus, I give up the spear. Exterminate the Beast! Drops of water pelted him like black rain...

The Captain would never be the same again. He had seen a vision, and it disturbed his very being, what American history books say notwithstanding. Captain Bethell heard the voice of the Spanish commander and his vision ended. He never had another vision for the rest of his unrestful life. But just one had been enough.

"That's my last offer, $900,000, take it or leave it; I'll throw in the palm trees and a few native girls," said the Spanish commander.

Captain Bethell said only three words, "Moby Dick lives."

"Who you calling a dick you Yankee swine!"

"Take him away boys. Book him. Read him his rights. We must follow the rule of law. Let's have a chorus of *Yankee Doodle Dandy*, boys," said the Captain to his men. "Stuck a palm tree in the ground and called it tourist money."

When Captain Bethell returned to America he was honored along with Admiral Dewey in a great outpouring of patriotism. Captain Bethell was aboard the *U.S.S. Olympia* with Admiral Dewey as it entered New York Harbor. The conquering hero returns. Lights were flashing across the Brooklyn Bridge: **Welcome Dewey**. Fireworks were heard as far as the Palisades. A triumphal arch had been erected of plaster of Paris on Fifth Avenue and Twenty-third Street by Madison Square. William Randolph Hearst greeted Captain Bethell. There was nothing Hearst could do for him. There's just so much baloney the public will buy. Bethell was out of the question, it would be Teddy or Dewey. In the end it was Teddy, and Hearst discovered that the public would buy any baloney it was sold. Hearst sold the public on Roosevelt because Hearst saw that Bethell had nothing to offer the American newspaper reading public. A dreary little man who has of late started talking mystical gibberish. No presence. Hearst joked to Bethell about the front page of tomorrow's *New York Journal:*

CAPTAIN BETHELL RETURNS
WAR HERO WHO TOOK GUAM

It was Hearst's little joke for the sad little man. "Enjoy what you've got out of all this. Dewey's the next President." Captain Bethell had no interest in politics. Not since the vision, anyway. I'm not going to be just another fat American tourist reading a Hearst newspaper!

He resigned from the navy. Roosevelt tried to dissuade his old friend, but after a short interrogation that was held at Sagamore Hill, Roosevelt concluded that Bethell was a madman, an anarchist, a mystic fool, had lost his way, and was obviously manifestly unfit. After all, you could tell one just by looking at one. And it wouldn't look very good to have a madman come out for you during a political campaign. Roosevelt washed his hands of the Captain.

When Bethell said to Roosevelt that Rooseveltian reform is just a matter of taking a stale piece of bread and throwing it to the birds, and that a proper revolution required snatching the whole loaf fresh from the propertied classes, Roosevelt was simply aghast; this, by God, was Anarchy!

Beware of a rich man's crumbs; Bethell quoted an old French aphorism. And Roosevelt was enraged! French nonsense. The nightmare of the Commune. That mad Jefferson's influence!

Bethell beamed at Roosevelt and Henry Cabot Lodge, also present, who sneered back like a Boston terrier. It was Lodge who was behind getting Roosevelt the assistant secretary of the navy post. It was their belief in a strong navy that prompted Lodge to make every effort to secure him that position. And when Roosevelt was president, Lodge would support him on Panama, the Alaskan boundary dispute, and the acquisition of the Philippines. Lodge was a senator for thirty-one years. He was Boston. He spoke like an Englishman but he hated the English at a time when it was fashionable to do so; before the threat of immigration reversed that policy. "Oh they're so stupid," he would say of the English, in English.

When the conversation between Roosevelt and Bethell came to an end, champagne was passed around. Roosevelt lifted the glass and said, "Here's to the capture of that Sitting Bull, Aguinaldo, and to the suppression of the insurrection in the Philippines." Alice barged into the room, for a third time, and said, "How d'ye do?"

"Alice, if you disturb us again, I shall have to throw you out the window," said her father, and he and Lodge shrieked with full-bellied laughter. Edith followed Alice into the room. Edith clasped her husband around the wrist, preventing him from taking a second mouthful of champagne. "Why Eee-dee! I'm drinking to the occasion of Aguinaldo's capture."

"You know what the doctor says. It doesn't agree with you."

"But the capture of Aguinaldo does agree with me." None of this agreed with Captain Bethell. Edith showed him to the door. Many more guests were arriving at Sagamore Hill on that day to congratulate the new vice-president. Colonel Leonard Wood, Winthrop Chanler, Gifford Pinchot, and other ex-Rough Riders. Bethell shot by them in haste. He had a sense of some force of ludicrous power taking shape, not unlike what Henry Adams thought shaped history and there was nothing to be done about it.

After Bethell departed, Roosevelt turned to his guests and said, "Mad. Utterly Mad. And sad. Such promise that Bethell" Then Roosevelt and his cohorts entered upon a rather narrow debate, a crude parlour game, from which none strayed from basic agreed upon assumptions: that the military life was indeed the greatest thing a man of honor can offer to his country; that the United States unfortunately will always be unprepared for war; that had America not announced that "peace was her passion," but instead was made ready for war in order to avert war, there would have been no War of 1812; that the most use-less citizen is the peace-at-any-price arbitration type; then the discussion turned to books: books such as Admiral Mahan's *The Influence of Sea Power upon History*, and a recent book published by Roosevelt's friend Owen Wister, *Life of Grant*. Arguments were put forth on ranking certain military leaders, to accord them their place in history: indeed, there was no dispute about the great geniuses, Alexander, Napoleon, and Hannibal. But the nit-picking began over Cromwell, Wellington, Marlborough, Washington, Lee, Sherman, Sheridan, Charles of Sweden, and Conde. Roosevelt claimed that Sheridan was a greater general than Conde or the "Swedish Madman." And so it went; superlatives and platitudes spouting like Old Faithful.

Captain Bethell met Henry Adams on one occasion. It was a daffodil pale day in early April 1901, in Washington, at Adams' house. Adams was anxious and restless. He was leaving for England on the 1st of May. He wanted to get this over with. Four of the five hearts were present in the flesh, one in spirit, Adam's wife, a suicide. They gathered around the Chinese bronzes, a Turner landscape, Japanese lacquer ware, and William Blake's Nebuchadnezzar, the king of Assyria who had restored his country to prosperity, rebuilt Babylon, and erected a new palace, but Theodore Rex, as Henry James would dub Roosevelt, wasn't quite on the throne yet, it was only a premonition. Adams, who had yearned for power, but had never gone out to get it tooth and nail because, according to Oliver Wendell Holmes, he wanted it handed to him on a silver platter. And now Adams was handing the corrupt democracy, the fledgling Empire, its head on a silver platter, with scathing pessimism and bitterness. They had christened themselves the "Five of Hearts." John and Clara Hay, Henry and Clover Adams, and Clarence King. They were very American and very elitist. The masses were to be educated to the extent that they can be educated to bear an unstriking resemblance to their superiors, these Anglo-Saxon aristocrats of good breeding and good taste. Beware of the bankers, the financiers, the

Jews; beware of the immigrants, unionists, socialists and anarchists. In spite of their pedigree The "Five of Hearts" were not conventional snobs. They were discreet and discriminating, but wealth, appearance, one's station in life, did not matter. For the hearts a spade was a spade. They relished in the *mot juste,* in correctness and form, in aesthetic cyphers, in aversion to boredom; *ennui* and pessimism were put right by charm and amusement, if only fleetingly. In the end, as Hay would write about King's death, alone and suffering in a California tavern, *ça vous amuse, la vie?* When even life is amused by death, by the spectacle, it must give us pause, this collaboration of life and death, this conspiracy of nothingness, a suicide note written every day, addressed to the god of farce and tragedy.

John Milton Hay was standing near the blazing fire of the hearth; at present he was Secretary of State to President McKinley. He had been the assistant to Abraham Lincoln's private secretary, John G. Nicolay. Together they collaborated on a 10-volume history of Lincoln, published in 1890. Hay had been a journalist and editorial writer for the *New York Tribune,* had covered the great Chicago fire and with ornate prose employing references to Greek myth had perpetuated the myth of "Our Lady of the Lamp" and her cow that kicked the lamp... that burned Chicago. He had published a collection of popular doggerel called *Pike County Ballads*, ditties in belittling dialect, benefitting from Bret Harte's popular "The Heathen Chinee," and other such xenophobic tales of the Wild West, written in "plain language." William Dean Howells, born by the banks of the Ohio, editor of the *Atlantic,* encouraged those robust and vigorous Western scribblers to send their "realists" brogues and burrs back to the East, to the civilized other side of the Mississippi, where a virtuous Boston Brahmin might divert himself by vicariously slumming in the purlieu of strenuous pages. Theodore Roosevelt, an Eastern dude, fled to the Bad Lands to invigorate his well-heeled, well-equipped body with sharp spurs, to inflict harm upon any beast that stepped in his righteous path. In his book *Ranch Life and the Hunting-Trail,* Roosevelt tells the tale of his encounter with four or five beasts, Red Indians, who took their guns out of their slings, and set their horses running full tilt toward Roosevelt, war whooping, and Teddy, upon his trusted horse, with one shot, chased off the Indians. The courageous Roosevelt meets face to face with the Injun, who says, "How! Me good Indian." How indeed! How much of this is false bravura? Roosevelt boasts that his cowboy friends are ripe for war, and that they didn't much care with whom. They were very patriotic. He adds that on the day those anarchists were hung in Chicago, he and "his men" celebrated by burning them in effigy.

Hay and Adams were born in the same year, 1838, the same year John Muir was born in Scotland, an otherwise uneventful year in American history: Martin Van Buren was President, and rolling hoops was the latest fad among ladies on the Washington Parade Ground in New York City.

Seated in a chair next to the short and thin Hay was his obese wife, Clara, one of Washington's ladies, who stood a head taller than her husband. The "Five of Hearts" were all short. Standing and bending and gesticulating and coughing and passionately talking was Clarence King, looking slightly mad, on the verge of death; Adams and the others virtually at his feet in admiration. King was en route from New York to California and Arizona, seeking some relief from the pangs of his tubercular lungs filling with fluid.

The table was scrupulously set. Captain Bethell would be arriving unaccompanied. Bethell told Hay that he preferred it that way. The truth is that he could find no one to come with him; even to the Adams' house. It was Henry Cabot Lodge who had arranged the meeting, anticipating a private execution that would finally debunk Bethell's growing reputation for once and for all. Lodge was at Sagamore Hill the same day that Bethell had his last audience with Theodore Roosevelt. The day that Roosevelt decided that Bethell was a madman.

And now just a week or so after his meeting with Roosevelt, Bethell is in Henry Adams' study in the company of certainly greater minds than that display of bombast at Sagamore Hill, but, though these men had lost the faith, unlike Roosevelt's, nonetheless, they still believed. History was the decision maker. And History had chosen America. Westward Ho! Oh Aryan tribe...

It had become known that Theodore Roosevelt, the recently elected vice-president, had had a falling out with Captain Roger Bethell, the war hero and now author of curious books on Zen Buddhism and bonsai trees, and that Roosevelt was issuing proclamations of Bethell's "madness" in private. Henry Adams was interested to ascertain for himself the extent of Bethell's "madness." Adams had read Bethell's books and enjoyed them. Bethell had read the travel books of Henry Adams. Captain Bethell would have the opportunity to discuss with Adams the latter's trips to Japan in 1886 and following trips to the South Seas. That was long ago, over fifteen years, and Adams didn't care to discuss it. This did not prevent Adams from expressing his revulsion of the Japanese. The women were ugly, awkward, their joints clacked, their voices were metallic, they were badly made and repulsive, the green tea undrinkable, the food poisonous, filthy rice fields, the places had a fetid odor, it's a children's country, all is toy, laughable, nothing serious, the Japs are monkeys, and as for sex, it does not exist in Japan, it's for scientific classification only, sex begins with the Aryan race! Clarence King disagreed with Adams and reported that the women were free of inhibition. Perhaps it is guilt and prudishness and all its fancy delights that begins with the Aryan race? Adams scoffed at King. The geishas were hideous. Though Adams did become aroused by a pretty girl of sixteen with a round figure and white skin who was drying herself, with her back turned to Adams, in a Tokyo bath house. But the exceptionally pleasing virgin walked away. Yet they are primitives, monkeys. Adams did managed to buy trunk loads of mementos.

After a long discussion on bonsai, Buddhism, Oriental art, and natural history, which pleased Adams, there ensued a rather more lively discussion centering (Bethell slightly more left of center) on politics, which did not please Adams. Simply insane, just a bore, thought Adams, and Bethell was presently shown the door. The trouble began when Bethell brought up the name of Mark Twain during the conversation. In February, Mark Twain's "To a Person Sitting in Darkness" was published in the *North American Review*, a journal for which Adams once served as editor, too long ago as far as Adams was concerned, and the quality of the magazine has certainly declined. Twain's article "defended" the benefits reaped by a Civilization bent on war and dedicated to the raping and exploiting of other lands and their inhabitants, and the Blessings of Civilization that were thus bestowed upon the Person Sitting in Darkness. It was an ironic and fierce attack on Empire and Imperialism. Bethell defended Twain's views. Bethell disagreed with Adams and his opinions on Japan and predicted that a future war and a paternal relationship will ensue because of America's imperialism, and how America will then come to demonize and indulge their childlike culture. After all they are children! Henry Adams spoke of power as an abstract law of nature; Bethell tried to refute him by saying that such power and powerful men were inextricably linked, and that man could be an agent influencing the course of human events, as Mr. Jefferson so aptly describes it for us. Adams said that Jefferson was trying too hard to persuade words that they could bend to a necessity which he himself acknowledged: When in the course of human events it becomes Necessary! John Hay was outraged by Bethell's views. Hay had published a novel in 1884 called *The Breadwinners,* in which he defended the propertied classes against the demands of labor, which were "dangerous." When Roosevelt became president and he asked Hay to stay on as secretary of state, Hay would jest about Roosevelt's dangerous tendencies to favor labor over capital. He would only jest because he knew better. Roosevelt, like many hypocrites to follow, placed human rights above property rights, placed the National interest above special interests, as they would come to be known, binding himself to the Constitution, when the two rights conflicted. No, Captain Bethell could not possibly be a guest in Adam's house for the night. There are young ladies present. Certainly he had made other arrangements. Indeed. Goodnight then. At the door Adams said to Bethell, "The efficient shall inherit the earth." And he was almost correct. The Nazis were indeed efficiency experts.

It was a hot Friday afternoon, on September 6, 1901, in the Music Hall of the Pan-American Exposition at Buffalo, New York, that President William McKinley was shot by a small young man named Leon Franz Czolgosz, who twice fired a short-barreled .32 caliber Ives-Johnson revolver that he held hidden in his handkerchief-bandaged hand. One bullet struck McKinley in his rotund stomach; the other bullet glanced by his chest. In the Exposition's emergency hospital, surgeons sewed up the wounds. No vital organs had been damaged. The bullet was not located. Vice-President Roosevelt came immediately to Buffalo, but after an uncertain fevered weekend McKinley seemed to be out of danger. Roosevelt tramped off into the Adirondack Mountains. Late in the evening the following Friday, McKinley died. Taken by gangrene. Roosevelt rushed back to Buffalo to be sworn in as the Twenty-sixth President of the United States.

When Leon Czolgosz professed to be a devotee and disciple of the anarchist Emma Goldman, she was apprehended in Chicago and taken into custody. The authorities asserted that she had formulated the plot to kill McKinley, perhaps conspiring with Spanish-Cubans who sought revenge for what McKinley had done in Cuba. But the Secret Service found no connections between the Anarchists and the Spanish-Cubans, and conceded that Czolgosz had most likely acted entirely on his own. Roosevelt declared that Czolgosz was "inflamed by the teachings of anarchists... by the reckless utterances of those who on the stump and in the public press, appeal to the dark and evil spirits of malice and greed, envy and sullen hatred."

Leon Czolgosz was the child of a Polish immigrant family. He believed that America was to blame for keeping his parents living in dire poverty. When the police asked Czolgosz who he was, he replied, "Fred Nieman." Fred Nobody. Everyman. Nobody. Nemo. *Persona non grata. Jedermann Niemand. Der gemeine Mann.*

President Roosevelt

Though Roosevelt had been born into the highest eminent echelons of New York society and aristocracy, it was said that he did his best to live it down. Roosevelt avoided the first circles that his brother Elliott once belonged to, setting the fashions and manners for New York's genteel and elite, frequenting the Knickerbocker Club and Meadow Brook, playing polo, going yachting, attending horse shows, living in a staffed brownstone in Manhattan's Thirties, ordering dresses from Palmers of London, and just more or less aping the English. Theodore Roosevelt claimed that his home was "modest" if compared to the Vanderbilt and Rockefeller mansions. He didn't compare it to the domiciles of the lesser breeds.

Theodore rebelled against his class; he didn't want to spend soporific afternoons among the dainty denizens of five-o'clock tea, or pursue the aniseed bag over the meadows of Long Island. He wanted to "do things." He claimed that he had been a sickly, rickety, and asthmatic child. His father urged and encouraged him to develop his body to be the equal of his mind. Theodore must have thought very highly of his mind because he engaged himself in a strenuous fury of activities and exercises to build his body into a staunch mound of hard forceful fluff and rubble and rubber-like elasticity. He believed that he had emerged fit and hale in both body and mind, due to his tough exercise program, his Harvard days, and his rustic apprenticeship. A predatory and flexible mind and body, alert, decisive, so sure of its powers. A natural and civilized creature unfettered by endowment or condition. A lion of will. A shark of the whale's way. King of the Jungle. Ruler of the Seas. Animal Empire. American Empire.

The grand metaphor of power. The dream. The desire to act. The deed. Great white hunter.

He wouldn't just hunt helpless foxes like some effete English lord; he would go for the big game, as suffices a big country: elk, buffalo, deer and antelope in the Dakotas; elephant and lion in Africa. Roosevelt wanted to appeal to the Everyman in every man as the all-embracing Everyman of America. A comic that appeared at the time, captioned *Our Versatile President and his Summer Friends,* shows Roosevelt entertaining various guests on each day of the week. Monday he entertains a tennis player. Tuesday he entertains some old Rough Rider comrades. Wednesday he entertains some fellow L.L. Ds. Thursday he entertains a couple of old-time hunter friends. Friday he entertains a few fellow politicians. Saturday he entertains some brother historians and authors. Sunday he rests.

He tried to embody in his legendary Herculean brawny body (which in fact only reached a rather precedented height of 5'10", was hard as rubber, more huskily fat and flabby than muscularly defined) the protean desires of the common man. If the name of the new American Empire could be semantically sequestered in the green camouflage of high-minded idealism, in expansion of Anglo-Saxonism into Americanism with one faultless burdening twist of the knife into the Republic's unbeseeched bowels, Christendom marching on, blood on the black buntings slung over the arms of the cross, then certainly Theodore Roosevelt could be made to appear as a white knight without a snobbish bone in his well-nourished American made body. But whence this body?

Claes Martenszen van Roosevelt was either a Dutch burgher or a rogue, maybe both. He came to New Amsterdam from Holland in the 1640s, established himself among a small enclave of about 800 settlers who lived in 80 houses at the base of Manhattan. His progeny would prosper: bankers, financiers, and two presidents of the United States of America. Johannes, a third generation Roosevelt, took to real estate, which ultimately brought him to Oyster Bay. After the Revolutionary War, James Roosevelt founded Roosevelt & Son, a hardware business. James's grandson Cornelius van Schaack Roosevelt became head of the firm, and was listed as one of the richest men in New York. Cornelius had a son whom he named Theodore, who was to become the father of President Theodore Roosevelt. The Roosevelts were a titled family in the economic and aristocratic sense. They held the titles of ownership, and they held degrees from Groton and Harvard. They kept to standards of honor, conduct, prestige, and status; correlated to appropriate lifestyles and living manners. They also kept to standards in the market, economic attainments, and influence. Some were into moneymaking; others expected to be treated with deference, regardless of their economic achievements. But if you had both money and position you had that best of all things: power.

Early on the Roosevelts changed church affiliations from Dutch Reform to Protestant Episcopalian, but Theodore Roosevelt carried the reform part with him into public service and civic duty. In order for Roosevelt to establish his version of Americanism, and the genesis of a new ruling oligarchy, he had to wash his hands of the old world caste-like system. The leaders of the new world had to be of America, by America, and for America. But what about the Americans? Who exactly qualified to be an American? One of those glorious creatures mythically invoked at Gettysburg by Lincoln: the People? There must be only one America, one language, and one people. A new birth of... and Roosevelt would have to prove it all by himself, by being every man, by doing every thing, to lead by example, this is Teddy the American. The American Way. So he had to live down his natural birthright, his glorious ancestry, and his family's distinction. He had to become a self-made man; he had to make the country believe it to be so. A natural aristocrat by virtue of one's natural talent, genius, determination, cunning, wheel-and-deal scrappiness, plucky bartering, individualism, aggressiveness, good old American know-how, American ingenuity, American smarts. Roosevelt could feign a distaste of his own affluent background, even his "good breeding," what was left to him then but power, energy, empire, domination... but wealth was always one step ahead. After all, the meaning of America is the meaning of money, the making of money, but what makes money mean?

An early purveyor of snobbism, William Makepeace Thackeray, wrote, "He who meanly admires mean things is a Snob."

The traditional snob believes merit is irrelevant; title is all. Not reality but appearance matters. And appearance is reality. Such is the nature of a social hypocrite. But Roosevelt would bring reality to bear. And bears to the reality of death. Folksy sincerity was a more attractive virtue than wisdom. The people won't vote for an educated man, the people vote for a... what does it matter who the public votes for, as long as the people, the public mind... as long as there is a crisis there will be leaders; there must be decrees, acts, there must be a sovereign party; therefore, there must always be a crisis, in order to convince the people that they must have leaders, willing to act, to make the big decisions, that the affairs of kings... state, are too complex, too inaccessible for the common man; the common man prefers his baseball to Bach; the lowly common denominator, apathy, idleness, but is that not irrelevant to what the common man is truly capable of in regards to social and political thinking: a bit of honesty, common sense? We are not discussing arts and aesthetics, this is not a community of craftsmen, we are not back in the age of Mary-worship, as Henry Adams, that contemptible decadent, would have us. We must hide that fact from the common man, so I must promise them a Square Deal; maybe it's a dangerous precedent, but I have preached the strenuous life to them (though I would have rather called it the Vigorous Life, as suggested to me by a translation of my book *The Strenuous Life* into Italian; my book has also been translated into German and Japanese, two countries where it has been much in demand). Empire is a crisis of nerve. We cannot fail. The crisis of democracy. The public mind must be lauded, flattered, praised. We must not let dissension foment, the damn muckrakers, the lunatic fringe; we must nip it in the bud. The common man cannot be brushed aside as if he weren't even there, like a fly from the rose of our glory. They must be given a square deal, no more, no less.

Not reality but appearance matters. America had all the appearance of a republic. Is appearance a reality to the common man? Will it be high words or bread? What we tell them is reality. They vote for a man with the common touch, not overly educated. We must present ourselves as such. A good man to camp out with, to be trusted in a crisis. Men of property are the most responsible, most patriotic, quite naturally, they have the most to protect, but if they appear too regal to the public? Yet do the people not like pomp? Look at England. Men of property, in the first generation at least, tend to be malefactors, malefactors of great wealth; but distance cleanses, more hand washing in the genealogical bowl of blood; rewashed distance, renamed as history, pure water, breeds a lineage of the anointed few and select, the established benefactors of hegemony and a proud fortress nation. But there are dangers. For instance, a demagogic mob-manipulating maker of public opinion (a madman like William Jennings Bryan or that traitor William Randolph Hearst; or Joseph Pulitzer, who is even more dangerous than Hearst) could, say, exhort indirectly the masses to rise up and act. This is a democracy, you know, at least in name, in appearance. But history tells us that new powers, revolutionary powers, take more power. The rise of the Fourth Estate could sway popular opinion. We have to be more careful; more pandering to the common man so that, God forbid, mass popular movements do not spontaneously erupt and blight the land. More cunning leaders. There must be cultural persuasion; tell them what it means to be an American. Therefore we must consolidate the wealth and power of the few, the men of property. Many are called but few are chosen. Few are called and fewer are chosen. There is something to be said for government by a great aristocracy that has furnished leaders to the nation in peace and war for generations, but there is nothing to be said for Plutocracy, for government by men very powerful in certain lines and gifted with the money touch. Henceforth there shall be segments of the ruling class, of government and big business, of military and media, dueling and squabbling over niceties, but the basic assumptions of our liberty shall be agreed upon.

Theodore Roosevelt wasn't a snob, at least not an "effete snob," as he called the expatriate novelist Henry James. Roosevelt wanted James to be the chronicler of the American West, not decadent Europe; picture Henry James in boots and spurs with sombrero? Yet Theodore Roosevelt got the poet Edwin Arlington Robinson a job in the New York Customs. It was that or starve. Roosevelt's son Kermit had an English teacher at Groton named Henry Richards, who admired Robinson's work. Kermit told his father about Robinson and the President looked into it. The Richards family had aristocratic connections and that did Robinson's cause no harm in the eyes of the President. It is doubtful that Roosevelt would have acted on behalf of a poet without such a crème de la crème recommendation. Robinson worked five years at the New York Customs House, doing less work than his literary forebear Hawthorne did in his corresponding position. So Roosevelt was snob enough even when it came to "effete" poets of the parlor type ("...is drawing-room a more appropriate name than parlor?" writes Roosevelt in his autobiography, referring to a room at Sagamore Hill, being conscious of fashion, or sarcastic?), as long as the poet and the words mattered to those who "mattered," who "belonged." For example, Rudyard Kipling's "The White Man's Burden," a poem that "mattered," first published in *McClure's Magazine*, in 1898, just after the Spanish-American War, in which the poet exhorts America's leaders to take up the White Man's Burden, and "send forth the best ye breed," to Cuba and the Philippines, for the coming of the light, for justice and civilization, "for the hate of those ye guard." Ah, hate envy greed. Emotions of a "half-devil, half-child." But could those same emotions and desires be attributed to the sullen peoples of America? O America, where would hypocrisy be without you? Hypocrisy is king. Woe unto you, scribes and Pharisees, hypocrites! Keep the doors of the temple of Janus open! Theodoric draws his sword at the feast of imperialism. The torch is passed on.

For the traditional snob, appearance is reality. One is what one appears to be, to those who matter. And only those who matter, matter. Nothing else exists. A snob lives outwardly toward the eyes of those who matter. The artist lives inwardly toward the eyes of a god, so how can he be a snob? God doesn't matter, God minds. But a king must have his court; he must have his subjects, his navy, and his dominion. Not that the people matter very much, not at all, in fact, but in a country as large as America, reality tends to expand beyond the confines of appearance. It vaults its own fences. Even God becomes real, literal, fundamental. Things crack, break, and rupture. There is a tendency to extreme behavior and un-natural violence. A straining of the sky toward endless night. Ivy rots the bricks upon which it clings. Roosevelt grasped some of this between his gritty teeth. He could play Theodore Le Grande, *Le Roi Soleil*, welcoming titled men of art and science, even the despised Henry James, to his palace, to courtly ceremonies, stately pomp. He could also be the man swiping punches with the illiterate champion boxer John L. Sullivan. He was the purest form of American hypocrite. Like Nietzsche's Zarathustra, he was a man for all and none. Mud sits on a throne stuck in shit. The smell of the state. In the axiomatic strictures of the self-defining idiomorphic world of the privileged few, hypocrisy is considered to be no greater a nuisance than the unconventional; it's just ignored. Certainly it doesn't rank as high on a moral level as committing a social *faux pas,* nor is it as provocative as a giggle behind a delicate white hand bejeweled with sparkling minerals. Some of the privileged few might have concurred with Samuel Johnson that "patriotism is the last refuge of a scoundrel," but a refuge consisting of what? a refuge from what? The only reply to such an accusation is action. It is a refuge of one's duty as a man of property and responsibility; it is a refuge of "doing things," a refuge from decadent society. In the end it is no refuge at all; it is noble and honorable. It is the glory of the fight. It's not having, it's making. It's making it that really matters. Making money, war, time, peace, history. History in the making. But decadent society, high society, oh how they loved not to do things, thought Roosevelt. But they did do things: they had fun. They were frivolous. No, Roosevelt meant real things! Things that really matter! Matter to whom? not to those who matter, who belong, but to the marginally enfranchised? So it must matter to the people, the Nation, the State. The State and the People are One. I am the State, therefore I am the People. Supposedly in England, in the Middle Ages, an undergraduate student who came from a non-titled family was marked with the words Sine Nobiliate. Eventually abbreviated S.nob. The etymology is questionable. But fashion speaks the present, with a raised eyebrow glance toward the past, to peer for peerage and blue blood in veins for those in line for the snob's throne, unspoiled, undefiled by the feces of that other subhuman species, the People. Those mysterious people invoked by Thomas Jefferson in the Declaration of Independence. We the People means we the Anglo-Saxon tribe. Every tribal people called themselves The People. The Oxford English Dictionary's definition of snob is "a person with exaggerated respect for social position, & a disposition to be ashamed of socially inferior connexions, behave with servility to social superiors, & judge of merit by externals." Compare an American dictionary's definition of snob with the OED's restrained and understated definition: a snob is "one who blatantly imitates, fawningly admires, or vulgarly seeks associations with those he regards as superiors." Adverbs do matter! Roosevelt detected all of this... the crisis of democracy, the common man who thinks he belongs in decision-making processes! Not belongs to those who matter, but who belongs to things that matter, dangerous things like democracy! In America we have no superiors, not even the President and his specially selected, unelected cabinet are better than we are, nobody in the world is better than we are... We, the People... they may be better off, but that is another part of the story, and in this story envy greed and hatred rear their common hyphenated heads... "the dark and evil spirits of malice and greed, envy and sullen hatred." Who is the half-child, half-devil, is it you, America? Not those brown brothers in Cuba and the Philippines? But men of breeding, property, culture, civilization, are above all that, not susceptible to being afflicted by such common feelings. Roosevelt thought so and said so after McKinley was shot. See what the public does! It kills Presidents!

1902

Theodore Roosevelt invited Henry Adams and John Hay to a dinner at the White House. The new president lectured his guests. His guests were quiet. Roosevelt railed about everything under the sun. "A-i-eee have always been unhappy," Roosevelt whined, "that A-i-eee was not severely wounded in Cuba… in some striking and disfiguring way." Adams flinched at this remark. Nevertheless, Roosevelt amused him. "Anarchists, socialists, that demagogue Bryan…" Adams told Roosevelt that his brother Brooke had once said that Bryan was the first slap in the face the new aristocracy had ever had. Roosevelt jolted at this remark.

1905

Captain Roger Bethell was born in the early hours of an April morning in 1861, when the first bombs fell on Fort Sumner, inaugurating the Civil War, and he died on August 6, 1945, at the moment, we can no longer speak of hours, when The Bomb fell upon the city of Hiroshima. That journey in time (can we speak of time?) began with Theodore Roosevelt's expansionist policies.

During the Spanish-American War Bethell became something of a hero. After the Philippines had been won, it was forward sail to the small island of Guam, where Bethell was among the first to go ashore, and where, it was later reported, he experienced some kind of strange vision from which he never recovered. Many thought he had lost his mind.

In 1899 a statue of Captain Bethell was put up in the village green at Oyster Bay. There were objections, even from Roosevelt, who was governor of New York, and at the time was still undecided about Bethell's "madness." Roosevelt and Bethell had been friends at Harvard. After Harvard, Bethell, influenced by Commodore Perry and the books of Dana, received a Navy commission from Roosevelt and went to sea. The Navy was at a low point, but Bethell and his friend Teddy wanted to change all that. Bethell later changed his mind; Roosevelt did not. Captain Bethell went on to write books that have become classics in their field, about bonsai and Zen Buddhism. The Long Island League of Lady Bonsai Growers was particularly fond of them and used them at all their gatherings. The League was disbanded on December 8, 1941.

The statue of Captain Bethell was removed from the village green in 1903 and re-located to an area by the bay, near a marsh land dump, which one day would be filled in and converted into a park, to be named Theodore Roosevelt Memorial Park. This time Roosevelt, now president, and certain of Bethell's madness, made sure of it, and soon enough the Captain's statue would be long gone and Roger Bethell forgotten from history.

In 1905 the statue was once again removed, this time from the dump-side marsh and brought to its final resting place, in the basement storage room of the Town Hall, a building which stands right next to the village green where the statue was first set on its cold trapezoid plinth. When the statue was removed in 1905, once again it had been removed by orders of Roosevelt. He didn't want the statue mentioned at all by the press, because Roosevelt was holding a summit with the envoys of Russia and Japan, and they would gather aboard the presidential yacht, *Mayflower*, in Oyster Bay Harbor. The little village would be filled with sightseers, press, etc., and Roosevelt didn't want the Captain to be seen in any form.

On August 4, 1905, the day before the dignitaries were to meet, Yukio Yamada was taking a stroll along the shoreline. He was a photographer who had a studio in the nearby village of Northport. He had come from Japan just before the turn of the century and had been a friend of Captain Bethell. Yukio Yamada stood on the shore and watched the statue of Captain Bethell being dismantled and taken away.

Captain Bethell was married the year before to Clara Klankenhorn, a first cousin of the renowned beauty and socialite Agnes Babs Widdlesworth, daughter of William Widdlesworth, the millionaire and friend of J. P. Morgan. On that August day William Widdlesworth and his friend Sir Dudley Gower would also be in attendance at the ceremonies when the Russian and Japanese delegates arrived. Yukio would come to take photographs. On that hot August day in 1905, Oyster Bay was in the national spotlight, not that the spotlight shined as far then as it does today, but people got the story eventually. The story was that Theodore Roosevelt was holding a summit at the highest level. This is quite high. Can you hear that you common little folks down there, can you hear us if we shout? Never shout; speak softly and carry a big stick. Sticks and stones. Bow and arrow. Guns and cannon. Rockets and missiles. A-bombs and H-bombs. That's the evolution of those arrows in the American eagle's talons on the dollar bill. But what has the olive branch evolved into?

227

Well, on that hot day in August 1905, Teddy Roosevelt invited the Russians and the Japanese to pluck at the olive branch. And on that hot day in August 1905, Yukio Yamada came seeking the olive branch of peace. But Yukio didn't have in mind what Teddy had in mind in dealing an olive branch to the envoys of Russia and Japan, whose countries were presently at war.

The harbor was filled with yachts, decorated with bright red white and blue buntings. Cannon were thundering a salute, 19 blasts for each envoy, and 21 for the President of the United States. The marching bands were playing the national anthems of Russia and Japan. A month later the Treaty of Portsmouth was signed. There were a few dissenting voices. Mark Twain was one: "Russia was on the high road to emancipation from an insane and intolerable slavery; I was hoping there would be no peace until Russian liberty was safe." Roosevelt thought all "slavs" were barbarians.

Yukio Yamada walked along the beach. He carried his camera and tripod in a battered suitcase. He is also carrying his umbrella, even though there is no threat of rain. He is dressed to the gills in a dark brown suit with a high white collar. His hair is cropped very short to the skull; the veins in his head can clearly be seen throbbing. He wears a large downy mustache that completely covers his upper lip. He seems distracted by all the hoopla and fanfare of the day. He is also ashamed. No, not because he had an affair with Clara, the wife of the good and wise Captain Bethell, but because he did not return to Japan to fight for his country when he was called upon to do so. And now he fears some kind of reprisal. He did not do the honorable thing. He did not serve his country and now does not deserve to live.

He sets up his camera on the shore and takes one picture of the presidential yacht, the *Mayflower*. He leaves the camera sitting on its tripod standing on the shore, and he walks away. He goes to the railroad tracks and continues walking the rails, passing by the marsh on his right, which in the future will be filled in and provide the location for Heemskirk's Shipyard. He walks across the trestle, until he is well down the line and out of sight. He is singing Yankee Doodle: "Stucku a noodaru inu hisu hato andu cawreda itu macaloni..." He slides down the pebble rail embankment and stumbles into the woods. Here he takes a note out from his breast pocket, which he had written earlier in the day. He looks it over:

Document 1.9.7

My dear Clara. Forgive me doing this thing. I can't stand it no more. I can't explain. This will end all. Sayonara. Goodbye. Give my love to Captain Bethell. Forgive me. Forgive me Clara.

Yukio's body is discovered eight days later. His umbrella is by his side. His hands peacefully folded over his chest. He had taken a lethal dose of morphine sulphate mixed with atropine sulphate.

Yukio Yamada came to America just before the turn of the century. He worked as a steward for the Seawanhaka Corinthian Yacht Club on Center Island, where he first met Captain Bethell and Clara. Established in 1871 the Seawanhaka was the first Corinthian yacht club in the world. It seemed only appropriate that a Corinthian yacht club, with its large Victorian Clubhouse, would emerge just across the harbor's inlet from the ruling class president and his large Victorian Clubhouse, within which walls President Roosevelt has been entertaining other members of the club for the summer of 1905, including Baron Kaneko of Japan. The Baron has been much impressed by the simple life that the Roosevelts lead at Sagamore Hill, how the president puts out the dog, doing things like that before it became the "thing to do" for presidents trying to portray themselves to the public mind as just one of the good boys in the Clubhouse, and there ain't no such thing as a bad boy. After Baron Kaneko left, the bad boy Serge Witte of the Czar's government arrived. Roosevelt and Witte did not like each other. The Russian bluffed, and Roosevelt called, and American Pressure, euphemistically known as International Pressure, was applied by Roosevelt, taking the envoys of the belligerent parties by their pointed ears and pulling them together with his muscular Christian hands, Roosevelt white-robed and winged like an angel of mercy, as a cartoon of the period depicts the scene during the negotiations.

At one point during the summer of 1905 the peace negotiations were getting bogged down because the Japanese were demanding an indemnity from the Russians. The press was declaring the conference a failure. Roosevelt then ordered *The Plunger,* one of the United States Navy's first submarines, to Oyster Bay. The president, eluding the reporters and Secret Service men, boarded the submarine, and as legend would have it, on that day there was such a fury of wind and rain the likes of which had never been seen in the quaint little harbor. On that day, Poseidon's anger surpassed that which he directed toward Odysseus for blinding his son Polyphemus. On that day the fearless President, like the famed American Mailman who will not be deterred by either sleet or snow or rain from delivering the news, delivered the news, a prerequisite to delivering the goods. Roosevelt's Jonah adventure, which had supposedly eluded the press, in the raging wild waters of Oyster Bay Harbor, nevertheless managed to become known. It was all very well managed indeed. When President Roosevelt emerged from the submarine after being on board for three hours, one hour of which time submerged, he stated, "I've had many a splendid day's time in my life, but I can't remember ever having crowded so much of it into such a few hours." The *New York Times* was horrified that a president would dare to do such a thing and wrote an editorial on "Our Submerged President." But Roosevelt was only immensely amused at the fuss. He was our Corinthian President. Not in the profligate, licentious sense of the word, of course; he was too much the Dutch Calvinist puritan for that, but as a sportsman, fair and honest, don't foul, and don't shirk, and hit the line hard. A man who defined American Manhood for years to come. The term Corinthian was coined in order to distinguish Seawanhaka Yacht Club as more than just "horse racing for boats," as more than just something to do for those type of yacht owners who wagered large amounts of money on their vessels without having either the interest to race them or ride aboard them during a race. The club was concerned with developing sportsmanship and dedication and nautical proficiency, things wholly to be admired in the serious manhood worldview of Theodore Roosevelt. Theodore Roosevelt, always the great nautical man, frontier man, pioneer man, expansionist man, had no regrets, had only pride and the great virtue of duty, to enlist the American men of great manliness, his genteel roughs, to make out of a land that was once spacious and void, a great civilization, break the chains of the barbarians and uplift them if they wished to be uplifted by Roosevelt's strenuous hands, and to give a name to that which was without name. We didn't ask the name, we just took it.

It was in 1905 that Roosevelt sent the Great White Fleet on tour across the Pacific Ocean. Aboard the ship were William Howard Taft and a large delegation that included Roosevelt's daughter, Alice. And Captain Roger Bethell, who had somehow got invited without Roosevelt's knowledge.

In Japan they were lauded and celebrated. When the fleet arrived in Korea the emperor of Korea warmly greeted them. Taft and Alice toasted the emperor.

Captain Bethell had overheard the secret ploy that Taft, by orders from Roosevelt, had conducted with the Japanese, a secret pact that allowed the Japanese to expand into Korea. The fleet returned to Japan and was not so well greeted. They were angry because Roosevelt had rebuffed Japan's claim for an indemnity from Russia. After the fleet started out on its return voyage, the American embassies in Korea were soon closed. The Japanese marched in. The appeals of Korea's emissaries for help fell on Roosevelt's deaf ears. Korea was now part of Japan. Make your appeals through Tokyo. And with this planned betrayal the bloody stage was set for the twentieth century, a better and brighter day to come.

Yukio Yamada left his job as steward after five years. He bought out a local photographer in Northport and opened a studio in January 1905. Over the next several months of his life, the last several months of his life as a matter of fact, he took many pictures of village street scenes. One picture shows an eight-year-old Johnny Bacigalupo standing with his father in front of his fruit and vegetable store in Northport.

The sign overhead reads:

GIANCARLO BACIGALUPO
CIGARS, CANDIES, FRUITS
C. MASPERO'S PURE OLIVE OIL

Giancarlo Bacigalupo, the brother-in-law of Giuseppe and Maurizio, prospered, in ways that Giuseppe only dreamed of. He invested the profits from the store and the rents from the apartments into real estate and land. Giancarlo would later sell the store and establish a block and cement construction company that would build many of the houses and small bridges in the area. Yukio Yamada lived the last month of his life in one of the apartments that Giancarlo rented out above his fruit and vegetable store. It is the same apartment that Yukio's son Frank Yamada will live in, years later.

Yukio was now nearly bankrupt; he had to sell the studio, where he had lived in a back room, which is why he had to take the apartment in the last month of his life. He left many glass plates of photographs in the apartment, and Giancarlo took them as a final rent payment and stored them in an old barn. Yukio couldn't pay the rent for the last month, and

Giancarlo expropriated the belongings that he had left behind; little did Giancarlo know that to Yukio it really didn't matter one way or the other, because Yukio would be dead, and Giancarlo was just doing what any good capitalist would do, and Giancarlo considered himself a good philanthropic capitalist, just like his son Johnny would become, it was Johnny who donated an ambulance to the fire department and an organ to the Catholic church and a building to the Historical Society, and who never cashed his Social Security checks, among other noble deeds. Years later Johnny Bacigalupo would discover the glass plates that his father had hid in the barn and he would donate them to the local historical society. No one knows why Yukio Yamada killed himself. No one knows the real reason.

Clara Klankenhorn was a plump, frumpy, homely girl, quite unlike her cousin, Agnes. Yukio had worked for three years as a steward at a local yacht club. It was there that he met the Captain and Clara. It was not long afterward that Yukio began a short and intense affair with Clara. A child was born. Yukio was the father. The Captain's disgrace was mounting, abandoned by TR, and now a cuckold, un-mounting too, you might say, as his statue came down. Yukio had watched it come down. He had set his camera up on the sand, to get a fixture on the place. He was preparing for the festivities. The offspring of Yukio and Clara's illicit coupling was named Frank Yamada. The boy was lucky in a way. He was accepted by the Widdlesworths and managed to survive with a silver spoon in his mouth, usually because he stole it. Frank ingratiated himself into the Widdlesworth's family, and was allowed to stay at their mansions and houses and flats for as long as he pleased, until Sarah, Clara's aunt and Agnes Babs' mother, who had taken the boy in, had decided that his behavior was, shall we say, intolerable. Nevertheless, Frank had advantages. He was educated at Harvard and later Cambridge, where he fell in with a group of notable characters who later gained fame as spies and reds.

The last pictures that Yukio ever took, the ones of the presidential yacht *Mayflower* in the harbor, on the day he committed suicide, were never recovered. The pictures are not lost though. In a novel by Roger Bethell, the time-traveler Aliaspun is in possession of a picture of the *Mayflower*. It's not a picture of the presidential yacht *Mayflower*; it's the other *Mayflower*, the one that landed at Plymouth in 1620 with the Pilgrims. What a strange transformation! How did that get there? Roger Bethell predicted in his novels that the strange new world of modern physics would reveal alternative worlds. Roger Bethell cautioned us with a word, repeated, beep-beep. Aliaspun was there. He was on the *Mayflower*, with the pilgrims. He was a kind of inspector. The Pilgrims didn't pass the inspection, but that didn't stop them. They were a law unto themselves. Aliaspun has taken the tour of the world in all kinds of ships, space ships and rocket ships. Ever since the 17th century he's been circumnavigating the oceans and exploring the world with his gunpowder musket and his printing press in the hull, disseminating leaflets into the technological void of the future. He didn't come over on the *Mayflower*, but he was on the ship. His application for membership in The General Society of Mayflower Descendants has been rejected. Ah shucks. What a disappointment not to be a part of an organization whose creed is "to perpetuate the memory of the Pilgrim fathers, to maintain and defend the principle of civil and religious liberty as set forth in the Compact of the Mayflower, to cherish and maintain the ideals and institutions of American freedom." Aliaspun doesn't quite have the same memories of these most glorious and cherished illusions. Poor misguided cynic and fool; Aliaspun didn't see too much liberty, civic or religious, around in those good old days. Actually, only forty of the *Mayflower's* one hundred passengers signed the famous compact. Aliaspun has signed many documents and contracts in his life; Aliaspun put his X right there on the dotted line; but it didn't count. But whose counting? One little two little three little Indians, four little five little six little Indians, seven little eight little nine little Indians, ten little Indian boys...

When Theodore Roosevelt took the oath of office in March 1905, on the East Portico, the grand entrance to the domed Capitol, and put his hand on the bible, he was standing next to a huge statue called *The Rescue*. The statue depicted a recoiling woman with a baby nestled in her protective care. Over her loomed the savage Indian in loincloth, wielding a hatchet. The savage is restrained by a male figure wearing a robe, a white savior. The statue represented "the conflict between the Anglo-Saxon and Indian races."

According to Theodore Roosevelt only the Aryans, the great White race, retained The Holy Mission in the north of Europe. Out of the north came the highest form of race to appear on this earth. They came out of the forests to spread freedom and individuality across the globe. The great Teutons migrated south and conquered and mixed with the natives and tainted their pure blood with a darker skin who possessed half a rational mind, and thereby lost part of the great impulses of freedom and the newly evolving standards of rights and law. The Teutons crossed the waters to the group of islands to the west, following the course of the setting sun, and slaughtered the natives, and then these Anglo-Saxons again with "all the pulses in the world... with the Western movement beat..." beat on, the pilgrims, the pioneers, and westward the course of empire takes its way, and there would have been no history of the great race, of the civilized world, because that "would have halted," exclaimed Roosevelt, if not for "the Teutonic conquests in alien lands."

1908

Giuseppe and Maurizio, the two brothers who walked into a small town on Long Island with their knapsacks containing a few bottles of red wine, singing, *"Io mi sono un poveretto, senza casa e senza letto; venderei i miei calzoni per un sol piato di macheroni..."* I am poor and homeless and without a bed, I'd sell my pants for one plate of macheroni.

Giuseppe worked hard all his life. He built the apartment buildings and shops on South Street, opened a fruit and vegetable store, and put his two sisters-in-law in charge; they worked in the store, collected the rents from the tenants, and swept the sidewalks in front of the shops. Giuseppe and his wife Fiorenza had five children, whom they named Silvia (after his mother), Francis Lincoln (after Abe), Stephen Roosevelt (after Theodore), Luisa (after Fiorenza's mother), and Joseph John (after himself and his halfwit brother). Nicknames were soon established, Toots, Butch, Chubby, Luzie and Babe. All the while the strange Maurizio climbed to the flat, tarred rooftops over the apartments and shops and carved his ugly rock sculptures among a horde of pigeons. The local authority, in the person of one Jake the Cop, was slightly concerned about Maurizio's unsocial behavior, but Jake the Cop left him alone because Giuseppe was a good friend and good citizen; Giuseppe was an outstanding member of the community; an immigrant who became Fire Chief of the local volunteer fire department; who owned property and a thriving business that sold fruits and vegetables to the likes of some of the richest families in America, including the Widdlesworth family... but above all else, Giuseppe had shook the hand of President Theodore Roosevelt, his neighbor, so to speak. America was truly a melting pot. A land for big dreams. Giuseppe

Cazzaza believed in the dream. Until a hot Memorial Day in 1927 when his dream of happiness turned into a nightmare. Into doom.

But until that day Giuseppe believed in the magical process inherent in the diverse properties of the alchemy of the American Way, whereby one enters the melting pot without even a pot to pee in and exits with a pot of gold. His brother Maurizio didn't believe it though. Maurizio believed that if you shit in a pot you would only find shit in the pot. After Memorial Day 1927 there was nothing left to believe in, except money and Babe Ruth.

Yes, but Giuseppe had shook the hand of President Theodore Roosevelt. That was in 1908... and yes Giuseppe believed... like Henry Ford's pageant of big melting pot clones uttering "I am a good American... I am a good American..." We have all we need, guns and a bible, beep-beep... keep them rolling off the assembly line...

Incident on South Street

Theodore Roosevelt was in town to dedicate, in a brief ceremony, two cannon that had seen service in the Spanish-American War. The cannon were to be placed where a statue of Captain Roger Bethell, the Spanish-American War hero, had once stood, on the village green. The statue of Captain Bethell had been removed from the village green in 1905 by orders of President Theodore Roosevelt. An executive order was not necessary. Roosevelt wanted the statue out of sight; he considered Captain Bethell an unpatriotic lunatic fringer and something of a traitor.

But at today's festivities, a September day in 1908, Roosevelt will be dedicating the two cannon in town. The past months have been busy for Roosevelt; Taft was safely nominated and Roosevelt was planning a hunting trip to Africa, a "mere holiday."

After the ceremony at the village green the president took his young son Quentin for a walk through the hamlet of Oyster Bay, the town where he made his home, and where the summer white house was located, but not quite in the hamlet, more in the outskirts. Quentin was insisting on getting a chocolate sundae from the soda fountain in Saunder's Pharmacy; he showed his father the nickel, holding it in his dirty hand. His father warned Quentin about his weight and health, but in the end relented, and Quentin ran into the soda fountain. They were accompanied by Secret Service men and surrounded by local citizens who revered and adored Roosevelt. His entourage passed by Schwartz and Horowitz's Stationery on

South Street, where Roosevelt's aide stopped to purchase a handful of New York newspapers, including Hearst's Journal, and some Havana cigars.

Giuseppe Cazzaza was standing in front of his fruit and vegetable store, with his sisters-in-law, Leonora and Teresa, and two of his children, five-year-old Silvia and seven-month-old Frankie. The president wobbled over to the baby and picked him up and shook him violently. He never kissed the little creatures. Everyone applauded and smiled with simple pleasure. Giuseppe proudly stepped forward and stammered in broken English, "Dear mizda prezidenta, my nexta babiboya aia willanaima hima Roosavelta!" Everyone enthusiastically cheered and smiled a small town smile. The president visibly cringed and recoiled at Giuseppe's mauled English pronunciation, but zestfully he took Giuseppe's hand and shook it strenuously.

"Bul-ly! Dee-lighted!" Roosevelt gleefully uttered, his whole body radiating ardor and delectation. Giuseppe and Theodore Roosevelt stood eye to eye, both men were very similar in stature and physical frame, bulky, ox-like, bull-necked, brawny, stout, with tightly arrayed facial features facading large round heads, made vegetatively fecund by the presence of prolific mustaches. Giuseppe's lineaments and mannerisms, excluding his speech, didn't seem very Italianate at all, his hair and mustache were a brown-reddish luster, the tip of his nose was turned up, the nostrils primly exposed, his eyes pale green; both men wore their hair precisely alike, but who didn't in those days, parted near the top on the left side, under derby hats, and both men were dressed in brown suits with vest and floral ties; though Giuseppe wore his suit under a white smock, which he had vigorously removed before he approached the president, and Giuseppe's suit had been sewn by his sister-in-law, Leonora, while the President's suit had come from Brooks Brothers. Giuseppe was not bespectacled like Roosevelt, with his pince-nez over fierce twisted eyes, around which wrinkles drew inward to the intense focal point of his eyes the stretched skin of his massive head. Roosevelt was all boyish buoyancy, the epitome of virile American manhood. And he stood shaking hands with the epitome of an ideal immigrant, healthy, fervently patriotic, with no interest in what little or preferably nothing left behind in anarchy-muddled and mass-huddled decadent Europe, come to these shining shores of freedom to begat hyphenated Americans, who were hardly Americans at all in the eyes of Theodore Roosevelt, one of whom Roosevelt had held, little

Frankie Cazzaza. "America needs good honest businessmen, good citizens, but above all else good Americans." The crowd of good Americans felt exalted, the Big Chief has come down from his hilltop castle to bless a baby, one of the common multitude. The "multitude," about twenty-five village dwellers, rejoiced with triumphant shouts, many of them hyphenated Americans of one sort or the other, while the pure legitimate un-hyphenated Americans were regaled and glittering like diamonds in the mansion depositories of their large estates in the wooded coves beyond Main Street, where they lorded over a patrician Arcadian America: the Gold Coast.

Roosevelt handed the baby to Giuseppe, and Giuseppe in turn offered the president a business card. Roosevelt took a furtive disinterested glance at the card:

Cazzaza Fruits & Vegetables
Groceries, Confectionery, Cigars, Tobacco
105 South St. Oyster Bay. L.I. Phone 200

Roosevelt's face shone gleeful and winsome. He chuckled like a woodchuck in the woods. It must have struck him as such for he remembered that he had planned to spend the afternoon chopping wood in one of his haunts north of Eel Creek on the face of Mt. Olympus, better known as lofty Sagamore Hill, where, in an old-world abode, dwelled the New World's leader. A camera crew will be waiting there for him.

Theodore Roosevelt spoke in a plain folk's tone to the plain folks. "Today I'm a choppin' some wood..." He paused to reflect, and then non-sequiturally imparted some Rooseveltian wisdom to the folks, "When you come to the end of your rope... tie a knot and hang on." The multitude nodded their heads in agreement. Georgie Dumpson Thompson was standing in the crowd, thinking to himself: Good advice for a nigger about to be lynched. Georgie had seen lynchings as a boy in the South; had seen his own father lynched; had seen bystanders join lynch mobs with small provocation. Roosevelt stuffed Giuseppe's business card into the inner pocket of his brown tweed jacket; a camera light bulb popped, the official photographer said, "Thank you mister president."

"Happy to oblige," said the president; and for a brief moment, Theodore Roosevelt, with his hand inside his jacket, looked all the world like another Napoleon, Emperor of the United States, and not only leader of the New World, but also manifest destined leader of The World. While

Roosevelt posed with his hand inside his jacket, his hand was touching the handle of the pistol that he always carried on his person, just in case. The pistol had once caused a president of Harvard to exclaim that Roosevelt had a lawless mind.

Roosevelt walked away with a staunch stride, but luckily for him not staunch enough, because all of a sudden Georgie Dumpson Thompson came charging through the crowd and barreled into the barrel-chested president, bowling him over onto his bowler hat; at that very moment a large chunk of brick and cement smashed on the sidewalk. It had broken off from the top of the building, Giuseppe's building. The Secret Service grabbed Georgie and wrestled him to the ground. A local policeman, Jake the Cop, rushed into the fracas and whacked Georgie over the head several times with his billy club. Georgie was knocked unconscious and blood was streaming from his head. It took a hectic moment but Roosevelt and the Secret Service finally realized that Georgie might have saved the president's life. Unruffled, the president stood up and dusted himself off. "Not to worry. No panic. As I've stated before: Keep your eyes on the stars and your feet on the ground." The multitude nervously laughed. If not for Roosevelt's unabashed humor and alert wit the multitude may have turned into an ugly mob. The president looked up at the building. "I believe some repairs are in or-dah," he said in his familiar rasping whine of Duchess County accented tones.

Georgie Dumpson Thompson was dragged into the alleyway next to Giuseppe's fruit and vegetable store to shouts of nigger. The nigger did it! Some bystanders had yet to realize what had happened and had to be restrained by the Secret Service. Theodore Roosevelt climbed into the back of his horse-drawn carriage, flanked by a Secret Service man and the presidential aide. "What shall we do with him, Mr. President?" said Mr. Wilson, the Secret Service man.

"Find out where the darkie lives and dump him there. No more talk of this. We don't need any brave darkie heroes now." Roosevelt remembered the trouble caused when he invited Carver to the White House. Roosevelt took a quick glance at the *Journal* in the aide's hands and shook his head, "If that damn Hearst caught wind of this incident, why that dirty coward and liar... would blow it up all out of proportion... look at your hands, man, all that ink and dirty printed matter. You must wash them..."

Roosevelt and his entourage began their trek back to Sagamore Hill, located in soon to be incorporated Cove Neck, which, if not exactly a "sundown town," incorporation managed to have the desired results, to keep out undesirables, blacks, and the more recently arriving Italians and Jews.

Children were permitted to run alongside the carriage, waving small town parade flags. A new Model T Ford, occupied by several members of the Secret Service, led the procession. The "machine" churned up dust from the dirt surface of East Main Street. A plague of dust-motes speckled Roosevelt's pince-nez and gray flurry mustache and settled in the furrows of his brow and face that he crinkled into a grimace disguised as a smile, the full set of teeth clicking together like Morse Code.

"Damn that Ford and his unholy machine. Silly sport for bankers only; and lazy Secret Service men," he roared out with laughter. "I tire of rich men; they bore me; they don't know anything outside of their own business. I can listen for hours on end to my friend Jack Abernathy, a fine man and great wolf-hunter, what a range of knowledge; or to Bill Sewall, a hunter and guide; I found the boxer John L. Sullivan a delightful conversationalist, very amusing... he was amused when I suggested we put on the gloves and spar a few rounds; I think I could have taken him; I was a champion light-weight at Harvard."

Roosevelt gazed at his son. Quentin was gazing elsewhere. Roosevelt coughed, but through the coughing he tried to force words together. He was relentless in speaking, undaunted by the fact that no one could hear him but his son, and Quentin wasn't listening. Oh the noise from that machine! Quentin wanted to ride in the machine, the Model T, but his father disapproved of separating father and son for the un-strenuous luxury of a moving machine. Ten years later, in July 1918, Quentin, now a fighter pilot in France, his father having approved rather vigorously of separating father and son for the noble cause of a war that would end all wars and make the world safe for democracy, is killed in another one of those new-fangled, moving machines.

"I want to walk. Stop that ungodly machine." The president took ten-year-old Quentin by the hand and with noble ease they both hopped out of the carriage like two boys playing together by themselves, jumping over fences in a bright meadow, with no spectators but the birds. The birds chirped and the spectators wildly applauded. He had had enough of riding

239

behind a symbol of the sport of bankers. Roosevelt knew about manly sports: ranch life in the wild west, charging up foreign hills on horseback while bullets whizzed by his ears, and would come to know other sports, big-game hunting in Africa, which he was now making plans for, and expeditions in jungles down unexplored rivers... so he would not be belittled and humiliated by the dust from a machine that was priced out of the popular market, beyond the popular desire of the common man, and Roosevelt, an uncommon man, knew exactly what the common man desired. At that moment, they desired to be near their emperor, and many of them were slavishly trotting beside his carriage like just another horse to pull Roosevelt's proud weight and ego.

In 1908 there were only 65,000 "machines" produced in the United States. Buicks, Fords, Cadillacs... sport for the uncommon few. By the early 1920s Ford produced more than two million in one year; a sport for the uncommon few was becoming a life for the common many. And by 1927, on the last day of May, the day after Memorial Day, the last Tin Lizzie rolled off the assembly line, number 15,003,007, and General Motors was in ascendancy... beep-beep...

Roosevelt was begrimed in dust. He wanted to spit, but when he looked up at the throng of worshippers, and had noticed that he had alighted on East Main Street with the First Presbyterian Church on his right, up on a hill, built in 1873, and the Episcopalian Christ Church on his left, built in 1878, where he himself worshipped on occasion, he refrained from spitting and swallowed his saliva and pride. The Model T pulled alongside the Oyster Bay Free Library, a building to which Roosevelt had laid the cornerstone. Roosevelt and followers walked in the center of the street. It would be an hour walk at least, as all school children in the village would come to know during their annual pilgrimage, even if all energy were strenuously exerted to its fullest degree, to the wooded retreat of Sagamore Hill. The town populace, with some friendly coaxing from the Secret Service, strategically dispersed along the trial, the winding road up the cove, and retreated back to the humble hamlet. Giuseppe, who had left Leonora and Teresa in charge of the store, followed Roosevelt as far as Sandy Hill Road, a winding dirt path up a hill, at the top of which he and some other Italians occasionally converge in a field known locally as Schiff's Field. In fact, all this wooded property from the bottom of Berry Hill Road to... who knew where it ended, was owned by someone name Schiff and was always referred to as Schiff's Woods or Schiff's Field. Giuseppe, Maurizio, and their friends, little Rocky, Pasquale, Elia, Stephano, Luigi, reverted back to old-world ways and boisterously enjoyed themselves, hidden in the woods near the unoccupied fire tower, drinking home-brewed wine, eating cheese and singing and dancing until the crows complained and darkness fell. Now does that sound like the doings of a group of raving anarchists or gangsters? For years, Jake the Cop had a hunch it did.

The president, now alone but for his son and his aide, and the Secret Service men, paused by an artesian well, where he and his aide washed their hands and faces and drank huge gulps of water. A path next to the well led down to the water of a small cove. The carriage pulled up to the president and, boarding the carriage, Roosevelt peered silently and contemplatively at Youngs' Memorial Cemetery, across the road, and at the long path leading up to the top of the hill, knowing that this will one day be his final resting place. If such a pure active spirit could ever rest. "Power when wielded by abnormal energy is the most serious of facts," Henry Adams wrote. Roosevelt was gazing into the serious fact of death. Roosevelt had no time for death; he was abundant energy and life. On January 19, 1919, death would have time for Theodore Roosevelt.

The president's carriage proceeded along Cove Neck Road, skirting the water of Oyster Bay Harbor, en route to his Victorian Mansion.

The following day Giuseppe was firmly admonished by the Secret Service. He made immediate repairs to the building's facade. But there was no official investigation. In fact, the Secret Service didn't even go on the roof, where they would have found several of Maurizio's sculptures and loose rocks of various shape and size. Jake the Cop knew all about Maurizio's rocks and sculptures and disliked him and them. He had to be an anarchist.

The Secret Service was housed in a building on the corner of South Street and East Main Street, the upper floor of this building served as presidential offices. A round turret was built into the corner of the building; all ship bottom rust-color with a dark olive-green trim. The turret protruded out from the second floor to the top third floor and was crowned with a comical, conical oil-funnel cap, which in turn was crowned with a dark olive-green dunce cap. The building was an annex to the "summer White House" which was "up the cove" at Sagamore Hill. When the president came to town, or his wife and children, the Secret Service were stationed on the roof of this building or on the roof of Saunder's Pharmacy, which was across the street from Giuseppe's building. The roof of Giuseppe's building was blocked from view by a large square clock tower on the corner of the roof of Hodman's Hardware Store. So Maurizio went about his sculpturing in pigeon-cooing privacy. The ex-pigeon-chested president and his pigeon-messenger Secret Service knew not of Maurizio's presence. Hardly anyone knew for the next twenty years, until Memorial Day 1927.

Document 1898-25

Dear Comrade Maurizio   1908

I am living in London. In a place called Stepney Green, in the East End of London. I live now in a big Victorian monster of masonry called Dunstan Houses. Ah! You would like the masonry, dear Maurizio! So now my address is 33 Dunstan Houses, London... C/O Mr. Rocker, but I will move soon but still please write to this address. We all have our mail sent to Mr. Rocker. You should see White Chapel Road and London Hospital. I am so surprised here they have many women getting too much drink. They fight in the street at night. They have many pubs. Such women! They are called Cockneys. I don't understand their English. They yell. The streets are so busy and buildings so big. Dunstan Houses is five stories! It has ivy on the walls, iron railing on stairs, and turrets! But you must of course have big buildings in New York... the skyscraper! Here there are many Jewish. Mr. Rocker he works with them. He makes a newspaper with them. I help to set type. I am a typographer! Mr. Rocker has a picture of Bakunin on his kitchen wall. Do you know Bakunin? Do you know Kropotkin? You must read them. But soon I am moving to Soho. That is where our brothers live. They live in Fitzroy Square and on Tottenham Court Road. I am leaving here to be with our brothers. I go with Mr. Rocker to the bookstalls on Charing Cross Road. There are many side streets with many bookstalls. In Soho there are many Italians, French and Germans. But Mr. Rocker will stay in the East End. He works with the Jewish. Mr. Rocker says I should move, to help my people. Our brothers work as shoemakers, tailors, and waiters. So I go. I meet *il signor* Malatesta at Soho! He is our hero. He seems so kind. He is short like me. He is dark with a grey beard like me! He is my brother. He is quiet and modest, not so exuberant and boisterous like our brothers back home. He is mechanic and he sells ice cream! He has little shop in Islington. He is kind to children. He gives them candy and toys. Somedays we march. We marched on May Day. We march from East End to Hyde Park. Mr. Rocker makes a speech there. He is great speaker. He gets big crowd. He makes speech by the big Marble Arch. The police watch us. The Scotland Yard has two detectives following *il signor* Malatesta. He so easily eludes them. It's so funny. Mr. Rocker calls the police the Lump. The Lump! Our brothers have all been coming to London for many years. London has become our refuge. In the heart of the Lump we live, is that not strange? After Bismarck they come here! After King Umberto they come! After Alexander they come! After the bombs in Paris they come! After Fatti de Maggio they come, when police and soldiers shoot and kill us! And now after King Alfonso they come! O the damn Lump!

Please write Comrade Maurizio
Your brother Francesco

What a better and brighter decade it has been! In the aftermath of our "splendid little war," and the drubbing of that candidate of Populism, William Jennings Bryan, the new century is ours! It belongs to us. Great confidence, great relief from class conflict, the great regeneration of the ruling class race, success, progress, and prosperity, the bloody nineties are over, rejoice, America, those foul and destitute men who marched on Washington, the false rise of socialism, the terrors of anarchism, the farmer's protest, the depression of 1893, the chaos in our cities, the flood of immigrants, are gone and now Teddy is leaving the White House. From the Alien and Sedition act of 1798, to the growth of Empire in 1898, a great hundred years, overcoming the atrocity of 1901, when the crazed Czolgosz shot McKinley... from that moment onward we have stood tall, and the ragged, unwashed, long-haired, wild-eyed fiends, with revolver and dynamite, with dagger between his teeth, Roosevelt's Square Deal dealt with them, the Anarchist Exclusion Act of 1903... but how does that explain that the Socialist Party had 10,000 members in 1898 and had over 40,000 by the time Roosevelt was done in 1908. Roosevelt said that the socialist threat is "far more ominous than any populist or similar movement in the past." Roosevelt sent federal troops to the mining town of Goldfield, Nevada… but what was the worry? Another recession? There were unemployed worker demonstrations in major cities in 1908. There were rent-strike protests in New York. The police used their clubs freely and many heads were broken. Anarchists were "worthless as rats and far more dangerous." Then Roosevelt ordered barred from the mails the anarchist newspaper *La Question Sociale,* on grounds that the paper had published an article advocating murder and arson. These "enemies of mankind." Police on horseback and wielding billy clubs dispersed a crowd of over 10,000 from Union Square. The Conference of the Unemployed. A bomb exploded in a man's hands. The Red Scare of 1908… but don't worry America, there won't be anymore Red Scares!

1917 - 1919

Theodore Roosevelt with his nerves on edge, was ready to fight the Huns. He went to the White House to confront President Woodrow Wilson.

Roosevelt pleaded his case. He had to get in the fight. Wilson was not moved. Roosevelt felt a sudden vertigo. The wolf rising… his eyes filled with blood. Roosevelt stared at Wilson. Roosevelt saw Wilson's mouth move very slowly. Wilson went pale. A strange voice in a strange tongue discharged from Wilson's mouth. There was foam on his lips. Roosevelt saw Wilson transform into a Russian Count… there seemed to be a mask on Wilson's face. Roosevelt heard Wilson utter a guttural and harsh tone; he was speaking Russian. Roosevelt saw Count Leo Tolstoy standing before him. And then the face and body began to alter itself again. Roosevelt saw a man standing before him, dressed in a suit, a man with a beard, and Roosevelt spoke to him. He said, I know you. Yes, the man said, you know me. But you are dead, said Roosevelt. Crosby… is that you, Ernest? The man said, "Listen Roosevelt. I was born into a New York patrician family, as were you. I was a member of the New York Legislature, as were you. In fact, I succeeded you in that position. I became a reformer, a temperance man, and I was involved in the social welfare of New York City, I worked diligently for the single tax, for the labor unions, for the Italian immigrants, for Filipino progress, for anti-imperialism, for anti-war…"

"That Tolstoy, that pacifist, that mad man… you were swayed by him… and by Howells, you had a weak mind, Crosby, you betrayed your class," spouted Roosevelt.

"The days of chivalry are over," said Crosby. "We have mass slaughter of combatants and noncombatants. There are no more swashbuckling adventures. You have to grow up, Roosevelt. You can't be a boy forever. We live in the modern world. We have modern warfare. We fight in mud and blood-soaked trenches. There are tanks and there are aerial bombardments. There is poison gas. It is total war. Mechanized war. The soldier is just a cog, a spinning gear. Our wonderful leaders come from Harvard and Yale and do not forsake their heritage, isn't that correct President Wilson? But you did, Roosevelt. You ran off to the west. To play Cowboys and Indians. Then you went to fight your little war in Cuba. You and your volunteers. Killing and dying for fun. There will be no more volunteer armies. No more Rough Riders, no more Yale and Harvard men playing soldier, no more cowboys... those Rough Riders, are you Walt Whitman? Are you Melville? Who are you in Washington, who are you to declare me the enemy of anybody? I deny your authority to sow hatred in my soul. Did you see what the English and that Maxim gun did to those poor souls in Africa. Ripped them apart in minutes. But I suppose that would have pleased you. That's what this war is about. All out war."

And now the voice faded. The mask melted. Wilson returned. "The days when an anarchist with a stick of dynamite could have threatened the state is over. They missed their chances. The fools. If they act, instigating more violence, marches, they will be throttled, suppressed efficiently and totally. I know you agree. This is a world war, Teddy, to save the world for Democracy! The new order is deeply embedded in absolute history. It will come to an end in fewer than a hundred years. We will win. The state is becoming all powerful. You are childish, but you have a sweet kind of charm. I like you Roosevelt. But do you wish your own death? You and I agree that the white race created the best of civilization, and that the masses must be led by men who come from that Anglo-Saxon tradition, from the rule of law, but we can't cast aspersions on races, you know that, you've said it in print, we need a labor force, we need true Americans, we need them to believe in this country, you and I believe in that together, but the future requires statesmen, rational leaders, not impulsive and unpredictable actions just for the sake of glory and duty... it's over Teddy, go back to that house in Oyster Bay and write some more books, your *Winning of the West* is a fine book, write something about hunting, go back to Africa and kill some more big dumb beasts..."

1923

Captain Roger Bethell was on a tour of the Far East. He was a guest of the Japanese writer Junichiro Tanizaki, and stayed with him at his home on the "Bluff" in Yokohama, during the hot days of August in 1923. The "Bluff" was the foreign quarter of Yokohama. The Captain and a group of Japanese and gaijin listened to Tanizaki as he held forth on numerous seemingly incongruous topics ranging from Charles Baudelaire and Edgar Allen Poe to Commodore Perry and the black ships, from bunraku and bushido to the nature of cruelty and the aesthetics of evil, from kabuki and Noh to the indecencies of Tokyo and the merchant class. Tanizaki seemed to Captain Bethell to be filled with ambivalent emotions, caught in the Japanese shadows of the past and the Western lights of the future, praising and berating both with equal vigor. He spoke of his plan to move to Osaka or Kyoto, to get back to the old ways. The Captain understood that Tanizaki, like Japan, was in the modern murk of a transitional crisis. But Tanizaki had more immediate plans: tomorrow he will be leaving for the Hakone mountains, and Captain Bethell will also be leaving tomorrow, for Nikko...

It was not a coincidence that Captain Bethell would be taking a house in Nikko that had once been occupied by Henry Adams and John La Farge. A house near a temple and garden, where Adams had once strolled about, reading Dante's *Paradiso*, while searching for an elusive Nirvana. Henry Brooks Adams was the great grandson of President John Adams, was the grandson of President John Quincy Adams, was the son of the diplomat and politician, Charles Francis Adams, and was himself a writer and historian. Henry Adams was searching for that inscrutable power that keeps peace in the heart. But whose power? The power of the dynamo? The power of nature? The power of the Virgin Queen seated atop a perfect unified world? Adams was small of statue and sympathy, large of mockery and bitterness; a hurt man, but it was difficult to put your finger on his precise wound, on the exact purport and intention of what he said often in excess of its true meaning. When Theodore Roosevelt departed from the White House, Adams sent him off tersely and pointedly, he said, "I shall miss you very much." This was a rare reversal of his formula. What exactly was he going to miss? A buffoon? An example of his obsession with force and energy? Roosevelt's mitigation of the will-to-power with the will-to-optimism? Adams was a little man with an elongated head such that El

Greco may have put to canvas on a stormy gray and black night in Toledo. A bright bald dome of cosmic significance carried Adams' forehead into geological time, a forehead that ridged slanting eyes, alert and searching; his head rooted to the earth by a pointed beard that made him look all the world (all the hell) like Goethe's Faust, a likeness he would have disdained, having judged Goethe a novice, an imitator, and highly overrated. Certainly Voltaire was the greater intellect, he claimed.

John La Farge was a New York painter who had for a time lived in a hut that he himself had built on the Paradise Rocks on the Hudson River, in which he painted and meditated. La Farge was a Catholic in the guise of a Chinese sage; he loved Confucius and Buddha. He and Adams set out for Japan in 1886; it was their first expedition together; directly from it came La Farge's book *An Artist's Letters from Japan*, and indirectly from it, years later, by way of La Farge's influence, came Adams' book *Mont-Saint-Michel and Chartres*. Their second journey took them to Tahiti and Samoa, a trip that resulted in La Farge's *Reminiscences of the South Sea*, and Adams' *Memoirs of Arii Taimai*. Their last trip together was to Ceylon, where Adams heard the monkeys howl in the Bo Tree of Buddha. A later visitor to Ceylon, D. H. Lawrence, couldn't bear the noise at night. But for Adams, Washington D.C. was all noise and his travels his deliverance from public life and history. Oh to sleep under the many-colored sky, on the shore of a South Sea island, where the trade winds blow, under the southern stars, forever. Yet, in the end, he returned to Washington, "as a horse goes back to its stable."

It was Adams' cherished and beloved friend Clarence King's phrase about "Old-gold girls tumbling down waterfalls" that had enchanted Adams and started him on his extensive travels to the South Seas and elsewhere. But there was another more plausible motivation for getting away. In 1884, Adams and John Hay had adjoining houses built in Lafayette Square, in Washington D.C., red brick houses designed by the American architect H. H. Richardson. It was to his new house that Adams had hoped to convene his familiars, a quiet place where they could come and gather around him. Familiars such as La Farge, Alexander Agassiz, and Henry James, who was usually indisposed to American soil. But above all else, this would be where the "Five of Hearts" held court. The "Five of Hearts" was the self-given title of a small circle of more than just friends, which included John and Clara Hay, Clarence King, and Henry and Clover

Adams. But on a Sunday morning in 1885, while Adams was out for a stroll, his wife committed suicide by swallowing potassium cyanide. Adams was distraught. He could not stand to live in the new house all by himself. So he burned many of his letters and diaries, and the following year was off to Japan with La Farge; thus began twenty years of restless journeys to the ends of the earth.

Clarence King was the most restless of all. John Hay held him to be the best and brightest of his generation. The Ideal American. King was a brilliant geologist and mining engineer. Adams thought him a "radiant" personage. La Farge, Hay, all of them admired King. He was everything that the others wanted to be. Hay was envious of King, more so because Adams was so envious of King. King knew more of poetry and art than Adams, Adams believed; and judging by Hay's own works of poetry, King must have known more of poetry than Hay. He knew the West; he had surveyed the Yosemite Valley and had first set out its boundaries. King went to Yosemite as an assistant to Josiah Whitney. King and Whitney wrongly rejected the views of "that shepherd" John Muir, who had expounded the theory of "glacial erosion" to explain the origin of Yosemite Valley. John Muir arrived in San Francisco in 1868, and not long after headed out for Yosemite afoot, searching for anywhere that's wild. It was April when Muir made it into the valley and the melting snows from the High Sierra were feeding the waterfalls; the foothills were covered with wildflowers, Lupine, Indian Paintbrush, Miner's Lettuce, and the California Poppy; the Steller's Jay and Brewer's Blackbird, suspicious and curious, warbling and clucking, were just learning to adapt to their human company. Living on three dollars a month from watching sheep, "hoofed locusts," and building a sawmill, Muir constructed a hut made of sugar pine near the base of the lower Yosemite Fall, which thundered in three cascades over varieties of granite and ran off in rivulets of shed water, cold and stark. He hung a bed from the rafters, and wrote at a table by a window where the ferns climbed over. It cost less than four dollars, cheaper than Thoreau's cabin at Walden. Ralph Waldo Emerson visited Muir in 1871. Together they stood in Mariposa Grove, where Emerson planted a tree to commemorate his visit. Muir turned to him and said, "You are yourself a sequoia." In 1903, Theodore Roosevelt visited Yosemite Valley. Muir accompanied him on a camping trip that lasted three days. Surrounded by the massive redwoods Roosevelt remarked with unoriginality that it was like a great solemn cathedral. Muir set a fire from some dead pine and Teddy blurted out, "This is bully!"

John Muir lived for six years in the Yosemite. His was not the idle restlessness of the Yale graduate and Newport boy, Clarence King. And though John Hay had lived just east of the Mississippi, the West to him was a barbarous place where there was no room for genius. It was Clarence King who had given Mt. Tyndall and Mt. Whitney their names. He was more an Adam than an Adams. He had studied with Louis Agassiz; he was charming, infectious, and irresistible; Adams was much impressed that King knew women, American women, even New York women! In Cuba together, Adams saw how King spent his nights at Voodoo dances, how he walked and talked with the lowly and oppressed, speaking to them in their native dialect. John Hay was shocked to learn after King's death that King had been "married to a negress" and sired five children with her. There were secrets that even the "Five of Hearts" did not know about each other. In his life King made and lost each of his fortunes; he destroyed his health and died alone in a tavern in Arizona. The Ideal American.

Captain Roger Bethell was made of the same restless fiber. Yet he was of a different order of knowing. Tonight Captain Bethell is an honored guest in the Tanizaki home in future efficient and far-away Japan, along with the others who have gathered to meet Roger Bethell. More sane minds than those Bethell met at Sagamore Hill or those met at Adams those many years ago when Bethell was ostracized from their ranks.

One of the guests was a young poet from Ireland. He had heard a rumor. He was pleased to make it known, that William Butler Yeats, the Irish poet, would most likely be awarded the Nobel Prize for literature. Tanizaki wondered if a Japanese writer would ever win this coveted prize of the West, and whether a Japanese writer should be infected with such an envious wish. "We have many good writers in Japan who can win Nobel Prize. Many though have died. Natsume Soseki is dead. Mori Ogai died last year. Arishima Takeo committed suicide with his mistress this year; very Japanese, *ne*? And poor Aktugawa who tries to kill himself. One day he will do it. We have many disagreements. He prefers style, the structure of a story. I prefer the contents. Nagai Kafu is living, but he is still young, almost fifty. I am only thirty-seven years old myself."

Tanizaki read from some notes that he was preparing for an essay that he was working on, translated to English for his guests. Tanizaki went on in a rambling manner to speak of many things. He tried very hard to pronounce the English words as clearly as possible, which made him appear to be affecting an aristocratic air, his mouth and tongue and teeth wrestling in a pool of saliva. "*Ano ne...* is it not significant for you writers in the West in 20th century that when Dante wrote of inferno... *nandaka...* you call it hell now I believe, when Dante wrote of poet and lover being in hell, he wrote of poet and lover spending eternity in hell... *ano ne... ga...* but when Rimbaud wrote of hell, he merely wrote of spending season in hell. Dante saw fixed and finite self. Rimbaud saw ever-changing seasons, other selves... for us artists this must be revelation, *ne?* Ground is moving like earthquake. There is no center. Things fall apart, as the Mister Yeats has recently said in poem. But which to prefer? The closed circle? The culturally dogmatic 'this is our way?' which has maybe spiritual wholeness... though vastly more narrow. Or the broken circle that has more of the idea of the freedom for the individual? Not very Japanese, *ne?* It is like our Sumo, for example, which is very... *nandaka...* rich and splendid with ritual, yes, but there is brief moment of spontaneous action in ring... that moment is our freedom, *ne?* Beyond necessity... or like our tea ceremony... *ano ne...* where master maybe seem to uninitiated eye to be doing nothing more than same old thing. But whose spontaneity and freedom is perfectly obvious to the adept. Are we not blinded by so much electrical light? Here and in America, in England... in Germany... so much waste. It is the whiteness on dark soul that evokes the shadows." Here Tanizaki dramatically paused and slid open the shoji, the paper window, and let in the moonlight. "This light and shadow is the illumination of our soul. But the illumination and industrialization of our cities will destroy soul, *ne?* The West produces nothing but more and more rubbish. We shall do the same in the future, we are copy cats, *ne?*"

Early the next morning Roger Bethell and Tanizaki stood on the street, on the hill of Ichikawacho, near the *gaijin bochi,* the foreigner's cemetery, and bowed a farewell to each other. In the distance Mt. Fuji stood hovering over Yokohama, or thus it seemed, for Roger Bethell had discovered that everything about Mt. Fuji and Japan just seemed. Sometimes seemed earthy, sometimes seemed ethereal; sometimes large and looming, sometimes small and cowering; sometimes a specter of wispy cloud, sometimes a solid seed of the earth. Roger Bethell was much impressed by Mt. Fuji. "Is it real, I wonder, or not just a figment of Japanese mind?"

"Yes, but you are not Japanese and you see it," replied Tanizaki.

"I see it because you see it; because Hokusai saw it, because Bashō saw it... we see it differently because they saw it before us, and created it before us, all of us envious of that first Fiat, that first Let There Be Light..."

"Ah, your Bible...

"Not my Bible..."

"Yes, and yet Western writers always quoting from Bible that you say is not yours. Fujisan will stand when cities of Tokyo and Yokohama fall. Fujisan will stand when cities of London and New York fall."

They bowed to each other and went their separate ways. Roger Bethell and Tanizaki reached their respective destinations, Nikko and Hakone, later that day. The following day, September 1, on a Saturday morning, Captain Bethell looked out from his hotel window. He saw the sky blacken over the mountains and heard thunder and heavy rain pounding the roof. The sky grew darker and darker over Lake Chuzenji. Then just before noon a tremendous earthquake destroyed the cities of Tokyo and Yokohama. A natural disaster? Earthquake, thunderstorm, fire and father. The four great forces of nature. That was an old Japanese proverb that Tanizaki had told Captain Bethell on the night before they had parted. *Jishin, kamanari, kaji, oyaji.* The earthquake provided the Japanese government and the military the excuse, if they needed one, to ascend to power. Martial Law was declared. The death of the Japanese left was decided. Suppression, arrests, and murder followed in the wake of the disaster. Japanese vigilantes killed Koreans. They killed two Japanese students of a school for the deaf because they could not answer that they were Japanese. They made lost wandering souls repeat a phrase of Japanese to see if they pronounced it properly, *ju go en*, fifteen yen, and not *chu go en* as Koreans pronounced it. The infamous Amakasu, a captain of the military police, had strangled to death the anarchist leader, Sakae Osugi, and his lover, Ito Noe, and his six-year-old nephew. Their bodies were thrown into an old well. The Japanese movie *Eros + Massacre* was made in 1968, based on this story, it's in Stephen's Top Movie List, he'll provide it later...

"How big, how effective, is the H-bomb?"

"Big enough," said Admiral Lewis S. Strauss, chairman of the Atomic Energy Commission under President Eisenhower, "big enough to take out any city in the world, even the largest, New York and London..." A man-made disaster? *Human beings never learn.*

In the News: Document 068-2001

Admiral Lewis S. Strauss has returned from observing and supervising the H-bomb tests in the Pacific... the most recent thermonuclear explosion surprised the scientists and got out of hand... that is "exaggerated and mistaken," said Strauss. The Japanese fishing trawler, the *Lucky Dragon*, got alarmingly sprinkled with radioactive dust, because the planes which were sent out to survey the area before the blast was let loose just naturally happened not to see it. A kind of human error, and random chance, for which no one can be particularly blamed. The Japanese depend heavily on the fish and those bomb-shocked people don't want to think they might glow in the dark after eating them. Elugebab, the H-bomb test island, is one geographical place we don't have to remember. It isn't there anymore. But we don't have to ask the name anyway, we just took it! It isn't there anymore!

Memorial Days 1927 (1933) Decoration Days or whatever-whenever

Fiorenza Cazzaza sat in her designated chair at one of the windows in the "front rooms" overlooking South Street. Across the street, from a third story window of Saunder's Pharmacy, under the eaves of the long pitched roof of a gable, the window's bottom half of six panes lifted up in front of the top half's six panes, mild May air entering the room, circulating and convening with the dust under the foot pedals of a grand piano, the sunlight distorting into rainbow fragments that illuminated the white piano keys and the short fat fingers of Luigi Bollo, smearing garlic scents on the black A flat and B flat, came the voice of Silvia "Toots" Cazzaza, molto lento, her left hand placed on her chest, feeling the aching fremitus like the physical rapture of the heart, her right arm extending like seven gut strings from the pharyngeal depths of visceral sensation, a viola d'amore, stretching out beyond the physical origins of sound to the spiritually luminous voice of silence that rests at the edge of infinity, where the guts are cut and snapped back to earth with a humble hum drum hum drum hum drum...

"Ave, Ave! Dominus tecum. Benedicta tu in mulieribus, et benedictus, at benedictus fructus vendris, vendris tui, Jesu..."

Toots' voice carried across the street, where her mother and two aunts sat at the windows in the front rooms, surveying the streets, listening to Toots' pearly gate's rendition of Schubert's Op. 52, No. 6., and waiting for the Memorial Day parade to march by, the American Legion Band to lead the way, as pre-ordained, with Toots' brother Frankie playing his trombone, just about the time Luigi Bollo shuts his windows, the bass drums booming and the real humdrum beginning.

Was it the breeze or the tremulous vibrato of Toots' voice that caused the red, white and blue banners and buntings to sway and flutter? Or the striped awning unfurled in sections with a long metal hook-tip rod twisted by Mr. Saunders himself, to pop up and down in a blustering of thumps? Each store had its own flag, which was patriotically displayed on the sidewalk in front of each shop respectively, slipped into specially prepared hollow tubes in the cement at the street curb near the gutter swept clean every morning by civically conscientious shopkeepers, flags teased by the wind, flapping out to smack the twigs of maple saplings planted two years ago in 1925 as part of this decade's town beautification project, then curling about their poles, limp and morose, as if unaware of the vocal beatification being cast down in volumes from the window of Luigi Bollo's studio above the drug store to the blessed multitudes gathering below.

Centered beneath the acme of the roof was a double window with a narrow strip of pediment, uniformly placed about twelve inches higher than the two single windows that flanked it on each side; at the middle of the two subordinate windows, measured out level to the edge of the roof, the long incline of the roof dropped vertically to the flat tarred roof overhanging Saunder's Pharmacy, encircling and conjoining the second floor, with three more windows, a double window flanked by two singles again, between which hung all the red, white and blue trappings of national pride and identification, long and triangular, tapering to a point, with some curls of black drapery to boot. If you were to drop a plummet from the peak of the double-sloping roof, suspended in air over the sidewalk, the string would hang bisecting the two double windows, one right above the other, straight down through the center of an entrance door, the lead weight of the plumb-bob scratching the center of the cement stoop occupied by little Rocky, small in stature and deformed from birth, the town's Quasimodo, twenty-five years old, behaves like a ten-year-old, sucking on the straw of an ice cream soda purchased for seven cents in Saunder's soda fountain behind the glass door that he is sitting in front of, obstructing customers, who have to walk on either side of him to enter

Saunder's, not daring to confront the ugly lump before them, until Mr. Saunders chases him away.

Rocky peered into the dark alleyway across the street. To the right of the alleyway, beneath a tin canopy held up by iron rods, was the Cazzaza Fruit and Vegetable Store; to the left of the alleyway were Schwartz and Horowitz's Stationery, Herman's Dry-Goods store, and Van Heffer's Meat Market; those were the stores in the Cazzaza building in 1927. That's what Rocky saw. Fiorenza and her sisters saw Saunder's Pharmacy, which took up most of the block. But it wasn't a day for building-watching; it was a people-watching day. There was holiday stillness in the air. Only two shops were open this morning, Saunder's Pharmacy and the stationery, open until around noon; people needed their newspapers. Also open was Luigi Bollo's studio; national holiday or no, he needed the money; Verdi must go on! A continuous pre-parade of men went in and came out of the stationery, newspapers in hand, wearing straw hats, puffing on cigars, jacket-less, white shirts and crossed suspenders. Good mornings were exchanged among the men, parade talk, weather talk, sport's talk, the Yankees won again and it was going to be a hot day for May; but Charles Lindbergh was still the main topic of conversation, people actually had something to say, to talk about in public, however briefly, a national hero, a vicarious adventure, pausing longer than usual on the sidewalks, eager to go but bending an ear, cracking a smile, for the civic decorum of the day, feeling almost a commitment to say something, to listen to something, besides the mundane, trite utterances, but this morning pridefully to acknowledge the national effluvia of sentiments that equated him with us.

"Up there all alone, my God..."

"Something, huh?"

Each passing hour saw more people mingling on the streets. Some wore uniforms, some wore pins on their lapels, ribbons on their chests, hats cluttered with badges: American Legion, Daughters of the American Revolution, Knights of Columbus, members of the Masonic Temple, volunteer firemen, auxiliary nurses, Boy Scouts, Girl Scouts, Cub Scouts, Brownies, Campfire Girls, baton twirlers, 4-H Club, Red Cross, little league ballplayers, marching bands, local politicians, policemen, assorted vendors, wow look at those balloons! Rocky wanted a red one. All of them converging at the south end of South Street, from where the parade will commence, in front of the American Legion Hall, Quentin Roosevelt Post

#4, a large two-story brick building with six rows of brick steps leading up to the black doors on the left hand side of the building, three small windows in the front of the building on the first floor, capped by stone lintels, and four of the same on the second floor, with a small arched window in the center at the top. On each side of the building were five tall windows, through which sunlight shone on the wooden floor of the large meeting hall presided over by a portrait of Colonel Theodore Roosevelt, decked out in Rough Rider gear, mounted on a horse, inspecting a row of his troops, also mounted, ready to take San Juan Hill, though in fact most of the horses were left behind in Florida, and the cowboys and college-boys went on to make history, neatly tidied up into sensational purple prose of yellow journalists in newspapers around the country, especially William Randolph Hearst's *Journal*. The famed First Regiment of the U.S. Calvary Volunteers, organized by Teddy Roosevelt but commanded by Roosevelt's old crony Colonel Leonard Wood, who by 1919 was leading troops in breaking up strikes in Bolshevik-threatened America, and was being considered for president in 1920, but that honor went to Warren G. Harding. The glorious adventure of the Rough Riders was fought mainly on foot, on Kettle Hill, not good copy, and sounds too much like an English tea party, Teddy in Wonderland. I'll fix that, said the newspaper magnate Hearst.

Frankie Cazzaza came out of the alleyway carrying his trombone case, followed by nine-year-old Luisa, and six-year-old Joe pulling a red wooden wagon in which little Stevie sat, holding tightly to a rope, crutches by his side, a new pair, which he received two weeks ago on his birthday when he turned twelve. He has never been able to walk without a crutch, a cane, or a limp. Yet his handicap hasn't affected his spirits, or his drive to stay as active as other children; he is one of the ablest swimmers among the younger boys of the village. Last year Stevie was in the New York Hospital for the Crippled. He was operated upon by the son of the world famous Dr. Aldoph Lorenz of Berlin, the surgeon whose "bloodless operations and cures had startled the world's greatest scientists." Since the operation a marked improvement has been shown in the defective foot and though further developments were anticipated Stevie walked with the use of crutches until he died in 1977.

"Faster! Faster!" yelled Stevie, and Luisa and Joe obliged, pulling the wagon so fast that it toppled over, sending Stevie careening into a telephone pole in front of Van Heffer's Meat Market. He dragged himself to his feet, clinging to the telephone pole, and hopped over to pick up his crutches. Frankie righted the wagon.

"My turn... pull me," said little Luisa, who also walked gimping along with her left hand curled into a permanent fist, the arm held close to her body. A childhood victim of spinal meningitis she would spend most of her adult life as a recluse, caring for her mother and Stevie, watching the world from the windows above South Street, or from the porch overlooking the backyard at the rear of the Cazzaza building, watching delivery trucks come and go, drunks stumbling home from the alley, drunken brawls, feeding a dozen stray cats that took up residence in the abandoned work-shed, always more kittens, what to do with them? Frankie, after he and Joe sold the bar in Northport, took a job for Van Heffer's, so it was Frankie who had to dispose of the new litters, usually by drowning them, though when some of the kittens crawled up into the engines of Van Heffer's delivery trucks to stay warm in winter they were ground up by the radiator fans, just like the beef ground up in Van Heffer's to make hamburgers. And every morning before the sun began to glimmer over the tall steeple of the large white wooden Presbyterian Church on a hill just beyond the end of the laneway that led down to the backyard, Luisa would be out with her broom sweeping the macadamized surface of the backyard, gathering the scattered rubbish left errantly blowing in the cold morning breeze by the garbagemen riding on the runners of a truck with a huge revolving lawnmower blade which would one day fascinate a young Stephen Cazzaza so much, sitting up in the window of Aunt Luisa's, that he wanted to be a garbageman when he grew up... first garbageman, then fireman, then astronaut, then trumpet player, then baseball player...

Luisa climbed into the red wagon and Joe and Frankie pulled her into the narrow alleyway, the wagon just fitting through the opening; the wagon had been built to specifications by Giuseppe so that it would make it through. The children pulled the wagon at breakneck speed through the 60 foot long alleyway, Luisa holding on firmly with her one good hand, leaning back on Frankie's trombone case, her mouth and eyes agape, while Stevie followed behind, chugging along on his crutches as fast as he could to keep up with his siblings. They came charging out of the alleyway and into the backyard, turning right on two wheels, nearly flipping over, avoiding a passerby who shunted to his right, and they came to a screeching halt under a forty foot high water tower. Joe ran over to the passerby and asked him for a few pennies. Emile Baldazzi dug into his pockets and gave Joe two cents. The children in town know that Emile was good for a few pennies once and a while. Luisa got out of the wagon and Joe climbed in; and off they went through the alleyway again, Stevie chasing behind them, again.

Seated at a table in the kitchen located on the ground floor behind the fruit and vegetable store, Giuseppe with pencil in hand pondered over his financial situation. It made him happy to hear the racket his children were making outside. Giuseppe glided the point of the pencil down the page of his account book. What he saw did not make him happy: April 2, 1927... balance $1,148.58... April 20, 1927... balance $562.01... May 4, 1927... balance $685.13... May 23, 1927... balance $650.21.

He flipped the small brown book closed and tapped the cover with his finger, where it read Oyster Bay Bank in Acc't with Giuseppe Cazzaza, and opened the other small brown book containing the names of customers who were in account with him; a list of names representing some of the affluent families of high social standing in the North Shore Gold Plush Territories, who must have considered themselves exempt by some blue-blood decree of snobbism from having to pay such measly debts owed to Giuseppe, because many of them never did settle their accounts with him or with Leonora, who was a fine seamstress, and sewed dresses and suits for some of the fine ladies and gents and debutantes of the New York "Social Register"; they never once even gave her a dime for her services rendered. Every so often those to the manor born deployed their servants into the village to procure on credit (the masters having no cash in hand, how dirty that would be!) some life and liberty sustaining commodities, necessary for the pursuit of happiness, at the same time bringing along a few evening gowns, selected to be worn at the next dinner party or charity ball, which were flung over the store counter and neatly gathered up by Giuseppe with a courteous smile.

"Mrs. Whitney would be must grateful if..."

"Sure thing... you bet," said the obliging Giuseppe. Fiorenza scowling in the back. Teresa came downstairs, leaving her perch at the window in the front room, and entered the kitchen. "You must get dressed soon or you will be late for the parade." She was carrying Giuseppe's fireman's uniform draped over her arm.

"I never be late yet!" Giuseppe barked. He was to march in the parade with the Atlantic Steamer Fire Company.

"Leonora has patched the hole. You will look splendid," said Teresa.

Giuseppe said nothing, but nodded his head in quick jerky motions.

"Why notta the richa peeples pay me?" Giuseppe complained.

"Maybe they are too busy and forget. They are rich, what can we do?"

"Soma forgeta!"

If Leonora was good with a Singer sewing machine, Teresa was "good with numbers," and managed the books, keeping a record of the financial transactions in her head, reluctantly writing them down, Giuseppe having to keep after her to do it.

"Looka here," Giuseppe pointed at the brown book.

"I know, I know, I don't have to look at what I wrote down," snapped Teresa. Giuseppe stared at the names and numbers.

Townsend	$ .48
Burr	7.72
Schiff	32.76
Roosevelt	2.50
Weekes	1.17
Moore	3.46
Doubleday	33.35
Whitney	12.24
Taylor	21.78

"I almosta killa myselfa puttig fire outa ina Taylor kitchena... Taylor justa laugha lika idiota... da cooka burna da meataballa for spaghetti... Taylor saya to mea whya notta you be my cooka you Italiano... *imbecille buon a nulla...*" Taylor had come running outside with a flaming pan of meatballs and tossed it on the grass.

Giuseppe rose from his chair; there were more names and numbers on the list but he couldn't stand to look at it. He took the uniform from Teresa.

"Ah but looka da buttona is fallin offa!"

"Leonora must not have noticed. I'll take it back upstairs to her right away."

"No! No! It'sa too late," said Giuseppe, and he tore the button off and put it on the kitchen table. He sighed. Giuseppe had joined the fire department in 1905, a year after settling in town. The all-volunteer fire company was founded in 1896, and by 1905 had one truck and seven members, Giuseppe became the eight member. Giuseppe took his wallet out of his back pocket and removed an old photograph of himself and seven others posing on a fire engine. Two large headlights popping out in front of the engine's meshed grill where the letters F. D. are attached. Beneath the grill a crank, behind which runs an axle connecting two thin tires with 12 spokes in each. On top of the wheel-guard sits the puppy mascot, a growling mutt with a chewed-off left ear. Giuseppe is seated at the wheel in the open compartment, a large spotlight on the dashboard, and next to the spotlight a hand-cranked siren. Three large hoses are strapped to the side of the truck, and above the hoses there are pipes and dials and switches and knobs and lanterns all cluttered together. On top of the pump a fireman sits holding a nozzle. Everyone is attired in his dress uniform: a narrow white shirt collar encircling above the wider stiff collar of a long black jacket, with a row of six large brass buttons. Oh look how shiny and new my brass buttons looked then! Giuseppe looked at the brass button on the kitchen table. He picked it up and held it. It felt cold, very cold. And he picked up his fireman's badge, which he pinned to the front of his hat. OB FD. He suddenly felt a cold shiver run through his body and had to sit down. A sweat broke out on his forehead. Just like when mama died he thought to himself. That was back in Orero, in 1888, when he was eighteen. Something bad is going to happen. Giuseppe looked one more time at the photograph before he stuck it back in his wallet. Each of the firemen was wearing a flattop round hat, with a shiny black brim and above the brim a strap and above the strap a badge signifying membership in Atlantic Steamer Fire Company. In 1912 Giuseppe was made fire chief. He got a new uniform and a special badge. Giuseppe is going to wear the same uniform today to march in the Memorial Day parade for the 9th time. He will march in front of the procession of firemen, which now numbers twenty-four, with two trucks, an ambulance, and the addition of a hook-and-ladder. The hook-and-ladder would bring up the rear of the Memorial Day parade for the next forty years or so, when it was retired to a fire truck museum in upstate New York.

The children were sitting together on the red wagon that they had strategically placed in the street gutter, thereby earning squatter's rights in lieu of a view to the parade. This was at a time when police barricades were uncalled for, the crowd was small, polite, familiar, and there was no chance of a fire truck having to leave the parade route in a hurry because of a brush fire started by some mischievous teenagers, as was often the case by the 1950s, when juvenile delinquents and Rock and Roll music were listed by the Town Fathers as public and parade enemy #1, and was certainly the case on an October day in 1962, when Stephen and his sister Sylvia set fire to a heap of garbage piled like a talus of rocks in front of Food Town supermarket; or on Memorial Day 1965, when Stephen, chasing his friend Jimmy across South Street, running out from the alleyway, wearing a "Rough Rider" toy sword strapped to his hip, purchased for one dollar from a man dressed up like a clown, was suddenly hit by a new shiny Ford Mustang being driven by a eighteen-year-old, some rich kid who got the car for his birthday. Stephen was knocked into a slight concussion, lying prostrate in the center of the street, looking up at Uncle Frankie, who had followed in his father's footsteps up a ladder and became a fireman. Uncle Frankie had raced over from the backyard where he was working for Van Heffer's Meat Market, washing the meat fat from the stinking bee-buzzed barrels. Uncle Frankie, all fuzzy and blurry in Stephen's eyes, bending over him, trying to soothe him. It was the only thing that Stephen would remember about the accident in later years.

Stevie, Luisa, and Joe pushed against each other's shoulders, trying to squeeze more comfortably into the wagon. Frankie, who was nineteen at the time, the oldest boy, walked across the street to meet Rocky, who was still sitting in front of Saunder's Pharmacy.

"Shut up with that noise up there!" Frankie spurted out; he and Rocky laughing, and then Rocky aped Frankie shouting the same. Toots, who was six years older than her brother, recognized Frankie's voice, and thought to herself: I'll get him! Toots was at the moment ecstatically twisting and distorting her face into operatic configurations as if to mimic a clef under attack from a brigade of confused quarter notes, con molta espress, as it is written on the sheet music that Toots is reading. Verdi's Requiem. Toots's singing: *Lacrymosa dies illa! Qua resurget ex favilla Judicandus homoreus. Huic ergo parce Deus...* and then Luigi Bollo singing in a not quite deep enough for bass voice, bowing his head firmly, lowering his chin, pressing his throat down upon his breast bone, forming hillocks of flabby jowls and double chin, and then opening his mouth, the lips pouting into an oval suction cup, emitted what could only be described as a series of hammering burps from the depths of God's black bowels, as if to spew up all the tiny black notes and markers on the page of sheet music... *Lacry... LA-cry-mo-sa! La-cry-mo-sa dies illa!...* Frankie had heard enough. He opened his trombone case and took out the instrument. "I think I should rehearse a bit." Rocky laughed again, knowing full well Frankie's intentions. Frankie blew and blurted out long sliding insults hurled upward at the open window, at Luigi, at his sister Toots, at Verdi... Whhaaaaaa! Whhaaaaaaaaaaaaaaa! humble hum drum hum drum hum drum...

"*Ave, Ave! Dominus tecum. Benedicta tu in mulieribus, et benedicta...*"

Roosevelts

A car pulled up to the curb in front of Saunder's Pharmacy; a long, low, sleek car, with deeply drawn "Flying Wing" fenders, white-wall tires, two-tone colors, and smooth rounded edges, it was a stylish car, the kind of car that pleased so many famous personalities and moving picture celebrities of the Jazz Age. Frankie lowered his trombone to his side. Rocky seemed to be gazing intently at the car, but one could never be certain about what Rocky was looking at because the distorted cloudy pupils of his eyes always flickered high in the recesses of his wide-open eye-lids. Toots came to the window and Luigi Bollo looked out from over her shoulder, placing his hands delicately upon her waist. Across the street Fiorenza and Leonora sat beneath the pressed tin ceiling embossed with segmented squares of fleurs-de-lis and a convex molding of oval egg-shapes tacked around the corners of the ceiling. They trained their eyes on the doors of the car.

"Get Teresa. She's downstairs. Hurry!" Fiorenza ordered her sister. Both sisters were inclined to listen to her, after all, her husband owned the place; she was the woman of the house. Leonora shuffled down the hallway, her apron fluttering in front of her. She stopped at the top of the stairs and called down, "Teresa! Come quick! Hurry! Come on! Rose-velts!" She whispered the name Roosevelt out of some the-walls-have-ears deference and humility. Teresa hesitated; then let go of Giuseppe's hand, slowly. She went upstairs and down the hallway to the front rooms.

The door on the driver's side opened and out stepped a tall and dignified Negro chauffeur. Walking around the front of the car, he ran his hand up the long black glossy "Flying Wing" fender, touched one then the other silver headlight, and ran his hand down the fender on the other side. He swept his right hand off the fender and placed it on the spare tire clamped to the side of the hood. A lower portion of the tire protruded through an opening cut in the fender at the edge of the running board. A small spotlight was strapped to the top of the tire. The chauffeur tilted forward and grasped the handle of the rear door with his left hand. He pulled the door open and back, retreating a few steps, and stood behind the end of the door, next to the wheel and its unhubcapped metal crossed spokes, and removed his chauffeur's hat. The front door on the passenger side opened of its own accord, unchaufferized, and simultaneously disembarking from front and back door, were mother and son. Teddy Roosevelt, Jr. offered his hand to his mother, Edith Roosevelt, who got out, squinted her eyes, and straightened her hat. Teddy, Jr. buttoned his jacket. The chauffeur walked around the rear of the car, passing the chrome sheen of two contoured strips of burnished bumper, which came in contact with his trousers, rubbing together like a magnetic connection, as if he were attracted to the car by a compelling force, a bee drawn to nectar. He stood in the street with his massive frame and traffic came to a halt, a Chevrolet Model K and a Buick "6" idled, vibrating like tin kettles about to burst. The chauffeur opened the door and there emerged from the plush interior the white frilly plumes of an out-of-style banana boat hat which lifted its unfashionable hull on a wave of elegance, revealing the haughty eyebrows and darting bowsprit grey eyes of Alice Roosevelt Longworth, eldest daughter of the late great President. Princess Alice adjusted her quills and feathers and retrices and all in brocaded saffron and white lace she glided like a swan in the direction of her stepmother and stepbrother. Mr. Saunders was holding the door open, attendant upon the regal arrival. He had chased Rocky away from the stoop. Rocky and Frankie were standing to one side, knowingly staring. Alice paused and reached into her large flowery handbag, removing a compact and cigarette case. She looked at Frankie, his trombone in hand.

"Give us a toot." Alice requested a command street performance in demanding tones of imperial imperativeness.

"Alice, dear, the crowd, in public, you mustn't encourage..." whimpered Teddy, Jr., eldest son of the late great President, with a simper on his face.

"Encourage nothing... nonsense. The crowd loves it. I love it. Play!" Alice was forceful.

"What shall I play?" Frankie was the moveable object.

"You must know something! You must know... do you know "There'll Be a Hot Time in the Old Town Tonight?" Of course you do. Here goes,

'Come on along, Come on along... well? Get you ready, wear your brand new gown, la la la la... for there'll be a hot time in the old town tonight. Eh, Ted? A hot time?'"

"Yeah, I know it. We're gonna play it today in the parade." Frankie was nervous.

"Yes, quite rightly, but I shan't be present, you see." And turning to her stepbrother, "Maybe if they'd build a grandstand for dignitaries to observe the parade..." Alice's pale gray eyes were suddenly adrift at sea, gazing into the vortex of dull confinement to Oyster Bay. "You should take it up at the next village meeting, Teddy, if they do that sort of thing here." Alice giggled sardonically, shaking the dust and boredom of Sagamore Hill and Oyster Bay from her ruffled feathers.

Luigi Bollo grabbed Toots by the hand and jerked her over to the piano. "Come! Come! Sing! You musta singa. Louda, so they heara." There was a knock at the door just as Toots was opening her mouth as wide as a cottonmouth's unhinged jaws, on the verge of injecting from her fangs a dose of Verdi venom, into the neck of a disgruntled Luigi, who slammed his clawed fingers on the ivory keys and shouted, "Ahhh! Mama mia! Whata for now... justa momento waita momento pleasa! I coma nowa..." It sounded as if he said, "I come in a hour," which caused the knocker to knock twice as hard. Toots had closed the window to the studio to prevent this outburst from being heard outside on the street and disturbing the placid holiday atmosphere. It certainly would be disgraceful if the Roosevelts heard such accented commotion. My word, what would they say? Luigi, standing at the door, turned to face Toots. He was nearly beside himself again. "What! What! What for you close the window?... *Questo gabinetto puzza!* What smell in here now... open window please again..." Why so upset? Toots realized it was because of the person behind the door. Toots opened the window. Luigi opened the door. The frightened eyes of Mrs. Zipper and her son stared into the dark wrinkles of Luigi's brow. He clasped the top of his nose between his fingers; this is how Toscanini must have felt like. Luigi said, "Waita one momento pleasa; I hava udda studenta... justa momento pleasa... tankayoua..." He closed the door and turned around to face Toots. Toots was walking toward him, carrying her handbag and pulling her hat down over her piled black hair. Luigi was shaking his hands in front of his face as if an electric current was running through them. "Itsa thata litta boya wita hisa mama... sucha biga moutda...

she wanta thata hera sona be anudda Heifetz!... every Jew mama wanta sona to be a Heifetz... mama mia... I can no do the miracle... if no talenta, itsa impossibile... *fa schifo*... I saya to the mama maybe he can be anudda Gershwin!... Oh she go crazy angry at me... what I saya... I saya joke... funny thinga... *mama mia*... *testardo*!..." Toots kept putting her erect finger to her mouth, tapping her lips. "Shhhh... hush... she will hear you. Then you will lose a student. And money."

"I no care... I am the pride hava..."

Toots said hush once again and then opened the door. She nodded politely to mother and son. "Goodbye Mr. Bollo. See you next week," Toots said and gave a wink.

"Ciao," said Luigi.

Luigi greeted Mrs. Zipper and son. The boy opened his violin case. "Pleasa beginna wita scales," said Luigi to little Herman. Mrs. Zipper then proceeded to take ten minutes of Herman's precious instruction time informing an exasperated Luigi of her precise itinerary over the next hour just in case of some unforeseen disaster requiring her immediate presence. "What can happen?" said Luigi, "maybe hisa fingers get stucka in the strings." Luigi cackled. Mrs. Zipper looked into his eyes in utter belief. In Mrs. Zipper's eyes, for a single brief horrible moment, Luigi had been transformed into Chico Marx, one of those Marx Brothers whom her husband had taken her to see on Broadway. It was awful. She shuddered at the vile possibilities. Luigi nearly had to extract her from the studio like a decayed tooth. Finally, she relented and reluctantly reached the door. Luigi held the door more than slightly ajar.

"Practice hard Herman darling... You'll be another Heifetz!" And with that weekly exhortation and prognostication out of the way, she sneered at Luigi and left the room. Luigi smiled at the boy. "Very good..." he said, and whispered, "very good, Mista Gershwin..."

Herman dragged the bow back and forth, scratching and screeching; and in spite of the stuffy smelly room, Luigi went over to the window and shut it. Little Herman would grow up to become a traveling salesman. In the 1950s he became a good friend of the Cazzaza family, especially Fiorenza, who was laid up in bed by that time. She only purchased a few items but he still came around. He also befriended Joe Cazzaza and Torhild. They bought some furniture and stuff, and Herman came around with lollipops for the kids. On several occasions Herman invited the family on boat trips up the Hudson River to Bear Mountain. Joe and Torhild and their children were on board a boat with a hundred elderly Jewish couples, all dancing to a brass band playing everything from *Havah'n'gilva* to *Hello Dolly*. And Joe Cazzaza always pointed out West Point and Sing Sing prison from the boat for Stephen… on the Hudson River…

Luigi stood at the window, looking down to the street. He saw Toots cross the street and enter the dark alleyway. The shiny roof of the car was glittering below. Alice Roosevelt Longworth opened her cigarette case. Abruptly snapped it shut. "Horror. Nearly depleted." She looked at Frankie, and smiling suddenly snaggled-toothed, dipped into her purse with nicotine fingers. "Be a noble boy and run over and get me a pack of cigarettes. I prefer Lucky Strikes. But Viceroys, Chesterfields, Pall Mall will do. Whichever. Do hurry."

Alice had appeared on the cover of *Time* promoting Lucky Strikes. "It would be an honor," said Frankie, disbelieving that he had said such a ludicrous thing. Frankie took the money and scooted across the street. A car honked its horn as he dashed in front. He was nearly struck.

"Oh how awful," said Edith Roosevelt, "such commotion, really Alice." Edith turned tail, performing a sudden volte-face, and entered the pharmacy.

"Good morning, Mrs. Roosevelt," said Mr. Saunders holding the door. Edith walked into the store, passing the telephone on the wall. She looked at the repugnant device with disdain. The first telephone in Oyster Bay had been placed in Saunder's. Edith Roosevelt did not appreciate the far-reaching social implications of a telephone. Serenely cloistered behind the purple pedestal of her ringleader husband, his big stick in hand, taming the upstart lions of the world, she had purred while he mewed and mewled and yelped and roared, driving his fist into the imperialist stigmata in his palm. Theodore Rex threw logs on the fire of the new Empire, dictating the White Man's Burden to the lowly, and threw logs on the tribal campfires in the meadows around Sagamore Hill, reading stories to his children. He had gravitated toward glory and honor like a crafty politician toward a baby. And though Alice had fanatically doted on her father, defending him with her unretractable claws, carrying his vainglorious torch ever onward after his death, Edith just plainly adored him, indulging his boyish excesses, soothing his boo-booed ego, humoring him as a spirited boy who whines that he wants to go out to play, playing cowboy in the Badlands, playing soldier in Cuba, later coming home scratched and bruised and bloody. And when he did come home such one time, little Alice screamed and ran, while Edith, distinctly bored, calmly urged him to do his bleeding in the bathroom.

Edith Roosevelt was making a rare appearance in town. One of her essential stops was Saunder's drugstore. Saunder's was established in 1881, as the sign hanging out over the door indicates in chemical blue lettering. The Roosevelts have been regular clients since its pestle and mortar inception; and the noble patroness of Sagamore Hill continues to confer her meretricious patronage to the local shopkeeper for the sake of historical contiguity and future amenities.

When the telephone was installed in Saunder's it had the distinction of being the numerical progenitor and Ur-sprache generator of all the subsequent staccato series of numerically induced discourses that disembodied forth in the village like steam from a hot tarred roof after rain. Saunder's telephone number was simply 1. The Cazzaza Fruit and Vegetable Store was 200. In such a way had egalitarianism and technology taken root together in a garden of tomatoes and grape vines by a brick wall, a concrete and steel pedogenesis, and the ever-spreading vines, a pedigree of mutts; and between 1 and 200, somewhere in that circuitous rigmarole of wires and sounds, numbers propagating ad infinitum, numbers of the people, for the people, the number of the Roosevelts was listed with all the hyphenated Americans, only another series of hyphenated numbers.

Edith Roosevelt detested the clanging, clicking, clacking, clattering, clamorous object; makes one wonder how she ever tolerated her husband, whose mental persona embodied the very dialectic of the telephone, to be where one is not, the incarnation of multitudinous natural forces being joined together at an eruption point of verbalized volcanics, spewing forth steam, venting a network of streaming lava across the jungles of the world. To be where one does not belong, selling glass beads and crucifixes, emitting the Word through a whirlwind of savior speech and a holocaust of brimstone, turning the tides of history, to the eternal credit of muscular Christianity and the ultimate profit of capitalism. A telephone had been installed at Sagamore Hill, in a pantry filled with large barrels of sugar and flour, after Roosevelt ascended to the presidency. Previously, the messages had been relayed by means of bicycle from Oyster Bay. After Roosevelt left office Edith rallied 'round the telephone pole for the telephone's removal, but the children voiced objections and the telephone remained.

Alice got back into the car and powered her nose. Frankie went into his father's store to buy the cigarettes. He didn't exactly buy them, which is why he went into his father's store instead of the stationery; it was easier to steal them from papa's store. He also stole a pack of Chesterfields for himself and Rocky. He ran back across the street to the parked car and handed two packs of Viceroys to Alice, who had rolled down the window, taking the cigarettes into her now gloved hands.

"Two packs? I asked for one. I gave you the money for one pack." Alice was brusque.

"Ah... ah..." Frankie faltered. "A gift from my father," he plucked up his courage. "That's his store." Frankie smiled, returning her the money.

"Well, thank you for that bit of news; I'm sure it's a fine store too." Alice wasted enough words on this... this... nameless, or if he has a name it probably ends in a horrible vowel; she took the packs of cigarettes and quickly rolled up the window. Frankie was taken aback. He had expected a small token of her gratitude but got short changed to the going rate of zilch.

"The bitch," he muttered to himself, turning away from the car, "and why not say it, that's what they call her in Washington, right? That's what Uncle Maurizio said." Such was the assumption and assessment regarding Alice by the everyday folk on the public pedestrian thoroughfares of Oyster Bay; that's if anyone even happened to mention her name; she and her hat being old hat by now. With Babe Ruth, Jack Dempsey, Charles Lindbergh, Bill Tilden, Bobby Jones, who gave a hoot or a deuce about anything that smacked of politics and smug, snooty, society bores. Working-class, lower middle-class downtown Oyster Bay hamlet was surrounded by these aloofish hoity-toity ritzy wood's dwellers who lived on something called estates; and the plain folk in the village were too caught up in sports, crime reports, and adventure stories related in tabloid newspapers and magazines; singers and comedians on radio; movie stars on the big screen in the movie house located on Audrey Avenue, called The Lyric, to listen to the dull rooty-toot-toot of a Calvin Coolidge and his ilk.

The tall chauffeur looked down at Frankie. "Nice try, kid."

"Babe Ruth wuddinov dunit. He wudda given me the loot, huh?" Frankie whined.

"Sure thing, kid. And hit a homer for ya too," said the chauffeur. Frankie's original plan was to steal just one pack, pocket the money but for a nickel in change that he would have given to Alice Roosevelt. Then he thought that maybe if he brought her two packs and returned to her her money, saying that the two packs were a gift from his father, maybe she would have told him to keep the money anyway, not having to give her the change back.

"Fat chance," thought Frankie.

"Fat chance," thought Alice, detecting his ploy. "Scheming little street urchin. Riff-raff." She rolled down the window just far enough to stick out into the rarified air the tip of her cigarette, unclenched from her never-sealed lips.

Alice made a sucking sound to draw the attention of the chauffeur.

"Yes, madam." He snapped open a lighter and held it up to the cigarette. Puffs of smoke billowed over the roof of the car. "How nice," said Alice.

Frankie Cazzaza put his trombone back into its case. He and Rocky were greeted by their friend Elia, who was carrying a bunch of bocce balls in a burlap sack. The three of them crossed the street and entered the stationery, from which Rocky stole a black squirt gun from off the metal-spoke spinable rack while Frankie and Elia distracted Sid Schwartz.

Alice, who was sitting in the car, gestured to Teddy, Jr. with a slightly noticeable come-hither hand mannerism. Teddy, Jr. noticed and went thither to the window of the car.

"Don't forget er... you know... now that your mother... before she returns... you know what to say now, don't you? Is Greta home?" Alice punctuated her truncated sentence with hard drags and puffs on her cigarette, and emphasized the words "your mother." Teddy, Jr. closed his eyes and took a deep breath, held it longer than the prescribed duration, then exhaled dragon flame from his nostrils. "If the Speaker is to speak," added Alice dryly, or perhaps, wetly, "he must be fortified; and the magazines and newspapers, don't forget." The Speaker in question is charming, bald, mustachioed Nick, Alice's lecherous hubby.

Teddy, Jr. crossed the street, smiling and bidding "Good morning" to all and sundry. He was the only Roosevelt who made frequent excursions into the village, buying a newspaper, posting a letter, becoming a familiar fixture in town, as Alice had become a familiar fixture in Washington, to her sometimes dismay. Teddy, Jr. was to inherit Sagamore Hill, but by 1937 he and his wife had been married twenty-seven years, tired of living in rented houses. They decided to build a Georgian styled house in the old apple orchard on the Sagamore Hill property. Like his father, he served as Assistant Secretary to the Navy, but unlike his father he never had the opportunity of fitting out Dewy's squadron of ships in the Philippines; he only got the chance to serve in the unheroic post of Governor of the Philippines. He was planning a Field Museum expedition to Asia in 1928. To escape loss and defeat? A Roosevelt trait. Like his father. He was always being compare to his father. Hadn't Theodore escaped from the loss and sorrow of his first wife's and mother's death by taking to the wilds of North Dakota? Back in 1924, Teddy, Jr. had been nominated to run for Governor of New York by the Republicans to oppose the incumbent Democrat Alfred E. Smith, who had been nominated by none other than that traitor and renegade and maverick, Franklin D. Roosevelt. Smith had won the election in New York despite the Republican landslide in the presidential election. Calvin Coolidge (he looked as if he had been weaned on a pickle, observed the ever observant Alice) defeated John W. Davis, a former congressman from West Virginia. There developed more bad blood between the Roosevelt tribes. Alice's husband, a poker-playing chum of Teddy, Jr. and the late President Warren Harding, had added his two cents to the feud by calling Franklin a "denatured Roosevelt."

Ticky-Tacky in Babylon

Alice Roosevelt Longworth was sitting in the car parked in front of Saunder's Pharmacy. She was thinking about the rumors that have been going around Washington that Warren Harding had had an affair with some mid-western tart that had bore Harding a child.

"Revolting..." said Alice, furiously to herself, speculating about the woman who allegedly had been the mistress of President Warren Gamaliel Harding, and who allegedly had given birth to his daughter, out of wedlock, and who allegedly spent many moments exploring old Warren's body in a large closet in the White House. "Disgusting, a humdinger for the masses. Revolting," Alice pronounced her verdict on the rumor that she knew was certainly true. Alice's father may have explored Amazonian rivers, his hands may have explored the cold contours of a gun, but certainly never

269

the warm flesh of a woman, a mistress, it's just unthinkable. Though there were rumors of that one time in Albany when he was Governor...

"Harding! That indolent slob!" said Alice, the insolent snob. "I still believe he had nigger blood... like that professor wrote, you know they destroyed his book and burned every copy... and he had many a dalliance unreported..."

In 1927 the dregs of the Teapot Dome scandal were dripping on newspapers like so much spilt coffee. They vomit their gall and put it in a newspaper, said the German philosopher Nietzsche. There was a lot of political puking going on in Washington. Legal action was under way. The story was coming serially and sensationally to yellow light. Harding's drinking binges and gambling sprees, his adultery, his bastard child, his peculiar death (a Broadway play based on a novel speculated his death was a suicide), his Ohio gang of poker playing corrupt cronies, secret liaisons and trysts, low intrigue, all good copy for newspaper fodder, and dirt, much more awaited, that Alice, despite herself, ardently wished for and the press was certain to deliver. Of course, Harding significantly lowered taxes for the rich.... that, at least, was a good and decent thing to do.

Hail hail the gang's all here... my God how the money rolls in... yes, we have no bananas... but we have plenty of rotten apples: Daugherty, Fall, McLean, Sinclair, Doheny, Forbes, the gang's all here. You scratch Harding's hump, Harding scratch yours. The spoils system run amuck. Harding got the Republican nomination in Chicago in 1920, while the back room boys and the big oil men maneuvered for their candidates, one of which was General Leonard Wood, Theodore Roosevelt's old buddy from the Spanish-American War, who was discarded as too fickle, that is he couldn't be bought, unless the price was patriotic, and proselytizing for war preparedness when the country was exhausted from war and tired of the idealist Wilson and needed some time to get back to business, make some normal money... but not at the risk of putting the country's oil reserves at risk, so Wood unleashed his riding crop from under his arm and chased the men with the money touch out of his room. He was done for. The oilmen knew for certain that Harding was their man. Harding could easily be distracted by cigars and poker and women. Chicago was the right place for the convention. The Volstead Act and the Black Sox scandal brought a dubious recognition of the city's charms. Harding kept his mouth shut and sat on his log like a turtle until his handlers pushed him into the water, and he then fled to his assignation with his twenty-three-year-old mistress, Nan Britton, in a hotel room. When the checks were written and the oilmen delivered the verdict, Harding was hung-over and messily attired. He was cleaned up and was asked once and for all: do you got nigger blood?" He defiantly and proudly intoned: No, I am a Caucasian! And Harding was whisked away from his hotel, leaving his mistress and illegitimate child in a room, to step into history, such as it is. Harding got the nomination and was subsequently elected President by a landslide over the Democratic candidate, Governor James Cox of Ohio, whose running mate was the Assistant Secretary of the Navy, Franklin D. Roosevelt of New York. Harding had promised a "return to normalcy." No more archangel great men for America, only a gang of men behind the genial, urbane front-porch speaking man from Ohio.

Woodrow Wilson had unwillingly led isolationist America into a foreign entanglement, and tried to entangle America even more in an unnatural alliance called the League of Nations. Alice Roosevelt Longworth led a self-proclaimed Battalion of Death, anti-leaguers, Republican stalwarts, warts and all, which included among its ranks Warren G. Harding and the ancient Senator (and in this case the origins of that term fully applied) Henry Cabot Lodge, who had been Theodore's best friend, against Wilson, and by extension through panic-stricken logic, against Bolsheviks and radicals, now that the Hun was demolished. The Battalion mustered all its cunning like a hunting pack and chewed up Wilson's league like so much grizzle, voting it down in the Senate. Wilson and the Democrats were defeated. If Theodore had still been alive, he would have swung from the rafters. The Battalion of Death led by the Great White Hunter Henry Cabot Lodge and his pack of dogs had put upon the wolves and brought them down like the vermin they were. And with radicalism in the air, with 3,000 strikes in 1919, the wolves would soon be on the run. "The beast of waste and desolation," Roosevelt called the wolf, no doubt the same could be said for the radicals that roamed the land, inspired by such vermin as Leon Trotsky and Emma Goldman. Unions and strikes. International inspired bolshevism, no doubt. And now strikes and bombs and riots... something's awry. True patriots saw red. The Red Scare of 1919. The Red Menace. Wilson's Attorney General, A. Mitchell Palmer, aimed to inveigle himself into the good auspices of the big capitalists by badgering and marauding the radicals with total disregard of legality, habeas corpus, search warrants, and especially radicals of foreign birth. Hundreds of United States Department of Justice agents were broadcast throughout the land like so much seed. They recruited local police and judicial authorities and super-patriot groups such as the American Legion and Daughters of the American Revolution. "Save our institutions from the Bolsheviks! Our institutions are in danger! Save the flag!" Palmer was a confessed Quaker, certainly one of the most darkly vehement in the annals of the Children of the Light.

As the Attorney General, Palmer was first law officer of the United States. He became a paranoid witch hunter; he commanded and condoned raids on magazine offices, union headquarters, private homes, public meeting halls; attacking socialists, freethinkers, atheists, social workers, liberals, and anarchists with frenzied "fighting Quaker" oxymoronic gusto. The hysteria led to sharp sudden revisions of the immigration laws; the pace of immigrants from eastern and southern Europe slowed like a redneck's molasses from a shotgun barrel. Deportation from Ellis Island surpassed in numbers those immigrants who were coming into the country. The innate Anglo-Saxon-Aryan Christian panic syndrome bred the resurgence of the Ku Klux Klan. The newly elected Harding promised to hunt down the Reds. Normalcy.

And then there was oil. Oil entered the world stage of international barter and booty during the conservationist movement of Theodore Roosevelt's presidency, with the likes of Gifford Pinchot and those other conservationists like Madison Grant, a friend of Roosevelt and author of *The Passing of the Great Race*, a book that Hitler called his bible, but Hitler had blood and soil, the Americans had to plant the flag in soil and make blood flow in order to believe in their American Ideals, these men who when peeling back their green shirt revealed a little too much brown shirt underneath. Liquid gold (America already had all the real gold) was essential to the bedrock of a modern navy. And Theodore loved his navy. Roosevelt's handpicked successor William Howard Taft, by executive order, in 1912 created an oil reserve for emergency use by the navy at Teapot Dome, Wyoming. In 1915 President Wilson set aside another reserve at Elk Hills, California; rather that than give up for quarry all the petroleum resources of the West to predatory private exploiters. Not much came of it until someone struck it heavy on the edge of the Elk Hills reserve. Congress acted by placing the management of the region in the hands of the Secretary of the Navy, that almost signature post of a

Roosevelt; his name was Josephus Daniels, who belonged to Wilson's Cabinet, and who was considered to be a feeble-minded pacifist. But before Daniels could take a shot at it, his navy duck quacked its last, because Wilson was out and Harding was in. Harding replaced Daniels with Edwin Denby, who turned out to be a naive numbskull who was easily convinced by Albert Fall, the Secretary of the Interior (Harding at first wanted him for Secretary of State), to cede the lands to Fall's department. Harding signed an executive order in May 1921 and the lands were transferred. Assistant Secretary of the Navy, Theodore Roosevelt Jr., acted as a messenger between the Navy Department and the Interior Department. Roosevelt Jr. had been a director at Sinclair Oil. Roosevelt liked Albert Fall, reminded him of his dear old Pa. Fall was a Stetson wearing frontiersman with a six-shooter strapped to his waist.

Denby didn't want to have to deal with such vast oil reserves, with no war in sight, except possibly with Japan. Throughout the 1920s the Navy Department feared that Japan's ambition was commercial and political dominance over the Far East. If America stuck to its course, to its commitments in the Pacific, the two countries seemed aligned for some serious imperialistic battleship head butting. The Navy Department was both suspicious and honorably attentive of Japan. But a war with Japan seemed as unlikely as a war with Mars, said the skeptical Senator Thomas J. Walsh of Montana as late as 1928. Nevertheless, American admirals positioned most of the fleet in the Pacific. This was no Teddy Roosevelt Great White Fleet Tour of the World in the service of rendering the American peace of righteousness to the world. This was the American Presence delivering a message to the Japanese. Though in fact Roosevelt delivered the same message with his navy tour, that the Pacific was as much America's waters as the Atlantic, and that our fleet could and would at will pass from one to the other of the two great oceans. "In private I said that I did not believe Japan would so regard it (as a threat) because Japan knew my sincere friendship and admiration for her and realized that we could not as a Nation have any intention of attacking her; and that if there were any such feeling on the part of Japan as was alleged that very fact rendered imperative that that fleet should go." Ah the subtle pre-emptive reasoning of righteousness!

So the fleet went to the Pacific and the Admirals coyly appealed to a somewhat historical bias in the Congress by hinting that the money was needed as defense against the British. Didn't we just fight a war alongside them? To save the world for democracy? Or was Trotsky nearer the mark in saying that we fought it to save J. P. Morgan's loans to the allies?

Anyway, it was Albert Fall's intention to hand over Teapot Dome to private developers in return for both a cut of the oil and storage tanks, to be built and filled when the Navy required them for their hypothetical war. Albert Fall promptly leased these defense properties to private oilmen. If the Navy needed them, they were there. Preparedness. Ready for any threat from a potential enemy like Japan. Made even more potential because of the Immigration Act of 1924 that excluded the Japanese from citizenship and provoked "Hate America" demonstrations and a "Humiliation Day" in Tokyo. There were oil storages in Pearl Harbor, must be careful... but haven't we had enough of war and leagues... can't we just have some plain old normalcy. Let the back room boys and the good folks of America make some hard honest cash. So Fall's shifty shifting of the two oil lands into the private sector was overlooked. But oops! Fall had taken a slice off the top of the American apple pie for personal profit: thousands from Teapot, thousands from Elks Hills.

He who owns the oil will own the world, said a French oil commissioner. The allies floated to victory on a wave of oil, said Lord Curzon, Viceroy of India. "Standard Oil, Standard Oil, turns the darkness into light," went the ditty, sung by the fat Colonel Stewart, president of Standard Oil of Indiana; he had been one of Teddy's boys, another former Rough Rider, the supreme business showman: Colonel Bob. Oil was on everyone's mind, spurting from a dunce cap of greed, and lubricating every grubby white palm.

Warren G. Harding had been churned out from Mark Hanna's political machine in Ohio. Assisted by the mighty organization of Senator Joseph B. Foraker, which had connections to Standard Oil Company, Harding had won two terms in the Ohio Senate. He was tall and handsome, with fine oratorical skills. Harry M. Daugherty, a lobbyist, became his private groomer. In 1915 Harding was elected to the U.S. Senate, where he remained until he was nominated for President in 1920. Chosen in a "smoke-filled room," as the legend goes. In that year, the nomination meant certain election. He was a "dark horse" winner over the more likely General Leonard Wood and Governor Frank Lowden, but both were eliminated when it became known that their campaigns had been heavily financed by big corporations. Harding's Cabinet was called the "Oil Administration." Gulf Oil's owner Andrew Mellon as Secretary of the Treasury; Standard Oil attorney Charles Evans Hughs as Secretary of State; Sinclair Oil attorney Will Hays as Postmaster General; and Albert Fall as Secretary of the Interior and keeper of public lands.

In 1923 the Senate called for an investigation of "irregularities" in the Veteran's Bureau. It had been cheated of hefty dollars by its chief administrator, Charles Forbes, a builder from Spokane, Washington. Forbes had been awarded the Congressional Medal of Honor, was an apostate Wilson Democrat who shifted allegiance to Harding. He had misdealt into his own and his chums' grasping hands millions of dollars, peddling surplus war supplies, drugs, and hospital equipment. He was the only hood to publicly emerge during Harding's lifetime. "I have no troubles with my enemies," said Harding, "I can take care of my enemies all right, but my damn friends! That yellow rat... double-crossing bastard..." as Harding so aptly described his friend, before sending him off to Europe, where Forbes resigned. He was later imprisoned. Harding was surrounded by small time hoods, swindlers, cheaters, bilkers, con men, chiselers, and scoundrels of sycophantic ilk. The Goths and the Vandals took the handles. American Normalcy. When the general consul to the Veteran's Bureau, Charles Cramer, shot himself in the head... something was certainly happening here but you don't know what it is, do you, Mister Man in the Street? It was Senator Robert La Folette of Wisconsin who asked for the Senate investigation. Senator Walsh of Montana was assigned the job of checking into the "irregularities." Meanwhile other friends from Ohio that Harding had brought to Washington filched from the tills. The number of lesser pork chops was legion. The fat just trickled down. The bitter leaves of the Teapot Dome scandal were infused through a secret mesh of government; and the teapot would not be left to steep in its own muck. It was shook like a beehive, and the bees came out stinging themselves and each other like suicidal kamikaze pilots. There were accusations, double-crossings, and battles in court, confessions, slanders, lies and more lies. At first the teapot simmered, but then it boiled, and all Washington broke loose over the placid Calvin Coolidge. Spillage and seepage, a blood letting that flooded the streets of the unholy capital city. But it wasn't blood or water that flowed from the sliced veins in the arms of the accused, it was oil and greed and profit... normalcy. Larceny on a grand scale. Good old boys, poker players, that old gang of mine, repaid in kind for their patronage of Harding. Other players included Jesse Smith, a dry goods dealer from Ohio, a fixer, a buddy of Hardings, a sidekick of Daugherty, a thief in the Justice Department, and a runner with the rich and powerful. He also shot himself in the head. Not very Roman. Very American. They behaved more like a gang of bankrupt shopkeepers. Harry Micajah Daugherty, once a chairman of the Ohio State Republican Committee, who had nominated McKinley for governor in 1893, and had lost an election for governor of Ohio, now a lever on a fulcrum of ambition, a man behind the scenes for other more eligible candidates, a proxy man. Harding made him the Attorney General. Daugherty in turn made the extremely corrupt William J. Burns head of the Bureau of Investigation. A determined Theodore Roosevelt inaugurated the Bureau of Investigation in 1908. He believed that there should be a Federal device by which the government could enforce Federal law. The Bureau of Investigation (renamed the Federal Bureau of Investigation in 1935) didn't become effective until 1924, when the anti-vice device J. Edgar Hoover was made director by the Coolidge appointed Attorney General, Harlan F. Stone.

Edward L. Doheny and Harry Sinclair, dough bosses, not doughboys, were two of the oilmen who were awarded the leases by Albert Fall and the Interior Department. Doheny had taken a lease on Naval Reserve Number One at Elk Hills, and Harry Sinclair had taken a lease on Naval Reserve Number Three at Teapot Dome. Both were brought as witnesses before the Senate subcommittee headed by Thomas J. Walsh. Walsh would later run for president in 1928. An Irish Catholic Dry Democrat... from Montana! A westerner! That freed him from the tag of urban corruption that Alfred E. Smith carried, being from New York, and the legacy of Tammany Hall. But as was said at the time, "Al Smith is head of an organization that has collected much more graft than that involved in Teapot Dome." But the honest man Smith had risen through Tammany. Smith trounced Walsh in the California primary, and that was that. And then Herbert Hoover trounced Smith, and that was that. 21,391,000 votes for Hoover; 15,016,000 for Smith; and 300,000 for Norman Thomas, the Socialist candidate, and that was that. And then Wall Street laid an egg, and that was that.

Doheny and Sinclair declared that the leases were in the best interest of the government and the Nation. That was that. The usual ploy. No one questions that interest unless he dares to be called un-American; no one dares suggest that just possibly it's in the interest of special interests. Unthinkable questions! The Senate hearings got stuck in a quagmire. But then Fall was asked to make some reckoning of the sudden money-spending ardor that he was displaying on his ranch, Three Rivers, in New Mexico. Fall used the tactic of the establishment's scoundrel, he stalled for loopholes; he than sent the subcommittee a letter explaining that he had borrowed $100,000 from Ned McLean, and adding that he had never approached Doheny or Sinclair... nor received from either, one cent on account of any oil lease. Ned McLean owned the Washington Post; his wife owned the Hope Diamond, with the curse. McLean was another poker playing crony. A dandy. And (surprise) none other than the notorious anti-red red-baiter himself, A. Mitchell Palmer, was McLean's lawyer. As it turned out McLean had yesindeedy given Fall checks totaling $100,00. The only problem was that they were returned uncashed. No loan. The truth was out. Doheny and Sinclair had paid off Fall for their leases. Fall, fell. He was ultimately fined $100,000 (prosaic justice), and spent around a year up the river. Through the whole scandal, 1923-1930, there had been ransacking and hounding and harassing and harrying; frame-ups, tampering, perjury, suicides. Enumeration sins to enumerate to enumerate. Could be Harding had been killed after all. A loosely veiled picture based on Washington gossip about the "Ohio Gang," called "Revelry," was published in 1926, after all was not said and not done, written by a flapper and dime novelist, in which Alice Roosevelt Longworth appears as Edith Westervelt, who endeavors to reform the tactless chief of state. But he was simply a slob.

In 1923 Harding dropped dead in San Francisco. He suffered an attack of embolism from crabmeat that others had eaten without becoming ill. He had a high fever; then he rallied; and suddenly death. Did his friends poison him? Did his wife do it to save him from disgrace? She refused to let an autopsy be conducted on her husband. The medical examiners report said that he died of a cerebral hemorrhage. He had been on a tour of Alaska, spreading the future ghost of oil over the cold snows. Much of the Teapot Dome scandal had not been disclosed at the time of his death, and the newspapers eulogized him as another Abraham Lincoln. I eulogize this space for words that I am inscribing here as another useless and pointless detour... ah history. Stuck a feather in his... why is any of this important?

American Kitsch and the Vulgar

The parade is coming... it won't be long now.

Alice Roosevelt Longworth turned and looked out through the small rear window of the car. In the empty air above the intersection of South Street and East Main Street she imagined that she was seeing three large banners hanging from one telephone pole across the street to another pole. Each telephone pole had three cross bars one above the other toward the top, with small round knobs spread across the bar like... like nothing else; no referent in nature; new metaphors would be needed for an artificial, alien, machine world. In 1912 Alice had indeed actually seen three banners strung across the street: a large oblong piece of cloth hung high above two other banners. Portraits of two men wearing glasses stared across each other's field of vision from the confines of oval frames side by side in the middle of the banner, which was trimmed by a black edge and had two brightly painted American flags, simulating a waving motion, emerging from the outer edge of each framed portrait. The middle banner was a long thin strip of cloth with white letters that read:

FOR PRESIDENT   FOR VICE-PRESIDENT

WOODROW WILSON   THOMAS R. MARSHALL

The lower banner, another long thin strip, read:

FOR GOVERNOR   FOR UNITED STATES SENATE

SAMUEL TILBURY   WILLIAM McCOMBS

The banners had been put up for a parade during the Woodrow Wilson presidential campaign of 1912. The original Atlantic Steamer Fire Company's horse-drawn carriage marched in that parade, fully regaled with flags and flowers. Giuseppe had held the reins of the two gray workhorses. Giuseppe was a Roosevelt man all the way. It was the year Roosevelt formed the "Bull Moose" party, the National Republican Progressive party, advocating a "New Nationalism," a platform whose purpose was to place the complete power of the federal government behind a wide program of economic and social reform. It was the year that Roosevelt said, "My hat is in the ring." Wilson won, Roosevelt finished second, and William Howard Taft, with whom Roosevelt had had a fallen out, came in third. Eugene Debs, the Socialist, managed (or mis-managed, as a laughing capitalist might have it) a meager million votes. Debs would later be imprisoned, in 1918, for having made the outlandish suggestion, in an antiwar speech, that "the master class has always declared the wars; the subject class has always fought the battles." Such disloyal freedom of speech was not permitted under the Espionage Act of 1917. Debs was sentenced to a ten-year prison term. In 1920 he ran his presidential campaign from prison, running as convict #2273. Debs was released from prison on Christmas Day, 1921. He had been pardoned by Warren G. Harding. In the 1912 election the incumbent Taft was considered by Theodore Roosevelt to have good intentions but a feeble will. The mighty will of Roosevelt roared again and broke the Republican platform in two; he formed the Bull Moose Party. Toward the end of the bitter campaign Roosevelt was shot. The manuscript of his speech and his metal spectacle case diverted the bullet, preventing it from puncturing his right lung. But there was enough air in his mighty lungs and Roosevelt made the speech despite the undressed wound. He just had to talk. "It takes more than one bullet to kill a Bull Moose!"

Alice stared into the empty air over South Street. Banners for Wilson. Democrats! Of all the nerve. She never forgave the traitor town. Alice had been against Wilson as much as her cousin Eleanor had been for him. And now Eleanor and her disabled husband are plotting to get Alfred Smith elected President in 1928, and Franklin elected Governor of New York. Traitors one and all.

Mr. Saunders held the door open for Edith Roosevelt, who bid him adieu and reiterated her patent reminder to all local shopkeepers in general: "Remember to send it to the Roosevelts of Sagamore. None other."

"Of course, Mrs. Roosevelt. Thank you very much. Good day." How many times has Mr. Saunders heard her say it? As if he didn't know by now which Roosevelt was which. There were many Roosevelts living in the area at the time. Edith had even taken care to have all her towels monogrammed with "R of S," Roosevelts of Sagamore, just to be on the safe side, when the laundry was sent out.

The chauffeur took Edith's hand and led her to the car. He opened the door and Edith sat down beside Alice. "Where's Ted?"

"On an errand," replied Alice, in a tone both demure and abrupt, reluctant to provide any more information.

"Oh. What kind of err-..." But Alice cut her off.

"Dear cousin Eleanor has written an article for a magazine and I want to read what she has to say. Poor deluded misguided Eleanor wants Mr. Smith to be our next President. She's even quoting father to the effect that he looked forward to the day when a Catholic or a Jew would be president. Balderdash. Isn't it?"

"Oh," said the serene Edith, "I hope Mr. Saunders remembers to deliver the goods to the Roosevelts of Sagamore."

Alice, annoyed, "He hasn't made a mistake yet, has he? So don't worry."

"Oh, but you are mistaken child, there was that one time, when was it, Thee was President, possibly in 1905, 6, difficult to say... but..."

Alice, even more annoyed, "Do you realize that Mr. Smith could be president if Eleanor and her husband have their way!"

"Oh."

"Oh no, is more like it." Seeing that she was getting nowhere discussing politics, that in fact, Edith was quite beyond politics, and cared only for the management of her home, as she always has, even when her husband was president, Alice changed the topic. But talk she did. "I am thinking about the book. I'll just glance at it when its published… but who would publish it? The book by that woman with the child."

"Which child dear?"

"Harding's, naturally. Or maybe not so natural!" She chuckled.

Edith, stern of face, replied, "Oh."

"I must get back to the muck in Washington. I do miss it you know."

"Where's Ted?" said the protective mother of her natural child.

"I told you... he's on an errand, for me." said the stepchild.

"For you?"

"Magazines. Do you want to read it?"

"A magazine?"

"No! The book. The book about that slob Harding and his... mistress."

"Don't be so harsh. He was our President. And no thank you, I do not want to read that book."

"Of course, I forgot, you prefer your Gypsies." Edith Roosevelt had a fondness for the novels of an obscure English travel writer and philologist, George Borrow, who had written several semi-autobiographical fictional accounts of his wanderings with the Romany Gypsy. Edith's favorite, *Lavengro*, was published in 1851. *Lavengro* relates the vagabond travels of a young man who becomes intimate with a band of Gypsies. In fact, Edith had traveled to the Yucatan in 1925, and just this past February had returned from a trip to Argentina and Brazil, complaining of "heart problems."

"I hope all this sordid business with Harding will be done with soon, once and for all," remarked Edith, daring a topical comment. Edith and Alice were silent a moment, both reflecting on the fact that Teddy, Jr. and his brother Archie, an employee of Harry Sinclair's company, had both been inadvertently sprayed by the tea from the Teapot Dome scandal. And also Alice's husband Nick Longworth, who had played poker with Harding and his "Ohio Gang."

"His wife is dead," said Edith, out of the blissful blue.

"The Duchess, he called her," added Alice. "Florence Kling de Wolfe. She was so Midwestern, like him. German background, superstitious, shabby, overbearing, punctual, except for one occasion: when her son was born just six months after her wedding..."

"Oh." Edith continued her one word barrage against a gossip's onslaught. Alice could string adjectives together like the pearls around her neck.

"...with her first husband that is; not Harding."

"The poor woman is dead. Let's not speak ill of the dead," said Edith. There was a pause in the noise.

"Flesh and The Devil," said Alice.

"What?" asked Edith. What is she talking about?

"Didn't you see the marquee at the Lyric Theatre? It's a new photoplay... moving picture, with that foreigner Greta Garbo. Her real name is Gustaffson. Do you know that she's romantically involved with John Gilbert, her co-star. The so-called perfect lover. I know for a fact that Gilbert was once so poor that he had eaten out of garbage cans. They are both uneducated. To be expected from the vacuous poisons of Hollywood. Jews and Reds. Palmer tried to clean up the Reds; and Mr. Hays is cleaning up morals in Hollywood; I don't believe he will be able to clean up the tainted money. Money buys morality in Hollywood, whichever way you want it. Gilbert is twice divorced. A drunk. Conceited. Uncivilized. Immature. Spoiled. I have heard it for a fact. Shall we see it? I hear they make love on a raccoon coat! Very racy."

"No thank you. I prefer my racy Gypsies, as you know. Anyway, the stage is more to my liking and..."

"Father preferred Sarah Bernhardt," chatterbox Alice interrupted. "Real name: Rosine Bernard."

"Oohh," said Edith, extending the length of the vowel sound into a tone of curiosity. Alice had finally touched a nerve.

"Father always saw her when he went abroad. Isn't that correct?" Alice prodded at the nerve.

"She was a good friend," was all Edith had to say on the matter.

"She was his oldest and best friend there... do you remember what she said?" Edith was more concerned that Mr. Saunder's remembered which Roosevelt was which. But Alice didn't let up, "Sarah Bernhardt said that father and her could rule the world if they... ever uh... got together, shall I say."

"Your father wasn't interested in ruling the world," Edith's voice heightened in pitch, "contrary to what the anti-imperialists were saying at the time, or getting together with... with..."

"The Divine Sarah?" Alice suggested.

"He just wanted America to take its rightful place as leader of the world." Edith's words halted Alice's stampede and turned her mind to other more pressing matters.

"Quite right... and if Wilson's type and Eleanor and her husband have their way, America will lose her liberty and her rightful voice as leader..." On that point mother and stepdaughter agreed and silence reigned for a moment, as they both contemplated the vast amorphous glories of American liberty. Henry James once remarked that Theodore Roosevelt was the "monstrous embodiment of unprecedented and resounding noise." Roosevelt referred to James as a "miserable little snob." Alice was both noise and snob. In Washington she had delighted in brandishing her wit like a royal sword. She and the Duchess Harding had been on none too smooth terms. Duchess Harding didn't want Alice near the White House. All that Rooseveltian noise. But the Duchess Harding never advised the heedless "Alice in Washington" as another Duchess had advised Alice in Wonderland: "Take care of the sense and the sounds will take care of themselves." Only the tactful Edith minimized the noise level and kept sense in her own domestic vision, while her husband made all the noise and disregarded the sense.

Sid Schwartz stood in the doorway to the stationery, hands in pockets, rattling coins. "Good morning, Mr. Roosevelt," said Sid Schwartz to Teddy, Jr. Nothing more was said, nothing more was required or expected. It had become a custom that those who lived in the village never said anything more to a Roosevelt than a simple civil Good morning.

Exiting the stationery with several newspapers and magazines under his arms, Teddy, Jr. looked across the street into the eyes of Alice. Alice nodded her head. Teddy, Jr. understood the unspoken signal. He turned around and went into the dark alleyway. He walked pass the water-tower and climbed up an enclosed stairway built onto the exterior of the building, and reaching the top, knocked three times on the door and said, "Is Greta home?"

Alice was fidgeting with a nervous mantic energy. Unable to be still, unable to be quiet. The unflappable Edith said, "Have you been to your dentist lately?"

"What do you mean?" Alice bit back. It had been rumored that Alice had become addicted to cocaine that her dentist proscribed for her in pain-killing doses. Edith didn't pursue this line of questioning.

"Why does Ted take so long to buy a few newspapers and magazines?" Edith asked herself.

"He likes to mingle with the people. They like him... speaking of newspapers, this new tabloid *The Daily News*, well not so new anymore, about six or seven years old now I guess... anyway, it has all the dirt on this murder case..."

"Oh," said Edith, automatically.

"That woman... that Snyder woman... Norwegian background, Viking blood I suppose, ruthless woman; oh her name is Ruth, Ruth the Ruthless, good spreadhead, yes, I must suggest it to a publisher. It's in the papers everyday. *The Daily Mirror*, the new Hearst paper, oh that wretched man, with his Ziegfeld girl, she's always in his newspapers, every edition, he ordered his papers to do it; he's a dictator. Pompous. Arrogant. A yellow-belly rogue... but she has a stutter, poor girl, and now that the moving pictures will have sound, you do know about this, or so we are told, something with Jolson, her career is caput, as they might say in Hollywood, Jews and Huns and Reds..."

"I don't read newspapers."

"Of course, only Gypsies... anyway, the *Daily Graphic*, another recent New York paper; they call it Porno-Graphic; they are all vying for the trash. Publicity." Alice twittered like a parrot of private opinion, like a parrot on the shoulder of a pirate. "Everything public is polluted," Alice ventured.

"Oh."

"Ruth Snyder has a lover, a corset salesman of all things. She and her lover bashed in her husband's brains, tied a wire around his neck and..." Alice got excited relating the details.

"Don't be so graphic yourself. Alice Graphic."

"I'd make a hell of a reporter, would I not? I wonder if Hearst would hire me? No, I'd never betray father to that hound from hell."

"You are brutal today," said Edith.

"No more than usual. Fight fire with fire."

"What's the difference?" Edith queried, unexpectedly.

"My fire is righteous fire. My fire illuminates. His fire consumes."

"I see." Edith thought that about said it all, but it didn't, obviously, and Alice continued.

"And there was an insurance policy on Albert Snyder's life, that's Ruth's husband; it was discovered in a safe deposit box. The box was registered under her maiden name. She had a little book that listed the names of over twenty men. They arrested a man named Judd Grey. He is her paramour and co-murderer. And they both confessed. Both blamed each other for the murder. And just a few weeks ago the so-called bloody blonde, a flapper, and her lover, were convicted of murder..."

Edith wasn't following very closely the loose threads of Alice's words. But she heard enough to heave a heavy sigh and say, "What's this world coming to." Alice became morose.

"They'll get the chair," said Alice, somberly.

On January 22, 1928, Snyder and Grey got the chair. They were electrocuted at Sing Sing Prison. A photographer sitting in the front row had tied a camera to his ankle. He snapped the picture at the moment the switch was thrown. The next morning, the photograph covered the entire front page of the *New York Daily News*. "Ruth-Judd Bare All. That was one of the headlines, a double entendre, aren't the newspaper people clever, so witty," said Alice.

"So informal. As if they were on a first name basis with the public," offered Edith, suddenly alert.

"But that's the point, you see. That's how they sell papers. Dumb bell murders."

"What?" said Edith.

"Dumb bell murders. Runyon called it the 'dumb bell murders.'"

"Run what?" Edith was adrift.

"Oh I am shivering suddenly. Death. It's so cold."

"Death is cold did you say?"

"Goose bumps. Look. I'm cold." Alice held out her arm. Edith rubbed it gently. "Do you remember the bomb that went off at the Palmer house?" said Alice.

"Yes. The year your father died."

"That most horrible year in the history of our country. All those radicals; strikes, riots, dynamite. I thought it was the end of our shining Republic. Thank God we'll never have to face that again. Even Eleanor and her husband could never be that bad, I don't think."

"Of course not," said Edith.

"I hurried over to R Street. I wanted to see Eleanor and Franklin; if you remember they lived across the street from the Palmer house..."

"I remember," said Edith. There was a long pause.

"There was a leg in the path... and another leg all the way down the street... and a head... a head was on the roof of a house. Just bloody hunks of human flesh being strewn everywhere. The man had been blown to butcher's meat."

"Alice, please. So gruesome." said Edith.

"Yes, but it was gruesome. I can't forget it. Sometimes I have nightmares..." Alice began to cry softly.

"Poor dear, now, now you mustn't..." Edith tried to console her.

"It's the head I see in my dream... but it's not the head of the anarchist... the dead man... it's... it's..."

"What is it?

"It's father's head. I see father's head. And he speaks to me. Like a Sybil at Rome. He says, 'Come nearer dear Alice. Come nearer to me, my dear girl.' So I go nearer and nearer to him. And then he says, angrily, 'who are you? You are not my Alice! You are not my wife! Who are you?' And I run away. I run through the streets of Washington. It's like a great maze; and I can't get out. I can't find my way out." Alice put her head on Edith's shoulder and wept. Edith looked up and saw Teddy, Jr. coming out of the alleyway.

"Here's Ted now," said Edith, relieved. Alice lifted her head and quickly gathered her composure. "What was he doing back there?" Edith wondered.

Teddy, Jr. met the chauffeur in front of the entrance to the alleyway.

The chauffeur was standing with some children. Little Stevie Cazzaza was standing with his crutches by the red wagon. Little Luisa Cazzaza and her baby brother Joe were sitting in the wagon.

"Used to be the time I'd pick you up, son," said the tall chauffeur to little Stevie, "but you a big boy now." Stevie smiled and said nothing. "When you gonna lose them crutches?" said the chauffeur.

"I don't know, sir," said Stevie.

"You wanna run like the other children in the village, don't ya?"

"I'm a good swimmer."

"You can swim? I'll tell you a secret." And the tall black chauffeur bent down and whispered into Stevie's ear, "I can't swim. A big man like me." He tousled up Stevie's hair. "Don't you go and tell nobody. It be our secret. OK?" Stevie nodded.

Rocky filled his squirt gun with water drawn from the artesian well under the water-tower in the backyard. Then he chased Frankie and Elia into the alleyway, squirting water at them. Elia swung the burlap sack of bocce balls over his shoulder; and Frankie, running through the alleyway, accidentally smashed his trombone case against the brick wall. When the three boys came dashing out of the alleyway they saw Teddy Roosevelt, Jr. and the chauffeur standing on the sidewalk with the other children; the boys came to a frozen stop forthwith and stood at attention like statues. Rocky quickly hid the squirt gun behind his back and looked to see if Sid Schwartz was coming out of the paper store to catch him, perhaps having realized that Rocky stole the squirt gun. Teddy, Jr. looked at Frankie's trombone case. "For which band do you play, young man?"

"American Legion." answered Frankie.

"Do you now. That's splendid."

Frankie dropped out of high school three years ago; he had been a member of the high school marching band. The American Legion recruited him to play for them. He wouldn't be going to college; he wouldn't be leaving town; so why not do something to serve the community. He agreed, reluctantly, and his father had insisted. Frankie has been working part-time in his father's shop and part-time as a bartender in Hoffman's speakeasy at the top of the enclosed stairs behind the water tower. Giuseppe approves; these are hard times, and that Volstead Act is the most ridiculous thing; the one and only thing that ever caused Giuseppe to say a negative word about his adopted, and adoptive, homeland. Frankie also has a strong inclination to play poker and shoot craps and spends most of his nights in the basement of Belsen and White's, a large architecturally corrupt Victorian house on the corner of Hamilton Avenue and South Street with a wide encircling veranda and a convoluted rococo roof of numerous lewd long-tongue gargoyles that were commissioned by the management to be carved by Maurizio. There are slanting gables and dormers with always drawn curtained windows. There is gambling in the basement, drinking in the parlor, and whores upstairs. If the "summer White House" at Sagamore Hill was no longer representative of the White House in Washington, with its presiding puritan president, Calvin Coolidge, then Belsen and White's house was very much representative of the White House in Washington during the Harding Administration. Sagamore Hill had been replaced in national spirit by the Belsen and White's summer White House. The times were a-roaring.

Teddy, Jr. was looking at Frankie's trombone case nearly as intently as Frankie was looking at the rolled-up newspaper under Teddy, Jr.'s arm. Frankie knew exactly what was contained within the newspaper. "And what do you young men think about Mr. Lindbergh's airplane flight all the way to Paris across the Atlantic Ocean all by himself?" Teddy, Jr. asked.

"Wow," Rocky blurted out, "dat muss be as far as Connedakit." Rocky has never seen the ocean, only the Long Island Sound from the beach in Bayville. Rocky can't swim, in fact he fears the water, but sometimes he has an odd need to pour cold water over his head, after which he will laugh hysterically and jump about like a dervish.

"You stupid or sumptin," said Frankie to the dull-witted Rocky. "It's alot farder den dat. Ya can't see it if ya look over da wawder."

"I guess you boys have to make your way up to the Legion Hall; the parade will be getting under way soon; it won't be long now. So long children." said Teddy, Jr.; that was quite enough conversation with these dim-witted children of immigrants.

Teddy, Jr. and the chauffeur crossed the street together. The boys waved goodbye and walked up South Street. They began humming and whistling and then singing the words to a popular song: "Pack up all my cares and woe, here I go, singing low, bye bye blackbird..."

Rocky pulled out his squirt gun and chased Elia down a path and into the woods behind the shops on South Street. Rocky refilled his squirt gun in the backyard and ran up the laneway looking for Elia, who was hiding.

Rocky couldn't find him and after a few minutes didn't bother to look anymore. Rocky walked back down the laneway, on the side of which was a trellis of grapevines reaching from the top of the laneway down to the artesian well beneath the water tower. Under the grapevines were chickens behind chicken wire in chicken coops. Rocky squirted water at the chickens. Frankie continued walking on to the Legion Hall, whistling "Bye Bye Blackbird," one of the songs that the band will play in today's Memorial Day parade.

It was just two Fridays ago, early in the morning, too early as far as Frankie was concerned, that the American Legion band, specially selected for the occasion, played at Roosevelt Field, for some airplane flying competition. Frankie didn't even want to go. It was such crummy weather, damp and raining, and having to wake up a 4:30 a.m. didn't make him feel any better about it. He had been working in Hoffman's until two in the morning and didn't get to sleep till three. The band arrived at Roosevelt Field around six o'clock. The place was crowed with reporters, photographers and policemen. The band started by playing John Philip Sousa's "Stars and Stripes Forever," not once but five times! Some of the reporters kept requesting it. That's enough thought Frankie to himself, and began playing "Bye Bye Blackbird" on his own. The band took up the cue and joined in. Mr. Luckybeak, the bandleader, showed a disgruntled face to his band members but piously pumped his arms back and forth, baton in hand. As they were playing, an airplane covered in a shroud passed by them, being towed through the mud of Curtiss Field to the airstrip at Roosevelt Field. The band played on, a bouncy death march; it's like a funeral procession, thought Frankie, cold and damp, bouncing on his mud caked shoes, trying to keep warm. It was Friday, May 20. It was now 7:54 a.m... while he played Frankie heard the words in his head. "No one here can love or understand me, oh the hard luck stories they all hand me... blackbird, bye bye." Finally, we can go home now, thought Frankie. The plane was airborne; it had just barely cleared some high-tension wires at the end of the runway. There goes the flyin' fool, someone said. Just cleared the wires, lucky you, thought Frankie, now let's get atta here.

Alice opened the window and took the magazines and newspapers from Teddy, Jr. She placed the rolled up newspaper on her lap and placed the other magazines on top of that one, nonchalantly and carefully, as not to arouse the attention of Edith. Alice paddled through the pages and pulled out a magazine. "Here. *Success Magazine*. Let's see what the high minded Eleanor has to pontificate about." Alice riffled the pages, too anxious to look in the index. "Here it is. Oh no. Listen to this title: What I Want Most Out of Life. By Eleanor Roosevelt. How like a proper schoolgirl. So noble. Sophomoric. Allenswood you know. Dear Aunt Bamie survived Souvestre, that freethinker, whatever that means, and she defender that Jew Dreyfus, her religious views were problematic. Father skirted the issue with Aunt Bamie. But Eleanor must wear the pants on that side of the family now it seems. She is becoming rather opinionated. And urging women to vote... really, if God meant for women to vote He wouldn't have given us so much more wisdom and wit than men possess.

"I have voted," announced Edith.

"Oh," replied Alice, indifferently, reversing single vowel roles.

The chauffeur started the engine of the car and pulled away from the curb, making a U-turn, circling around in front of the Cazzaza Fruit and Vegetable Store, and proceeded to the intersection about 50 feet away, where he stopped to check traffic. Alice was reading the magazine article silently to herself, but not for long. Something caught her eye. "Listen to what she writes: '...and so if anyone were to ask me what I want out of life I would say, the opportunity for doing something useful, for in no other way, I am convinced, can true happiness be obtained.'" If Eleanor wants to do something useful she would not support Mr. Smith for president. I'll put a whammy on him, like I did to Wilson when he returned from Europe."

"Are your famous whammies, as you call them, do they..." Teddy, Jr. began to speak but was derailed.

"Whammies, hexes, curses, murrains, all the same," said Alice, rubbing the ugly jade ring that she wore.

Teddy, Jr. added, "Are they always against people? Never for?"

"Not against all people; only those people who are Democrats."

"What of the Socialists and Communists and Anarchists?" Teddy, Jr. was having her on.

"They are cursed by God," Alice emphatically proposed, and, by God, deposed. "They are a higher evil. Doomed. But Democrats are only nuisances."

"And how great a nuisance are Mr. Smith and Franklin?"

"Mr. Smith is a Catholic," Alice seemed to consider that an obvious answer; no more had to be said.

"Cursable?" asked Teddy, Jr.

"Damnable! And dangerous!"

"And Franklin? Now that he's crippled..."

"Not my doing; I don't dabble in black magic..."

"But he'll never be president now..."

"There is and always will be just one President Roosevelt. It is ordained. Franklin had his fling with Lucy Mercer. She's married now. No more trouble from there I'm afraid. If only the noble Eleanor had divorced him. She was willing. But the children you know. And Lucy was Catholic. Franklin knew a divorce would be the end of his political career. He would never have had a chance at the presidency. A divorced cripple. Never. But he's had his good time, he deserved it, he's married to Eleanor. But president. Never. Hoover shall be the next president."

"Hoover!?" said Edith.

"But what about Nick?" questioned Teddy, Jr.

"I have had a premonition. Coolidge will take his hat out of the ring. Hoover will be president, and our new hero, Mr. Lindbergh, will come out for Hoover. Lindbergh is actually his real name. Refreshing. Nothing secretive. All up front. From Minnesota. Swedes. But Lindbergh has rubbed the sordidness out of the headlines. Harding, scandals, gangsters, murders. We can hold our heads high once again. So Smith hasn't an Ave Maria chance." There was no traffic and the car turned right.

By simply stating the racial background of a man, or woman, and the State, or country, from which he or she hails, Alice believed she could convey all that one needed to know about a person, to persons who were in the know, that is.

"And look at this," Alice pulled out another magazine, the *Atlantic Monthly.* "Can you believe the audacity of Mr. Smith and this article. How pompous. His creed as a Catholic! All these I believes... I believe this, I believe that, a Catholic and patriot, isn't there a contradiction?"

"Will Franklin be governor of New York?" Teddy, Jr. asked Alice the fortuneteller.

"The wrong Roosevelt. You should have knocked off Smith in '24. That would have buried him. The Empire State shall have its first queen regent, I'm afraid."

"I'll be in Asia next year and well out of it," said Teddy, Jr.

"I'll hold the fort. The barbarians shall be slain by my terrible swift sword. They are at the gate... Reds and Jews and Italians and Japs and Chinks and anarchists and... and... and..." Alice's mind seemed to lose track, her engine derailed; she turned her head to look out the rear window of the car.

"What do you see?" said Edith, startled by the silence.

"Oh nothing." But she knew exactly what she saw; and this was real fortune telling.

"That car? Is it the car?" asked Teddy, Jr.

Alice was ashen. A Rolls Royce had passed them and turned left onto South Street. Rich is as rich does. Widdlesworth. Real name. Alice knew money and pedigree when she smelled it where it counts. This was castles and titles in Europe money. This was ethereal other-old-world money. This was way way way up on the ladder money. This was elbow rubbing with Kings and Queens and Dukes and Duchesses money. Real Duchesses! Not some frumpy midwestern wife of a slob who fell off the front-porch to become president. This was property money. Gentry money. Ancient money. Old World pedigree property money that made the Roosevelts appear as a chihuahua's bark on the evolutionary scale of dog eat dog capitalism. But this was beyond capitalism, beyond democracy, the American's prideful boast. This was pure unmitigated blood and soil. Alice didn't want to discuss it. Snobs, she said to herself. She changed the topic. She had seen the marquee of the Lyric Theater, FLESH AND THE DEVIL, down the street when she watched the Rolls Royce go round the corner. So it was the first thing that came to her mind.

"Gilbert's the next Valentino."

"Sorry dear, what was that?" said Edith.

"I said John Gilbert will be the next Rudolph Valentino."

Edith and Teddy, Jr. ignored this comment. Valentino had died the previous year. His funeral was held at Campbell Funeral Parlor on Broadway and Sixty-seventh Street. It had caused quite a sensation. One hundred thousand people had viewed the body. Outside the funeral parlor the crowd waited in the shimmering sun and sticky August heat; then a sudden cloudburst dumped sheets of rain on the crowd. The crowd struggling to find shelter stampeded through mounted police; some of the crowd was pressed so hard against the glass in the windows of the funeral parlor that it shattered, slicing into the flesh of screaming women. Reporters and photographers had a field day. This was real news.

"Real name: Rodolpho Alfonzo Pierre Filibert Guglielmi di Valentina d'Antonguolla," said Alice, to the amazement of Edith and Teddy, Jr.

"Times, please," said Teddy, Jr., weary of patronymic word games.

"Yes, of course." Alice handed Teddy, Jr. the newspaper. She took the hint and remained subdued and silent, slightly insulted. Edith sighed. Alice was thinking about her husband. The affable apathetic alcoholic Nick Longworth. She tightened her grip around the bottle wrapped in the newspaper as if it were someone's neck; Nick's? Did she know about his affair with a Senator's wife? No one said another word on the ride up the cove to Sagamore Hill.

They Were Here Already

Morons and the manifestly unfit...

The Rolls Royce parked in front of Saunder's Pharmacy. Monday morning was moving on to Monday afternoon. More people were mingling on the sidewalks. There were men dressed as clowns pushing makeshift dolly-like contraptions with large vertical boards covered with black felt. Buttons, ribbons, small toys were attached to the boards, and bundles of helium-filled balloons flying aloft were tied with strings to the forearms of the clown-men. Miniature American flags were sticking out from everywhere all which way, fluttering in the self-generated breeze, and pin-wheels were spinning, and children were running, and the sound of lone rehearsing instruments were heard up and down South Street. The bell in the clock tower above Hodman's Hardware Store rang twelve times, and Sid Schwartz was pushing his broom across the wooden planked floor. "Don't dirty the floor. Don't dirty the floor," he said to Emile Baldazzi, who had dropped a dime on the floor.

"Get ya balloons'ere. Balloons. Balloons. Get ya balloons'ere," barked the balloon man. Rocky opened his hand, revealing five pennies.

"Which color?"

"Red," said Rocky.

"Here ya go, son."

It was then that Sid Schwartz saw Rocky through the store window and came bolting out into the street. He grabbed Rocky by the arm and twisted it back. The balloon floated up into the sky.

"My balloon! My balloon! You're hurting me!"

"Good... I saw what you did. Don't think I didn't. You stole a squirt gun from my store. Now give it back. I know you got it." Sid Schwartz reached into Rocky's pocket and pulled out the squirt gun.

"You dumb little guinea moron," Schwartz whispered. Rocky stood eye to eye with Schwartz. They were both no more than 5'4". Rocky, though in his mid-twenties, appeared to be half his age, and acted that way too. "You're a damn moron, ain't you? Just a moron." Sid Schwartz let go of Rocky and pushed him away. "Get lost, kid." But Rocky didn't get lost. He lunged at Schwartz and grabbed the squirt gun. They wrestled and jerked and yanked back and forth. Then Rocky, in what would later prove to be one fateful effort, pulled with all his might and got the gun away from Schwartz. Rocky ran around the corner.

"Get back here! I'll call the cops. Moron!"

"You won't call nobody," said Emile Baldazzi, who had been watching the whole incident, "and the kid ain't no moron."

"Mind your business ya guinea bum!"

"And mind your business, kike."

"I know who you are. You're just a bum. You live in the flophouse on Hamilton Avenue. You're not from around here. You came in from the city with the rest of them. Go back where you belong."

Emile Baldazzi had come to this town from the city, but for a reason unfathomable he has never left, except when he went off to fight in the Spanish Civil War, otherwise he has remained in this town, a bum. What went wrong? Emile has plenty of theories about what went wrong. What went wrong with the whole country. Emile was born in lower Manhattan in 1895, and saw action in France in World War One. He was discharged in 1916, and found himself hanging around the employment agencies, worked his way east to west and back east again, doing every odd job. In 1922 he went to sea with the merchant marines as a mess boy; after three years of seeing the brutal treatment and the sabotage and the waste and fed up with all of it, he returned to land, to New York, and hopped on a train completely by chance. That train took him to Oyster Bay. Even before the train pulled into the station, he knew where he would go for a job, Heemskirk's Shipyard, because just before the train pulled into town, it passed by the shipyard. Emile Baldazzi knew right away that that was his first stop. He was hired on the spot.

Rocky ran around the corner into the backyard. He climbed up the ladder on the water tower and hopped onto the roof of Hoffman's Building. He walked along the coping-stones until he came to a spot where he could step down onto the Cazzaza building. He looked up at the sky and saw the red balloon moving north toward the harbor, a speck in the sky. "My balloon," he said and sat down to cry.

It was ironic that Sid Schwartz had called Rocky a "moron." The word, from the Greek for "foolish," had been in vogue as an epithet of derision and abuse ever since H. H. Goddard invented the term to be used to classify people found to be mentally deficient and manifestly unfit. The defective, inferior, sub-human, and feeble-minded. The main targets were Jews, Italians, Slavs, Turks, and Greeks. The lazy, dirty, dumb peasants of Southern and Eastern Europe. As for African-Americans, that went without saying, it wasn't even necessary to test them. They were here already. The "facts" were already known about how shiftless and lazy they were. They were here already. But Marcus Garvey, a Jamaican, planned a "back-to-Africa" movement, and had commended Warren G. Harding for a speech Harding delivered in Alabama in 1921 against racial amalgamation; it was Harding who later supported a back-to-Africa bill sponsored by a racist Senator from Mississippi. No wonder Harding was eulogized as another Lincoln when he died; both Lincoln and Harding had considered colonization as a solution to the "African problem."

To stifle the breath and depth of the influx of undesirable yearning masses it was found necessary and expedient to devise an "objective and scientific" means of verifying if such newly arriving inferior races would threaten the sacred preservation of the pure Anglo-American stock, and stock market, as it has existed in a perfect master-slave symbiotic relationship with those other inferior races, who were here already, the Native American and African-American. Goddard identified his "morons" arriving at Ellis Island with such rigorous scientific and intuitive inquiry (you could tell one by just looking at one, in fact, he claimed) that his success amazed even himself. He came to the not unexpected results, through his moron-detecting system, that 80% of those tested, Jews, Italians, Slavs, Russians, Turks, Greeks, were of feeble-minded type. Sid Schwartz and Rocky were in the same boat, had come on the same boat, so to speak, so it was ironic that Sid Schwartz was now adapting to his new-found land by adopting the competitive cut-throat characteristics of its true-blue owners, it was Us versus Them, assimilate or go home, call a spade a spade or get out of the game. Goddard's influence was so pervasive and strong that restrictions based on racial quotas were established by the Immigration Act of 1924, in order to keep the established order, just as it had been prior to 1890, before the sluice gates were opened. Quotas were set in proportions according to the percentage of nationalities who were here already, which of course favored the northern and western European, and as for the Negroes, well, Colonel, they were here already, the problem was keeping them down; thus protecting the pure American gene pool from further deterioration. Let's dive deep into that pool. Here we find a true holy pearl. She sat in the backseat of the Rolls Royce that was parked in front of Saunder's Pharmacy.

Agnes Babs Widdlesworth sat between Captain Roger Bethell, formerly of the United States Navy, and Rear Admiral Sir Dudley Gower, of His Majesty's Service.

"Felix," said Agnes to her chauffeur, "just a bottle of Bayer Aspirin will do. I've such an abominable headache."

Felix got out of the car and went into Saunder's.

Brent Widdlesworth, Agnes' eleven-year-old brother, moved over to the driver's seat and, clutching the steering wheel, pretended to drive the car. Like Stevie Cazzaza, Brent was also a victim of the infantile paralysis epidemic of 1916; disease having no respect for class distinctions. Last year he nearly died from a bout with pneumonia. Brent had only one desire in his short life, to drive a car and drive it fast. Chauffeurs drive so slow, he complained.

It was an unusually cold night, May 17, 1938, when Brent, now twenty-two, drove his sports car along the shore road that skirted Oyster Bay Harbor. With him in the car was Frank Yamada. Passing under the railroad trestle, Brent was going too fast to make the turn left and skidded straight into the Mill Pond. His steel leg brace got caught; unable to free himself from the car, with its specially designed hand-break and accelerator controls on the steering wheel, he drowned.

Frank Yamada managed to escape from the car. Frank panicked; he screamed for help, but there was nobody around. He stood among the rushes a wet midnight figure.

Frank Yamada screwed up his courage and flopped into the water again; he could barely swim. He made it over to the car and crawled on top. The water was but inches over the roof but it was deep enough. Frank pounded the roof with his fists, but he was too frightened to enter the water again. He reached around into the opened window of the car and felt for Brent's body, as he had a hundred times under the sheets of his bed. He touched Brent's cold soft face. He felt Brent's hand clutch his arm and then let go; he gasped, and then he grabbed Brent's jacket and pulled; it was in vain; he couldn't budge him. He scrambled out of the water splashing like a giant night bird, and reaching the tall grasses around the pond he stumbled through them until he reached the side of the small side road. There were no cars, no help. There was a large upright rock with geological scars enhanced by frost and the ambiguities of moonlight to reveal the preciousness of life in the quietness of a beetle's contemplation. Frank Yamada saw the beetle as the devil himself and he crushed it with his hand. If he only had a knife he would do what his father had done, the honorable thing.

The large upright rock marked the spot where the Quaker George Fox had preached a sermon in 1672, on May 17th, this very night, over two hundred and fifty years ago; the Quaker's words still hung in the air, too light to touch the earth. In the darkness Frank Yamada closed his eyes to both light and darkness and slept till morning. He dreamt that a dark naked man who called himself Aliaspun came out of the woods and lay down next to him and just then, in the quaking shock of emission, Frank saw Brent walking on the water, a pale apparition of Jesus; Brent was smiling, holding out his arms, bathed in a celestial light, quaking like a leaf. A young girl was standing on the railroad trestle, watching everything, but the dead cannot act. Her name is Elizabeth, and she is waiting for her Indian father so that they might return together to Hog Island to live in peace among the dead. Aliaspun walked towards Elizabeth.

They were here already...

Aliaspun is reclining on his back, his right leg bent back with the knee pointing toward the smoke hole in the dome-shaped wigwam, his left leg is turned upward and crossed over, the left foot resting on the cap of the right knee. His fingers spread and rub his smooth brown chest and dally over the hard belly reaching the black hairs. There is a mixture of blood and dirt. His eyes are burning and are blinded by the cloying smoke. His naked body reeks a foul odor of prophecy. Speaking is a play at death.

Nobody shall hear what he shall say. Nobody shall understand. His hand manipulates the bloated tube of flesh and blood. It grows hard. He draws the bow, releases the arrow... another play at death. Death comes in small doses. Aliaspun's village shall become a dead end. He shall tell the people what he has seen of tomorrow. Seven days has he fasted and sweated and wept toward a vision for his people. But his dreams have been punctuated with curious configurations and disturbing symbols of which he has no remembered knowledge. Slashes and dots and marks that carve deep scars in the memory of his dream. The sound of his voice is an actual happening, a force of personal power and episode. The sound of his voice is evanescent; an arrow clipping the moon's edge that cannot ever return to earth, it has reached the sacred land of his forefathers. It passes in the root of saying and spring. It is in silence and winter that he hears the dead voices waking in the wind's song. His words and voice are one. He is speaking out of the memory of the future. There is as much immanent presence in the spoken word as in the act of hunting, in the planting of maize. Are you listening? Aliaspun will not be interrupted by a fat American tourist reading a newspaper.

Men of strange appearance have come across the great water. They have landed on this island. These are strange fluid translations of time and space. His dream is no boasting of power. He is but a soothsayer. He is a wordsmith. Power is lost as readily as won. Dangerous encounters mark the path to destiny. He is old but his dreams are always young. Lately he has heard of a curious dream; he hasn't been able to disentangle its threads, to interpret a single bead of its intricate interlineations. It is so unusual, so unfamiliar to his tribal experience, dealing with things beyond his vision, things unwarlike yet certainly of evil potent. It was the young girl's dream, not Aliaspun's. It was she who spoke of things fearful, of coming disasters and the plague of white rabbits and the hairy bears with human faces unsuited for consumption but well suited with dapper jackets and ties and tails and spraying smoke from long tubes not peace pipes that roared at the birds that fell over Madison Avenue, where all the tallest trees stand now on that cheap island with the erratic meandering cow path down the center, speckled with chips, droppings, road apples, shit... they call it Broadway now. The smoke is everywhere, unlike the smoke from Aliaspun's pipe; his pipe is silent between speech. But Schwartz in the paper store on South Street, he talks constantly with his fat stub of a cigar in the corner of his mouth. Sometimes someone drops a dime on the floor and he grumbles, "Don't dirty the floor. Don't dirty the floor." Aliaspun says to him, "Don't dirty our land." Aliaspun used to speak well. He had the whole tribe staying up late on a Saturday night, sitting out by the marsh, and listening to his tales. The marsh is gone. It's been filled in. There's a park there now. Theodore Roosevelt Memorial Park. A gang of teenagers hang out there. They park their cars in the parking lot, where the marsh used to be...

Aliaspun is reclining on the hood of a 1963 Chevrolet Impala, white with a red stripe down each side. His right leg is bent back and his left leg is crossed over, the left foot resting on the cap of the right knee. He is looking out over Oyster Bay Harbor. Captain Roger Bethell has summoned Aliaspun from history. He wants to make of him a fictional character for his new series of sci-fi novels. About a time-traveler. Jules Verne and H. G. Wells have lately influenced Captain Bethell. The Captain continues to write books on Zen Buddhism and bonsai, his main interests, the other being merely a diversion, an entertainment.

Captain Bethell
Welcome to the Boondocks
Young Brent Widdlesworth was turning the steering wheel of the Rolls Royce parked in front of Saunder's Pharmacy.

"I've had these headaches ever since India. The climate I suspect," said Agnes Babs Widdlesworth, opening the window to let fresh air in.

"Too severe. Too severe, indeed," echoed Sir Dudley.

"Hot as hell huh? Never been myself, but I'd bet hell it is," said Captain Bethell, laughing at this once unfamous play of words on his name.

In 1904 Captain Bethell married Clara Klankenhorn, a first cousin of Agnes Babs Widdlesworth, and settled in Northport, Long Island. He became a world-renowned authority on the propagation and cultivation of bonsai trees, and wrote several books on bonsai and Zen Buddhism. He also wrote several proto-science fiction novels dealing with time-travel. Some of his works include: *Zen and Bonsai* (1899), *The Zen Way* (1900), *Bonsai for Ladies* (1901), *Zen in Japan* (1904), *Bonsai Techniques* (1905), *Approach to Zen* (1910), *Adventures Where Time Ends* (1912), *The Saga of Aliaspun* (1914), *Zen and Western Art* (1919).

Captain Bethell, who is now nearly seventy years old, looked out the window of the Rolls Royce parked in front of Saunder's Pharmacy on

South Street, and took Agnes by the hand. Agnes, thirty-five years his junior, smiled endearingly. The Captain never speaks of Clara, his deceased wife, and Agnes respects his wish. The same year that Clara married the Captain she began the affair with the Japanese photographer, Yukio Yamada. At first Yukio was only interested in the Captain's bonsai trees, until he became more interested in Clara. She had married the Captain when she was twenty. He was more than twice her age. They got on splendidly at first, that is until the night she came to his bed and put her hand on his abdomen and went searching. The Captain was furious and aghast. She had nearly groped him and pinched him to death in the dark, searching for the missing object. He pushed her from the bed and rushed out of the room. Later she found him in his arboretum among his bonsai trees.

"Captain?" Clara whispered, entering the arboretum.

"Moby Dick lives," was all he replied.

She never knew and the Captain never told anyone what had happened so long ago and far away on that island in the Far East, where the object and its appendages and a belief system were lost forever.

Widdlesworth

Agnes Babs Widdlesworth was born in New Orleans. She remembers very little of the city, only that there was much gaiety, Mardi Gras balls, French opera, wonderful restaurants, but her mother told her about those things, and she only remembered her mother's gay memories. Her mother, Sarah Barbour, always described things that she like as gay, and Agnes would always do the same. Her father, William Widdlesworth, had his business in New York, and he often took his family with him, staying at the Waldorf or the Grosvenor.

When Agnes was five her father decided to move the family to New York. He bought a house on Center Island, overlooking Oyster Bay Harbor. Agnes counted among her ancestors seven Presidents of the United States: George Washington, John Adams, John Quincy Adams, James Madison, James Monroe, Andrew Jackson, and Zachary Taylor; and a congressman from Virginia who had helped negotiate the Louisiana Purchase; and a Captain John Widdlesworth, Indian fighter and explorer of the Mississippi River; and a Brigadier-General who commanded a division of the army in the War of 1812; and Patrick Henry, who was a distant cousin; and a great-grandmother who claimed to be descended directly from William the Conqueror, Alfred the Great, and Charlemagne! Agnes Babs Widdlesworth was indeed a holy pearl, the very highest incarnation of European Civilization. Of course, none of this was ever authenticated.

She has spent most of her thirty-three years attending parties given for the likes of the Prince of Wales (Edward VIII), the Duke of York (George VI), the Duke of Connaught, the Aga Khan, King George V and his wife Victoria Mary, the Crown Prince of Sweden, and the King of Spain, who delighted her by wearing a purple suit, brown shoes and a homburg hat. She has attended receptions given by the likes of Lady Astor, Mrs. Vanderbilt, and the Rothschilds; there were gay seasons in New York, London, and Paris; there was polo and tennis and fox-hunting and race-horsing; she sat in the royal box at Ascot. There was bullfighting in Spain; skiing in St. Moritz; casinos in Biarritz. Cannes was gay, Paris was gay, London was gay; everything and everywhere and everyone was gay gay gay. And there was always the next gay place; and offers to take up residence in this or that ancestral house or castle. Just dropping in, actually, to name drop.

Agnes Babs Widdlesworth met Alice Roosevelt Longworth but one time. It was in 1921, at Washington D.C. The occasion was a dinner party given by the actress Louise Brooks. Their short conversation amounted to nothing more than, what else, name dropping. Count them Counts. Royalty and riches. No politicians were mentioned; Agnes wouldn't dare drop a brick like that; though Alice might have.

"Do you hunt?" asked Agnes, knowing that Alice's father was a famed killer of furry objects.

"Always on guard," answered Alice with ambiguous airs.

"I myself shall one day hunt tiger in India," Agnes stated.

"My father, as everyone knows, hunted in Af... ri..."

"Pardon me dear but the Major is an old friend," said the young Agnes, looking over Alice's shoulder, acknowledging the Major's presence by returning a smile.

"...in Africa..." Alice's voice trailed off into darkest jungle. Agnes abruptly went hunting for the Major, leaving snubbed Alice stunned and staring into her reflection in a glass of whiskey (illegal) that her husband held in his hand. Her husband's eyes watched the wiggle in the aspect of Agnes' derriere as she went her red carpet way. Such was the only meeting between Agnes Babs Widdlesworth and Alice Roosevelt Longworth, an event of little worth. Whether Agnes ever met Mr. Longworth again is open to speculation. But the Congressman was known to partake in carnal assignations at the highest level. And when Alice saw Agnes today, her car passing by the Rolls Royce, it did cause Alice to become that which a Roosevelt is not by nature, quiet.

"...and two weeks aboard the *S.S. Rawalpindi,*" said Agnes, who was telling Captain Bethell and Sir Dudley about her hunting trip to India in February. They were still sitting in the Rolls Royce parked in front of Saunder's. "It was very comfortable," Agnes continued, "Large state-rooms and..."

"How did you occupy your time? I'm always curious to know what a woman... is... prprpr..." Sir Dudley faltered on precarious argumentative ground and withdrew his nascent commentary into a puttering of Oxford fluttering lips.

"Why, Sir Dudley, we simply sleep in the day and dance and play bridge in the evening. What on earth else could you possibly imagine us doing?" Agnes tittered and pressed the tops of her thighs, rubbing her hands over her dress to smooth it out.

"Bridge? Yes, of course. What else indeed." Sir Dudley had no intention of revealing what little imagination he had to offer to Agnes.

"You say you slept in the day. I for one would like to know what you dreamed. I never had the same dreams on land as I had at sea. Nor the same in the day as in the night. And I've recorded every dream that I've had since my... the..." Captain Bethell was about to say vision, but thought better of it in present company. All this talk of dreams and imagination was making Sir Dudley rather uncomfortable.

"Two weeks at sea you say..." Sir Dudley guided the rudder of conversation back into a secure, impersonal, and unemotional harbor.

"Yes, from Marseilles to Bombay," said Alice. "The first week was quite cold. Sunsets were gorgeous. Splendid stars in the night sky."

"Did you notice Venus and Jupiter cradled together? Stunning at that latitude," said Captain Bethell.

"I noticed many stars; but which were which and which were where... I'm afraid I haven't the sense... is it science or poetry? Why all these names?"

"It's science, a kind of classification, same as looking through a microscope," said Sir Dudley.

"Poetry. All poetry," said Captain Bethell, "a kind of expression, same as playing a violin."

"Either way, it was beautiful. And such wonderful views passing through the Straits of Messina. I saw Mt. Etna and Stromboli. We passed through Port Said and the Suez Canal... around Aden..." Agnes journeyed in her mind.

"The very same route that brought by caravan the Queen of Sheba unto her King Solomon," Captain Bethell waxed historically sentimental.

"I wasn't aware of that. History's not my strong suit you know," said Agnes. But not to be outshone by the Captain's knowledge, she stated, "Besides dancing and bridge, I'll have you know, I did do some reading."

"Guide books? Swashbuckling romance?" Sir Dudley mocked.

"Yes, some," Agnes confessed, "but not only. I read *Passage to India.*"

Sir Dudley raised an eyebrow; E. M. Forster was not in favor, but Sir Dudley pretended a slight interest in literature, so as not to seem too provincial, or worse, parochial, as Henry James might charge. "I am partial to Mr. Kipling's verse myself," said Sir Dudley. He recited: 'Each to his choice, and I rejoice the lot has fallen to me, in a fair ground, in a fair ground, yea, Sussex by the sea!'" Sir Dudley was born in Hastings and always maintained the unverifiable claim that his ancestors had died fighting toe to toe and vis-à-vis and hand to hand and tête-à-tête against William the Conqueror and the Normans.

"Have you read it?" Agnes turned to face Captain Bethell.

"I have read it. What did you think about Adela's hallucination in the Marabar Caves?" Captain Bethell asked Agnes. My God, thought Sir Dudley to himself, first dreams and now hallucinations! Is there no privacy of thought in America? So frank and forward!

"I found Mrs. Moore's experience in the caves more, how can I say, more realistic, truthful. That echo of all that is worthless... of... life... and..." Agnes found it difficult to articulate what she was trying to say. "But I also had such an experience. In a Hindu temple. A temple dedicated to the Mahatama Devi."

No no no... no more talk of personal experiences, Sir Dudley's mind raced with the velocity of the earth spinning. But the Captain was fascinated. "Mahatama Devi," Captain Bethell said, curling his voice around the syllables like a cobra. "The Goddess of small pox and destruction."

"Truly?" said Agnes with sudden illumination in her eyes. "I had no idea. Yes, it makes perfect sense." Though Agnes had little sense of scientific eventualities in the patterns of nature's fabric, she had a keen sense of intuitive connections in the patterns she encountered in her own experience. "It was in Central India. So much of the temple was in ruins. I attended a service. Great brass doors... behind it was the sacred image. They were ringing bells and beating drums. I had been hunting the previous week. I had ridden an elephant. And there you stay holding a rifle. And wait to shoot something if it appears. I saw a red deer, fired, missed; I was very disappointed. I saw hyenas and big sambars, but at too far a distance to shoot. For one week I hunted... saw two bears with cubs, too far; the last day there was a clatter of monkeys and birds, this I was told meant that a panther was near, but I saw nothing. My friend Captain Steward shot a wild boar that morning. I wanted to shoot something, anything. Then she came... a tigress... I had waited all week and now at the last moment she was mine. A panther had been shot previously, a marvelous beast over seven feet, a superb cat... but a tigress! Then suddenly it started to rain and thunder." Agnes stared silently into her mind.

"And..." said Sir Dudley, "did you kill the beast?"

"That's when," Agnes continued, "I don't remember... I was in the temple... I saw the tigress, the panther, the wild boar, the peacock, the sambar, the monkeys, the birds, the bears, the hyena, the red deer, the black partridge... a terrific thunder storm... the animals were in the temple, they were devouring a human, not another animal... I moved nearer. I was not afraid at all. Not of the animals anyway. I was afraid to see whom it was that the animals were eating. The bells were ringing, the drums beating, the animals so noisy... howling... the human face was eaten away... I screamed and ran out of the temple."

"I must have misunderstood. What happened to the tigress?" asked Sir Dudley, matter-of-factly. "So you didn't kill the beast? Did you get a shot off?" Sir Dudley avoided the ramifications of hallucinations and turned back into safe seas. Once again securely anchored.

"No... I mean I don't remember. No."

"I see. Not a woman's place..." Sir Dudley was brave, but Agnes made no rebuttal; she rested her head on the Captain's shoulder.

"My headache is killing me," Agnes said.

"Have you ever hunted with a pack?" Sir Dudley spat out the words.

"With a pack of what?" Captain Bethell retorted.

"Why dogs of course. Fox-hunting."

"I do not hunt. I don't find any pleasure in killing a helpless, defenseless creature."

"But surely it is great sport..." Sir Dudley had his own big hunting stories to relate, the outcome of which was quite different from Agnes'. First, he thought of relating a foxhunting tale, but then went for bigger game, more likely to impress the voracious and vigorous American appetite for bigness. "I once hunted in Nepal. There was a large party of us, and the elephants, shikari, attendants. There was a great tigress also, very much like yours, which had killed a buffalo. Alarm calls went out from a sambar and birds... boiling hot it was... I heard the tigress moving in the brush and palms where the buffalo had been killed... didn't see her... the next day we returned to the spot, the buffalo was missing, only a tigress could have moved it, not a panther... we found the buffalo about 200 yards away... the tigress had eaten all but the head and the fore quarters. I was in my machang... I waited... it was nearly 7 p.m. when the tigress returned to her kill... she approached it... the day was growing darker... we took our places... we set the elephants charging and roaring through the brush... the tigress bounded into the open... an enormous beast... she was making for the jungle... I had to fire now... I got her in the haunch... she turned to face me and snapped with terrible pride... I shot again, into the shoulder... everyone in the party started firing... a wild cannonade... she roared magnificently... I took aim at the head... hit her!" Sir Dudley jumped up and hit his head on the car's ceiling; then settled back, pausing dramatically, and said, "That finished her. She was mine. I had hit her first. I drew first blood. She was over 11 feet, at least 800 pounds, about ten years old. I was so terribly pleased." Sir Dudley inhaled and exhaled with terrible pride, quite satisfied that he had defended the honor of the King to the two boasting Americans.

"Riveting stuff old chap." Captain Bethell was taking the mickey, needless to say.

"Fancy that!" said Agnes, adding her two pence.

"Goodbye my fancy!" Captain Bethell crossed the Atlantic in a ship of slang, adding his two cents.

"Hello my Nancy boys!" Agnes rowed ahead. The Captain and Agnes letting go a stream of consciousness through American green valleys and back alleys.

"Over here my Doughboys."

"You can bring Nan with the old dead pan but don't bring Lulu..."

"OK by me."

"Well I'll be dang."

"What a lot of bunk."

"I've been gypped."

"That's the dope."

"My sister sells snow to the snowbirds..."

"My father makes bootlegger gin..."

"My mother she rents by the hour..."

"My God how the money rolls in..."

"My Bonnie Prince lies over the ocean..."

"My Bonnie Prince lies over the sea..."

"Bring back bring back O bring back my King's English to me to me..."

Agnes and Captain Bethell finished their rollicking chorus. Sir Dudley was not amused. Even upper class Americans lack aristocratic distinctions, he thought to himself. How could he ever get on with these simple folk? He saw no other recourse but to defend the honor and purity of the King's English. With a stiff upper lip, he said, "Americanisms. Slang. These innovations are surely unnecessary and are to be deprecated. There are more than enough words, quite satisfactory words, capable of encompassing all manner of detail and elaboration of thought and experience."

"I s'pose we just don't know our place old sport," said the Captain. This really irked Sir Dudley, who expected to be treated with the dignity afforded to someone of his position in society.

"You must know that Europe is being divided: Communism, Fascism in Italy, and Nazism in Germany. Of course neither of you are a Communist but..." Sir Dudley let the "but" deliberately hang in the air like a cold icicle to be grasped by a contentious party. Sir Dudley wanted to get to the heart of the matter. He was startled when the Captain fired back a reply. Is this chap serious?

Captain Bethell said, "But... speak for yourself!" Sir Dudley had heard rumors about this odd chap named Bethell who had become a pacifist and author of some slight repute, but he never expected the Captain to be "dangerous," which conclusion Sir Dudley was coming to; he was certainly over the top.

The tension was snapped when Agnes spoke. "I certainly am not a Communist. The Captain merely jests."

"Does he now?" said Sid Dudley, chagrined. Why did I come? Bloody tradition; bloody duty to a dead friend. But this is the end. I shant come next year.

"I am a Buddhist," suddenly said the Captain.

"Then all the worse for you," said Sir Dudley, at wit's end. "Nevertheless, you will have to be one of the others. You must be something. You will have to choose."

One of the others, the Captain wondered one of the other what?

"You forgot Americanism. I will choose Americanism," said Agnes pridefully. Is that one of the others, wondered the Captain to himself?

"And what will England choose?" asked the Captain.

"England is England. Our position is clear. The British Empire is civilization. We are the last bastion. Will America stay the course?"

"But you said that one will have to choose from one of those -isms. Why must America choose at all?" said the Captain.

"But surely dear Captain you don't consider England to be a part of Europe." Sir Dudley was severe.

"Nor do I consider America to be a part of the British Empire." Captain Bethell was stern.

"The choice is yours. Civilization or anarchy."

"To be or not to be," said the Captain, "I am a Buddhist."

Bloody fool, thought Sir Dudley. But he played the Hamlet theme. "Hamlet failed to act until it was too late. He was weak and unprepared. The Buddhists in Japan will dominate in the Pacific. We may be damned in heaven if we don't disarm but we are certainly damned on earth if we do disarm. We need more warships. You need another President Roosevelt. Mr. Kipling has told me personally that he has put his ear to the ground and he hears the war drums not far away."

"The militarists in Japan, not the Buddhists. Roosevelt, my blowhard ex-friend," said the Captain, "let the Japanese have Korea if they'd promise to leave the Philippines alone; that is quite an indication of acting expeditiously for the peace of righteousness, as he so elegantly put it, the hypocrite..."

"No more talk of politics," said Agnes, "I abhor all this intrigue."

But the Captain wanted to duel it out to the bloody end. "Did Hamlet fail to act or did the actor fail to act, that is the question," the Captain said, cryptically.

"What are you saying?" answered Sir Dudley without answering; the London Times crossword wasn't his cup of tea.

"I am merely suggesting."

"Yes, I know... but suggesting what!" Sir Dudley did not like having the piss taken out of him. Some silly Punch and Judy show. This is a bloody pantomime. He thought about Hamlet. Two can play at this game. He saw the skull under Bethell's flesh, and said, "Equivocation will undo us. Let us speak to the card." Aha! That'll get him. Touché!

"Lies and deceit and hypocrisy will undo us!" said the captain, raising his voice for the first time. But Agnes raised her voice even louder.

"My headache! Gentlemen, please, enough."

Captain Bethell and Sir Dudley eyed each other. Of the two of us, who is not a gentleman? They twiddled their thumbs. They were silent. They were gentlemen.

Brent, who had been quiet all this time, the perfect little gentleman, pretended to be driving the car, noticed Stevie Cazzaza get up from the red wagon and walk with his crutches. His little sister Luisa pulled Joe in the wagon. Joe climbed out and Stevie climbed back in; his siblings usually deferred to Stevie because of his handicap. Luisa and Joe pulled their crippled brother across the street. The red wagon, picking up momentum, got out of control. Luisa and Joe dropped the handle. The wagon crashed into the side of the Rolls Royce. Brent opened the window and shouted. "Stupid, stupid slow pokes!"

Felix arrived with the Bayer Aspirin. He pulled the wagon out from under the car. "No harm done," he said to Agnes, who was hardly bothered by the incident.

Captain Bethell got out of the car and picked Stevie up from the street. The Captain dusted off Stevie's pants and shirt. "All right, son?"

"Yeah," said Stevie, adjusting the hinge of his steel leg brace.

"Waifs. Urchins," muttered Sir Dudley to Agnes.

"No, they're just kids," said Agnes.

"Kids! Kids are young goats!" Sir Dudley despised what he presumed to be an Americanism.

"Not here!" said Agnes, more harshly than she would have liked. The Captain was back in his seat. Felix situated himself behind the steering wheel, and Brent took a last look at Stevie. The Rolls Royce pulled away from the curb. Brent and Stevie continued to stare at each other. At the last moment Brent held up his crutch so that Stevie could see it. Stevie and Brent smiled at each other.

Sir Dudley Gower had been an old friend of William Widdlesworth, and for the past several years has represented the British at the Decoration Day services held in small Townsend Park on Audrey Avenue. He also was in attendance, at the request of William Widdlesworth, for his first time here, in August 1905, when President Roosevelt, who had once flexed his muscular Christian voice for war with England over a boundary dispute between Venezuela and British Guiana, held a "summit" at the highest level (before they were called summits), with the envoys of Japan and Russia, aboard the presidential yacht *Mayflower,* which was docked in Oyster Bay Harbor. William Widdlesworth died in January 1927, just one month before he was to accompany his daughter Agnes on the hunting trip to India. Sir Dudley has already informed Agnes that this will be his last trip to America, now that William was gone it just wouldn't be the same. He did not wish to encounter anyone as balmy as Captain Bethell again.

As the Rolls Royce turned right on West Main Street and proceeded in the direction of Townsend Park, Agnes continued to tell her account of her "world tour."

"Lucknow was hot, frightfully so; temperatures of 110 degrees in the shade. At least Nepal cooled off at night. I was relieved to feel the sea breeze again when we returned to Bombay."

"Where did you stay?" Sir Dudley was being conversationally polite and trite, as he believed was proper when a gentleman talks with a lady.

"Taj Mahal Hotel."

"And how was the sailing back to Europe?"

"We had a head wind in the Red Sea..."

"Ah," said Sir Dudley, "jolly good luck I'd say. Rare indeed. Otherwise, it would have been stifling."

"I decided to take an excursion to Cairo... from Suez... and rejoin the boat again at Port Said. I saw all the discoveries of Tutankhamen. Rode a camel; not at all disagreeable. Though I'd prefer an elephant. The Sphinx. Thrilling. The desert was lovely. The bazaars. Must go again."

"Agnes, dear, tell Sir Dudley all about your courage in Spain."

"The bullfights? I have become quite an *aficionada*."

"Sorry?" said the bemused Sir Dudley.

"*Aficionada*. A fan. No. Not that kind." Agnes waved her hand in front of her face. "I've always harbored a longing to try my hand at it. Bullfighting."

"And did you?"

"In a manner of speaking. I attended a school outside Seville. I learned the passes... with the cape... *Mariposa* and *Veronica* and I got in the ring... but only with baby bulls. That was it. I enjoyed the bullfights immensely. Eating little scrimp in paper bags like peanuts at a baseball game. What do you call them... *gambes*... that's it. And drinking sherry between *corridas*. I sat in the front row, the *berrera*. The bulls have been known to leap over into this part of the grandstand..."

The Rolls Royce parked by the side of Townsend Park. A grandstand had been assembled for the occasion, for the people. And a bandstand was already there for speakers and dignitaries. Agnes and her entourage took their places on the platform. A Navy destroyer was anchored in the harbor. The Navy band was playing a selection of appropriate patriotic tunes, among them the Star-Spangled Banner, which had not become the National Anthem yet, not for another four years; therefore no one was standing for that reason. They were standing because they were chatting and greeting friends and colleagues. Many children were playing and climbing about the large rocks that had been erected in memory of Theodore Roosevelt, whose spirit was never far away, even if Alice had no intention of showing up. The first speaker was Reverend Sowles of the First Methodist Church. He began with a solemn invocation and then followed with the Lord's Prayer. In front of the American Legion Hall the parade was about to get under way.

The Last Pearl on the String

When Sir Dudley Gower arrived at the Widdlesworth home on Center Island earlier in the week he had found the household in a disrupted state. William's death drove his shipping and cargo insurance business into disarray. Sarah Barbour Widdlesworth wanted nothing to do with her husband's business affairs; she had enough to do just trying to keep the family name from falling into disgrace and disrepute. Sarah had become reclusive ever since her niece Clara had had the affair with Yukio Yamada. A child had been born in 1905; there was no doubt about the father's identity. It certainly wasn't Captain Bethell, Clara's husband. Both of Clara's parents, Anne Barbour and Edward Klankenhorn, died when Clara was twenty years old, in 1900, and the Captain would have nothing to do with Clara when it became known that she was pregnant; in later years he regretted the way he treated Clara, denying her a home and banishing her completely from his life. Sarah accepted Clara and the child into her home, and when Clara died in 1918 of "Spanish" influenza, Sarah became the sole guardian and provider of thirteen-year-old Frank Yamada. By the time Frank was eighteen he was living on his own. He had no cash on hand, but he had plenty of places to stay, scattered properties of the Widdlesworths that at some time or the other were unoccupied and available. Frank availed himself of every opportunity, and occupied them, and invited his latest bright young man to share the lodgings and his bed. On weekends he and his lover visited Brent on Center Island. In the daytime they would go sailing in the Long Island Sound, and in the evening Frank would don a black mask and go preying on the large estates of Oyster Bay Cove, Cove Neck, Laurel Hollow, Mill Neck, Center Island, Muttontown, and Brookville. He came to know the wooded grounds of the estates better than the grounds-keepers who mowed the vast lawns and cleaned the fallen leaves from the long driveways that led up to the mansions on the hills. He became quite an accomplished cat burglar. He only took cash and jewelry and sometimes he took nothing, and never as much as disturbed the dust under the Aubusson carpets and Tiffany lamps and Chippendale furniture as he filched the Cartier jewelry, which he took to New York City and exchanged for cash. As a young boy he had come to know the area and the back roads, all the roads with the private property signs swinging from a chain. But it was the other roads, the entrances for delivery boys and servants, that Frank found to be the most accommodating for his line of work. Work? Frank had inherited a playground to test his wiles and wit. He was an accident. Never meant to be. Never meant to belong. Never meant to matter. He drifted, light as a feather, a feather falling from the highest nest, and the only way to go was down, slowly, darkly, and then go out, out like one of those green lights that blink from the ends of the docks around the rim of the harbor. Sarah sent Frank off to Harvard and Cambridge.

Sarah was far from pleased with Frank's unorthodox lifestyle, whatever she imagined it to be; she had not the slightest notion of his burglarious doings; yet she became wary about his influence over the still impressionable Brent, because she was suspicious of Frank's sexual proclivities. Frank and Brent would often go racing at breakneck speeds down some of the new motorways on Long Island, from the hinterlands of Brooklyn, Bay Ridge and Coney Island, to points out east, Montauk and Orient. Finally, Sarah insisted that Frank stay away from Brent. She cut him off. No more Widdlesworth's apartments. No more visits to Center Island. Frank found an apartment in Northport and paid the cheap rent with the money that he stole. That was fair enough, he thought. They never accepted him into their little world. I'm a half-yellow Jap bastard.

If Frank Yamada had not been enough infamy to blotch the good name of the Widdlesworths, more was in store. If one bastard in the family wasn't enough, then the humiliation of a second illegitimate child, the product of her own daughter, was to prove too much for Sarah. In 1920 Agnes gave birth to a boy whom Sarah named Charles William. She had to name him because her daughter, Agnes, would not reveal the identity of the father and Sarah insisted that Agnes relinquish any claim to the boy. Sarah would take care of any arrangements.

Giancarlo Bacigalupo had two sons, Johnny and Anthony. In 1928 his eldest son Johnny Bacigalupo married Silvia Cazzaza, his first cousin. They had no children; two babies had died at birth (the hyphenated peasant version of Theodore Roosevelt's "theory" of Anglo-Saxon Race Suicide). Johnny's brother, Anthony, was the lazy one, so everyone said, even though he had fought in France during World War I, and returned manifestly shell-shocked. When he came back from the war he worked as a delivery boy for Van Heffer's Meat Market in Oyster Bay. He liked to drive the road, the winding Route 25A, from Northport to Oyster Bay each morning to go to work. Working for Van Heffer's he delivered to all the large estates around Oyster Bay. He delivered to the Widdlesworth mansion on Center Island. One day in late 1919, Anthony met Agnes Babs Widdlesworth in the kitchen. What happened? Who seduced whom? Week in and week out they carried on in the large larder, plain and fancy fornicating. Then she became pregnant. Then she said that she had been raped. She never said by whom. Anthony was killed in 1922 when his delivery truck crashed conveniently through the wooden railing that went along the edge of the bay on the shore road from Oyster Bay to Bayville. Some speculated that the death was a suicide. Some speculated that it was murder. Charles William was born in December 1920 and Sarah, long suffering Sarah, had a second bastard on her hands.

Inevitable Paris beckoned. Now that William was dead, Sarah saw no good reasons to stay on. Sarah's ancient spinster Aunt Stephenine had plenty of room in her large home on the Rue de Varenne in the 7th Arrondissement. Sarah would leave America in the spring of 1928, next year, and she would take Charles William with her. Agnes would have no say in the matter; if she wanted to go gallivanting around the world, by all means do it, but Sarah would have no more to do with her daughter, and Charles William was coming with her to Paris. Agnes didn't protest. Brent did. He wasn't going anywhere. Fine, said Sarah. I've put up with all I can. Stay here and do as you like. Brent was only thirteen, but Brent did what he liked. Frank was a big brother to him. Frank would watch over him.

Agnes would never see her mother again. In April 1928 Sarah Barbour and seven-year-old Charles William boarded the *SS Paris* in New York, bound for Liverpool, England. They stayed at the Widdlesworth flat at Smith Square in London for two weeks before crossing the Channel to La Havre. Leaving the coal-stained buildings of La Havre behind them they took a train through the blighted, tired landscape, passing grim, grimy and sooty cities, and arrived at Gare St. Lazare, to be greeted by a Rolls Royce, which contained an English chauffeur.

Sarah died in 1935, two days shy of her sixtieth birthday. In those brief seven years since she had fled America, Charles William had disappointed her so. He ran away from home on many occasions. He fell in with the wrong crowd. He had rebel against the proper French language that he had been taught by a private tutor. He had rebelled in every possible facet of proper decorum. He was picking up the parlance of low-lifes, bums, thieves, and street people. Charles William started calling himself by different names, searching for the one that clicked; he was Zachariah, Jacob, Judas, Elijah. He acted like an outcast; he became an outcast. He told people that he was a Jew. An evil buzzing Jew. He wanted to pile on all their hatred. He lived on the streets. He slept on benches. He huddled over the heating vents at the Place de la Contrescarpe with the *clochards,* where young flower girls dyed their flowers on the pavements, where men and women got drunk and stayed drunk on cheap wine. When he was fifteen years old Charles William was living on the streets; he never again returned to the house on Rue de Varenne. He slept at night in the deserted Place St. Sulpice; he haunted the bars on the Rue de Buci; he walked among the dirt and squalor near the Place du Combat and Rue St. Denis; he snuck into the Cine du Combat to see the latest American movie; Charlie Chaplin's *Modern Times* was his favorite. He sat on the benches with the insane and old and infirm around the Square de Furstenberg and Eglise St. Germain; he climbed the stairs of Notre-Dame to gaze at the gargoyles; he attended to the whores on the Rue du Pasteur-Wagner and at the corner of Rue Amelot; he preferred the older whores; he frequented the Cafe de L'Elephant where the whores gathered in droves; he stumbled along the walls of the Cimetiere Montmartre and entered the Rue de Maistre, climbing the hills of Montmartre, up the Rue Lepic, to the Place du Tertre, and then downward into the frosted lights of Place Pigalle and Place de Clichy, to the bars and dance halls and cabarets; there were always two whores waiting at the corner of the Rue des Dames. The piss smelling blind alleyways were filled with whores, alleyways where dogs smelled the crotches of prostrate drunks. If on some cold night he managed to scrounge enough money, say five francs, Charles William would get a room on the Boulevard Beaumarchais; but if Frank were in Paris he would put Charles William up with him in a hotel on the Rue Bonaparte. Frank would take Charles William to the Dome, or Café de la Rotonde, and nurse a aperitif in the early evening and enjoy ridiculing all the orating and intoxicated American *poseurs*; it was quite a change from the sweat and poverty of the Cafe des Amateurs.

Under his torn overcoat Charles William carried his personal library. In one pocket was a battered copy of Gide, Cendrars, Baudelaire or Rimbaud. In the other pocket always a different book that he had stolen from a bookstore. One day it was a new novel called *La Nausée*, and then next week it would be another. Frank Yamada would visit Charles William several times in Paris. One day in 1938, in the Place de la Contrescarpe, they met Samuel Beckett. In the Jardin du Luxembourg they met Jean Genet; at Cafe de Jockey on the Boulevard du Montparnasse they met Jean Cocteau and Marchal Duchamp. Charles William actively sought out "names." He wanted to collect them like objects, to put them in a menagerie of his own design. He took notes. In February 1936 Charles

William stood outside the bookstore Shakespeare and Company, in the cold night air, on the Rue de L'Odeon, and waited for a glimpse of Andre Gide, who was to give a reading. Charles William saw a man wearing a black patch over his eye, him he couldn't place, but he could place Stephen Valéry. In May 1940, Charles William met a young journalist for *Paris-Soir*, who showed him a manuscript of an unpublished novel that he had been working on that morning, called *L'Étranger*. Can one be happy after an evil deed? In theory? Is he another Raskolnikov? Reading the first page made Charles William think about his mother for the first time since that day in April 1928, when he left her on the dock in New York and kissed her and waved goodbye from the ship. He was a stranger to mother love; a stranger to love. He wasn't sad and he never cried. The others cried… *cris de haine*.

After the war he met Jean-Paul Clébert and frequented the cafés around Saint-Germain-des-Prés, most regularly Chez Moineau, where a younger crowd gathered and a group that called itself the Letterist International promoted themselves, exclaiming: never work and drift. *Dérive*.

Charles William Mouche's memoir of the 1930s was published privately and became an instant underground classic. Although the book was suppressed for indecency and obscenity when it was published in America in 1964, the book was eventually carried along in the ever-changing tides of legal and cultural opinion that swept through the various lower court judicial decisions that permitted the publication of Allen Ginsberg's *Howl*, and William Burroughs's *Naked Lunch*, and a Supreme Court decision in 1966 that Henry Miller's *Tropic of Cancer* was protected by the First Amendment's guarantees of freedom of speech and press. Charles William Mouche's book is now a crumpled paperback of faded cover and yellowing to brown paper. It's on my desk beside me even as I write these words. It's called *O Vers!*

Brent Widdlesworth traveled with Frank Yamada to Paris in the spring of 1937, the year before Brent drowned. It was also the year that Frank returned to America and stepped-up his activities and sharpened his prowling prowess as a cat burglar, stalking the grounds of the large estates on the green-glowing North Shore of Long Island. He lived in the small apartment in Northport, over one of the garages in the backyard. The place looked exactly like the Cazzaza buildings in Oyster Bay. There was a good reason for it. None other than Toots Bacigalupo was his landlady. Her opera career didn't pan out like Frank's life of theft did for him.

Agnes Babs Widdlesworth never married. She became inordinately fond of Captain Bethell and when she wasn't somewhere else in the world, she was at the Captain's house in Northport. The baby remained a secret and Agnes had no desire to see him after her mother took Charles William to Paris. She didn't attend her mother's funeral in Paris in 1935. But when Frank Yamada told Agnes that he had been meeting Charles William in Paris for the past several years, her motherly instincts got the best of her. She had to see him at least one time before she died. She had only a few close relatives left; her mother and father were dead and she and Brent haven't spoken to each other in five years. When Brent died in 1938, Agnes was in Paris, and became more despondent than ever when she heard the news. Despite the growing dangers in Europe she had come to Paris in the summer of 1936. Her son Charles William was all of sixteen years old by now and was already calling himself by his *non-de-plume*, Charles William Mouche.

The Anarchist of South Street

"Are you waving the flag at me?"

Maurizio Cazzaza closed and locked the door to his room and walked down the long dark hallway. Behind him in the front rooms, his three sisters-in-law sat in their chairs by the windows waiting for the Memorial Day parade to pass by. Maurizio didn't turn around to see if they saw him as he quietly made his way down the hallway to the landing at the top of the stairs. As he descended the stairs he turned around to look beyond the dusty thick curtains that were hung in the doorway instead of a door at the other end of the hallway; his eyes peering over the top step; nobody saw him leaving. He went down the wooden stairs; at the bottom of the stairs he turned right, entering the kitchen; it was dark and cold. On the kitchen table was a large picnic basket filled with sandwiches, cheeses, nuts, fruits, and homemade wine. Next to the picnic basket was the brass button that had fallen off of Giuseppe's fireman's uniform at the last moment as he was squeezing into his jacket. Leonora didn't have time to sew it back on. He would have been late for the parade; and Giuseppe has never been late. Maurizio looked at his brother's brass button as if it were more than a button, as if it were a piece of gold. Maurizio took an apple from the bowl and went out the door, down the concrete steps, into the dark alleyway and then out to the bright light of South Street.

The streets were crowded with people by now, all lined up on the sidewalks; children sitting on the curbs or on the shoulders of their fathers. Men wore white cotton pants and short-sleeve shirts, suspenders and straw hats with white bands, standing akimbo, or with arms folded, leaning on cars and telephone poles. Boys were dressed in baggy short pants, white shirts, marching in place and saluting every time that they saw their fathers saluting to the flapping flags fluttering by. The women wore flowing frumpy dresses with thin belts, skirts well below the knees or lower, flopping wide brim summer hats with flowers, many of the women sat in cars, watching through the rolled down windows, or sat in folding chairs placed under the awnings of shops, protecting themselves from the sun. A few daring women wore their skirts tightly around their hips, hems at the knee, no hats, short hair. Emile Baldazzi had his eye on these young creatures of fashion. For Emile, seduction was the only attainment left for a leftist revolutionary to accomplish, and advertising and flaunting their wares didn't hurt none, arise and subjugate the bourgeois! "Get a load of that piece of pook, Henry. Ya didn't think a small conventional dead-end town like this had any action; and you want to go to Paris! Ya just wait until tonight, it's all here Henry, right here in small town America, you just wait until tonight, wait and see, ther'll be some real rough ridin' for the boys in Teddy's town tonight, don't cha know..." Emile smoothly shifting to singing... "there'll be a hot time in the old town tonight..." what else? Did you expect *Vesti La Guibba* or somethin' like that for land's sake? Did you expect Luigi Bollo to throw open his window and join Emile in a duet from his beloved icon Verdi, from Rigoletto perhaps?

Maurizio is silent. But he is not a mute. He tries to follow the conversations that Emile has with his friend Henry. Maurizio sculpting on the roof, Rocky playing with the pigeons, Emile holding forth on Anarchism, Sacco and Vanzetti, Emma Goldman, Dostoyevsky, Nietzsche... Maurizio and Rocky taking it all in. The charismatic intonations, the gesturing, the vibrancy, the scatological interjections, the felt passion, the apocalyptic and apodictic diction of death and resurgence, the bone scattering energy, but none of the structural articulation of transcendent meaning that seemed absent now and forever on a spring day in 1927. It's all nonsense anyway, thought Maurizio; sometimes he saw himself as more the passive nihilist than anarchist.

The drum and fife corp of the American Legion Band was playing "Yankee Doodle Dandy" in the couple-of-blocks-distance. The smacking, hacking ratata ta ta of the snare drums approaching. Frankie Cazzaza was in the sixth row of the main body of the band, holding his trombone at his side. This was the traditional start of the parade. The parade will follow the accustomed route up South Street, turn left onto Audrey Avenue and proceed on to the future site of Theodore Roosevelt Memorial Park, where a destroyer of the U.S. Navy is anchored in the bay. The Navy Band will play the "Star Spangled Banner," and a memorial wreathe will be thrown from the destroyer and settle on the water, followed by a 21-gun salute blowing the seagulls off their perchments. The bugles will blow taps and then the politicians will blow hot air.

On its own the American Legion Band marched down towards Townsend Park. Ratata ta ta the sharp snare drums sneering a monotonous languid lullaby of taut precision. Twenty-five spiffy sailors all in white with long swords hanging from the hip are waiting in the park, having disembarked from the destroyer. The American Legion Band will meet them and then accompany the navy men back the same route from which the band came. The crowd proud as peacocks applauding the shining white examples of preening strutting pre-eminence in the world.

Maurizio walked through the crowd. He crossed East Main Street and continued north on South Street. He turned around to watch, as the American Legion Band turned left onto Audrey Avenue, passing around the corner where the Oyster Bay Bank stood. The band marched passed the smiling-as-if-toothless brick facades of small town shops; now passing Powyrs Plumbing, the Five & Dime Store, now passing Razzini's Fruit and Vegetable Store; the Razzini's were later Italian arrivals to town and became friendly rivals of Giuseppe's store (Giuseppe does the better business); now passing the Lyric Theater and the Post Office, now passing, bearing right, for the road bends that way down to the railroad station, the bandstand with two flanking cannon in a small village green called Townsend Park. Behind the bandstand surrounded by some shrubbery is the concrete pedestal upon which the statue of Captain Roger Bethell once stood, now deposited in the basement of the Town Hall, which stands opposite the Post Office.

After enough Italians had arrived in Oyster Bay by the early 1920s, mostly coming from the city on the dead end train tracks, to this dead end town, finding quarters on Irving Place, a cul-de-sac on a hill beneath the Catholic Church, an Italian Club was organized, with twelve original members. They found a small room to hold meetings on Audrey Avenue, near the railroad tracks, exactly where the band is now passing. Later, a Knights of Columbus was organized, with six original members; they found a spare room above Powyrs Plumbing shop. And no member from one club ever attended the other club for some private tribal reason no doubt. But these meeting rooms were rather modest compared to that other club in town, the Masons, Theodore Roosevelt was a brother, who were well-heeled in a large two-storey wooden shoebox building with a large piazza and decorated pillars holding up a fancifully carved sign with gold lettering that read: Masonic Temple. This Anglo-Saxon-Dutch tribe had no discourse with the two Italian town tribes, only on occasion a bit of intercourse, daughters of the Masonic aristocracy breaking the taboos set forth by the big chief White Hot Panic and degrading themselves with the plebs. Eventually, of course, it was neither discourse nor intercourse that became the interface of the tribes; it was a business course learned at the school of individual enterprise. And eventually, the two Italian tribes, the earlier immigrants to town representing the Italian Club, speaking mostly in Italian, and who were primarily interested in bocce ball and wine, and the later immigrants to town, representing the Knights of Columbus, speaking mostly in English, and who were more interested in business and civic matters, got together to form a St. Rocco's Feast. The Italian Club taking care of the more festive matters and the Knights of Columbus taking take of the more financial matters. St. Rocco's Feast was held every summer for two days on the streets surrounding the small village green. On the second night of the feast a firework's display was held in the empty baseball sand-lot by Heemskirk's Shipyard, the crowds having to make their way over to the firework site by walking on the sunken pebbled path next to the railroad tracks, but over the years the crowd became so big that some people had to walk on the tracks, therefore the Anglo-Saxon-Dutch tribe of Town Fathers stipulated that the fireworks couldn't be shot off until after the last train pulled out, at midnight, for safety reasons. Town Fathers cared about things like that in those days.

The American Legion Band returned to the Legion Hall with its sparkling and spangling members of the Great White Fleet in tow. Now the parade was ready to advance in full measure, from engine to caboose, from American Legion Band to hook-and-ladder fire truck. Boom ba boom ba boom. Many of the people who had gathered in the park to hear the speeches and see the Navy destroyer in the harbor, were walking back to town to see the parade. The speeches were still going on, much longer than anticipated. But the parade couldn't be held up any longer. The crowd had been kept waiting long enough. The parade will begin without the town administrators and elite. Without Agnes Babs Widdlesworth, who had no intention of seeing a parade anyway (if Alice Roosevelt Longworth knew that Agnes Babs Widdlesworth was at the ceremony in the park, would she have attended also? To be in the same company as such an illustrious personage! Both of them twiddling their thumbs and forefingers around their pearl necklaces; isn't that what being royalty was all about, rubbing elbows with your executioner?). The parade will start without the ministers from the Presbyterian Church, the priest from the Catholic Church, etc., they were still sitting in their folding chairs on the podium in the park, with their hands folded together and their heads tilted. The politicians were now taking turns making speeches, the leaders of the business community having just completed their big speeches. Everyone spoke of the great sacrifices, the great martyrdoms of the past, of freedom, of country.

The parade passed by the Cazzaza building; Frankie waved up at his mother and his two aunts in the windows in the front rooms. After the American Legion Band passed by, it was followed by the naval brigade, as white as Agnes Babs Widdlesworth's splendiferous European and American-kept-custodianship soul, from Charlemagne to Alfred the Great to William the Conqueror, rekindled on the teat of American independence.

The Atlantic Steamer Fire Company took up the rear of the parade, with proud erect Giuseppe marching in the first row. His proudest moment, every year, was that moment when he passed by his fruit and vegetable store, looking up to the windows in his building, seeing Fiorenza, and hearing his children call out to him from the curb, seated in the little red wagon that he had built.

The parade turned right onto East Main Street and continued boom ba boom ba boom on up toward the cove, passing the firehouse and churches and library and new high school; now the road narrowing, no more sidewalk, fewer houses with front yards and gates opening directly onto the sidewalk and street, now great majestic elms and oaks and beeches and spruces and lindens spreading out over the road, the purple pebbled driveways leading up to the manor houses on the private estates, roads frilly with azaleas and rhododendrons and dogwoods and Japanese cherry trees and magnolias and crab apples and many other flowering trees bubbling with blooms this warm day in May, and here and there a Cedar of Lebanon and a Sargent Weeping Hemlock in the middle of a spacious lawn, a carpet to the mock-Elizabethan architecture, the landscaped gardens, but of course you cannot see any of this from the road where you stand in front of the large 18th century iron gates imported from England, maybe you are a little boy, and your father is taking you for a walk "up the cove," pushing you in the stroller, and you wonder why these pebbles are purple and who lives in those big houses up there that you can see slightly but only in winter when the falling leaves reveal them, and Stephen picks a stick up from the ground and his father turns back into town, pushing Stephen passed the high school, the library, the churches, and through the big lifting doors of the firehouse, where the trucks are being washed and shined and where Uncle Frankie picks Stephen up and puts him in the driver's seat of a big red fire truck... gonna be a fireman one day...

Frankie is playing his trombone now, and the parade marches on boom ba boom ba boom toward the wooded recesses of Cove Road, and as it does the crowd becomes more sparse; the parade now passing the new Oyster Bay High School, which is under construction, to be opened in February 1929, from which ten years later Joe Cazzaza will be graduated.

At this point most of the parade turned left onto Ships Point Lane, which leads down to the harbor, where there is a small beach, where Joe and Frankie and Stevie like to go swimming. It wasn't too long ago that the fashion was for young Anglo-Saxon swains to build human pyramids here to the delight of a bevy of onlooking bathing beauties, before the riffraff from the city moved in and started using the beach.

At Ships Point Lane most of the parade disbanded and the old dispensation of clans reunited with their familial contacts. At this juncture the American Legion Band and the Navy brigade, like one of the train engines down at the revolving turntable by the dead-end railroad station, were disconnected from the trailing passenger cars, and continued on their own up the cove until they came to the base of Cove Neck, where a road leads up to Sagamore Hill, where Alice Roosevelt and Edith Roosevelt are having tea in the Drawing Room. Edith's small eyes are staring into the polar bear eyes of a polar bear rug, a gift from Admiral Peary after he returned from the North Pole. Alice is staring into a painting hung above a Beauvais tapestry screen, a scene from a Louisiana bayou. Nick is staring into a glass of whiskey. Everyone is silent. Everyone is somewhere else. Edith is on the North Pole, Alice in the Bayou. And Nick in the arms of his mistress. And Alice's little daughter, Stephenina, born on Valentine's Day two years ago, lies on the carpet, and Nick searches her features for some resemblance to him, but in vain.

Frank Yamada is on a train heading for the station at Oyster Bay. He is contemplating a crime, the next victim of the servant's entrance cat burglar. Giuseppe is walking home, where Fiorenza and her sisters are making some more sandwiches for the picnic basket. Frankie is thirsty and wants to get a drink of water from the artesian well located across the road from Youngs' Cemetery. The band paused here, ratata ta ta, Youngs' Cemetery on the right, with its wooden white crosses at the base of the hill, where a plaque in stone indicates that these crosses are In Memory Of The Faithful Slaves Of The Youngs Family Whose Graves Are Marked By Wooden Crosses. That was so nice of them to be faithful. "Where are the stones that mark the bones of those who die in Oyster Bay? There are no stones to mark the bones of those who die in Oyster Bay." -Samuel Youngs 1800.

Up twenty-six steps, at the top of the hill, within black iron bars, is the grave of Theodore Roosevelt, comprised of an upright grey gravestone arched at the top with two pilasters at each side and rosettes at each point, and just beneath the arch is the great seal of the United States, the one on the back of the dollar bill, the eagle with his olive branch and arrows. The ground is covered in ivy. And now a navy man is laying a wreath, and the minister from the Episcopalian Church is saying a few words, speaking softly, the birds darting through the trees. And now a wreath is being tossed onto the water of the cove at the end of the dirt road across the street from the cemetery, near the 18th century homestead where George Washington slept one night in 1790, and a navy chaplain is saying a few words, speaking softly, the sea gulls gliding over the bay. Frankie finally gets to take a drink of cool running water from the artesian well. This artesian well, like all the other artesian wells in the town, had dried up or, more often, been shut down, re-routed onto private property, or plugged with cement, within the next fifty years. Notice the wasteland motif.

The north end of South Street was quiet and empty. Maurizio crossed the street and took a drink from another artesian well. He continued walking, taking a short-cut through a small wooded area with a narrow path until he came out on Hamilton Avenue. He could see the colored tanks of the Commander Oil Company at the end of South Street, standing on the edge of the harbor. Across the street from Belsen and White's was a long rambling flophouse. Maurizio entered the house and knocked on the door of room 6. Emile Baldazzi opened the door and greeted Maurizio by offering him his gnarled and mutilated hand to shake. Two fingers were missing due to carpentry related accidents; another half of a finger was missing due to non-accidental union organizing activities at Heemskirk's Shipyard, where Emile had worked as a carpenter. He doesn't work there anymore. Maurizio looked around Emile's room. A bed, a night stand, a pile of books on the floor, including Emile's collection of Victorian and other types of "pornography": *Justine, Fanny Hill, Venus in Furs, The Autobiography of a Flea, The Lustful Turk, The Mysteries of Verbena House, Love on the Sly, Peep Behind the Curtains of a Female Seminary, A Night in a Moorish Harem, Life and Loves, Ulysses,* and *Count Bruga,* a gift from Emile's friend Henry. Thrown around the room were photographs that Emile had taken of some of the prostitutes in Belsen and White's. Cindy, a Chinese girl with a "scent of crushed and perfumed butterfly wings hovering over her Jade Gate," as printed on the bottom of her photographs, was the subject of most of the photographs. Emile made a few dollars selling these pictures. Frank Yamada bought some and brought them to Paris to sell.

Maurizio and Emile walked down the street. At the end of Hamilton Avenue they turned right and were in sight of the railroad station. Theodore Roosevelt Memorial Park was on the other side of the tracks and station. Officially it was not yet called Theodore Roosevelt Memorial Park; it wouldn't be designated and dedicated as such until next year, 1928.

The station was busy; the park was filled with people. Many of them leaving, many of them still arriving, hoping to see the navy destroyer. Many had come on the ferry that ran from the pier at the end of Bay View Avenue, and crossed the Long Island Sound, to Stamford, Connecticut. Maurizio and Emile sat down on a bench on the station's platform and waited for the arrival of the train that would be carrying Emile's friend Henry out from the city. Over the park the loudspeakers carried the voice of Reverend Sowles: "...That they have not sacrificed their lives in vain..."

The train carrying Emile's friend Henry passed along the ridge overlooking the pond at Beaver Dam. When covered with ice in the winter the pond is a favorite spot for ice-skating. The Beaver Brook runs down from the south... "Papaquatunk, it is called by my people, Papaquatunk," said Aliaspun in a novel by Roger Bethell. "Here our thirty families lived on common land. My families are dead. The founders say that the land is now waste and vacant. Everything that they do not own they call it waste and vacant. After the Waste Land the Vacant Lot. Postmodernism. The train is coming; I must hop the train and ride outta here. Can't let the bulls catch me. They'd beat me with a club. Oooh dem bulls are mean. I'm a card-carrying member of the I.W.W. I won't work!"

Mr. Van Voorhis and Mr. Tomlin are on the train, sitting next to each other, both reading the financial section of the New York Times. "Look!" says Mr. Tomlin to Mr. Voorhis, gazing out the window. "What do you make of that?"

"It's a wild Indian I dare say."

"It's a hobo."

"It's an anarchist!"

"We shall be scalped!"

"We shall be begged for a handout!"

"We shall be blown up!"

"Oh dear."

"How will this affect the stock market?"

"Not to worry. Look. They've got him. Splendid. The bull clubbed him. No more trouble from him."

"Bully for you, old boy, bully for you. Hip hip hooray!"

Aliaspun rolled down the embankment like a bag of potatoes. The train disappeared like a dark wedge between the trees. Aliaspun got up from the mud and grass, his face bloody, and waved his fist at the train. "Damn you fat American tourists reading your newspapers!"

The train's whistle was blowing a long crowing whaaaaaa as the train came around the bend and crossed the trestle over Shore Road by the Mill Pond. The ticket collector passed by the large St. Bernard that sat between coaches. "Hey, Butch boy, that's a good dog," said the ticket collector and Butch stuck out his tongue and lapped up the drool from around his mouth, his tail wagging playfully. Butch had boarded the train in Glen Cove and was riding to Oyster Bay on his daily excursion. When he gets off at Oyster Bay he'll head straight into town in the direction of Van Heffer's Meat Market. The butchers there are good to Butch. They throw him slabs of fatty meat edges. When he's finished he heads back to the train and returns to Glen Cove where he frequents the local meat market there, and he'll sleep the night in the train station; it's the same routine everyday; it's a dog's life. It's a wonderful life.

The train approached the railroad crossing, where red lights were flashing, bells were ringing, black and white bars were lowering in place to prevent cars from passing over the tracks, and a father was holding the hand of his little boy, waiting for the steel soot-black blast of air to dust their faces. The train's whistle blew two short hoarse honks that reminded the father, holding his little boy's hand, of migrating geese, the Canadian Honkers that the father will take his little boy to shoot one cool day on a trip upstate. Down the track by the station, two boys, one black and one white, had put a penny on the rail and were now waiting for the results of their experiment. What if the train crashes? Said one boy to the other. The other boy just shrugged. The train passed between Heemskirk's Shipyard and the leafy green arabesques of the woods, where Yukio Yamada's body was found, over twenty years ago. "We had some trouble here," said Mr. Van Voorhis, referring to Heemskirk's Shipyard, "with union agitators. But we put them down. You never know what those anarchists' bastards will be up to next. Dynamite. Sabotage. It's a real war. But we ran them out of town. They won't give us any more trouble. You can rest assured." Mr. Van Voorhis and Mr. Tomlin began singing Yankee Doodle: "Plucked a feather from his hat and called it ca-vi-a-ri... ha ha ha..."

Emile's friend Henry looked up from the book he was reading; he closed the book; he had reached page 268 of Dostoyevsky's *The Idiot*. He looked out the train's window. He was unable to focus his eyes on the blur of branches that the train speeded past. He placed his fingers, like two pinchers, on the ridge of his nose, shoving his glasses up over his brow, and rubbed his eyes.

"They found my father dead there," said a voice. This surprised Henry, for the man who has been sitting next to him the entire trip had said nothing at all previously. "He killed himself with poison. In 1905. Before I was born. He had the courage to do it. To act. I am a coward. I am like Strindberg running in and out of the icy sea." At this, Henry smiled. Must be a literary man. Frank Yamada was not especially a literary man. He was

324

the poet of cat burglars, that he would admit to. He only mentioned Strindberg because he saw that Henry was reading Dostoyevsky. He wanted to break the ice. Henry for the first time looked into the eyes of the young stranger, saw his dark features and black wavy hair. Henry thought that the man might have some Native American blood but wasn't presumptuous enough to ask him. He didn't have to ask. "My father was Japanese. He wanted to be loyal to his country. It was the time of the war with Russia. He also wanted to be loyal to his friend. He was disloyal to both. So he killed himself."

"My ancestors were Germans," said Henry, "Germans are loyal Americans. I think they make the best Americans, but they are also loyal Germans, unfortunately. They have been known to kill also, like most European nations."

"My name is Frank. Frank Yamada. It's a very common name in Japan, Yamada, it means Mountain Ricefield. It's like Smith or Jones. But it's a samurai name too."

"Miller. Henry Miller. From Brooklyn."

The train whined to a halt in the station. The two boys who had placed a penny on the rail, raced to the track and searched for the defaced penny. It was not to be found. Disappointed but undaunted by the results, the two boys ran down the pebble path and hopped up on the station platform. "Hey mister dy'a got anudder penny," said one of the boys to Emile Baldazzi.

"What happened?"

"I'd'n't know. We can't find it."

"Well look harder. Ya think I'm rich or somethin'."

The boys ran over to the turntable to watch the engine turn around.

Emile paced back and forth on the platform. "Henry will bring a batch of books with him. Just you wait'n'see."

"Yes yes. Good good," said Maurizio, disinterestedly.

Back and forth, a nervous nellie, Emile paced in front of the bench where Maurizio sat in unflappable repose, which was unusual for these nervous and flapper times. His hands were folded over the knob of his walking cane that was held erect before him between his legs, the fingers of his left hand patting repetitively the knuckles of his right hand, one finger flapping after the other, pinky-ring-middle-fore fingers, thrud-thrud-thrud, that was the extent of his nervous energy. Maurizio stuck out his chin, his

325

eyebrows raised and alert, his nasal tracers sniffing out over his mothish mustache for the scents that surrounded him, within reach; his nose hairs like spores whiffing over warm air. Maurizio had a formal dignity that in no manner contradicted the insouciant spriteness in his playful beguiling eyes. Women simply adored him for his charm. But for some reason Maurizio wouldn't lay a hand on them. He just attracted them like bees to nectar, and that was the sport to him, attraction. He didn't shun the low class or high class. Maurizio doffed his hat, twinkled his eyes and mustache and the ladies were charmed beyond comprehension. At least Emile couldn't comprehend it. It was one of the reasons that Emile sought out Maurizio's company. Emile has been dying to get his hands on a high-class wench, as he not so fondly calls them. Maurizio may provide access through that impervious membrane of silt and swill that makes a pearl smooth and sparkle, the highest and holiest pearl. And little did he know that one of these pearls was sitting on a platform not far from him, in the park, attending today's ceremonies, a shining white pearl who goes by the name of Agnes Babs Widdlesworth. But sitting on a rung so high that no matter where Emile places his social ladder he will see only the bottom of her public shoes and not her private pubic hair, ever. Not that he wants to move up in life; not that he could possibly be a social climber. There was no rung low enough for him to hop on in the beginning. And yet, he told Maurizio, it is his "proletarian challenge and revolt in defiance of an oppressive class system; a revolt to circumvent the concentrated heritage of the plutonic hermitage of Roman antiquities that fettered the least enfranchised class with the duty of procreating in droves the labor force of a slave state. In the end it is only a matter of economics. Sex, pure and simple. I need to perform this duty, to prevent the Anglo-Saxon race from its own self-inflicted demise. Race Suicide. I want to help them procreate, to create a stronger and smarter race of mutts."

He was telling this to Maurizio but to no avail. Maurizio didn't catch the sarcasm and irony in his discourse. One day he'll get one of these moneyed wenches. But tonight he'll settle for his Cindy Chinchin.

As for Agnes Babs Widdlesworth, unbeknownst to Emile, she's already been penetrated by a member of the working classes, one Anthony Bacigalupo, now deceased, a former delivery boy for Van Heffer's Meat Market, and she has begat a new product, a stronger and smarter mutt, who will prove unmanageable, six-year-old Charles William, who right now is staying with his grandmother in the mansion on Center Island.

Maurizio sought only the platonic company of women; he loved to be the only man in a room filled with women and perfume fragránces, which is why he spent so much time in Belsen and White's. Maurizio has not been with too many women over the years. He remembers fondly one particular time, when he was fifteen years old, and his distant cousin who lived in Genova (Maurizio was never certain that he actually was a blood relative) invited him to stay at the University of Turin. (Maurizio was surprised that any relative of his could go to a university!) But Maurizio's father insisted that he go along with his cousin.

"So this is what you study at university? Prostitutes!"

"Maurizio, it's a three, four, five-hundred-year-old tradition, don't worry; the Pope knows! All the Popes knew."

So Maurizio lost his virginity in the halls of the University of Turin, in a traditional rite of passage also upheld at the University of Naples, where Maurizio's nephew Joe, Giuseppe's youngest son, would sleep, not with a woman, but with a hundred American soldiers who had just crossed from Oran to Naples in a British ship during World War Two.

When Maurizio and Emile met for the first time, in Belsen and White's, they had been attracted to each other by that mysterious chemical reaction activated by sex, words, silence and music. Emile talked and took photographs of Cindy Chinchin, that was the name he gave her; and Maurizio listened and hummed Italian songs. But he never took part in a physical sense, and he hardly looked; he wasn't a voyeur as you may well imagine under the circumstances. Sometimes Maurizio waited in the foyer, while Emile closed the door. Maurizio smiled at the women walking down the hallway, going in and out of the doors, and they smiled back at him, alluring and perfumed, unbuttoning and peeling back a portion of their blouses, exposing large luscious breasts. "Yes, yes. Good, good," said Maurizio, approvingly. After a night's debauchery, Maurizio and Emile would either go and sit up on the roof with the sculptures and pigeons or go back to Emile's room in the flophouse across from Belsen and White's, and then they would discuss politics and art and philosophy. Sacco and Vanzetti was the current topic, revitalized after a seven-year debasement in the hollow basement of the American judicial system.

A trail of black smoke from the train's engine twisted upward like a black burnt rope and spread out like a hangman's cloak. The train let out a sigh of steam, pshodddd, and came to a halt in front of the station. Henry was lost in vague thoughts of suicide and escape. A hand clasped his shoulder a bit too gentlemanly, a bit softer than public decorum allows.

"Getting off? Coming? This is it. The end of the line. Dead end," said Frank Yamada.

"I know," said Henry, brusquely. Henry gathered up his books. Frank touched Henry's elbow.

"You do like to read. Are you meeting anyone?" said Frank.

"Yes. I'm meeting a friend. Emile Baldazzi. Know 'im?"

"Sorry. Don't believe I've met him. You look pale. Are you sick?"

"I'm fine. Go ahead." Frank tilted his head to the side slightly. He got the message. Nonplussed, he disembarked, followed by Henry, who was followed by Butch the St. Bernard.

Emile greeted Henry as he stepped down from the grated steel step to the cement platform, steam gushing up from under him. "Ah heh," said Emile as a greeting, and clasped Henry around the shoulders in the proper friendly and manly fashion, ironically a very Rooseveltian gesture.

"Ya made it. I doubted you'd come for a moment."

"Just about. So what kind of a town do you got here?" asked Henry.

"You'd be surprised to find out what goes on in this town. That guy bother you? I know him. We do a dirty picture business. A local fairy."

Emile made a beeline for Frank. "Forget it," said Henry. "Don't cha'know, let 'em go. He reads Strindberg. He said he didn't know you."

"Not by name. Anyway, Strindberg, all the more reason to kick his ass," joked Emile. Strange, isn't it? That having read Strindberg saved Frank's balls from being battered black and blue, whereas it has probably caused a lot of Swedes to commit suicide.

Emile introduced Henry to Maurizio. "Here's the guinea anarchist I was telling you about." They shook hands.

Arthur and Wayne headed up Hamilton Avenue. The parade was over but the fire trucks would be on display in front of the firehouse. The children were permitted to climb on them. "Hey, let's go see the fire trucks," said Wayne. The two boys crossed South Street and went into the dark alleyway. They took a drink of water from the artesian well in the backyard.

"Hey! That's our waawder," shouted little Stevie Cazzaza, leaning forward on his crutches. "You got to ask permission from my papa first." Wayne went over to Stevie and pulled a crutch out from under him. Stevie fell to the ground.

"You got two cents?" said Arthur to Stevie. "Let's have it."

"I ain't got nothin'," said Stevie."

Giuseppe and Frankie were walking down the laneway together, returning from the parade. Luisa ran to them and cried, "papa, papa." Frankie handed his father the trombone and ran down the laneway. When Arthur and Wayne saw him running towards them, they both ran into the alleyway. "Hey you two!" Frankie yelled.

"Hay is for horses!" shouted Arthur Macarthur and Wayne Payne together, as they vanished into the dark narrow alleyway. Unfortunately, for Arthur and Wayne, Butch the St. Bernard was coming through the alleyway in the other direction, heading for the backyard and Van Heffer's, looking for some leftover fat to lick out of the meat barrels. There was no room to get around Butch. The boys had a choice. Let Butch clobber and slobber them, or take cover in the pee-stained corner halfway through the alley.

In the kitchen downstairs Fiorenza and her sisters are putting the final touches on the sandwiches for the picnic, wrapping them in wax paper, placing them in the picnic basket, snug and cozy next to the bottles of homemade wine. Sandwiches made of homemade bread with slices of cold cuts from Van Heffer's Meat Market: liverwurst, pepperoni, bologna, mortadella, and pancetta. There are sesame breadsticks, bruschetta, olive rolls, and hard rolls sprinkled with poppy seeds. There are cheeses: romano, parmesan, pecorino, fontina, mozzarella, provolone, and cheddar. Leftover cold pasta. Baccala and anchovies. Salads doused in olive oil. Spices of basil, parsley, oregano and garlic.

In one of the garages beneath the apartments Giuseppe is starting up the large dark-olive REO truck. The long canopied flatbed truck has removable wooden side-slats that are shaking about as Giuseppe revs up the engine and pulls the truck out onto the macadamized surface of the backyard. With the exception of special days like today, the truck is utilized only twice a week, on Mondays and Thursdays, when Giuseppe wakes up at 3 a.m., gets dressed, and quietly creeps out of the house, careful not to awaken anyone, usually in vain, because once he starts up the truck, the pounding engine acts as an alarm clock, the children open their eyes, realize that it's only papa and his truck going off to the city, and fall back to sleep. Giuseppe begins his journey about 3:30 and travels the narrow meandering route 25A, which becomes Northern Boulevard in Queens, then down to the Williamsburg Bridge, crossing over into Manhattan, up Delancey Street, to the old neighborhood, where he loads the truck with crates of vegetables and fruits from one of the outlets. Maurizio, loyal as ever to his brother, goes along to help.

Giuseppe takes the large picnic basket from Fiorenza and places it down in the back of the truck. Fiorenza grabs hold of Giuseppe's hand and he pulls her into the back of the truck. Leonora and Teresa are next to be helped up into the back of the truck, then the children climb up: Frankie lifts Stevie and hands him his crutches, and then lifts little Joe; Toots lifts Luisa into the truck. Giuseppe's oldest friend, Elia Preggo, Sr., sits in the cab with Giuseppe, and Elia Preggo Jr., carrying his burlap bag of bocce balls, hops onto the back of the truck. Luigi Bollo arrives with his accordion; Stefano Carducci arrives with his violin; they both climb into the back of the truck. *Como sta?* Hi. Hi. *Como sta?* Howayooa? *Cos, cos.* O.K. O.K. Yes, yes. Good, good. *Andiamo...* we're off...

The children spot Butch the dog and call to him. C'mon Butch, c'mon. Butch runs to the truck as it pulls out of the backyard. Frankie and Elia Jr. grab hold of Butch and pull him up into the truck where he lets out a lazy breathless bark of happiness at his success. The truck stumps and stamps up the laneway; the rattling tailpipe blows carbon monoxide fumes, visibly swirling around the grapevines and chicken coops. The truck turns left onto East Main Street, passing the firehouse, the fire trucks outside on display. Arthur and Wayne are climbing on a fire truck; Frank and Luisa see the two troublemakers and blow raspberry cheers at them, who reply in kind with the added emphasis of middle fingers vigorously thrusted into the air. "Ooooo see what they did," said Luisa to her mother.

"Sit down before you fall down."

Giuseppe and the others on the truck wave to the firemen, who are sitting out in front of the firehouse, and the firemen wave back. Then Wilbur Waters, assistant fire chief, pulls out a large knife, smiles at Giuseppe, who smiles back. Wilbur and some of the firemen go over to the laneway behind the firehouse, steal a chicken from the coops, string it up, slit its throat, and prepare it for cooking. The firemen will be shooting craps late into the morning and eating chicken with greasy fingers. The chicken thefts, which began five years ago as a practical joke, are all done with Giuseppe's half-hearted approval and what-are-ya-gonna do consent. It's become a tradition.

The REO truck turns left onto South Street and passes between Giuseppe's fruit and vegetable store on the left and Saunder's drug store on the right. At the end of South Street the truck turns left again, onto Berry Hill Road, a tree-lined dirt road winding its way through the woods. Beyond the top of the road where it curves sharply to the right and joins up with the top of Sandy Hill Road, there is a large rectangular field, where occasional pickup football games take place. For a while, the high school football team played its games here; Giuseppe's son Joe would play here, and by the early 1960s Joe's son Stephen would watch black men dressed in white outfits play cricket here. By the 1970s the development started, and the field was no more, just suburban houses. In the woods behind the field a firetower crowns the treetops. The REO truck enters the field, bouncing along, and stops on the other side, at the edge of the woods. The children jump down and run into the field, heading for the firetower. The adults spread blankets on the grass. Luigi Bollo plays his accordion... jammo jamma jammo jamma...

Maurizio and Henry are with Emile in his room.

"So how's your wife doing?" Asked Emile.

"June's in Paris," replied Henry.

"Paris you say. Paris, as in Paris, France? How's that?"

"Look..." Henry took some postcards out from between the pages of one of the books he was carrying. A postcard of the Eiffel Tower, one of the Arch of Triumph, one of Notre Dame. "She wants money," said Henry, "tell me where am I gonna get money? I'm a goddamn gravedigger. And yet I send her what I got."

"Gravedigger?"

"In Queens. It's got me feeling suicidal. I work for the Parks Department."

"As a gravedigger?"

"I was out in the field for a short while but now I'm behind a desk again," said Henry.

"Henry, I've been a gravedigger, a bartender, a carpenter, a printer; I've worked in furniture and steel, in a shoe factory, on farms and ranches; in restaurants, stone quarries, automobile plants, construction, on the docks, on ships... the list goes on. But I've never been a writer, like you. I'm a stiff. A working stiff. That's what they call the likes of me. Always on the bum. I've accepted it; I'm a class-conscious proletarian."

"D'ya think I'm a writer? I'm a failure at that and everything else don't ya know."

"Society's made you believe you're a failure. How can an artist be successful in this country unless he carves dollar signs of clay with dynamite stuffed inside? Sabotage. You want to be some dilly dandy like that crowd in the Catacomb in Greenwich Village. I don't know why I ever let you drag me down to that place. Effeminate velvet and silk swine. Bovine Bodenheim and his lot. Some of the pussy was nice though. Why do you let them fawn and fuss over your wife like that? *Count Bruga* indeed. Oh, by the way, here's the book back," said Emile, handing the novel *Count Bruga* to Henry. "It's a piece of shit."

"You're telling me it's a piece of shit. It's got my wife crazy. You know she went off to Paris with a woman."

"A woman! What is she a lesbian or what?"

"She thinks she's Rimbaud. They made this Count Bruga puppet that dangles from the bedpost like a voodoo idol, they're both possessed. It's all misery out of Dostoyevsky."

"Ah ha!" said Emile, "don't give the game away with literary talk. Sounds like you like it, you like the literary comparisons. You love it, don't ya? Good material for a book, huh? Now don't get upset. I just think they got that puppet dangling from your prick, Henry, and if you don't put an end to it, they're gonna eat it up with the rest of ya, like vampires. Self-indulgent decadence. I know their kind. Rimbaud shit! *Merde!* Ubu – what? *merdre!* See, I read... I know stuff... I'm not preordained to read, not someone like me, but I do. That Bruga book is a satire of these avant-garde ghouls. Cheap art. Confessions. It's art as luxury. In this country the common man can hardly afford life's basic material needs. And on top of that, the goddamn capitalists, with their advertisements and salesmanship, are driving the salacious appetite for worthless luxuries to the point of orgasm, and what a useless orgasm it is, transforming their useless products into necessities. And if you ain't got it you're made to feel like an outsider, as if you're poverty-stricken, a failure, like you said. Nothing wrong with being an outsider. I try to explain this to Maurizio but he thinks all Americans are capitalists. But Thoreau and Whitman. Lincoln too...

Lincoln said government of the people, by the people, for the people. Now isn't that anarchism or is it just some more rhetorical American Dream nonsense of the ruling class to keep the dimwits keeping the faith. You ever read Kropotkin or Bakunin? Well, I ain't gonna beg for a job no more. I want the whole fucking thing to collapse. I want to see the big capitalists shit bricks. Gold bricks. That's what it'll come to. If that's what it takes to make profits, the greedy bastards, they'll eat us up for fodder and shit gold bricks. And I ain't got no use for racketeering or unions or nothing anymore but... self-indulgent pleasure. I guess we're back to where we started. When all else fails, try decadence. Why not? There's no way out as I see it. Civilization's got to be razed to the ground. Starting with those national blooms of the Renaissance: oceanic exploration, empire, the printed word, and weapons... renaissance men, culminating in the apotheosis of Theodore Roosevelt, our glorious Everyman, who lived up the block from here, more or less, as you may know, and a sly pecker he was too, bringing the military and industry and government all together in the name of the people, creating a band of ruling-class thugs, in the name of the nation, profit hounds, trust-busting my ass. Ya see socialism was strong and spreading, he wanted to keep all the power in the executive branch of the rotten tree of evil, take three tyrannies of empire, the president and his unelected band of thugs, his cabinet, the military, the big corporations, and bring them all together in the name of the people, the nation, and then with power of unprecedented proportions impose the whole conglomeration on all the poor suckers of the world who haven't the brains to see that the American Way is The Way, the civilized Christian way.

"There was always gangs in the cities before the capitalists started employing criminals to keep down the proletariat, small gangs no doubt but effective, pick-pockets, bandits, tough-guys, gunmen for the powerful industrialists, organized on a large scale by detective agencies, ya know, Pinkerton, hired out, protecting their property and their scabs, attacking strikers, later the unions played the same nasty game, paying for strong-arm men to fight back against the scabs and managers and foremen... by the time of Prohibition there was already well established rackets in protection and gambling and hooch-running and dope-peddling. We're all a bunch of saps to these Capones and Morans and Rothsteins and Schwabs and Fords, they're all heroes now one way or the other because they've made it in the

American way, any way, just bring in the loot... payment and debt, that's what Saint Paul preached to the merchants of Rome, the goddamn business community, that's what made America great, doom and happiness, yeah well I'm not buying it see, I sympathize with the dynamiters and the saboteurs, don't get me wrong, it's no worse than the methods of the capitalists, wasting the natural resources, dumping cargoes of goods into the sea, I've seen it, burning cornfields and cotton and wheat, throwing trainloads of potatoes to mush, all for higher incomes, profits; mixing chalk into flour; Vaseline into candy; sulphuric acid into vinegar; eggs and milk stored away in order to raise prices; all kinds of shit, Henry... I'm not taking too much shit on the shovel no more; I'm not breaking my back; I've wised up. Tell ya what Henry, tonight you'll get fixed up good. A good night on the town, even this shitty little town, will cure you. Will cure anything. Forget about this crap. Look at the stuff you read!"

Emile picked up Henry's books, tossing them one by one onto the bed as he read off their authors. "Spengler, Joyce, Dostoyevsky, and a Funk and Wagnall's dictionary! What depressing shit! My God, no wonder you feel suicidal!"

Suddenly Maurizio spoke, having grown impatient with Emile's long hobbyhorse speech. "We go now... my famiglia no home now."

"Leave your books here Henry," said Emile, "we'll pick them up on the way back."

"Where we going?"

"To see Maurizio's sculptures."

Maurizio's famiglia was in Schiff's Field. Several cars have pulled into the field and parked by the REO truck. Giancarlo Bacigalupo, wife Gina, and son Johnny got out of one of the cars, a new colored car of Mr. Ford, "a deep channel green." Giuseppe greeted his brother-in-law. Fiorenza greeted her sister-in-law. And Toots greeted her first cousin Johnny Bacigalupo. There were also Mr. Nocciola, the "chicken man," he sells chickens; Mr. Bruno, the barber; Mr. Carroccio, the bookie; Mr. Medicio, the oil man; Mr. Ficcino, the ice man; Mr. Santi, the bootlegger; and then there were the women, the housewives. Fiorenza opened the picnic basket. Elia Preggo Jr. opened the bag of bocce balls, dumping them on the grass. Stephano Carducci played his violin. Luigi Bollo played his accordion. Dancing and games and eating and singing and laughter ensued. Italian descendants of the Italian Renaissance you might say... sort of.

Walking along the street Emile Baldazzi noticed the "coming attractions" at the Lyric Theater. *Nanook of the North* and a Harold Lloyd comedy. Maurizio mentioned how much he likes Harold Lloyd. VE-ry MUD-ch. How about Charlie Chaplin? He's the best. Yes, yes, Maurizio said. Maurizio entered the alleyway first, and Emile and Henry followed him through the alley and into the backyard. They climbed the wooden stairs that clung to the exterior brick wall of the paper store. The stairs led up to a long porch, in the middle of which was a door that opened into a hallway, at the other end of the hallway was a window, outside the window you can see Saunder's Drug Store across the street. There were four doors in the hallway, two on each side; the four apartments are occupied by sundry emigrants and refugees, the poor, tired and huddled masses from, no, not Europe, from New York City.

Maurizio takes a stepladder from the clutter of boxes and brooms in the corner of the porch. He climbs over the porch's twisted steel bar railing and pulls the stepladder over behind him. He walks on the slightly inclined tarred roof, an extension of Van Heffer's Meat Market built five years ago to accommodate a meat packing room. Maurizio places the ladder against the wall of another building; this building was the last building that Giuseppe added to his property. There is an apartment on the second floor and four garages on the ground floor. In one of the garages Giuseppe keeps his REO truck. Another garage serves as a slaughterhouse for Van Heffer's; another houses supplies for the paper store, and in the other garage, behind the large double doors with six small windows at the top, Giuseppe breaks his grapes and makes his wine. The wine is kept in barrels in the low-ceilinged basement beneath the fruit and vegetable store.

Maurizio, Emile and Henry climb up the ladder. They walk along the edge of the roof of Hodman's Hardware Store. Henry wants to take a look at the clock tower with its mock battlement, crenels and merlons, and crazy cock weathervane atop. He walks over to the corner of the roof and looks into one of the small windows in the clock tower. Suddenly a face appears in the window, staring back at him. A voice howls like a demon. The face disappears. A bell rings. "Holy shit! What the fuck is that? It scared the hell out of me." A small door on the side of the clock tower opens and out steps Rocky. Emile and Maurizio are laughing like the Dickens, or laughing like the Hugos. "It's the fuckin' Hunchback of Notre Dame," says Henry.

"Henry, meet the REAL Quasimodo," says Emile.

The four of them cross over to the roof of the Cazzaza building. Henry is interested in Maurizio's sculptures. Mostly they look like lumps of distorted ugly shapes. "I like ugly things. I no like pretty stuffa," says Maurizio.

"And here is the ugliest of all," says Emile, walking over to the edge of the roof where the large figure of a dollar sign, which had been shaped by Maurizio's hands, stood on the coping stones, precariously balanced, like Capitalism, standing like a sign, facing toward God and presiding over South Street and small town America.

"The great idol. Mammon..." And now Emile is talking again, no stopping him. With his hand placed on the top downward curve of the \$ figure, he gushes forth a veritable history of class-conscious rebellion in America. The Molly Maguires, the I.W.W., the riots of 1877, the Gilded Age, Theodore Dreiser, Upton Sinclair, Jack London, the Haymarket bombing, the Homestead strike, anarchism, Bakunin, Guillaume, Emma Goldman, Kropotkin, Marx, Engels, Luxemburg, Elitism, intelligentsia, Nechaev, the Socialist Labor Party of Chicago, the Freiheit, Johann Most, Exterminate the miserable brood! Let us rely upon the unquenchable spirit of destruction and annihilation which is the perpetual spring of new life, the joy of destruction is creation, dynamite, sabotage, street-fighting, Die Arbeiter Zeitung, Alarm, Science of revolutionary Warfare, a manual of Instruction in the Use and Preparation of Nitroglycerine, Dynamite, Gun-Cotton, Fulminating Mercury, Bombs, Fuses, Poisons... Dynamite! of all the good stuff, that is the stuff! Mother Jones, the Noble Order of the Knights of Labor, Storm the fort, ye Knights of labor, Battle for your cause; Equal rights for every neighbor, Down with tyrant laws! Jay Gould, I can hire one half of the working class to kill the other half, Frick and Berkman, Gompers and Debs, J A Wayland, Appeal to Reason, Proletarians, unite! muckrakers, Lincoln Steffens, Ira Tarbell, the Wobblies, Joe Ettor, Joe Hill, Arturo Giovannitti, Clarence Darrow, John and James McNamara, the AF of L, the Ludlow Massacre, Mooney and Billings, steel strikes, Centralia killings, racketeers, gorillas, Americanize, Sacco and Vanzetti...

"Yes, yes. Good, good," Maurizio repeated this locution to himself throughout Emile's big spiel. Henry has been thinking about his wife and Paris. Rocky has been playing with the pigeons.

In Schiff's Field, Elia Preggo, Jr. has just led his team to victory in bocce ball, a clean sweep of his father's team. 12-4, 12-5, 12-8.

Bong bong bong bong bong the bell in the clocktower.

"You mentioned Theodore Roosevelt," said Henry, "well I once tried to live the strenuous life that he propounded. Went to California in 1913 or thereabouts, worked on a cattle ranch, gave up writing, met Emma Goldman, but I've never been able to reconcile politics and art, society and personal freedom. I can't rail against the capitalists and politicians as I did back then, to hell with systems and theories and organizations, we need the stuff that builds men, individual men, that kind of stuff... not dynamite to blow the fingers off a maid like what happened in Washington a few years back... but dynamite to awaken the soul. On second thought, maybe it would be better to spit in the face of God and Beauty and Man and Art and Poetry; have it all done for and start from scratch, start by singing and dancing over the voices of the dead. Ambiguities, do I contradict myself? I am large, I contain multitudes..."

"God, don't quote me Whitman; that brazen nationalist and warmonger and fairy," said Emile, but Henry was off in forethought and didn't hear what Emile had said.

"These past days I've had a sort of revelation. It all came to me recently. That I would write a book about my life. An honest book. A really honest book. I doubt that it's ever been tried. Maybe Nietzsche came the closest, or Rousseau, or Augustine, but they smudged it all with philosophy and religion."

Maurizio was humming. Pigeons were cooing. Rocky was mumbling some private pigeon-talk with the pigeons. Emile and Henry were singing and dancing like jesters, like mystic fools, waltzing out the old *weltanschauung*, a dance of death, a *danse-macabre*, a dance of joy, the dance of Shiva, dancing to the far off fiddling of the Neros of the world.

In Schiff's Field, Luigi was playing his violin; Lincoln his trombone; and Luigi Bollo was singing *La Donna é Mobile*, while accompanying himself on the accordion.

And Rocky is singing: Ring around the rosy, pocket full of posy, ashes, ashes, we all fall down...

"Crashing down, crashing down, let the dollar come crashing down, down on the heads of the greedy and mean..." sings Emile. And the image of the crashing dollar flashes in Rocky's mind. Henry says that it's time to go. "Sabotage and dynamite. How else can the proletariat fight back against the institutionalized conspiracy against them? It's the machines, the weapons, the navy ships, the propaganda..." And now Emile and Henry are leaving, climbing down the ladder, going down the stairs, through the alleyway, and Rocky is standing on the edge of the roof, looking down, waving to them as they cross the street and walk up South Street to Belsen and White's. And there, look down to the street, directly below, in front of the Cazzaza Fruit and Vegetable Store, standing on the sidewalk, two fat American tourists reading their newspapers, one has come down from the heights of the small Jewish enclave up the block, and the other has come down from the Anglo-Saxon Arcadia up the cove... are they talking to each other? What common ground have they reached? On the common ground under their feet, on the sidewalk, it is written, not in stone but on stone: **Sacco and Vanzetti Must Live!** The work of Emile. Earlier in the day he had written it with chalk on the sidewalk, and now one man is trying to wash it away, cleaning up the mess, the heresy, and with him the other man, looking down at the man on his knees; it's a position of authority that the man-looking-down is quite familiar with; and what a rare appearance for him, a holy pearl from the happy gilded days of yore, those happy days of unassailed capital accumulation, Mr. Jay Tiffany Morgan Vanderbilt Gatsby Gould Townsend III, and the other man, the merchant, scrubbing the sidewalk, is Mr. Sid Schwartz. "Don't dirty the floor, don't dirty the floor." Don't dirty the public sidewalk... they are both standing on the sacred spot. The Splot. Get away from the ledge, Rocky, you may fall; yes, he is the man who twisted your arm; he is the man who made you lose your balloon, and the other man, what of the other man, they are together; put your water pistol away, don't play games, oh you want to squirt water into your mouth, you are thirsty, be careful walking on the edge of the roof, don't push too much against the sculptures, the big dollar sign, and no, not that, Rocky, surely you don't intend to... an accident, crashing down, the dollar sign crashing down on their heads, just like Emile said, and falling, my God, the screams in the street below, the crash of the large dollar sign sculpture, the two men lying together on top of the fruit and vegetable stand, all smashed up, splat splot, all bloodied up among the old-fashioned tomatoes and Long Island potatoes, the Irish cabbage, the beet red, and the blue blood, and do they see you, Rocky? The two people in the street are pointing to the roof... run, Rocky, run...

Maurizio grabs Rocky by the arm and pulls him along. They hurry over the roof and down the ladder. They run up the laneway passing the cock-a-doodle-do of the chickens in their coops. "Cock-a-doodle-do," says Rocky. "Come, come," insists Maurizio. They go through the grapevines and into the woods and climb the hill to the top, now they must go out into the street; they run down Summit Street. "Cock-a-doodle-do... twenty-three skidoo... where we goin'?"

"Come, come... *ah cervello di gallina.*"

"I'm tired," says Rocky.

"*Anch'io...* yes, yes, me too... come, come, you must come."

"O.K... I'm comin'"

"Good, good... *benissimo...*"

"Cock-a-doodle-do...Yankee Doodle came to town, riding on a pony, stuck a feather in his hat and called it macaroni... I'm hungry."

"Here, here... in here."

"No... I don't want to go in there," said a suddenly frightened Rocky.

"Come, come... in here." Maurizio dragging Rocky by the shirt.

Jake the Cop comes running out from the alleyway. He has been up to the roof. Didn't find anyone up here. He stands over the two mangled, dead bodies. Wilbur Waters approaches him, and whispers in his ear, "It's that guinea bastard, that crazy brother of Giuseppe. I saw him on the roof before, as usual, all those damn weird statues up there."

"I know," says Jake the Cop, "but he's not there. I just checked."

"The whole lot of them was in the truck going to their picnic..."

"Yeah, I know where they go; I just feel bad for Giuseppe if that nitwit brother of his is involved in this, and I believe that he is," says Jake the Cop.

"Where do you think he went? To them?"

"I'dun know. Maybe."

A small crowd of shocked observers had gathered. This kind of thing just doesn't happen around here. And on Memorial Day of all days. The parade has been over for several hours and most of the spectators have gone home, only a few stragglers were walking around town. Angular shadows were descending on the brick buildings like guillotine blades. Jake the Cop was keeping his composure, collecting his wits about him, plotting his personal glory and revenge. But official business first. He grabbed

Wilbur Waters by the shoulder. "Here's what we gotta do. You go get Doc Cooper. I gotta call the county police in from Mineola... and the coroner... hurry..."

Rocky leaned against the stone buttress of St. Dominic's Roman Catholic parish church, looking up at the large circular colorful window above him. Maurizio grabbed him by the arm and pulled him through the archway and into the church. Rocky remembers coming here with his father when Rocky was a boy, before his father was killed by a large steel plate that had broken loose from the chain riggings of a crane at Heemskirk's Shipyard. Rocky had been enrolled at St. Dominic's Catholic School just three months before his father died; in those three months Rocky had suffered the nuns' beatings, his hands thrashed with a ruler, palms up, knuckles up, his head bashed against the blackboard. If his father hadn't been killed, Rocky would have never been able to get out of the school, but with his father's death he was sent to public school; Rocky's mother died when he was four months old; there was nobody left to provide for him. Rocky left school at thirteen and found work loading boxes and sweeping floors for some of the shops in town.

"I'm afraid," said Rocky.

"Whatta you'fraid?" said Maurizio.

"The black ladies. They hurt me."

"Here some water. Drink."

Maurizio cupped his hands and drank water, holy water, from the font. Rocky filled his squirt gun with holy water. Maurizio lay down on one of the pews, tired from running; he placed a hymnal under his head and took another book from the slot. He opened the book, randomly, and read: *In manus tuas commendo spiritum meum, redemisti, me Domine, Deus veritatis...*"

Maurizio shook his head and muttered something under his breath, as if to say: NO! Into MY hands thou commend Thy spirit!"

"Whad'ya say?" asked Rocky.

"Nut-ting."

"What's that book?"

"Nut-ting," said Maurizio.

"Watch this," said Rocky, and he ran down the aisle. He squirted water at the tiers of candles and doused their flames. The water, the candles, had no meaning to him; he was being playful; and it was so quiet in the church.

"Come, come, we must go now," said Maurizio.

Rocky ran up the aisle and once again filled his squirt gun with holy water from the font. Maurizio gazed around the edge of the buttress.

"Coas's clear," said Maurizio, using one of the few expressions that he's bothered to learn in English. They crossed the street and ran along the side of a wooden fence, on the other side of the fence were two levels of tiered playing fields at the bottom of which the construction of the new high school was about to commence. From the top of the hill they could see the work in progress on the building at the bottom of the hill, located on East Main Street, which leads "up the cove," to the homes of the wealthy. Maurizio and Rocky entered a wooded area and stumbled down a hill. On the other side of a narrow dirt road they hopped a split rail fence that marked the border of Schiff's Field. They came to a bridle path and followed it through the woods, avoiding stepping on the clogs of horse manure that speckled the path. After a while they came out into an open field, the setting sun was flashing kaleidoscopically through the trees. In the middle of the field was a large ash tree, and in the middle of the ash tree was a tree house. They climbed up the ladder and crawled inside. They sat there leaning against each other and Rocky squirted water into Maurizio's mouth. Rough air struggled in and out of Maurizio's nose. When Maurizio's loud breathing subsided, he heard the world breathe its scratchy silence upon him. Then he leaned his face forward and tilted his head. "Shhhhh... listen, you hear?" Rocky aped Maurizio by leaning his face forward and tilting his head. Rocky shook his head. He didn't hear anything. They both focused their ears on the apparent sound. Their eyes met. Well? Recognition? A smile broke over Maurizio's mouth. He heard the sound of an accordion and a violin and a human voice... the words were muted and unclear, but Maurizio knew the melody.

"Ave Maria..." he whispered. "Silvia. Come, come..."

They climbed down from the tree house. They stood knee-high in the grass, quiet and unmoving like two feline predators; Maurizio tightly held Rocky around the elbow. "Shhh... quiet... this way! Come, come." They ran through the field like two naked angels, toward the edge of the woods, their faces glowing like neon signs on the humblest street of the biggest city, Maurizio pointing "that way," and they ran in the direction of the transcendent music coming out of the trees.

By now Jake the Cop has alerted the county police. A squadron of police cars and paddy wagons and Harley 74's were roaring towards Oyster

341

Bay. A row of four shoulder-squeezed-together policemen sat on a bench in the back of the paddy wagon, staring across at another row of four policemen. Garbled larynx-rattled voices spouted profuse "legalized" obscenities directed at this or that ethnic group moving in on the Irish turf. One red-faced cop was reading a newspaper. The sport's section. The Yankees were in first place, as usual. They won yesterday. The cop checked the box score, reading out loud each player's name, but checking the batting results silently to himself. "Combs...hmmm... Koenig... Ruth... wow... Gehrig... wow... Meusel... Lazzeri... hmm... Dugan... Collins... Hoyt... what kind a name is Gehrig?"

"That's a German, see."

"A Hun, huh? Lazzeri's a guinea name, yeah? Whattabout Koenig?"

"How da hell do I know," he said, and read the funny papers to relax.

"D'ya lissen to Amos and Andy last night, did ya? Funny niggers dey are."

"Dey ain't niggers. Dey made up by white men. No nigger's dat funny, dat smart," said the addressed cop and he gave a tug on the sides of his long cossack-like coat with two rows of brass buttons. There was a Thompson machine gun on his lap. Jake the Cop had made it sound as if a whole gang of mad anarchists were assembled in Schiff's Field planning to overthrow the American government. The alleged anarchists were playing bocce ball, eating hero sandwiches, and engaging in the traitorous and treacherous activity of a communal sing-a-long, to the jamma jammo of Luigi Bollo's dangerous accordion.

"How many you think is there?" said cop to cop.

"All with guns and bombs! This ain't funny." And he put down the funny papers.

When Maurizio and Rocky appeared at the edge of the field, Giuseppe saw them, and waved to them to come over to him. Toots had finished singing and was off into the woods with Johnny Bacigalupo. The children tried to follow them but Toots chased them back. It all happened so fast and unexpectedly. Who could have foreseen the events of the next several minutes? Who could have prepared his or her memory to remember what really happened that day? Sirens were heard. Police cars pulled up alongside the field. A machine gun fired. Ceased. Panic ensued.

"He had a gun. I saw it," the cop who read comics said afterwards. "It was shiny and black like a... it looked like a real gun... he was deformed, he looked crazed like a... Cho... Cho... gots... ya know, the nut who shot McKinley, how was I s'pose to know it was a squirt gun... like from a comic book or sumpthin'."

Rocky had drawn his squirt gun, filled with holy water, like Billy the Kid. The cop saw the gun and fired, spraying bullets like dots of ink. Periods. Full stops. Plugs. Luigi Bollo was dead. Shot in the heart, right through the accordion. He fell on the accordion and both the accordion and Luigi exhaled their last breath of air in the minor key of death. Giuseppe was dead, his mouth filled with the chewed morsels of cheese and bread soaked in red wine. The others survived. Rocky was slightly wounded; a bullet grazed his left arm. Maurizio was cuffed and thrown into the paddy wagon, shouting, *"Sono innocente!"* Teresa went into hysterics and shock. Fiorenza tripped over the picnic basket and broke her hip. The children screamed and cried. Butch the dog ran off into the woods.

Emile and Henry were in Belsen and White's. Emile was being entertained by Cindy Chinchin. Henry was waiting. The carpet was a deep burgundy red. Cindy Chinchin shuttered like shutters on a window in a storm. Emile withdrew and squirted, like a squirt gun filled with holy water. The missile screaming through the air.

"Just keeping the Open Door of China open," said Emile.

"How will this affect the stock market, Emile?"

"Why don't you give her a shot and find out for yourself."

Henry heard the bell in the clock tower strike midnight. He thought about Rocky. The Hunchback of Hodman's. Henry entered the room of Cindy Chinchin. The sheets of the bed were white. It was now Tuesday, the 31st day of May 1927. The day that Henry Ford's last Model T Ford rolled off the assembly line. Beep-beep.

The evidence was collected and interpreted by the judicial authorities of the State of New York, and Maurizio Cazzaza was found guilty of premeditated homicide. The investigation brought to light reams of "subversive" literature that was found in Maurizio's bedroom. Magazines, broadsides, and newspapers, such as *Il Proletario, Appeal to Reason, N.Y. Call, Jewish Daily Forward, McClure's, Everybody's, Atlantic Monthly, Pearson's, Red Book, N.Y. World, Harper's,* and such books as *The Menace of Privilege, History of Socialism in the United States, The Jungle, Sabotage, The Great Steel Strike and Its Lessons, Le Avventure di Pinocchio, In Morte di Madonna Laura, La Vita Nuova, Sonnets of Michelangelo to Vittoria Colonna and Tommaso Cavallieri,* some of this literature was found in a trunk stuffed with stuff that Maurizio had scavenged from Manhattan book stalls, and from the print shop where he worked in Manhattan, most of it he couldn't read, and had put in the big trunk that had come with him and his family from Italy. This is the trunk that would take several more transatlantic trips and carry with it strange and fateful encounters with others.

But all this literature was evidently incriminating items that were not used explicitly as exhibits A to Z, but nonetheless were used against Maurizio in a court of law. The judge pronounced the verdict. Guilty. It was as if the judge had said, mockingly, "There won't be any free trips to the ice box for some cold macaroni any time you want it anymore ha ha ha."

"Stuck an electrical prod in his head and called it Mar-co-ni."

beep-beep

The radio gave the news out on August 22, 1927, that Nicola Sacco and Bartolomeo Vanzetti had been executed in the electric chair by the State of Massachusetts. Maurizio heard about the executions while in his cell in Auburn Prison in upstate New York. Later he was able to read an account of the events in the *New York World*. It was at this time that he took a pen to paper and wrote a letter, a kind of confession.

Giuseppe Cazzaza's funeral was held in the front rooms of his building. The coffin was placed in front of the windows overlooking South Street. Giuseppe was laid out in his fireman's uniform. Leonora had sewed on the brass button. It was the last thing that Leonora ever sewed. Three days after Giuseppe's funeral, Leonora committed suicide by throwing herself on the tracks in front of an incoming train at Oyster Bay Station.

Maurizio's letter was addressed to Teresa. She put the letter in a secret compartment in the trunk that once held Maurizio's papers and magazines and books, which were never returned to the family. The family did not want them. Not long after the funeral Teresa began acting strangely. She was caught burning money. She was placed in a mental institution at King's Park. She would remain there for the rest of her life.

"Ave Maria! gratia plena, Maria, gratia plena..."

Toots was standing to the side of the closed coffin, singing. They were ready to carry Giuseppe away. Carry me off to the burying grounds. Outside in the backyard Rocky had opened the valve on the water-tower. He climbed down and danced around. The water pouring over his head.

He then climbed up to the roof, entered the clock tower, and with a hammer hit the bell again and again... bong, bong...

"*Ave Maria, gratia plena, Maria...*" Toots was singing.

Bong Bong Bong Bong Bong Ave Maria Bong Bong Bong Ave Maria...

Then Rocky threw himself off the roof. Cars came to a halt in front of his small deformed body.

Beep-beep

Ave Maria, gratia plena...

1929

Maurizio Cazzaza sat in his cell at Auburn Prison. It was in this prison that President McKinley's assassin was electrocuted on October 29, 1901. It took three jolts, 1800 volts each, to kill Czolgosz. They burned all his letters. Maurizio has not received any more letters from his friend Francesco in London. It would be impossible now! And the letter that he wrote to Teresa, his letter of confession, did she ever receive it? Was it burned? Discarded?

It was two years ago that Sacco and Vanzetti were executed in Massachusetts. Maurizio had read that Vanzetti's ashes were sent back home to Italy and were buried with his mother in Villafalletto in the Piedmont, not far from Maurizio's birthplace in Liguria. Maurizio was certain that Vanzetti was innocent. But that Sacco, not so certain, he was from the south of Italy. And Maurizio didn't have any connections with the Galleanisti. They were violent and advocated the "propaganda of the deed." What Francesco told about in his letters from Paris, *propagande par le fait,* which Francesco and his group vilified as a useless and immoral act.

On a cold December day when the streets of the city of Auburn and the prison grounds were covered in snow, Maurizio walked in lockstep with other inmates back to his cell. The Auburn System was a punitive system. The inmates wore a uniform of horizontal black and white stripes. They were compelled to work. And the prison took the profits of their labor. They were kept in individual cells. The charity organization The Mutual Welfare League provided newspapers and candies, Oh Henry! and Baby Ruth. Maurizio chewed on a Tootsie Roll. It's just like capitalism in here thought Maurizio.

He was reading a newspaper when the terrible silence of his confinement was shattered by the sound of a gun being fired. Maurizio startled, stood up from his cot, and heard some commotion coming from the main yard. The warden, six guards and a foreman had been taken hostage by a group of twenty armed inmates. The Principal Keeper was shot dead. The convicts had got the guns from an earlier riot in July and had concealed them. The inmates set fire to buildings. State troopers were called in. They scaled the prison walls with ladders. They wore long heavy overcoats, tall black boots and furry hats. A detail of the Army National Guard arrived. The inmates were ordered to surrender. They fled from the main yard to the main hall, where they barricaded themselves. By nightfall, under cover of the dark sky and twenty-foot high walls, the troopers and guard members took the main hall. The warden and the guards were liberated from the clutches of the rampant inmates. Eight inmates were dead. Some of the inmates escaped to a cell block. By dawn the smoke had cleared. The inmate who had instigated the take over of the prison refused to give up. He was shot and killed by a trooper. The last holdouts were overpowered and restrained and many were lying on the cold concrete with gunshot wounds. Afterward one of the troopers complained that the inmates were coddled and pampered. That's why there was a jail break. They can listen to the radio, watch movies and smoke tobacco… it's like they are hotel guests… they had knives and were throwing them… they came at me several times and I remember clearly shooting one of them in the head… you see this watch fob, I think it's gold, I picked it off their spokesman, Sullivan, after he fell dead, the bastard had the gall to raise his hands and say I surrender, but he got what he deserved.

1937

Guernica burning…

Monday, 26 April 1937, a Nazi squadron of warplanes, the Condor Legion, flew in the direction of a small Basque village in Northern Spain. The Junker and Heinkel aircraft bombarded the village of Guernica with incendiary bombs. In the village market square the scorched and charred bodies of women and children smoldered, surrounded by a wall of fire.

If you had turned the page you would have seen a photograph of a mother and her two children. On her left side, the mother held her little girl's hand; on her right side, she held her little boy's hand. They moved forward, slowly. The mother was frightened, apprehensive. To her left and right was a line of people, behind her were more lines of people, men, women, and children; they were moving forward, together. It was a sunny and hot Sunday in Chicago, as gray as steel. It happened to be Memorial Day. The people, most of whom were workers at Republic Steel South Chicago plant, and their families, moved slowly toward the factories. The police were waiting for them, double file with billy clubs in hand, some of the clubs and also tear gas were obtained from Republic Steel. The people drew up near the police line. They wanted to set up their picket line. A confrontation of words ensued, and then a few sticks and stones, then the police hurled tear gas. The workers turned and ran; the police shot at them. Ten were dead and many wounded. They were shot in their backs, as autopsies later proved. It became known as the Memorial Day Massacre of 1937, and is mentioned in history books on the labor movement. It is marginally mentioned in some minor history books. It does not appear at all in any grand theory history books, the big picture subsuming all the little pictures; if you had turned the page you would have seen one of the pictures: the mother and her two children.

The Memorial Day Massacre of 1927 cannot be found in any history book. In the 1930s, the streets were filled with hungry people waiting in breadlines. It was the worst of times. There was hardship brought on by economic upheaval. Strike activity was at an all time high in America. There was harsh conflict between Labor and Capital. From 1933 to 1937 there had been around 10,000 strikes. Between September 1936 and May 1937, there had been a half million workers participating in sit-down strikes across America. If Emile Baldazzi were still in America he certainly would have joined the strikers in a show of solidarity, though he didn't have a job. In January 1937 he was standing in one of those breadlines, and by February he was on his way to Spain to fight the fascists of General Francisco Franco. If Agnes Babs Widdlesworth were still in America she most certainly would not be joining any strikers; in any event, she had gone to Europe in July 1936 and has remained there through 1937. Captain Roger Bethell was once again traveling in the Far East. At seventy-seven years old he remained vigorous, adventurous, inquisitive and unperturbed. His first port of disembarkation will be Nagasaki, where the women wicky wacky woo, in Fujiyama you get a mama... the lyrics of a popular novelty song stuck in Captain Bethell's head. From Nagasaki he will travel by train to Hiroshima and Kyoto. Frank Yamada and Brent Widdlesworth were visiting with Charles William in Paris in 1937. This was Brent's first trip to

Paris; his handicap did not thwart nor prevent him from going; he would do just fine getting around Paris on crutches; Frank encouraged him and Brent was emboldened. Agnes Babs Widdlesworth, not having located her son as of yet, and Frank and Brent keeping their promise to Charles William not to reveal his whereabouts, telling Agnes only that Charles William is somewhere in Paris, destitute but happy, like another writer living in Paris at the time, Henry Miller, whose address Emile Baldazzi has tucked away in his war battered coat pocket, and maybe he'll pay him a visit one day at 18 Villa Seurat. Emile received a letter from Henry while Emile was still living in the flop house on Hamilton Avenue in Oyster Bay; Miller asking for money as usual, "Ain't got no dough..."

Ten years ago, in 1927, twenty-five-year-old Charles Lindbergh flew across the Atlantic. The next day he was famous all over the world. He made the decade shine like newly minted coins. His female counterpart followed his shining example the very next year, when Amelia Earhart flew across the Atlantic. But this year, 1937, on July 2, while circling the globe, her plane vanished somewhere between Lae, New Guinea and Howland Island. She was lost in the Pacific, never to be found. The shine of the 20s was wearing off; the coins were tarnished; paper money was just paper after all. Steel and iron and concrete were replacing tin and tinsel and glory. Lindbergh may have put a glow in the lives of average Americans, and that glow may have lived in their minds like an imagined reflex of themselves, like a reflection of fame and fortune, but many Americans still felt the reflex of hunger in their stomachs and the reflection of desperation in their souls.

In 1927 the Mayor of New York was the irrepressible Jimmy Walker; in 1937 the Mayor of New York was the irascible Fiorello La Guardia. There was a change of moods, from mass giddy to mass gloomy. In 1927 the governor of New York was Al Smith. In 1937 the governor was Herbert Lehman, who as the incumbent defeated the Republican Robert Moses in 1934, in a race in which Moses' attacks upon Lehman grew so feral and virulent that the man who brought beaches, highways, parks, and toll booths to Long Island had even antagonized a supportive press. He went so far as to call Lehman a liar. It takes one to know one. He lost the election. He never ran for public office again. The public be damned. But the public will love me despite their ignorance, for I will give them beaches and parks and highways and bridges and beauty... Moses was referred to as a public official. Moses had come up through the Tammany machine along with Al Smith. He was the governor's aide. They masterminded the art of bill-drafting. When Moses wanted to put a highway right through the North Shore of Long Island, right through the estates of the wealthy, for the sake of The People and their cars, their freedom to commute to work and to parks and to beaches, the estate dwellers would not have it; so they put the highway right through some farm land and booted the farmers off. That is an act of a public official. The 1930s would see acts of grandiose construction not seen since the Pharaohs tiptoed across the pyramids. It was a prelude to the cosmic destruction of the war that was being heralded by rhetorical trumpets playing ying for yang notes in the tone-deaf ears of public officials.

From the 1920s to the 1960s Robert Moses changed the shape of Long Island from a smooth scaled fish whose flukes flapped toward Europe, into a spiny shark whose sharp-toothed mouth chewed up and swallowed Manhattan's flotsam and jetsam and then spat it out upon the Anglo-Saxon and Dutch landowners. We don't want those people out here. I am one of those people, roared Moses. The rivers, the marshes, and the ragged edges were shored up against nature's ruin with concrete and steel. He re-formed the landscape: parks, bike paths, fields, overlooks, roads, buildings, bridges, trees, bushes, and more leaves of grass than could be found under old Walt Whitman's boot heels. But he was no reformer. He was a transformer. Moses wanted his Shea Stadium to resemble the Coliseum of Rome. His was the dream of Empire, the Empire State, the empire's statesman, and the master builder.

In a far away land called Germany, another public official, another statesman, named Adolf Hitler, who with his master builder and architect, Albert Speer, were also proposing the building of gigantic majestic structures and the beautification of the land. In the name of *Die Folk*. And on Long Island the Nazis also marched. The German-American Bund set up camp on a lake near Yaphank and called their 45-acre settlement Camp Siegfried. They lived in bungalows and tents and named the streets after Hitler, Goering, and Goebbels. They wore swastikas on their uniforms and high-stepped in their jack-boots. They sold *Mein Kamf* and other Nazi merchandise, anti-Semitic pamphlets and books. Photographs of the *fuhrer*. And beer and frankfurters. Martial training. Nazi indoctrination.

Italian Radicalism had symbolically died in 1927 with Sacco and Vanzetti. The Mafia and Mussolini were now the icons of Italian-Americans... but why the tolerance of gangsters but not the anarchists?

The shimmering swerving shine of the 1920s was wearing thin. People were becoming thin. It made their skin thicker. They melded with their tyrants. Defensive measures. Fat armies armed to the hilt. It was time to lay it on heavy. When Moses was offended by that 20s flapper, Jimmy Walker, he promptly demolished the Casino in Central Park for the sole reason that Walker frequented the place. In the 1930s, depression or not, sit-down strikes or not, somebody was putting brick atop brick and bolting steel girders together, the Empire State Building was completed in 1931, the Golden Gate Bridge and Hoover Dam were completed in 1937-38, the Triborough Bridge was opened in 1939, from whose toll booths the people's coinage was collected and gathered in the dark pockets of Moses' Triborough Authority. In Germany, Hitler and Speer had ideas about a bridge for Hamburg exceeding the Golden Gate, a Zentralbahnhof in Berlin that would dwarf Grand Central Station, a dome of a Meeting Hall that could contain within it the Capitol in Washington. Hitler even dreamed of world conquest. Oh the dreams of public officials.

In 1937 the president of the United States was once again a Roosevelt, a distant cousin of Theodore, Franklin D. Roosevelt, who won his second term in a landslide victory over Alfred M. Landon of Kansas. As for Theodore's happy little village, nothing's changed much, not much for Moses to do here, in this little out-of-the-way village, unless someday they decide that a nice big bridge might free Long Islanders from the hazards of passing through New York City, release them from the traffic jams that Moses brought unto them, disdaining and eschewing the socialist influenced contrivances of mass transit. Anyway, no one remembers much about what happened ten years ago; the Memorial Day Massacre of 1927. The Cazzaza family is still around. Fiorenza sits in her window in the front rooms overlooking South Street. These days her eighteen-year-old daughter Luisa joins her most of the time. Toots married Johnny Bacigalupo in 1928 and moved to the town of Northport; Toots rarely if ever keeps in contact with her mother and sister. There was a fight over Giuseppe's will back in 1928. His brother-in-law claimed that he should have been in it. Frankie would marry a girl from Ireland in 1938, her name Mary, from Tipperary. Not Typhoid Mary, who also worked in Oyster Bay. Frankie works for Van

Heffer's Meat Market. He didn't want to take over his father's fruit and vegetable store, and therefore that was the end of Giuseppe's American Dream, squandered by lazy and unambitious sons. Stevie worked part-time that summer as a watch repairman and jeweler in a store in town. And Joe, still in high school, is a big New York Giants' fan. The Giants won the pennant back in 1933 and this year looks promising. They still got some good players like Mel Ott and Bill Terry and Carl Hubbel.

One day Joe and some other students protested the comments of a rich "cover" who said the high school was too good for "blacks, Italians and pollacks…" But the new roads of Robert Moses led to the Promised Land, and more refuse was filing out from the city, more Italians were moving to the village, settling on Spring Street and Irving Place. Jews came too…

Stevie Cazzaza went out to buy the newspapers every morning, despite having to walk with crutches and having to struggle down the stairs and then out through the alleyway where his knuckles sometimes scratched against the brick walls. He had more courage than his two brothers, more perseverance, fortitude and ambition, despite his handicap. And more brains. He had taken study courses through the mail to learn jewelry and watch repair, and would even manage to attend one semester at Rider College, where he was scorekeeper for the basketball team. But the demands and the strain on his body and mind proved too much and he left Rider to return home. He got the job as a watch repairman in Smith Jewelers and worked there for several years; the shop was adjacent to Saunders Pharmacy, so Fiorenza and Luisa could watch him carefully cross South Street every morning to go to work and come home for lunch.

This morning, Tuesday morning, as Stevie Cazzaza took his early morning journey to the stationery to buy the newspapers, he was on a special errand for Luisa, because yesterday the radio reported that Jean Harlow had died. Luisa was beside herself; she was troubled with disbelief. Jean Harlow, her idol, her favorite movie star, dead. She took out the scrapbook for which she has been collecting newspaper and magazine articles and pictures for seven years, ever since the movie *Hell's Angels*. She wept as she leafed through the scrapbook. She was a member of her fan club. She had received an autographed photograph and a thank you note from Harlow.

Stevie was carrying the newspapers up the stairs; the newspapers were tucked under his arm as he placed both crutches together on his left side and used the railing to climb the steps. Luisa was waiting on the landing. She seized the newspapers, the *Daily News*, and the *Daily Mirror*. A picture of Harlow was on the cover of the Daily News, her head flung back, smiling. Beneath the picture was printed:

Born Mar. 3, 1911, Kansas City, Mo.

Died: June 7, 1937, Hollywood, Cal.

The Cazzaza family gathered around the kitchen table. Joe wanted to see the back cover of the Daily News, see how the Giants made out. They beat the Pirates 5-2; that's all he wanted to know and he collected his books and started out for school. It was warm outside, already 70 degrees; it was suppose to go up into the mid 80s today. Joe walked to high school on the sidewalk along East Main Street. It was a quiet morning, so unlike a September day the following year when the wind and rain battered Joe as he walked home from school during the big hurricane of '38.

Jean Harlow wasn't the only headline in the news today, subheadlines:

Youngstown, Ohio, Steel worker shot;

Albany, Lehman vetoes 2 school bills;

Berlin, Nazis attack Vienna Cardinal;

St. Louis, Africa, Amelia Earhart lands after ocean hop;

Hendaye, Spanish Border, Franco rushes troops.

In Spain, there had been an insurrection led by Franco in July 1936. Franco declared war on the legally elected government in Madrid, the Popular Front, which had been formed of left-wing and liberal and Communist forces to fight fascism. After the voting was over on Sunday, February 16, the Popular Front had elected 257 deputies, the Right 139, and the Center 57. The new Prime Minister was Manuel Azana. The victory of the Left caused the Right to panic. There had been several months of strikes, expropriations and battles between the Civil Guards and peasants that led up to the Franco insurrection. Largo Caballero, a left-wing Socialist leader, insisted that the workers be armed, but Azana refused his demand.

Emile Baldazzi was ready to go. He had read an article in which Spain's elected Republican Government was asking the world to volunteer and come fight against Mussolini, Hitler and Franco. But first he needed a passport. He headed straight to the new Oyster Bay Post Office. A man in a hut was carving sea horses at the base of the flagpole on the grass in front of the Post Office. It was an art project that he was commissioned to do by the W.P.A. The man's name was Leo Lentelli and he was a native of Italy.

In January Emile got his passport. He opened the passport and saw the big stamp: **NOT VALID FOR SPAIN**. We'll see about that.

Emile took one last look at the mess of books and papers that was his room in the building on Hamilton Avenue and he walked out. Would he ever be back? It was a few minutes walk to the train station. The first thing that he did in Manhattan was meet up with his old friend Sal at his digs down on Canal Street. Sal was staying at a flophouse. The soup kitchen was just down the block. They stood in line, shivering in the cold. In the middle of the night Emile woke up sweating and burning. He lit a match and saw the bedbugs crawling all over him. He jumped up and yelled, and beat the blood-sucking bastards off him. He woke up Sal who was sleeping at the other end of the room lined with rows of beds. "I'm gettin' outta here." Sal went with him. They slept in the park. Two cops with billy clubs bashed the bottoms of their feet in the morning and told them to move on. They made their way to Union Square. The usual crowd was there, talking, arguing, ranting, and fighting with fascist sympathizers. Emile picked up a few leaflets. There was going to be a political rally in Madison Square Garden sponsored by the League against War and Fascism. W. B. Du Bois was one of the speakers. Vito Marcantonio, a leader from the American Labor Party, spoke... and Paul Robeson sung "Let My People Go" and "Old Man River."

Emile spoke with the others who were going over to Spain, and none of them was disheartened or discouraged by the stamp's words. Toward the end of February Emile boarded the *Ill de France*. There were at least 1000 passengers and of them some 200 were heading for Spain. The ship docked in Le Havre. But just before they disembarked, the loud speaker broadcast the names of passengers who should meet in the stateroom. Emile was on the list, and not coincidently most of the other men who were going to Spain had heard their names announced. A man from the U. S. Consulate stood on a box and asked everyone to settle down. "It has come to my attention that most of you have the intention of traveling to Spain. This is illegal. Read your passports. Not Valid for Spain. The French government has shut off the borders to Spain. It is impossible to pass through to Spain. If you are caught trying to cross the border, you'll be arrested. If you are caught with no money in France, you will be jailed and deported. Do I make myself clear? I am offering you a chance to return to the United States, and at the expense of the United States government. Think clearly about this. You must decide now. Please raise your hands if you wish to return. Just one?"

Just one hand when up. Damn, obviously a plant, thought Emile to himself.

Emile stood in line while each of the men was questioned. "What is your purpose? Business or pleasure? Where are you staying? Where are you going?"

Emile said, "Paris... I have a friend there."

"Who is your friend? Do you have his address?"

"I'd rather not... say"

"How much money do you have with you?"

Emile showed the man $175 in cash, more than sufficient funds. Emile told the man from the consulate that perhaps he would go to Germany and Switzerland too. A sightseer. Some of the men were young enough to claim to be students, but not Emile; he was forty-two years old. It took nearly three hours for all the men to get off the ship. They were surprised to learn that the train to Paris had waited for them. French custom's officials asked some of the men a few harmless questions, and all the men where whisked quickly through customs and onto the train. They didn't even search my baggage, pondered Emile. Perhaps they know what we are up to and they sympathize with the Republican cause! *Viva la France*, said Emile, as the train pulled out of the station. One French custom's official gave him a brisk salute as the train raced along.

Emile stayed for nearly a week in Paris. His hotel overlooked the Seine and he watched the boats go back and forth. He could see part of Notre Dame from his window. He walked along the Seine and stopped at the bookstalls, and watched the artists sketching the river and the people. He had onion soup at the market places, or wine and a baguette. Sometimes he had a cognac at a café along the Champs Elysees. He thought many times: Fuck the war. I should stay in Paris. He thought about going to see his friend Henry.

Emile took the Metro from Montparnasse Station to Alesia Station. The area was slummy until he came to a bright bourgeois-styled street of merrily hued stucco houses. Always merry and bright. He found Henry at home in his studio on the second floor of 18 Villa Seurat. The house was occupied by writers, poets, painters, photographers, clowns, astrologers, magicians, weather forecasters, it was *La Vie Bohemian* but without a demure Mimi. Henry had company, a man named George who held a handful of brochures. George was a designer and has designed some of the brochures for the World's Fair. Emile looked at different samples.

L'Exposition Internationale de Paris 1937
Exposition Internationale des Arts et des Techniques
Paris 1937 Plan Officier
Paris invites you to her exhibition May – November 1937
Arts et Tecniques dans La Vie Moderne
Arts, Crafts, Sciences in Modern Life
Paris Plan Monumental avec Carte Imagée des Environs
1937 Mai – Novembre - Exposition Internationale

That evening they took a long walk along the rue de la Tombe-Issoire toward the outer boulevards and returned along the rue de la Fontaine a Mulard. They stopped by the Café Zeyer that was near Villa Seurat.

Henry spoke: Orwell was here. You know him? English chap. He liked my Cancer book. But not *Black Spring*, my latest. He said some rubbish about how I had left behind the ordinary world of two and two is four. Yeah, that was the point. He was here around Christmas… on his way to Spain. I told him that all causes are idiotic. Civilization is doomed. See, this is a new French translation of my cancer book. My book, *ce n'est pas un livre au sens ordinaire du mot…* this is the way I put it to Orwell, *le temps continuera a etra mauvais, dit-il… des calamites, encore de la mort…* Orwell said he felt guilty about having served as a cop in Burma… so why join another damn police force! And you, Emile, why you of all people… I gave Orwell my old corduroy jacket… yeah, I gave it to him, but not as a contribution to the Republican cause. You can have this copy of my book, Emile, take it to Spain. Do you know Cendrars? He came to see me a few years ago. Spent a day and night in his Paris. He knows the ropes. Whores all over him."

"How are you able to stay in Paris for so long? Don't you need to show proof that you can support yourself?"

"Sure," said Henry. "I've been able to muddle through so far. I know there's a scheme that some of the Jews use. They have a 1000 franc note that they pass around to each other… they are a cunning people."

"And the French authorities don't mark the note so these intelligent Jews can't swindle them?"

"C'mon Emile. At least pay them a compliment for their resourcefulness. Give them some credit. I think it's inspired. Hell, I'd join their arrangement if I could…"

Emile sat at a café table and read the *Herald-Tribune* that a fat American tourist had left behind. The time had come. He met up with about twenty-five men from the ship. They took an early morning train to Arles, in the south of France, not far from Spain. They got into cars and drove the straight road toward the border. At the end of the road they fled into the woods and were met by Spanish guides. French soldiers, ordered to uphold the embargo against Spain, were patrolling the border. They made it across the border. The French guards didn't seem to be paying much attention. Emile looked up and saw the Pyrenees. Over the mountains was the only way to go... he was on his way, at last... with his comrades.

Agnes Babs Widdlesworth left New York for Europe on a hot humid Saturday in July 1936. She had booked passage aboard the *S.S. Rex*; the trip lasted a pleasant week and she arrived in the South of France. She stayed at her usual hotel in Cap Martin. She rested in the way the rich rest. She enjoyed swimming and seeing old friends, mostly English nobles. The Riviera was gay and she was sufficiently amused. She took the pilgrimage to Lourdes. Beneath the Pyrenees and beneath the cathedral on the hill she offered a prayer, silently and demurely among the demonstrative Catholic pilgrims: she prayed that she would find Charles William in Paris. The healing waters flowed from the simple grotto and the impression that Agnes took away with her would not be soon forgotten. She had had long discussions with Captain Bethell about religious and spiritual matters of the sort that cultivated leisurely time provides; the Captain's Buddhist precepts could not penetrate Agnes' core of bloody and ritualistic inclinations. If she would be anything she would be Catholic, she told the Captain. She liked the rituals, the symbols... but spiritual matters or no, the main thing was her appearance, that was reality. For the benefit of her appearance and health she traveled to Salies de Bearn, where she took the "cure" under the care of Doctor Faustus Von Bleinbern. As she took the "cure" she could hear the guns blasting over the Pyrenees, booming in the air over the cloistered retreat. There was a war in Spain, she was told. Oh, how awful. She left for Biarritz. Her usual hotel, the Helianthe, was closed. This was due to the war in Spain. How inconvenient this war has become. In Biarritz the guns were heard blasting into the night. She felt as if she were at the front. San Sebastian was under bombardment. There were refugees coming into Bayonne. Biarritz was not gay and carefree and she was not amused. Nevertheless she managed to play golf and swim in the Cote d'Azur.

Nevertheless the tea tables were filled at the clubs. Though the Americans were conspicuously absent in both their presence and their consumption. In September, before the coming of the storms over the equator, she left for London. She had planned to go to Paris first, but she grew fainthearted at the prospect of having to comb Paris in search of her long lost son.

Agnes' mother died last year and Agnes has been guilt ridden for not coming to Paris to make peace with her mother. She wasn't sure she could have handled the emotions that would have descended upon her in that city. She wasn't strong enough yet. She preferred to see her friends in London, distract herself from the inevitable confrontation with her self doubts and a too killing meeting with Charles William in Paris. If there would ever be a reunion, if she would ever see her son again.

Emile and the men made it to Albacete, official headquarters for the International Brigades. Albacete was about 100 miles southwest of Valencia, the provisional capital of Republican Spain. Emile started training with sticks instead of guns. Would FDR drop the embargo and aide the Loyalists? Emile became a truck driver. Later he drove an ambulance. He knew a little about fixing engines, but not enough to stay behind at the camp as a permanent mechanic. He drove out along the roads, saw the orange groves and olive trees, the donkeys and carts and peasants... they shouted *"No Pasaran!"* In the towns children gave him flowers and oranges and the town's people gathered to sing "The Internationale."

Emile drove food to the front, to Brunete. He drove an ambulance to Barcelona, where he walked Las Ramblas, with its large trees, bookstalls, newspaper stands, and cafés. In Barcelona, Emile had seen the visible remnants and heard stories of what the revolution had achieved since July 1936, about how the factories were taken over by workers, how they then elected managers, who were always subject to recall, and who always made decisions with the direct involvement of the workers. Emile wondered if he could try this at Heemskirk's Shipyard if he ever went back to America? Emile was amazed to hear stories about how food unions had been established by workers who along with restaurant and hotel workers, opened communal dining rooms to feed the populace. It had been a mainly spontaneous revolution. The anarchist's and socialist's workers of both industry and agriculture had worked together. The counter-revolution, as Emile saw it, was under Communist direction. And between the Communists and the Nationalists, the anarchist cause would be smashed.

357

Either way, the anarchists would be blamed for most of the violence. But that was last year and things have changed. Revolutionary songs were not blaring from the loud speakers along Las Ramblas. Class had returned to Barcelona, and fancy clothes. Not all the barbers were anarchists anymore.

Emile left Barcelona in April 1937 and arrived in Madrid just in time to meet Ernest Hemingway in one of the trenches that were dug around the city. Emile was slightly taller and bulkier than Hemingway and had a fist as hard and as large as a sledgehammer. This seemed to annoy Hemingway, who kept staring at Emile's hands and the half missing fingers. It also annoyed Hemingway that Emile had never read any of his books except the first chapter of *The Sun Also Rises;* something about Jews and Princeton, and couldn't get beyond that. They had a brief discussion, or more precisely, an exchange. Emile urging Hemingway to support the revolution, the true revolution of the anarchists and the CND. Hemingway challenged Emile to arm wrestle. They were both drunk. But no fingers or half fingers Emile drove Hemingway's fist six inches deep into the mud.

In April 1937 Frank Yamada and Brent Widdlesworth were searching for Charles William in the Cimetière du Montparnasse. They had to begin somewhere. Charles William had no address and the only way they could find him was to haunt those usual places that Frank remembers Charles William frequenting during Frank's two previous trips to Paris to meet Charles William. Today Charles William was not among the dead. Was he still among the living? wondered Frank. They found another Charles instead: Charles Baudelaire. They found his withered gray tombstone in a concrete clutter of mausoleums by the edge of the cemetery. There were fresh flowers lying on the cold slab. Frank picked up a hyacinth and broke it off; he stuck it in his jacket pocket. "Another flower of evil," said Frank. He had earlier tossed away the dead crumpled remains of a hyacinth taken from Oscar Wilde's colossal limestone tomb in Cimetière du Père-Lachaise.

"Oh very clever," Brent replied.

"Here, put it in your pocket... for my Greek boy..." Brent turned away. On the last Sunday afternoon in April the world was marching towards evil, with or without flowers. Frank wanted to keep in lock step. Last year Italy had finished its march through Ethiopia. Frank admired Benito Mussolini and his fake Roman orderliness and lunatic posturing; though he didn't appreciate Mussolini's flare for buffoonish journalese, the way he threw himself into a sentence much in the Theodore Roosevelt manner, with Napoleonic honor and glory and duty and obedience and manliness. Frank appreciated more the lyrical outpourings of amoral passion in the writings of that other supporter of the Fascist Party, Gabriele D'Annunzio, who was dying in Italy, who would not live to witness the Grand March of Hitler and Mussolini through Europe.

"The world of the future will be small," said Frank to Brent, "the Fascists, the Communists, the Chinese, the Japanese, and what will America's role be when all these mill stones start their inevitable grinding together. All will be dust and ashes and anarchy. And what do we care on a Sunday afternoon in Paris?"

"We don't care. Do we Frank?" said Brent, who nearly fell down trying to step over the gravestones with his prodding and plodding crutches.

"Because the stronger evil will always be on top," said Frank.

"And the weak shall fall down and be stomped upon," said Brent, collapsing to his knees and tossing his crutches against one of the gravestones. He was crying, huddled up into a small object. This didn't surprise Frank. It has happened often in the past. Brent was very sensitive to Frank's pessimistic ruminations, his death-speech, his signature of doom written across Brent's heart. Frank sat down next to Brent and held his hand.

"There, there dear chicken," said Frank, "You didn't come all this way to sit in a graveyard and cry, did you?"

"I want the world to become as small... as my hand. I want to touch everything. I want to go to all the cities. I want to be in all of them at the same time. I don't want to miss a thing. I have to keep going. I can't return home. Don't you see... that would be a living death for me? We have to keep going. Paris. Rome. Athens. India. China. Japan." Brent reached for his crutch leaning against the tombstone. His face turned suddenly pale; blood had drained from his head and he felt himself spinning. "My God," said Brent, "look, Louis Barbour, Marie Barbour, Vitalie Barbour, Paul Barbour... and Sarah Barbour. My mother, Frank, it's my mother's grave."

"Sarah Barbour," said Frank, reading the gravestone, "1875-1935. So it is. It must be. So you have found your mother and you weren't even looking for her. Your sister searches and searches for her son and she can't find him. Of course we are of no help. But we must be faithful to Charles' wishes. He doesn't want to meet his mother."

"It looks as though I've met my mother again," said Brent, "the world indeed grows smaller... and fatalistic."

"Smaller with death and destruction," said Frank, unrelentingly morbid. Brent's tears were flowing steadily again. Paris has been a catharsis for him. "That's my roger chicken, bah bah bah, get it all out, cry over the old bitch," said Frank, brutally.

"The old toothless bitch. She hated me. I know. Hated me the day I was born. She was almost forty when she had me. An accident. I almost killed her, she told me. I feel a strange kind of victory by out-living her. The world is yet mine. I can breathe the air of Paris."

"You can indulge your bodily passions," said Frank, somewhat opportunistically.

"I can laugh and cry and..."

"Shit, piss and die, yes, yes…" Frank said with finality.

"Let me have this moment of strange joy, please. My revelation. You throw dirt on everything," Brent was almost showing anger, an emotion he rarely revealed to Frank.

"They threw dirt on your mother, literally, I mean. And she threw dirt on you; and now you want to clean it up in a symbolic sense. Dear Brent, in five years Paris may be buried in dirt. Let us suck the marrow from her old bones while we can. Come, we must find Charles."

Brent wiped the wetness from his face. In his mind a red hot thought of self-inflicted vengeance and self-loathing and abhorrence formed an image of himself striking and pummeling the tombstone with his crutches, lashing out with twenty-one years of anger against the mother who conceived him, who brought him into this world, this abomination, *cette dérision. Ah! Sa mère.* But he was too weak, both physically and emotionally, to lift a hand against the cold stone that stood there silently mocking him. Brent stood up with his crutches and he and Frank departed from the cemetery, with the evil *bénédiction* of Baudelaire hanging over their heads.

They walked down Montparnasse Boulevard, stopping briefly at a café, Le Jockey, and then continued on to the Luxembourg Gardens; they may find Charles there.

On their first day in Paris they not only found Brent's mother's grave but they found the boy that Sarah Barbour had taken away from America at the age of eight. Charles was sitting on one of the benches; next to him was an old woman feeding pigeons. He was wearing his dirty overcoat, even though it was a warm day. The same overcoat that he was wearing the last time Frank met him in Paris. He was also reading a book, as usual, but it wasn't the same book that Charles was reading the last time that he met Frank in Paris. Charles was reading a thin volume, *The Immoralist,* by Andre Gide and on the bench by his side was another book, *Voyage au bout de la nuit,* by Céline. Charles was meeting someone, he told Frank and Brent. He couldn't be disturbed now. It was business. They made a plan to rendezvous at the Café de la Rotonde later on in the day. They parted from Charles and returned to Montparnasse Boulevard.

The world that day proved to be even smaller than they could have imagined. Maybe the destruction had already begun and the little pieces that held civilization together were already falling from the museum and library walls. A piece of the small world that was coming fell right on their heads on the Rue Delambre. They met Emile Baldazzi. Frank noticed Emile first and stopped him. "We know each other from somewhere?"

Emile stared at Frank. He couldn't place him. Frank was impeccably dressed, as usual, wearing a pinstriped suit with a diagonally striped bright tie; Emile noticed the hyacinth in the pocket. Frank appeared to Emile quite urbane and dandyish. Why would I know someone like that? thought Emile. And the young boy with him. No doubt a couple of fruits.

"We know each other..." Frank thinking as he spoke very slowly, "from... from... yes... I know... Oyster Bay..."

This was not the best of news to hear. It implied that Frank knew that Emile was a town bum. Of all things to be recognized as, while in Paris, of all places. But Emile finally remembered. And when he did he wasn't too concerned anymore about his reputation, considering the reputation of the person to whom he now knew he spoke.

"The man who bought my dirty Chinese postcards... doing business in Paris I see," said Emile.

"So you do remember? Yes, that was quite lucrative. But I'm not in that business anymore."

"Yeah, I remember you from Belsen and White's. You met my friend Henry on the train, remember?" Frank did not. "We almost had a problem that day," Emile continued, trying to throw it up in Frank's face, "you know, with your inclinations, what, advances toward Henry. At least that's what Henry told me. See, I remember. It's funny, but I remember all the little things. We met that same night in the bar, this must be eight, ten years ago, well enough of that. No hard feelings. I didn't beat you up, did I? I don't always remember that sort of thing. After I get through with the faces sometimes there's no face left to remember. You can't guess how many scabs and punks I've knocked down and out for the count. And with these dukes, no fingers and all."

Frank and Brent stood stoically erect, mildly intimidated by the sheer presence of Emile Baldazzi and his truncated hands that were formed into fists and sparring with the empty air, nicking the buttons on Frank's jacket. Like an Italian McGlaglin. "Pardon my appearance, but I've just come back from the war," said Emile. This statement sent Frank into convulsive bursts of laughter.

"Pardon me for laughing. It just sounded so ludicrous," said Frank, not really knowing why, but Emile stared back at him with unforgiving eyes. Emile may have to beat up this poofter yet.

"Of course, the war, then you deserve a cigarette," said Frank, sensing that he'd better give Emile the benefit of the doubt. He opened his cigarette case. "Pall Malls okay?"

"The war," Frank became encouraging, "you must tell us all about the war, but first we must meet our friend Charles at a café. You may join us if you wish. You would honor us." Frank would just love to sit out on the terrace of a café with the well-dressed American tourists and the Jews and the Parisians and the artists with this hulking presence of a man who smelled and dressed like he just crawled out of one of the graves in Montparnasse Cemetery.

When they arrived at the Café de la Rotonde, Charles was already there, reading his Gide. Frank was pleased, two proletarian men wearing dirty smelly overcoats in the company of two well-dressed and debonair gentlemen; how scandalous. And one of them a cripple. Another with a hyacinth in his pocket. Emile was talking as they first sat down together.

"As I was saying, my friend Henry is a published writer now. Lives here in Paris. I've got his address. I saw him before I went to Spain. Maybe we can all pop over and visit him later. I don't think he'll mind, as long as you don't come on to him again, Frank." Emile laughed.

"Paris changes people. Maybe there is hope," said Frank.

"No hope in hell. Henry's a pussy man all the way."

"Not a Nelly pussy?"

Emile winced.

Frank liked the sound of that: pussy. This conversation should become very vile and vulgar; he hoped. He may learn some new slang words.

The waiter stood over Frank's shoulder. "This is my treat, gentlemen. So I hope you don't mind if I order for us." Everyone nodded obsequiously. Lack of money does that to you. Emile thought about it, and hated to be that way. It was a rare occasion for Emile to act servile. Frank ordered a sparkling Vouvray and a platter of oysters.

"What's that?" asked the diffident Brent.

"You know what oysters are? You're from Oyster Bay! We eat in honor of our town. Three cheers for Oyster Bay!"

Emile said, "Bullshit, that town can go to hell."

Brent said, "I second that. To hell with that town."

"Why, gentlemen, you disappoint me. Your beloved village. It's been good to me."

"Yes," said Brent, "Because you are a thief. And there are fine diamonds and pearls to go along with all the oysters."

"I don't remember much," said Charles, and returned to his book.

"I know what oysters are, what is the Vouvray?" Brent asked again.

"An excellent white wine from the Touraine." And when the wine came, Frank sipped and pronounced it "exceedingly pleasant."

Emile was once again on the subject of his friend Henry. "He's written a dirty book you know. Maybe he'd be interested in some of our dirty Chinese postcards, eh Frank?"

"This Henry has completely slipped my mind. Maybe if I saw his face."

"Like I said, bald, glasses, we can pay him a visit sometime later, I got the address," said Emile.

"Where does he live?" Brent quietly whispered.

"I take the metro to the Alesia Metro Station and walk to Villa Seurat. By the way, Frank, you haven't properly introduced me to your two pals."

Pals, thought Frank, what a word, so inappropriate. He chuckled at the notion. My pals. "Yes, by all means, I have been remiss. Let me introduce you to my dear little chicken, oh don't be so coy, Brent Widdlesworth."

"Widdlesworth!" barked Emile, "as in very fucking rich Widdlesworth?"

"Very fucking rich," said Frank. Oh the joy of vulgar language. A chill ran up his spine. It did no such thing for Emile though, for whom obscenity was second nature.

"Please refrain from calling me that," said Brent, and knocked Frank in the leg with one of his crutches. Nobody mentioned the crutches.

"Calling you what? Chicken? Oh don't be so delicate."

"I'm not delicate," shouted Brent.

"I apologize," said Frank, "Look, the oysters have arrived, ahh."

"And..." said Emile, "the silent one with the book?"

"That would be my other little dear, Charles William Barbour, if he still uses that name."

Emile was fascinated by the possessive way Frank called Brent and Charles "my" this and "my" that, as if they were his property. They looked so young. In fact, Brent was twenty-two and Charles only seventeen, and whereas Brent looked innocent and naive, Charles seemed all street-smarts and cunning; after all, the poor parts of Paris was his home turf.

And how much older was Frank? thought Emile. He must have been at least in his thirties.

"Charles was born in America, by the way. Lives in Paris. A street urchin. A waif. He's just adorable," added Frank.

"I live *in*..." said Charles, finally abandoning his book, which he carefully placed on the small round café table. "I live on, in, over, under, through... every way I can live, in Paris. I try to remember my English prepositions. They make no sense."

"When did you come here?" asked Emile.

"When I was eight. With my grandmother."

"Brent is uncle to Charles," said Frank.

This was getting interesting. Emile speculated. How about Frank, was he related in some way? Frank read his thoughts. "I know what you're thinking. That we are some sleazy *ménage e trois*. Sorry to disappoint. In fact, Charles and I are both bastards."

Emile said, "There are a lot of bastards around these days."

"I don't mean that kind. I mean illegitimate."

"I know what you mean," said Emile. "That's pretty rare for your breed, blue-bloods and all."

"My father was Japanese. So I am not quite a pure blue-blood. I got some yellow blood. Charles had an Italian father. Some peasant in the village. At least we think we know the person. But he's dead now anyway. A mere delivery boy for a meat market. He crashed his car and died."

"That's right," said Charles. "My grandmother told me. She said he was a delivery boy. I'm very proud of that, working class."

"The delivery boy did it, huh, knocked up your mother," Emile said to Charles, "and your sister," Emile said to Brent," and your..." Emile looked at Frank, well, related?

"Yes, my, what?" said Frank, "My mother's first cousin..."

"So this is a family reunion of sorts then," said Emile, laughing. "Agnes Babs Widdlesworth is Charles' mother."

"How did you know her name?"

"I've seen her around, in her Rolls Royce. Can I make a confession? I've always wanted to seduce her." This really sent a chill up Frank's spine. And a hot lick of anger up Brent's, who thought that perhaps he should defend the honor of his sister. But didn't. And as for Charles? After all, it was his mother Emile was talking about; he didn't seem to care.

"No wonder your grandmother took you to Paris and escaped. The shame of it. A daughter with a bastard and a what, niece... with a bastard, oh the fucking rich..." said Emile. The more Emile uttered his casual profanities the fewer chills went up Frank's spine.

"It was indeed my grandmother who took me to Paris. But she is dead now. Buried nearby, in the Cimetière du Montparnasse," said Charles.

"Yes, indeed, as Brent discovered this morning, unfortunately. He had one of his scenes," said Frank.

"And I have never seen my mother," said Charles, "but she is looking for me. Correct?" Charles looked at Frank and Brent. They nodded in agreement.

"Yes, she is looking for you right this moment perhaps," said Brent, "she came to Europe last year to find you. You may pass her on the street and not know her."

"She didn't come to Europe to meet me. She would have to come to Paris for that. Not some grand tour. I am incidental. Illegitimate and incidental. Like music. Anyway, I don't really want to meet her. She is a rich American lady... so perhaps I've already met her. Perhaps I've already robbed her jewelry, perhaps I have already," and here he paused, "fucked her."

Even Emile cringed at that one. "Are you a thief?" asked Emile.

"I am a writer; a thief when I have to be," said Charles.

"So you survive by stealing?" asked Emile.

"I steal," muttered Charles, with a crooked smile, remembering Paul

Muni's last words in that chain gang movie. Frank knew the reference and smiled too.

"I do what I have to do. A hotel job is best for me. Yes, Frank knows..." said Charles, and Frank smiled again, knowingly.

"Very easy," continued Charles, "what I do. I become lover to a chambermaid and she steals the jewelry for me. That's one way. There are other ways. Sometimes there are old men who come looking for pretty boys, pretty errand boys, so I can make money that way too. I've been waiter, errand boy, even dishwasher... but usually I don't bother to work so hard. And then I might go three or four days without a crumb. But food is easy to steal. I walk and sleep on the benches. When I'm fed up with the hotels. How much can you wake up at 5 am and put on dirty clothes and hurry into the streets when only the lights shine in workmen's cafés. And the pavements being swept by slow men, and the men and girls with their baguettes and croissants and chocolates in their hands, all going to the metros... pushing, fighting for a place on the train, oh their stinking faces and wine and garlic breath, then into the hotel basements, into the darkness, and not out until evening, and then the only thing for me to be not going crazy is to find a little bistro at midnight to eat with dogs and cats..."

"Where is everyone staying tonight?" asked Emile.

"A hotel on the Rue Bonaparte," said Frank, "Charles will stay with us tonight. Yes, Charles, no objections."

"No, no, no, no... no hotels. I will sleep somewhere," replied Charles.

"I have a room here on the Rue Delambre. Is it true that there's a big whorehouse on the Edgar-Quinet?" queried Emile.

"The Sphinx. I will introduce you," said Frank, "but first, more food and wine. Crepes Suzette and... did you know that Proust masturbated to two rats in a cage tearing each other apart... and to posing boys... whorehouses had such style in those days." Frank reminisced.

"No more for me," said Emile, "I'm gonna visit my friend Henry. Anybody want to come along? No... but let's meet again sometimes, yes?"

"Where?" said Frank, "In Paris or Oyster Bay or in the coming hell?"

"I'm going to London for the coronation," said Emile, half-jokingly.

"Oh now there's a splendid idea," said Frank. "Let's meet in London. Let's arrange it now. But first Brent and I shall take our tour of the Ile-de-France. So we can't leave right away."

"Why such a foolish and stupid... tour, as you say?" commented Charles.

"Because the City of Mud is full of it, sometimes, and I have promised Brent that we would see more of France. I can't let the boy down," said Frank.

"That's all right," said Brent, "I'm perfectly happy to go to London now. We can come back after London and the Coronation."

Charles was suddenly cackling. "Coronation? Off with their heads! The German barbarians!"

"Oh, I love the pomp," said Frank, "and don't be so drab, Charles, and don't talk about politics, for God's sake. Brent and I are going to explore the Ile-de-France and we shall do it by bicycle too. It is lovely and gentle country. How can you appreciate the paintings of Corot, Monet, Renoir, unless you have seen the light dancing at twilight on an autumn day?"

"Simply," said Charles, "I don't appreciate."

Frank pretended to be shocked. "Don't listen to him, Brent, he is jaded. Think of it, Notre Dame de Chartres, the most beautiful of all cathedrals, Gothic... and Beauvais, with the great high Gothic arch; Amiens; Soissons; and others, many, many, and the chateaux, Malmaison, Fontainebleau, and, of course, Versailles."

"And don't forget Invalides, here in Paris, where you can kiss the ass of Napoleon," said Charles, with bloody dreams of 1789 and storming the Bastille in his head.

"Not to mention the Louvre," said Emile, interrupting the exchange between Charles and Frank, looking for a chance to get away. "Which I believe is the largest palace in the world. I was there yesterday to see the Mona Lisa. I really have to go now. Shall we make arrangements to meet in London?"

"How will you get there?" asked Frank, and then offered to purchase a ticket for Emile and Charles. They would meet Monday at the train station and together travel to London. Emile was overjoyed. A free ticket and another day to spend in Paris.

"But you haven't told us about the war?" said Frank.

"By bicycle?" Brent said to Frank, belatedly. "How am I going to ride a bicycle?"

"Never mind about that, Brent. The war, Emile, tell us about the war." Frank implored Emile.

The war. Emile told them a few stories. "You say that you're a writer, Charles? Then let me tell you a few literary stories from the war. You know Hemingway, right?" Emile told them about the arm wrestle in Madrid, and then he told them about the time in Valencia when he had been ordered to pick up two reporters at their hotel. One wrote for the New York Times, and the other was Hemingway. Hemingway sat in the back of the car. The reporter and Hemingway talked about the war and bull fighting. Emile looked in the rear view mirror. He couldn't understand why Hemingway had not recognized him from the arm wrestle in Madrid. Too drunk?

Emile took them out to an abandoned town that had been devastated by the fighting. Emile parked by a long trench on the main street of the town. The street was filled with dead cats and dogs, boots and uniforms, and rats. The reporter and Hemingway took pictures and jotted notes. Then back to Valencia. The reporter and Hemingway busily writing on the trip back.

"But I'll tell you something else," said Emile, "something quite unbelievable. But I swear it's true. It happened back just after we had crossed the border into Spain. It was in the mountains, in the Pyrenees. We had to climb over... it was steep and dangerous and we held on to each other. It was fucking treacherous I tell you. Rocks were falling, and men were slipping. We would come to a plateau and boy what a relief, but then some guy drank water, and the Spanish guides yelled not to, but he did it anyway, and got the most horrible stomach cramps. We tossed a blanket over him. And left him there. His anonymous death, that was my first taste of war. And that poor bastard's first taste of war was a fucking taste of water. How absurd. Absurd. The whole fucking world's becoming so god damn absurd. But nothing to be done. We went on without him. And our loads were too heavy. We had to get rid of stuff. Toss stuff away. Lighten our loads. I think everyone had some books and they were the last to go. But eventually we had to throw them away. It was sad. I was near the rear and I passed by all these discarded books. Books in all kinds of languages. English, Italian, Spanish, German, French, Russian... and I walked by Shakespeare, Dante, Cervantes, Goethe, Hugo, Dostoyevsky... just one after the other... it was like we were throwing civilization away. But we had to do it in order to save civilization, don't you know?"

"No," said Frank, "I don't know."

Emile took leave of his newfound friends' company and went off to visit Henry. This time they met at the Dome. Henry was sitting at his favorite table on the terrace. He was tending to a *café-crème*. This was the place where Miller had sat just a few years earlier and wrote his begging letters to friends asking for money and this is where he fished for suckers to pick up the tab. Henry was reading a long narrative poem by the American poet, Robinson Jeffers. It was called *The Women at Point Sur*.

"You know I sometimes slept in the loo here, in the sawdust," said Henry.

They sat among the crowded small round tables under the canopy. There were plants in long rectangular containers at the edge of the canopy. Salt, pepper, straws and a menu on the table.

"This is the most incredible thing I have ever read. Do you know Jeffer's poems?"

Emile was not familiar with Jeffers. Conversation turned to Orwell and war and literature.

Agnes Babs Widdlesworth arrived in London in October 1936. She stayed at the American Women's Club on Grosvenor Street. She distracted herself from thinking about Charles and Paris by going to sporting events; she took the racing train from King's Cross Station and went to horse racing; or she played bridge at a club; or she strolled through Hyde Park and went to museums. Toward the end of November she visited her father's old friend, Sir Dudley Gower, who lived in Lewes, Sussex. He had forgotten about the time he spent in a car with her and Captain Bethell. The weather was mild and she enjoyed motoring and strolling through William the Conqueror's country, as she saw it; historical references were like little blue angels of truth rowing a boat through her blood, also blue. But there were moments when she saw red.

It was rumored that the Prince of Wales, the future King of England, Edward VIII, was presently romantically linked to an American woman, a divorcee, Wallis Simpson, who Agnes knew was carrying on with another man. He confessed to her that he never wished to be King. But Agnes had her doubts. Was he just using her to get out of all this messy business? All this love of my people and country and heritage and duty? The thought of it made Agnes' English ancestral blue blood boil red. Or did he really love her? Just think of it! Agnes felt under the weather for a few days. She had heard rumors that the King would not consent to it. Once again Agnes became sick with fever and chills. Why such a reaction? She later heard rumors that the Prince was involved with another woman. An English Lady. Agnes was told by one in high places that "they" did not consider it proper that an American woman marry the Prince and that the English people would not approve. This angered Agnes no end. She was seriously questioning some subtle use by which the Monroe Doctrine could be newly invoked. Of course, this was mere bluster. After all, whom exactly would she be if she were not Agnes Babs Widdlesworth, direct descendant of Charlemagne, William the Conqueror, and Alfred the Great! She was just an American cousin, a member of a large family, who had traveled afar and made good, still owing a duty to the folks back home, like loans to win wars. The last several months of this year have provided ample excitement, and much gossip, about Edward VIII and his friendship with Mrs. Simpson. Wherever Agnes lunched she heard the talk, and she and the visiting Americans seemed to be more *au courant* than the King's subjects. The American newspapers and periodicals have been carrying the story ever since the death of beloved George V in January. And when the abdication announcement came in early December, Agnes felt relieved now that all shall be resolved and no matter what changes have been taking place, all too rapidly as far as she was concerned, nevertheless, the old order endured; she was assured of this by many a Duke and Duchess and Lady and Lord with whom she attended luncheons.

After she listened to the abdication speech on a radio, she was curious to know what kind of unkind words and otherwise were being spoken by the crowds that had gathered around Buckingham Palace; therefore she took to the streets and walked and listened and rubbernecked among the rabble. There were throngs of people on Oxford Street who were bunched together around bulletin boards where the latest news was posted. Many of the remarks that she overheard were rather hostile, she thought. Agnes has long been cultivating friendships with the upper-crust English who are sympathetic to Italian and German fascism. Certainly Edward VIII and Wallis Simpson were pro-German supporters. Edward remained loyal to his Hohenzollern royal bloodline. Agnes walked over to 10 Downing Street, where she got a glimpse of Prime Minister Baldwin. A crowd had gathered and chanted, "Edward's right, Baldwin's wrong! We want Edward!" When she got to Buckingham Palace, she saw the fascist Sir Charles Mosley's blackshirts out in force. The London police and riot squad were also present. Agnes listened to their singing: "For he's a jolly good fellow…" Agnes wasn't sure if the words were "For he's a jolly good fellow" or "Fuhrer's a jolly good fellow." Agnes walked passed a small man who barked loudly in her ear as she passed, "We want Eddie and we want her Missus!" The situation remained tense until the ex-King was whisk out of the country and was once again together with the woman he loved in a castle in Austria. And the people once again raised their voices: God save the King. Edward VIII had reigned for 324 days, the shortest in five hundred years of British history.

Frankie Cazzaza has never been so happy. He told his mother that he has met a charming girl. He had met her while delivering a pot roast and a leg of lamb to the Moore Estate, where Mary worked as a maid. She wasn't Typhoid Mary, another Mary who had worked in these parts as another invisible servant girl.

Frankie has been a driver for Van Heffer's Meat Market the past several years but never had anything like this ever happened. Mary was from Ireland. She had dark red hair. She had an Irish brogue. And her face turned beet red when Frankie kissed her. He courted her for only three months and then he popped the question one day when they were sitting together in the front of the delivery truck in the back courtyard of the Moore Estate, with the smell of raw meat in the air. The wedding day was set for May 21, 1938. Frankie sat at the kitchen table telling his mother about the girl he met a few weeks ago. Today's newspaper, dated June 8, 1937, was spread out on the table and Frankie's elbows were resting upon it. Luisa kept reminding Frankie to be careful with the newspaper because she wanted to cut out the pictures and articles pertaining to Jean Harlow's death. Frankie felt too happy to bother to tease her and said that he would be careful with the newspaper, so don't worry. Frankie scanned the page. He was thinking about buying a used car; he wanted desperately to impress Mary.

"I've narrowed it down to several," said Frankie, and he read from the newspaper: "Chevrolet 1931 Sport Coupe, rumble seat, good tires, glossy finish. Ideal for economy. $95.00. Or this one, Chevrolet 1931 Coach, $135.00. Or a 1934 Chevrolet Sport Coupe, snappy, $110.00... let's see... De Soto, 1930 sedan, wonderful condition, $95.00 down, drive away. Graham 1931 Sedan, reconditioned throughout, $50.00 down, $4.00

weekly... I don't know what to do..." Frankie looked up at his two brothers, Stevie and Joe, who were fiddling with the dials on the radio. Stevie, at 22, has taken a keen interest in his older brother's romance. Stevie has never been involved with a woman; he was very shy, and having to hop around on crutches didn't help his confidence. Joe wasn't interested in girls, yet; his main interest was sports. He liked baseball, basketball and football. He especially liked to play basketball. He was already taller than his older brothers. He had a good two-handed set shot. But he excelled at baseball. He had even hit a few home runs over the fence at the baseball field behind the high school.

"Whadda you think?" said Frankie to his brothers.

"I like the Sports Coupe with the rumble seat," offered Stevie. Joe kept fiddling with the radio dials. It was nearly seven o'clock. Joe was trying to tune in station WEAF 660 Kilocycles. Amos and Andy were coming on, followed fifteen minutes later by Uncle Ezra. Frankie insisted that he be allowed, at eight o'clock, to listen to the Dorsey Brothers' Orchestra on WEAF, but Joe wanted to listen to Fibber McGee and Molly on WJZ, but if their mother has her way, she will listen to the Lombardo Orchestra on WABC. Luisa and Stevie wanted to listen to the Lone Ranger on WOR. Fiorenza will decide when the time came. It's been so difficult for her these past ten years taking care of her children without a husband and the loss of her two sisters, one to suicide, and the other to a mental institution; and then there were the troubles with Toots and her husband Johnny.

After Giuseppe was killed, Fiorenza asked Toots and her husband to take care of young Luisa for a while, Fiorenza had enough on her hands with the boys. Toots was furious. She had just married and didn't want Luisa getting in the way. Luisa was very demanding and required much attention, both physically and emotionally. Johnny was even more furious and never forgave Fiorenza. Luisa proved to be too much of a burden for Toots and after six months Luisa returned home. But the damage had been done and for the rest of their lives there were strong feelings of animosity and resentment between Fiorenza and her two daughters.

Joe tuned in 660. It would be on this same large upright Philco radio that Joe would hear about the Japanese attack on Pearl Harbor in 1941; and when Bobby Thompson hit a home run to win the pennant in 1951 for the New York Giants, Joe would hear it on this radio as it happened, tuned in to 570. Giants win the pennant! Giants win the pennant!

Fiorenza roosted herself on the comfortable chair in front of the radio and her children gathered around. Fiorenza was quite pleased that she might have a first daughter-in-law in Mary. Of course it was too early to tell, but Frankie seemed to be smitten indeed. She had almost given up on her eldest son ever getting married; he seemed to be a confirmed bachelor. And she remained concerned that Frankie would continue to be the confirmed gambler and drinker that he's been since the age of fifteen. Maybe Mary can straighten him out. Frankie told his mother that Mary was a good Catholic girl. Fiorenza was pleased.

They listened to the radio, except for Luisa; she was in mourning; still brooding over the passing of one of Hollywood's glamour girls. Luisa would never be a Hollywood glamour girl. Her nose was too big, and she was short, her body was slightly deformed; her only outstanding feature was her bright green eyes. Once again she read the newspaper, the stories about Harlow. "Jean Harlow, Glamour Girl of the movies, whose death yesterday shocked the make-believe world in which she had been one of the greatest figures..." That was from the *Daily News*. Then Luisa read from the *Daily Mirror,* and from the *Evening Journal.* And then she began cutting out the clippings, articles and pictures. A voice said, "Don't open that door McGee!" and the sound of things crashing made her smile for a moment. Joe had got his way and was allowed to listen to Fibber McGee and Molly. His mother told the other children that it was his turn. Luisa noticed Joe's schoolbook on the table: *History of the United States.* She opened it and read what Joe had written on the back of the front cover. There was a heart with an arrow piercing it, and Frankie and Mary was written inside the heart. Beneath the sketch of the heart was a curious list of sorts.

Document 3.9.3

I.   No body can part these two. "Horse Feathers"

II.   Oh! What a school girl complection!

III. We will step right on their bunions because we know our onions.

IV. Act your age kid! How about it.

V.   Three cheers for the Irish. Notice!!!

VI. Children over fourteen should be aloud out!!!

VII. Do your stuff boyfriend.

VIII. Hows chances kid?

IX. To day isn't field day.   feel

X. I live down the East River drop in some time.

XI. You're the only one.

XII. Do teachers pet. You bet.

XIII. Oh! boy lets go.

It was all rather cryptic to Luisa, but it would appear that Joe was also interested in his brother's romantic involvement with Mary. Luisa couldn't resist and began reading the list out loud. Joe got up and tore the book out from her hands. "Leave my book alone."

Frankie looked over to see what all the commotion was about. When he saw that the newspapers were all cut up and spread over the table, he said, "Wait a minute, I'm not through with those papers yet. What are you doing?"

"You said I could," said Luisa.

"But I have to check something first."

Frankie wanted to check what was playing on Broadway. He wanted to take Mary to a show. He filtered through the newspapers and found what he was looking for and told Luisa that she could cut up the rest. He sat down next to his mother and asked for her advice.

"I don't know, ma, I can't decide between a musical or a drama," said Frankie.

"A musical, a romantic musical," said Fiorenza without hesitation.

"I don't know, I was kinda wanting to see *Tobacco Road.*"

"Some guy pees on the stage," interjected Stevie.

Frankie stared defiantly at his brother. How could he say such a thing? Mama wouldn't approve. Before his mother could say a word, Frankie said, *Anything Goes!* He was now reading from the newspaper. "*Anything Goes!* William Gaxton, Victor Moore, with Bettina Hall. New York's No. 1 musical hit. At the Alvin, W. 52nd street. That's Cole Porter, isn't it?"

Fiorenza frowned. Porter was too, what's the word, sophisticated. She preferred Eddie Cantor. Frankie kept reading. *The Great Waltz... The Old Maid... The Children's Hour... Three Men On A Horse...* that's a comedy... um... Gilbert and Sullivan... Earl Carroll Sketch Book, cast of hundreds, laugh revue, Winter Garden, Broadway and 50th... how about that one?"

"That's more like it," said Fiorenza, "and you can change the station now."

The Call of the Sea, a drama, was coming on the radio. Joe said, "I don't wanna hear this." He once again started fiddling with the dial. He paused when he heard the announcer speaking; "...greatest gang of talent you ever saw, in one mad, gay, exciting movie! *New Faces of 1937*, with Joe Penner, Milton Berle, Parkyakarkus, Harriet Hilliard, William Brady, Jerome Cowan, Thelma Leeds... a RKO-Radio picture..." and the music peaked and stomped a final chord.

"We have to see that when it comes to The Lyric," said Joe.

"That Joe Penner is funny," added Stevie.

"Yeah, do you wanna buy a duck?" said Frankie and they all laughed.

Except Luisa, who was still busy cutting clippings and pictures from the newspaper. She had the trash receptacle positioned by her side now; and as she cut out the clippings she tossed the rest of the pages of the newspaper into the trash. She clipped out the article with the headline: **INHALATOR CREW FAIL TO SAVE JEAN HARLOW.** And the rest of the sheet of newspaper went into the trash. There it goes... swooning lightly into oblivion, with the headline: Steel Pickets Disarmed on Strike Battlefront. And then Luisa trimmed another clipping with the headline: **LIFE OF JEAN HARLOW, FLAMING METEOR OF SCREEN WORLD.** That went into her scrapbook. Shakeup In Navy Due To Oust Reds went into the trash. **JEAN HARLOW DEAD AT 26 IN HOLLYWOOD** went into her scrapbook. Color Line Drives Pair From $20,000 Home went into the trash. Everything went into the trash but Hollywood and Harlow. Luisa was an American girl. She wasn't even interested in the brief mention of Amelia Earhart: Amelia Hops S. Atlantic. St. Louis, Senegal, Africa, June 7 (UP). Amelia Earhart arrived here tonight in her "flying Laboratory," after a 1,900-mile flight across the Atlantic from Natal, Brazil, and sat down to a hearty dinner with French air mail pilots... that went into the trash can. Something about the Duke and Duchess of Windsor... rather than trying to live a hermit's existence in their quest for tranquility they asked after their marriage, the Duke and Duchess have chosen now to "taper off" on publicity... that went into the trash.

Frank, Brent and Charles were waiting for Emile at the Gard du Nord. He arrived just in time to catch the train. They made the crossing on the Night Ferry, a train service that was launched last year. The sleeper trains were built by the famous *Compagnie Internationale des Wagons-Lits,* the sleeping-car company that had built the trains of the Orient Express. The Night Ferry traveled between the Gare du Nord in Paris and Victoria Station in

London. The ferry crossed from Dunkirk to Dover. The train ferry transported the passengers while they were sleeping.

It was early Tuesday morning, May 11th, the day before the Coronation. They walked in Trafalgar Square. Emile was looking toward the National Gallery. Hordes of pigeons swarmed around his feet. He turned and looked at one of the lions that guarded Nelson's Column. A small piece of the lion's left ear was chipped off. They crossed the road and entered an alley. A young girl approached them. "Good morning, gentlemen, feed the birds, penny a bag." She held small bags of stale bread in her apron. She was selling them to the tourists to use to feed the pigeons. Emile spoke with her. She said her name was Mary. She told Emile that she gets the bread from the rubbish bins behind the big houses in Wykeham Place. From 5 a.m. until 6 a.m. she rummages through the refuse in search of stale bread. Ten pieces of bread makes about 6 or 7 bags. "Penny, sir," said Mary. Emile gave her a penny and took a bag. Mary skipped out of the alley and crossed over to Trafalgar Square. The alley was busy with gentlemen going to their places of business. Bowler hats composed on their heads, and black umbrellas swinging with well-ordered meticulousness. The alley was filled with people selling all kinds of wares. But the austere gentlemen walked by briskly. They bought nothing. No good mornings were exchanged. I'm not in Paris anymore, thought Emile. Commerce surrounds us. Little Mary got bumped about quite rudely.

On Thursday they took the Underground to Camden Town tube station. They followed Frank. Camden Town was a poor area of London. He led them to a small rather poorly maintained café. The table was grimy. The seats were rickety. Even so, Frank seemed to know the area and the café. They sat down together at a table, on an unknown street. The pomp and crowds were too much even for Frank. He wanted to show Brent a bit of the squalor portrayed in the novels of Charles Dickens. The police have been watching over every corner of London, following and pestering any suspicious looking strangers and any dangerous looking chaps who reeked of foreign influence, and who could be the cause of possible embarrassment to the royal ceremonies, or worse a possible assassination attempt. Charles with his tattered clothes and French accent may draw attention. There were multiple small Union Jacks and bunting strung across the street. Frank said, "Charles Dickens lived here when he was twelve years old. His father had been tossed into a debtors' prison. Dickens had to leave school. He said that he was cast away at a tender age. He worked in a shoe-polish factory to support his family. He worked ten hours a day."

Emile was surprised by this show of concern for the downtrodden. "Frank, I wouldn't have thought your sympathies were so large. I rather thought you were a nihilist and doomsayer."

"It's only because it is Dickens. Any other ten-year-old factory worker does not concern me. It is genius that counts. I am not a nihilist. I'm a Nietzschean."

"I would not advise looking too long into that abyss," said Frank.

"Or the abyss looks back... the gaze? Well then, as I was about to say, Rimbaud and Verlaine stayed here in 1873, in a flat over on College Street. We can walk over there if you wish. No? Not interested? I'm ready. I got my Baedeker, my cigars, my Wellington books and my umbrella. I'm ready for the London fog, the unreal city. So let's go. Shakespeare, Keats, Coleridge and Carlyle walked here."

"Carlyle was a Fascist!" blurted out Emile.

"Of course. And Hitler and Mussolini. Hero worship. Slavery kept the order. Democracy's a sham. The ablest men. The lesser breeds. Well, nevertheless, let us see the houses of the great and famous men. Their monuments await us. Let us go then you and I and see the houses of the great poets. Keats lived in Hampstead. We can walk on the Heath. Marx took his family there. That might interest you, Emile, no?"

"Sarcasm does not become you," replied Emile. "Did I invade your soul? Did I speak the Devil's language?"

"Mock on..." whimpered Frank.

"Sorry," muttered Emile, "I really should just thank you. You purchased my fare for the train and ferry. I am in your debt."

"Then I must be the doom merchant. Well then, off to debtors' prison with you," playfully snarled Frank.

"Let's just go," said Brent, exasperated.

"Yes, *allons-y* ... I want to see Rimbaud and Verlaine!" said Charles.

Emile returned to America aboard the *SS Champlain*. The others returned to Paris. They wanted to attend the *Exposition Internationale*, the World's Fair. The exhibition promoted Peace and Progress united under the banner of Arts and Techniques. Pavilions were dedicated to railway, to flight, to refrigeration, to cinema, to radio, and to printing. But the winds were already stirring up the dust and ashes. There was great uncertainty in the air and colossal clashes of ideology lurked underneath the appearances of these massive presentations. Paris and the Provinces, Art and Science, Communism and Capitalism, France and its Colonies, Fascism and Democracy, International cooperation or Nationalist fervor, Workers and Peasants and the Bourgeois, Artisans, Craftsmen and the Artists, Art and Technology, the Universal and the International, Art as Artisanship, Science as Technology, the New Criteria of the Usefulness and the Social Utility of Art and Technology, the confinement of Art and Science to the practical, to the pleasing, to social enrichment and advancement, to decoration that is both practical and beautiful, something acceptable to both the left and right, a tidy liberal consensus. But is it not condescending? Is it not tantamount to saying that we, in power, and the intellectuals, are so right about what we believe that we can tolerate your little dissenting words. Backed by institutional force.

Painters and sculptors would not appear with the lower mechanical arts; they displayed their work at salons where patrons entered into the higher level of aesthetic beauty. There was a rift. The Post-Modern is born. Arts and Techniques should be separated... Art and Industry...

How lovely Italy has become under El Duce. The Soviet Union pavilion shows a map of Mother Russia made of gold and rubies and other precious stones, the most expensive display of all; well, the workers' money had to go up to someone, just as in Capitalism. The Nazi Pavilion was directly across from the Soviet Union, facing each other with severe resolve across the fountains spraying water; these massive fortifications of ideals presented to the world the heroic workingman and peasant woman brandishing hammer and sickle, and on the other side the German Eagle, its talons clutching a wreath, encircling a huge swastika with a massive and naked Teutonic couple positioned on the concrete platform.

The Great Railway Pavilion was designed by four French architects, a great Art Deco masterpiece, the facade of the building showed a marginally abstract mural of looping tracks and trains weaving in and out of each other like an Escher print. The official book of the exhibition, *Le Livre d'Or,* makes no reference of the artists who created the mural. After all, why mention them, unless one also mentions the designers of pull-down beds, or every man who helped to build it, to lay bricks or attach steel beams.

Maurice Chevalier was singing "La petite dame de l'expo." The Spanish were preparing to display Picasso's mural *Guernica*.

And when *Guernica* arrived in July, Frank, Brent and Charles stood before it. Amazed and dazed. Is this shrieking of despair rendered in the name of the artist or in the many unknown names of the workers? Did Picasso sign his name to it? And what are the names of the women and children who were killed, smoldered, surrounded by a wall of fire?

I Am in the Best of Health

Man makes history and history makes man. Man makes a text and a text makes man. Man makes a war and war makes man. Man makes money and money makes man. A word points to infinity and a sentence points to itself. A book points to infinity and a book points to itself. Literary narrative points to infinity and narrative history points to itself. Which came first, the subject of experience or the object of experience?

Newsreel: In the summer of 1942 there were approximately 15,000 involuntary inductees bound for the 88th Division of the Army. The 88th was the first all draftee division to enter combat in World War II. Joseph John Cazzaza was at Camp Upton on Long Island, but not for long.

Postcard: Post Headquarters, Camp Upton, Long Island, New York

Dear Mom,

Don't expect to stay at Camp Upton long. When we get settled in our camp I'll write more. Your son, Joe.

Newsreel: They were working-class boys from the east. Most of them had never heard the sound of gunfire, let alone held a gun in their hands. They were just draftees. Let's take a look at one of these young men. His name is Joe Cazzaza. Joe is from a town on Long Island called Oyster Bay. He is tired and confused as he is jostled through the induction station. Before he knows it Joe is on the long train ride to Camp Gruber, Oklahoma. He is assigned to his unit, the 351st Infantry Regiment. The infantry, the toughest job, because after the bombers and the artillery are done, the infantry man rises from his foxhole, seeks out the enemy in his hiding place, and with rifle and grenade and bare hands, takes on and holds the ground. Man to man, killed or be killed. The infantry takes most of the casualties in the war. Good luck Joe, and good luck to all our boys over there.

Postcard: Will Rodgers Tomb and Garden, Claremore, Okla.
July 30, 1942
351 Inf. Co. B APO 88th

Dear Mom,

It is pretty hot here. The army ain't so bad except we have no laundry yet. I'll be able to go to town in a week or two.

Your son, Joe

Postcard: Oklahoma Indians, Muskogee, Okla.
August 3, 1942

Dear Toots,

How is Grandma Luise doing? I went to the movies Saturday night. I go to church every Sunday. The beads you gave me broke. Write and let me know how everything is.

Your brother, Joe

Newsreel: Basic training began in early August. The sun was hot and the air dusty. Joe learned how to make a bed, mop a floor, police an area, stand at attention, march, and they learned basic first aid and discipline. In the field they learned map reading and navigating with a compass during night marches. The obstacle course, long hikes, gas-mask drills, and firing .30 caliber bullets from an M-1 rifle. By November basic training was over and new recruits from the south and mid-west were arriving at Camp Gruber.

August 8, 1942

Dear Toots,

How are you? How is Grandma Luise coming along? I am way out in the Wild West. Frankie wrote and told me that Mary's brother Jim is in the same camp with me. I go to the movies pretty often. I haven't met anyone from Oyster Bay yet, but I met one fellow from Glen Cove. The weather here is warm. It was a long train ride. It took two days and nights. If Mr. Miller is there tell him I was asking for him. We have good eats in the camp. I hope everyone is well. Your brother, Joe.

August 25, 1942

Dear Joe

Received the cards you send us and we all thank you. How do you like to do your own washing. We had rain for one week. It's nice you have a Day room. I send you the local papers and I will mail it every week. Stevie still goes to work but no license yet, he didn't get the air tank yet. We are all pretty well now. My feet are the same as usual. Harry goes shopping for me but he still goes to the doctor. I got a nice letter from your Chaplain Day B Werts you are in good care. Mrs. Zipper thanks you for the books of Oklahoma. It must be a beautiful place. Hope some day you come home to tell us all about Oklahoma. We all waiting to see your pictures. The kittens are so cute. Short Tail climbs on Lu's back and climbs up the drapes. Will write again soon. God bless you all.

With love, Mom

Postcard: Alice Robertson Junior High School, Muskogee, Okla.
Nov. 2, 1942

Dear Luisa

Hope you are well. How are all the kittens? We have it pretty easy here now. I hope to get a furlough soon.

Your brother, Joe

Nov. 12, 1942

Dear Joe,

I hope you get your furlough in December so you will be home for Christmas. I am still working in the shipyard and one minesweeper is finished. They took it out the other day and it was away all day, nice looking boat. I worked all night from six to six the next morning then came back at 8 o'clock the same morning. I made $67 bucks that week. Did you hear about Nicky's father, he had an operation on his head and died last week, I think it was a tumor on the brain. And Nicky is in the marines you know and was stabbed by a Jap in Guadalcanal and in the hospital and in bad shape. There are about 45 draftees going away tomorrow, there won't be anybody left soon. So how is Oklahoma? Is it very cold? Hope you have plenty of warm clothes. If you need anything Babe let us know, we will be only too glad to send them to you. We are praying that this war will be over soon we can't even use our cars! I don't know what this old world is coming to. I guess we will just have to keep smiling and hope better days are coming with the help of God... I was doing pretty good in the meat market getting $35 a week but the shipyard work took all my time. The boys in the meat market are kept busy trying to get more meat to sell, chop meat is .35 a pound. We were in Northport a few weeks ago, Grandma Luisa didn't feel very well, and now Toots wants us to take her to the empty apartment on South Street, who can take care of her there? She's going to be ninety years old soon. Oh my God. We just took a chance taking the car out but we didn't get stopped. If you have a picture of yourself send it out I will put it in the Drug Store window, they have all the boy's pictures in there. I guess you get the best of everything to eat. We are going to be rationed to 2 pounds of meat a week. Can't pay for much more than that anyway. Well we must make the best of things till you get that machine gun and knock over a few japs and germans.

Best regards, Frankie and Mary

Nov. 15, 1942

Dear son Joe,

Received your letter of Nov. 10, didn't you get a carton of Camel cigarettes you didn't mention them in the letter. We went to Grandma to hear the record it didn't sound like your voice, some one else was speaking for you. Toots wants to send Grandma here. My poor mother. She should have stayed in the city. She lived so many years at 235 Mercer Street. I grew up there. If my brother John didn't die so young he would have took care of her still. I am sending you the Pilot. We shut the front rooms, and we are sleeping in the dining room to keep warm. We can't get much kerosene. We still have the cats. Stevie went to get his tests 2 weeks ago and didn't get no answer yet. Let us know how you are getting along is it cold there, so long for now. With love Mom

-----

Newsreel: Unit training began in December and lasted through to February 1943. Early in December Joe went on his furlough and appeared in his hometown bearing the blue clover leaf insignia of the 88th on his uniform.

Joe returned from his furlough and immediately set about viewing a full schedule of training films, motion pictures from the front lines and battle zones, and learning about new weapons and tactics, hearing lectures on history, the propaganda of why they were to fight. But a rumor was spreading that they would never leave Gruber, that they were just a replacement unit.

United States Army
Camp Gruber, Oklahoma
Jan. 13, 1943

Dear Toots,

I received your letter today and was glad to hear from you. The weather out here is swell. It is just like the spring time out here now. We have lots of recreation here. I go to the movies a couple times a week. We even have stage plays here. Last Monday I saw the play *Claudia*. They show the latest movies here. The other night I saw *Yankee Doodle Dandy*. I didn't know Jimmy Cagney could sing and dance. Mom sends me the hometown papers every week. Give my regards to everyone and don't forget Mr. Miller. Tell Louis I was asking for him and tell him to save that drink for me. Well, I'll say so long for now.

Your brother Joe

Jan. 18, 1943

Dear son Joe,

I received your letter and pictures was nice of all your buddies and you. I am sending you the sweater and gloves. I did not know the size of the gloves. The gloves was $2.75 and the sweater $2.50 I hope they fit you. Two boys brought Stevie home sick last Thursday he is home yet, he beginning to feel a little better. But he didn't want a doctor. Your sister Toots must be busy singing in choir, I am sending you some cookies. So long for now, and God bless you all, your Mom

-----

United States Army
Camp Gruber, Oklahoma
Jan. 25, 1943

Dear Mom,

I received your package it was swell. The sweater and gloves fit me fine. Thank Harry for his candies and Chubby for the box of cigars. As I was opening the package my friend Joe Imbraico comes in. He's in the MPs driving a truck. Give my regards to Mrs. Masini, Mrs. Zipper, and Emily. How is Lu and her kittens? Well, everyone in Camp Gruber is the same. Well, that's all for now.

Your son, Joe.

PS I'm going to read the local papers now.

Feb. 2, 1943

Dear son Joe,

I am glad you received the package sweater and gloves and they fit you fine. Stevie didn't go to the bank for the money I paid for them. Stevie is better now and goes to work again. We had a snowstorm and it's fine weather here today but we still have snow on the ground. Lu and I went to movies last night we saw *Springtime in the Rockies*, it was funny. I guess you see lots of movies there. I am sending you the *Newsday* and *Pilot*. Cats and Lu are all right. Mrs Zipper is right here while I write this letter and she is going to mail the letter for me and sends her best regards, your ever loving Mother

-----

United States Army
Camp Gruber, Oklahoma
Feb. 20, 1943

Dear Toots,

I received your letter and was glad to hear from you. You're sure having some cold weather out there. We are having wonderful weather here. We can walk around in our shirtsleeves here. I go to the movies often here. I go two or three times a week. They show the latest pictures here too. Sunday night I am going to see *Star Spangled Rhythm*. I was sorry to hear that Grandma was worse. Frankie and Mary wrote and told me that they were over to see you. Give my regards to Mr. Miller when you see him. Well, I'll say so long for now. Your brother Joe.

PS Tell Theresa I'll still buy her that pizza.

United States Army
Saturday, Feb. 27, 1943
Camp Gruber, Oklahoma

Dear Mom,

Well this is Saturday afternoon and there is nothing to do but write. I just had a nice dinner. We had liver, mashed potatoes, mixed fruit and coffee. I got fooled one day I thought I was eating mashed potatoes and it was squash. We been eating a lot of pork lately. The weather is fine here. We had a very good winter. We only had a few real cold days. I go to the pictures often here and see some pictures before they get to New York. I'll be a year older Wed. March 3. I'll have to pay my income tax this year. I hope everyone is well at home and I'll write again soon.

Your son Joe

United States Army
Camp Gruber, Oklahoma
March 2, 1943

Dear Mom

I am writing you a few lines to let you know that I made out my own income tax. I figured I made $571 and it cost $4. We are inside today because it is snowing out. It is the first snow we had this winter. It was some change in the weather. Well, how is everything at home? I hope all is well. I got paid March 1st and got $39.65. I got $50 saved. That's because I don't go to town. I went to the movies last night and saw *Reveille with Beverly*. It was a swell musical. I am going to the movies again tonight and see *Random Harvest* with Ronald Coleman and Greer Garson. Well, that's it for now.

Your son, Joe

Newsreel: Full division reviews were held by early April, and then on April 18, armed guards were placed in all buildings and along the roads. Telephone lines were cut off. Something big was happening. A reviewing stand with a special auto ramp was built on the west side of the main parade ground. At 5 p.m. a special train pulled into Camp Gruber with President Franklin D. Roosevelt aboard.

Tourjours Pris
351st Infantry
Easter Sunday April 25, 1943

Dear Toots,

I received your very nice Easter Card the other day. I went to the 10:30 Mass this morning and after Mass they had Benediction. We have a very nice Chaplin here his name is Father Luis. I am in the best of health and hope you are all well. We are having nice weather here, but it's a little dusty. We go out in the field tomorrow for a whole week. I don't know when I will get another furlough. There are quite a few fellows here yet that didn't get any furloughs at all yet. I'll let you know when I get my furlough again. President Roosevelt was here last Sunday. We had a parade for him. Give my regards to everyone.

Your brother, Joe

Newsreel: In June the 88th traveled south to Louisiana for maneuvers. For two weeks Joe and the men marched through swamps, and across rivers, and on land with snakes, bugs, chiggers, ticks, mosquitoes, hogs and dust. The 351st Infantry marched with full gear for 62 miles in 42 hours, 29 hours actual march time, every man going the full distance. This march brought praise from General George C. Marshall.

The 88th had done so well on maneuvers that it drew Fort Sam Houston, San Antonio, Texas, as its new home, one of the choicest spots in the Army.

Fort Sam Houston, Texas
Sunday Oct, 10, 1943

Dear Toots,

I got back to my camp Thursday morning. I stayed in town Thursday and saw a good movie. I saw *This Is the Army*, with Kate Smith and Irving Berlin. It was sure a long, train ride but we had lots of fun. The weather is pretty warm here during the day. But at night and when we get up in the morning it's pretty chilly. Well, I'll say so long for now and I'll write again soon.

Your brother, Joe

Newsreel: In November the first Liberty ships left Newport News, packed in the holes were soldiers of the 351st, starting on their longest journey yet, across the Atlantic in a slow convoy. They were on their way finally, headed for Casablanca, French Morocco, in North Africa.

United States Army
Friday Dec. 24, 1943

Dear Toots,

I received your letter and was glad to hear from you. I am in North Africa. I am in the best of health and hope everyone in Northport is well. It sure was a long boat ride here. I was sick the first day on the boat, but after that the trip was swell. When you see Mr Miller and Louis give them my regards. Merry Christmas. Well, I'll say so long for now and I'll write soon.

Your brother, Joe

Newsreel: Joe sampled the sidewalk cafes, saw the camel caravans, wondered about the off-limits Medina section, and saw his first glimpses of war in the wrecked French battleships in the harbor. He bought a ring and had it inscribed with "CAZZAZA CASABLANCA 1943," and he bought a brown leather wallet.

Before long they were off again, this time by French boxcars to Oran, Algeria. Joe slept in his pup tent and considered the latrine rumors: that the 88th would never leave Africa, that they would remain only to police up, that they were to be converted to MPs, but with the Fifth Army in Italy in bad need of replacements, it was only a matter of time before the action began. By February they were on the move again. Joe Cazzaza was on his last water lap of a long journey that began in Camp Upton, and proceeded through basic training, and on to a combat zone and action. He sailed on the *Lancashire,* an English ship, and landed at Naples, where the units bivouacked for the night at the Italian Collegio Constanza Ciano, formally used as German headquarters prior to the fall of Naples. The following day truck convoys moved the troops to the general area around the village of Piedimonte d'Alife, where Division Headquarters had been established in a former agricultural college. After four months on the move the 88th Division was together again and at last in its first combat zone.

United States Army
Friday Feb. 25, 1944

Dear Toots,

I am in Italy. I visited Naples. I saw Mt. Vesuvius it's very high and always smoking. I am in the best of health and hope everyone in Northport is well. I guess Johnny is always keeping busy doing something. Tell Louis to stop making a pest of himself and get into the Army. Give my regards to Mr. Miller. Well, I'll say so long for now and I'll write again soon.

Your brother Joe

Newsreel: Vesuvius blew its load on March 18th, and Naples had been quarantined since the beginning of the year. The city was being deloused with DDT. American hospitals were filling up with VD patients. A new drug, penicillin, was available by the middle of February. The 88th were outside Naples. Joe could hear the sound of gunfire in the distance at the front, and at night he saw faint flashes over the mountains to Cassino, and he wondered about when they would move up. The weather was cold and rainy. Soon into the front lines, and this was no movie… the waiting was killing. Lets lick these Germans so we can get out of the Army. There was talk that the 351st would be sent to the Anzio beachhead, where after initial success the attack on the beach had bogged down, and was under attack by Nazi units. The 351st was sent as far as Naples, was outfitted and equipped and ready to move on the beachhead, but then orders were changed. The regiment was sent back to its old area.

Then they were on the move. They moved north to Minturno. They maintained a three-regiment front; the 350th was assigned the left flank on the seacoast, the 351st in the center sector, and the 349th on the right flank. It was May and the days lengthened, the Big Push was coming soon. The 351st moved back into the line in the Minturno-Tufo area. Everything was set. They waited for the hour. The 88th was ready. Joe Cazzaza was ready too.

It was May 11, a spring day, scarlet poppies shook in the sea breeze, smell of Mimosa filled the air, and as the light of day faded stars blinked in the sky. The whining sound of an incoming shell pounded the dirt with a distant muffled crash. Then just before midnight a long sheet of flame erupted along the front, a massive artillery concentration exploded and shattered the night. Tons of steel shot from guns along the long-dormant front. Joe Cazzaza took his first steps into battle, following closely behind the fierce barrage of artillery.

The 351st arrived near Santa Maria Infante, and started up the slopes under a hail of German fire. Small-arms, tanks, machine guns and mortar fire were exchanged. The Germans held the devastated village, now a mere rubble heap. Eventually, the relentless attack of the 351st cracked the German line, and the town was taken.

On the afternoon of May 14th Mt. Bracchi was occupied with A and B Companies by nightfall. Joe Cazzaza led his squad up the hill and a hot piece of shrapnel ripped along his back. They pressed on. The 351st then took Mt Passasera and drove on to the north and Rome. Rome and home was the battle cry. The 351st moved on and seized Mt. Valletonda. The 351st was ordered to push forward along Hwy. 101, enter Rome, and seize important bridges over the Tiber River. But they ran into German resistance about one mile east of the city. They detrucked and took on the German strongpoint. At long last, behind three tanks, they marched into Rome.

Soon they were on the move again. Laiatico, Monte Foscoli, San Romano, Volterra, Gesso, Verona, Borgo, the Brenner Pass...

To Mrs. Silvia Bacigalupo
Main Street
Northport, Long Island, New York
From PFC Joe Cazzaza
Co. B 351st INF APO 88
CENSOR''S STAMP
Friday Sept. 15, 1944

Dear Toots,

I received your most welcome letter of Aug. 25 and it was swell hearing from you. I received your cigars and chewing gum in Mom's package and I appreciate it very much. I visited Rome here and I saw St. Peter's it sure is a beautiful cathedral. I visited lots of other interesting places there. I am in the best of health and hope everyone there is well.

Your brother Joe

To Mrs. Silvia Bacigalupo
Main Street
Northport, Long Island, New York
From PFC Joe Cazzaza
Co. B 351st INF APO 88
CENSOR"S STAMP
Monday Dec. 16, 1944

Dear Toots,

I am sorry that I haven't written you sooner but I have been kind of busy. I want to thank you for the cigars and gum you sent me. Chubby sent me a watch in the same package and it's a pip. Well, how is everything in Northport? I guess you and Johnny are still running from one store to the other. Give my regards to everyone. I am in the best of health and hope everyone there is well too.

Your brother Joe

To Mrs. Silvia Bacigalupo
Main Street
Northport, Long Island, New York
From PFC Joe Cazzaza
Co. B 351st INF APO 88
CENSOR"S STAMP
Italy
Feb. 17, 1945

Dear Toots,

Just a few lines to let you know I'm in the best of health and I hope everyone in Northport is well. I'm sorry I haven't written sooner but I been kind of busy. I guess you keep pretty busy yourself. The weather has been swell here but the snow is melting now and making things muddy. Well, I'll say so long for now and I'll write again soon. Give my regards to everyone.

Your brother Joe

Italy
March 29, 1945

Dear Toots,

I received your most welcome letter of March 18th and it was swell hearing from you. I'm in the best of health and I'm glad everyone over there is well. I want to thank you for giving Mom some cigars and chewing gum to send me. The weather has been pretty fine here, but we had some rain the past few days. I've been seeing some swell pictures and USO shows here. The other night I saw *A Song to Remember* with Paul Muni and I thought it was a pretty good picture. Well, I'm going to say so long for now and I'll write again soon. Your brother Joe

-----

Document 4.5.2

Joseph John Cazzaza, 805th Replacement Battalion, Sergeant, Machine Gunner, on crew of 30 caliber machine gun with 88th Division; Squad Leader, in charge of 30 caliber light machine gun squad of 5 men with 88th Division in Italy. Inducted on 6 July 1942; departed 23 Nov. 1943 for North Africa, arrived 10 Dec. 1943; departed 2 Feb. 1944 for Italy, arrived 6 Feb. 1944; departed 21 Aug. 1945 for the USA, arrived 6 Sep. 1945. Date of separation: 2 Nov. 1945. Battles and Campaigns: Po Valley, Rome-Arno, North Appenines. Decorations: EAME Theater Ribbon w 3/ Bronze Stars, American Theater Ribbon; Good Conduct Medal...

Home from war he returned to his old bedroom; the room at the back of the house overlooking South Street. He was born in that room. He showed his family the souvenirs of war. There were postcards and books. There were objects of war, a canteen, an ammo belt, a folding shovel, a jacket, and a gun, a M1934 Beretta. He put everything away in the closet and sat at the edge of his bed and exhaled.

The next day his brother Frank came to see him and welcome him home. He brought along his wife Mary and their son little Frankie.

While they were sitting around the kitchen table they heard a loud metallic pop. It came from the bathroom. They ran to the bathroom and there stood little Frankie with the Beretta in his hand. And there stood Fiorenza, frozen in front of the mirror over the sink. The mirror was shattered from the bullet. Fiorenza was not hit, but the bullet missed her by inches. Little Frankie was scolded.

Joe opened the old trunk that stood in the corner of a storage room. It was the trunk that his father Giuseppe brought from Italy in 1893. There was a secret compartment in the trunk. Joe wrapped the gun in cloth and slid the secret door open. There was some old yellow paper in the compartment but he was not very curious about it. He placed the gun inside the secret compartment and slid the door closed.

In 1921 Nicola Sacco and Bartolomeo Vanzetti, a shoemaker and a fishmonger, were condemned to death for an armed robbery at a shoe factory in Braintree, Massachusetts. They were executed in 1927. This event has been sited by leftist historians as the death of the Italian radical Left. America preferred that admirable Italian gentleman Mussolini, who from 1922 to 1935 was well-regarded by the American press, by American business leaders, and by the American Roman Catholic Church. The Facisti are to Italy what the American Legion is to the United States. Mussolini and the state corporate model, and the mob, and their astute business practices. We can understand that. That congealed well with our institutions. Then the final blow. In 1943 the anarchist and anti-fascist Carlo Tresca was murdered, shot by a mob hitman, and there was no more left of the radical Italian Left in America. There were now real Americans. There were the Sons of Italy, and Fiorello La Guardia, a progressive Republican like Teddy Roosevelt, and there was Lucky Luciano, a gangster who helped the government during World War II, when the US government made a secret deal with Luciano, who was in prison at the time. The American government was concerned about sabotage on the docks in New York City. The government knew the mob controlled the waterfront. The Navy, the State of New York and Luciano settled on a pact. Luciano's sentence would be commuted if he promised to assist with providing intelligence to the Navy. The deal was made. And with the added promise that no dockworker would strike during the war.

And there was Joe DiMaggio, and there was Frank Sinatra. Middle-class Italian-Americans that made it. Respect. This was a better and brighter and more appropriate mirror of the USA than radical mad anarchists! This is the entertaining reflection the ruling class could abide. So let's say goodbye to all that. We writers don't do so well in that regard… just as well… and true enough… it's a better, brighter day when you read the *New York Times!*

Agnes Babs Widdlesworth stayed in Paris for the duration of the war. She never did have a reunion with Charles William. She never saw Charles William again. She never saw Captain Bethell again. She had become the mistress of a German officer. She had become addicted to the morphine that the German officer had supplied her. When the Germans retreated from Paris, she holed up in her room at the Hotel Ritz. She sat by the window and looked down on the Place Vendôme, watching the soldiers come and go. The hotel had been occupied by the Germans and had been the Paris headquarters of the Luftwaffe. The officer left her a gun. He placed it on the bed table, and smiled at her, and walked out the door.

How will she be treated after the war? She's not a French woman. I can't be accused of *collaboration horizonatle?* Can I? I am not Arletty! I may have had dinner with her at Maxim's, with her lover, that German officer, Hans, but I am a wealthy American woman. I must get to London… but she was too afraid to leave her room. She shot herself that night.

From the Ends of the Earth to the End of the World

At 6:10 p.m. on August 5, 1945, Captain Roger Bethell entered his arboretum in his garden at his Northport home and tended to one of his most prized bonsai trees. The Captain gently snipped a tiny twig from the one hundred and thirty-two-year-old bonsai tree, a species named *Goyoo-matsu* in Japanese and *Pinus pentaphylla* in Latin. It was a Japanese white pine. When on a tour of Japan in 1923 the Captain had received the bonsai tree as a gift from the Japanese writer Junichiro Tanizaki, who was familiar with the Captain's books on bonsai and Zen Buddhism.

In his arboretum in his Northport home, Roger Bethell accidentally scarred the tender beautiful bark of the bonsai tree with his small pruners. A natural or man-made disaster? The result of natural law or human intervention? Determinism or chance? Roger Bethell is old now, eighty-five years old, his hands are not as steady as they once were.

There was a narrow tiny piece of white paper folded and twisted around one of the branches of the bonsai tree. It is a custom of Shinto, the indigenous religion of Japan, to choose a piece of paper or wood plaque with a fortune written on it, and tie it to a tree at one of the Shinto shrines.

Roger Bethell has never looked to see what was written on the paper, and even now if he had the desire to do so, his eyes would not be strong enough to read the no doubt very small print.

It was now 6:15 p.m. August 5, 1945. Roger Bethell felt a sharp sudden pain in his heart. He collapsed on the table, slid back, and fell to the floor. Straining and striving to get up, he reached for the table's edge. His fingers dug into the potted soil of the bonsai tree, breaking the delicate covering of moss, pulling the bonsai tree to the floor, where its clay retainer smashed into pieces. Roger Bethell saw the tiny piece of white paper in a pink glow of light. There it was there, like a message, like ancient runes in rock, the human ability to see the structure of a human message in the natural world, somehow mirroring the mind, and saying come and decode me, come seek me out, I am not just rock and tree... it would be an inhuman act not to look. Let the mystery rest, Roger Bethell thought, I am old. Roger Bethell has been searching for enlightenment ever since the vision on the beach at Guam, the island that Magellan just happened to bump up against on March 6, 1521, after crossing the Pacific, the island the natives called Umatac. Magellan didn't have any visions of Moby Dick or Atomic Bombs. Magellan was killed in the Philippines, on the island of Mactan, while fighting on behalf of a native chief. Of the five ships that had set sail from Spain in 1519, only one returned, thus completing the first circumnavigation of the globe. Aliaspun, a character from a Roger Bethell novel, was on board the returning ship, carrying a message that he had been ordered to read to the King of Spain, Charles V, the slave sender...

Unlike the Kafka parable in which all the people of the world wish to become couriers with messages for Kings who do not exist anymore but in legend, and therefore all the messages were meaningless, Charles V did exist, and Aliaspun was a courier, and his message was the same message that Sputnik I sent back to earth in 1957, beep-beep... pika-pika-boom-boom...

And now Roger Bethell was staring into another beep-beep. He desired to read the message on the tiny white piece of paper, but he desired enlightenment above that revelation. Above all he didn't want to be disappointed and disillusioned by something trivial.

The promise of Enlightenment. *Satori*. The promise of the Word. Communion. This has been a major conflict in his mind for many years. The Void and the Logos. The endless and infinite search for the bibliography of God, the un-findable alpha book in the library constructed beneath the ruins of Babel, all the solutions and destinies, every arrangement of words and sounds, the fallible script of life's dictionary illuminated by the infallible underwritten word. But if you could locate the supremely comprehensive, totally coherent Bibliographical Book, it would have nothing in itself to say, but direct you and guide you to a shelf where meaning resides in decimal proximity to history, languishing in the dust of dissemination through time. And so Roger Bethell turned to the Void... so why bother to unfold the paper? Because somehow it seemed unavoidable... the mind would not let go its grip. Most likely it was just a note from his old friend Tanizaki, possibly it said nothing more than "To my good friend Roger Bethell." But that was not what Roger Bethell desired at that moment. He desired enlightenment, if enlightenment can be desired. Possibly the paper was blank. Something always absent, missing, a white moon emptiness. That would be satisfactory. Possibly there was written on that paper a haiku, the most exquisite, the most beautiful ever written. Possibly there was a Zen koan, the most elaborate, logic-halting, mind swamping. Possibly there was a philosophically suggestive phrase, elliptical and elastic as words, saying it all. Possibly there was a mathematical equation, an axiom, a unified theory of the universe, saying it all. Possibly there was a political idea exploding off the page into Utopian dialectics. Would Roger Bethell run the risk of being disappointed? Possibly there was nothing more than a schoolgirl's wish.

He unfolded the paper. Like a flower. Like a crystal. Like the Tower of Babel falling. Like the folds in the human brain unfolding and revealing mind. It was written in Japanese because Japanese eyes had first seen it, first perceived it into being, in the idiolect of the philological labyrinth.

はじめに言葉がありました

Roger Bethell tried to recall the Kanji, the ideograms derived from the Chinese, which he had studied many years ago, and the Japanese Hiragana characters, the signs and sounds of which he has never forgotten. Roger Bethell whispered a word and some sounds. "...ha ji me ni... beginning..."

"Beginning... in... language... no, word... word... ko to ba... there is... there is... arimasu... mashita... there was... atta... there was word in the..." and Roger Bethell lifted his head, "In the beginning was the Word." He was profoundly disappointed. There would be no enlightenment. "Hajime ni kotoba ga atta... in the beginning was the Word..." When is the beginning?

No when. What language is the original language of God? No what. Deep diver there is no pearl of knowing... nothing to bring to the surface... no whole. No word for word translation. No word in the midst of the word. No rumbling there is... there was... why would it break? A fall from Grace? Paradise? Eden? Experience? There is no communion. No sacrament. Barely communication anymore... dada dada dada pika-pika boom-boom beep-beep... but that was not all. He unfolded the paper some more. And each time that he unfolded it he unfolded it again and again. The means of the unfolding seemed infinite. But our world is finite! How can this be? The words went on forever. The paper went on and on. And the notations, the marks on the paper went on and on. And this is what Roger Bethell saw as he unfolded the paper, written in every language ever written... the translation of objects into other objects... here and gone... the Word bringing the urge of translation into the World... lest there never be an end to this endless lack...

In the beginning was the Word...

In principio erat Verbum...

No princípio era o Verbo...

En el principio era o Verbo...

Nel principio era La Parola...

Au Commencement était la Parole...

Im Anfang war das Wort...

In den beginne was het Woord...

In begynnelsen var Ordet...

Na początku było Słowo...

La inceput era Cuvantul...

Baslangicta Tanrisal Soz Vardi...

...

...

...

...

...

...

... (It is at this ellipsis that Roger Bethell died)

Letters from Buddies

Sept. 21, 1946

Hi Joe

I'm sending you back the pictures I got when I visited you quite a while ago now. A lot has happened since then. I left school and decided to come back in the Army. I was getting restless and sick and tired of everybody in general. I got a gsl's rating anyway. I'm shipping out of here tomorrow. I'm going to the Pacific for a while. I'll write you soon when I get a permanent address somewhere. Thanks for the use of your pictures. Your pal, Bob

-----

Dec. 25, 1946

Hi Joe

I've nothing much to do right now so I thought I'd answer your letter. I should have before but was too busy with xmas shopping, that's over now and I'm damn glad of it. I'm not working right now but am going to see about a job after the New Year. So Bob joined the Army again. I guess it isn't too bad seeing the war is over. They get $75 per month now. I might try again myself but I doubt it. I haven't heard from Conrad in a long time. I did get a xmas card from Adams. He gives me hell every time he writes for not going to visit him. I would like to see him or any of the old gang. We had about two inches of snow but we got a rain last night and turned warm so it's all gone. I was hunting rabbit twice in the snow. We used 22 rifles. We saw seven and got three of them. That isn't too bad with a rifle. I suppose you'll hang one on New Year's Eve. I might myself. I don't drink much anymore, it cost too damn much. I never did write to Stanley after you sent his address. Then I lost it. I suppose he's a married man a long time ago. Well Joe it's about time I sign off for tonight. Write when you have time. Your buddy Blaine

-----

March 19, 1947

Hi Joe

It's about time I answer your last letter. I knew I was a little slow in answering but not as bad as it is. I looked at the date today for the first time in weeks at least it seems that way. The weather has sure been nice since the first of March. We haven't got much snow left. I hope the bad weather is over for this spring. We had our share of it. I haven't heard from any of the boys lately. I want to go down and see Adams some time this summer. He's been giving me hell in every letter he writes for not coming. You know Joe I'm a busy man, when you're working the afternoon shift and there is half women working there then you put in another shift with one of them and it's a rough deal. I was shacking up with one of the girls for a month. She got P.O.B at me so I'm working on a new one. It costs a lot but it sure is fun. I had one I lived with for six months before that, what the hell is the use of getting married when you can do that. You should move to Michigan and get some of that too, just like good old Army days. Well Joe I'll cut the bull for this time. Write whenever you have the time. Your buddy, Blaine

And as the years passed there were fewer letters and then fewer Christmas cards and then nothing.

1947

The Golden Age

Torhild Andersen stood on the deck of the transatlantic steamer *SS Stavangerfjord*, sailing into New York Harbor, and looked up at the beat blue sky, exactly where the Verrazano-Narrows Bridge would be one day, but the bridge wasn't there yet, not in the year 1947. She took a deep breath when she saw what she believed to be the Manhattan skyline, in fact it was only the Brooklyn skyline, but Brooklyn was her destination anyway, at least to begin with. Torhild saw the Statue of Liberty. And finally the Manhattan skyline was pointed out to her. So that's it. The skyscrapers didn't reach into the clouds as she had pictured them in her mind a hundred times before. She was disappointed that they weren't as tall as she had imagined them to be. But that was of no importance.

Torhild held a piece of wrinkled paper in her hand. Her mother's address was written on it. Torhild read it for the thousandth time: 822 54th Street, Bay Ridge, Brooklyn, New York. Her uncle will be waiting for her at the docks. He has come up from Baltimore where his ship is in port, just to meet his niece. His father had ordered him to do so. Her uncle is the captain of a Norwegian cargo ship. Torhild will be seeing her mother for the first time in her life with remembering eyes. That's the main reason she has come to America, not for some vague "better life." She never imagined for a moment that there could ever be a life better than that of her first nineteen years of her youth spent growing up with her grandmother and grandfather on a farm on the south coast of Norway, even during the war, but such is the enfolded rose of memory.

Torhild saw the Brooklyn Bridge. People are the last thing that you see when you come to New York. Thereafter people are the only thing that you see in New York. Before the Brooklyn Bridge, Walt Whitman crossing Brooklyn Ferry, from shore to shore, seeing the tall masts of Mannahatta, the beautiful hills of Brooklyn.

Torhild did not disembark to Ellis Island. The immigration men boarded the ship and checked the passengers' papers. There was a time when Norwegians jumped ship and stayed in New York, and never left and were never caught, and Torhild met many of them over the years.

Before the Verrazano-Narrows Bridge was constructed, Torhild crossed on the Staten Island Ferry to picnic with her mother in the park near the cemetery where Torhild's mother will be buried one day. The Brooklyn Bridge, the river coursing under it, the cars crossing it, a two-way causeway to human events on both sides of the river, over to the Bowery and Broadway, up Delancey Street and Mott Street, and then to Mercer Street and Houston Street and Wooster Street where Giuseppe and his family had lived and celebrated the feasts of the many saints, parading the painted lady through the streets, to honor the old country's local saints, Santa Rosillia, Sant' Agata, and the Neapolitan festa of San Gennaro, but back in Orero it was Saint Ambrose; and across the Brooklyn Bridge, over to the other side, through downtown Brooklyn, where Torhild had seen her first American movie, across Fulton Street and Atlantic Avenue, up 5th Avenue and 8th Avenue, where the Norwegians paraded on the 17th of May to celebrate the old country's independence, where the Jewish shopkeepers tried to entice Torhild into their stores, "Something nice for the beautiful lady, you are so beautiful, just like Sonja Henie, come in, come in..." and along the streets, 41st and Sunset Park, where Torhild's father had been found dead on a forgotten Columbus Day; which is why her father wasn't there to meet her at the dock; she never met her father... 14th, 27th, 54th, 62nd, 86th, 92nd... each street had a memory, right up to the end of the 69th Street pier from where Torhild and her family could take the Staten Island Ferry.

Family and Births

Torhild had come to America from a farm in Norway at the age of 19 in 1947. From the beginning she watched television and went to see movies. In Norway her grandfather would occasionally let her go to town and see a movie, usually a Swedish or German movie; she had never seen an American movie until she came to this country. The first movie that she saw, in that downtown Brooklyn movie house, was *Dear Ruth*, starring William Holden and Joan Caulfield. Like everybody else in America she quickly acquired a compulsion for going to the movies. She had her Hollywood idols. She looked at the pictures in the movie magazines. It was difficult to read the words, but that didn't matter. She followed the lives of the famous. Her sister-in-law Luisa had collected movie magazines and movie star's photographs over the years; she had several scrapbooks, one had only Jean Harlow pictures and newspaper's clippings. Luisa kept the scrapbooks locked away in her bedroom, and rarely did she take them out, and never did anyone ever go into her bedroom. Torhild thought her a bit strange. But one day she did take the scrapbooks out and let Torhild see them. The one scrapbook in itself was dedicated like a shrine to the actress Jean Harlow who had died in her twenties in 1937 at the peak of her career.

Torhild saw the endless display of merchandise on television. She shopped on credit and coupons. Green stamps. She learned the ways of the natives. She was re-created in the corporate media images of the 1950s in America. She wore her large wide-rim hats and high heel shoes. Television, refrigerators, washing machines, patios, barbecues, all new and improved, consumerism as a national sport, General Electric, General Foods, General Motors, General Eisenhower... she had never seen anything like it before in Norway, all those famous generals who won the war and beat the Nazis and Hitler. It's true, she hated Germans. It's also odd that Americans, who can hardly recognize an irony in life, should live with a million little and big ironies everyday. Torhild's first "best friend" in America was a German woman, who was her neighbor.

America was riding the crest of the post-war boom. General Motors' post-war market forecast was for economic activity and growth to increase in the future as it had in the past, stimulated by scientific knowledge and technological progress related to an expanding population, with expanding demands for products. General Motors was the "world's largest manufacturing concern." Such concerns included such "defense business," the supplying of steel and titanium rocket-motor cases for the Minutemen missile program. Another concern was "responsibility for bombing navigational computers." Another was an inertial guidance system, designated "ACchiever," which was successfully flight tested in the air force's Thor long-range ballistic missile in 1957. Other General Motors divisions undertook projects for the nation's "new defense program and space activities." In 1955 General Motors appointed a nuclear scientist as vice-president of research. President Eisenhower's Secretary of Defense from 1953 to 1957 was a former president of General Motors. He once said that he thought that what was good for the country was good for General Motors and vice versa. And the cars kept rolling off the assembly lines: Chevrolets, Pontiacs, Buicks, and Cadillacs... beep-beep... beep-beep... boom-boom.

Torhild sat in a Chevrolet at a small amusement park and watched her son Stephen going round and round in a little blue car, turning his steering wheel left and right, honking his horn, beep-beep... and she felt the blood ooze from her vagina.

In 1947 her family bought her a ticket for the New World. A ticket that would permit her to see the never-seen mother who had abandoned her at birth on a farm in Norway; her mother leaving Torhild behind with her grandparents so that she could return to America without the excess baggage of a baby. A ticket that would permit her to see her father but it would prove too late for he was to be beaten to death in a Brooklyn park as he wandered about in a drunken stupor. She had a ticket to America and crossed the Atlantic on a great ocean-liner. She was just another immigrant, another pilgrim with a quest. She had a ticket to New York to see the legendary tall skyscrapers that reached into the clouds. The tall buildings were not as tall as she had imagined them to be; but when is anything exactly as one imagines it to be? She wouldn't have to worry about that anymore. Everything would be imagined for her. She just had to sit back and watch. She had the best view. A television and movie theaters.

Torhild knew only a few words of English when she arrived in New York; but soon she knew what she wanted. She wanted what most women wanted in America in the 1950s: a husband, a house in the new frontier of suburbia, and babies, precisely in that order. So she left Brooklyn behind; on the other side of the city was green suburbia, Nassau County, Robert Moses' paradise for the "right kind of people," those taking flight to greener pastures, who desired to have four bedrooms and three bathrooms and a swimming pool and two cars to drive along all the new parkways leading to thre new parks and beaches.

After leaving Brooklyn, Torhild lived with her aunt on Long Island; her aunt found her a job working as a chambermaid for a wealthy family who lived in a mansion on Center Island that had been built by William Widdlesworth, a shipping magnate tycoon and friend of J. P. Morgan. Torhild was a nice, clean, Norwegian maid, the kind the old world wealthy could tolerate. Better than an Irish girl with her horrible crucifixes hanging over the bed. It was Torhild's aunt who had introduced Torhild to Joe Cazzaza, on Memorial Day in 1948, and on a cool October day in 1949, they were married. Joe was no tycoon, but surprisingly his family did own some property in the center of town, a legacy of Giuseppe Cazzaza's hard work. Yes and no can go a long way in attaining the American Dream. Torhild had no need to consult the archives. The future was open. She was beginning tabula rasa in America. But it didn't take long before her clean slate was etched with stretch marks. In the 1950s having babies was the new national past time. Torhild had her first baby in 1951, a girl named Sylvia. Sylvia Teresa Cazzaza. Unaware of the popular American names of the time: the Sandys and Barbaras and Patricias and Lindas, she opted for names from her husband's side of the family, with his family influencing the not so democratic decision making process. Torhild had wanted to name Sylvia after a movie star, Judy Holliday, because she had won the Oscar for best actress in *Born Yesterday*. Her sister-in-law Luisa suggested Jean for Jean Harlow. That's how caught up in the movies she had become. But Sylvia it was. And Teresa. Teresa was the name of Joe's aunt, his mother's sister. At the time she was residing in a mental institution, Joe informed Torhild. That moment lasted for the rest of Teresa's life. She was committed in 1927, after a tragedy struck the family. She just lost her mind. She was found burning money. That will do it.

Torhild would spend most of her free time taking Sylvia to the movies. Wives in the 1950s had plenty of free time, what with all those household gadgets to make life so much simpler. All Torhild knew of her husband's father is that he came from Italy, settled in Manhattan's Little Italy, and then made it out to a small town on Long Island. Her husband didn't really know much more than that. The story goes that he and his brother walked into town one day with knapsacks on their backs containing some old clothes, twenty-five dollars, and two bottles of red wine. They entered the town singing an old Italian song. They liked the town and stayed there; the year was 1904, eleven years had past since Giuseppe arrived in America. That was the story, anyway. Giuseppe was married in 1902 to a neighborhood girl who lived at 235 Mercer Street, with her two sisters and two brothers. Fiorenza Maggio was her name, and in 1903 she bore their first child, a girl named Silvia, whom everyone, except her father, would call Toots, because she was a young and tough tomboy.

When they moved out to the small town on Long Island, Giuseppe at first did some masonry work. But he had saved up enough money from doing numerous odd jobs in Manhattan and with the financial aide of his good friend Giancarlo and his wife's family he was able to open a fruit and vegetable store. His two sisters-in-law helped with the store and Fiorenza raised the children. Teresa helped with bookkeeping and Leonora sewed dresses for local ladies of means. There was no going back for Fiorenza. Teresa and Leonora would go back, eventually, as far as Queens, to lie in the family plot, with their father and mother and two brothers.

Document 1.6.3

Cemetery Deed
Maggio
Sect. 27 Range 10 Plot G Graves 02-03
Calvary Cemetery
49-02 Laurel Hill Blvd.
Woodside, New York 11377
Deed of Mr. Antonio Maggio
Residence 235 Mercer St, New York City
Charles Vespa
Sexton, Undertaker and Embalmer
Offices 26 1-2 Mulberry Street
New York City
Received from Antonio Maggio
Fifteen dollars
For the privilege of burial in one grave, No. 2
In Plot G Section 27 Range 10 in Calvary Cemetery
Dated, New York, October 23, 1905

Fiorenza's mother would be the last of her side of the family to be interred there. Her mother died in 1949. Luise Maggio was ninety-five years old when she died. She lived her final years in Northport and Oyster Bay. She never wanted to leave Mercer Street where she had lived all her life. But after Antonio died and her son John died, she was moved out to Long Island. Her other children, Leonora, Teresa, Harry were all dead when her son John died. There was only Fiorenza to provide for her. Toots helped at first. Put her in an apartment in Northport. But her husband Johnny complained, as usual. When an apartment opened up in Oyster Bay, she was moved there, to 105 South Street, and there she would die.

Several months after moving to the small town Giuseppe bought some property right smack dab in the middle of the town. There was an old building on the property and Giuseppe had it torn down. He cut down the last of the trees, a large oak, cursorily glancing at the word carved into the bark: ALIASPUN; couldn't find it in the dictionary, and so forgot it. Tore off bark and put it in trunk. He used the wood from the tree to build a forty-foot high water tower over an artesian well near where the stump of the oak tree stood. He then proceeded to hire a few cheap Italian laborers that he brought in from the city and they constructed a two-story building, which was completed in 1906. And in the years that followed, Giuseppe opened his own fruit and vegetable store, rented out apartments to Italian and Polish and Irish immigrants on the upper floor, and rented out to German and Jewish shopkeepers on the ground floor. But the Dutch and English patrician families that lived on the outskirts of town, and expensive skirts they were too, didn't mind too much because they could use the cheap labor, and the dirty foreigners were confined to the center of town. The rich wasps did get a bit peeved later on when the Italians started recruiting black laborers to work for them. But they were quickly hidden away in shacks by the railroad tracks near Hamilton Avenue, where there was also located a flophouse for down and outs and where many of the cheap immigrant laborers lived. In one of the rooms lived Emile Baldazzi, who had come out here from the city in the early 'twenties looking for work and found it at Heemskirk's Shipyard. He worked there until he tried to organize a union; after that he didn't work there anymore; but for some reason, he didn't leave the town, a town he grew to hate.

Torhild thought that she was marrying into a little money. But her husband and his brothers didn't have their father's knack for business. It was handed to them on a copper platter and they just didn't want it. They were ass-kissers to the Jews and wasps in town, it was said of them. The Cazzazas were considered a strange family. Not the usual extroverted Italian family. There was something introverted and sinister and secretive about them. They weren't ambitious; they kept to themselves. They were obliging doormats, as if they kept a dark secret. Torhild discovered the secret; but it was too late.

So the new girl baby addition to the Cazzaza clan was given a name from Joe's side of the family. He was born in this town, grew up here, went to school here, worked here, and yes, you guessed it, will probably die here, and be buried in the same plot with his mother and father and brothers and sisters. The baby was named to honor his family. This placated the furies, his mad rosary clutching relatives, dressed in black and festooned in draperies of shawls, who screamed and cussed and sang in Italian as they charged around the kitchen cooking spaghetti. When Joe brought his wife to an Italian restaurant in Manhattan Torhild thought spaghetti was worms and couldn't eat it. And when her in-laws served her corn for the first time, corn! that's what you feed to animals!

God what a scene on Sundays! Torhild had never seen anything like it before in Norway. But she did her best to be a dutiful wife; after all, she had to live in this town and get along with them. Of course both families had been against the marriage. A Lutheran and a Catholic marriage in 1949 was looked upon with a crooked eye. Actually, Torhild wasn't Lutheran. Her aunts and uncles in Norway were Lutheran. That was the state religion, and it invested them with middle-class respectability. But Torhild's grandmother and grandfather were rural people, and they were prayer-meeting types who for the most part eschewed the ceremonies and class-consciousness of the state church, except for funerals and Easter and Christmas, when they attended the Lutheran church near the graveyard.

A blonde-haired blue-eyed Norwegian and a dark Italian. It just won't work out. They're too different. She's not even American! Will she convert to Catholicism? Joe halfheartedly tried; he took Torhild to see a priest. Torhild listened carefully to the priest and tried to understand the slurred words emanating on his alcoholic breath, and then his grubby paws were petting her hair and shoulders. Oh how beautiful, just like Sonja Henie! He is a *toulbul* man said Torhild, which is how she pronounced terrible. No, she had never seen anything like this before in Norway. On the drive back from the church she made her husband stop the car on Bayville Bridge; she stepped out on the bridge, blocking traffic, and flung all the catechism papers and pamphlets the priest had given her into the water. That was that. But there was no Lutheran church in town; so they compromised and went to the Methodist church. His family was furious. Let's move to another town, Torhild begged her husband; let's get out of this apartment; get away from your family. It took seven years but finally they moved to a near-by town, Hicksville, where they found a brand new suburban house on a tree-lined curling sunny street, Narcissus Drive, and everything went all right for a while; but then the Jew moved in next door, and then the snobby second-rate wasp couple moved in across the street, and Joe couldn't stand them. So he moved his family back to his town, to the apartment building and stores that his father had built. A good Italian-American boy never leaves his mama or his hometown. And Torhild cried and cried because she had lost a piece of this wonderful American Dream.

The pieces would keep falling and breaking, along with the knick-knacks and dishes, as the family moved in and out and kept moving to different houses in town, and inevitably moved back to the apartment building in the center of town; Joe could not only not leave his hometown, he could hardly leave his family's bosom. How did he ever make it through a war? North Africa and Italy... how did Torhild ever make it through a war, on that farm in Norway? And now both of them together in Joe's family's building where the rent was free at least, except that her husband did have to tar the roofs to appease the complaining tenants. The flat roofs always leaked. The place was becoming old and decrepit. The family hardly raised the rent payments in fifty years. One of the Cazzaza brothers worked in the meat market that the family rented out. They owned the place but they worked for their tenants. This was something new in capitalist America. There were three brothers and they just didn't care. Torhild couldn't understand how she ever got stuck in this mess. What a strange family. They are so peculiar, she would say. Peculiar became one of her favorite English words. They let everyone in town take advantage of them. Why? No backbone. No drive to make it, to be successful. They keep the doors of their rooms locked, and the rooms are so dark. It's as if they're hiding something; such were Torhild's thoughts. But it wasn't that bad, she thought positively, as she always did... this is still America, and there's television and movies and cars and shopping and my children... thank God for my children; I don't know how I would have made it without my children. In 1956 Stephen was one of the 4,244,000 babies born in that productive year. The happiest year in American history! Stephen Knut Cazzaza. This time she managed to stick a Norwegian name in there. Torhild and Joe decided to give their son the middle name Knut in order to honor, as it were, the legendary head football coach at Notre Dame, Knute Rockne. Torhild knew nothing about football but she had seen the movie starring Pat O'Brien as Rockne and Ronald Reagan as George Gipp; though she couldn't stand that Reagan guy; a bad actor and wasn't much to look at; now Charlton Heston, that was a real man. She liked Richard Widmark, always a bad guy, but nice in real life, is how she put it. And because Joe was a football fan and Torhild was Norwegian, this choice in a name pleased both of them.

As Saint Augustine related his birth in his confessions may Stephen break in at this point and fix in space an interruption in the continuity of this narrative, this shuddering of time, an unreasonable linearity as paradox in the absence of time. His mother told Stephen that the doctor complained that she had interrupted his golf. It's quite certain that St Augustine's mother did not record such a complaint. Stephen's mother told him the story about her pediatrician, an older woman named Wicker, and how on the table little baby Stephen, naked and cold, suddenly peed upward and splattered her in the face. Awful. Dr. Wicker and her husband were big time local Republicans and she was a Daughter of the American Revolution. Disgraceful. Well, what else can he say but his aim was true.

Another girl was born in 1960, named Susan. After Susan Haywood, best actress in 1958 for *I Want To Live*. And in the last year of the baby boom, 1964, another girl was born, Simone. After Simone Signoret, best actress in 1959 for *Room at the Top*. Torhild saw some significance in naming her girls with a name whose first letter began with S. Surely it could be fortuitous. A sign of good luck. And Sylvia's name began with an S, though she was against naming her Sylvia at the time. But everything works out in the end, she believed. Torhild brought all her grandparent's superstitions with her from that little farm in Norway. But old world superstitions don't hold up against the hard grain of capitalism, the biggest superstition of them all.

The Bar on Main Street

It was early in the morning. There was a light mist in the air. Toots was sweeping up the yard, collecting the debris, bits of cardboard and newspaper mostly, that the negligent garbagemen in their haste to depart, amid the tin clangor of garbage cans and tops of garbage cans, personalized with family initials, being banged about, and accompanied by churning truck stomach noises caused by digesting all manner of filth, and shouts of dawn and cries of cats, had disregarded as unworthy of their collective attention, and that now swirled around in small eddies with the sand and pebbles and puddles and the hungry cats. The cats moved in and out between the legs of Toots, who reproached them with shoves from her broom. The broom's yellow straw was dark and wet from sweeping through the rain puddles, rippling no moon image, only cloud and narcissistic cat faces with protruding snapping tongues lapping at clouds, breaking the sky open, revealing the blue that mirrors infinity, but without the faces, sense of self, or words to cobweb the right angles of un-meeting integers, and so began another post-Newtonian day, Friday, September 11, 1959.

Toots was sweeping along the bottom edge of the garage doors. Her husband of thirty-one years, Johnny Bacigalupo, who was also her first cousin, was having his coffee, sitting at the kitchen table, reading a newspaper. A cat jumped up on the kitchen table and shit in the litter box that was on the table. Johnny Bacigalupo didn't bat an eye; then Johnny sneezed. Mucus and snot went all over page 5 and the AP photo, in the lower left hand corner, of clashing students and police at Yale University. It seems the New Haven police had charged the demonstrating students with nightsticks and fire hoses. The student's "grievances" had been directed at the St. Patrick's Day parade. The students had hung swastikas and Japanese flags from their windows and taunted and jeered the parade with cries of "God Save the Queen." Johnny Bacigalupo closed the newspaper and flipped it over to its back page and the beginning of the sport's section. There are many for whom the back page is the front page, who read newspapers back to center, front to center, center to front, center to back, top to bottom, bottom to top, here and there, in the dotted grid of news reality, skipping the business section, the obituaries, skipping the gossip column, the editorials, skipping everything but the pictures, their captions and the crossword puzzles... there are many possibilities in the probable world of axiomatic selves freely subscribed to and circumscribed by an internal dialectic of self-defining block-building hierarchies; and Johnny knew all about block building, how to put one block on top of another and still manage to create some object that will, *mirabile visu,* stand and not fall; so a million eyes can witness that same event through one eye. Johnny codified his morning with structural certainty: front page, page one, page two, back page, sport's section, picture spread in center, and if time allows, a glimpse at the obituaries. From pictures to big print to progressively smaller print; the smaller print he will get to as the day wears on, if time allows he will make an allowance for the details, the contents, the message, the meaning, pre-interpreted according to his cultural stack of blocks, the foundation of which was laid precisely a priori upon the foundation that was laid precisely a priori upon the foundation. Because a newspaper contains gutter information, Johnny has manifold pipelines taking the words out with the waste. Of course the newspaper is not left behind; it accompanies the workday and is resurrected at lunchtime, comics and crossword, another run over the sport's section, a mystified glance at the stock market numbers... one is not a tourist in one's own country, though one could conceivably be a tourist within the formal system of a newspaper, reading about a fat American tourist reading a newspaper, the American Presence outside of every system but the system with the final rules on how to control and change the other rules, inside the front page looking out from the headlines, and you are the newspaper, and the American Presence, at the top, is reading you.

Johnny turned to the obituary page. Time allows it. In here the dead live in you and you live in the dead, then you step back, and breathe a sigh of relief; but there is a pit behind you, and you fall in, and the next day someone is reading your obituary, if you rank, if you are notable. Oh dear, another little inconvenience in our miserable little lives. Time allows it. Johnny sneezed again. This time he filled his hand with mucus and snot. He didn't want to defame the memory of the dead by snotting on the paper. The dead have somehow become part of his memory, uninvited, and have taken up residence in the comprehensive sum of his brain sump, an image burning in a neural blast-oven. Johnny knows all about blast-ovens. He's shoveled enough coal and garbage to fill the belly of all the poets in Hades, and still find some mysterious soul seeping its drainage into the basement. Newton's laws still built houses in Johnny's world. But the blocks weren't impervious to curious leakages coming from an undemonstrative source; news source or God source or spaghetti sauce? What's the difference? It all comes down from above. Johnny sneezed again. The cat looked at him as if in expectation of an "excuse me," but none was forthcoming from the rude man. The cat licked his paws clean. The cat had no name. Johnny and Toots didn't like to name things. The cat was cleaner than the house. The Irish curtains hung everywhere, but this wasn't a direct act of defiance aimed at the future ruling class Yale-birds roosting on their golden eggs, shining their Yale padlocks, used to barring access to the top level, rather this was the flag of cheap labor, emblematic of the sweat shop profit-mongers and greed-breeders, a flag waving freely in the undeveloped lands of the un-free south of the border, dollar bills waving freely; but Johnny's hands can't reach that far, his blocks don't pile that high; he can't exchange currencies and trade at that level, but Johnny's all for development, new homes, old homes renovated, investment, capital, and American families to occupy them and live happily ever after. Yet Johnny can't keep his own house in order. The rooms and the house are always dark, an inbred darkness of black candles. Toots always answers the door with a flashlight. They have never traveled. Never took a trip back to the old country. This is my country, Johnny says. And yet Johnny and Toots had some property and some money. They were supreme hard working folk. The kind that work because if they don't work they say that they will go crazy. Hard work. They worked hard all their lives. Damn hard too. Johnny's block and cement company has built a good chunk of the town. Johnny has donated money to the fire department to buy an ambulance, donated a house for the town's historical society, and money to the Catholic church to buy an organ, to which of a Sunday Toots can be heard singing Ave Maria. Johnny has achieved a hard working "middle" class respectability. He has become a cornerstone of civic pride.

Johnny scanned the obituaries. "Raymond Chandler... author of *The Big Sleep*... never hurd of 'em." Johnny yawned. Johnny didn't read books. He read the *Reader's Digest* and he looked at the pictures in *National Geographic*, both of which he subscribed to. "Howard Ehmke, baseball player, he pitched the ball that gave Babe Ruth his first homer in Yankee Stadium... whadayoukow... that's interesting..." Johnny had a habit of reading aloud, softly, his lips slightly opened. "Daniel Francis Malan... died Capetown... hmmm... made use of the Boer word apar-apar-hade... what the hell is that, a disease?" Johnny was not a dictionary man; if he didn't know a word, he didn't know it, and it wasn't worth the effort of knowing. "Jack Norworth... who's that? song writer... vaudeville... Ziegfield Follies... best known song is 'Take Me Out to the Ball Game'... I'll be! I didn't know that... I guess somebody got to write them songs." Now you know, Johnny. Now you know Johnny. Johnny got up from the table whistling "Take Me Out to the Ball Game." Johnny leaves the house through the front door. The back door and the back yard and all that, seems to be the domain of Toots and the Cazzaza branch of the family; the front door and beyond is for a Bacigalupo. Hyphenated respectability. Real American. He made it. Made money. Money in the mainstream. He still sensed that the Cazzaza's were peasants. But Johnny had pride and resourcefulness and ambition. He just didn't have any class or taste. It wouldn't be long before all of Long Island is run by such, Italian politicians and businessmen and hoods, and some Jews; the parting of the sea by Robert Moses. "Look! Long Island! The Promised Land! Exodus! Follow me!" Dante, thou should'est be alive today. We have need of thee.

Between the Bacigalupos and the Cazzazas an almost total disregard for each other's clan has existed for years, perhaps predating the arrival in America, a kind of kinship warfare prevails at the level of gross indifference, as if the only rung in the class ladder was the one below yours, where you can put the boot down, and kick off the lower sorts, even if they are family, in the land of the free, in the land of the dream, where the New World begins and the Old World ends, that competitive interface where Americans become Americans all in all, completely. The Cazzazas never amounted to much, that's one way of putting it, where the parts are less than the sum of the father, where the sons are greater than the parts of the dismembered father. Burnt offerings on the altars of indecision. Bottles of pills thrown in the faces of the husbands. Back-page people. Backstage people. Like most people. Like Abe and Grace who live in one of the apartments in the Bacigalupo buildings.

It was early in the morning. "Abe, you bastard, I hate you. You're not a man. You're a weakling... so run away why don't you... go to your damn bar with all the rest of them bums, you can't even put up a good fight with me. You coward. Get out! And don't come back. Go ahead hit me, why don't you. You ain't even got the guts to do that. You don't give a damn about nothing. You'd just watch the whole world go to hell. Let it all fall down.

And you'd be sitting there with that dumb look on your face. The wall paper peeling, the roof caving in, rats running around, when will you do something, when will you act, look at this goddamn dump!"

"Shut up or you'll wake up your kid."

"Oh my kid is it now. You're his father. You never even take the kid fishing or camping or take him out to a ball game or nothing."

"Shut up Grace!" Abe slams the door behind him. Izaac wakes up, crying. Poor Abe. Grace shouts at him from the porch as he walks out the alleyway. "You poor dumb bastard. I hate you!" Poor Abe. Another poor dumb bastard. Abe goes through the alleyway, whistling Take Me Out to the Ball Game...

Toots and Johnny are awoken by the shouts of their tenants. Johnny turns over and looks at the alarm clock. 4:56am. He gets up, puts on his robe, slips into his slippers, and goes downstairs. Toots gets up from her bed, they have separate beds, and follows Johnny downstairs. She puts on the hot water for coffee. The cats follow her around, rubbing against her legs. Johnny is sitting at the kitchen table reading the newspaper. The cat shits in the litter box, right on top of yesterday's newspaper... Johnny sneezes... time loops around...

Toots is sweeping along the bottom edge of the garage door. Something's wrong... an unpleasant smell... where are Grace and Izaac? Grace is usually on the porch this early in the morning having a cup of coffee, and Izaac is usually playing with his toys, throwing down wooden building blocks from the porch into the yard, trying to hit the cats. The wooden blocks were a Christmas present from Mr. Bacigalupo, hand-made. The cats want to be fed. They circle around Toots as if she were their kill, and in a way she is; she is a provider, a human sacrifice, she offers food so that she may live, for not to offer is to die of boredom, is not to work hard, is to think about things, is to remember death, time does not allow it. "I've worked all my life, damnit, and hard too!" That's her usual boast when her brother Joe asks to borrow a hundred dollars now and again.

The backyard has come alive as the day moves on, the sun has now moved directly overhead...

A delivery truck for Siegfried Beer Company drove through the narrow driveway between two cement-rendered buildings that both belong to Johnny and Toots. The wall on the truck's left side being the wall of the duplex, half-of-house, where Johnny and Toots live; with Mrs. Grass and her son Pete occupying the other half. Mrs. Grass is part-time cook and bartender in Joe and Frankie's bar, which is located on Main Street in one of the Bacigalupo buildings, in back of which is the back yard, to which you gain access through an alleyway from Main Street or the driveway from Scutter Ave., from which the Siegfried Beer truck has just entered the yard.

Mrs. Grass opens up every morning and the boys come in around twelve. It takes them about 30 minutes to drive over from Oyster Bay. Sometimes Joe takes his young son Stephen along; Stephen is learning the names of the towns as they drive along Route 25A; Joe keeps repeating them as they drive through each town... "Cold Spring Harbor... Huntington... Centerport... Northport..."

The delivery truck has parked in the backyard behind the shops and tenement buildings. It was a humid Indian Summer day in September and the stench of cats' and drunks' urine deposited on the walls of the alleyway and the stench of large raw slabs of meat that were being butchered was vile and saturated the foul air. Several metal barrels contained globs of meat fat around which swarmed flies and yellow jackets. A procession of butchers, using big shiny hooks, pulled lamb carcasses from a delivery truck and carried them over their shoulders, the lambs' blood staining their white aprons. There were four delivery trucks of various sizes parked wherever they could fit in the yard crowded with cars belonging to tenants, shopkeepers and customers. Cars were constantly being moved from one spot to another spot to accommodate the delivery trucks. The regulars in the bar were interrupted every so often by a pounding on the bar's backdoor with shouts of Hey Whip, move it! Hey Snipe, move it! Hey Cosmo, move it! to which the regulars replied by throwing their car keys into the alleyway. This alleyway being on the opposite side of where the alleyway is located in the Cazzaza building at Oyster Bay; all else being equal. A bar, a paper store, a meat market, and a small grocery store. The same effect holds true for Joe Cazzaza, in a sense, he being the bartender in the Northport bar and patron in the Oyster Bay bar, he and his family being the owners of the Cazzaza building at Oyster Bay, Johnny being the owner of the Bacigalupo building in Northport, except for one missing image in the mirror, Johnny never goes to the bar in Oyster Bay and never visits his relatives on that side of the family; in fact, he has nothing to do with their business. He wants nothing to do with them. Toots collects the rents and takes care of the accounts and taxes for both buildings. Johnny plays with his developmental blocks.

A dark fat man in the back of a small flat-back truck cleaved a big square chunk of ice from a bigger bulk of ice. He covered the bulk of ice with tarpaulin and grabbed the chunk of ice with large tongs; he moved the ice to the back of the truck. He then held on to the side of the truck and turning his body around stepped down on the runner and then on to the worn gray pebbles. He started chopping the chunk of ice into smaller and smaller cubes, directing an ice-pick with fierce accuracy.

The Siegfried Beer delivery man, wearing a uniform of brownish-gold pigment, rolled a barrel of beer to the side door of the truck and stood it up at the edge; he hopped down to the ground and carefully eased the barrel unto a dolly. He tilted the dolly backward, using his right foot to gain some leverage, and pushed it forward into the stinking alleyway. A half-size door opened unto the basement of the bar. The deliveryman lowered the keg through the door and into the hands of Joe Cazzaza who placed it down on the raised wood planks and connected it to the tap-line. An overpowering smell of stale beer exuded from the damp basement.

"One more to go Joe," said the deliveryman.

"One mort glow Joe," said Stephen, standing next to his father.

The Siegfried Beer deliveryman briskly pushed the bouncing dolly over the bumps and dips in the gravel yard where puddles of rainwater had collected from last night's thunderstorm and downpour.

Shuffleboard plastic pins snapped back, sounding like shattering glass. A man flung a silver disk with a red insert along the smooth boards once again and hit nothing but the rubber backstop. The metal disk bounced back and slid into his hand; he angrily shoved it again and grumbled, "Dirty cunt!"

"Watch your fucking mouth," said the other man holding a silver disk with a blue insert, "there's a child in here."

GAME OVER GAME OVER GAME OVER flashed on the scoreboard. "What a fucking game, huh...bowling for drunks."

"Speak for yourself, asshole."

"Fuck you!"

Suddenly a silver disk with a red insert was flying through the air, coming in contact with the mirror behind the bar's counter. The mirror and two bottles of whiskey shattered into shards. The man who threw the silver disk with the red insert ran out of the bar. The man holding the silver disk with the blue insert, shouted, "Jackass!"

The Siegfried Beer deliveryman rolled another keg of beer to the edge of the truck. But this time he placed the keg too far over the ledge and leaning his hand on the outer rim exerted too much pressure while jumping off the truck, sending him and the keg of beer tumbling to the gravel surface. The keg smashed opened, bursting its beer belly. Lush foamy suds spouted up like a geyser. In no time at all the news spread and the bar emptied of its patrons, faster than piss from a drunk's bladder. The regulars charged through the narrow and low backdoor, slamming toes and bumping heads, cursing and stumbling into the hot sun. They held their beer mugs high, one in each hand, and crowded around the holy fountain to get their fill. They then formed a bucket brigade, passing on beer mugs and tumblers and shot glasses and wine glasses, anything to save the beer from seeping through the gravel.

"I guess it's on the house, boys," said Joe Cazzaza.

"I guess it's the louse, boys," said little Stephen.

A screen door opened and seven skinny cats came bolting out from the darkness of a kitchen, followed by a woman with short-cropped black hair with specks of gray. Toots wore a headband pulled back over her forehead so that her hair stood up straight. She was fifty-seven years old, short and stocky, with masculine features. She wore a smudged black rag of a dress and she carried a broom. She always carried a broom. She used it to sweep up the yard before dawn and to chase cats and drunks away at night.

Instantly all eyes turned to her, because they all feared her. She was as sharp and tough as they come. She owned the bar and she ran it and kept things under control, ordering her two brothers about. The regulars hailed her with raised goblets. "Hey Toots! How ya doin'?" She didn't respond to their felicitous inquiries, but instead began to rave with her Italian mannerisms in full swing.

"What the hell happened here now... if it's not one damn thing it's another... Jesus, Mary and Joseph." She would not take the Lord's name in vain, without good cause. She was a good Catholic.

The beer keg was pooped of popping forth and now only dribbled down its chin like an old drunk. "Don't just stand there like a bunch of bums, get back into the bar, you're blocking business, don't you have homes to go to, some of us have to work you know, damn bums, you'll be the death of me, I'm not long for the world you know, I don't know what the hell you're gonna do when I'm gone, oh carry me off to the burying grounds, Jesus, Mary and Joseph."

Toots looked at her nephew and then turned to her brother and said, "Why the hell didn't he stay home, Joe?"

"He wanted to come with."

"What the hell dya mean he wanted to come with. Make him stay home. This ain't no place for a kid for Christ's sake."

"No place for ribs cripe's steak," said little Stephen.

Frankie is making sandwiches and a ham omelet in the bar's kitchen, slicing the ham and bologna and cheese. Frankie and Joe have had the bar and grill since 1950. But now they want out. They're trying to unload the business. It's getting too rough, too many fights, too many drunks. In 1962 they'll end up selling the business to Mrs. Grass and her son. And after that, Frankie will take a job with Van Heffer's Meat Market. Joe will find work as a janitor in an elementary school. Before they got the bar, both Joe and Frankie worked briefly for Johnny's block and cement company. Joe was honorably discharged from the army in '45, having served in North Africa and Italy. Johnny gave him a job when he got out. The army made him an offer to stay in, told Joe they'd fix his teeth, but Joe was through with the army life.

It was hard labor working for Johnny; chipping cement off a million old bricks; pulling nails out of a million old boards; shoveling sand, mixing cement, learning shoveling techniques to save your back, like digging and sliding the shovel along the ground and not lifting it until the last moment. Joe got along well with Johnny Bacigalupo; but Frankie and Johnny didn't see eye to eye. Frankie was a nasty practical joker and his exploits became famous. There was that one time when the boys were renovating a large old house, 12 rooms, 6 bathrooms, up Asharoken Road, where a lot of well-to-do and well-known people had homes at one time or another; for instance, New York's flamboyant mayor Jimmy Walker, King of Graft and Tammany, whose unseemly doings would have put President Harding to shame. Well, while Johnny and some of his workers were cleaning house, taking everything that wasn't nailed down and some of that too, like copper and brass fittings, Frankie was taking a shit in a brown paper bag that he afterwards carefully placed up behind one of the beams in the ceiling. Johnny thought that he had finally struck gold! He always knew that one of these crazy rich bastards had hidden a bag of money somewhere, and Johnny couldn't wait to get his hands on it, or in this case, in it. A handful of shit.

If it's not clear to you, let me remind you that we are not in Oyster Bay but in Northport. The buildings are nearly isomorphic, as I have said, though inverted like a mirror image; the buildings having been built by Giuseppe Cazzaza and his brother-in-law Giancarlo Bacigalupo. And here comes Giuseppe's son; Joe is walking into the bar, going behind the counter, and pouring one from the tap. And damn if he isn't singing "Take Me Out to the Ball Game." ...buy me some peanuts and CRACK-erjacks...

And Stephen is right behind his father, singing: buy me some peanuts and crackers jack...

And now the whole bar is singing. Crack and Whip, Floral and Cosmo, Snipe, Tommy Vine, Zippy the Mayor, Old Bean... I don't care if we ever get back for it's root root root for the home team... if they don't win it's a shame...

Every bar has its preferential team. And in Joe and Frankie's bar it use to be the New York Giants. But they went west to San Francisco; so there's a void. But there's Tommy Vine. Tommy Vine plays shortstop for the Philadelphia Phillies' single A farm team in Buffalo.

"God, I don't know," said Toots, "I smelled something funny, gasoline fumes or something, I don't know, and when I opened the garage door it was all smoke and... and I saw them in the car, Grace and Izaac, and I called Jerry, the deliveryman over, and Vinny, what's his last name. I forget, damnit, you know, the ice man..."

"Yeah, yeah, yeah..."

"And he ran over to the fire house and got an ambulance... my God, I gotta sit down."

A policeman approached Toots. "What can you tell us Mrs. Bacigalupo about the husband? Do you know where he might be?"

"Oh God, how the hell do I know. He's a bum. They're all bums around here. They were always fighting and shouting this and that, oh God what a mess... I don't need this, Joe. Papa should've never gotten involved with this. Oh God Johnny's gonna be mad as hell, Jesus, Mary and Joseph."

"What happened?" Joe asked the policeman.

"Seems to be a suicide. There were rags stuffed under the doors. The carbon monoxide fumes suffocated them. They'll be a full investigation of course. We'll have to speak to Mr. Churchyard if we can find him."

A man in a gray coffee-stained suit and black-banded fedora, a cardboard cutout man just like the sun-faded advertisements in the display window of the stationary, with pen and pad in hand and drooping cigarette in mouth, advertised himself to Toots and Joe with a swaggering overture that revealed the silver gun in brown leather holster against the sweat-stained armpit rims of a blue shirt.

"Dadadadetective Abe Dedededesurd," said Detective Abe Desurd, offering his stuttering voice and shaking hand to Joe to shake. The detective had a firm grip that negated his nervous twitches; but if he could only avoid those damn D's and terrible T's that came out like New York D's, not to mention the DT's that came out like hallucinated DaDa's.

Frankie unassertively stepped up alongside Joe. Frankie had a habit of muttering indecipherable random melodies under his breath, while jingling the coinage in his pockets. "Uppa duppa uppa duppa uppa duppa hummm bi dum bi dum bido," said Frankie Cazzaza. "Clinkydee clankydee clinkydee clankydee," said Abe Lincoln and Company. With his right hand Frankie shook hands with Detective Desurd, introducing himself, while with his left hand he continued to shake hand with Abe Lincoln and Company.

"I've got a few questions. All right," said Detective Desurd. That came out all right.

"Fire away," said Frankie.

Toots and Joe deferred the answering to Frankie. None of them were adepts at social discourse. The men were always willing to please anyone whose station in life was perceived to be above theirs, addressing "authority" figures with the honorific "Surely sir, yes sir, surely, surely..." O men without faith, men without reason, indecisive men, conditioned men, men without wills, men without dreams. No power, no wisdom, no hope, no love; unless power is impotence, wisdom is foolishness, hope is madness, and love is hatred of oneself; and greatness is the tragedy of life sacrificed to itself... for nothing... all for nothing...

"How could she do it?" said Toots to herself, "it's so absurd... I don't get it... how could she kill her own kid? She's gotta be a monster to do something like that. What a tragedy. Jesus, Mary, and Joseph."

"About dddis Abe. Ddda husband and faddder. Ddddoes he dddarink in your bar?" It sounded like rapid fire.

"Yeah. He comes in after work every day about four o'clock or so."

"Dddarinks alot?"

"Three or four boilermakers. Quiet guy, doesn't say much."

"He dadadarives a cccc... taxi, I take it?"

"Do you take it?"

"No, I mean he dadadarives a taxi, I've been told."

"Yeah, he does." The taxi was the car in which Grace and Izaac died.

"Will ya keep an eye out for him? Let us know if he shows up."

"Surely sir," said Frankie and Joe, in unison.

"Surly slur," said little Stephen, holding onto his father's trousers.

"Hail Mary, full of grace," said Toots to herself.

"Hairy Mary, full of grapes," said little Stephen.

The ambulance pulled out of the yard. Heads bowed, the crowd filed back into the bar. Voices commingled: This calls for a drink... I need a good one after that... I gotta take a leak..."

It was early in the morning. Grace sat at the kitchen table, head in hands, crying. Izaac came out from his bedroom, wearing his pajamas, rubbing his eyes. He was barefoot. He touched his mother. She grabbed him and pulled him against her breast. As she was holding him, he fell asleep in her arms. Grace carried Izaac back into the bedroom. As she tucked him in, pulling the blanket up to his chin, he opened his eyes.

"Go back to sleep," said Grace.

"Where's Daddy?"

"Shhhh... count sheep."

"Tell me a story... a nursery rhyme."

"Mary had a little lamb, its fleece was white as snow."

"Why did Mary have a lamb?"

"As a pet, I guess."

"Why did she lose the sheep?"

"That's a different story... Little Bo Peep has lost her sheep and don't know where to find them..."

"Will God give her a new sheep if she prayers for one?"

"Yes, God will give her a new sheep... now go to sleep... count sheep..."

"Where's Daddy?"

It was early in the morning...

Grace said, "Where are you going?"

Abe said, "None of your business."

Grace said, "You don't know, do you? You can't decide. You can't make up your mind. You can't act. You have no backbone. You're a mouse. Look at you tremble. Look at the fear in your eyes. Like an animal."

Abe said, "I'd rather die than justify or explain myself to you."

Grace said, "Damn you!" and sneezed.

Abe said, "Bless you."

Grace said, "You're absurd."

Abe said, "I'm leaving... I'm going up that mountain alone."

Grace said, "Take the boy with you... don't leave him here with me."

Abe said nothing.

Grace said, "Say the tragic word, be a hero, test your faith..."

Abe said, "I have no faith."

Grace said, "No tragedy, no passion, nothing. You have nothing."

Abe said nothing.

It was early in the morning...

Grace carried the boy down the cement stairs. Out into the rain. She opened the garage door, struggling to hold tightly to the boy and not drop him. The taxi was waiting. She put the boy down on the front seat. He slept. She gathered rags and stuffed them in the cracks at the bottom of the garage door. She got into the car and started the engine. Izaac opened his eyes. "Where we going?" He put his head on her lap. "We're taking a little trip... go back to sleep. I'll wake you up when we get there."

Grace kissed Izaac, her pride, her joy, her hope for all time.

O taxi O taxi, with death for a destination.

Right on time, quarter past four, Wookie Jones was the first through the door. "Grandma's pants will soon fit Willy," said Wookie Jones, and he sat down at the end (beginning) of the bar, where the counter curves around and ceases to exist at the wall. Joe poured Wookie a beer, nimbly spun the coaster onto the counter and placed the beer down on the flopping coaster, the foamy head running over the edges of the glass. Wookie put a five-dollar bill on the counter and Joe sized it up, snapped it up, figuring the change (this is appropriate enough, because the word "counter," as in "bar's counter," derives from the Middle Latin word meaning "computing place.") Joe rung out the cash register, took out the change and put the money in front of Wookie's beer. Wookie left it there; took a good hard look at it; gonna drink it all up tonight.

At the other end (beginning) of the bar, Snipe eased himself off his stool and zigzagged into the toilet, just as Cosmo was coming out of the toilet, zipping up his fly; they brushed against each other and grunted muddled words at each other. "Thwaya druwwound..."

"Canna man PEEin PISSinPEace." Whip and Crack, Cosmo and Floral, and Snipe... they were all there. Still there.

"Ain't youse got no homes to go to," said Toots to the regulars everyday, drinking the usuals everyday.

A group of five clammers have come in, dragging muddy boots across the floor. They are joined by three Norwegian workers from the scows, the flat-bottomed boats that are used for transporting sand and gravel. They all gathered around the bar counter where it curves, this is the least frequented space along the bar's counter, changing faces often, reserved for small clans of clammers, or lost dreamers of the whale's way, sitting alone, isolatoes, and late comers, beach combers, and fishermen; this turning point in the counter held the structural pressure of the psyche's identity, the breaking point, the storm and stress, the bend in the bow where the arrow is held in taut equilibrium, uniting the rest of the counter, a fulcrum of an unrelieved point of tension, where a crowd can drown out the noise of the strain of a single consciousness, or where an isolato finds himself to himself completely withdrawn, in the crow's nest, drinking Old Crow, thinking about the old crow at home, but the myth ends here, cry of the corbie, caw caw caw... thar she blows!

The door is opening; some eyes are averted, a head nods, a hand waves; it's Stan and Ted, the twin brothers, the Polish plumbers.

"What shall we have to drink, brother Stan?"

"Let me think about it, brother Ted."

"Well, brother Stan, we could have a beer."

"Sounds good to me, brother Ted."

"Then two beers it shall be, brother Stan."

"Two beers it is, brother Ted."

Pause

They drink, say ahhh

"I still say that should have been a 1/2 inch pipe, brother Ted."

"Indeed. But it just didn't fit, brother Stan, it just didn't fit."

"Well it should have fitted, brother Ted, it should have fitted."

"You can't make it fit if it doesn't want to fit, brother Stan."

"Look at it, brother Ted, just look at it." Stan puts a piece of copper tubing on the bar counter.

"Yep, that's the rascal, brother Stan, doesn't fit."

"It should have fit, brother Ted, it just should have fitted," said Stan, dreamily.

The door is opening, here's Smiley Jack the Harmonica Man, flashing his white teeth from a jet black face, talking to himself, playing improvised harmonica Charlie Parker like, or so he says; the harmonica playing annoys a few of the clammers, so one of them walks over to the jukebox at the back of the bar, drops a coin in the slot and pushes L-7 and soon that old gang of Mitch Miller's is singing "That Old Gang of Mine."

Gee but I'd give the world to see that old gang of mine...

Zippy the Mayor (an unemployed "touched in the head" type of local character, who walks around town all day as if he runs the place, therefore the name) is playing shuffle board with skinny Fats Wallet, the shopping cart collecting man, also "touched" according to town tradition, who also walks around town all day collecting shopping carts and returning them to the supermarket, pushing long train lengths of carts with his long thin ungainly legs taking loping striding motions; a big fat wallet prominently sticking out from his back pocket, therefore the name. School children returning home pick-pocket the wallet at least twice a day, and empty its contents on the street, a wad of paper Monopoly money; but Fats Wallet never gives chase, because that would entail abandoning his train of shopping carts.

As you enter the bar, the counter is on the right, like a long barrel pistol laid on the floor by a gangster movie's right-handed hood. Wookie Jones takes the butt of the handle on the back of his head. The clammers are cocked. The regulars are scattered bullets that have missed their marks. The booze behind the bar like triggers.

Across the bar's counter, lined up against the wall, are the amusement games. Immediately to the left as you enter the bar, is the pinball machine, followed by the shuffle board game, followed by the pool table. In the back of the bar is a slightly raised platform with a few tables and chairs on it, a dark unvisited place, except for the dark figure in the corner, who is reading, or pretending to read, a paperback book. What book? Let me look.

It's *The Big Sleep* by Raymond Chandler. And the man is detective Abe Desurd. To the right of the tables and chairs, against the wall, is the jukebox, and next to the jukebox is a set of small toy drums. On the front of the bass drum is a picture of two dancing youths, the girl wears a poodle skirt and has a long pony tail in her blonde hair; the boy is holding her hand and they are swinging around a large black quarter note which is in between them; and arched over their heads the words Rock'N'Roll are painted in black. On the top of the bass drum is a small metal triangle suspended from a wire; also a small cymbal propped up on a metal spike. Two other small drums are on each side of the topside of the bass drum, and Stephen is sitting behind the drums on a small stool, banging away.

The door is opening; here's Frank Yamada, who never stays at the counter. He orders scotch and water and goes to a table at the back of the bar. He sits at the table next to Detective Desurd, gives him the stranger's eye... drums pounding... temples flaring... pool balls clattering... Mitch Miller and the Gang on the juke box... Smiley Jack's harmonica... voices and sudden shouts... and now Joe is turning on the television...Wagon Train, Gunsmoke, Perry Mason, Father Knows Best...

"Damn shame they took all them quiz shows off the air," lamented Whip.

"They were rigged; it was a racket," responded Crack to his wife, "just a big advertising scam for you dumb housewives... not that you're much of a housewife, baby... anyway I kinda like these western and detective shows. To hell with that phony-baloney jack-pot shit... $64,000 Challenge, Dotto, Twenty-One... just crap..."

"Crap, listen to him, from someone who shoots crap all night... anyway, that's because you're stupid and ain't got no education you don't like them shows," said Whip as she whipped her hand across the back of Crack's head. "CRACK" shouted Snipe and Cosmo, as usual, in unison; attuned, as usual, to the marital bickering.

"Don't you get it. It was fake. Dishonest. They provided the answers... you just kinda like that Van Doren guy." Crack defended himself, skewly.

"He's good lookin' and smart as a bee sting, baby, can't say as much for you."

"They only wanted him to look good so people like you would watch. Marshall Dillon would shoot his ass out of town... scoundrel... Perry Mason would have sent him up the river... to Sing Sing... where a canary can sing for his bread and water... and Jim Anderson would spank his ass and send him off to Sunday School... I tell ya it's them Communists behind all this... that's where the money goes... to the Communists... I bet it goes to Cuba... to this new guy with the beard... what's his name? Help me here Snipe, uh..."

"Castro."

"Yeah, Cas... Castro oil..." Crack spit on the floor, "taste like shit... Commie shit..."

"That's CASTOR oil, stupid, Castor... you disgusting pig," said Whip.

"Who you calling a pig, you bitch... why I oughta..."

"You oughta what? Go ahed... just try it... see if I don't knock you on your ass."

Crack got off the stool and stood there shaking and wobbling; like Gary Cooper in High Noon. "You dare me... I'll sock you I will. Just because you're a woman don't think I won't do it, baby... bitch... I know, I know about you..."

"You know what about me?"

"I know about her; I know who had you on your ass... she did... she had you on your ass... you queer bitch..."

"Shut up you godamn drunk."

"I saw it, both of you... kissing her right here," and Crack grabs for Whip's cunt. They wrestle each other to the floor. Joe and Frankie are pulling them apart. The clammers are hooting and hollering. Stephen is wide-eyed banging on his drums. Mitch Miller and the Gang are singing a medley of "There is a Tavern in the Town" and "Show Me the Way to Go Home."

"Hey baby... I'm tired and I wanna go to bed..." sings Crack.

"I hadda a little drink about an hour ago..." sings Whip, and then half the bar is singing... "And it went right to my head..."

Toots appears from the back door. That quiets things down in a hurry. She is carrying her mop. That's a sign for peace or else SMACK! And she'll use it too if she's got to. Later in the evening Toots brings out the mop and the black hose to give a signal that it's closing time; she'll start sweeping out the bums. She'll whip them with the black hose too.

The door is opening... David Chaseman comes in... this guy's no bum, this guy's got plenty of dough, lives up Asharoken Road. He's quite a well-known painter; mainly portraits; was once married to a famous actress.

He's also a drunk. He greets Joe and then goes right over to Toots whom he spots at the back of the bar. He likes to butter her up with promises. They both have a mutual love of opera, and David's been promising Toots that he'll take her to an opera one fine day. They sit down at a table and talk shop. Toots has never been to an opera, a real opera. Her dreams of being an opera singer and taking her Papa to an opera are long gone. Toots has never been anywhere much.

The door is opening again... who's this guy? Here's our first stranger of the night. "Seen him around a coupla of times," says Frankie to Joe. "Don't know his name." The clammers seem to know the stranger. They call him over and he joins them.

"If it ain't the famous writer," shouts a clammer.

"Fuck famous. Set me up a beer and whiskey chaser."

"Hey Jack, you buyin'? What with all those books you sell you're makin' enough dough to buy a few rounds for us working men."

"What's with you? You don't think I work? I work as hard as your head is square."

"Hey, I'm not a square-head," said the clammer.

The Norwegian scow workers turned around to see who this fellow was that was employing this term of abuse for those of the Scandinavian persuasion.

"*Ja*, you say something to me?" said a big broad red-bearded Norwegian named Olaf.

"No, I didn't say anything to you, Ingemar," said Jack, abrasively.

"Who is dis Ingemar?" said Olaf.

Ingemar Johansson had become the world's heavyweight boxing champion when he KO'd Floyd Patterson in the third round at Yankee Stadium back in July.

"Don't you know your own kind? Wookie here knows who Floyd Patterson is. And Joe Louis. Rocky Marciano. Jersey Joe Walcott. The great American champions." Jack emphasized American.

"Johansson is Swedish, we are Norwegians, dere is big difference," said another big bearded Norwegian named Alvig.

"Where's the difference? Blond, blue eyes, only chicks should look that way, man," Jack blurted out. Things were becoming tense. Fists were being formed. Fuses becoming shorter.

"Have you not heard about one thousand Swedes went through the weeds chased by one crippled Norwegian?" said Alvig; that drew some laughs and defused slightly the growing international crisis.

"There's never been a Jew champion," offered Jack for consideration, out of the blue. Everyone considered it and nodded his head in agreement. There were no Jews in the bar, none they knew of. Jack was still steaming from what he saw on television a few nights ago. Some Jewish comedian was performing a parody of Jack. Calling him "Jack Crackerjack," as if Jack were some raving lunatic, an Abraham-man, an imposter begging for attention and money and fame. It was tough being Jack Kerouac.

"There's plenty of kike comedians though... but there's never gonna be a Jew heavyweight champion," Jack said almost self-congratulatoringly." But not all Jews are kikes. Ginsberg's a Jew. But he's kinda pinko. I hate Commie rats," Jack mumbled to himself.

"And not all Negros are niggers," said a clammer, and took a quick glance at Wookie to see if he would react. He didn't.

"Where's the fuckin' logic in that!" said Jack, gallantly defending reason.

"You know what I mean," said the clammer, "there's good one's and bad one's."

"I don't have to listen to this hateful shit," said Jack. The clammers and Jack displayed aggressive postures.

"What shit?" said a clammer. But Jack just walked away, clearly outnumbered. He sipped from the flask of whiskey that he kept hidden in his jacket pocket. That was not a prudent thing to do in this bar, any bar. And yet nobody made a big deal about it.

"I don't have to listen to this Mitch Miller shit," and Jack pointed to the jukebox. He got outta that trouble. He walked over to the jukebox. His face glazed by the flickering lights. He swayed back and forth, reading the song selections; his beer spilling onto the bubble-glass case.

Toots put a beer and whisky chaser on the table in front of David Chaseman, and she sat down on the other side of the small round red and white Formica-top table. She tore open a bag of Planter's Peanuts and shook out a few on a napkin advertising Canadian Club.

"October 26 is opening night for the Metropolitan Opera. You want tickets?" asked David.

"What day is that?" said Toots.

"It's a Monday."

"Johnny ain't gonna go... he's too busy."

"I'll take you. But I can't make it opening night. You're gonna miss the debut of Giulietta Simionato."

"Oh yeah, never heard of her, in what?"

"Il Trovatore. Verdi, your favorite."

"No kiddin' heh? Boy, I'd like to go..." Toots paused to reflect. "But maybe some other time... how the hell can I get away from here," her tone of voice became harsh, "I gotta watch this place... I have to work you know. I've worked hard all my life, mister, it's not the life of Reilly for me bub, not like all the bums you see around here." Toots rationalized an excuse. "Ah it doesn't matter... some other time... all those rich folks."

Jack couldn't find anything that he liked on the jukebox. A clammer approached him and challenged him to a game of pinball, winner buys drinks. Jack saw Stephen sitting behind the drums and went over and kneeled down beside him, thus extracting himself from the proposed competition.

"Can I play?" said Jack softly. Stephen said nothing and handed over his drumsticks to the stranger.

"Let me show you how to play a jazz beat." Jack started drumming and humming. "Here, now you try." Stephen took the sticks and proceeded to bang away.

"Yeah man, go go go, that's it, you're wailing now... what's your name kid?" asked Jack.

"Stephen?" shouted Toots from the table, "tell the man your name."

"Stephen," said Stephen.

"Stephen Cazzaza. His daddy is the bartender," said Toots to Jack, who turned around to look at the bartender.

"Go on, play some more," said Jack to Stephen. "Jazzy Cazzazy."

Detective Desurd was sitting silently in the corner. Frank Yamada was tapping his toe nervously. He rotated the swizzle stick between his thumb and forefinger. He looked at it, and read the gold print on the red stick.

FRANK & JOE   commercial rest.   NORTHPORT,   L.I.

The swizzle stick had a round knob at the top and earwig-like pinchers at the bottom end. Frank tried to clasp his finger with the pincher but his finger was too large to fit. Detective Desurd looked up from *The Big Sleep*. Frank picked up his drink and went over and sat next to the detective.

Frank listened to Abe Desurd. The detective said that he had been an FBI agent for twenty years. That was a lie. That he had been a good friend of J. Edgar Hoover. That was less than a lie. In fact, Abe named himself after the FBI director, which was true, Abe Edgar Desurd. Everyone on the force called him Edgar, and not just to please him. But the sarcasm was lost on him. He always wanted to be a G-man. But A. Edgar Desurd just couldn't make the grade, couldn't cut the mustard. Too many physical and mental disabilities. "I'm retired now. Though sometimes I'm called in on special assignment. I'm working on something now. Can't say anything more about it though, you understand, top secret stuff, something to do with the Russkies and Khrushchev. You know he's coming here for a visit next week... well, I can't say anything more, of course."

"Of course," said Frank Yamada, the North Shore's most famous cat-burglar. Detective Desurd eyed the room, watching for the other Abe, the mysteriously absent Abe Churchyard, husband and father of the dead wife and child.

Jack, perspiring and out-of-breath from playing the toy drums, sat down on the floor. He took a napkin from a table and wiped the sweat from his brow. Toots was telling David about what had happened earlier in the day, about finding Grace and Izaac dead in the taxicab. Jack overheard their conversation. As he listened he began drawing on a napkin, tortured scenes of crucifixions and strange Pietas. A child in his mother's arms. Jack looked up and saw the group of clammers heading for the door, exiting en masse. "Hey! Wait up!" Jack howled. As the clammers were crossing Main Street, Jack lay down across the old un-used streetcar rails in the middle of the road. The clammers kept walking. "Don't shut me out!" Jack screamed. Ignoring him, the clammers kept walking down the street until they came to Skipper's, one of the other bars on Main Street.

"C'mon, I'll mother ya!" screamed Jack, and he crawled to the sidewalk and vomited in the gutter and passed out...

...Around midnight, Jack opens his eyes and has a vision. He is hearing Toots singing "Ave Maria"... the bar's door is open to let in some cool air, and Toots has had a few too many... after all it is a Friday night...

"...Ave Maria... gratia plena... Ave Maria... Maria..."

And Jack hears a voice: Verily I say unto thee, today shalt thou be with me in paradise.

Jack Kerouac is in heaven.

Document 59-759

We call the joint Joe and Frank's Piggery. We got a logo of an angry pig with a beer mug in his hand and a shirt that reads Joe's Pigs. We are the regulars. We drink late and we get a bit sloppy. Frank and Joe's Piggery. The bar with the High School education. The next annual meeting of Frank and Joe's Pigs will be Friday night. We will be at the pleasure palace from 5:37 to ...?

The Wandering Pig

When we go a boozing
Across both land and sea
We always seem to wind up here
In the Cazzaza boy's old piggery.
We wander here, we wander there
But no matter where we go
We're greeted from a fist from Crack
And a song from little Cosmo.
Little Cosmo can hardly hold a chord
Old Crack can't hurt a flea
So we just play the shuffleboard
Until the clock strikes three.
Good fellowship is what we seek
In a cold glass of brew
So next time you're passing by
Stop in and have a few.
The lights are dim the smoke is thick
And Frankie's behind the bar
But oh what fun we always have
Just being where we are.
When it comes to shuffleboard
Old Beaner knows the rules
He thinks that all the rest of us
Are just a bunch of fools.
Old Babe, that's Joe, is on the wagon
He hardly takes a drink,
To look at him so very thin

His Norwegian bride knows not what to think.
Old Wookie never shuts his mouth
He never stops his breath
Though no one knows just what he says
He'll talk us all to death.
Joe he likes the Giants
Both the baseball and football teams
But now the baseball team is gone
And he just wants to scream.
Our song is just about to stop
Cause the Cazzaza boys are about to close,
Toots has just brought out her dirty mop
And her big black rubber hose.

It was early in the morning... around 2 a.m., the regulars remained; and Frank Yamada and Detective Desurd, still in the back corner, getting rather drunk and chummy.

"Right now the FBI is investigating all them beatniks, commie sympathizers and homos," said Desurd, drunkenly.

"Is that a fact?" said Frank, eyebrow raised with delight.

Joe was clearing off the tables. Toots was sweeping up. Stephen was fast asleep on the couch in the backroom, left alone in the dark.

"How about a card trick?" said Frankie, which was his way of setting them up for poker. "Or maybe just a few hands of showdown poker?"

"Yeah I'll take your money," said Cosmo.

"Me too," muttered Snipe.

Whip and Crack were asleep, or passed out, in each other's arms.

"No you don't," Floral bellowed, and grabbed her husband by the ear. Cosmo smacked her arm down.

"Lay off!" Cosmo said.

"Well, you in or out?" said Frankie.

"Deal me in," said Cosmo.

"How 'bout you Joe."

"Yeah, why not." Joe threw a dollar bill on the beer counter. The others followed suit. Frankie dealt five cards, one at a time to each player, face up. That's it. No bidding, no discards, no new cards. The highest hand wins half a dollar; the highest spade wins the other half a dollar. A flash in the pan game. Bang. Frankie has a pair of nines, Joe a pair of trays, Snipe is a brick high, and Cosmo is jack-of-hearts high. Frankie has the highest spade, a queen. He takes the whole pot: $4.00. "The buck stops here," said Frankie, "c'mon, ante up."

"That's it for me," said Joe. He had lost enough money playing showdown poker in North Africa and Italy during the war.

"That's it for all of youse... go home... go home... damnit..." said Toots to the regulars in a tone of voice that one uses when addressing a stray dog.

"Crack! Whip! Wake up!" shouted Toots. She poked Crack in the arm with the mop. Detective Desurd got up from his table and went to the toilet. The door is opening... in walks Abe Churchyard... he is drunk and babbling... "Wha'em I gonna do?"

Joe looked around for Detective Desurd but he's gone off somewhere.

"Hey, do you wanna see a card trick?" said Frankie to Abe Churchyard. "Abracadabra," said Abe, "can you make me disappear? I want to go far away. I understand nothing." The jukebox is playing the final selection of the evening, Mitch Miller and the Gang singing "Let Me Call You Sweetheart." Joe's choice. He used to sing it to Torhild before they were married; he didn't sing it much afterwards.

"I know a trick; watch," said Abe Churchyard. "Abracadabra! Presto!" And Abe pulled a .22 caliber pistol out of his pocket. He walked to the back of the room and leaned against the wall.

"Do something," said Toots.

"Do what?" answered Joe.

"Somebody do something," said Toots.

"D'what?" answered Joe.

"Something! Anything!" said Toots.

"D'wa?" answered Joe.

"Useless..."

"Yeah, well, fuck..." Joe wouldn't dare say it to Toots. Curse and turn away. Run away. Where you gonna run to? You're already in the bar! Abe Churchyard has gathered all you cowardly pissbrains here for a shot of reality; he's gonna drown you in your mothers' wombs. He's gonna rearrange your alphabet soup of life; he's gonna shed his animal skin of human language; shut ins... that's what you are... shut inside yourselves... shut the world out... condemned buildings... falling down... let it all fall down around you and lie in the shit and rubble... let it grow familiar... rank and foul... adapt to the dirt... peasant minds... Mother, for love of grace... do you not come your tardy son to chide?... father died when he was but a boy... father was shot by cops... it was a mistake... an accident... it was not intended... I dreamed that my father was Abraham Lincoln, and in my dream he was weeping weeping... he said to me: All I am or ever hope to be I owe to my angel mother... there's a divinity that shapes our ends... and he told me to remember the Gettysburg Address, and I told him that I had remembered it, for I had learned it at school... and then he held a long black knife in his large hand; he was dressed all in black, black eyes and tall black hat... and he said that God required it of him... and he held the knife above me, prepared to thrust... and then I shot him in the head... I killed the president... my father... it was the last thing I ever did... I could never act again... there is no resolution... no thought on this matter... I was an honest workingman, no trouble... I was no prince... no king... a peasant... I can't fiddle while Rome burns... but I twiddle my thumbs while my house and home is falling down... to say something is rotten in the state of... my state of mind... state of exile... smell of decay... to hear my son talk of suicide... the future... no one speak to me I don't speak to myself... language is a chain... my little boy is sleeping in the backroom... my little boy is dead in his mother's arms... we are forging them a chain with words and deeds... we don't talk to them... they have their own language... we'll never talk to them... because we can't stand behind our words, we'll hide behind them; we have no words to stand on... news sports and weather... beep-beep... We can't stand ourselves... we hate ourselves... we hate life... whatta gonna do? Whatta gonna do?

"Do something," said Toots.

"Do what? What are you gonna do?" said Joe and Frankie, and all the pathetic weak-willed men in the room.

Abe Churchyard waved the gun in the air. "Ask me if I have any last requests, any last words, just like a firing squad, go'hed, ask me," said Abe Churchyard.

Snipe drunkenly nervously laughing uttered, "D'ya got any last words before you die ha ha ha."

"Yes," said Abe, and put the point of the gun in his mouth and tripped the trigger. BLAST! Abe Churchyard falls back and slides down the wall... what happened? Nothing... all eyes are fixed on his pale drained face, mouth gaping... nothing... nothing happens... his eyes wide open... he slouches over slightly... what's gonna happen? whatta ya gonna do? Is this it? No one moves an inch... is this infinity? is this the ultimate paradox? Death is nothing at all... empty and void... but then... what then? His mouth opens and a torrent of blood is gushing forth from his mouth...

"My God," says Floral... and she is vomiting... "Abraham's bosom," says Snipe... "Jesus, Mary and Joseph," says Toots... Whip and Crack are in each other's arms, shocked faces... jookbox: "...let me call you sweetheart I'm in love with you..." Stephen is still sleeping in the back room... Toots softly is singing Ave Maria to herself... Detective Desurd appears from the toilet... his gun drawn... Cosmo bends over and clutches his stomach... "I can't hold it in..." and he is shitting his pants... jook and Toots: "...in your eyes so blue... *Maria... Ave Maria*... let me call you sweetheart... *gratia plena, Maria*... I'm in love with you..."

Stuck a feather in his hat and called it macaronic verse... vomit of ham omelet... om and hum, alpha and omega, humdrum and humlet, abrahamlet, and the shot rang out from the hamlet of Northport to the hamlet of Oyster Bay... and little Stephen slept through it all, as they say when they say that a child slept through it all... left alone in the dark...

Later... Torhild called, worried, where are you so late? How's Stephen? Stephen woke up. Alone. And because he was alone he cried. He cried out. No one came. And because no one came he ventured forth, curious to discover the meaning of this aloneness. To find meaning where there is no meaning. Stephen found his father on his knees washing the blood from the floor, doing the dirty work, moping up. The ambulance and the police have come and gone. Everyone has gone, gone to wherever they call home. Stephen and his father are the last to go.

Joe finished cleaning up the mess; moping up. Blood and shit and piss and vomit. Then he turned out the lights, locked up, and carried Stephen out to the car, a green and white two-door 1957 Chevrolet Bel Air, an American classic... the sun was rising... it was early in the morning... the car headed west on route 25A... the sun was rising...

The Day the Town Stood Still

Stephen's first hero was John Glenn, the astronaut. The first American to orbit the earth. It happened on February 20, 1962; it happened on television; right before our eyes. Stephen watched the Atlas booster rocket thrust upward in an explosive, engulfing mass of flame and smoke, surging skyward and spaceward. He heard the magical backward countdown 10-9-8-7-6-5-4-3-2-1-BLASTOFF! Every boy in America learned the magical formula and repeated it; and then four hours and fifty-five minutes after blast-off, after three orbits of the earth, after piercing the atmosphere with a sonic boom, the Friendship 7 capsule splashed-down in the water off Bermuda in the Atlantic Ocean just three miles from the *SS Noa*. Little strange creatures called frogmen were jumping into the water, the hatch was opened, and the hero emerged from the spaceship and removed his helmet. And Stephen saw it all on the television, and America was made one in deed, as America would be made one in death watching the funeral of John F. Kennedy; Stephen watching the black horses pulling the coffin covered with the American flag, and there would be no division, no disagreement, the entire nation, his whole family rejoiced in the great deed and mourned in the great death; so we believed. But then one day four lads from Liverpool appeared on the television, and Stephen's father said, That ain't music! And Stephen's mother said: They must be wearing wigs! And suddenly a tiny voice of dissension was heard in the land of national heroes. Stephen's sister shouted, She loves you yeah yeah yeah! Stephen's father shouted, Turn that down! Sylvia was five years older than Stephen. In 1965 when she was fifteen she had a nervous breakdown. She was taken to King's Park and received shock treatments. Technological advancements in the service of society... and the Friendship 7 capsule floats down on its parachute... SPLASH! SCREAM! SPLASH! SCREAM! SPLASH! SCREAM! And society is redeemed. And the mother sits in the back seat of the car and watches the children on the rides... the small planes and boats and rockets spinning and splashing and the children screaming and her flesh bleeding and the music blasting she loves you yeah yeah yeah and troops are sent to Vietnam singing yeah yeah yeah yeah and the flesh is bleeding and yeah he said yeah I will fuck her fuck her uh uh uh yeah yeah yeah and the jungles are burning orange fuck me yeah and the bombs are falling fuck me yeah yeah and the images the flesh the blood the images on the television the flesh the blood yeah yeah yeah she loves you yeah yeah yeah and the Friendship 7 capsule splashes into the water and the hero emerges yeah yeah yeah... no... no... no... it ain't me, babe...

Stephen takes out his crayons and draws a picture of the rocket, and then he draws a picture of the splash-down, and then he takes another piece of paper and draws a circle: That's the earth and the earth is round,

Columbus said the earth was round but nobody believed him. And in the middle of the circle he draws the outline shape of the United States: That's America but it looks more like an elephant, Columbus discovered America. And around the earth he draws another circle: That's the orbit of the rocket. And then he draws another circle in the upper left-hand corner of the paper: That's the moon! President Kennedy said that we shall land a man on the moon this decade! And Stephen cuts clippings and pictures from the *New York Daily News*, his father's favorite newspaper. His mother saves all the front pages with the bold headlines and pictures of big stories, of big events, of deeds and heroes and deaths of heroes... there is a picture of Douglas MacArthur in full uniform with all the medals and corncob pipe, and Stephen hangs it on the wall over his bed. It was an age of heroes. That is, Stephen was at an age when heroes appeared to him in the radiance of Manhood. The light came unto him, and he was made one with the light. But it was not a pure light. It was an image, a reflection on the wall of the cave. It all began in darkness, but it was the eyes that released him, and Stephen saw as far as his eyes could see, and what he saw was the light, the night-light that kept the bogeymen away, until the heroes arrived, and every Saturday afternoon the heroes arrived. Stephen entered the dark temple and saw the light; he and hundreds of other children, casting their eyes toward the shining icons, as the popcorn of absolution rained down on their heads from the balcony above. They entered the darkness until the light was unveiled; they entered the darkness on bright sunny Saturday afternoons, forsaking the baseball field, the woods, the rivers, the streets... and they emerged from the darkness of the temple into the streets at early dusk, and the world was somehow different, and the light stayed with them. In the beginning was the image and the image was made flesh. And for Stephen, as a small boy in a small-town, everything began in America, everything was invented in America, everything was discovered in America, everything was advertised and sold in America, and everything was America and America was Hollywood.

Heroes lived in the world of light, bigger than life, daring to risk death, to battle darkness, and what was darker than the night sky? And what was brighter than the moon? And what was more pure than an American hero? It was an age of heroes because youth is the sacrificial age; and Stephen was at an age when heroes summon you forth to go and do battle in the dark forests against the forces of evil. The heroes take you away from school and society and family. A power leads you into that dark forest and it's exciting and frightening and wonderful. But then the heroes betray you. You stand before the dragon and his greed with your sword unsheathed... but the heroes betray you. They say: It's time to grow up! The heroes give you away, turn you back into the hands of a school principal, teachers, instructors, society, family, flag, uniformity, and uniforms... you fall back in line. And father returns in all his glory and power, to place the load on your hump, and if you're man enough you'll make it, make a living, make money. Father will instruct you in the achievement of American Manhood, and then you will be released, then you will have to let go, be on your own, but created in the image of your father and in the high interest of society. Just when you are about to slay the dragon you are brought back, the light has shifted, the heroes remain, but now they are just tales in books and movies, icons and symbols without vital life. They are nothing but the maturity myth of Manhood, of atonement with the status quo. Stand up and be counted... I have to keep busy or I'll go mad... go about my father's business... funny business... the dragon is in the temple... the outlaws are in the cave... the judges sit on the bench, admonishing the boy... fat cat Juno Moneta sits on her heap... she has piles... she had a large litter... housekeeper who sweeps the dirt under the rug... and consumes her kittys... brought back to do the things that are expected of you; don't let me down boy. And the dragon of greed returns to his throne in full regalia, and the fire he breathes burns the dark forests, burns the sky, burns the sea, burns the soul, and leaves nothing but ashes.

Stephen returned from the dark forest to a silent father and a burning house, so he kept going back to the forest, kept crossing the borders, kept getting lost. Those cunning heroes, where are they now? They are images, excuses, rationalizations, justifications, and expediencies. Father says, be a man. But some fathers are silent... so you return to the forest in search of him, but not him. The images stay in your vision for ten seconds and then make their way to the heart. But they never completely captured Stephen's heart. The constant bombardment of images was deflected in a broken mirror where he saw his father's face. The heroes had Stephen set for slaughter. But his father did not have the faith of Abraham and the knife trembled in his hand. Lord Mammon turned his back, but his truth keeps marching on... the truth is marching around and around, circling the altar, the ambitious ones are here, and Stephen stands inside the other to see only one side of his face, but Stephen broke through the circle and saw the otherside of his face. And when he turned around he saw the death, the blood, the bones, and the flesh.

On March 1, 1962, Stephen watched the parade on television. People lining the streets and crying, waving little flags. And John Glenn, the astronaut, the hero, the ticker tape raining down on him like popcorn in a Saturday matinee. He is riding in that long white limousine, license plate 50-NY, flying a gold-ruffled flag, one of America's great ships of honor and prestige, taking up space, moving through space, round 'em up, the covered-wagon, the automobile, the airplane, the battleship, the rocketship, the missile, the spaceship, entrepreneurship, taking up space, energy and space... and John Glenn is sitting with a man and a woman; who is that man with the big ears? Some guy named Johnson, who is he? How dare he sit in the same car with our hero! The ticker-tape parade is heading up Broadway. The marching bands and baton twirlers whirling their batons into space. And there he is, on television, the hero who fought the powers of evil in heaven. American Manhood. And the paper is falling... paper and paper... *Life Magazine... Time Magazine... The New York Times...* paper and paper... *Look Magazine... Saturday Evening Post... New York Daily News... Reader's Digest... New York Herald Tribune... Wall Street Journal...* and the Manhattan telephone book... paper and paper... news and numbers... falling and falling... blowing in the wind... blowing off the streets... words and images... words and images...

Beep-beep means: only a self-referential word and sound made by the vocal cords in conjunction with the tongue, teeth, lips, and mouth... with air, not spirit, Breathe in! Breathe in! To represent the sound, to signify the sound, of electronically conveyed information... from the logos of neurons firing in the burning bush of the brain, to the algorithm of formal systems smoking on the mountaintop of the mind... from the story of our time, to the story of our mind, narration and history to blips and beeps on a screen, from in search of God to in search of the Machine...

And the movie ends... one of Stephen's favorites, it's always on channel 9 on Saturday mornings, *The Day the Earth Stood Still.*

"All right, you saw the ending, let's go," says father to son.

Joe Cazzaza and his son Stephen came out of the alleyway and briefly surveyed the scene from the sidewalk. It was the same. Ever since Joe and Frankie gave up the bar in Northport, selling it to their former dishwasher and part-time cook, Mrs. Grass, who, with her son Pete as bartender, made a real go of the place, preserving much of the old clientele, the regulars, the old timers, clammers and fishermen, but at the same time bringing in a new younger crowd, Joe has been unemployed for the most part, except for three short stints, working one month as an usher in the new movie theater up in Pine Hollow, two weeks as a furniture delivery man, and two months working as an outside mechanic in Heemskirk's Shipyard, where Frankie also worked for a while, back during the war.

Sometimes in the evening, Emile Baldazzi will walk along the beach and sit on the rocks and watch the welding sparks falling from the tugboats in the shipyard. Subordinated fools, he would mutter. Capitalist swine. Emile still lives in the flophouse on Hamilton Avenue, across the street from what was formerly Belsen and White's, which changed management back in 1957, and was renamed Burr House, eventually changed into a comfortable Bed and Breakfast establishment. Burr House on Hamilton Avenue, there was bound to be some dueling going on. And there was. The proprietor of Burr House, Mr. Haywood Burr, has been trying to clean up the street, trying to force out the residents of the flophouse and the few blacks who live at the end of the road by the railroad station. But Emile is fighting back, a losing battle of course, he can't afford that capitalist commodity called freedom, freedom of speech, no one is listening. Emile is 67 years old, he's about had it, and in the free market he's considered damaged goods, just another town bum in small town eyes. But Rocky remains a good friend. Poor little Rocky. He survived his jump from Hodman's clock tower back in 1927. They put him in the state mental hospital at King's Park. He was released after three months. He was given a job as a member of the ground's crew, working for the county school system. He had to rake leaves and shovel snow, clip hedges and pick up scraps of paper, and hang out the flag the first thing by dawn's early light.

Joe and his brother sold the bar business because Joe finally found work that he would keep until he retired. Frankie became a butcher for Van Heffer's Meat Market. He and his family owned the place, they were the landlords collecting the cheap rents, yet his peasant mentality prevailed, and he worked for them. As for Joe, he became a janitor. It so happened that the town was building two new elementary schools to provide for all the baby boomers coming of age in Oyster Bay. Joe signed up, took the civil service exam, failed, but was hired even though several local blacks scored higher on the exam. This was before affirmative action, and Joe had some friends with connections. So he registered (an unofficial prerequisite) as a Republican (he had voted for Nixon in 1960 anyway, though in later years he told his son that he had voted for Kennedy) and began his days as a toilet bowl cleaner. All the kids thought him a nice guy. The kids would tell Stephen, "Your dad's a nice guy."

And it also so happens that, today, October 27, 1962, one of the new elementary schools will be holding its dedication ceremony. The new elementary school has been named, don't hold your breath, Theodore Roosevelt Elementary School. And today is also the anniversary of Theodore Roosevelt's birthday; that's no coincidence. And today is also the day that President John F. Kennedy has challenged Nikita Khrushchev to remove his missiles from Cuba or else, and that was no coincidence. Theodore Roosevelt would have been proud of Kennedy's macho humiliation of the Soviet leader, who was making an offer of mutual withdrawal, Soviet missiles from Cuba, American missiles from Turkey. It was the classic American confrontation, the Big Walk Down, right off the pages of *The Virginian.* That's the title of a 1902 novel by Owen Wister, a book dedicated to Wister's friend Theodore Roosevelt, and subsequently made into several Hollywood movies and a television show.

The prototype of all future western good guys, the unnamed Virginian embodied many of the attributes and ideals of Roosevelt. The bad guy Trampas gets riled up by the nameless hero, and in a poker game Trampas accuses the Virginian of cheating and then insults his forebears, so our hero places his pistol on the table and replies, "When you call me that, smile." In the climatic pistol duel the Virginian blows Trampas away. And now we have Kennedy putting his pistol on the table and saying, "Americans may long for the days when war meant charging up San Juan Hill, or when our isolation was guarded by two oceans, or when the atomic bomb was ours alone, or when much of the industrialized world depended upon our resources and our aid. But they know that those days are gone..." and so Kennedy places his big pistol on the table: We're the poker players, they're the chess players, and Cuba is blockaded by U. S. Navy Task Force 136, which consists of sixteen destroyers, six support ships, three heavy cruisers, and the carrier Essex. Task Force 135 is made up of a ring of ships protecting Guantanamo naval base, including the nuclear-powered carrier Enterprise. Five Army divisions are mobilized in Florida, prepared for the invasion of Cuba. A Cuban division led by Che Guevara holds Mariel Bay. The 101st Airborne is ready to go in and take them out. Nearly 200 vessels are deployed and ready to strike Castro's island. Thousands upon thousands of Marines are set to go ashore; over 100,000 Army troops are ready to land. Who will blink first? The world stands "at the brink" of nuclear confrontation. Will Khrushchev yield to the young President's machismo posturing? So the Big Walk Down is being counted down... just like the countdown back in February when the Friendship 7 capsule carried John Glenn into orbit... 10-9-8-7-6-5-4-3-2-1 BLASTOFF... but this time the countdown and the BLAST may carry us all into orbit... you can see it on the faces of the people on South Street, the tension etched in our age, the Modern Death Age.

Joe Cazzaza said "Hi" to Hy Horowitz, and Hy stuck a big stale cigar in Joe's shirt pocket and said, "Enjoy it, it may be your last." Joe bought the *Daily News* and gave a nickel to Stephen to buy a Hershey Bar. Back out on the street, right in front of the paper store, Joe stood and opened the newspaper. But he didn't exactly read it; it was just sort of a habit. He flipped through a few pages and then folded the newspaper and stuck it under his arm. He lit the cigar. He stood on The Spot. The exact spot where Sid Schwartz had been killed thirty-five years ago by a falling chunk of rock sculpture shaped like a dollar sign; the exact same spot where a falling chunk of cement and brick had nearly killed President Theodore Roosevelt back in 1908, another falling missile from the sky... but now real missiles are about to fall from the sky, those Russian missiles arcing over from Cuba.

Stephen saw the old man with the long gray beard approaching, the long gray overcoat dragging on the sidewalk, it was Georgie Dumpson, out foraging for a meal, searching through the green KEEP OYSTER BAY BEAUTIFUL receptacles that line the sidewalk, and from the other end of town, came Jake O' Toole, former town cop way back when, who was out for his morning stroll. Jake the Cop, who had dragged Georgie Dumpson into the alleyway and clobbered him, Jake and Georgie, two old timers of the town, converging on The Spot. They walked right pass each other, they didn't even recognize each other. Joe said "good morning" to Jake, and Jake stopped, shook Joe's hand, and shaking like the bones that he was, looked down at Stephen and said, "This your boy, Joe? Why I knew your granddaddy son. And a good man he was too. And..." The stooping Jake straightens himself up and looked at Joe. Jake had forgotten so much but it all came back to him just then. Giuseppe riddled with bullets from Thompson machine guns. Maurizio fried in the chair, or was he? Jake didn't say another word. He smiled at the boy and his father. He went into the paper store. He mumbled a few greeting words to Hy Horowitz and he bought the *Daily News*. Then he opened the paper, rippled the pages, closed it and folded it and stuck it under his arm.

Stephen and his father crossed the street and stood on the corner of Saunder's Pharmacy and looked back up to the windows. There they were; forever a fixture in Stephen's world. Grandma Fiorenza and Aunt Luisa and Uncle Stevie. Fiorenza in her wheelchair at the window, Uncle Stevie at the window in the other room, his crutches leaning on the chair, and Aunt Luisa, paralyzed hand in her apron pocket, sitting in the other chair. How could a missile ever disturb such a secure fortress as this building on South Street? Bombproof, fireproof and shockproof. The stores have changed very little over the years. Van Heffer's Meat Market, Biggs' Grocery, Horowitz and Gilman's Stationery, (the alleyway), Old Harbor Bar and Grill, and a Modern IGA Market.

The firehouse whistle blew the noon hour. One long small town sigh. A few hearts trembled thinking that it might be an air raid warning but the fear soon subsided. Was there fear in the hearts of small Russian towns? Fear of those American missiles in Turkey? Those obsolete missiles in Turkey that were about to be replaced by Polaris submarines. So the world is being brought to the brink in order to make it perfectly clear that the United States can keep missiles on the border of Russia but the converse is unthinkable. The Big Walk Down. The Big Count Down. The build-up of arms, and the flexing of muscles.

A cloud was passing in front of the sun. South Street darkened. Stephen looked up to the sky, beyond Hodman's clocktower, from which little Rocky had jump off of over thirty years ago. Stephen wasn't stunned or surprised. He saw plenty of these things in the movies and on television. This one looked somewhat like the one in the movie, with the robot that never moves, and the soldiers and tanks surround it, and then everything stops, the cars and trains and machines all over the world. The movie he just saw at home. Something in Stephen stood still also. Something that doesn't run on fuel or electricity. It was more of an arrestation and epiphany; Stephen saw his world, his future. His imagination was enthralled. His first thought was: Why are the other rockets shaped differently from this one? The Mercury rocket, John Glenn's rocket was tall like a lighthouse, like the picture he drew in his kindergarten class, this one is flat and round, a flying saucer. Stephen was confronting the paradox of science and religion. However far science went, faith had to go one step farther. Adam named all the animals and man made the wheel. Ezekiel had his assembly line of prophets, Henry Ford his wheel of profits. And Stephen turns to his father and says, "Daddy, I just saw a spaceship."

The flying saucer, the UFO, whatever it was, lands in a small clearing in the woods behind the Mill Pond, not far from Council Rock, where Quakers once held outdoor meetings three hundred years ago. The Mill Pond is just up the road from the new elementary school, where, on the narrow lawn, a crowd has gathered for the dedication ceremonies. A cool breeze blows through the crowd, the ladies hold their hats on with one hand and hold their skirts down with the other hand. A thin old man in uniform who is seated on the platform removes his gray sombrero. The sun appears again as the lone cloud passes...

Stephen and his father are walking up West Main Street. From the other side of the street, Jimmy Pushin, standing high on the mound of an arched sidewalk, behind him on the hill the Baptist Church from which he has just departed having attended his bible study class, calls to Stephen, and hops over the fence, jumps down to the street, and runs over to meet Stephen.

"Com'ere. I gotta show you sumthin'," says Jimmy. And as Stephen's father walks on ahead, Jimmy opens a brown bag. Stephen looks inside. "Wow!" he says.

"I'm gonna need them when the war comes, with the Russians... firecrackers, lady fingers, cherry bombs, ashcans, M-80s, I'm gonna need them, my daddy said so," says Jimmy.

"Where'd ya get them," asks Stephen.

"My daddy got them for us. We can't use guns yet, so we will fight with these. Hey your father wants you, I'll see ya later, bye." and Jimmy runs down the street.

War, thinks Stephen, what war?

The hatch of the UFO opens... Alisapun and Geronimo step down from the space ship, no longer to be classified as a UFO because the space ship has been identified as No Rule II, descendant of the sea-faring ship No Rule I, which was the ship that Aliaspun commandeered from a fleet of

Spanish warships off the Spanish Main sometime in the late 17th century, the ship with the printing press in the hull and the single musket hanging on the wall, though in the year 1829 Aliaspun did obtain a cannon, a relic of the French Navy, purchased on the black market operating out of the Barbary State of Algiers; and in 1809 he replaced his old Gutenberg printing press, which also doubled as a wine press, with a new all metal press. Using his printing press Aliaspun continues to disseminate subversive anarchist leaflets from his space ship. It's just so much more thorough and efficient than a sea-faring ship. The No Rule I was scuttled off the coast of Cape Hatteras in the waters that are known as the Graveyard of the Atlantic. Just like an elephant burial ground, thought Aliaspun, and so sailed his ship there and let it die and its bones lie with the others. Several years ago, the No Rule II had been working in a mutual effort with the 30-foot ketch, Golden Rule, in attempting to stop test explosions of nuclear weapons. In protest of which the Golden Rule sailed toward the area around the Bikini and Eniwok atolls in the Marshall Islands in the Pacific where the U. S. intended to begin a series of nuclear bomb tests. The Golden Rule protest was non-violent, based on the spirit of Gandhian passive resistance and the creed of the Religious Society of Friends, the Quakers, that stated that God is in every man, the Holy Experiment of non-violence. The four-member crew of the Golden Rule was arrested by the Coast Guard in March 1958 and was detained. The government's report of its UFO sightings in the area at the time has not been declassified and remains Top Secret. The nuclear bomb tests proceeded as planned. The No Rule II has not been entirely innocent of violence but makes no claims in the matter either way. A recent success for the No Rule II was the sabotaging of several SAMOS satellites (SAMOS is an acronym for Satellite and Missile Observation System) that were developed and built by Lockheed Missiles and Space Company for the U.S. Air Force, to be used for military reconnaissance from space. The launchings took place in 1961. SAMOS I, II, and III all failed. At the time a spurt of UFO sightings were reported in the area, just the usual stuff, a few drunken red-neck fundamentalists crawling out of the backwoods to frighten the petunias out of god-fearing people and get a little publicity for Jesus, as if He needed anymore in God's land, I mean Paul and his minions are a hell of a PR team, and then say you all come down to Jim-Bob's general store and we'll shoot the breeze over a little evil brew that I'z done mixed up in my moon-shining distillery up in back behind the hogs, by the way, maybe one of you fellows can help me trim the hogs, taste mighty fine all fried up and finger-lickin' good... no thank you, says Aliaspun... Aliaspun's only concern is that one day the whole U.S.A. is gonna be filled with red-neck back wood's mentalities and then something might be done about the UFOs, and other types of "aliens," if it hasn't been done already, and Jim-Bob's General Store looks more like General Electric and General Motors everyday, but instead of shotguns we gots nuclear missiles.

The No Rule II was nearly shot down two years ago while flying over the Soviet Union. A few days later a U. S. U-2 aircraft was shot down at nearly the same coordinates. The U-2 pilot, Gary Powers, was captured and sentenced by the Soviet government to ten years in prison. He was exchanged for a Russian spy a year later. President Eisenhower called all this spy business a "distasteful but vital necessity." He blamed the Soviet Union for their "fetish of secrecy and concealment." The U-2 was soon replaced by the Midas I, a new line of military reconnaissance satellite. The No Rule II remains on alert.

Aliaspun and Geronimo smoked a cattail together, and then ate a cattail spiked with a certain ingredient, a type of cannabis paste, called majoun, that Aliaspun had picked up for 20 pesetas while wandering around the medina and casbah in Tangier last summer, when he also came in contact with several American expatriate writers, with whom he shared a kif pipe.

Aliaspun and Geronimo sat down in the tall grass, not far from the granite Council Rock, where Quakers and Anarchists are scheduled to meet later on in the day. A meeting of Quakers and Anarchists is not as unusual as it might appear at first. After all, as Aliaspun has written, even an anarchist must have manners. Aliaspun spread the majoun paste on the roasted cattail and offered it to Geronimo; he then poured a cup of Japanese green tea and placed it on the tatami mat before them. The ceremony commenced.

Geronimo is the one who was called Goyathlay, the One That Yawns, by his own people, who called themselves The Dineh, meaning The People, who were called Apache, meaning The Enemy, by other people.

Geronimo was a Chiricahua Apache who conducted guerrilla raids against Mexican and U.S. troops in the American Southwest. He was signaled out as the chief enemy of the U.S. authorities who, in their efforts to systematically consolidate if not exterminate all Apaches, called for the capture and hanging of Geronimo. The Apaches were not subdued until the 1880s. In 1885 Geronimo and 38 warriors, 8 boys among them, and 100 women and children, escaped into the Sierra Madres in Mexico. The U.S. government then breached a treaty whereby the Chiricahuas would be removed to confinement on a reservation in Florida for two years. Geronimo fled again, this time eluding 5,000 U.S. troops under the command of General Nelson A. Miles, who, with the help of a network of heliograph stations, tracked down Geronimo and his band of followers using Morse Code. That same summer Sitting Bull was touring with Buffalo Bills's Wild West Show.

In 1886 the warpath came to an end for Geronimo. The Chiricahua Apaches were transported to Florida, where Geronimo was imprisoned, and where many died from the humidity and consumption. The children were taken from their parents and sent to the Indian School in Carlisle, Pennsylvania. There they died, far from the place where Geronimo was born, the place the white people have named Arizona, whose people refused to accept the Chiricahuas back, into their land of birth. Geronimo was later imprisoned in Alabama; then in 1894 the Chiricahuas were removed to Oklahoma, where Geronimo became a rancher.

Last Aliaspun heard from him, Geronimo had joined the Dutch Reformed Church, was selling souvenirs at the Louisiana Purchase Exposition of the St. Louis' World Fair in 1904, and rode in a Locomobile touring car in Theodore Roosevelt's inaugural parade in 1905. If Aliaspun were going to recruit Geronimo to his ranks, it would require a lot of rehabilitation. So Aliaspun began by removing his clothes, his deerskin breechcloth and his moccasins. Geronimo, his hair cut short, was wearing a suit and tie and top hat. That wouldn't do. As the cattail began to take effect, Geronimo and Aliaspun entered the inner space of the New Frontier.

"Do you remember the old frontier, Geronimo? As far as I'm concerned the New Frontier can't be any worse than the old frontier."

There was a rustling of leaves and grass. Aliaspun walked down the path along the pond. He saw a naked man with his arms wrapped around the granite Council Rock, his buttocks flaring, his head was tightly bent back and his mouth open like a cuspidor of dripping saliva. Another man stood behind him and was also naked and like two crescent moons had joined together to make the coyote howl. Aliaspun returned to Geronimo, who by now had removed his clothes and was whirling around in the high grass tying baskets with his pounding feet to hold the spirit of the slaughtered flesh of the bison.

Aliaspun and Geronimo reentered the space ship, the No Rule II; inside it was completely dark. It was hot and beads of sweat soon formed on their dark skin. In the center of the circular chamber a pile of rocks was red with the heat of screaming birth. As Aliaspun and Geronimo heated themselves by the fire they were joined by other men until they were all wet and supple and prickly with expectation of a drama extreme and forbidding and ready to be played out in the desire-scorched sand that stuck to their bodies like the first flesh of the sacred mushroom, the very flesh of God. Aliaspun held the plant in his hand. It resembled a mushroom, but it was not a mushroom; it looked more like a carrot or a radish; in fact, it was a cactus. Captain Bethell examined the plant in the red light, but Aliaspun shook his head and said, *"Has comido el peyote?"* To which the Captain replied, *"Has comido carne de gente?"*

The plant has many names: teonanacatl, hikori, kamaba, ho, xicori, huatari, seni, wokowi, mescal beans, mescal buttons; as well as the Nuhuatl name peyote; and the white man's name Lophophora williamsii.

Aliaspun placed the peyote on a tray and passed it around. Take more, take more, take as much as you want. A circle of dancers broke loose and bodies were flung about, in the dim wine-red pall, falling from exhaustion, moaning and chanting, stabs of bloated penis in greased loins, crying and praying, mouths and tongues searching in the dark, standing and shaking, foreskin folded in a brown crevice, sitting and staring, hands directing dizzy flying hearts, and then the women came, came with sticks and ropes, slashing with corn stalks, filling cups with corn liquor, screaming and deriding, small and sinful, inadequate manhood, men chewing at the women's' breasts, beaten down, humiliated, and the dawn of colors a blast in the head, shattered rainbow, serpents falling from the sky, arrows piercing swaddling babies in the snow, claws ripping the walls, small rays of white light, cold streams of air, flutter of eagle wings, white bears, black cats, low clouds, and Captain Roger Bethell saw the burnt melted flesh hanging from the arms, and Aliaspun his hands wedged between a split oak, crushed and then eaten alive by bull mastiff dogs, and Sitting Bull crawling off to die on the hill, and Geronimo thrown from a helicopter over Vietnam and hearing an American soldier's voice laughing shout

GERONIMO!... and a young man has sharp sticks driven through his breast, and is hung over the fire with ropes tied sticks to pole, and he slowly dances backward, the rope tightens and pulls the nipples pointing forward, and he dances backward until the sticks are torn through his breast and blood spurts and runs down his body... and men beating themselves, ejaculate a milky arc of morning dew, and women rub the syrup on their breasts and the men lick it off and bite the nipple, the peyote button, and the women climb upon the men on all fours, beasts of burden... and he crawls to the light, and pushes against the small opening in the wall of the space ship, pushes, and the woman holds his feet, then reaching under his ass grabs his balls and yanks him back, his head breaks through the membrane, a sword about to fall, she pulls his penis back, his shoulders breaking through, his hips, his legs, her arm extending into the world, and he has come through, and the sword falls and severs her hand; he runs into the pond... and Christopher Columbus stands there with the bloody sword in his hand... Christopher Columbus standing on the edge of a new frontier, as we stand on the edge of a new frontier, the vines of Dante's Paradiso growing heavenward from the soil through his translucent skin and winding around his purple veins; yellow grass growing up like a cage around him to capture his murderous soul; the rocks melting beneath his feet to drag him hell bound... his hands reaching upward to the woman's breast, his mouth yearning for the nipple of the earth, the roaring, thundering waters of the Orinoco River about to engulf him, sailing downward into history, and Aliaspun Atale, on board the ship that sailed around the world, that took Magellan under South America and into the Pacific, returned to Spain with a message, Paradise unfound, Paradise an unfounded rumor, and Aliaspun Atale the words of which went Beep-beep, the sound of the voice of the modern world, the technology of the crowded space filled with corpses, spinning the universe out of the sun, moved by his words, moved the earth and the sun and the heavens, Copernicus and Galileo Galilei, the impetus of the divine, double-crossed on a cross of gold, monument of time and pain, in the beginning was the Beep Big Bang Beep, and the sun was excommunicated, harnessed to the horses of the apocalypse, the machine language, the Beep peeB, the recursive maelstrom, the swallowing and spewing of entropy, the juxtaposition of beep-beep, the translation of beep-beep on the island Columbus named San Salvador, the replication of DNA in the alphabetical terrain of his voice, he comes across the water, speaking his bones to flesh his flesh to spirit, he calls across the water, caught by a hook with a line leading to a neuron, to a terminal connection, to a pencil moving over the paper, he crawls across the sand, come forth, and have faith, in the beginning was the Beep-beep...

They have gathered in a circle around the tall straight tree. Aliaspun sitting, leaning on the Council Rock, his right leg bent back, his left leg turned upward and crossed over, the left foot resting on the right kneecap.

"I speak and you listen. O Christ-bearer. O glorious faith in God. O persistent one. O indomitable will. O master of the sea. O master of enslavement. O master of dispersion. O master of decimation. O master of genocide. In the Name of the Holy Trinity. In the Name of the Father, Son, and Holy Ghost. In the Name of Gold. In the Name of God. In the name of the Word. In the Name of Names. In the Name of Kings and Queens. In the name of Defense against Aggression. In the Name of Preventive Intervention. In the Name of Divine Intervention. In the Name of Preemptive Strikes. In the Name of Life, Liberty, and the Pursuit of Happiness... speaking language from the mouth, speaking violence from the hand, what did they say to him when he came ashore like a lion into the mouth of a language?"

Stephen is with his father, walking down West Main Street. How did this happen? Shall we make a map designating the course of all events and arrive at the place that we had set out to discover? Do we find it? No, not exactly. True places are not down on any map. We sight land. By the light of the moon. Then, at 2 am, on October 12, 1492, or thereabouts... we land. Aliaspun steps off the pages of one of Captain Bethell's sci-fi novels. Does that mean that time stood still? How did the town stand still? What caused the machines of life to cease and bark like dogs in the dusk of a small town going to sleep? We have landed... what sort of gold awaits us on the moon? In the New Frontier? He has found the Orient of Marco Polo. He dies believing it. Deluded to the end. I speak language. I am telling you this because I speak language. And language speaks Aliaspun. I know this because I have arrived at the place where the poets are silent, where they die believing it, but is this the place where we had set out to be? Where else can we be but where we are. Or can we be where we are not?"

Aliaspun completes his speech. To the Quakers and anarchists he introduces Captain Bethell, who is sitting next to him; Captain Bethell introduces Molly Light, a Quaker, who is sitting next to him; Molly Light introduces Geronimo, who is sitting next to her, Geronimo introduces... and so on...

In the middle of the circle is a tall straight tree. A fire is lit at the base of the tree. Wet clay is packed around the tree to control the flames. The green wood burns slowly. When the tree is ready to fall, Geronimo and others whack at it with stone axes. The branches are removed. The tree is hollowed out by the use of fire and axes. They craft a canoe. It holds up to 25 men. The canoe is set upon the Mill Pond and the men climb into the canoe. Other men run through the woods beating animal thighbones together. Frightened deer flee the woods and dash into the water, where the men in the canoe grab the deer around their necks and drag them onshore. After they have cooked and eaten the deer, a circle is formed around a man. A new fire is burning. Christopher Columbus has his arms held straight out by a rope tied to a branch above him in the tree. The sword comes slashing down and severs both his arms with one swing. The body falls to the earth. The eyes are extracted, scooped out by sharpened tortoise shells. The chest is slit down the middle, the heart, the lungs, the stomach, the liver, are removed. The ribs are then caked with clay. The body is set upon the water of the pond... and thousands of Arawak Indians enter the disemboweled torso, and are carried to the other side, to the land of the Fountain of Youth, where the body of Ponce de Leon is set upon the earth, and more of the people who are called The People climb aboard, and are carried to the river, leading to the Terrestrial Paradise, where the body of Hernando de Soto is set upon the Mississippi River, and more of the people who are called The People climb aboard, and are carried to the desert, to the Seven Cities of Gold, where the body of Francisco Vasquez de Coronado is set upon the sand, and more of the people who are called The People climb aboard, and are carried to the Word, of the Father, Son, and Holy Spirit, but the Word meant not life but death; so they are carried to the words of the Founding Fathers, We, The People, but the words meant death, not life, for all the people who are The People because a new People have arrived...

Frank Yamada and Augustine O'Deedless are swimming in the Mill Pond. The two men whom Aliaspun saw by the Council Rock. Augustine is Frank's new lover, a 20-year-old Irish redhead whom Frank met at the Shore House Bar. Frank, in his mid-fifties, has found his fountain of youth in Augustine, whom he has dubbed Saint Augustine, and together they pursue pleasure, a need refined in a most extravagant manner by Frank.

In the middle of the circle, Molly Light, the Quaker, held her newborn baby, just a few hours old. The men in the circle chanted: Kill! Kill! Kill!

Aliaspun stood and spoke: If you let it live a moment more you will have experienced the baby in time, in life... then it will be too late... remember the pain... remember that life is pain...

Aliaspun knows pain. He died experiencing pain. Aliaspun had been captured and tied to a tree. The tree had been split and Aliaspun's hands were wedged between the split tree and then the tree halves were snapped back, crushing his hands. Then mastiff dogs were set upon him, tearing him to pieces, eating him alive. All this was done for the security of the frontier. America's first defense against aggression.

And now Sitting Bull is leading two horses into the circle. "This horse is the only living creature to survive the victory at Little Big Horn, where the Long Hair stood like a sheath of corn with all the ears fallen around him. And the other horse is named Blackjack. America will know this horse that no warrior shall ride when America's warrior-and-chief shall fall. My warriors, my people, crawled away in the snow to die at Wounded Knee. America's warrior-and-chief shall die in Dallas and be taken away in a long black car, his woman crawling away. There is no eternal flame for my people in America's cemetery. That flame burns in the heart of my people. And the flame of history has been extinguished. From that day when the horses first stepped upon our land; until that day when the warrior-and-chief Theodore Roosevelt charged up San Juan Hill on horseback, I laugh to contemplate it, a circle had been formed and broken, and a new birth of empire, a fledgling empire, a Pax Americana, to our day when all the fires of hell have burnt the cities of the world, blinding light, unholy mushroom, the man-made missile-arrows arcing from bows held by and released by...? Shall I say Nature? Nature's Laws? History? Man? Shall I speak or shall I be silent? Am I telling you this because I speak language? Shall I ever arrive at the place that I set out for? Shall we journey together? And if the journey is all that there is, all that is the journey, shall we go on?

And now Captain Bethell, who speaks, is carrying a young child into the circle: And now on the eve of battle the warrior-and-chief performed a war dance. His troops gathered around him, and with his Big Stick in hand he jigged and hooted and bellowed and howled. And upon the echoing light he felt the glory of his race, *Supériorité des Anglo-Saxons*, as a French writer proclaimed at the time, and the warrior-and-chief romped and rollicked under Florida skies, encamped with his boys, his Rough Riders, oh aren't we going to have fun in Cuba, kick a little Spanish butt, good practice for the army and navy boys, good fun for the cowboys and Indians, hunters and prospectors, broncobusters and Ivy League lads, all the good trumps, yachtsmen and tennis players of the Knickerbocker Club and Somerset Club, all good men to camp out with, and the Colonel looked real smart in his uniform, ordered to fit from the expensive New York clothier Brooks Brothers, the world is my market, and in this world the nation that has trained itself to a career of unwarlike and isolated ease is bound to go down before other nations which have not lost the manly and adventurous qualities, and can anyone doubt that the result of this competition of the races will be the "survival of the fittest?" and thusly Darwin and science were invoked dogmatically by ideologues, a lethal injection, the world is my market, and the English and Americans would occupy all those uncivilized places immunized against the Rule of Law, democratic institutions and commerce... see this child whom I carry... (And Captain Bethell removes the blanket from the child and reveals the small body scarred with death) this child and many others were murdered, you might call it biological warfare, he and his people were infected with the disease, the pox, because they had been intentionally given infected blankets from a hospital where the English were dying, the same people who set the mastiff dogs upon the people of Aliaspun, disease, the mighty random ally of the conquistador Cortez, disease, death, syphilis and potatoes, slaves and corn, gold and silver, Sevillian merchants, Charles V, *Viva l'Espana!* Empire of a global economy, the world is my market, *mas y mas y mas y mas y mas y mas...* and then it came to an end, the full circle, from Columbus to the Spanish-American War... the manifest destiny of America, Monroe Doctrine, Ostend Manifesto, the Roosevelt Corollary, and in 1893, a celebration of Columbus, the World's Columbian Exposition in Chicago, the new Empire built upon the machine, modern industry, the first Ferris wheel, Machinery hall, wonderful American engineering feats, the first long-distance calls to New York and Boston, Edison's Kinetoscope, a peep-show device on celluloid, the electric dynamo, Westinghouse's alternating-current generator, a 125-ton steam hammer, the Palace of Electricity, the glories of the American economy, the White City, the world is my market, more and more and more and more and more and more and more... then the following year, pro-American interests with the help of the U.S. Navy and a contingent of marines, staged a coup in Hawaii which overthrew the nationalist Queen Liliuokalani; leading to the annexation of the islands in 1898, thus a naval and commercial base was realized, a desired goal of policymakers since the 1860s. The course was charted. But unlike Columbus, America was well aware of its manifest destination every step of the way...

The White Hunter in the White City, went on safari in Africa, Roosevelt with his nine extra pairs of eyeglasses, took aim at the same time as three other hunters, just to make sure, and the conservationist president proceeded to shoot five elephants, nine lions, seven hippopotamus', thirteen rhinoceroses, and sundry other game, accounting for almost three-hundred trophies.

On the eve of the battle the warrior-and-chief danced for his troops, on the sands of Florida, by the light of the moon reflecting in the thick telescopic glass of his pince-nez, yes we shall go to the moon and beyond, but first Cuba, Roosevelt's dream of glory and history: We know not whither we are bound, nor what we are to do; but we believe that the nearing future holds for us many chances of death and hardship, of honor and renown. If we fail, we shall share the fate of all who fail; but we are sure that we will win, that we will score the first great triumph of a mighty world-movement.

Sitting Bull speaks: O Molly Light, Quaker woman, do not kill your baby. I will slit the throats of the horses. Let them die. Let the baby live.

Captain Bethell carries the baby in his arms, wrapped in a blanket...

Captain Bethell places the baby on the bamboo raft in the river Otagawa...

Joe Cazzaza and his son Stephen meet Uncle Frankie and his wife, Mary, at the dedication ceremony. Rocky comes up and greets them. Rocky says, "How's your mama doing? Is she doing all right?"

"She's fine," says Joe and Frankie.

Stephen sees an old man in a gray uniform. The old man is standing on the platform that has been erected for the ceremonies. He is wearing a sombrero and carrying a sword. He is none other than the legendary Winthrop Overkill, former Rough Rider. For an introduction to the life and times of Winthrop Overkill, let's first refer to an entry in J. M.

Maxburg's *Encyclopedia of American Military History and Literature,* in 45 volumes, 36th Edition (1990), which contains thousands of concise but comprehensive biographies, and covers the complete canon of American literature dealing with the vast topic of war.

Document 9-786

Here is the entry:

Winthrop Scott Nichols Mason Overkill (1870-1962), historian, editor, essayist, memoirist, biographer, novelist, journalist, adventurer.

Out of Harvard in 1892, he traveled widely, being financially independent (his father was a banker millionaire who built the Overkill Estate, completed in 1890, a 75-room mansion at Glen Cove, New York, which, in 1963, became, ironically, the headquarters and residence for members of the diplomatic corps of the Soviet Union).

One of Overkill's early adventures found him in the North African city of Marrakesh, where he was arrested for raising a riot against him for an "indiscretion" that he committed, the nature of which has never been disclosed by Overkill; he forthwith protested his apprehension to the local authorities and threatened the local government, such as it was, to the effect that the American government would not stand to see one of its citizens treated harshly and would at all costs protect him and any other American citizen abroad with utmost force if need be. To the Sultan, Overkill declared, "Sir, it's me alive or you dead!" Overkill was a good friend and fanatical admirer of Theodore Roosevelt, at the time Governor of New York, and had friends in high places, though he himself held no official position in the government. Nevertheless, he proclaimed to the ruling Sultan that the American government would hold any foreign power that caused harm to him or any other of its citizens to "strict accountability."

The Sultan of the North African nation apologized profusely, even offering to decapitate those responsible for the inconvenience and discomfort caused by this misunderstanding, but Overkill suggested that that wouldn't be necessary and declined the offer with Christian charity and an American sense of justice, and Overkill was released. Such was the estimate of American power in those heady days following the Spanish-American War. Overkill told the story to Roosevelt after he returned home and Roosevelt later used Overkill's strenuous phrase in a similar situation when he was president. In that context an American had been kidnapped in Morocco, his name was Perdicaris, and his abductor's name was Raisuli. The president said, "Perdicaris alive or Raisuli dead!" Roosevelt included this quote in a message that he delivered to the Republican convention when he nominated himself for president.

After private conversations that Overkill had had with Roosevelt at the president's home at Sagamore Hill, Overkill formed a band of twenty-four fellow Freedom Fighters and made a secret and unsuccessful raid on the shores of Cuba in 1897, with the intention of liberating Cuba from Spanish repression. The following year he volunteered to serve with Roosevelt's Rough Riders in the Spanish-American War, and during the First World War he was appointed to General Pershing's staff. He covered many of the so-called "Banana Wars" as a journalist for the *New York World* and later the New York Sun. His military historical writings include *The Glorious Taking of San Juan Hill: An Account of the Spanish-American War* (1902*); In The Name of Civilization: The Philippine and Moro Campaigns* (1913); *Bombing the Bananas and Blasting the Bamboo in the Boondocks: Interventions in Nicaragua,* 1912, 1927-1932 (1935); *Hotter than Hell: Nicaragua* 1912 (1913); *An Affair of Honor, Mexico 1914* (1915); *The Big Stick in Defense of Freedom: Accounts of Interventions in Santo Domingo* 1904, 1916-1918 (1920); *Blood Crazy: Haiti* 1915, 1919-1920 (1922); *The Big Stick in Defense of Freedom, Vol. 2, Guatemala* 1954 (1955); *The Big Stick in Defense Of Freedom: The Collected Writings of Winthrop Overkill* (1960); *Indochina: Let Freedom Ring!* (1961); *Cuba under Red Castro* (1962); *The Walk Down: Democracy Versus Communism: Selected Writings* (1965); Overkill has also written biographies of Admiral Dewey, General John J. Pershing, General George S. Patton, and Senator Joseph McCarthy. His portrait of Roosevelt is titled *TR: My Bully Buddy* (1920); and his letters are collected in a 5-volume edition, *Letters of Winthrop Overkill 1897-1962* (1965). For a time Overkill was editor of the magazine he started in 1919, *Run Red Run, See Red Run,* dedicated to fighting the spread of Bolshevism everywhere in the world; at first the magazine advocated preparedness and supported Billy Mitchell and air power, and later the development of atomic weapons and nuclear missile systems. In 1973 it was disclosed that the Pentagon, C.I.A., F.B.I., and State Department had subsidized the magazine. The magazine was bought and incorporated into *The People's Digest* in 1975.

End of entry.

When Joe Cazzaza and Stephen arrived at Theodore Roosevelt Elementary School, the dedication ceremony was just getting underway. Programs were being handed out. Joe Cazzaza took a program and looked at it. On the cover, in the center, was the architect's sketch of the new school. Three sections of brick structures: on the left the Gymnasium, in the center the main offices, on the right two floors of classrooms, connected by passageways; it still wasn't big enough for the glut of baby boomers and in a few years an annex had to be added on. Behind the school a playing field, and beyond the field Theodore Roosevelt Park and Oyster Bay Harbor, all prettily sketched. Inside the program, on the left hand page, a portrait of Roosevelt; on the right, listings of the events and speakers for the day, and on the back page the names of members of the Board of Education, the Superintendent of Schools, and the architects. The ceremonies began with the playing of the National Anthem, played by the Oyster Bay High School Marching Band. Everyone rose from his or her gray folding chairs. The dignitaries were standing on the platform, from left to right, Father Don of St. Dominic's R. C. Church; Rev. Stephen of St. Paul's Methodist Church; Rev. Townsend of Christ Episcopal Church; Mr. Medicio and Mr. Levy, members of the Board of Education; Mr. Weeks, President of the Board of Education; Dr. Howard W. Irving, Superintendent of Schools; Hon. John Stephen Burnsides, Supervisor, Town of Oyster Bay; and the honored guests, Ethel Derby Roosevelt, daughter of Theodore Roosevelt; and seated next to her, dressed in his original Rough Rider's uniform, with medals and sword, ninety-two-year-old Winthrop Scott Nichols Mason Overkill, historian, editor, essayist, memoirist, biographer, novelist, journalist, adventurer.

To the surprise of many, Winthrop Overkill was saluting the flag in what seemed to be the Nazi salute, except for the fact that his palm was turned up instead of face down. His lips quivered as he sang... the bombs bursting in air... his mind lost in time had tricked him back to the turn of the century. The flag, the sacred icon, waved as it ascended to the big brass ball atop the flagpole. None other than Rocky was pulling the rope down as the flag went up. Standing across the street and watching, was Emile Baldazzi, thinking to himself: What a lot of crap. Emile probably knew more about American history than any one of the assembled crowd, Winthrop Overkill included. Emile knew that all this flag business was a patriotic ruse perpetrated by some of the dumb broads in the Daughters of the American Revolution, who were so in fear of the hordes of immigrants coming to these shores that they expediently formed a "natural" alliance forever with Britain, one blood, one tongue, one purpose, in order to set in cement the background of the Founding Fathers and to make certain that the foreign blood would pledge absolute loyalty and allegiance to America as enshrined in the sacred icon of a flag. Though in fact, as Emile was thinking, their forefathers were too busy fighting for their new nation to worry all that much about so slight a gesture as saluting a flag. But during the Spanish-American War, in 1898, the people were instructed to salute their flag with arm extended and palm raised, and so there we see Winthrop, saluting such like, while all about him every man, woman and child held hand over heart. Suddenly Winthrop remembered where and "when" he was, and saluted the flag. The hand over heart salute wasn't adopted officially until World War II, when the extended arm salute was dropped for obvious reasons... oh say does that star-spangled ba-a-an-ner ye-et waa-ave. Rocky pulls the rope and all eyes and hearts are lifted... (Emile knows that schools weren't even required to fly the flag until 1890) the flag has reached the top... Father Don leads the people in the pledge... I pledge allegiance to the flag of the United States of America... (Emile knows that the pledge of allegiance wasn't adopted until 1892) under God, with liberty and justice for all... everyone on the platform takes it for granted that the flag and the Constitution were conterminous expressions of the Founding Fathers... and Father Don speaks the invocation... "Dear God, protect our Christian nation from evil empires and give her strength in this difficult time... (And Emile knows that the word Christianity does not appear in the Constitution, and that the Declaration of Independence speaks only of "Nature's God")... "Amen... you may be seated" says Father Don and then Mr. Medicio of the Board of Education steps up to the microphone and says "welcome." After a few political and commerce related words he sits down as Mr. Levy steps up and speaks a bit more on commercial enterprises in the community. Mr. Medicio ran for the Senate as a Republican candidate several times during the sixties and seventies; he was defeated each time. The highlight of his career was realized when he was selected to be one of the escorts for his political hero, Richard M. Nixon, when Nixon visited TR's home at Sagamore Hill. This was after Watergate. Mr. Medicio was killed in 1985 on a fact-finding mission to Indochina, in search of missing POWs. He was blown up by a bit of old unexploded ordnance, property of the U.S.A., along the Ho Chi Minh Trail on the Laotian border. The metal from the ordnance was then sent to Japan where it was reused in the manufacturing of Toyota cars that were exported to the United States. One of which cars was involved in an accident in Manhattan in 1987 in which the said Toyota rammed into a limousine whose passenger list included none other than former Secretary of State Henry Kissinger and ex-president Richard Nixon. Dr. Kissinger and Mr. Nixon sustained only minor abrasions, but the chauffeur of the car, who was uninjured, reported hearing, and I quote, "The metal from the Toyota car, that rammed into our window, I swear I heard it screaming and it looked like flesh being ripped open, it was like I heard women and children's voices crying and screaming... I still have nightmares..." When questioned about the remarks made by the chauffeur, Dr. Kissinger responded by saying, "Vi hurd nooo such scleaming." The chauffeur continues to undergo psychiatric treatment at Bellevue Hospital.

And so the Oyster Bay High School Marching Band breaks into its rendition of the Sagamore Hill March. Toes are tapping and hearts are racing. The band conductor stabs his baton in an upward curl and a final resounding Ba-Boom and then applause. At the microphone we see the Hon. John Paul Burnsides, Supervisor, Town of Oyster Bay, a retired Lieutenant Commander in the U. S. Navy. A veteran of World War II, he was aboard the U.S. Lexington during the battle of Coral Sea, when carrier-based aircraft shot down 43 Japanese planes in the determining battle. Thirty-three American planes were lost. The American fleet under Admiral Fletcher had found unexpected support from bad weather that hid the carriers from Japanese bombers. In the end the slight margin of victory was soured because of the heavy damage that the Lexington had undergone from torpedo and bomb strikes. The Lexington was scuttled only hours after the battle's end.

The Hon. John Stephen Burnsides gingerly taps the microphone and clears his throat. He stands tall; looks left and then right, looks down at the prepared speech on the lectern, looks up, looks up at the flag flying and smiles a gritty clenched smile.

"I have been asked to say a few words about Theodore Roosevelt and the legacy of the man as it relates to this village. Certainly the legacy is great. But even greater is the legacy that President Roosevelt left to the entire nation, the aggregate of all the little villages just like this one, containing smiling school children, proud and true, the future of our great country. So let me speak not only of this village but also of the nation as it relates to the legacy of the man who made his home here. I want to speak of the nation as a whole because we are now in the midst of a grave crisis, a crisis that strikes at the heart of freedom, at the heart of our nation. That crisis is the dagger, the communist dagger that points at the heart of each and every one of us, and at our nation, from just a stone's throw away from our proud free shores. If President Roosevelt were alive today, his most urgent concern would be over the terrible crisis that at this moment is taking place. And it is at this most important hour in our nation's history, while our great naval fleet is arrayed like a laurel of freedom around the communist bastion of dictator Castro's Cuba, that we cannot overlook the great debt that we owe to Theodore Roosevelt, who above all others sounded the reawakening alarm of freedom and defense of that freedom in the nation's unprepared heart. For it was Roosevelt who said, 'Build! Build! Build! Build a strong and efficient navy, a great sea power'.

"TR was very fond of this his beloved little village. If he were alive today I think that he would still be proud of the boys and girls of this village. He would be proud that we are building two new schools where boys and girls can learn about our history, about nature, about our nation's resources, the forests and land that Theodore Roosevelt loved so well and helped to preserve for posterity, helped to preserve for you, the children of America. In this new school you will learn of the basic building blocks that make up strong minds and bodies, the virtues of our American character, the glories of our War of Independence, the great Civil War, all the great battles in defense of freedom, freedom for all. And we must never forget the words of George Washington in his farewell address to the people of the United Sates on September 17, 1796, when he said, 'Of all the dispositions and habits, which lead to political prosperity, Religion and Morality are indispensable supports....' In Oyster Bay there are many fine churches, and each of these churches has Sunday school classes, and I'm sure that you are good children and will attend Sunday school regularly as you attend this new school regularly. And then you will grow up to be strong moral adults, good American citizens, for we must all do our duty to God and our country. In this regard I have discovered a speech that President Roosevelt gave at Arlington Cemetery in our nation's capitol, Washington D.C., it was delivered at the unveiling of the Soldiers' and

Sailors' Monument at Arlington, erected by the National Society of Colonial Dames, to honor the memory of the men who fell in the great war with Spain in 1898. Theodore Roosevelt wrote, 'What we need most in this Republic is not special genius, not unusual brilliancy, but the honest and upright adherence on the part of the mass of the citizens and of their representatives to the fundamental laws of private and public morality....' Oh how true, children, oh how true.

"And now a little history lesson. President McKinley appointed Theodore Roosevelt Assistant Secretary of the Navy in 1897. TR had always taken a delight and keen interest in the navy. His first book was *The History of the Naval War of 1812*. Still considered the essential work. Roosevelt wrote the book when the navy had hit bottom. In his autobiography Roosevelt writes candidly about the total incompetence of the American navy at the time, the 1880s this would be, to fight a naval war with any of the other major sea powers, especially Spain, at a time when there was much war talk about liberating the Cuban people from the horrors and degradations of Spanish oppression, but little action. The duty of liberating the Cuban people from the clutches of another more sinister power, communism, may be our duty once again, a duty that we cannot shirk. It is the American duty, to keep freedom alive in the world.

"Roosevelt, in his autobiography, recalls the fuss that was made over the efforts to gain a strong navy. He cites the books of Admiral Mahan as a determining factor, playing a large part in facilitating the gradual change. Alfred Thayer Mahan was a naval historian and a naval officer. He published his book, *The Influence of Sea Power upon History, 1660-1783* in 1890, this book greatly influenced Theodore Roosevelt. Mahan claimed that a nation could only achieve greatness if that nation has a strong navy that can control the seas. And so with the help of Roosevelt we started building the great battleships of our great fleet. With our battleships we could engage the enemy on the open seas. There would be no more concentration on coastal defense and raids on commercial shipping. There would be expansion. There would be empire over the dominion of Neptune. And even today, when the aircraft carrier has replaced the battleship, Admiral Mahan's thinking speaks to us across the years; we still employ many of his strategic ideas.

"First we built cruisers, because battleships were believed to be wicked by many in Congress who were influenced by men with the "money touch," and cruisers would be enough to protect our commerce, but Roosevelt knew that cruisers were nothing without a battleship to back them up. Then we built more powerful fighting ships, but still we did not call them battleships because that was somehow suggestive of violence. Roosevelt thought that all this name playing was silly. The new ships were called armored cruisers. Finally we built some battleships. But we called them 'coast-defense battleships.' Then we called them 'sea-going coast defense battleships.' Today we know better. Today we know that our nation has a duty far beyond our coast. And it was Theodore Roosevelt above all others who first taught us that we had this duty, which brought with it the peace of righteousness. We are right. Let there be not mistake about it.

"The evolution of naval vessels and naval war has developed steadily since the late 16th century when the manly might of oars gave way to the finesse and force of the sail. Then in the 19th century with the advent of the industrial age, we see the power of steam and iron and steel, followed in the 20th century by aviation, guided and ballistic missiles, submarines, and nuclear propulsion. In 480 B.C., during the Greek-Persian War, the Battle of Salamis was fought in the Mediterranean; from that time until 1571 A.D., when Spain and Christian forces defeated the pagan Turks in the Battle of Lepanto, the major naval engagements were fought in the Mediterranean, fought in galleys propelled by men with oars. The Mediterranean, that beautiful and bloody sea... but a change occurred in the early 16th century when England's Henry VIII had powerful cannon placed aboard his warships. The big guns became the standard bearers of naval warfare. It was the time of the great classic sea battles, Trafalgar in 1805, when the British destroyed the French and Spanish fleets, to the great victory of the *U. S. S. Constitution*, with its 44-guns blazing, over the British *Guerriere* during the War of 1812. Which brings us back to Theodore Roosevelt's first book, *The History of the Naval War of 1812*. Let us recall the now famous words of one of our great naval heroes of that war, John Paul Jones, during the great victory in battle, of his ship, *Bonhomme Richard*, over the British vessel, *Sarapis*. When asked if he'd surrender, John Paul Jones bravely replied, 'I have not yet begun to fight!'

"Though great sea battles have been fought in all the seas and all the oceans of the world, let us return to where it all began, the Mediterranean, but not to the 5th century, let us return to the 19th century, and the

Tripolitan Wars. For over three hundred years Barbary corsairs, pirates, were the scourges of the Mediterranean, inflicting harm on commerce and taking Christians as slaves. These ruthless pagans attacked English and French ships and even American ships. The English and French shamelessly paid tribute to the pirates. But at the close of the War of 1812, American naval vessels under the command of Commodore Stephen Decatur attacked many of these marauders at their own ports, destroying their warships and insisting upon submission from the leaders of the pagan countries of Tunis, Algiers, and Tripoli, thus ending the barbaric raids on American commerce. In a biography of Stephen Decatur published in the 1930s, we are told that at a dinner party held in honor of the great naval officer, certain toasts were made, one of which goes, 'The Mediterranean! The sea not more of Greek and Roman than American glory!' And there you have it. Another toast was made by Decatur himself, the most famous toast ever made. He said, 'My country, may she always be successful, right or wrong.'

"Theodore Roosevelt would have entirely concurred. My country, right or wrong. But let there be no mistake. We are right. If there is a battle off the coast of Cuba, if there is war with the Russian Empire, let there be no mistake about it, America is defending freedom. We are right because we are virtuous and righteous; we hold in our hearts that beautiful expression of Theodore Roosevelt, the Peace of Righteousness, and we know it to be true. Thank you my fellow Americans."

The crowd stood and applauded. John Paul Burnsides returned to his chair on the podium.

The group applause abated and terminated in the singular sturdy clapping of Mrs. Frederic Major Laidlaw Down, illustrious member of the National Society, Daughters of the American Revolution, who has ascended the podium, the demiurge of democracy, the spinner at the wheel of homestead and hearth and country, a gray and wrinkled apparition of an elementary school teacher, prudish pursed lips, haughty demeanor, horn-rim eyeglasses resting on the point of her nose, with looping beads affixing them and dangling round her neck and ears, she is stooped as if to write upon a blackboard, lessons in good citizenship and patriotism, her left arm securely placed behind her back, covertly holding a thunderbolt of judgment, gazing out from under her flower-festooned hat, her right hand demurely touching her chin and fingering her pearl necklace; she addresses the assemblage of students and parents... "Greetings..." and continues to speak in greeting card idioms about the hallmarks of American freedom... "Greetings and a heartily welcome to you, my fellow loyal and law-abiding American citizens..." speaking as if she were addressing a new flock of immigrants, of hyphenated Americans, as if it were necessary to make a clear distinction of the distance between her and Them, a distance of time and ancestry, for she knew that many of the crowd were hyphenated-Americans, town-dwellers, not estate-dwellers, Italian, Polish, Irish, German, Jewish, African, Norwegian, Swedish... "So when the Flag passes by one does it honor by standing at attention or saluting..." thirteen stars white on a field of blue, representing a constellation, red and white separating mother country from son of liberty, white stars and blue heaven, a union indivisible, one nation, but most of Them were born here, indoctrinated, insulated, vaccinated, under God, fought in wars, faces in the crowd forming a constellation to be approved of by Mrs. Frederic Major Laidlaw Down, still suspicious of Them and their intentions, motives, pursuits, a constellation that has added space and states, configurations of stars dipping over the continent's edge, in myth and symbol and blood, like a neuron belt firing, weighed down by sheer number and exhaustion of resources, not race suicide, but a nova suicide, a shooting star in a net of minds, connecting happiness and doom... "Above the public school flies the Flag of the United States of America. The best system of free education to be had in the world, under its protection... use it... it belongs to you and your children..." as Mrs. Frederic Major Laidlaw Down nasally whines to a fervent pitch.

The two brothers, Joe and Frankie, are standing in the rear of the crowd, aloof, too slavishly humble to sit down, letting the ladies and their community involved assertive husbands sit down; Joe and Frankie were nevertheless greeted felicitously and replied solicitously to inquiries made pertaining to their and their mother's and family's well-being by a number of the town's minor luminaries, proprietors of local businesses, the funeral director, liquor store owner, grocer, postman, and old school chums. Rocky, who was no more than five feet tall, with the black hair protruding from his nostrils and ears, the dark rings around his gentle eyes, the black teeth, the stubby gray hairs on his unshaven face, a low husky voice, unsure, stumbling, inarticulate, hesitant, grasping, faltering, anxious, humble, too humble to speak or sit down, stood next to Joe a foot taller and Frankie a half foot taller than he and all three mumbled, doodled humming and whistled nervously, their eyes reluctant to meet and fix upon the eyes of any one of the town's prominent desirable citizens and well-heeled denizens, avoiding conversations that may tax their vocabulary, their knowledge beyond the rudiments of civility, their peasant mentality in the stratified caste system of small-town capitalism, their streak of yellow down their backs, their nice walk-all-over-me image, and Rocky puts his hand on Stephen's shoulder and asks, "How's your grandma doing?" It was always the same question that he asked. And Stephen didn't answer but turned away shyly and clung to his father's pants. Rocky then directed the question to Joe and Frankie. "How's your mother doing?" They answered, "She's fine."

Joe, Frankie and his wife, Mary, hands folded humbly in front of them; the brothers huddling together and awkwardly bumping into each other, oops, ha ha, each at a loss for words, and Stephen starts complaining that he wants to go home, pulling at his father's pants... stop that will ya... and Joe signals surreptitiously to Frankie with eye and hand movements that it's time for a quick one, just a shot and beer and we'll be out, lickety-split, but Mary, Frankie's wife, has caught on to the treachery, and in a deep-Dooley Irish brogue, "Oh no you don't, we're going straight home we are," and Frankie chuckles it off, "And not a one," says Mary, but nonetheless they are saying goodbye to Rocky and leaving the ceremonies and walking up West Main Street, en route to the Old Harbor Bar and Grill, right under the rooms where Fiorenza, Luisa, and Stevie are sitting at the windows; and coming up the street, Joe asks about Augustine, "Oh he's fine," says Mary, "he's off to the city for the weekend as usual." Augustine is Mary's nephew; he's the son of her brother, Sean O'Deedless, who was killed in London in the summer of 1944 by a German V-1 rocket buzzing over and greeting Sean as he was coming out of the underground station at Archway, on his way to work, wearing his tweed jacket with elbow patches, to clean up the streets of debris. Augustine was raised by his mother, who died in 1959, and a year later Augustine came to America to stay with his Aunt Mary. Mary and her brother Jim had come from Tipperary in 1930, it's a long way from Tipperary to Florida, where she came first and worked as a maid for a family in Miami, where on occasion she had a glimpse of the gangster Al Capone; later the family moved to Center Island and took Mary with them. At the time, Frankie Cazzaza, when he was not gambling or bartending or taking bets as a bookie, was working part-time as a deliveryman for Van Heffer's Meat Market, bringing the goods around to some of the rich people. His cousin Anthony Bacigalupo, who died ten years earlier than when Frankie met Mary, had had the misfortune to deliver the goods to the Widdlesworth mansion one winter day in 1920, a series of back-door assignations followed, which culminated in the issuing of a baby boy named Charles, who, as we have seen, was taken to Paris by his grandmother. There are not many Widdlesworths left, the much dreaded Anglo-Saxon race suicide bringing the family to its demise, with the help of a little southern European peasant blood, and some Nazi cohabitation, but no misfortune would await Frankie and Mary, like the peasant marriage of a potato and sugar beet, there would be no thoughts of race suicide, now in America, land of opportunity. They were married in 1938, and a son, an only child, Edward, was born in 1941.

Augustine and Frank Yamada are getting into the car, leaving the Mill Pond, where Brent Widdlesworth drowned in 1938, with Frank in the car with him, but Frank escaped through the window, and now Augustine is driving, speeding, like Frank and Brent used to do, speeding around the dangerous curves of the Shore Road, passing the very place where Anthony Bacigalupo crashed into the bay in his Van Heffer's delivery truck, carrying meat to the rich, and now Frank and Augustine speeding, speeding like a missile...

Joe and Frankie, halfway through the alleyway, enter the side door to the bar, and stand, do not sit on the stools, drinking a beer and whiskey chaser, while Mary and Stephen continue passing through the alleyway until they come into the backyard, and climb up the cement stairs that lead up to Fiorenza's house; they are greeted at the door by Luisa who had seen them coming from the front window and had descended the many wooden steps, carefully holding to the railing with her one good hand, limping downward, moaning each step of the way, to unlock the door and let them inside the dark and peasant monastic sanctuary, private and secretive, strangely Italian, strangely American, but somehow neither.

Meanwhile, back at the dedication ceremonies, Mrs. Frederic Major Laidlaw Down is still delivering her standard birth of freedom speech: "...freedom is a very old idea. It all began in the forests of northern Europe where a people called Teutons lived. A free and independent people. They had elections and voted for chiefs by voice. They had respect for women and homes. Some of these tribes were called Angles and Saxons..." Emile Baldazzi is coughing and crossing the street at the traffic light in front of the new school. He sits down on the lawn behind the last row of folding chairs. Not far from him, in the center of a triangular green where the flag pole stands, is a spruce tree sapling, prepared to glorify the event, wrapped in the ball of a burlap bag and three shovels are positioned around it, stuck in the earth.

Emile coughed and cleared his throat with exaggeration, interjecting a visceral commentary of disgust, peppering the speech of Mrs. Laidlaw Down with unseasonable spices from the new world, new frontier, new whatever, but trouper that she was, she persevered; she had the platform, she had the support of the crowd, so she vigorously cleared her throat and raised her voice to a higher level of ruling class audibility: "It was from the discovery made by Columbus that the country later called America, was settled... most of the colonists came from England..." Ahem went Emile, clearing his throat... AHEM went Mrs. Laidlaw Down... "The English made their first permanent settlement at Jamestown, Virginia, in 1607... they sailed in three little ships called the *Sarah Constant*, the *Goodspeed*, and the *Discovery*... the ships carried one hundred and five settlers under the leadership of Captain Stephen Newport..." ahem went Emile... AHEM went Mrs. Laidlaw Down, with the aid of the public address system. "Later the settlers were commanded by the brave and famous Captain John Smith... no one lived in that country but savage Indians and wild beasts..." ahem went Emile Baldazzi rising to his feet... "AHEM and it was evening and the settlers cut down a tree from a grove of trees for an altar..." ahem went Emile picking up the small bundled spruce tree... "AHEM and they held a religious service..." ahem went Emile carrying the burlap bag with the small tree swinging about... "AHEM and thus began the first permanent English settlement in America with the formation of a government and a religious service..." Ahem went Emile walking down the aisle toward the platform carrying the spruce tree... "AHEM Americans abhor the kind of revolution which destroys and overturns, which murders, loots, and burns..."

A policeman and several other men were converging on the scene. Emile reached the platform, standing disheveled just below the podium where Mrs. Laidlaw Down was standing, a dismayed and disgruntled look on her face, what to do? Emile drops the tree in the grass, looks her in the eye... but then a light breaks from a dark passing cloud, reflecting from a silver metallic object in the sky... what? The missiles? Could it be at last? The end? Everyone freezes... a broad parabolic light shoots down in a cylindrical cone, shimmering with a visionary gleam from the object in the sky, the spaceship *No Rule II*... everyone in the crowd is frozen, unable to move, literally, except for Emile Baldazzi, who walks back up the aisle and the light suddenly lifts while another stream of light shoots down next to Emile... and then that light lifts like a concentrated fog being sucked upward into a vacuum... and "AHEM this is the meaning of the American Revolution," says Mrs. Laidlaw Down, "Thank you..."

The crowd applauds, unaware that anything has happened, that a moment of time had stopped. Rocky is standing behind his friend Emile. "C"mon, let's go," says Rocky. "Wait a minute, what's this?" There is a package next to Emile. The words DO NOT OPEN UNTIL YOU ARE READY 1893 are scribble across the top. Emile picks up the package and he and Rocky walk up the street.

"One more thing," said Mrs. Laidlaw Down, with an apologetic smug smile on her face, "I just want to read a few announcements. John Gipp, Commander of Quentin Roosevelt American Legion Post No. 4, wants to say that the next scrap and paper drive will be held next Sunday, November 4th, beginning at 9:00 a.m. All local residents and businessmen are requested to place all sale-able material including paper, rags and metal at the curb in time for collection. Also, Edward W. Thatcher, president of the Oyster Bay Republican Club, announces that the November meeting will be held in the Quentin Roosevelt American Legion Hall on Monday evening, November 19th, at 8:30 o'clock. Also, if I may beg your indulgence a moment more, Lester H. Weeks, president, Board of Education, Union Free School District No. 9, announces that a special meeting of the Board will be held on Tuesday evening, November 20th, at 7:30 p.m. Just a few more, bear with me, selections from "Tocqueville" and "Democracy in America" will be the topics under discussion at the November 22nd meeting of the Great Books Group to be held in the public library, Thursday evening at 8:00 o'clock. And last but not least, William G. Blake, president of the Oyster Bay Square Club No. 704, announces that the next regular meeting will be held at Matinecock Masonic Temple on West Main Street, Friday evening, November 23th, at 8:00 o'clock. Marvin Platt, a science teacher at Oyster Bay High School, will be the guest speaker and discuss "Magic in Science." He is presently associated with the Atomic Energy Commission. One further announcement that was just handed me. The annual Theodore Roosevelt Pilgrimage will be held at the Temple on November 25th at 2:00 p.m. That's it. Thank you once again. I would now like to introduce the first of our two special guests; she was the guiding force in the efforts that were made to preserve Sagamore Hill as an historic site. I give to you, the daughter of President Theodore Roosevelt, Ethel Roosevelt Derby. "Thank you. Thank you. You know that there is a quote of my father's that is my favorite of all. He said, 'In the long fight for righteousness, the watchword for all of us is spend and be spent.'"

Joe says "Good health to ya," and Frankie says "Yep," and they both down their third whiskey chasers. Ever since they gave up the bar in Northport, Joe has worked weekends off and on as a bartender in this bar at the times he's been in-between regular work, but now with the school job all lined up he seems to be set for a good many years to come. He never did like bartending. Frankie's been at it since he was sixteen and worked in the speakeasy at the top of the stairs in the old building next door, which, by the way, isn't there anymore; the building that is, not the speakeasy, the speakeasy was transformed into this very bar, the speakeasy owner Adolf Hoffman went legit and started the business the year prohibition was repealed. The old Cazzaza Fruit and Vegetable Store went out of business, what with Giuseppe dead, Leonora dead, Teresa in the nuthouse, having burned most of the cash that was kept in her care, and Frankie not interested in taking over the business, it went to the dogs. So the store was partitioned and Adolf Hoffman set up the Old Harbor Bar and Grill, the name never changing but the ownership changing hands several times. Adolf Hoffman sold the business to Adolf Brenner who sold the business to Adolf Steiner who sold the business to Adolf Spies... all Adolfs, all Germans, funny thing huh? Then in 1960 the old "Hoffman Building" next door was demolished and in its place a huge concrete block Food Town supermarket had arisen from the dust and rubble, blocking the windows in the south side of the Cazzaza building, but the family didn't protest, they still had the windows in the front rooms overlooking South Street... and that's where we go to now. Stephen is running down the long dark corridor, being followed by his twelve-year-old sister Sylvia, who is being followed by their mother Torhild, who is carrying two-year-old Susan.

Mary is smiling with her Irish eyes, rolls of oscillating flab under her chin. The family exchanges aloof pleasantries with Torhild. They never did want her in the family, maybe because she wasn't Catholic, maybe because she wasn't American, but then neither is Mary an American, but she is Catholic, and that counts for something when familial bonds are being forged in the new world's springtime ashes. Torhild goes over to the ancient Fiorenza and gives her a kiss on the cheek. Fiorenza is the only one who has ever shown any affection or acceptance of Torhild.

"Torhild... the boys are downstairs... been there an hour now... maybe one of us should go down and get them out..." says Mary, slyly trying to coax Torhild to the task of summoning the boys from the bar. This sort of gab goes on and on.

"Oh those boys," says Luisa, with a chuckle.

"It's the life of Reilly, isn't it? Torhild," says Mary, and Torhild just smiles.

"Oh those boys..." continues Luisa.

Mary says, "How long has it been now... over an hour... right Luisa? I don't know what's the matter with him... he's not suppose to drink you know, Doctor Cooper told him to lay off the stuff, I don't know, and Friday night up in the firehouse till three in the morning, shooting craps... gambling he was... I kept telephoning but they said that he wasn't there... I knew he was there... the liars... oh for the love of Pete... I don't know what I'm going to do with him... and with my heart condition..."

"Oh those boys..."

"Oh carry me off to the burying grounds," says Fiorenza, disgusted with the jabbering.

"Can we go out and play in the yard?" Sylvia asks her mother.

"All right, but stay around the stairs," says Torhild.

Sylvia grabs Stephen by the hand and they run down the long hallway. Uncle Stevie by this time has heard enough talk; he never really liked Mary anyway, and has lifted himself from his chair, reached for his crutches, and chugged off down the hallway to his room where it's safe and quiet and no one ever goes in there. Stephen tries to peek into the room as Uncle Stevie goes in. An entire life spent in one room. Can you pursue happiness in there, Uncle Stevie? Do you agree with Pascal when he wrote that all the unhappiness of men arises from one single fact, that they cannot stay quietly in their own room? What diversions have you found to keep you from your misery Uncle Stevie? Have you found God in there? What are we hiding from in this family? What is our sin?

At the entrance to the alleyway, on the pavement, Sylvia finds a book of matches with only three matches left in it. Sylvia leads Stephen out of the yard and they go around the corner of the new Food Town supermarket. The parking lot has about ten cars in it, scattered around at different points. In front of the supermarket is a pile of cardboard boxes and garbage, high enough to block the lower half of the four large windows with thirty panes in each.

"You do it," says Sylvia. Stephen strikes the first match; it flares up and burns out in the breeze. He strikes a second match. It also goes out. For the last match he hunches down low, and he and Sylvia cup their hands around the flame. He blows on it. A little smoke. A little more smoke. A fire. "Step on it! Step on it!" But it's too late. Stephen and Sylvia run around the corner. "Don't say a word or we'll get in trouble." They run through the yard and up the stairs and down the hall. "What's the hurry," says Aunt Luisa, "going to a fire or something?"

Jimmy Pushin has positioned himself under the protective covering of a large tree with long branches leaning on the ground, in the yard of an 18th century house adjacent to the new school. From there he can see the crowd, who, in this case, is the enemy. Jimmy Pushin, retard, for that's what they all call him in town, has engaged the enemy on all sides. He can see that horrible Mrs. Reardon, whom he smack in the face when he was in her 1st grade class. They put him in a "special school" because of that. Jimmy has blackened his face, like they do in the war movies, for the sneak attack. He has a box of long wooden kitchen matches, one of which he lights, and gazes at the dying flame, thinking about this morning and the gift that his father promised to give him, if he came down in the basement; Jimmy went down in the basement and was sexually assaulted once again, but this time his father wasn't lying, he got something for it, he got a bag of firecrackers, cherry bombs, ash cans, and M-80s.

Emile and Rocky are walking down Maxwell Avenue; at the street corner there is a small red Italian hotdog stand, where Rocky treats Emile to a lemon ice. They lean against the maple tree in front of the hotdog stand and spit pits into the trashcan. The hotdog stand is usually crowded on a Saturday afternoon when students gather here before and after a high school football game, football star seniors parking their new convertible coups with the top down and the cute bubbly cheerleader in the front seat to buy her a hotdog and show off and then go hang out on the front stoop of Saunder's soda fountain. There isn't anyone at the hotdog stand now, just Emile and Rocky; the students are all at the game. On a normal Saturday afternoon the high school marching band gathers at the high school and marches down East Main Street with the cheerleaders leading the way, followed by baton twirlers, and the band playing the inevitable "We're From OBHS Don't You Forget" and "There Is A Tavern In The Town"... In fact, at present, there are five taverns in the town, and Joe and Frankie are on their fourth beers and whiskey chasers when none other than Mary herself comes through the side door of the bar, and the patrons let out a big "Uh oh Frankie here she comes!" but as usual and inevitably and normally as everything goes in this small town, Mary is cajoled into staying and having a drink herself, and, against her will, of course, she orders an Orange Blossom, but just a one and then we have to go home.

The band is marching down to the football field, which is located behind the new elementary school. If this was a normal Saturday afternoon in cool October. But it's not. Today the band is over at the dedication ceremonies, and it's almost halftime at the football game. The dedication ceremony is running overtime, and Winthrop Overkill hasn't even made his speech yet. Ethel Roosevelt Derby is speaking and from the other side of the new school building comes the muffled sound of student body cheers, punctuating her speech. A cool October wind, a few leaves loosed from the summer of '62... blowing in the wind... innocent eternal small town America waking early Saturday morning with the threat of annihilation hanging over our heads... but Billy Warren has just run 25 yards for a touchdown, his girl Betty jumping for joy, pom poms flaking off, she dreaming of riding in his new convertible, going to the soda fountain, she the homecoming queen, she voted most popular girl, cutest couple, one day married, children, our own house, O happy happy happy, O American future, O American Dream.

Emile and Rocky are standing on the corner of Main Street and Audrey Avenue. Emile is holding the package in his hands. They are standing in front of the Chinese laundry, a white-washed cement-rendered building with all the windows and doors wide open, through which are seen and heard the sight and sound of shields of steam brandishing the air. Emile stands and stares through the windows; Chinese women are standing in sweat-drenched blouses lifting coffin-lid-like dry-cleaning presses, placing the clothes across the convexed rectangular cushion and pressing down sossshhh... sossshhh... The Chinese workers come in from the city on the train; many stay and sleep in the small back rooms, sleeping on mounds of dirty laundry. The train brought them all here... Emile remembers back to the 1930s just before he went off to Spain, when a small back room was an opium den; he remembers when he and Frank Yamada used some of Frank's father's old photographic equipment that Frank had found in the closet of the apartment in Northport, to take pictures of the Chinese workers having sex with each other in the back room, and made "dirty Chinese postcards" that Frank took with him to France, selling them on the streets of Paris. Emile met Frank the evening of Memorial Day 1927, when Henry, coming out from the city on the train, was occupying the window seat next to Frank, who tried to get too chummy with Henry, and on the train platform Emile volunteered to beat Frank up but Henry said forget it. They met again late that night under more relaxed conditions in Belsen and White's, when Frank suggested the idea of the photos to Emile an idea about "dirty Chinese postcards," and persuaded Emile to participate, just a little clinical screwing is how he put it, and that's how Emile met Cindy Chinchin, and that's how she became a prostitute in Belsen and White's, and later became the head Madame, an American success story. Emile is thinking about Cindy now, his mind racing through images caught in the cobwebs of his memory... staring through the windows of the past and through the windows of the laundry. New faces, old ways... Look at me! Look at me! But they go right on working lifting pressing steam engines, steam engines, trains rolling along the rails of fate, ghouls out of Jay Gould, steam engines churning churning churning turning sossshhh... life in a small back room the promise of America, and those inevitable normal usual lying words of Mrs. Laidlaw Down have stuck in Emile's mind: Americans abhor the kind of revolution which destroys and overturns, which murders, loots and burns... burns... burns... burns...

The pile of cardboard boxes and garbage stacked in front of Food Town burns burns burns...

Emile and Rocky cross the street to the triangular village green. A Victorian bandstand is situated in the center of the green, the bandstand is flanked by two commemorative cannon, relics of the Spanish-American

War, one of which stands on the spot where the statue of Captain Roger Bethell once stood, until it was removed by order of President Theodore Roosevelt. Across the streets from the village green on one side is the post office Building, and on the other side the Town Hall Building, where the statue of Roger Bethell collects dust in the basement. And there is a plaque on the side of the building with Joe Cazzaza's name inscribed, hero of World War II. And from the top point of the triangle of the village green directly down the street, is the railroad station, within view. Emile and Rocky enter the bandstand and sit down, eating the hotdogs that they bought at the hotdog stand. Slowly Emile unwraps the package that he found next to him, the package appeared as if by magic. "What is it? Where d'ya s'pose it come from," says Rocky. DO NOT OPEN UNTIL YOU ARE READY 1893

"I'm ready. Why in God's name have I stayed in this town for most of the last forty years, why? I went to fight in the civil war in Spain, but I returned here, I have no hope, this is why, Rocky, this is my destiny, inside this package. How can a man get so beat down that he just doesn't give a shit? Stuck here... I came on that train a long time ago... that train... and I'm gonna leave on that train... it would have been so easy to get back on it and return to the city and from there go anywhere if I had wanted to... but... in the city I was a nobody and didn't know it, here I've been a nobody and did know it. I could have stayed in Spain or Paris… that damn shipyard took so much out of me, damn I tried hard to organize a union, but they cut off my fingers, that's what they did, the bastards. And they killed your father Rocky... letting those big metal sheets swing around just to get the job done fast... for profit..."

Emile looks inside the package. There is one stick of dynamite. Holy shit! The too late forever stick of dynamite.

Amid the applause and an occasional disassociated hurrah from the football field, the Hon. John Stephen Burnsides is returning to the lectern as Mrs. Ethel Roosevelt Derby takes her seat. "Ladies and gentleman, students of all ages. I have a very special guest speaker whom I would like to introduce to you at this time. Mr. Winthrop Overkill was born ninety-two years ago and is in as fine a fettle as any man half his age. And what a life! Oh children if any one of you but lives half the adventurous full life of Mr. Overkill you will not have under lived. Ha Ha. Mr. Overkill is not only a veteran of the First World War but he also fought alongside his good friend Theodore Roosevelt in the Spanish-American War. Yes, children, Mr. Overkill was one of the famed Rough Riders! (Children ooh and ahh). So without any further ado I give to you Mr. Winthrop Overkill."

The high school marching band plays "There'll Be a Hot Time in the Old Town Tonight." Winthrop Overkill, with cane in hand, is helped to his feet. The crowd stands and applauds. Wild hurrahs come from the football field. Billy Warren has just scored another touchdown. Jimmy Pushin, huddled under the hanging branches of a tree, selectively lines up his ordnance on the dirt; when you are ready Jimmy, you may fire. Winthrop Overkill leans his ancient frame on the lectern and begins his speech, "What is American history? It's the story of our great country. It's the story of our forefathers who crossed the mighty Atlantic long ago and settled in the New World. Our ancestors built homes and gathered food from the good land and sea, made their own clothes, founded states, and became united as one people, the American people, who won their freedom and founded the government of the United States. It is the story of the western frontier, of the people who took the land from wild animals and savage Indians, until, finally, our destiny was fulfilled, our Manifest Destiny, a great new nation reaching out from sea to shinning sea." Winthrop Overkill's voice cracks and breaks and rises and falls. The crowd applauds. There is a tear in the corner of his eye. He wipes it away with a finger. A soft breeze flutters his sombrero, which he removes, revealing a shock of gray hair.

"Our nation grew richer and stronger, with hard work and the aid of machinery, building the railroads, the growth of the factories, using the bounty of the abundance of our natural resources. Also we see the story of America becoming a land of schoolhouses and churches, because Americans believe in education and religion and virtue. We see America becoming a world power, a power righteous and free, so big and strong that other nations listen when it speaks, so rich that it has business in all parts of the earth, and so unselfish that it is helping to make the whole world a better place in which to live." Once again the crowd breaks into applause. The breeze ruffles the papers on the lectern, but Winthrop Overkill firmly holds onto his papers and his sombrero.

Inside one of the back rooms of the Chinese laundry, Mr. Wu has dropped his bong and a lighted match that he can't find among the mounds of dirty laundry.

In front of the Food Town supermarket, there are now large flames building up in the cardboard boxes and garbage.

Joe and Frankie are downing whiskey chasers number five and beers number six, and Mary is sipping her Orange Blossom number two. Torhild, holding Susan, joins them in the bar; Torhild asks for a Tom Collins, and Sylvia and Stephen, who get Coca-Colas. Up above, in the front rooms, Luisa and Fiorenza sit silently gazing out the window on South Street. Suddenly the fire whistle on the top of the firehouse is screaming, and Luisa runs down the hallway to the back of the house, looks out the corner window and watches the firemen racing into the parking lot in their cars with red lights flashing. A minute late Stevie comes out of his room to join her. Small town excitement. People are rushing over to Food Town. Luisa can now see the smoke. Jesus, Mary, and Joseph.

The fire whistle at the top of the telephone pole located by the basketball courts on the other side of the new school is blaring and drowning out the cracked weakening voice of Winthrop Overkill, who steps away from the lectern and waits for the whistle to blow its seven whistles and fade. Winthrop finds this a good time to blow his nose. The ambulance, which had been parked by the football field in case of an injury to a player requiring immediate transportation to the hospital, has pulled through the wire gate and is traveling up the street, passing Emile and Rocky, who are still seated at the bandstand. "I'm gonna see where it is," says Rocky, who, when he can get away, follows the volunteer firemen and the fire trucks to fires. "No, not this time," says Emile, "stay here, I need your help."

Winthrop Overkill is speaking again as the fire whistle has whirled to silence. Several volunteer firemen who were in the audience have booked out to the fire, much to their speech-rattled relief. Winthrop Overkill is speaking about Gatling guns, gunboat diplomacy, the hottest places this side of hell, Cuba, Nicaragua, Mexico, Dominican Republic, Haiti, banana wars, America's honor, Vera Cruz, Medals of Honor, blood crazy garden of Eden, Las Canitas, Guardia Nacional Dominicana, the Haitian president Vilbrun Sam who was publicly dismembered and his heart eaten by crazed mobs, gruesome voodoo rituals, eerie noises blown from conch shells, the war cries of the Cacos, the Gendarmerie d'Haiti, Augusto Cesar Sandino, the specter of a Mexican-fostered Bolshevistic hegemony intervening between the United States and Panama, the Machos, the redbugs, lice, mosquitoes, the Guardia Nacional de Nicaragua, the red and black hatbands of the Sandinistas...

"In the end it was a job well done... classic counterinsurgency campaigns..." At this point even so patriotic a crowd as is assembled for today's ceremonies was beginning to get restless; yet being together they felt some sense of duty, courage, unity, comfort, when at any moment atomic war could break out with those Russians.

Emile can't get the words of the orgulous Mrs. Laidlaw Down out of his head: Americans abhor the kind of revolution which destroys and overturns, which murders, loots, and burns... wild beasts and savage Indians, a recurring theme of today's festivities. A new school, education, education... a new school... but if truth be told, thinks Emile, if the truth were ever told... would it make any difference? Who was actually destroyed? Who was overturned? Who was murdered? Who was burned? And by whom? And now Emile is talking, counterpoint to everything Winthrop Overkill is saying, as if Emile could hear him, but the sound of Overkill's voice coming from the loudspeakers is flattened and elongated in meaningless echoes of itself, mixing with the hurrahs from the football field, filtering down from the lost source, trickling over stones in the riverbed, mouthing the lines into the mouth of public opinion, carving the man-made canal, the Panama of the public mind, not the mind of the people, and Emile is talking about the sinking of the U. S. battleship Maine, Yellow Journalism, Rudolph Dirks, Arthur Brisbane, Isolationism, Platt Amendment, Ostand Manifesto, the secret service uncovering espionage plots and networks during the Spanish-American War, the Message to Garcia, Boxer Rebellion, Open-door policy... "Yeah Rocky, then it was *Cuba Libre*, but do you know what they are writing on the walls in the cities of Cuba today? They are writing *Cuba Territorio Libre de America... Patria O Muerte...* back then even as astute an observer of human nature as Joseph Conrad was writing in his letters *Viva L'Espana,* did you ever hear of the Generation of '98, no, of course not, Spanish writers, deeply troubled by Spain's defeat in that war, Antonio Machado, Jose Martinez Ruiz, there's a big world out there Rocky, beyond all that dribbling salivating sugar and mish-mash that is being spooned out over there in those speeches... America, America, America, that reminds me, there's a poem by Neruda, goes like this, Jehovah divided his universe: Anaconda, Ford Motors, Coca-Cola Inc., and similar entities: the most succulent of them all; The United

Fruit Company Incorporated. Ha Ha. Do you remember when we, when was it? 1938? 1939? When that Orson Wells' radio program, what was it? "War of the Worlds," ya remember late that night we set off some dynamite up in the hills of Pine Hollow, in the woods, scared the hell out of the whole town, they were in the streets scared to death, thought the Martians were coming, yeah, we sent them a message then, that was a meaningless message, the Martians are coming, what about the Russians? It wasn't exactly a "Message to Garcia," no, now there's great American literature, I mean it, that's the real thing, real American, a little sketch of Americana, man on a mission, then the businessmen hung it on their walls, in a gold frame, and distributed it to their workers as an inspirational creed, do your duty! Follow through to the end! Take your Message to Garcia! I swear to God it's great American literature, the great American novel boiled down to a few pages, all the truth of America right there, just like the Constitution, it is what they say it is, and the institutions say this and that's final, interpreted according to Doyle, get lost in the shuffle, that's us Rocky, lost in the shuffle off to Buffalo, I'm babbling now, seditious babble though, according to Holmes, no, not Sherlock, you know, Schenck versus United States... clear and present danger... that's me, I'm a clear and present danger, in ordinary times, normal, usual, the 1st Amendment does not protect a man in falsely shouting fire in a theatre and causing a panic... but what about the actor on the stage? The audience can distinguish fact from fancy you say? What if you're on opium? When the English brought large amounts of opium to China, were the Chinese demanding it? Hell, no. That was the free market working... open new markets, open the door... did you hear what she said, about Americans not liking those kind of revolutions that destroy, murder, loot, burn... that is the essence of American history! How could the victims of all that shit even be accused of ever shouting fire falsely in a theatre? Who exactly is the false one here?"

Emile had said enough. Rocky didn't understand a word of it. Never has. After thirty years of listening to Emile he has no idea what has been said... but who else can Emile speak to these days? And who else will speak to Rocky like that, so passionately, so engaged with him? Emile picks up the package and walks down the street. The time has come. He is ready. First Heemskirk's Shipyard, then the Commander Oil Company, then... they can blame it on the Russians! Oil! Oil! Oil! It's all about the oil!

There is a fire burning in the Chinese laundry; the fire whistle is blowing again. The fire is still burning in front of Food Town. Joe and Frankie and their families have come out to watch the fires, everyone except Fiorenza, Luisa and Stevie, who are watching from the windows. Unfortunately for Stephen and Sylvia, someone had spotted them playing with matches in front of Food Town. Joe Cazzaza is told about it, and the police and fire chief will be up later to see them. Joe is angry, real angry; he drags Stephen upstairs while Luisa watches, and Joe takes out his belt and spanks him.

Winthrop Overkill is acknowledging the applause as Father Don steps up to the lectern to say a final quick prayer to end the ceremonies. The marching band has dispersed and is running down the walkway next to the school in order to get to the football field in time, where they will reassemble and lead the way back up to the high school, with cheerleaders and baton twirlers and some students in tow. Billy Warren scored three touchdowns and OBHS won the game 34-6.

Suddenly... there is a bang and a boom. Then another bang and a boom. The crowd is startled. Jimmy Pushin is heaving cheery bombs from inside the cover of the tree's drooping branches. He lights the ash cans, lights the M-80s... even bigger bangs, but the explosives fall short of the crowd, Jimmy can't throw that far. Then there is a boom... an incredible massive boom, gusts of fire shoot up in the sky from the north, is it over the bay? A ship? No, it's the shipyard, then even bigger booms, from the direction of the oil company... a tugboat is engulfed in flames, the brightly colored oil tanks are shattering in fantastic explosions and fire rages and black smoke is drifting over the town... the crowd is panicking... there are screams, screams and shouting that the MISSILES ARE FALLING... THE MISSILES ARE FALLING... IT'S THE RUSSIAN MISSILES FROM CUBA... THE RUSSIANS ARE COMING... IT'S THE END OF THE WORLD... people scatter in all directions... but the high school marching band plays on, they play "There'll Be a Hot Time in the Old Town Tonight." They keep marching right through the intersection of South Street and East Main Street... cheerleaders and baton twirlers... Luisa and Stevie are rushing back and forth down the hallway from the front rooms to the back of the building, trying to see it all from their narrow perspective... Joe is whacking Stephen with his belt, Stephen squirms and cries on the couch... the Chinese laundry is burning, Food Town is burning, the shipyard is burning, the oil yard is burning, the lumber yard is burning, the whole area along the bay where the companies are located is burning... black smoke covering the town... and Winthrop Overkill has drawn his sword and is charging down the street, shouting, "Remember the Maine!" He charges up the street and comes to the village green with the bandstand and two cannon; he is waving his sword... "Charge! Charge!" He sees Theodore Roosevelt charging down the street from the other direction. Winthrop is trying to fire the cannon; he drapes himself over the cannon like a flag and dies, his sword falling from his hand, his sombrero dropping from his head.

And there is a plaque with names carved in stone of the boys from Oyster Bay who served in World War II... and there's Sgt Joe Cazzaza's name.

And Rocky is standing on the platform of the train station waving to Emile, who waves back from the train window, having caught the last train out of town on this day, riding out of town at last... heading west into the sunset...

Crowds are descending on the village green, trying to break into the Town Hall where the yellow sign bolted to the brick wall indicates a fall out shelter. The door is smashed in. The forgotten statue of the forgotten war hero, author of sci-fi novels and books on Zen Buddhism and bonsai, the forgotten statue of Captain Roger Bethell that has stood in the basement of the Town Hall building in a cold damp corner, why... it seemed to smile. The people stood frozen, the large crowd inside and outside stood frozen; and then they moved aside, divided, forming a passage between themselves, because the statue of Captain Roger Bethell was ascending up the stairs. It ascended the stairs and went out the door and up into the sky. It floated over the burning town, over the bay. The people watching from the ground in disbelief.

The statue was being held up by cables, held up and carried through the sky by cables attached to the spaceship *No Rule II*, with Aliaspun in command and control. Aliaspun, just a character from a sci-fi novel written by Roger Bethell.

1964

One day in the late summer of 1964 Joe Cazzaza took his family to the Bayville Rides, a small amusement park for children located across the road from a beach on the Long Island Sound, with a view over to Connecticut.

The last time Joe Cazzaza took his family here was on the Fourth of July, when he parked by the beach and the family watched the fireworks shooting up across the sound from Rye Beach.

His wife Torhild sat in the car and watched two of her three children enjoying themselves on the rides. It was a hot muggy day. She felt uncomfortable. She was three months pregnant. Little Susan sat next to her in the car. Torhild was cutting out paper dolls for Susan. Sylvia and Stephen were spinning around on a ride called The Whip; their father was standing by the ticket gate. Through the glass windshield Torhild watched the world go round in the carefree play of the children with their implacable energies concomitant with the subatomic particles intermingling among the physicality of the steel rides and the flesh of the children and the world and her own flesh and blood daughter and son and her husband and herself who watches but cannot see through mimesis or catharsis the meaning and value creation imports to creativity with words or signs when creation itself is bleeding toward birth or death unknown to her, in her own womb, in her own being. The next moment she is lying on a stretcher in the ambulance and her mind is flashing images of the past... on the deck of the transatlantic steamer *SS Stavangerfjord* sailing into New York Harbor...

During the previous summer of 1963 the father had taken his family to Washington D.C. As a young married couple they had honeymooned there in 1949. Harry S Truman was president then. He had reigned over that golden period of post-war peace when Torhild arrived from Norway. But Eisenhower was her favorite president. She saw him standing in a car and waving in Oyster Bay... and now John F. Kennedy was president. The father had bought a Bell and Howell 8mm movie camera just for the trip. It was the first and last time that he ever used it, which was typical of him. It had been Giuseppe's dream to see Washington D.C.; he never made it. But now his son was leading his family around the nation's capital. And everywhere they went Stephen marched in step and saluted the flags; a good little trouper. Susan was in the baby carriage most of the time; and Sylvia frolicked and romped around the huge mall.

The National Archives Building is in Washington D.C., and on the facade of the building these words are carved: "This building holds in trust the records of our national life and symbolizes our faith in the permanency of our national institutions." The Declaration of Independence, the Constitution, and Bill of Rights are on permanent display in the National

Archives Exhibition Hall. To preserve them for posterity, the parchments are sealed in bronze and glass cases filled with helium and protected from harmful light rays. In the event that a national crisis might arise that could endanger the treasured documents the display case can be lowered into a large safe that is fireproof, shockproof and bombproof. At the National Archives Building genealogists can trace a shoot in a family tree by consulting census schedules, military service records, or veterans' pension applications. Joe Cazzaza had no need to consult the archives for family roots, just military service records. And Torhild had no roots here at all.

Now it was the summer of 1964. Lyndon Johnson was president. Was the country as fireproof, shockproof and bombproof as those documents in their bronze and glass case? There were riots and fires in the cities. Fireproof? John F. Kennedy had been assassinated in Dallas. Shockproof? How about bombproof? Was that next?

There were two seeds in Torhild's stomach; one of them was Simone, the other burst in blood on that hot summer day at the amusement park. It was a premonition of things to come, after 1964 the national birth rate decreased. What happened to the baby? Stephen wondered. Is the baby dead? Will he go to heaven? Yes, he will go to heaven, said his mother. America's first bestseller declared that the unbaptized shall be sentenced to hell. But times have changed. We have moved beyond such superstitions. But unbaptized or not, in the next few years, the young would be sentenced to hell in, and bring hell to, a far away placed called Vietnam.

The mother did have a name picked out if it had been a boy, if it had lived. He would have been called James. Stephen wanted a brother to play catch with. One day, the day Simone was born, he came home hoping to hear the announcement of a baby brother, but when he was told that it was a girl, he ran upstairs crying. Not long after his sister was born, Stephen discovered a new friend whose name, ironically, was James. Everyone called him Jimmy. He was slightly disabled mentally and went to a special school. He was four years older than Stephen. Jimmy had no friends except for Stephen, briefly. Jimmy had a father who beat him without reservation, and a mother from Louisiana who had dedicated most of her life-force to Jesus; the tiny amount of life-force that remained she used to torment her only child. She dragged Jimmy off to church almost every day when he would have preferred to be playing toy soldiers with Stephen; but he learned to sing some swell songs which he taught Stephen. "If the devil doesn't like it, he can sit on a tack, sick on a tack, sit on a tack..." and other such profound Baptist hymns.

When Jimmy and Stephen spoke to each other over the telephone they used their own lingo. Jimmy would say, "Big ones or little ones?" Which meant do you want to play big soldiers, life-size, with gear of Stephens's father's old Army uniform, a belt, a canteen, a shovel kit, or little soldiers, plastic toy green soldiers sold in plastic bags, or maybe even the tall and realistic G.I. Joe doll, which was not really a doll, it was an "action figure." It was the golden age of toys. Every Saturday morning between the incidental war movies and cowboy movies and cartoons, the national myths gave way to what it essentially was all about: the other manhood myth of business. The toy commercials assaulted the children of America, and Stephen yelled out in unison with a million other boys on a Saturday morning, "I want that! I want that!" Stephen wanted rockets and missiles, and Jimmy wanted guns and bazookas. The world was crowded with heroes and adventures. And at the end of the day a nice home was waiting beyond the green lawns where mommy was cooking and daddy was coming home from work in his shiny new car. But why did Jimmy always want to come to Stephen's house and not go home? Because his father beat the shit out of him, that's why. The story goes that Jimmy's father punched his pregnant wife in the stomach when she was carrying Jimmy, that explained it, why Jimmy was "slow," and when Jimmy was born he kept punching him. Another story that Jimmy told Stephen but which Stephen was too young at the time to understand, was that Jimmy's father often took Jimmy down in the basement and stuck his penis up Jimmy's ass.

On an October day in 1957 the Russians launched Sputnik, a small round satellite, into orbit around the earth. It went beep-beep; and America drew a soft dark curtain over itself; and that curtain smothered Jimmy and smoldered in Stephen. On Christmas Day 1962 Stephen was playing with his new toy, the X-500 Missile Defense Base and Rocket Launcher; on the same day, his friend Jimmy was being dragged down to the basement and Jimmy's father closed the door behind them. In 1964, at the Bayville rides, Stephen was going round and round in a little oval space ship, shooting the red flashing ray gun. It went whoo-whoo like sound effects in a sci-fi B movie. His mother was watching him from the car, and then she was bleeding.

Newsreel:

Goodbye *Sputnik I.* That's the first big headline of 1958. You made such a big noise, you will never know how big. You gave us a shock. The shock hit us as hard as Pearl Harbor. Though not as hard as Hiroshima and Nagasaki? You see, comrade, a nation can grow fat and complacent. Certainly when it knows itself to be number one in everything. But you taught us something about ourselves that we didn't know, until now. You taught us something about the Russians that we didn't believe possible, though many earnest and patriotic men have been warning us about Russian peril and power. But now the President has put a burning light on our need: missiles, rockets and satellites. Now we shall put scientists in positions of power and get the results that we need to protect our freedoms. Now we know it's there: Russian ambition. Now we know that what we thought was a peasant country is a highly developed scientific country, whose ambition is world domination.

The radio signal was heard again today, loud and clear. The Soviet newspaper *Pravda* confirms that *Sputnik* has been transmitting information by code. What is the meaning of beep-beep? It is the sound of radio signals transmitting information from space to Russian scientists. What is the meaning of beep-beep? Beep-beep means the Russians are coming. Beep-beep all around us. Beep-beep in the radio. Beep-beep in the television. Beep-beep in the toaster. Beep-beep in the schools. Beep-beep in the government. Beep-beep in Vietnam. Beep-beep in rock and roll music. Beep-beep in our heads... beep-beep in small town America...

The father opened the door of the car and pulled the seat forward, bending it down. Stephen climbed up into the backseat and crawled over to his mother and sat on her lap. Her lap was soaked in blood. Stephen's little sister was sitting next to her mother and sucking her thumb; an older sister was looking in through the window of the car.

"Stephen," the mother said softly, "Mommy's all right."

Son of a bitch. What a mess. It was his new car. His new baby. A 1961 Chevrolet Impala SS, white with a single red stripe down each side, six round taillights, and deep red seats; at least the color will hide the bloodstains a bit. He'd have to clean it up. The same shit. Story of my life. Mopping up shit, piss, vomit and blood. The father was deeply annoyed. It was the third car that he had ever bought brand new; it would be the last that he ever bought brand new. His first car had been a 1928 REO Flying Cloud, with the devil thumbing his nose with his fingers as a hood ornament; he had bought it from Jake the Cop in 1939; he was just out of high school. After that, in 1940, he bought a 1932 Model A Ford, with a rumble seat. In 1941, a year before he was conscripted into the army, he got a 1934 Ford V8, just like Bonnie and Clyde's. After he got out of the army he used his GI bill to buy his first new car, in 1947, a bulky black Dodge, with fluid drive. He had that car when he got married in 1949 and drove down to Washington D.C. on his honeymoon, taking old Route 1, starting out crossing the Whitestone Bridge and then the George Washington Bridge, driving through dots of small-towns between Trenton and Philadelphia and Baltimore. And then taking his new wife to a burlesque show in Washington D.C. on their honeymoon; Torhild didn't like it; she couldn't figure that one out. And then in 1957 he bought a spanking new green and white Chevrolet Bel Air, which he then traded in for the Impala. There were no more new cars after that.

Who exactly was bleeding? His wife or the car? That bit of his mind that had sensed that his new car was blood-stained was shattered into even smaller bits of incoherence when he heard his wife utter a doleful cry; his momentary loss of absolute consciousness returned to him like the image of his own father lying on the cold wet grass with a pool of blood on his stomach, lying right under the door of the big green REO truck; that was over thirty-five years ago; he was only six years old at the time.

His new baby; did she lose him? Her? Stephen was eight years old and stared blankly and helplessly; it was like something on the television; it was like President Kennedy being shot; it was like seeing all that on the television again, just last year, days and days sitting in front of the television, at home or at his Grandma Fiorenza and Aunt Luisa and Uncle Stevie's house; and Uncle Frankie was there too, with his wife, Aunt Mary, who had come to America from Ireland many years ago, and they were in a Catholic state of shock, or mere dumbfoundedness, or disbelief, or something that made the memory of it stick in the mind like stalactites connecting with stalagmites in the deepest cave after a thousand years of yearning; or like the space between God's finger and Adam's hand in Michelangelo's painting, that space being an eternity; or like the memory of the smell of flowers at his grandmother's funeral.

Sitting next to her mother in the back seat of the car was four-year-old Susan. She wasn't crying. She had been sucking her thumb, but now she held her golden-hair Barbie-like doll and a book in her hands; the doll was naked, both legs and one of the arms were torn from their plastic sockets. The father reached into the car and lifted Susan out; she dropped her Yogi Bear Little Golden Book but clutched fiercely to the torso of her doll.

"Come out, Stephen," said his father. Stephen positioned himself firmly against the far window. His mother devotionally smiled, but that did not relieve his anxiety at the sight of his mother's body stained with blood. Stephen's father walked around to the other side of the car and tried to pull the boy through the opened window. Stephen again retreated to the security of his mother's bloody lap. She hugged him tightly and uttered a sharp cry of hurt. His father, visibly angry, quickly picked Stephen up, grasping him under the arms, and swung him out of the car. Stephen's face was struck with horror and distorted with distress. His stomach was cramped like a white-knuckled fist. He started flailing his arms up and down like the paddles of a penguin rushing to the sea. He ran around in a circle and emitted a long slow cry that gathered force and whined with the vocal contortions of agony, just like the siren of the ambulance that at that moment was rounding the corner and entering the grounds of the small amusement park. His father shouted at his eldest daughter, thirteen-year-old Sylvia, "I told you to keep him away. I didn't want him to see." Sylvia stood speechless, with little Susan at her feet. Sylvia put her hands on Stephen's shoulders and tried to pull him away, but he spun around and smacked at Sylvia and pushed on her legs. Little Susan fell down and started crying.

Stephen screamed, "No... no... no..." The amusement park loudspeakers blasted music: the Beatles, that group of boys from England whom Sylvia is so crazy about: John, Paul, George, and Ringo. Her mom thinks they wear funny wigs. "That can't be their real hair. They must be wigs!" Her dad prefers to listen to Mitch Miller and the Gang and Lawrence Welk. When Sylvia plays her 45s, he shouts, "Turn that noise down!" An almighty directive that reverberated through many a home under teenage siege.

The music played on: "Yeah... yeah... yeah... she loves you... yeah... yeah... yeah..." Stephen screamed, "No... no... no..." The whirling red light of the ambulance glowed in their eyes. Joe Cazzaza picked Susan up and carried her over to her mom, who was strapped to the stretcher. She kissed her three children. "I'll follow you to the hospital in my car," said Joe.

The rackety gears of the slowly ascending roller coaster clanked and churned until the small coaster reached its apogee and then sped downward and streaked sideways along a sharp incline to the left. Children screamed, shouted and laughed. The clangorous calliope music played a marching tune, as wooden horses pumped up and down like pistons, greasing the frisson and excitement of the metallic atmosphere. The frenetic whirling around of the various rides: small airplanes being swung on chains; little sober boats guided by rusted iron bars in the water; trains on steel tracks; rocket ships with red flashing ray guns; everything turning and turning, whipping about in a desperate urgency to move, to go, to keep going, cyclic transport, flight to nowhere...chop chop chop... entrance, exit, get on, get off...get on, get off... beep-beep boom boom...

The mother's stretcher was slid into the ambulance. It drove off on the dirt road in a gallop of dust. The siren wailed. Children laughed and shouted. Stephen cried into his father's trousers. Dad fecklessly addressed his children. "Mommy will be all right," he just managed to say, but it was hardly consoling.

Torhild had told Stephen a hundred times that there was a baby growing inside her stomach. Stephen had placed his hand on his mother's stomach and felt the kicks; had put his ear to his mother's stomach and listened to the gurgling water; had put his mouth to his mother's stomach and spoke words to the baby in his mother's stomach.

Stephen made the connection between the blood and the baby in his mother's stomach, and he asked his father when driving to the hospital, "Why is the baby making blood on mommy?" His father did not answer.

1966

Joe Cazzaza carried a five-gallon can of heavy cement tar in his right hand and made his way up the ladder to the black flat roof. Stephen stood at the base of the ladder on another black flat roof. His father hoisted the can of tar up and placed it on the copingstones. He climbed up a few more rungs and stepped onto the roof. Stephen watched his father climb onto the roof and then Stephen went shakily up the ladder. He was afraid of heights, though the ladder was no more than ten feet high. It was a wooden folding ladder that was folded in and stood leaning against the side of the building.

It was placed on the slightly slanted roof of a building extension that had been added on to the two-story building that stood on South Street and that attached that building to the two-story building that stood perpendicular to it. The additional rooms of the extension served as a storage space for the stationary and the grocery store, and as a backroom for the meat market with a large walk-in freezer.

Stephen stood on the roof of the building that contained two apartments on the second floor and four garages beneath them. When he was about four years old his family lived in these apartments. He was ten years old now, and he lived on Summit Street, just a five-minute walk from here. He saw the parking lot behind Food Town supermarket, and beyond that he saw the trees on the hill. They lived somewhere up there, but he couldn't see his house. Stephen walked across the roof and saw the high white steeple of the Presbyterian Church that stood on the hill to the east. Yeah, that's where his friend Jimmy had his arm twisted by the Reverend. He saw the large colorful oil tanks and the water of the bay to the north. He heard his father say a curse word and saw him going back down the ladder. He forgot his trowel. Joe Cazzaza stepped off the bottom rung and walked across the roof to the metal railing that separated the roof from the porch. He lifted one leg over the railing and then the other leg followed and he stepped onto the concrete porch. A door in the middle opened to a hallway with two doors on each side, entrances to four apartments. Each apartment had two bedrooms, a kitchen, a living room and a bathroom. The porch had some chairs and a table. The residents included a Polish family, a Norwegian man who worked at the shipyard, an Irishman who worked in the meat market, and a widowed Jewish woman. Joe and his family had lived in one of these apartments when Stephen was about two years old. Joe had just moved his family back from a new 1950s style house that he had bought with his GI loan. It was to that house that Stephen was brought home as a baby. But his dad didn't like the neighborhood, the Levittown-like boxes of houses and the grass that had to be cut and all the up-keep... and the damn Jew couple next door and the snooty wasp couple on the other side... and it was too far from his family and home town, actually just a short drive, in a neighboring town called Hicksville. So what he couldn't do for himself he did for others, very obligingly, like a good peasant doormat. He tarred the roofs of the tenants. Someone had to do it. And being nice Italian landlords, the rents were never raised... and no money was made. Joe worked as a construction worker, a shipyard worker, a bartender, and a janitor... and never saved a dime. Shovel, tar and mop... same motion in life. Joe walked along the porch until he came to the wooden stairs that were attached to the side of the building. He went down to get his trowel.

Meanwhile, Stephen walked across to the edge of the roof. He looked down into a narrow space that separated one building from the other, that separated this building that his grandfather had built on property that he bought in August 1914, from another old building that stood at the corner of South Street and East Main Street. He stepped onto the copingstone and crossed over to the other building. A clock tower stood at the corner of this building overlooking the intersection. Below was the dentist's office, where Stephen had had his teeth looked at a few weeks ago. No cavities! He was proud. A hardware store occupied the ground floor of this corner building. Across the street he saw the cone-top of a building that once housed offices for the secret service when Theodore Roosevelt was President. Stephen walked back toward his family's building and stepped over the copingstones that divided the two buildings. He walked across the roof of the apartment building and came to the next building. His grandmother, uncle and aunt lived in this building. Stephen looked down between the buildings. He saw the entrance to the alleyway that led out to South Street, and saw the side door to the bar; after his father is done tarring the roof he'll be in the bar. Stephen walked on the roof, over the hot black felt paper and tar (how many layers of tar paper have been rolled over this roof; it must be a foot thick?) and came to the edge and got on his knees and leaned over the foot high wall capped by a coping stones and looked down on to South Street. He knew that his grandmother, uncle and aunt were probably sitting in the windows right beneath him and looking out over South Street. There were some old rocks and clumps lying about on the roof. Stephen always felt a sense of pride knowing that his family owned these buildings in the center of town. Stephen looked across the street and saw Saunders's Drugstore. There were high school kids hanging around the stoop, mingling in front of the door of the soda fountain. Stephen liked being up here, looking down.

Later...

Across the street from the Cazzaza building was Saunder's Pharmacy. Little Stephen was sitting on the stoop in front of Saunder's. He looked up at the windows across the street. He gazed upon the white painted facade of the Cazzaza building, seventy-five feet across. On the right side of the alleyway was the Old Harbor Bar and Grill, and to the right of that, a dry-cleaners. To the left of the alleyway was Horowitz and Gilman's Stationery, and next to the stationery was Biggs' Grocery Store, and after that, Van Heffer's Meat Market. They were the stores along South Street in the Cazzaza building, sandwiched between Hodman's Hardware on the north and the large white block building of Food Town on the south, in the year 1966.

Stephen saw his grandmother's face in one of the thirteen 2nd floor linear windows in the building that his grandfather had bought and restored and augmented in 1906. But his grandmother's eyes are clouded with cataracts and she can't see him clearly. Fiorenza sat in the third window from the right, as was the custom in the Cazzaza family. Luisa sat in the next window, fourth from the right, in the same room as her mother. In the second window from the right, in the other of the two front rooms, sat Uncle Stevie, his omnipresent crutches leaning on his chair. Giuseppe kept his promise to Theodore Roosevelt in 1908 and be-knighted his son with the royal name, and also, so it seems, the curse of Rooseveltian afflictions. Stevie Roosevelt Cazzaza was a victim of the infantile paralysis epidemic of 1916.

Beneath the fifth window from the right was the alleyway. A narrow twelve feet high passage with a basket-handle arch, leading to the backyard, a graveled area where delivery trucks unloaded their goods. The alleyway symbolized a passage to a secret and private world that few dared enter. To be sure, most people, visitors to the town and residents who lived outside the hamlet, saw this alleyway as a dirty passage, used by bums who frequented the bar and then pissed on the alleyway's walls, or as a shortcut to the parking lot behind the large supermarket which was built adjacent to the Cazzaza building. It was a magic passageway for Stephen.

Stephen sat on the stoop of Saunder's Pharmacy and inclined his head upward to greet Mary the Police Lady, who gave him a scowling reproachful look. She knew when a child had played hooky from school. She had a sixth-sense about such matters. But she also got cold hard evidence from simple observation. She didn't see Stephen this morning at the time he should have been seen walking to school, because he was late, and his father had to come home from his job as a janitor in the other elementary school in town, in order to drive Stephen to school. Boy was his old man angry, cursing the little bastard.

Mary the Police Lady has held the hands of over a thousand students over the years, crossing them safely from one corner of South Street and East Main Street to the opposite corner of South Street and Audrey Avenue, but this morning no Stephen; it never occurred to her that he didn't want to be hand-held by a brown-uniformed matron, which is one reason boys usually crossed the street in groups, and quickly too. Stephen would never approach that corner by himself, a feat of cowardly procrastination that had caused him to be late for school on numerous occasions. He would rather wait in the alleyway until he sighted some students and then he would appear, confident that Mary the Police Lady would not hold his hand, and then run like heck to the other side of the street. "No running! No running!" Shouted Mary the Police Lady.

Stephen sat on the stoop, looking across the street; he was eating from a Pez and biting candy dots off the strip of candy dot paper that he bought in the little red hot dog stand down by the village green. Stephen watched as shadows emerged from the alleyway and became recognizable people, entering the dim sunlight, shading their eyes, too long in the darkness of the bar. They came out of the bar's side door in the alleyway accompanied by cool air and a burst of stale beer and jukebox music and loud tangled voices. They came out of the alleyway and stepped onto the sidewalk, pausing briefly to orient their sloshed brains. Here's old man Ryan, town drunk, heading for a park bench, and here's... Stephen didn't know him... and here's Emile Baldazzi, another bum who lives in the flophouse on Hamilton Avenue... and here's.. Uh oh... Dad...

Stephen watched his father turn sharply to his right, swing around and lurch back in the direction of the alleyway, and walk between smudged glass display windows, up a slightly sloped ramp composed of small black and white tiles, and go through the doorway with a door held open by a bundle of newspapers, entering Horowitz and Gilman's Stationery, popularly known as the paper store, because its essential business was selling newspapers; it didn't sell much else, unless it sold some cheap new toy fad to Stephen and his peers, a $1.00 Spalding baseball wrapped in white tissue paper and enclosed in a box, or baseball cards that Stephen and his friends would flip, or a wiffle ball or a tennis ball to play curb ball, or a water pistol. The display windows were decked out with desk supplies, pipes and pocket watches, all covered in dust and loomed over by sun-faded cardboard advertisements, out-dated, showing pipe-smoking gentlemen in fedoras and gray suits. A Calderesque metal-spoke configured spinable rack stood just inside the doorway on the right, decorated with small cheap toys wrapped in crinkly plastic; Stephen was saving his leaf-raking money to buy a ninety-nine cent water pistol. Along the left side of the store was a counter of nickel and dime candies in tiered rows behind green-edged glass; at the end of the counter was a box of penny Bazooka Bubblegum wrapped in tiny comic strips; followed by boxes of baseball cards, and cards of the latest hit television shows and movies. Across from the candy counter all the newspapers were stacked, *New York Times*, *Newsday*, and the *Daily News*, the tabloid that everyone bought, or so it seemed; and above the newspapers was a wooden structure filled with slots for cover-page facing magazines, *Life, Look*, and movie and teen magazines, of which Sylvia has a vast collection; and high on top, so infinitely high, out of the reach of young boys, the seductive smile of Miss October beaming down from the cover of *Playboy*. At the back of the store were hundreds of *Hallmark* and *Norwood* greeting cards of every size and shape and for any conceivable occasion of Gentile patermaterfamilias togetherness functionarism. In the far rear of the store another metal-spoke spinable rack contained paperback books, bestsellers and other books of a more, but not that much more, sleazy "dirty book" nature and variety. Stephen found many occasions to loiter among the *Hallmark* cards and try to get a glimpse of female flesh arrayed with various swanky-spanky white silk or black leather accoutrements, dressed as nurses, school girls, French maids, bending over with ass held high, Stephen's heart racing to a speed of mach one. Who actually bought these books? What sex and dope fiend in our town? Stephen never mustered up enough chutzpah to touch one of the paperbacks, let alone open it, and well into his adult life he would often dream that he was in the back of the paper store, just within reach of the unattainable secret of desire, just about to grasp it, when the urgent voice of Abe Gilman was heard in all its here-to-serve glory, "Are we going to buy or are we going to look? Isn't it your sister's birthday? Don't forget Mother's Day?" Abe Gilman grinning like the patron saint of greeting cards. Abe Gilman made Stephen so nervous that he dropped his dimes. "Don't dirty the floor! Don't dirty the floor!" said Abe Gilman.

Each store in town had its Lingering Time. There was no such thing as browsing. You either knew what you came to buy or you had no business being there. Horowitz and Gilman allowed about 30 seconds Lingering Time for children, before they pounced on the young prey with No Sale and shoplifting apprehensiveness. The only other stationery in town, with a better selection of toys (newer and not covered in dust as they were in Horowitz and Gilman's, which was only good for a Spalding baseball or the latest small cheap fad, a Rat Fink ring or a Slinky), but with a selection of toys actually seen on Saturday morning television, including some wonderful model airplanes and ships and racing cars, which Jimmy Pushin bought whenever he had the money and was therefore permitted to enter the store on East Main Street, was Feldsky's. Admittance to which required proof of financial solvency. Children had to empty their pockets to reveal their net worth, with intent to buy, telling Feldsky the particular product or generic product under consideration for purchase. If the money could afford the said product Feldsky would let the kid come into his holy tabernacle, leading the child directly to the section of the store where the said product dwelt in market place limbo, just reaching out to little boys to save the toy from the hell of the mark-down basket (never happen in Feldsky's) where the unsellable souls of toys go to pine away in mercantile doubt. If Jimmy or Stephen wanted to choose from among the model airplanes and cars, there could be no consultation between them; Feldsky permitted only one child at a time to be in the store, while the other waited outside, sitting on the stoop, nervously counting his nickels and dimes.

Stephen sat on the stoop of Saunder's Pharmacy. He was counting his dimes; he needed 40¢ more to get the water pistol. Inside the paper store, Joe Cazzaza bought a pack of L&M cigarettes and White Owl Invincible Cigars and placed some coins on top of a glass case containing Ronsen lighters and Timex watches, behind which stood Hy Horowitz, ancient proprietor, who had opened the stationery with his late partner Sid Schwartz back in 1907, first paying rent to Giuseppe Cazzaza, and now paying to Giuseppe's five un-businesslike, to-be-taken-advantage of, offspring, shamefully cowering behind a Memorial Day scandal, the life-denying curse after all these years.

The eighty-one-year old futzer chomped on the short fat black stub of an unlit cigar in the corner of his mouth. He rolled the cigar from one corner of his mouth to the other. Hy Horowitz pulled a cigar out of his breast pocket. "How about a cigar, Joe?" Hy ran the cigar under his nose and inhaled and exhaled. "Go on, take it. On the house." Hy indicated with head-jerking upward motions that Joe should take the cigar, which he did, as he has done for the past twenty-years or more. Hy smirked an easy to be mistaken smile, as if to say: We take care of our ass-kissing guinea landlords around here. Ass-kissing Joe thanked his patron, and stuck the stale, un-smoke-able cigar in his shirt pocket, and then he walked out on the old creaking pine-planked floor, upon which he dropped a dime; he bent down to pick it up and Abe Gilman, who was sweeping the floor, something he did to occupy his idle time-is-money-time, mumbled his customary comment, inherited from Sid Schwartz, to his coin-dropping customers, "Don't dirty the floor, don't dirty the floor."

Stephen, still sitting on the stoop, watched his father leave the paper store and go back into the dark alleyway. Joe Cazzaza went through the alleyway and then turned right, coming to the front of his mother's house. He climbed the five chipped cement stairs and opened the door. He entered and walked up a flight of twenty wooden stairs, and standing at the top landing he could see, straight ahead, beyond a partially drawn curtain, at the end of the hallway, one of the four windows in the front rooms; in a chair by the window sat his brother Stevie, crutches leaning on his lap. Joe walked down the hallway; he walked passed four closed, probably locked doors, and entered the front rooms overlooking South Street. He greeted his mother.

"Grandma's pants will soon fit Willy."

Maybe it was an old Vaudeville song. Joe first heard it when he and Frankie had the bar over in Northport from 1950 to 1962. Wookie Jones would come through the door and introduce himself in his Alabama accent, every day at the same time, for nine years, the familiar black face of a stranger. "Grandma's pants will soon fit Willy." And he would hardly say another word the whole time he was there; until he left, and he never stopped muttering, and then he was gone until tomorrow. Joe never learned the origins of the song, or for that matter, the origins of Wookie Jones. The day Wookie died they took up a collection in the bar to pay for his burial expenses. It was known that Wookie had been working the past twenty years as a gardener on the 75-acre estate of Jacob Wernburg, whose first and last and only words to Wookie were, "Niggers don't get poison ivy, do they? Whatta think of unions? You got nothing to say about it? Good. You're hired."

"Thank you, mistah bossman."

"Grandma's pants will soon fit Willy." Joe said it again. "Go on home your mother's calling, your father got caught in the washing machine…"

Fiorenza looked up at her son from her wheelchair. "Oh shut up with that song, will ya?" As a young girl Fiorenza grew up on Mercer Street in lower Manhattan, that's where she had met Giuseppe, who lived several blocks away at Wooster Street. Fiorenza loved all that Lower East Side immigrant music born on the Fourth of July amid the rhythmic racket of ghetto hurdy-gurdy syncopation, the cadence of fruit vendors, the scream of fire engines, the barks of peddlers and dogs, the children playing in the streets, the roaring elevated trains, all the commotion of a crowded metropolis. She loved that humming tin trinket sound, Irving Berlin, George Gershwin; those voices of sooty city alleyways, Al Jolson and Eddie Cantor; listened to them all the time when they were big stars on the radio. Joe was but a boy but he remembers, every Saturday night, sitting around a large up-right Philco radio, with an orange-lit dial, tuning in Eddie Cantor and lisping Joe "wanna buya duck?" Penner. But she loved Jimmy Durante best of all.

And when Fiorenza Victoria Adela Luise Maggio was married to Giuseppe Stefano Cazzaza in St. Anthony's on Thompson Street by Father Camillus, on June 11, 1902, little Jimmy, or so she liked to tell it, but no one was sure, was waiting outside the church with his friends, Antonio the Hurdy-Gurdy Man, featuring Caruso the Monkey; Luigi the Mandolin Man, and Dominic the Accordion Man.

"Hello Miss Maggio. My friends play for you."

… De maggio e na rosella…

Fiorenza loved music and passed that love on to her children; two of them took music lessons. The oldest girl, Silvia, had the most talent, though her taste proved more refined than her mother's and they often quarreled over the comparative merits of Eddie Cantor or the opera singer Marion N. Talley; they nearly came to blows over that one. But Toots got her way; she took singing and piano lessons from Luigi Bollo, who knew his Verdi like no one else, or so the signs posted on the street poles claimed. His studio had been located in a room above Saunder's Pharmacy from 1905 to 1927, coming to an end, like so many other things, on that strange Memorial Day back in 1927.

"Grandma's pants will soon fit Willy," Joe crooned again; he was pretty drunk, had been down in the bar for two hours after work. Stephen was afraid to go and meet him; no telling how he would react to Stephen's playing hooky today.

"He's had too many drinks," said Luisa to her mother.

"Grandma's pants will soooon fit Willy."

"Damn liquor... you're drunk!" said Fiorenza.

"And you are deaf!" said her son.

"The hell I am. I can hear you and that stupid song can't I?"

"Go on home your father's calling your mother got stuck in the washing machine... take your shoes off Willy don't you know you're in the city... Grandma's pants will soon fit Willy."

"I'll give ya a Willy," Luisa said and giggled.

"Oh carry me off to the burying ground." This was Fiorenza's standard reply to anything. Joe looked out the window and saw Stephen sitting on the stoop of Saunder's Pharmacy across the street. "There's the little bastard... he played hooky again today."

"Again! What's wrong with that boy!" Luisa chimed in.

"Thaaat boy!" said Joe, in beer-sodden tones, referring not to Stephen but to Stevie, nicknamed Chubby; this was a kind of greeting to his brother, who responded with sharp short hiccup-laughs and various head gestures in the Ed Norton style. Stevie never said much. This was about as far as communication got even within the inner-circles of the Cazzaza family.

Joe took the cigar out of his pocket. "Another stale cigar from the Jew downstairs." He threw the cigar in the trashcan.

"Here comes that boy," said Stephen's Aunt Luisa.

Stephen got up from the stoop and crossed the street. He passed through the alleyway. They heard the front door open and shut, and then footsteps on the stairs and then footsteps coming down the long straight hallway, footsteps like years passing.... his footsteps all over this town, walking its streets, alleys, yards, sidewalks, stores, stairs, hallways, hills, rooms, roofs, beach sands, walls, fences, paths, piers, lawns, gardens, school halls... and then he stopped walking...

1969

The 1960s didn't arrive in Oyster Bay in the 1960s, the 1960s arrive in 1970, when on a spring day about fifty students gathered in front of the high school to protest against the incursion, though the students insisted that it was an invasion, of Cambodia, and the killing of four students by National Guardsmen at Kent State University the previous day. That was it. The 1960s arrived one day and left the next. Oyster Bay's stalwart conservative Republican old guard hardly blinked a reptilian eye. Theodore Roosevelt didn't even turn over in his grave. And on the forthcoming Memorial Day the biggest parade the town had ever witnessed was held. Someone did stick a bouquet of flowers into the tubular shanks of the old cannon, Roosevelt's Spanish American War artifact, a relic on the village green, but that wasn't to protest anything, that was done in memory of the legendary hero Winthrop Overkill, who died seven years ago defending the town against some plot of a crazed anarchist to destroy all that is good and decent in America.

But the good and the decent prevailed. On January 20, 1969, Richard Milhouse Nixon was sworn in as president, the nation's 37th. Two months later the secret bombings of Cambodia were underway.

It was the year of Woodstock: dreams of marijuana and LSD, free love and peace, and rock music; it was the year of Altamont, nightmares of violence, Hell's Angels and murder, amphetamine and heroin, and rock music; it was the year of the first reports of the My Lai massacre: Charlie Company and Lt. Calley, old Vietnamese men, and women, and children ripped apart by machine-gun fire down in a bloody ditch; and it wasn't the only bloody ditch; it was the year of the Vietnam Moratorium Day, to which Vice-President Spiro Agnew responded by saying that the whole thing was encouraged by an effete corps of snobs who characterized themselves as intellectuals; it was the year that America Indians occupied Alcatraz Island in San Francisco Bay; it was the year that thousands marched on Washington, gathering at the Justice Department building, only to be dispersed by tear gas, while Richard Nixon watched a football game on television in the White house; it was the year that men first walked on the moon, and that was the week that Jimmy Pushin was killed in Vietnam; and it was the year that Joe Cazzaza and his son Stephen went to Shea Stadium and saw the New York Mets in the midst of an eleven-game winning streak defeat the San Francisco Giants. Stephen's clearest memory of that game was the home run that Willie McCovey hit against the narrow scoreboard in right field, a line drive that went BAM ZOOM BANG so fast you could hardly follow the ball.

1969... what a year! Neil Armstrong walked on the moon! The Mets won the World Series! And Fiorenza Cazzaza died. She was eighty-six.

Joe Cazzaza was shaken. It was hard for him to deal with this kind of stuff. Joe liked to be left undisturbed. Anything that was a bother was too disturbing; even the CBS Evening News with Walter Cronkite was beyond the limits of small town America and Joe Cazzaza's place in it. He wasn't about to confront anything that would shake the foundations of his cautious and distrusting world. Wars, murders, riots, assassinations, student protests, rock music, Woodstock, Ted Kennedy, Charles Manson, Hippies, drugs. Unless he shook them himself, or let them be shook by neglect and habits of omission. And that's what was happening. The house was actually falling apart. The roof was breaking and water was leaking through; the roof in one room was caving in. The grass and the garden were let go to weeds and high grass. The house hadn't been painted in years. And one winter day while Torhild and her children were watching television, a rat ran across the floor. The rooms in the house were filled with boxes and clothes and sundry clutter. Only at Christmas time was the place put in order, because everything was piled up and hidden, giving the place a semblance of care. Things had gone wrong. The family was falling apart. But Joe Cazzaza refused to see it, refused to act.

When Sylvia had a nervous breakdown... what was that? Whatta gonna do? His entire family was broken down, crippled, insane... normal conditions, dese are the conditions that prevail, said Jimmy Durante. Joe's Aunt Teresa was still in the mental institution, had been there since 1927, but no one was concerned, no one visited her there in all those years, and then there was Leonora, she killed herself by throwing herself in front of a train. Joe's mother and his two aunts always sitting in the windows of the front rooms, and then his mother and his sister and brother always sitting in the windows of the front rooms... and now his mother dead; she who gave birth to him in one of these front rooms, and now it was in that chair in that front room that Luisa found her mother dead. Luisa, who administered to her mother all her adult life; she bathed her, brought her the bedpan, gave her insulin injections for her diabetes, and pushed her in a wheelchair back and forth down the long dark hallway to the front room where she could sit in the window and watch over South Street and all the goings on. On Memorial Day 1927 she sat in the window with her two sisters. They were waiting for the town parade to begin and the world to end.

Joe Cazzaza looked out the front room window and saw his son sitting on the stoop of Saunder's Pharmacy. Played hooky again. Stephen was heading straight for reform school and it was nobody's fault but his own. Would they really send him away from home? Torhild asked her husband. Sure they will, the fuckin' nut. That's what his father called him, when he got angry, fed up, announcing it to all his buddies in the bar. When he couldn't deal with it he went straight to the bar, after work, after payday, after an argument, a confrontation, after and before anything... how would he handle his mother's death?

At Fiorenza's funeral they filed in one after the other and all heads turned; flowers and death. The Cazzaza family was sitting in the front row. The coffin buried in flowers. An unforgettable smell; an unforgettable association, flowers and death. They came into the room, kneeled at the coffin, and crossed themselves in the Catholic fashion. They got up, slowly, turned around, and shook hands with the family, commiserating, mentioning a favorite recollection of the deceased. They continued to file in and sign the reception book. As they entered they looked around for signs of recognition. There were familiars like the Van Heffner brothers, Mr. Biggs, Tony Razzini, Luigi Carducci, Elia Preggo, Sr., Elia Preggo Jr., Mr. Hodman, Mr. Hoffman, Hy Horowitz, Abe Gilman, and tenants who had lived in the apartments in the Cazzaza building, people who had worked in the shops in the building, distant relatives, strangers to some, and there was little Rocky. And there was Fiorenza clutching her rosary; Stephen kept staring at it, as if at any moment she would move those long thin fingers that used to grab him by the shoulder and then hand him a dime or even a dollar from the little black purse she kept hidden under her pile of many pillows.

The next morning just the immediate family arrived at Da Vino's Funeral Home. It was a bright and sunny day, everyone said so. They came up to the coffin and stood there, sons and daughters, grandchildren, and then Mr. Da Vino said the Lord's Prayer, the Apostles' Creed, and three

Angelical Salutations. Hail Mary, full of grace, the Lord is with thee; blessed art thou amongst women; and blessed is the fruit of thy womb, Jesus. Holy Mary, Mother of God, pray for us, sinners, now and at the hour of our death. Amen.

They slowly walked out. The coffin was closed. She was gone from the world forever. The coffin and the procession rode up to the Catholic Church. Torhild and her children have never been inside here before. They've been going to the Methodist Church. But her husband's family is Catholic. The others in the congregation looked at Torhild and her children when they weren't making the sign of the cross. And why were they not repeating the words after the priest? Way up in back Stephen heard angels singing, crying, and making weeping sounds. And look at all those candles, if I only had my water pistol. Then the priest swinging a censer and walking around the coffin, and when Torhild and her children were instructed to leave the pew to take Holy Communion they just looked at one and other doubtfully, until Susan, gregarious lovable nine-year-old Susan steps out into the aisle and by herself leads the way for the others, and Stephen feels a tinge of embarrassment; again, Stephen hears the angels... *Agnus Dei... peccata mundi... Agnus Dei... dona nobis pacem...* who is this Agnes woman? Torhild couldn't understand any of it; her mind focused on her grandfather sitting by himself in the corner of the kitchen in the small white house back on the farm in Norway, reading his Bible, keeping his religion to himself. She always told her children, my grandfather was a good man, and he kept his religion to himself. His most austere ritual was praying every morning among the cows in the field, asking God to protect little Tulle, his pet name for Torhild.

Stephen wanted to be a pallbearer, but he was told that he couldn't do it because he wasn't old enough. He watched his father carry the coffin; don't trip dad... that would be embarrassing. Stephen often dreamed that his father was walking down a crowded street and fell into a hole and Stephen had to try to help him get out. Stephen had to protect him. But from what? From his father's tears?

Go, the Mass is finished. Thanks be to God.

Fiorenza was being carried out and placed in the hearse. Carry me off to the burying ground, she had always said so. The hearse drove pass the building on South Street, as was the tradition that had started with Giuseppe Cazzaza back in 1927; the hearse passing the alley, the bar, the front room windows. There were no eyes looking down on South Street on this day. All the eyes were looking up. Stephen was amazed at the size of space inside the black limousine. Wow, this car must cost a hundred dollars. They all laughed.

Stephen remembers the tears that were shed at his grandmother's wake. He remembers the wake for two reasons: It was the only time that he ever saw his father cry, and for the strange scene that was caused when Aunt Mary's nephew Augustine arrived with three of his friends. The wake was being held at Frankie and Mary's house. Frankie had rummaged through the attic and found an old reel-to-reel audiotape that he had made years ago of Toots singing in the Catholic Church in Northport. When he played the tape at the wake, Joe Cazzaza bawled like a newborn baby. Stephen never felt so embarrassed. Here was his dad crying, and Aunt Toots singing... *Ave Maria*... the church organ playing, the organ that Toots and her husband Johnny Bacigalupo had donated to the church.

And then Augustine came through the door with his friends, Frank Yamada dressed in a silk purple smoking jacket, followed by a black guy with an elaborate afro, followed by a thin blond girl, wearing jeans, a halter top, headband, beads, and orange bellbottoms. Augustine was bringing the rebellious sixties to Oyster Bay; maybe the 1960s did come to Oyster Bay in the 1960s after all. It was culture shock. The following morning when Augustine didn't come downstairs for the breakfast that Mary had prepared as usual, before Augustine went to work, it wasn't anything as small as culture shock; Mary called up the stairs but heard no answer, so she asked her son Edward to go up and take a look. Edward seemed nervous.

Lance Corporal Edward Cazzaza, 1st Marine Division, arrived home last August from Okinawa, where he was recuperating from shrapnel wounds sustained in fighting in the Battle of Hue, while wielding his 106mm recoilless rifle through the streets.

Augustine had lived in the room in the attic ever since he came from Ireland, where he had lived after his father had died in a German bomb that fell on North London. He has been no trouble at all since he came to live with Mary and she didn't suspect him of much of anything. Mary cooked him breakfast and dinner; that was about it. He had kept to himself. He worked in the machine shop at Grumman, was involved in the Lunar Module project, he often said, but not much else.

Augustine would disappear for the weekends, going into the city, but Mary never pried. Though there was that one time recently when he came back home with cuts and bruises on his face. He said it was from some skirmish in a pub in the Village was all. So now Mary nearly died when she saw him come through the door with that strange crowd during the wake. He had never brought anyone home before, had never even mentioned friends. Yet they seemed polite enough, though they giggled a lot. Augustine introduced his friends: Frank Yamada, and Alexander Ali Pope, "Call me Pope Ali," and Poppyseed, and they went upstairs. A few moments later Edward came home from his VFW meeting.

"How was the meeting dear?" his mother asked. "Did you see any old war buddies?"

"Yeah, we're gonna get together for a drink later."

"That's nice."

That evening after everyone went home from the wake except for Augustine and his friends, who were still upstairs, Edward was sitting in the living room with his mother and father watching television. It was just after 6 p.m. and the local news was on channel 5. What's going on up there? Edward pictured it in his mind, group sex, interracial sex, smoking grass, discussing the overthrow of the government, anti-war protests, this shouldn't go on in his mother's house! What was actually going on was even more subversive than Edward could have ever imagined in his wildest flag-kissing fervor: Alexander Ali Pope was reading his poetry aloud.

my people will have the power again
be made whole again a-men
the power that was in the beginning a-men
when the white man was a snow ball at the North Pole
when the white man couldn't walk or love or dance or sing
until the black man show him how to do those things
Africa, my Africa, where man was born, black and beautiful
young and free, until the white man come like a glacier
rolling over the earth, and took away our li-ber-ty
now we come to take it back-a, back-a, back-a
take it back-a to Af-ri-ca.

"That was beautiful, man," said Poppyseed.

And then they sang a duet, changing the words to the popular Civil Rights anthem *We Shall Overcome*. Augustine strummed the guitar.

We have all we need
We have all we need
We have all we need today
Oh guns and a bible
And the all-mighty dollar
We have all we need today.

Augustine and his friends came down stairs. When Edward saw Poppyseed and Pope Ali with his arm around her shoulder, words and images of interracial sex played in his mind: and Edward felt the heat rise in his face, his flesh reddening, his fist tightening, nigger lover, white trash, hippie shit, queer...

Augustine and his friends said goodbye and left the house.

"Aren't you going to meet your buddies, Edward?" said Mary.

"Yeah," said Edward. And Frankie and Mary sat down to watch the Lawrence Welk Show by themselves. Goodnight, sleep tight, and pleasant dreams to you.

And that night Edward and his Marine buddies followed Augustine and his friends in a car along the Shore Road, swerving precariously near the railing, passing the spot where Anthony Bacigalupo crashed his delivery truck years ago and died, and now bottles of beer are being flung out the windows of the car and into the bay, and they followed Augustine and his friends to the Shore House Bar, walked in and in a few moments realized that they were in a gay bar, so smashed a few tables and screamed fuckin' fags and queers. The cops were called in; Edward and his buddies scrammed.

Later Edward and his buddies found Augustine and his friends at the beach by the entrance to Center Island. They were smoking dope; so Edward and his crew came upon them stealthily, and the three of them dragged Pope Ali into the underground passageway that leads from the beach in the bay to the beach in the sound, and beat him bloody, leaving him with his big afro hair twisted from fists grasping and pulling, kicks to the face and stomach, rolling over, covered with sand, and then the girl, by the edge of the soft receding waves, harassed by Edward and his buddies while they held and taunted Augustine and Frank, C'mon fags, you do her, like a man, and left her on the wet sand by a dead horseshoe crab and a piece of driftwood, and then they stripped the clothes from Augustine and

Frank and encircled them and said let's see how fags do it, and Frank, who was past sixty years old, broke down crying, I'm an old man, and he and Augustine crawled to each other and held each other, and Edward said is that it? C'mon man, and they teased Augustine and then Edward kicked his boot into Frank's face, and a boot to Augustine's ribs, and they fell over on their sides, panting, sweating, and Edward's buddies picked them up and punched them in their stomachs repeatedly, and Edward kneeled over them and said, "Did you ever feel a bullet rip your fuckin flesh wide open, the shrapnel tearing the flesh off your bones, and then feel the blood running down your arms and legs and touch the warm blood with your own hands, here, feel it, you've been wounded Corporal, the VC cut your ass to the quick, man, and you're dead, I'm dead, and Jim's dead and Sal's dead, ain't that right? you guys are dead? right? We're all dead, you got fifty fuckin bullet holes in you and you're dead, we're in hell, boys, you can smell the fire and the burning flesh, and they just tossed us in a helicopter with the empty supply cases dropping right on top of us, hands and feet sticking out everywhere, flying with that angel of mercy out of hell, during the Tet, at Hue, about a year ago, a year ago in time, and space, I think about time and space, space, being here, being there, shadows moving between reality and death, strange to be here now, I'm here, I'm here, right here, see this sand, there's nothing wrong with this sand, is there a trip wire in it? Blow your fuckin legs off, does the sand feel pain? Does the water? I bet you feel pain, did you ever feel pain like this before? This is nothing, we only tickled your fag asses, you don't know pain, real pain, you don't know nothin, how could you, how the fuck could you know anything, how about I cut off your balls and stick them in your mouth, you're not a man anyway, ya fuckin fag, you goddam dinks... Sal and Jim pulled Edward to his feet and said let's get outta here, man, who cares about them, let's go...

Later that night Edward slipped into his mother's house and went to bed. His mom and dad had fallen asleep in their chairs after watching *The Tonight Show* starring Johnny Carson. Augustine came in a while later. How could he say anything? How could he tell her? About her son the war hero. It would drive her mad. And she's been so nice to him since he came here. He went upstairs to his room in the attic.

He didn't come down in the morning. Mary went upstairs. Edward followed. His mother entered the room. And there Mary saw Augustine hanging from his belt. "Cut him down," said his mother, calmly. Edward thought that she sounded like John Wayne in *The Longest Day*. You remember the scene: Soldiers hanging from poles. Red Buttons hanging from the church steeple. "Cut 'em down," says John Wayne. Edward helped get Augustine down and laid him gently on the bed. The police and the ambulance came. They put him on the stretcher. Detective Abe Desurd had a few questions.

On a spring day in 1969 Stephen was watching television. Outside in the world there were riots and war. Inside on the television there were riots and war.

On a summer day in 1969 Stephen was watching television. He was watching a rocket blast off to the moon.

On an October day in 1969 Stephen was watching television. He was watching the New York Mets win the World Series.

In January 1970 he went to a high school basketball game; it was the night before he was to be taken away to a home for children in upstate New York.

He never returned the book that he had taken out from the school library, *Twenty Thousand Leagues Under the Sea*. He took the book with him upstate. It was like a comfort object, as long as none of the pages were torn out...

Sentenced to hell. Sent to heaven. Guns and rockets. Guns and a Bible. Doom and happiness.

pika-pika boom-boom beep-beep

Was America really sealed and safe forever like those documents in Washington... fireproof, shockproof and bombproof?

Book Three

Vulcano Outwords 1969-1992

Willie McCovey Hits a Home Run

October 1969! What a great month, huh? What a great year! First, the Amazing New York Mets win the World Series, defeating the mighty Baltimore Orioles in five games. It was a miracle. When Buford, the first batter up for the Orioles, hit Tom Seaver's pitch over the fence, my father said: It's gonna be like playing a little league team. My father was a very pessimistic man. But, as was the clarion call four years later: ya gotta believe, right?

Then I get the shit scared out of me by appearing in Family Court. Probation papers I had to sign like some dumb oath. Oh but what a year! Man lands on the moon. The Jets beat the Colts in the Super Bowl. Broadway Joe over the great Johnny Unitas. Actually, I was pulling for the old guard. I was kind of a Colt fan; I was actually a Giant fan like my Dad, but they sucked. *Wait'll next year*, my Dad said, sarcastically quoting the Giant's head coach Allie Sherman. In New York sport's terms, my father had presented me with a moral dilemma of no little significance. Most of my friends were Jets/Mets fans or Giant/Yankee fans. I was a Giants/Mets fan. This got me into loads of trouble with my friends, and in none too few fistfights. How did this come about? Well, my father had been a Giant's fan, both baseball and football, since the thirties, and when the baseball Giants moved to San Francisco in the late fifties, becoming a Yankee fan was absolutely out of the question. Then the Mets arrived. To play in Robert Moses' Roman Coliseum called Shea Stadium. So it was football Giants and baseball Mets, an unnatural entangling alliance, perhaps, but those kids who were loyal to their father's sport's teams will understand. Well, loyalty goes so far. In December I was back in Family Court. I didn't keep my oath. Shows bad character. Judge Amberstein decided to throw the book at me. I caught it, and you are holding it in your hands. I was sent upstate to the Cayuga Home for Boys and Girls. This now puts me in mind of Henry Herbert Goddard, director of research at the Vineland Training School for Feeble-minded Girls and Boys. He had added another word to our ever expanding dictionary: **Moron**. This classification was used to designate children of ages seven to twelve as **Feeble-Minded**. The term **Idiot** included those children up to two years

504

old; and the word **Imbecile** included those children ages three to seven. Inclusion is a wonderful thing. I was fourteen years old. I was beyond the scale. What am I called? Goddard proposed, this is science remember, that two-thirds of mentally defective people inherited their feeble-mindedness. Paupers, criminals, drunkards, drug-addicts, prostitutes, and other ne'er-do-wells are obviously mental defectives. I love this word: ne'er-do-wells. What am I? What am I to be called? I am a writer. Do you really believe that? Therefore I would like to be classified as a **Ne'er-do-well.** A *Dekunobo*, a word we shall return to in the following pages.

The home was opened in Auburn, New York, in 1852 as the Cayuga Asylum for Destitute Children. In the fifties the home started serving the Family Court system. It also instituted the new cottage system of treatment. There were three cottages by 1961: May, Cowen and Emerson. I was appointed to Emerson Cottage in January 1970. Two boys shared one room, and there were approximately sixteen to eighteen boys in the cottage at any given time. My given time was a two-year period extending from 1970 to 1971. That was a cold winter. All it did was snow, like a funnel directed right on Auburn, and all we did was shovel the shit. The boys were ages seven to seventeen, therefore there were many morons and imbeciles, but no idiots thank goodness.

Document 9.3.1

Order and Conditions of Probation

To: Gottlieb S. Brandes

Name: Stephen Knut Cazzaza

Date of Birth: May 24, 1956

Address: 101 Summit Street, Oyster Bay, New York

Having been adjudicated a Juvenile Delinquent or Person in Need of Supervision, is this day on Probation under your supervision. While on Probation, he shall observe the following conditions of Probation, and any others which the Court may impose at a later date, and he shall also follow the instructions of the Probation Officer as to the way in which these conditions are to be carried out:

(1)　　Not to commit a new crime or offense.

(2)　　Obey his parents and all school regulations and directions.

(3)　　Keep all appointments with probation officer.

(4)   Attend school and all classes regularly, or be suitably employed in a job approved by the probation officer.

(5)   Be at home at night by the hour set by his parents and advise parents of whereabouts at all times.

(6)   Avoid any undesirable persons, places, habits or activities: drinking, use of narcotics, gambling, driving without a license... *see the rest of the list in the afterword.

(7)   Other conditions: treatment at a local mental health clinic.

Failure to comply with any of the conditions of probation will constitute a "violation of probation" requiring that the case be returned to court for "revocation of probation" and any other action deemed necessary. In other words: There won't be any free trips to the icebox for a glass of milk anytime you want it anymore!

The parents or guardian of the Probationer are expected to

(1)   Cooperate with the Probation Officer

(2)   Permit the Probation Officer to visit the Probationer at his home or elsewhere. Life is not elsewhere! There is no escape!

(3)   Take him fishing, camping or take him out to the ball game.

Official Classification: Ne'er-do-well.
Dated this 21st day of October 1969
Beatrice Slimeberg, Judge, Family Court, Nassau County
Witness: Ralph Dickman, Probation Officer

Well, I failed to comply.

1970-1971 Upstate

Uncle Chuck walked down the long hallway. Keith, a nine-year-old black kid who is always getting into trouble, or being blamed for all the trouble, and Bucky, a nine-year-old white kid who is always getting into trouble, were fighting. They never got along, but Uncle Chuck kept them as roommates, regardless of the hostility engendered by their close proximity to each other. They came from broken homes, as had most of the boys here. The boys were sent here because they were good kids deep down and still had a chance to make it. Classic misfits. They just couldn't get along with anyone. Not tough guys, not trouble makers, not gang members. Just loners and losers. Bucky was a fat bucktoothed kid from Albany. He loved two things: the Oakland Raiders and the TV show Star Trek. Uncle Chuck let the boys watch football games and Star Trek. Uncle Chuck was from Pittsburgh and was a Steeler's fan. Uncle Chuck liked to watch Jeopardy. "Shut up! I'm getting my education!" And he liked to watch the Hollywood Squares. "That Paul Lynde is a comedic genius!"

Star Trek came on at five o'clock, just after we finished our homework, and before we sat down to eat. That's what Bucky and Keith was fighting about, Star Trek. He started it, said Bucky. I did not, said Keith. Uncle Chuck sent Bucky back to his room. Uncle Chuck stood in the middle of the long hallway and took out a key that opened the door to the medicine closet, where all the boys' pills stood in bottles on the shelf. The closet contained other items. Uncle Chuck grabbed the wooden paddle that was hanging on the back of the door. It had been signed by many of the boys who have had a taste of its wood. Keith had to stand there in front of this door in the hallway dimly lit by recessed lights pulsing down.

"Pick a color, boy," said Uncle Chuck. Keith had to choose a colored tile on the floor upon which to stand and not move from. "Drop your drawers." There was a large assortment of colored tiles: red, green, blue, yellow... Keith stood on a red tile. Then Uncle Chuck gnashed his teeth and said, "five inches... ten inches... twenty inches..." and he whacked Keith on the ass with the wooden paddle pulled back away from his ass the distance in inches that he had said. "Twenty inches." Slam! Keith cried and ran back to his room. Uncle Chuck likes to distribute justice by measurement. He was very scientific and rigorous in his approach.

"I'm gonna kill you Bucky."

"I heard that. Get back out here." Uncle Chuck waited by the door, twitching his eyes. "Pick a color... thirty inches..." Wham! Keith ran back down the hallway, crying. The boys were now hooting from their rooms. "Shut up, Keith." But he kept complaining and crying. Uncle Chuck didn't like crybabies. He was a twenty-year Army veteran, a sergeant, a war photographer, a great patriot... the Vietnam War was being fought and he was reading a biography of George S. Patton and it was not a good time to be here. "What are you crying about, Keith? Better be quiet now. That's enough baby. Baaa-by. Baaaa-byy. Shut up or I'll give you something to cry about." Some of the boys joined the mocking choir. "Baaa-byy." Keith kept whining and crying. Uncle Chuck told him to come back out here. Keith slowly walked back down the hall, his face wet with tears, his pajamas down around his ankles. Did he enjoy this shit? Poor Keith. Uncle Chuck asked him why his elbows were so black. Darker than his skin. I don't know. I'm black. No, said Uncle Chuck, it's because you don't wash them. So Uncle Chuck made Keith wash his elbows, made him scrub and scrub and scrub until the elbows were raw and bleeding.

"Pick a color."

"You hate me. It's cus I'm black, ain't it?"

"Pick a color. Bend over. Forty inches." Slam! "Now shut up or I'll really give you something to cry about."

Keith knew what he meant. The boiler room. Keith had been down there before. All the boys have been down there before. Just last Monday we were all down there. We had returned from the YMCA swimming pool. I wasn't sure why we were all down there. But it was guilt by association. It was the usual; everyone gets punished unless someone finks on the guilty culprit. It had something to do with sex. Uncle Chuck implied this. When the boys got back to the home, to their cottage, emptying out of the red Ford van, Uncle Chuck told them to march downstairs and line up, toes on the yellow line. They stood on the yellow line in the recreation room and waited for Uncle Chuck to come down stairs. He came slowly down the stairs. He turned the corner and captured the whole room in a flash. The boys were quiet, toes on the line, terrified and apprehensive. Beads of sweat formed on Uncle Chuck's forehead, beneath the Richard Nixon contours of his receding hairline. Shit, I thought, can't we just go upstairs and go to bed. Uncle Chuck sat down in a folding chair placed in front of the boys. He spread his legs and leaned forward, resting his elbows on his thighs. He held the paddle in his right hand and tapped it in the palm of his left hand.

"Punks. That's the name for it. That's the name for you. Punks."

It turned out that Uncle Chuck had got himself all worked up over some veiled sexual advances that took place in the pool between some of the boys. When you put a dozen pubertal boys into a swimming pool who are discovering their first sexual impulses, genitals and buttocks tend to rub against each other in differing sequences and combinations. According to Uncle Chuck, this is the behavior of a punk. This was his obscure definition of the word punk. In the 16th century a punk was a whore. By the 1920s in America, punk meant nonsense or twaddle. A punk was also a young guy who works for a circus and thinks he knows everything. A punk is a thug, a hoodlum, and a ruffian. As an adjective it could mean low, inferior, rotten, worthless. In a few years time, by the mid seventies, the word would define a music and its lifestyle. And I would be a part of it. But that's for later. As Bill Burroughs use to say: I thought a punk was someone who took it up the ass. Polysemous semen punk. We used to call a cat-tail a punk.

Uncle Chuck suggested a sexual connotation to the word. Maybe Uncle Chuck knew what he was talking about. So Uncle Chuck sermonized to the boys in a loud, strident drill-sergeant voice. He stopped short of using too many expletives because Aunt Laurie was upstairs and he didn't want her delicate ears to be exposed to the sordid details resounding in vibrating echoes around the cement walls of the recreation room.

The boys were ordered down to the boiler room. We went down a few stairs to the basement, and at the back of the basement, in the dark corner, a heavy door led to the boiler. In here, Uncle Chuck let loose. Every word in the book. Sweat poured off the faces of the boys. And then one by one the boys lined up and passed in front of Uncle Chuck seated in his folding chair, pulled down their pants, and received a whack from the wooden paddle. Then we were sent straight upstairs to bed.

On a spring day in 1970 I was in my 8th grade science class at Auburn Central High School in upstate New York. It was the Home's policy to send the children to public school. I stared out the window to the softball field below, where students were carrying banners and placards with peace signs and ecology slogans emblematic of the first Earth Day. Beyond the field I saw the walls of the prison, the Auburn Correctional Facility. There were cops and barricades set up around the prison. Students were being escorted home. Rumors were that several prisoners had escaped and were at lodge, that they were members of the radical Black Panthers and were "armed and extremely dangerous." It was only a rumor. But later in the year the prison did erupt in riots, and a year after those riots Attica occurred.

Mr. Shelton, the science teacher, was writing at the blackboard, some axiom of Newtonian physics, pure mathematical slogans, while outside students chanted their slogans, and across the street cops with bullhorns directing traffic and pedestrians, barked their slogans.

"What is electricity?" Mr. Shelton asked, rhetorically for the moment. "Think of the connections to the word electric, electric battery, for instance, invented in 1800 by Alessandro Volta. From Volta we get the word volts. Electric generator, invented around 1830 I believe, by Faraday. Electromagnetic Telegraph, invented by Morse in 1837. Let's not forget Benjamin Franklin and his kite. Can you think of any other connections to the word electric? Hands, please. Robert?"

"Electric eel."

"Yes, any more? Greg?"

"Electron."

"Good, an electron is a particle of negative electricity. One more? Stephen?"

"Electric chair."

"Ah, very negative electricity, in a manner of speaking. Anyway, you get the point. Electricity is everywhere."

"Is the Atom Bomb negative electricity?"

"You might say that it is, in a metaphorical sense."

Mr. Shelton then proceeded to enact the classical example of the magnetic field by shaking some iron filings from a bottle onto a piece of white paper with a magnet lying beneath it. He asked the students to conjecture about whether the magnetic lines of force are still present when the filings are not there.

I walked out the front door of the school. There was a crowd of students carrying placards and encircling the field. A magnetic field containing lines of force, I thought. At the end of the walkway police were in the street standing behind barricades, more lines of force. They surrounded the prison. They weren't too concern with the student protest. It was peaceful so far, not too much anti-war sentiment. But the Black Panthers were "armed and very dangerous." I looked at the walls of the prison. It was in this prison that the first man was put to death in the electric chair. His name was William Kemmler. He axed his wife to death. On August 6, 1890, he died in the electric chair.

I looked at the walls of the prison and thought about Maurizio Cazzaza. He was my father's uncle. He was arrested in 1927; he was accused of murder. He was sentenced to die in the electric chair. Don't know what happened to him.

I sat in the back row at the end desk on the right hand side of the classroom by the large windows. If I were a chess piece I would be positioned like the white rook on the king's side. At the blackboard the enemy king stood and held court; the teacher tapped the slate with his chalk. He said, "To every action there is always opposed an equal action. That was it. That was the old law. Newton's Third Law; and by Godfrey it still works; it had better; we've been to the moon and back."

I thought about the book that I was reading, a biography of Charles Lindbergh, one of those American Biography series of children's books that made American myths out of daring men and women. Charles Lindbergh, the Lone Eagle, the Flyin' Fool, who flew solo across the Atlantic in a single engine airplane in 1927, a lone warrior conquering the air, defending honor and pride, old virtues too low for the dizzying concrete heights of skyscrapers and too near for the far expanding reaches of steel bridges. The people became the first mass of industrial waste, and things were cracking and rusting, and who could escape it all? And the machines groaned and the parties roared. We had not been saved by plastic yet. So one man went forth... but how many men had sent him out? One man could ride out on a horse but the horse will not evolve wings, like Pegasus, not in a country without imagination, not in many generations of life; but one man could carry a gun and a bibel. An airplane could evolve; it could even lose its wings and become a missile. And many men and women and children will be waiting at the other end, to cheer? Or to die? The people waited and he came back to us. On that day we cheered... on another day we died, we died in Coventry, Dresden, Stalingrad, Dachau, Buchenwald, Guernica, Rotterdam, Hiroshima, Nagasaki, Budapest, Algiers, Vietnam, Cambodia, and Laos... when one lets go, something must fall. Lindbergh didn't fall; his airplane didn't crash. The stock market crashed. Somebody let go; which group? Which powerful elite? But Lindbergh, a man, a name, a face, held tight. He had guided a machine, commanded and controlled a machine, single-handed. But who was the real hero, man or machine? He was America's first hero of technology; it was a brave new human experience, a personal, solitary experience, an experience of life, and it became a national experience only because he returned, and the people were waiting when he brought back the boon of vicariously experiencing a hero's adventure and a catharsis of a commonplace workaday world. But why bother to return? I was thinking at the time. Why not keep going? America's first flight of fancy. Away from the real world. It was in that year of excesses, 1927, when Babe Ruth hit 60 home runs, far surpassing the previous high for a single season. Yes, what a brave journey, I thought, but why return? Why not keep going? Why not make it a life's journey, not just an event for national consumption? And when John Glenn orbited the earth and returned to an ecstatic welcome home, that too was a fine journey, that too was an adventure, and John Glenn was my first hero. But when we landed on the moon, the balloon was already bursting for me. I watched the moon landing; I saw it with sleepy eyes on the black and white 12" screen of the General Electric television that my father had bought from Hodman's Hardware Store. I was sitting on the couch. I kept dozing off and waking up to the beeps and voices, beeps and voices, and fuzzy images and beeps and voices and beeps...

I could see the school grounds below, on the right was the other half of the school building facing over the grounds at a right angle; the main entrance was in the other side and I watched as students went in and came out, wearing their colorful beads and bright bellbottoms; it seemed as if everyone was wearing bellbottoms, except me. I was forbidden to wear them by the directors of the children's home where I was living now, having been sent here by order of the family court on Long Island.

We were down in the recreation room. A low ceiling room with florescent lighting, thick concrete pillars, a ping-pong table, mats, laundry room, photographic dark room, the exit door to the garage where the garbage is stored in bins, the steps down to the basement and at the back of the basement, the boiler room... a punching bag in the far corner, folding chairs, yellow lines painted on the concrete floor... the boys come downstairs and line up on the yellow line. Uncle Chuck commands the boys to put their toes on the line. Uncle Chuck slowly descends the stairs. Things have to be worked out; some conflicts have to be resolved.

Leon and Ronnie were told to put the gloves on... the mats were dragged to the center of the recreation room. There is a folding chair in each corner and a chair for Uncle Chuck, the judge and referee all in one... the boys stood around, about 16 boys watching, two about to fight... when they were ready Uncle Chuck said go, and the two boys came out swinging wildly like windmills, hitting and slapping, pummeling each other, Leon's scabby pimply face starting to bleed, Uncle Chuck yells stop and the two boys sit down winded, panting... Uncle Chuck evaluates the situation, and after a minute's rest the fight resumes... some boys are drawn toward one or the other, Barry, David, Jim, Stephen, Bucky, Keith, Peter, Dennis, Bobby, Doug, Joe... their ages ranged from eight to seventeen. The two boys fighting were both sixteen. I stood and watched; I did a play-by-play in my head; I called the action, like Frazier vs. Ali in March... I observed the spectacle... "A right cross to the head, a hook... a left jab..." It was just like when I was home, before I was sent here, when I played in the front yard, tossing a broken piece of Styrofoam in the air and hitting it with a broken broom handle. I did the play-by-play in my head, describing the action... it was the 1968 World Series, the Cardinals against the Tigers; I knew the lineup, Lou Brock, Curt Flood, Roger Maris, Orlando Cepeda, Mike Shannon, Julian Javier, Tim McCarver, Dal Maxvil, Bob Gibson... I was rooting for the Cardinals; I had to choose sides... even though I was a Mets fan.

I went to see my first game at Shea Stadium in 1967 against the Braves, Henry Aaron, Joe Torre, Felipe Alou, and Rico Carty, it was a double header on a hot summer day.... we sat several rows up behind home plate. And left before the end of game two, it was so hot... we got the tickets from Macy's out on route 110... but last year the Mets finally started to win and dad took me to several games, including a game against the San Francisco Giants, and my clearest memory of that game was the home run Willie McCovey hit against the small rectangular scoreboard in right field, Bam, Zoom, the ball went so fast you could hardly follow it... the Mets went on to win their first World Series in 1969, the only real miracle ever documented... I mean there were millions of witnesses... look it up in the big book of stats!

And now Ronnie has hit Leon so hard that his nose and mouth are bleeding. Uncle Chuck usually stops the fights when blood is drawn, but just before he yells to quit, Ronnie hits Leon one more time and drives him back toppling over and smashing his head against a concrete pillar... Leon lay unconscious... Leon was out cold. Uncle Chuck called upstairs to his wife and she came downstairs with some smelling salts and a cold towel. Leon opened his eyes and shook his head. He went upstairs and cleaned up. Leon complained of headaches for a week. I was his roommate. He couldn't play his Led Zeppelin album. He couldn't listen to *Whole Lotta*

Love as he always did, and really loud, until Uncle Chuck told him to turn it down. Then one day when Leon and I were in gym class at Auburn Central High School, playing softball in a field with a short right field fence with a pile of car tires behind it, and a view of Auburn Correctional Facility, Leon collapsed in right field and died of a brain hemorrhage. The gym teacher Mr. Adams ran over to him and told me to run for help. I ran. The boys were stunned when we heard the news... but we were told that accidents happen, and the boy's cottage is restricted from any more skateboarding until this incident is history. And Uncle Chuck read his book, a biography of Patton, and Nixon started bombing Cambodia secretly... secrets, secrets everywhere... and death death death. Ever since Richard Nixon said "Sock it to me," on television, we have had our leaders in our homes performing comedy like the guy next door, as if they are just regular guys, with no blood on their hands. My Methodist Sunday school teacher talks about us kids only having known war, death, and he got the reverend to play *Jesus Christ Superstar* in its entirety on a record player set up in front of the altar in church on a Sunday morning. The older people walked out. And we mocked them as they did.

Uncle Chuck had the radio playing one time when we were sitting down to dinner. The song "Lookin' Out My Backdoor" came on the radio. Uncle Chuck liked the song. He said it was a Hank Williams' song. And I, maybe for the first time in my life, stood up for my convictions, because I had the record, the 45, you know, I had the documentation, said, "No, it's not. It's a song by Creedence Clearwater Revival. I can get the record and show you." Uncle Chuck was mildly perplexed. I was always so obedient. He said, "Ok OK, sit down, I believe you."

Later when I got back to my room I took out the 45, and there it was, FANTASY on the green and red label, LOOKIN' OUT MY BACK DOOR and printed underneath (J. C. Fogerty).

I was sitting at my desk, looking out the window. I looked down to the school grounds where the grass, what there was of it, had been smeared and trodden by trampling feet the day before yesterday in the anti-war rally. The wooden fence in front of the school had been stampeded and was lying broken and battered on the ground. The police barricades had not been removed yet. They had been knocked over and scattered around the grounds. Torn banners and signs were dumped into the corner of the baseball field behind home plate, where older banners from last week's

Earth Day celebration were turning yellow and faded. In my mind I saw the New York Mets on the field, and Tom Seaver pitching, my second hero. Several students were sitting on the wooden bleachers behind home plate, eating lunch. As I looked across the field and down the narrow alleyway between a barbershop and a gas station, my gaze came in contact with a slither of the tall brick wall of Auburn Correctional Facility. It was in this prison that my father's uncle Maurizio Cazzaza had been incarcerated on two counts of first-degree murder in 1927. He was scheduled to die in the electric chair. A machine death. A technological death. Whatever happened to him? I walked out of the school building. I saw more of the the twenty foot high stone walls of Auburn Correctional Facility. A huge fortification of grey. It had gun towers and the strange figure of a man atop the building. I was told that this was "Copper John." I walked pass Fred's Service Station and down the street.

Every so often I saw a counselor or therapist. I wasn't sure what Mr. Simon was... Mr. Simon puffed on his pipe, inadvertently sprinkling tobacco all over his desk, and he stared at me, and said nothing. I said nothing and stared at the wall. If Simon didn't speak, I didn't speak. Just before our last session ended, Simon said to me, "Come over here." I stood up and stepped over to Simon's desk. "Bend down," said Simon, "I want to tell you some good news." I bent down to listen and Simon smacked me across the face. Simon said, "That's for being good. Oh, and by the way, you'll be going home next month."

At first I was angry that the idiot had smacked me, but then realized what Simon had said, about going home. That made me happy. Another fucking paradox in life... absurdity, irony, satire, ambiguity, ambivalence... these will be the themes of my life... and what is the meaning of all this shit? There is no meaning, no answer. I needed a smack in the face just for nothing to wake up. Anger and happiness, doom and happiness, beep-beep. Mr. Simon angered me and then rewarded me. Meaning resided in the operation of power. Without power there was no meaning. Power and violence. History has meaning because it has power. Violence, like a boxing match, a death, a lie to cover it up... and do you speak truth to power? That'll get you a smack in the face. Power lies in truth. And when Simon stared silently at me and I at him for a half hour, which of us held the power? Who had the answers? Simon's smack in the face was the answer to my silence, not my good behavior. The answer to my good behavior was my being released and sent home. My good behavior may have saved me, but my silence got me a smack in the face. Silence closes off the mind completely. My behavior lets them, the others, in, slightly. But they want to get in completely. No mental barriers. It's like they want me to swear an oath of allegiance if I choose to remain silent. What if I had been both silent and bad? Like some modern anti-hero who thought about writing a post-modern novel... but why the fuck bother.

He shuffled down the hall and stood before a door. He was a short man. He was very old. The door swung open and he entered a room. A man behind the desk told him to sit down. The man introduced himself. "Hello, Maurizio, I am Doctor Bitsen, the new prison psychiatrist." Maurizio stared at him silently. The prison in 1971 held about 1500 prisoners. They were mostly black and brown men. Maurizio was the oldest prisoner. He was referred to as that "old Italian gentleman." Some of the prisoners thought that he had connections to the Genovese crime family. He was respected. Maurizio told them to read books about anarchism. One crazy guy named Joe kept asking all these philosophical questions, directed to Maurizio. "Don't read Machiavelli," said Maurizio to Joe. "No Nietzsche!"

"You have been incarcerated for a long time, Maurizio, since 1927." The psychiatrist wasn't too worried about this inmate. He was not very intimidating. He wasn't like the big menacing black man that just left his office and had told him to shut the fuck up with his shrink bullshit. Dr. Bitsen kept his finger on the panic button under his desk the entire interview. But Maurizio was hardly a threat and the doctor could relax. The doctor opened a folder and looked over the pile of papers. "Hmnn... two counts of first degree murder... by dropping statues... that's a new one."

"Falling... not dropping... see the difference? It's the words!"

Some of the prisoners that the doctor interviewed were anxious to talk. These men were always the ones who were contriving and plotting and studying law books and court transcripts, in an attempt at engineering their own exoneration, even if only in their own minds. There were others who dabbled in books on the occult, weird sects, and conspiracy theories. There were others who were connivers, hustlers, wheeler-dealers, gambling, bartering, and who had a great aptitude for numbers... if they were honest they would have been good businessmen. Some of the men were painters, poets, and writers, and they couldn't wait to show their work to Dr. Bitsen.

There was much death and violence and blood. Dr. Bitsen encouraged them; after all, he told them, what's Macbeth and Hamlet without a little death, violence and blood. The standard reply: I tried to read that shit but it ain't in English. Others were quiet. They were near to their date of release and they didn't want anything to go wrong. Maurizio was mostly quiet, nodding and whispering a yes or a no. At the end of the interview he asked the doctor for a favor. "Yes, Maurizio, if I can help you but..." Maurizio said, "When I am dead I want my ashes sent back to Italy, to Orero, in Liguria... just like Vanzetti..."

"Who?" said the doctor.

"Not who... Vanzetti..."

"Oh, Sacco and Vanzetti... I see..." said the doctor.

"I see says the blind man..." answered Maurizio.

Document 5.8.2

Excerpt from *The Student Handbook*

Oyster Bay High School

The two main purposes of the English Department here at Oyster Bay High School are to familiarize the student with literature, both classical and modern, and to teach him to express himself clearly grammatically. The English teacher endeavors to teach his students skills which will aid them in other fields, skills such as taking notes, reading efficiently, organizing written material, speaking clearly and audibly, and cooperating with others.

A brief description of the work done by grade levels includes:

English 12th year: Gaining insight through literature into human behavior as well as into persons and experiences foreign to the reader; understanding modern writing; developing intellectual curiosity; recognizing apt, colorful words and phrases; reading thoughtfully and appreciatively; skimming intelligently; organizing and summarizing research material; recounting personal experiences and observations; becoming conscious of words; realizing that language is constantly changing; forming habits of courteous, attentive listening.

Curriculum:

Textbook: An Anthology of American Narration © 1966, Pukklesen Press

Contents:

1. Tales of Baseball, by Stanley Short

2. Tales of Democracy/Capitalism, is it either/or? by Wilfred Smatter

3.   Tales of Space Travel, by Werner Loophinder
4.   Tales of the Immigrant, by Urban Tennant
5.   Tales of the Automobile, by Shelby Goggle
6.   Tales of Columbus and History, by Aliaspun Atale
7.   Tales of Hollywood Movies, by Ihkabibble Babcock
8.   Tales of Theodore Roosevelt, by Roger Bethell
9.   Tales of the Great American Novel, by Al Abbot
10. Tales of the Cold War, by Learned Handsome
11. Tales of the Bomb, by Anot Hitz
12. Tales of Television and Technology, by Mewanna Moore

Graduation Awards: Julia L. Thurston Award- to the senior attaining the highest average in the study of English.

I didn't win any awards. In the high school literary magazine I published four poems, as Anonymous.

Thomas Pynchon also attended Oyster Bay High School, and in the "Purple and Gold" high school newspaper he published six short pieces in 1952 and 1953. He worked on the high school yearbook, "The Oysterette."

He received the Thurston Award. It was in the glass display case, with all the basketball and football trophies, near the auditorium doors, and in later years I was told that the award was "missing," and Mr. O'Donell, the school's truant officer, and an old friend of mine, didn't know what had happened to it when I asked him about it years later. Was it purloined?

Well, I'm back home and in my old high school. But not for long.

I worked as a landscaper for a while on one of the large estates up the cove. I lost the job when this famous fashion designer bought the place, and brought in Puerto Ricans from the city. He bought it for his wife. That was the rumor, a famous actress who was writing her autobiography there. But more and more I was taking the train into the city.

NYC 1975-1979

Greenwich Village. Long ago in a subterranean basement below street level there was a local watering hole called Pfaffs. It was a restaurant that served decent food. There were proper tables located in the front of the restaurant. But in the back you could find the likes of actors, poets, artists, and journalists, downing a few beers. Walt Whitman was a patron who gathered around him some of nature's darlings. They spilled out into the night and trampled up Broadway with the shoppers and theatergoers and prostitutes. They were called bohemians and regarded as such.

I hear the bells of St. Anthony's of Padua, where my grandma was baptized, bong bong, over Sullivan Street and Houston Street. Italian immigrants built the Romanesque artifice and it was consecrated in 1888.

There was a long line of bohemians, radicals, hipsters, beatniks, be-boppers, folkies, and punks... who passed through this welcoming but revolving door. There were many who fluttered in and out of the Village over the years: Edgar Allen Poe, Stephen Crane, Theodore Dreiser, Upton Sinclair, John Reed, Emma Goldman, Henry James, Eugene O'Neill, Djuna Barnes, Edna St. Vincent Millay, Mabel Dodge Luhan, Marcel Duchamp, Henry Miller, ee cummings, Frank O'Hara, John Cage, Dylan Thomas, W. H. Auden, Woody Guthrie, Jack Kerouac, Allen Ginsberg, William Burroughs, Bob Dylan, Andy Warhol, Patti Smith, and Stephen Cazzaza...

It was New York City and it was a cold December evening. I heard a soliloquy on 42nd Street. Listen: "So dis iz Chris-mas, ain't none of my biznus, hey Salva-shun Army, I need some of dat money. I waz in the army once too, dat's why I iz blue. War is over, but not for me, c'mon nummer ten, it's too cold for my men, it wasn't cold but it's a jungle here tonight, yeah yeah yeah oh yeah, hey John Lindsay, Abe Beame, and crazy I said crazy Eddie Koch... oh the steam I said the steam from the subway is warming my cold crotch. Hey crazy Eddie where are you tonight? Yeah yeah yeah oh yeah. I sleep in dah alley, where are you loo-ten-ent Cal-ly? WORE! What is it good for? Oh where are you Henry Kiss...Kiss in... kiss my ass, I can't find a rhyme for yo' stoopid name. Ain't dat a shame... here I am... green eggs and ham, yuck, watch out for that son of Sam... Hey! we won dah revolooshinery wore, we won dah wore of a etten twelve..."

...and a tourist with a tan, and a little old lady with her house in a bright red Macy's bag. Cabbies playing tag; but I'm waiting for a bus downtown, at least I know what direction to go; crazy people all around me! Here's the scene: at the back of the bus sat the black brown-bagger dressed in military green, lit up like a Christmas tree this Times Square night of holiday shoppers and NYC's finest coppers, hookers and off-track bettors and bookers, theatre goers and cock blowers, purple clad pimps with royal limps, smack addicts in ragged jackets, soldiers of vagrancy marching the streets aimlessly in the white sleet of a December 42nd Street. The black drunk begins to declaim on a nation's shame, punctuating each line with a swig from a bottle of cheap wine: "We won dah revolooshinery wore… we won dah war a etten twelve… we won dah ci-vil wore… yeah man it's in dah history books… den we won dah first wawrl wore… den we won dah sekin wawrl wore… den we won dah kohrin wore… but we lawst... we lawst in Nam... shit… shiii-it… I ain't no goddamn hero here in New Yawk Ci-ty tonite with the cold and snow comin' down hard real hard upon my black ass… no way man…" Pause of reflection in pain-stabbed eyes; bus stops... on off on off on off… "Yeah we won dah revolooshinery wore… we won dah wore a etten twelve… we won dah ci-vil wore… den we won dah first wawrl wore… den we won dah sekin wawrl wore… den we won dah kohrin wore… kicked ass… no shit… but we lawst in Nam man... man... MAN... YOU LISSININ' ta ME man I says we fuckin' lawst in VI-et SHI-et Nam… shit I waz in dere in dat fuckin' jungle. We never ever looz till we looz in Nam. Shit hole jungle. We jus wazint no good enuff brave enuff strawng enuff. Like dey waz back den man. George Washindon Ulysis S Padden Genral John Wayne. Shit… I know, I saw dah movies man. It's hisdory… American hisdory. It's the truth MUDDER FUCKERS!!!" Shouts... bus riders stare away; no eye contact... bus stops. Some get on, some get off. Sing: "Oh lord they shot George Jackson down, Oh carry me off to the buryin' ground, give peace a chance, save the last dance for me, I'm as happy as a kitten up a tree, look at me, look at me… Lord, Lord… we won dah revolooshinery wore… we won dah wore of etten twelve… We won dah ci-vil wore…"

An old man in Manhattan, with his 1940s fedora hat on; walking the alphabet streets of Sodom, with his inkling of a hard on. This old man in his damp room, with his damn rheumatism and his filthy fruit of the loom. This old man he play one, he play Russian roulette on his gun. Give the old dog a bone. Show him the way to go home. Dead hollowed-out fly twirls on a strand of cobweb in the window. Curtains with heavy shoulders of dust, cracked ceilings, passages for rats, ruins of neglect in time's decay, water stains and wild roaches run madly in the neon glow on the abyss of a silver sink, stale rust water leaks through roof and languishes in lavishing oceans of scum rings, swishing, swishing… this is about an-old-man-none-in-particular. This old man he play two, he feel so goddamn blue. This old man who is a shadow in the darkness of the street, who is a burden for the sunshine, a cloudy old man, a man with thunderstorms in his head, the rain falls through his head, the rain falls through his nose, on cold nights it freezes on his upper lip, and then the roaches like to skate on his face. This old man he play three, he play the horses at OTB. His hair is diseased, it's decayed, the landlords put THIS HOUSE CONDEMNED signs on his forehead (they nail it in good), the children like to play on his head, the cops chase the children away (it's very dangerous there), the old decrepit man might crash through the floor (someone could get killed), the old man might crumble into his shoes, with the holes, the sewer holes, the rats run through the holes in his shoes, they climb up his pants and go into his condemned head, they bite the children, the cops try to keep the children away the best they can (it's a difficult job), the children like to play in the old man's hair, they tie knots and pull so that the pus runs out of his bedsores; they enjoy making the old man squirm at night. This old man he play four, he play life's game at death's-door. Give an old man a dog food bone. This old man is all alone. What good is a condemned building? Once, of course, people had lived there, raised their families there, cried and laughed and shit and fucked there, kept their garbage organized in a nice neat pile of black plastic bags for the junkman to take away in the morning. One morning the junkman intrudes too deep into our private lives and takes us away too. This old man he play five, he shoot horse into his hives. We all go to hell, turn gray and rubbery, have dirty hair and muddy eyes, have sticky assholes and filthy toes and pee stains on our underwear. This old man he play six, he play slap-slap on little Johnny's prick. Give an old dog a new bona. A new trick. We become wise old men, experienced old men, teachers to the children, but the children can't play in the old man's head. This old man he play seven, he roll snake eyes in Bellevue bedlam. The children rather call him names and throw stones at him. Beware of this old man, children, do not throw stones at him, you may break a window in his head. This old man he play eight, he and his fly try to masturbate. See now, we have to board up the windows of his mind. He is inside there, don't you think? Somewhere? This old man he play nine, life sure ain't no nursery rhyme. Anyway, no one ever saw him again, called 911, they came and carried him out in a black plastic bag. They padlocked the door of his room, where a dead hollowed-out fly twirls on a strand of cobweb in the window... this old man he play ten, there just wasn't any more oxygen. Not for him.

My friend Tommy and I took a ride on the local RR subway out of Brooklyn to Greenwich Village. We spent the afternoon visiting art galleries in SoHo, seeing blood-evoking streaks and smears on huge canvases, portraying reenactments of the battles in Homer's Iliad, and one meditative soul sitting in the lotus position on the floor before one of the sprawling war scenes, praying for the deliverance of man from bad karma, and one attendant art aficionado, she was cute, trying to explain rather pathetically the nature of abstract painting and how it justs "speaks to you" or not. Later we popped into a bar with a loud band singing the line "the pope smokes dope" over and over, and I waited at the bar while Tommy made a few phone calls to some of his baby photograph-buying clients. Tommy spoke broken Spanish to his mainly Puerto Rican customers in Brooklyn. He needed the dough and he had to make a few deals. In Washington Square Park we smoked some grass, drank some beer, popped a few pills, goofed on a paranoid Burroughs expert, and generally played our parts in a Dostoyevsky story that we had conceived using characters from several of his novels. Tommy was the God-intoxicated man, seeing the Dostoyevsky world of evil all around him, predators and conspirators, obsessed with the nature of evil, and saying things out of the blue that would give you goose bumps. His sister was a nun and had told Tommy that John F. Kennedy is in hell. Tommy got a chill up his spine when she said it. But Tommy was a good card and liked to go along for the ride. Whatever I proposed, Tommy was up for. We'd spent the day in the village and then headed uptown. At Times Square we ate at Tad's Steak House. Tommy always carefully selected the choicest steak from the rack. That one, he says to a big black cook with a 45-inch chest, holding a pointed skewer in his hand. This one? No, that one... This one? No, that one... Then a slop of brown gravy and mashed potato. Then after dinner we attended a porn flick. We sat in the back row, a small theater, with only a few patrons of the art scattered about. In the front row, right in the middle, a fat white man sat, at least four hundred pounds, and when the sex heated up on the screen, the fat white boy has pulled it out and is wanking off, holy shit, it's an earthquake, the entire front row of seats is literally lifting off the floor, ka-boom, ka-boom... we fled the place in disgusted hysterics and found ourselves mindlessly crossing the street. Beep-beep a car horn honks... I'm walking here! I'm walking here, said Tommy, sounding like Ratso Rizzo in *Midnight Cowboy*. Don't step out, fool! Don't step out, fool, shouted a black guy from the window of a car speeding by. We walked down the block where we encountered a hooker and her pimp bouncing a tennis ball to each other on the sidewalk.

By evening we headed farther up town to Columbia. There's a poetry reading in McMillin Hall featuring Ginsberg, Burroughs and Corso, the usual suspects. Tommy listens and snickers. I don't even recall what year it was. We got back to Brooklyn about 3 a.m. in the morning. Tommy decided to show his slides from Vietnam. I don't know why and we were wasted. One slide showed a tower on the screen, and someone falling out of the tower, jumping off... it startled me, a hallucination? These damn drugs and booze? Tommy yelled sniper and fell to the floor, then got up and charged the screen. He ripped it to shreds, screaming kill the motherfucker, and collapsed on the floor. I picked him up and held him. He was soaked in sweat. It was only a damn cockroach that had crawled down the screen.

I remember a few years later Tommy saying, That fucking movie, that *Apocalypse Now* shit, you remember when the Viet Cong are out in an open field, that would never have happened, that would never have happened... they weren't that stupid. It's Hollywood bullshit... Hollywood is stupid.

When we first met we were surprised to discover that we were both reading the same novel at the same time, Dostoyevsky's *Brothers Karamazov*. The rest of our friendship seemed to be shaped by the white-hot contours of the metaphysical questions posed in that book. Even the devil makes an appearance. Tommy said that I was like Ivan Karamazov and that he was like Alyosha Karamazov, though I said that he bore a more striking resemblance to Dimitri Karamazov. He disagreed. I even called my father Smerydakov in a moment of cruel thoughtlessness; and Tommy laughed. I recall it to this day, and still feel the guilt. Every son wishes his father dead at some point, said Dostoyevsky, but not humiliated, that's worse than death. I had dreams about it. I also still had bad dreams about Auburn. I would wake up in the morning and for a brief, traumatic moment thought that I was still there. Not exactly a nightmare, but to me it was worse than that, because it came from a reality that I had experienced. I would wake up in a cold sweat and shaking... then would come the great realization that I was not in Auburn at the children's home but that I was home, my home, with my parents and sisters...

Tommy lined up customers for baby pictures and I worked at a car service. Murray Car Service on Fort Hamilton Parkway. One day I went to work and there was no work, there was no car service, there was no office. It had been blown up. It seems that some rival car service didn't like good old American competition and torched the place. Just as well. It had taken a toll on me, on my already flayed nerves. One time I had to pick up a woman outside of Maimonides Hospital. She was crying hysterically. Her husband had been shot and he was barely hanging on. I couldn't understand what she was saying, because her voice trembled so severely. I finally deciphered her stuttering Brooklynese accent. She wanted to go home. Yea, where's that, lady? She told me and I drove her there. I parked on the street and she told me to wait here, she'll be right back. Oh by the way, she said, my husband was shot right here last night, on the sidewalk. She pointed to the bloodstains and the chalk marks of the body figure. I waited, and waited, nervously looking around for some Joey the hit man to whack me, you know, like the guy who was on Tom Snyder the other night, with the black hood over his head. And Snyder says, what if I pull your hood off. And Joey says, you'd be dead. Tommy laughed so hard he almost cried. Yeah, so hurry up, lady, it's about time. She emerges from the door and now she wants to go to her mother's house in Bensonhurst, where I was invited in for cookies. I politely passed.

The biggest tip that I ever received was from a Jewish Princess in Williamsburg. It was young Henry Miller Country. I had to deliver flowers there. I drove up the road about five times, a one-way street, Bedford Avenue, because I couldn't find the address. Finally I found it and double-parked. The building was an old, shabby brownstone, but when the smiling and beautiful Jewish Princess dressed all in black opened the door, I could see inside: a mansion-like interior with a large chandelier. She smiled. I left with a two-dollar tip. It never happened before, said Patrick with the gimpy leg. Not from them Jews up there. I must have looked like a nice gentile boy. Needless to say, my sexual fantasies were well sated for a while.

It's easy to describe with precise terminology the abstract and physical attributes of a place. Our place. The apartment we shared on 5th Avenue in Bay Ridge. It was a dump, what a dump, a filthy, dirty, stinking dump. It was never cleaned, washed, dusted, or vacuumed. There were beer cans and wine bottles piled in a corner, and garbage piled in another corner, and dishes piled in the sink. There were old yellow newspapers and half-empty

Chinese food containers. Oh hello hello roaches. There were lots of roaches, swarms of roaches. And books, books about Padre Pio, the CIA, about conspiracy theories, multi-national bankers, big corporations, the mafia, the occult. Everything that you picked up had a roach hiding behind it. Those dirty little commie bastards infiltrated every nook and cranny, and perverted every book and god-fearing granny.

It's harder to describe what goes on in the mind, in the mind of a paranoid, of a schizoid.

Tommy attended a Jesuit school in his teens. He was there long enough for the rites of passage to take. Later, he enlisted in the army, because he thought it was the right thing to do, and ended up in Vietnam. He served in a parachute division from 1966-1968. He caught malaria and spent the rest of his time in the army recuperating in Japan. In Japan he discovered Zen and sex, and rediscovered baseball and Coca-Cola.

When he returned to the states he helped his friend Gordon sell cacti on the streets of Manhattan. Gordon would drive a van to Texas where he collected the cacti. Tommy also went to college for a while, at Hunter, to study law, but he soon dropped out. So now he's a salesman for a photographic studio that specializes in baby portraits, selling in mostly Puerto Rican neighborhoods, for which Tommy picked up enough Spanish to get by, and which also afforded him the opportunity to be mugged by a ten-year-old with a twelve inch knife and to be almost raped by a three hundred pound black woman who dragged him through the door after he was dumb enough to put his foot in it.

It was a long journey to the end of night. A hallucination. And the roaches were winning. It was war. Tommy became like some South American banana republic dictator with a hundred medals pinned to his uniform. Tommy placed his beer can down and rolled up an old newspaper, turning it into a bludgeon, and he furtively approached the enemy. Wham! Splatter! The war, or this hallucination of war, went on for months. In the early stages of the war, Generalissimo Thomasso, as he liked to refer to himself, but whom the roaches designated as Tommy D-Max, which means "demote maximally" in the euphemistic jargon of the CIA, but which really means, "kill the motherfucker," in plain old English, the good general utilized basic stone-age implements: shoes, fly swatter, magazines, books, and the aforementioned newspaper, most certainly the *New York Times*. Later he changed his tactics and his weapons (but not his underwear) and resorted to both chemical and biological warfare. Like most American folk heroes, we were largely outnumbered, with our backs against the wall, ready to come out fighting, had not yet begun to fight, I shall return, regretted that we had but one life to give for our country, and nuts to you roaches. Tommy D-Max imagined his kitchen as the Alamo, and himself as Davy Crockett, King of the Wild Frontier, fighting against hoards of roaches led by the indomitable General Santo Anna. The battles were fought all over the apartment. We shall fight them in the kitchen, we shall fight them in the bathroom, we shall fight them in the bedroom, and we shall never surrender. One must admit that the nature of the environment was advantageous to the roach cause. They were good guerilla-garbage fighters. The roaches maneuvered through the crumpled newspapers and food-stained couch and chairs. They fled up the walls and scurried along the baseboards. And then the ultimate transgression against freedom-loving peoples occurred. The Evil Empire of roaches invaded our dismal food supply. They contaminated the bloodline of the nation: they crawled into our Budweiser beer cans and nibbled at our McDonald's hamburgers. And none dare call it treason! No more pussyfooting around. No more yellow belly. This demanded more urgent action and advanced methods of warfare. One Saturday morning Tommy was watching television, and holding a canister in his hand. A roach ran across the screen. Tommy aimed and fired when he saw the slits of its eyes, sssssssssssssssssss the poison streamed through the air and splashed on the television screen, engulfing the roach and the image of Fred Flintstone in toxic fumes. The roach fell to the floor, squirming in his death throes. Yabba-Dabba-Doooo! Tommy saw another roach chasing the coyote that was chasing the roadrunner. Tommy fired from the canister a long semeny squirt. The coyote blew himself up with his own TNT and the roach fell to the floor. The roadrunner scooted off down the road. BEEP-BEEP

Night after night the battles raged on. Then one day Tommy discovered the ultimate biological weapon. An insect to fight an insect! How obvious. Tommy found a Praying Mantis at a local park. The insect took full control of the situation. He charged up the walls and devoured every roach in sight. He praised the Lord and preached the end of the world at Armageddon. Gog and Magog have arrived! Righteous bastard! Even Tommy was sick of it. He lit a match to the insect and it ran up the wall in a heap of flames. I believe the operative word is internecine. Tommy finally made the call to

Burroughs Exterminators. And there he was at the door. Mr. William S. Burroughs. The Exterminator. He dropped the bomb. The stink bomb of American Literature. A nice big American Shit. Tommy came out of the bathroom, grabbed a beer, and sat down to read some crazed invective about Kennedy and the Pope and all the rest. Meanwhile, a big rat crawled out of the toilet bowl. And I wrote some shit down in my notebook...

We were standing together on some street corner of 5th Avenue in Brooklyn. It was now the summer of 1980. I had been working at a shipyard on Long Island but I quit after three months. I couldn't take it. I was ready to leave. I was back in the city again, and we were trying to say goodbye. The 70s were over; my time in New York was over. Would it be the last time that we ever saw each other? Friends, buddies, pals. I wanted to leave for North Carolina and then head west to California as soon as possible, maybe tomorrow. Tommy was deciding whether or not to come along. I wanted the American buddy system to prevail. Jack and Neil. In the old west, in the frontier mentality, nobody was to be trusted, so when trust was found and mutual, the resulting loyalty was total and irreversible, therefore the American sidekick, the partner. In a country without blood and soil of ancient homogeneous heritage the blood brothers live and die in the immanent ideal of preserving and protecting the artificial home turf over which the banner of identity flies. No American ever put on a dirty uniform to enter the arena: soldier or athlete, janitor or ice cream vendor, the pride of the tribe depends on looking one's best when the buck and the buckshot exchange hands and hearts in a world too small for the two of us, pilgrim. These were our heroes, and they were cold-blooded killers.

"There's nothing out there for me. It's all here," said Tommy. "I was born in this city and I'm gonna die here."

"Die here!" I retorted, "You don't die here; you may get killed here!"

"You want to die a noble death? In the end it's the same. A gutter in Brooklyn. A mountain in Nepal. A rice paddy in Vietnam. It's the living that matters. There's a wild surreal pulsing energy in this city. The heart of the matter. The heart of matter itself. A spirit between the rocks. Words between the lines. Orgasms between flesh. Breaking down walls. Who am I? I don't know. Oh yes I do but I won't tell you."

"Your famous poem. Modernist's metaphysics," I said. Tommy laughed like a naughty schoolboy prankster who didn't understand what the teacher was getting at. So Tommy said, "What are you getting at?"

"I don't want to talk bullshit, Tommy. We may not see each other again, ever."

"You're right. But can't you see that it's just a game. And New York is the Big Bang of all games. The loudest sound in the universe, with the possible exception of a pachinko parlor in Japan, which sounds like popping popcorn made of steel in a pot the size of Madison Square Garden during a million decibel rock concert." Tommy paused. "Did I ever tell you about the time I stayed in Japan, in the hospital, because I got sick in Vietnam, malaria, there was this Japanese girl... we went out together for a while..." the subject faded into silence, which was a measure of its seriousness. He knew I heard the story already. Tommy rallied his memory. Came back to the game. "I don't want to go anywhere right now. You see I'm a religious man, and a realist," Tommy said ingenuously, "I'm looking for signs in everything. I'm looking everywhere in this city of cities. There are no effete whimperers in New York City. No middlings in the middle way through the mirrors. Only expanding black tides through zero loops of nothingness. Only the play of absence amid the exiled presence of the transcendent. The neon nights of theology. New York is the most faithful city in the world." Tommy began gesturing theatrically; this was his big farcical and absurdist spiel and he was going to let go. I'd heard it all before. "Not Mecca nor the Vatican; not Jerusalem nor Bombay; not Washington nor Moscow; those are cities without miracles, annunciations, communions, those cities are filled with apostates and heretics. But every bum in the Bowery and every bag lady in Bellevue can see the Burning Bush; every cocaine brain on Wall Street and every poor black child in the Bronx can see the Broken Tablets. Because in New York we truly believe, for we have touched the actual wounds of Jesus Christ; we have sat beneath the actual Bo Tree with Buddha; we have been chained to the actual rock on Caucasus with Prometheus, and we have witnessed the actual miracle of the New York Mets winning the World Series in nineteen hundred and sixty-nine." He paused and then added dryly: "Though I still have my doubts about that one I must confess." To which a passing nondescript bum reeking of a body odor of alcohol and every other scent that swirls around a New Jersey waste disposal site, smiled and nodded his head in accord. Tommy put his arm around the bum's shoulders and asked the grubby guy to give his recollections of that amazing year. "Where were you in October 1969, sir, do you recall? Could you tell us a bit about how it was like back then? Were you at the World Series?"

"I was in Vietnam..."

Tommy tore a can of beer from his plastic netted six-pack and gave it to the bum.

"What do you think you're gonna find in California, anyway?

"I don't know." I said.

"Good answer. What does any of us know," said Tommy.

"So you're not coming with me. You'd rather be a New Yorker than an American?"

"What does that mean?" said Tommy.

The bum, the earth moving beneath him, turned a drunken eye to me, and said, "Well I godda see my gurlfren, anway," the bum said proudly. "Sheza waytariss ober adda Alanic Cafe. Dey god dem good Norwigin pancakes dere... her namz... Sonje... like da iceskader... blona blu eye... not meny ov em lef here... all dese spicks n chinks movin in..."

"You got yourself a beer now fuck off," I shouted.

The bum fucked off.

"So what's this about wanting to be a New Yorker instead of an American?" Tommy wanted to get this one straight because this accusation interested him and struck to the heart of his New York City metaphysics.

"You never strayed from the ship. So now you can sink with the rats."

"So what are you saying? New York is sinking and California isn't?"

"The whole country's sinking. New York is the end of the ship that's going down first. And when Ronald Reagan becomes president it'll be a fast ride down."

"Down a Los Angeles freeway... a party all the way... I hope you enjoy the sun... come back with a nice tan."

Tommy concluded by returning to his primitive metaphysics; he said, "I am that I am. And I'd rather be an American than whatever it is you want to be. This is my hometown. I feel at home here. I know this city by heart. Can you say as much? Where do you feel at home? What do you know by heart? Something real! Not from a book!"

I was quiet. Then I spoke: "That's what I got to find out. Anyway, I know a bar out on Long Island where they've got the pitching rubber from Shea. These guys planned the whole thing in advance. They got this huge 300-pound fat guy to run out on the field at the end of the game and lie down over the pitching rubber until the other guys got out there to help dig it up. The actual rubber from the last game of the 1969 World Series, hanging in back of a bar counter with the dollar bills and the bottles of booze. We could take a pilgrimage out there and bow down before the holy object, and cry into our beers." I had heard this story from my father. I didn't know if the story was true or not.

"Did I ever tell you that I was at the last game? (Yeah) My friend Gordon got me the ticket." Tommy's thoughts turned to Gordon, who drowned last month off the 59th street pier. Tommy was with him. It was Tommy's idea to take a midnight dip. Both of them were drunk from drinking together at Clancy's. Gordon was disconsolate. Tommy was trying to cheer him up. It seems Gordon met his life long idol, the country and western singer Jimmie Bean, of *Big Bad Bob* fame, in the lobby of a Manhattan hotel. Gordon worked for a motorcycle delivery service and was tramping through the lobby with his cowboy boots. He approached Jimmie Bean and asked for an autograph. Gordon complimented Bean on his cowboy boots, to which Jimmie Bean replied, "They cost a lot mo' then you'll ever afford city boy." And walked right passed him. No autograph.

Tommy tried desperately to save Gordon, but being drunk himself couldn't hold on to him, and Gordon went under. Tommy got the cops and later the divers found the body. It's been a tough month for Tommy. His girlfriend of five months left him too. She was living with us for a while at our roach infested hole on 5th Avenue. How could she stand it? It was different for me when I lived there with Tommy. We were two boys living off our irresponsible wits with no commitments. But one day she came back from work. She was a waitress at the Atlantic Cafe. And Tommy was just heading for the toilet to take a pee. He had the urge, and as she came through the door he peed on her. She screamed and left. That was it. Tommy doesn't understand why he did it. He was just overtaken by an impulse and followed through with it. That's how he lived his life. He never seemed to regret the things he did on impulse. He usually laughed about them and said that man is evil, simple as that. I'm self-destructive, lazy, greedy, evil. I concluded that Tommy belonged in New York. He was the right person in the right place. But wait, maybe it was a hooker he peed on? My thoughts are not so clear today. When Tommy didn't return from his private thoughts for several minutes while a limp pizza dripped oil, I finished the last bite of crust from his slice of pizza and finished off his glass of red wine, and then I said, "So you were at Shea for the last game of the World Series?"

"What? Yeah. But I wasn't a big sport's fan; didn't even know the players' names. But it was the thing to do at the time. I had returned from Vietnam about a year and a half before that; I couldn't get into the music and all that hippie stuff at the time. That also was the thing to do at the time, that's how I saw it. I had dropped out of Hunter..." Tommy stopped when he saw the look on my face that said I've heard all this before. So Tommy said, "Aren't you forgetting something? You want to leave for California tomorrow."

"Tomorrow... yeah soon."

We were at Lento's having a pizza, sitting down in a booth, at a table covered with one of those red and white checkered tablecloths, the kind that many a Mafia hood find themselves sprawled over with blood streaming out of their heads and big cigars still stuck in their mouths. Tommy ate his pizza slowly and deliberately; he considered it to be the finest pizza this side of New Jersey, which by default would make it the best pizza in the country; a unique thin crust topped with the most scrumptious offering of home grown tomatoes and imported mozzarella cheese, with a secret touch of spices that Mario refuses to reveal to anyone, much to Tommy's delight, because then he can badger him more, "C'mon Mario, what's in it? You can tell me. Would I tell another pizza parlor? Never."

"Mama's dying words were to me she say never reveal the secret of my pizza to anyone or else," said Mario.

"Or else what?"

"Or else a curse, of course. I can see mama's face now."

Which was true. There were several portraits of mama hanging on the walls. "She had the power you know."

"What power?" Tommy probed.

"The evil eye, of course. Mal'occhio."

Tommy enjoyed his superstitions with the best of the Italian contadini. Tommy's parents had come from Poland, from peasant stock, and were very Catholic. Both his sisters were sisters. And two of his uncles were priests, one lived in Chicago, with whom he still held all-night discussions on spiritual matters, the kind that would drive me up a wall whenever Tommy and I would carry on all night; Tommy skating on thin ice and grabbing for every icicle in the cold mind of reason, but reason doesn't play that game anymore, not since the name of God packed his bags and went AWOL into SNAFU land. But Kilroy was here. The writing is on the wall. And the walls are tumbling down. There was nothing more to say. Tommy couldn't be persuaded to come with me. Out on the street corner we nodded our heads, shifted about nervously, kept our cool eyes to the sidewalk, shrugged our shoulders, turned up our collars, ran our fingers through our hair, stepped back from each other, stepped forward, stepped back, looked up, and I said, "Well, I guess I'll see ya 'round."

"Yeah, I guess. I'll see ya when I see ya," said Tommy.

"Yeah, I guess. Don't do anything I wouldn't do," I said.

"Yeah, and be good, and if ya can't be good, be good at it."

Tommy turned back and walked into the evacuated bowels of the streets of New York City, into the empty stomach of scarcity. Scar City. Scapegracity, the city that escaped from grace. Surrealisticity. City of the Surrealistic. The city that I always loved and wanted to live in forever... what happened? And soon I would be heading out for California (would it be tomorrow?) through a tangled and strangled land of roads and signs pointing the way to The Way or No Way and either way it's the same, a gutter in Brooklyn or a mountain in Nepal, and when the New York radio stations are fading into staccato static somewhere behind me in the buzz of New Jersey I will be tuning in Philadelphia and driving on... Jesus on the jukebox... rock and roll... the daily hog report... news, sports and weather, the holy triad of media... stop in 'n' see us we're just off exit 29... the sounds of freedom... and I will be all alone in my 1972 red Dodge Torino station wagon that I bought off an old retired tug boat engineer down by the waterfront where I worked at the shipyard that summer and where I met Saul, who is already in North Carolina, on the coast, near Croatan National Forest, and I was driving without my sidekick... and I had a beat vision of myself and Tommy: collars turned up, hands in pockets, eyes on the ground, dollars burned up, holes in pockets, fathers not found, roads with white lines flashing by like torpedoes, desire for mythic places only obscure need knows, it is not down on any map, true places never are, one-way the free-way, dirt roads and cross roads, girl in the alley, girl in the bus stop, girl in the bar, girl in the valley, girl on the hood top, and the boys in the car. Tommy didn't know how bad my mental condition was when I returned to live out on the Island. It pretty much came down to this: I tracked down the bastard, the school psychologist, whom I hadn't seen in nine years, not since I was sent away to the home for children upstate. I went from school to school in a manic rage, bursting into the main offices, feeling myself empowered by my anger, feeling confident and assertive... oh but how false... feeling the monomaniacal fury of Ahab searching for the white whale, the despised Moby Dick, the embodiment of fate...

I found him at Theodore Roosevelt Elementary School. I demanded to see him. I was let into his office and was greeted by a smiling Mr. Rawshock, his real name was Porco, who approached me with his hand extended; I kept my hands in my pockets as I had planned, to elicit fear, I suppose. He wore a grey beard and longer hair, not his sporty conformist crewcut from back then. Good to see you again... he offered his hand... I refused to shake, I tried to get answers from him, why was I sent away, neglected and no follow up... we don't do follow ups... what? He had good intentions don't you believe my intentions were good... I lost my family for two years... I lost friends that I never got back. I was suspect and ostracized... but you were in bad shape and your family was a mess... your father was... you lied you told me I could get out anytime, just send a letter... and my father had to pay, they came to the school where he worked as a janitor, and arrested him, humiliated him, brought him to jail and docked his pay, oh what a fucking scam between the state and private schools huh... with a goddamn school shrink as a middleman... the poor bastard is a janitor... oh I hate this fucking system capitalism... what swines... I'm not gonna be like him or all you hotshot Jews and Italians and rich fucks who run this place now, lousy bourgeoisie... give me the old guard, the Theodore Roosevelt kind... at least they stood for virtue and character... are you you're afraid of me? You think I might have lost it and that I have a gun in my pocket and I'm gonna kill you... you think you have the power and right to make that decision? You don't know what I'm feeling inside, I could know exactly what I am doing, this could be all planned out... I could shoot you and I don't care if I go to prison...

And then he says to me... he says to me... *you're already in prison*...

Oh the fucking prick... the fucking smartass thing to say... the clever motherfucker... well it's the wrong thing to say smartass... I took my hands out of my pockets... his eyes widened and his back stiffened... I raised my arm and pointed the gun at him...

The Sadness of the Janitor

Verse:
Threw my test paper on the floor
I got an F my teachers a whore
See my footprint stamped on it
Like ink that says its all just shit
Chorus:
Who cares, the janitor will pick it up
Who cares, the janitor will pick it up

Verse:
Jenny threw up on the floor
Shes my girlfriend thats for sure
Shes kinda messed up in the head
Shes under the desk hey slut thats no bed
Chorus:
Who cares, the janitor will clean it up
Who cares, the janitor will clean it up

Bridge:
I cant wait till im outta this school
They say ill be back ill be a janitor too!

Verse:
Billy took a piss on the locker room floor
The gym teacher smashed his head against the door
Gym teacher called the jan-i-tor
Bring your mop and bring your bucket
And this is what the kids all heard
"Clean it yourself you fuckin turd!"
Hey hey hey fuck it fuck it fuck it
Chorus:
Who cares, the janitor will mop it up
Who cares, the janitor will mop it up
Who cares, the janitor will mop it up
Who cares, the janitor will mop it up

Never Found a Pearl

Verse:
Never found a pearl in a pile of oyster shells
Never gave a damn about what buys and sells
Never goin' back to South Street and Main
I've shouted all my curses
I've said my few farewells
I've rode in long black hearses
That passed the front room windows
Filled with old Italian eyes
That passed by the alley between
The bar and the paper store
Never gonna serve a beer to a bum
Never gonna sweep the filth from the floor
I never found a pearl in that hamlet of humdrum
And now that I've been turned round and round
In this big sad world
I'm casting all my oyster shells to the swine
I'm sitting in Paris drinking red wine
Chorus:
I'm casting all my oyster shells to the swine
I'm sitting in Paris drinking red wine
I'm never goin' back to Oyster Bay
Hey Hey Hey Hey

The Janitors Carry the Keys

Chorus
The janitors and the porters oh baby
You know they carry the keys
The janitors and the porters oh baby
You know they carry the keys
Verse
The first thing in the morning baby
The last thing at night
The janitors unlock the doors

And the porters haul in the goods
The first thing in the morning baby
The last thing at night
The janitors lock the doors
And the porters haul out the goods

Chorus
The janitors and the porters oh baby
You know they carry the keys
The janitors and the porters oh baby
You know they carry the keys
Verse
The janitor can get you in anywhere baby
Anywhere you wanna go
The janitor can get you in anywhere baby
Anywhere you wanna go
The toilets of CBGB
The toilets of Studio 54
See Liza snort some coke
See Sid shoot some horse

Chorus
The janitors and the porters oh baby
You know they carry the keys
The janitors and the porters oh baby
You know they carry the keys
Verse
The janitor can get you in anywhere baby
Anywhere you wanna go
The janitor can get you in anywhere baby
Anywhere you wanna go
See the rich man and the poor
See the pimps and the whores
See Andy and Jackie and Truman
Theyre oh so pretty but they aint human

Chorus
The janitors and the porters oh baby
You know they carry the keys
The janitors and the porters oh baby
You know they carry the keys

The janitors and the porters oh baby
You know they carry the keys
The janitors and the porters oh baby
You know they carry the keys

Smartass Shrink

I don't care if I go to prison
Im going down with a gun in my hand
I don't care if I go to prison
Im going down with a gun in my hand
Youre already in prison
The smartass shrink says
Youre already in prison
The smartass shrink says
Wrong thing to say
So shutup
Wrong thing to say
So shutup
Wrong thing to say
So shutup
Wrong thing to say
So shutup
(improvised instrumental)

All Songs Copyright 1977-1978
Music by Tommy
Lyrics by Stephen
As recorded by The Filthy Floor, a seminal 1970s New York punk band

She had her first breakdown when I was in the third grade. I remember it in the following way. I was in my class at Theodore Roosevelt Elementary School, and my teacher announced in front of all the students in the classroom that there was one boy in class who was always a polite little gentleman, and that's Stephen. I was embarrassed. Yet I never have forgotten it. I also have not forgotten that the teacher wrote on my fourth quarter report card, "There's been a change in Stephen. He's not the quiet, shy, polite boy that he had been..." The "change" corresponded to my sister's breakdown at home. There was the ridiculous doctor who wanted to operate on her back, and the psychiatrist who wanted her committed. My parent's were lost. There was the car ride to King's Park State Hospital, and my sister vomiting in the back seat. There were the visits to Ward 22. Someone named Big Lips. There was the talk about electro-shock therapy, and about a drug called Thorazine. These are my memories and they could be wrong, and yet somehow there is something about these memories that must be right. She was fourteen. These visits to Kings Park both fascinated and mortified me.

And yet... there's always an "and yet" in life... I look back on these years as the happiest of my youth. There are memories that return like floating shadows on the edge of sleep. Those innocent moments in my unadulterated bed, just after my mother's goodnight kiss, were the only times in my life that I enjoyed a faint and static confidence in the future. When I awoke after these sanguine nights, I expected my resurrection, my transformation, and a reprieve from the false promises of the gone day. The dreams, moods, images and feelings of a past borne up on the mist of sleep and dissolving into nothingness... a delusion that the night had a mysterious power that could without my effort or will-power transform tomorrow and my life thereafter into a fresh green world absent of anxiety and fear. And yet... this is the negative side of "and yet"... it wasn't the brilliant reappearance of morning that greeted me, nor did I wake to find that I had metamorphed into a bug, it was plain old yesterday standing there and smirking at me. Nothing of my unease and apprehension were absent. I was absent, from school, and the telephone started ringing off the wall. I was nothing more than the same old self in the same old place. No modicum of post-modern decentering of the subject displaced or removed myself from myself. No Buddhist emptiness of the self, eliminated from the self, rendered the place as a renewed hope of dawn, as if to recognize the same place as a new place for the first time. It was old. Nothing changes the trappings of life. And therefore despair was the only way to keep it all together and not fall apart like the bindings of an old book.

So on the edge of sleep the memories surged up... variations on a simple theme... and I am playing baseball, a neighborhood pick-up game, and it's 1964, 1965, 1966 or 1967... my transistor radio is tuned to an AM station, 77 WABC, and *I Want to Hold Your Hand, Downtown, Wooly Bully* or *Light My Fire* are forever playing in the background. We played baseball in a rock-riddled field behind the high school on the upper tier of a stepped hill, the track field below, and the high school below that. We took our sleds there in winter. We played baseball in summer. There's a hill in right field. It has a fence at the top and the street behind it. I hit some home runs over the fence and almost hit the parked cars. I played first base. Sometimes I played catcher. That was my favorite position but we played a lob baseball game with a backstop so we didn't really need a catcher. My father took me to a sporting goods store in Huntington. I got the shin guards and chest protector. They didn't have a mask. They only had a softball mask. I got it anyway, but I was disappointed.

My father and I would drive out to a Macys at the shopping center on route 110, in Huntington Station. There was a counter with a large black and white aerial photograph of Shea Stadium on the back wall. They had a certain allotment of tickets for games. There were yellow, brown, blue and green tickets. They had a seat map to show us where the seats were located, and the salesgirl pointed with a pencil to the seats on the chart. I think she wore an orange and blue uniform, like an airline hostess, but I'm not sure. My father purchased the tickets. Our first game was a doubleheader against the Atlanta Braves, in May of 1967. The Braves had Henry Aaron, Joe Torre, Rico Carty, Felipe Alou and Clete Boyer. The Mets didn't have much. They had a rookie named Tom Seaver and my father's favorite player at the time, Tommy Davis. The Mets got him from the Dodgers. My father said that he was the Mets best hitter. He hit a few line-drive doubles down the left and right field lines. See, my father said, best hitter. The Mets won the first game 6-3 and Davis went 4 for 4 and hit a home run. We had seats about ten rows behind home plate. We would never get seats that good ever again. They lost the second game. My father wanted to leave in the seventh inning. It was a hot day and he wanted to beat the traffic.

In the summer of 1966 the New York State Fire Tournament was held at Oyster Bay. This was a competition involving different fire departments from around New York State. Oyster Bay had two volunteer fire departments. The Atlantic Steamer "Rough Riders" and the Oyster Bay Fire Company No. 1 "Teddy's Boys." A large metal arch painted bright orange was built on the side of the parking lot by the railroad tracks and the football field. My friends and I watched the hot rod trucks speed down the track. Each fire company had two jerry-rigged hot rod trucks. One truck was bigger than the other truck. They had loud engines that the driver revved up and zoom! Hit it! Wilbur! Wilbur was the driver. The truck raced down the track and screeched to a sudden stop, and the firemen, standing on the back of the truck and holding on to a rail, then jumped off and with the hose unwinding from the back of the truck, and the truck racing away without them, hooked one end of the hose to the fire hydrant and on the other end screwed on a nozzle and with the firemen falling flat on top of the extended hose sprayed at a round target that flipped up when hit.

The firemen participated in numerous events. They ran with a ladder and placed it against the arch and climbed up, one two three at a time. They also raced down on the truck with the ladder on back and skidding to a halt, planted the ladder and nearly before the ladder was in a vertical position a fireman would be climbing up the ladder as they raised it. It was great fun. The bucket brigade was the most fun. A barrel filled with water was placed next to a ladder leaning against the arch. An empty barrel at the top of the ladder was waiting to be filled with water. The firemen ran into position. They scooped water into their clothe buckets and handed the buckets to one man who stood at the bottom, lifting buckets of water up and getting completely drenched by water spilling out of the buckets. The buckets were passed up the ladder hand to hand and emptied into the barrel at the top of the ladder.

My friends and I were proud of our hometown teams. Some of us had relatives who were firemen. My grandfather was a fire chief and my uncle was a firemen. The "Rough Riders" had won the state tournament in 1950, 52, 53, 54, 55, and 64, and on the side of their racing trucks they had the results displayed in white lettering. The St. James "Wildcats" won this year. My friends loved the team names, East Meadow "Meadowlarks," North Bellmore "Rinky Dinks," Islip "Wolves" Elmont "Bangtails," Central Islip

"Hoboes," Port Washington "Road Runners," Lindenhurst "Snails," North Lindenhurst "Piston Knockers," Patchogue "Forty Thieves," Hempstead "Yellow Hornets," and the West Sayville "Flying Dutchmen."

We took a shopping cart from Food Town parking lot. We removed the top cage part, and the bottom resembled a racing cart with a few enhancements added later on. The sides of the cart had two rods on each side good enough to clutch and push, and the front was flat on which a hose or one of my brave friends could sit and be pushed at breakneck speed. We held a firemen's tournament that summer in my front driveway. The driveway was dirt but what the heck it was good enough for us. The garage had a series of windows and we succeeded in cracking or breaking every window, and my father as usual didn't seem to mind, which is why we used my front yard and not the yards of my friends. My father's wooden ladder was placed against the garage, and we raced up it. We struggled to get a barrel up the ladder to the roof of the garage. The barrel was taken from the back of the meat market. It stunk of meat fat. And we used several metal buckets collected from various places. We had our bucket brigade. We used the garden hose and its nozzle to squirt water at the round red circle I had drawn on the garage door. We all got soak and wet. Life was good.

In my backyard there was a small-enclosed porch extending out from the house. The slanted basement door was next to the back stairs of the porch. Under the porch my friends and I dug out a bigger space than the crawl space already there. We made the space big enough to bend down to enter and squat down around a small table. We used the rolling wheel conveyor that we commandeered from Food Town and we filled wooden boxes with dirt. We rolled the boxes of dirt down the conveyor and dumped the dirt on the side of the backyard. We built a casino in the space under the porch. We got an electric bulb on the end of an extension cord to light the small space. I remember pretending that we were in the movie *The Great Escape,* the scene where Charles Bronson is sliding on tracks digging a long tunnel to escape.

I had a small record player. We played the soundtrack from the movie *Casino Royale* over and over as loud as we could. We had seen the movie in the theater on Audrey Avenue. It was a wild surreal adaptation of the Ian Fleming book. Still my favorite Bond movie though regarded as a mess and too far out there for the too critically predisposed... a corny movie of the sixties... well, to each his own. We had a small plastic Coke machine for drinks. We invited kids from the neighborhood to play poker. When some of the kid's dads found out about the casino, we had to return their money.

Our backyard was an unkempt and untidy clutter of bushes and debris. My friends' romping feet summarily crushed down the grass that tried to grow up. The rosebush, the forsythia, the lilacs grew as awkwardly and as gracelessly as their nature's permitted. My father had no interest in cutting the grass, or trimming the hedges, or pruning the bushes. Years later, in my adult dreams, I often saw myself in the backyard trying to reshape the landscape, designing the layout, recreating the backyard into a manicured and beautiful garden.

My father also neglected the house. My first bedroom in the house on Summit Street was at the top of the stairs. It had a slanted ceiling. My father had built shelves. In third grade my teacher had us make seasonal adornments for the classroom corkboard. I remember making orange leaves and snowflakes and tulips. I did the same in my room, using the inside back of one of the shelves to paste my decorations. My sister took that room from me when she returned from Kings Park. I moved into the room next to my mother's room, where she slept with my other sisters. My father slept in a bed across from my bed. Sometimes he would sleep in my bed to help me fall asleep. He told me some nursery rhymes and the story of *The Three Bears*. He told the same stories over and over and over with no hint of a variation. I remember this because when I told stories to my daughter I would try to change the story of *The Three Bears* every time I told it, a scary version, a funny version, a version with added characters from other stories or people from so-called real life.

The house was falling apart. I next moved to a room downstairs. The old bedroom was leaking from the ceiling. It got so bad the ceiling was caving in. The room was moldy and had a terrible decaying scent. So I used the room to play baseball. I had a rubber ball that I threw against the wall and caught in my glove. It didn't really matter at this point the extent of the devastation that I inflicted on the crumbling room, because it was already beyond hope. I used to have nightmares about the floor of the room collapsing under me.

The downstairs room was not really a bedroom. It was a sitting room behind the garage. It had a big window that looked out on the stunted and scraggly purple lilac bush. I loved the smell of that lilac bush. The room also had a bathroom. I remember my father combing my hair in that bathroom, using Vitalis, that yellowish liquid in a glass bottle, or Alberto VO5. I hated the smell of those hair tonics. I'm not sure where my father slept at this time, on the couch perhaps. It was in this room that I had a small black and white GE television. I could watch the Mets and the astronauts walk on the moon and I could watch, with the door closed, a movie with Joey Heatherton, with her short cropped blonde hair, and wearing a very short mini skirt, running through a field of wild flowers. I don't remember the name of the movie, but I had my first inkling of pubescent urges.

But those years ended for good when I was sent upstate. And while I was away, the house and family had become damaged beyond repair. My mother told me that one night when they were watching TV a rat ran across the floor. They had to move. My father had not made any mortgage payments in six months. He never told my mother. They were being evicted. The new buyers came into the house and started painting while my family was still living there. Paint got on furniture and clothes. They just showed up and pushed their way in. My mother sobbed endlessly. My father did nothing. My father was at work. My oldest sister had moved to Brooklyn. I was in a home for children in upstate New York. My other two sisters were only five and nine years old. Not only things and possessions were lost in the move, but a lost innocence that would never return. An old set of baseball cards and an old sport's scrapbook that my cousin Frankie had given to me, with cards from the 1950s, disappeared. It was probably stolen. Even the clothes that I wore when a car hit me, and that my mother kept neatly folded in the closet, even those clothes disappeared. It was the last straw for my mother. Nothing would ever be the same. We moved back to the apartment on South Street. I came home from upstate and my mother tried to fix up the small apartment to welcome me back. But something was wrong. My father stayed at his sister's house across the yard. He slept on the floor in the cold front room, above the bar, in the room next to the room that he was born in. The music from the bar's jukebox blasted all night. But my father said he had no problem sleeping. He said, "I slept in foxholes in Italy, this is nothing."

And once again, I had dreams in my adult life about being able to be there when this happened. I dreamed that I would yell at the people invading the house before my family had even moved out. I would stand up to them and say stop or else I would physically throw them out. If need be I would viciously attack the bastards and kill them if I had to… someone had to do it. But I wasn't there.

And then the second breakdown in 1977. Stephen and his father drove down to Brooklyn to get his sister and bring her home. And out into the night life. Out to 5th Avenue in Bay Ridge, Brooklyn. She walked toward the poolhall on 70th street. Where you going? I've got to find Billy. Before it's too late. She walked around the block. Stephen persuaded her to return to the apartment. Begged her. Please please please. Billy was back at the apartment. Stephen drove down 5th Avenue. His father was getting angry. It was passed midnight and the streets were empty. Billy followed the car in the middle of the street, waving like an idiot. Sylvia in the back seat was looking out the back window of the car. Billy Billy Billy…

When they got her home they put her to bed. His father went across the yard to his sister's house. Didn't want to face it. He slept on the cold floor in the front room, next to the room that he had been born in, and that was his room through High School and after he returned from the war. The front room where his brother and sister sat and looked down upon South Steet. The room where his father lay in a coffin. The front room where his mother sat in her wheelchair at the window. The front room above which on the roof Maurizio made his sculptures. And met with his friends Emile and Rocky. The front room under which the bar blasted music all night but it doesn't disturb Joe Cazzaza… oh this stoic and adaptable peasant mentality. We suffer and we turn away from life, our unspoken self-disgust, our unspoken self-hatred, the incestuous tribalism, the lack of communicating even a basic emotion, the childlike simplicity of turning away… turning away from pain… we suffer ourselves, we endure, we decay, we cover ourselves in rags, we do not speak to anyone about our lives, we do not better our lot… and the mother found herself in the blood dream of her husband's future and in a fierce haze of hysteria threw the pills in her husband's face. Would he react? Would he do something? What ya gonna do? So she swallowed the bottle of pills and went to the bar and fell off the bar stool, had her stomach pumped. No wonder there were affairs with other men. Lots. You've come a long way, baby. Got pregnant by some guy, so faked sex with her husband, the first time in years and the last time, and did he really not know what was going on? When Sylvia had the breakdown in 1965, something changed... Stephen's third grade teacher wrote in his report card: There has been quite a change in Stephen during the last few weeks, his attitude about school is not the same. He hasn't been interested in his work and his behavior has become restless.

Restless. And now it was happening again. They were alone together in the apartment most of the time. Their father was working at the school, their mother at the nursing home, his sisters were at school, they didn't want to come home. His mother was good with old people. She was raised by her beloved grandparents in Norway. Her grandparents were the two greatest people who had ever lived. All her memories were of a variety of Garden of Eden myth. A lost paradise. It would become a forgotten paradise. How do you lose a paradise? How could America measure up to that? Only her children matter now. She would die for them. She would kill for them, she would say, I am a Viking! Torhild filled up her empty life with stuff. The apartment was cluttered. Most of the objects held no personal significance for her, except the memory of the place and time that they were bought at some yard sale. If she and her husband didn't have a pension and Social Security they would have ended up with nothing. She would have spent all that money on trivialities. Of course she was generous to a fault. She always wanted to make Christmas a happy time. She would buy many gifts. She would straighten up the place and cover everything with Christmas decorations. Stephen remembers it as the time he was happiest, when the place was cleaned up. But it didn't last. Once the decorations were put away, the clutter returned.

His middle sister was married at eighteen. Married to a lout. A bum. A drunk. But Joe liked him. He had found a drinking buddy. This made Stephen angry. You made your bed now sleep in it. There's the door. His father's favorite expressions. Neglect, turn away. Abandon. Younger sister drank. Jumped off a water tower. So Stephen and Sylvia were alone in the apartment most of the time. They both went mad. It took three Christmases to finish the job. When they brought her back from the city, she continued to neglect her apperance. She stood in front of the mirror. Her nose was crooked. Her back was crooked. They played cards. They played the radio. First insanity... then an unwanted baby is born, then a miscarriage... meanwhile Stephen locked himself in his room.

They couldn't find her. She would stand in front of the mirror bent over and complain that her back was falling down. She wouldn't leave the apartment because she couldn't leave the mirror. If she left the mirror she would get lost and nobody would ever find her again. She said the pidgeons on the skylight in the bathroom were spies, talking to her about what a bad girl she was and she had better be a good girl from now on. At one point she told Stephen that the problem was Billy. That Billy needed help because he was going to kill himself. It got so bad that Stephen didn't know what to believe. Billy saying, Stephen you know it's not me. I'm not crazy. It's her. She needs help. She's hearing voices. Stephen returned to the apartment one night and couldn't find her in the apartment. She hadn't left the apartment in a while, where would she go? They found her in the closet, cowering in fear, hunched down, naked. Why did she strip off her clothes and want to go out into the cold? Because she had no body.

She said that she had to find Billy. That it might already be too late, that he may have hurt himself already. She started to walk out the door. It was the middle of December. She had no clothes on. They tried to stop her. But they didn't want to use force. They covered her up with a jacket. They walked down the stairs. Please please please he remembers saying... please please please his voice crying...

oh selfish grab the mental break down nervous fling wash up in vanity mirror reflective trimming back seat barfing again the stomach ride to the institution the devil and the pablum notes and depression in the closet silence as noise in panic out the door no no no I must save him the immense difficult down stairs daddy daddy daddy blackbirds talk dark yard and the man in the black cloak is it him you know who you know who wavers over trap bingo bar and teenage forever child free to bingo bar flirt selfish remembering the soft baby madness before depression before the voices taking over the servile girl should always be this way we laughed sister mother you hitler you witch you bitch death to you don't wish anybody dead but oh she dead dead dead broken dishes punches and bruises and laughing enticing down the stairs the cement stairs don't fall save yourself halfwit save herself and his sisters laughing later in life recalling but Stephen never laughed why not she wants police she screams I want police she shouts for attention please please please he says again and again I told you didn't I the father the father's rage ya didn't listen to me she shoulda had an abortion ya know it don't you this baby madness she holding a knife to her stomach her pregnant belly drawing her belt tighter I'll kill it it I'll flush it down the toilet oh it's all my fault the mother in guilt it's not it's not nobodys to blame only got yourself to blame she made her bed outta here I gotta get out of here go to your fucking bar you useless bastard son to father there's the door ha ha like you always say mother to son outta here, screams voices go to your bums in brooklyn they ain't coming out here no more oh be brave daddy you shit ass coward be a big man now huh you can bet your bottom dollar on that ah the invalid return of morning and weariness on the first day of spring redeem the family or sleep forever till these tarred roofs bind me suicidal forever and never leak again the baby's first words are gonna be fuck you o christmas of madness christmas of horrible births christmas of miscarriage oh mommy just a chunk of meat came out of me a chunk of meat smiling o joy to the fucking world.

Document 19-3748

Dear Billy

How do I start this letter, I do not know. As you know I've been in the hospital for almost a month now. It hasn't been easy. Things just started to happen that I couldn't account for. After you came out for Thanksgiving I slept continually until one night I couldn't sleep. I was sitting in the kitchen and all of a sudden the form of the devil appeared on the wall. I know it's hard to believe, but it's true. There was nothing on the table at all. I went into the bathroom after that happened and when I came out a round piece of carved wood was left on the table with five empty cigarette butts attached to it. I screamed and woke my mother. I showed her but she barely looked at it and threw it in the garbage and put me back to sleep. She didn't believe me. But I tell you Billy, it is true. Other things have also happened to me in this fashion, but it's very hard to talk about this, you understand. I know I wasn't acting very nice when I was staying with you, but you've got to understand that wasn't Sylvia that was staying with you. Remember when you took me to the hospital that night how strange I was and when you came out for Thanksgiving how strange I was. That was the start of my haunting nightmare. I believe I am possessed by the devil. In fact I know that I am. I talked with a priest in the Catholic Church in Oyster Bay, and he said you are without doubt. It was like pulling teeth to go and see him. In the hospital while laying down at night strange things start to happen. The other night my body was floating in mid air, that was after I just finished praying to God to help me. As I was floating some hands were around my neck choking me and saying you shouldn't have done that repeatedly over and over. I was crying like crazy. I know you have been talking to Stephen about me. I don't know why the hell I am in this hospital. I am not a bad person. I have never done anything seriously wrong in my life so how do you explain this suffering. I never really sinned. I thought maybe I could be exorcized, does that sound strange? I will be coming home next weekend for good. The hospital will be releasing me. The hospital stay hasn't been that bad, in fact it has done me some good. I take all this medicine. We all missed you at Christmas time.

Love Sylvia

My Story of Saul Cellini

I found work at a shipyard. My uncle worked here during the war, building minesweepers. My father worked here after the war, but just for a brief spell, building tugboats. I sat down with my friend Saul on our lunch break. We were planning a trip south and then west… if Tommy won't come, Saul would, but Saul was going somewhere else anyway… he was a drifter. Saul was born in 1952. His father was an Italian beatnik from San Francisco, and his mother a Jewish poetess from New York City. They met at Berkeley. They met in a coffee shop called the Piccolo. She was wearing a black beret. He was wearing a blue fedora. That's all his parents ever told Saul about their budding romance.

Most of the laborers in Heemskirk's Shipyard were Polish immigrants. They spoke broken English, worked lots of overtime, until after midnight sometimes; late into the night one could watch from the beach the welding torches glaring and shooting down sparks from Moran tugboats in dry-dock. Heemskirk's has always been a non-union open shop. The workers had many horror stories to relate about this or that accident which nearly killed someone, and were more than happy to tell all about it… for example, the whistle blew and Saul and I came out of the engine room of one of the tug boats to take our lunch break. Stefan sat down to join us. He leaned over and showed us the scars and stitch marks crisscrossing the top of his head. He had fallen forty feet from a tugboat in dry dock and landed on the rusted scraps of metal that had been left under the docks like futuristic sculptures. Unfortunately for him, the tide was out, but he was lucky enough just to have survived. Stefan then told about how he was so amazed to see commercials on television selling food for cats and dogs! Cats and dogs! In Poland we have nothing like this. And he laughed and said to himself: cats and dogs, huh. He gave some advice to Saul and me: Never walk under the big cranes carrying sheet metal, many times they break loose, break loose and fall, very dangerous. And never get off your ladder, if you do someone will take it out from under you and leave you up on the side of the ship, no foolin'. Just then Gregory sat down to join us, and he began telling his story. He lifted his shirt and showed his scar; it ran down the front of his stomach and into his pants, just then he unzipped and showed the rest of the scar. He turned around, dropped his pants down over his ass and lifted the tail end of his shirt to reveal the scar as it continued right under his scrotum and up his back. "You wanna know how I do this. I fall on metal pole. Impaled is the word I think. It got up my ass and into stomach. No kiddin'. I stuck on pole for five hours. Yes five hours, the Pole on the pole ha ha, five hours to get me off pole, yeah I pass out you know, very much blood, doctors come, I wake up in hospital, I live, that's America, in Poland I dead, here I live, wonderful country." No union here yet. But who need! Solidarity was a union in Poland, yes, but…

Saul worked at Heemskirk's Shipyard for the past two years. I met him at the time that I briefly worked there, three months in the summer, as an outside mechanic. Saul quit after working a year straight this time and got on his motorcycle and headed south to meet a few old buddies who retired from the tugs a few years ago. A few days later I quit and headed down south.

Let Saul tell you why he quit and left: I take everything to heart, and things taken to heart can kill the heart. When my six-month-old baby was dying of a rare and fatal heart disease called Endocardial Fibroelastoesis, I knew that baby needed more love than I could have provided. She needed a miracle, and a second opinion, or both. She needed an infusion of hope in the plastic bags of blood hanging over her oxygen tent where she lay with needles stuck beneath her skin and taped to her temples. The doctors took so much blood from her, and had to find so many different places to take it from, temples, arms, feet, that her small body was one blue and yellow bruise.

We got a second opinion and perhaps even a miracle; she lived. Whether she gets any love in her life is another story, and harder to come by. The kindly nurses named her their little miracle baby.

I was thinking about not coming back to take the baby in my arms and carry her out of the hospital and into her own singular and special universe; I was thinking about leaving her behind, an orphan in a multiverse of empty stomachs and hungry souls...

Was she really my miracle baby? Surely the original diagnosis was wrong, when this seventy-year-old woman doctor, who was a locally renowned heart specialist on Long Island, said to me: You can't keep this baby.

What do you mean? I responded with no small degree of shock.

I mean she is going to die.

This may seem a cold and heartless way to put it, to impart to me what was just a bit of information, and the tone of the doctor's rasping, unequivocal monotonic voice would have corroborated such a judgment. She didn't want to pitch the big spiel; she blurted it out squarely on the chin. She was a tough old cookie. But she was the doctor, the professional, the expert, the specialist, and she should have known, and she was highly recommended by other doctors, and they should have known, but she didn't know a damn thing, because if she did know, the baby would be dead now, and if I had believed her, the baby would be dead, and then the baby and the baby's mother would both be dead...

Saul had never mentioned the mother of the baby.

Saul took everything to heart, and things taken to heart can kill the heart. I helped Saul write letters to all the major heart hospitals in America to obtain a second opinion. He explained his circumstances. His wife had died during childbirth, that he worked at a shipyard, with no insurance, no union... a few weeks later he received a letter from a hospital in Texas, which referred him to a doctor in New York City. Saul acted upon it immediately. The doctor in New York Hospital in Manhattan examined the baby and refuted the claims of the old doctor on Long Island. The New York Hospital doctor said that the baby required only minor surgery. She stated it simply: We disagree with her. The baby had something called Patent Ducus. A value in the heart that feeds the baby in the womb and closes at birth had not closed. Saul had no other choice but to believe her. At least this was a sign of hope. The procedure is not complicated, the doctor said, no big risk. The operation was successfully performed. And then Saul saw no other option than to put the baby in the custody of New York State. Cruel fate.

Would Saul ever see her again? Saul was twenty-eight years old and had lost his wife and baby.

This is the story of the mother. Saul had met the mother in Hong Kong. Her name was Ko. She didn't know much about her own background...

But I did some research.

It seems that when a certain Captain Roger Bethell was on a tour of the Far East in 1923, he fathered a child with a courtesan in an Ichikawacho brothel. The courtesan's name was Reiko. She was a renowned beauty. The Captain's friend, the writer Tanizaki, had introduced them to one another. The captain was sixty-two years old. It was his only child. The baby boy was named Masahiro and he lived in the brothel with his mother. Reiko wrote letters to the captain over the years informing him of the young Masahiro's life. Then one day the letters stopped coming.

The Captain was gravely saddened by the militarism that was sweeping Japan at the time and that swept Masahiro into the navy. His mother was too distraught to write to the Captain about the news. He never heard from her again. She committed suicide the day after her son had left for Korea. In Korea Masahiro fathered a child with a Korean "comfort woman," during Japan's occupation of that country.

The baby was named Kim and placed in an orphanage. When she was fifteen, in 1956, she became the mistress of an assistant of a French diplomat and was taken to live in Vietnam. After soldiers of the Viet Minh killed the assistant, Kim lost everything and lived the life of a peasant in a village. In 1961 Kim gave birth to a baby girl. The father was an American, perhaps CIA. The baby was Ko. Her "uncle" adopted her and took her to Hong Kong. She grew up there. He told her about her background. But he left her when she was 14 and he returned to the states. Several years later Saul met her at the Kitty Kat Klub, in 1978. She was a dancer, a seventeen-year-old stripper. They came to America. Saul went to work at the shipyard. They were actually happy for a short while.

Heading down toward the end of the dirt road on his motorcycle, Saul drifted in from the night and fog and backwoods swampy smell (if not back-alley sewer smell) like a row of rotten collards (if not like just plain shit) which infected the thick suffocating air (if not suppurating air) with a plague of odious memories, the smell trailing behind Saul from New York

City down here borne on the wind that his father blew, long ago, and flew away on, far away... where? And what is that smell?

"You're rotten inside!" Saul remembers his mother shouting this phrase at his father coming out of the "shithouse," as his father affectionately referred to the only place on earth where he found peace and contentment living with his wife.

"How rotten you must be inside to smell like that!"

"Ah leave it alone he says," he said.

"And don't say it's my cooking," she said, before he had the chance to get it out of his mouth, so instead he said, "Fuck it all he says."

"That's your father for you," she later told Saul when he was seventeen and his father had been gone five years. "That's your father for you. He used every word in the book. What a filthy mouth he had."

Saul remembers asking his mother if she could remember the last words that his father spoke to her. "I told him to get out and never show his face in my house again."

"And what did he say to that?"

"He said every word in the book," she said.

"You mean he cursed you out even at the end."

"That too."

That too? Thought Saul, perplexed. So what was she talking about if not some reference to a symbolic dictionary of swearing and verbal abuse?

When Saul remembers his father he remembers his father's Italian pasta and meatball and Parmesan cheese dinners that left an after smell of precisely timed and placed farts intended to antagonize his mother's delicate nostrils; her voice trilled in anger, and he was thrilled to see her react as if civilization, that is New York City bourgeoisie Jewish civilization, had come to an abrupt end with the irreconcilable clash of custom and instinct, deliberations in the dark anus of history, oh those post-dinner effects! Or was it the clash between working-class and middle-class? Or the clash between Italian Catholic boy San Fran born cum atheist leftist bohemian beatnik poet and Jewish Princess New York born cum intellectual leftist bohemian beatnik poetess who later (post-marriage) reverted back to being a Jewish princess bourgeois nagging housekeeper wife? Whatever it was the farts really got to her and brought out all the true feelings and resentments. "Rotten guinea smell!" Saul's mother calls it.

Saul's father cooked one meal a month and pasta and meatballs was it (sometimes with pork chops, sometimes with sausages). "I'm gonna do my spaghetti tonight he says," he said. And no matter what kind of pasta he used it was always called spaghetti, and he had the habit of tagging on "he says," usually timidly but as if to assert himself in some way, to the end of the sentence that he just said. But what is that smell?

If Saul didn't know where he was, and he doesn't know exactly where he is, geographically pin-pointed on a map anyway... he knows it's somewhere down this dark rural dirt road, lined with the gut-split corpse of a black-mutt dog, the stiff gray corpse of a possum, and the fluffed mound corpse of a raccoon, a road like a trophy-lined hallway in the house of a hunter who indiscriminately and blindly hunts with fender and wheels, reckless on the roads that lead to private places and as far as it goes in the public trust, along the decorous bordered secret lives, desires, and dreams, cross against the grain at your own risk, run off into the woods at your own risk, strut-of-the-cock to the other side of the street at your own risk, tell an ethnic joke at your own risk. "Why did that damn chicken cross to the other side of the road anyway he says?" Saul's father used to say; then his father answered himself, saying, "Because a Jewish mama was waiting on the other side luring him across with her charms like Susanna of old among the elders or whatever the fuck it was... and then whack, off with the head, like John the Baptist, another lovely fable from that Jewish book; she wanted to make the chicken soup don't you know, soup's on! How much does it cost? Your freedom. Your artistic integrity. What a rip off! Try to Jew 'em down. Jew 'em down..."

"Oh shut up with all that," shouted Saul's mother, "and anyway it's not Jew 'em down, it's chew! Chew! Chew 'em down."

"Chew Chew Charlie was an engineer. Chew! Not in my book he says," said Saul's father. The "he says" was always sort of whispered weakly and demurely but with a rising pitch.

"Oh who gives a damn about your book."

"You never did that's for sure."

"I was just being honest. It was trash. All those bad words. Self-indulgent and self-pitying. All that sex and filth. Roth or Mailer you were not."

Saul's father didn't reply to her criticisms. Ah the book! He was quiet. He was being severely reminiscent about the book.

Anyway what's that smell? If Saul didn't know exactly where he was... knows it's somewhere down South along the East coast, with vibrating tassels of crickets in the leaves, bellowing frogs, rattlesnake rattling, Hank Williams' loneliness in the moon through the pines, the full moon illuminating decay and decomposition, glowingly reflected in the transparent maggots crawling in the bloody innards (now outtards) ballooned out from the dead dog's stomach like a sack of gizzards stuffed into a supermarket-bought chicken, Saul's Jewish mother stirring the chicken soup, "You don't want to smell like your father did, eating that horrible pasta and pork chops, do you Saul sweet boy, such a good boy..." if Saul didn't know where he was, what with this smell, he could almost believe that he was back in New York City, slobbering in a stinking sticky alleyway again, his eyes and ears and fingers over the ledge of the large metal garbage container, like some misplaced Kilroy looking inward instead of outward, instead of greeting lost souls, greeting garbage, by the slamming screen backdoor of a restaurant, foraging with the flies and yellow jackets for stale moldy bread crusts, soft blackened vegetables, and red wine that looks like an oceanic mouthful in the bottom of the discarded bottle, better than Muscatel, when tipped sideways by a tipsy hand, and the full-rigged model ship sinking in the bottle to the bottom of the soul, going down, way down, no message in the bottle to be found on the island sands, the game of life is rigged, unfair, no S.O.S., and the Salvation Army Band marching past the alleyway's entrance, breaking off rays of sunlight, flickering and jabbing into Saul's foggy eyes looking nowhere, guided by a sense of that smell that Saul picks up everywhere he goes, even here, yet a native smell, but he picks it up everywhere, like picking up a cheap diseased whore, or picking your nose in public, or picking a fight, or picking a horse, or picking shit off your shoes, sometimes he just forgets where he is, it becomes unavoidable, he just has to do it, like a bad habit, unavoidable, like a frighten animal running across the street at night, cars braking, swerving, smash! Animals battered to a pulp in the land of pulp novels, dime novels, buddy can you spare a dime? What is that smell? Acidic tobacco? Saul saw a lot of tobacco fields while riding down here; or maybe it's the smell of fighter jet fuel trickling down from the sky? Camp LeJeune Marine Base is not far from here. Whatever it was it was there, the smell of the South, the smell of the North, uncivil war waging in the night, the Battle of Bullshit Runs...

Saul turned off the lights and engine of his 1969 black Triumph motorcycle, 750cc; whirling spouts of sand that had followed him down the dirt road caught up with him and engulfed him, settling on him like a cloud burst of dry tears; dry because Saul never cries you see. Never as he or anyone else can remember. He had something of a reputation back in his school days as being the one boy who made it through elementary school, junior high school, and high school, whom no one saw or ever made cry, not his father's spankings, not a teacher's scolding, not a bully's punch, not a gym teacher's shout, not a sport's injury, not a girl's rejection, not any kind of humiliation, nope, never.

Saul kicked the kickstand down. The door to the brick house opened and a fat man came outside. "Saul, my good man, you finally made it. Good to see you again. Glad you could make it. No trouble finding the place? Good. Huh? What? Loop Roads? Ha ha..."

"I asked for directions in a bar a ways back and they told me to take the next loop road, so I did, until I discovered that half the fuckin' roads have signs that say Loop Road."

"They were pulling your leg in the bar. The sign just means that the road loops around back to the main road. Ha ha."

"Rebel assholes."

"Hey Saul, come in," said Stanley, "how about we get you started off with a shot of... what'll it be, bourbon all right?"

"Sounds fine."

"Hold on a minute," said Stanley, concerned, "I godda call my dog... hey Rebel? C'mon boy."

"Stan... I saw a... sorry to say but there's a dead black dog on the side of the road... maybe..."

"Oh no. Oh shit," said Stanley, visibly shaken, and called to his wife, "Marge? Marge? Get me the flashlight, the long machete, the pith helmet, the netting, and my .38."

"The long machete? Pith helmet? .38?" Saul wondered aloud.

"That's right. Snakes, Saul, copperheads, rattlers. Cottonmouths. Mosquitoes. You name it. Maybe some escape convict nigger coming through the swamps..."

"Oh don't lissen to him, Saul," said Marge, "you know he's a good liberal democrat from New Jersey. Stanley, don't say things like that when you know you don't mean it."

"It makes me feel like I'm an auxiliary cop again, back in Newark, you know what the streets were like, Marge."

"Yes, dear, I know."

"Oh right, you were doing that on the side when you worked on the tugs."

"That's right, Saul. You know once a copperhead bit Rebel, that's my dog. Boy his head swelled up like a balloon. I'd never seen nothin' like it before in all my life. I was sure he was gonna die. But he didn't. No siree."

"Here we go, Stanley," said Marge, handing her husband the flashlight, the long machete, the pith helmet, the netting, and the .38. "And here's your snake boots too, you don't wanna forget those."

"Sure don't."

"That's some machete you got there," said Saul, still standing in the doorway.

"Bet you can't guess where I got that? Off a dead Jap on Guam. I'll tell you 'bout it sometime," said Stanley, spinning the barrel of his .38. "This is the gun I carried with me when I was a cop. Stainless steel. Tough as hell. Not a cheap Saturday night special. Won't blow up in your face. It's the real thing, Saul. It's never let me down yet."

"You've had to use it then?"

Stanley didn't answer right away, kept staring at the gun, head down, then a slight smile appeared on his lips. "Just once, just once. I'll tell you 'bout it sometime. I can use my machete to chop through some of that fog out there." Stanley changed the subject.

"You coulda used it to chop through some of the contaminated chemical air back in Jersey," offered Marge.

"Marge actually likes it down here."

"You don't?"

"Well you know how it is, Saul, they're kinda slow down here about getting things done. I've been trying to get a new firehouse built for our district, but they'd just as well settle for that tin shack they got."

Stanley got into his snake boots and went out into the night and fog and the swampy smell in search of his dog. Saul wasn't much interested in hearing Stanley's World War II stories or cop stories, not again. He was sorry he asked about the gun; he probably heard that story a hundred times but couldn't recall the exact details. Why does everyone always want to tell his life story to Saul? He's heard Patrick's and Richard's and Stanley's, all the old guys who have retired now from working on the tugs in New York Harbor, whom Saul met when the tugs were dry-docked for repairs at Heemskirk's Shipyard where Saul worked for, what, five years, and where he met Stephen.

"C'mon in Saul," said Marge.

BRMNN! BRMNN!

It was the sound of a foghorn.

"What's that?" said Saul.

"Oh just the boys," said Marge.

Saul knew what it was but why was the loud foghorn blasts coming from inside the house? Richard Stoutbender and Patrick Larkin were seated in easy chairs in the living room, listening to a record on an old record player, heads resting back on quilted pillows, whiskeys in hand, eyes closed, feet up on hassocks, shoes off... socks that reeked of... popcorn? Saul thought that they smelled of popcorn. Is that the smell?

BRMNN! BRMNN! CLANK! CLANK! GRIND! GRIND! Sounds of a tugboat... voice of tugboat captain...

"Well?" said Patrick.

"Hold on. I'll get it. I believe that's the Elvira Queen out of New Orleans," answered Richard.

"That's right," said Patrick.

CLANK! CLANK! BRMNN! BRMNN! GRIND! GRIND!

"Well?" said Patrick.

"Let's see... that's the... the Hornet Dove out of Boston. Am I right?"

"Right as rain." Saul had entered the room and was standing next to a painting of snow-capped mountains, astounded to witness this dreamy session of tugboat nostalgia and expertise.

"How the hell do you do that?" said Saul, to break the ice. Richard and Patrick opened their eyes. "Don't get up." Richard and Patrick shifted their glasses of whiskey from right hand to left, spilling a tinkling on their pants and leaned forward to shake hands with Saul.

"Hello Pat... Dick."

"You come down here on that noisy bike of yours? I didn't hear it," said Richard with his stentorian voice. When Richard cleared his throat the foundations shook.

"How could you with that noise!" Saul gestured toward the old console record player.

"Noise? That's music!"

"I'll turn it off," said Kay, Richard's wife.

"No, no, it's all right," said Saul, amused.

"Of course it's not all right," challenged Kay, "you can't talk over that noise. I can't hear myself think."

"Whadda mean can't talk," said Patrick. "We talked over that noise and a lot louder for years and years and heard every word that was spoken. Ain't that right, Dick?"

"That's right. It's when there isn't no noise and it's dead quiet in a room, that's when we can't hear a word being said, right, Pat?"

"That's right."

"Well, Saul didn't work in an engine room for 40 years like you guys," said Kay. "So he can't hear and I can't hear so I'm gonna turn it off. Help me up." Richard was sitting opposite his wife; they both reached out to grab each other's hands and started rocking back and forth. Richard weighed around 300 pounds, his wife nearly 200 pounds, so it's one two three to and fro and up we go, and they both pulled each other up and collided bellies together. Patrick had no problem getting up because of his weight; he was terminally thin, has been all his life. Patrick ran his fingers through his wavy hair; in his youth he had thick black hair, but the years have turned it completely gray. Patrick was tall and lanky, whereas Richard and Stanley were of medium height and built like two big old Buicks with big round hoods shining just like Richard's and Stanley's bald domed heads, with a clip of wiry hairs sprouting around the equatorial regions and lower. They were big men; wearing their Bermuda shorts you could see their muscular calves like quartered oak trees.

"Help yourself to a drink, Saul," said Marge, entering the room with a tray of various cheeses and crackers, followed by Betty, Patrick's wife, a short fat rotund woman carrying another tray of snacks.

"C'mon boys, eat 'em all up."

Patrick took a piece of cheese from his wife's tray. "Thank you Betty Boop."

"Where's Stan?" asked Richard.

"Looking for Rebel," answered Marge. "Saul saw a dog, dead, on the side of the road."

"Oh no," said Richard, with heaviness.

"Boss man's comin'," Patrick blurted out. Patrick didn't like to think about unpleasant subjects like death, man's or dog's. "Yeah dah bowz man's a-comin', here com' dah bowz man, here com' dah bowz man," Patrick mimicked Al Jolsen, minstrel show, black face, Uncle Tom; good Irish lad that he was from the streets of Brooklyn.

"Don't use that damn word," said Richard. "They all use that word down here. I hate that word. Boss man. My ass."

"You were always a good union man, Richard," said Kay.

"I can't say only good things about the unions but it woudda been a lot worse without 'em, I can tell you."

"So Heemskirk's coming," said Saul, not too thrilled to see his ex-employer, owner of Heemskirk's Shipyard. A non-union man if there ever was one.

"Comin' with Ralph Stronzo," said Patrick. "Ralph's somethin' else. What a card. Wait ta meet 'em Saul. Another Northerner. Grew up around my old stompin' ground in Brooklyn. But he's been down here a long time now. He was a hairdresser in Raleigh for 40 years, of all things. Did the hair of all the wives of all the big shots. Governors' wives, mayors' wives, senators' wives, businessmen's wives. Thinks he's hot shit," Patrick added with a titter.

"I for one thinks he's a bit peculiar," said Richard.

"Dick and I met him at a K of C meeting," said Patrick. "A few months back. At the time he was really sick. Wouldn't come oudda the house. He had the scales. Wouldn't talk. I use to bring him food or else he wouldn't eat. Eventually I got him out of the house and now he's all energy, non-stop, and a real little dynamo. Always got some deal going on. He'll tell ya 'bout it. Says he's been a millionaire four times over but lost it all each time. Hot shit."

"Full of shit is more like it," said Richard.

"Always scheming, huh? He's got some big deal going on now but I'm not sure what it's all about," said Patrick, wondering why Ralph hasn't let him in on it.

"He's too damn vague. Never talks straight. Talks in circles. I don't trust him."

"Maybe Ralph can do something for you, Saul. You're in between jobs now, right? Ralph knows everybody."

"Knows more people than you do," said Betty to her husband, hurting his civic pride; such pride amounted to knowing all the right people.

"He's been down here longer than me, Betty," replied Patrick, a bit defensive about this comment from his wife. Patrick's so good about worming his way into everything that's going on in a community, getting to know all the right people. Unfortunately for him, he usually ends up antagonizing everyone because he's your basic Know-It-All. Patrick, as he usually does to fend off a sulk, displayed his hackneyed wit. "Hey Saul, what's the best thing about the South?"

"I dun'know, Pat. What?"

"The trains goin' north. Ha ha ha." Patrick was one of those guys who could actually remember all the mundane stupid jokes that he's been told over the years.

"I hear Stanley," said Marge. "I'd bedder see what's up." Marge knew right away by the look on Stanley's face. "It's him," was all he said and went into the garage to get a shovel and cardboard box. Marge went back into the living room where everyone knew by the look on Marge's face that the dog on the side of the road was Stanley's.

"Stanley's gonna bury him," said Marge. "Stanley takes these things hard. He gets too close." Saul offered to help and went out to the garage. "That's nice of you, Saul."

Under some pine trees Saul dug a hole; the roots were relentless. Saul was twenty-eight years old; much younger than the others, who were all beating a path toward seventy. All his life Saul had found himself in the company of older people, maybe that's why they were always telling him their life stories. With a shovel, spade and axe, Saul chopped and battled the earth for a space, a hole, to place the carcass of a dog. The ladies remained inside and mourned and commiserated with each other, telling stories of old pets: dogs, cats, birds, children, for some reason children kept entering the conversation, even though none of them had ever had children. Oh they tried. There were miscarriages, stillbirths, and crib deaths.

"It was a man's job, to bury the dead," said Marge.

Stanley, Richard and Patrick stood around the rim of the hole watching Saul dig. Stanley held a flashlight; the hole in the ground was illuminated; it was eerie to see the light in the empty hole surrounded by the dark earth, with death in the air.

"Number four," said Stanley. "This is the fourth dog I've had to bury since retiring down here. In just five years. The first one got ran over. A snake bit the second. The third caught some disease. And now Rebel. In New Jersey I had the same dog for eighteen years. A beautiful Irish Setter. But down here they go in for mutts. When it comes to people they inbreed; but dogs are smarter down here, they screw around outside their tribe. I met a farmer down here who was bragging to me one day about how he screwed his niece; he claimed she wanted him bad. She was as hot as a firecracker, that's how he put it: she was as hot as a firecracker. I couldn't get over it."

Patrick perked up his ears. This was his kind of dirty old man dirt. Patrick's been helping out some of the younger girls he meets. He finds them jobs as waitresses, loans them money, all out of the goodness of his charitable Catholic heart. Dirty old man, his wife calls him. Sometimes his compliant wife will venture an opinion of her own, though rarely, and when she does Patrick forthwith rebukes her by simply stating in his best Brooklyneese: You're wor-awng Beddy, you're wooor-awng."

"Dogs just don't last down here in this heat," said Stanley. "Rebel just came into the yard one day and wouldn't leave." Stanley didn't mention that he had started feeding the dog right from the first time the dog came pathetically and submissively snooping into the yard looking for food and security, reason enough to stay. "He adopted me you could say." Stanley was unwilling to betray his manhood. Dogs and women come to men, preferably on all fours, and men, because they are strong and the provider, take them in, they can do the chores around the house. It's like one of those old Hollywood westerns, when the honest stranger knocks on your homestead door looking for work and a meal. Sure thing, buddy. But hands off my wife. And if you lay your hands on my daughter, you're as good as dead, he says, hands on gun. But Saul won't have to worry about daughters, and the wives he wouldn't want to touch with a ten-foot pole. So why the hell is he here? Actually he really wanted to meet Stephen, who hasn't shown up yet. But should be here soon. Maybe tomorrow. Saul digs the hole, doing his chore. "I named him Rebel because he had a confederate flag tied to his tail," continued Stanley. "Of all damn things. I don't know how it got there. Can you imagine?"

"Was he whistling Dixie, Stan?" said Patrick with his usual smirky chirpy HO HO HO laugh-at-your-own-joke Irish wit.

"No, he was barking the Battle Hymn of the Republic," jested Richard, not to be outdone. But Stanley wasn't laughing.

"Was he being chased by a Yankee dawg?" Patrick just didn't know when to quit.

"Damn roots," said Saul, dripping with mosquito attracting perspiration. "Damn mosquitoes." Saul smacked himself on the cheek and on the back of his neck.

"What was that? I heard something move over there." Patrick suddenly remembered that this was snake country.

"Could be anything. Possum. Coon. Snake. Bear," said Stanley.

"You got bears around here?" Saul was surprised. He's a city boy.

"Black bear. They come out of the forest. There's a 130,000-acre forest behind my house, Saul. Didn't you see it on the map?"

"What map? I just followed the road signs."

"Croatan National Forest. They got them Venus Flytraps in there, plus a whole lot of rattlesnakes, and some alligators."

"No shit," said Saul.

"Yes, shit, Saul," added Patrick, another city boy, for whom nature was pretty or it wasn't to be contemplated at all. Nature was a pretty veil that shined with God's handiwork. But nature was nature and heaven was heaven and never the twain shall meet, such was Patrick's metaphysical outlook. What he forgot to add is that sometimes they do meet, in hell.

"There's some lakes in there too" said Stanley. "Most of them are dead. Hot and dry and dead. But one lake is maintained, and I hear that there are fish in that one."

"So you can go fishing there?" said Saul, and dumped a shovel load of dirt on the rim of the hole.

"Why the hell go fishing there when you got the whole goddam ocean. The Gulf Stream is just 20 or so miles off shore and you can catch blue marlin and dolphin and big stuff," said Richard, who sometimes takes the chartered fishing boats out of Morehead City.

"Anyway, you can't go fishing in the lake even if you wanted to. It's private. There's some kind of campground there. Run by Uncle Earl."

"Uncle Earl?"

"Yeah, Uncle Earl. The Redneck Messiah," said Stanley with a booming laugh.

"The Redneck Messiah? What's that?" Saul was curious.

"It's just a rumor but they say that there's some neo-Nazi, Ku Klux Klan, para-military white supremacy group that lives and trains there. But it's just a rumor. Can't be true."

"Can't be true," Richard and Patrick echoed Stanley. But Richard and Patrick looked at each other when they said it, as if they knew more than what they let on.

"There it is again," said Patrick, to change the topic. "Shine your flashlight over there. On that pile of pine needles. Something moved."

Stanley shined the flashlight on the pine needles. A large green striped garter snake was lying on the pine leaves with a... rabbit? Squirrel? gobbled up within its jaws. One half of the animal was inside the snake, creating a huge bulge, the other half exposed. Stanley moved closer. "It's harmless. They're not venomous. It couldn't move even if it wanted to." Patrick and Richard moved closer, slowly; Saul climbed out of the hole.

"Sonofabitch, it's gonna swallow the whole thing. Look at that bulge," said Richard.

"Kill it," said Patrick. This was not pretty nature. Patrick did not like the sight of nature being so ruthlessly tooth and claw. It gave him a sick feeling in his gut. "Let me have the spade." Patrick took the spade and went over to the snake. He raised the spade in the air and brought it slashing down on the snake and nearly split it completely in half, the two halves held together by a slither of skin. The snake squirmed and writhed around in the pine needles.

"Look," said Richard. There was a nest of baby rabbits, all dead, in the mound of pine needles. "The snake was going to have a feast. Greedy bastard." Patrick whacked the snake again. And again. And then again.

"Take that you bully. Take that." He hit the snake again and again.

"I think it's dead, Patrick," said Stanley. But Patrick kept hitting the snake. Sweat was dripping from his contorted face.

"That's enough Patrick, calm down." Stanley and Richard grabbed the spade and put their arms around Patrick's shoulder. It's been a while since they saw Patrick lose control like that.

"Damn snake. Bully. It's like Khomeini and the hostages, damn Arab terrorists, Carter's doing nothing. Just wait till Reagan's president. He'll take care of those bastards!

"That's right, Patrick. Let's go inside," Richard led Patrick into the house.

"I'll finish up here," said Saul, smacking his bare chest. "Damn mosquitoes!" Saul looked at his hands and chest. He was covered in smears of blood. "Jesus Christ, look at this."

"Put your shirt back on," said Stanley. "Go inside and clean up. I'll bury Rebel. I should do it."

I followed Saul down south in my 1972 Ford Torino red station wagon. I arrived a few days later.

It was through Patrick, the old tugboat engineer, that I met Ralph Stronzo. Patrick said that he might be able to find Saul and me some temporary work before we took off to California. Ralph had owned a hair salon in Raleigh and he was a very popular hair stylist with the wealthy ladies and wives of politicos. Ralph did not seem the type. He was a small and burly guy, with a big mouth, who was raised in a bad part of Brooklyn. Patrick met Ralph at the only Catholic Church in town. Ralph had been laid up in bed with the shingles and hadn't left his room for six months. Later I would find out why he hadn't left his room. But he was all boundless energy and a go-get-'em American now. He had invented some secret device that involved a pink box and tin foil. It had the potential to make millions. But he couldn't tell me what it was, not yet. The FBI was bugging his house and had tapped his phone. The secret of the pink box and tin foil had to be kept secret.

Then one day he explained to me that it had something to do with the beauty industry. It would be worth millions because the beauty industry was the biggest industry in the world. Women are vain.

A few days later he asked me to drive him to western North Carolina, where we went to a Gyrocopter Gymboree event. He bought one and hooked it on back of the car. Then we met a Spanish man at the airport. He was Juan Vasquez. He was trying to attract tourism to Spain, to Torrelimos. Ralph had somehow inveigled himself into a meeting with the Governor. Ralph introduced Juan and then me as our chief mechanic. I didn't know a damn thing about engines, cars or gyrocopters. Juan had some idea about a honeycomb boat that would sail the Mediterranean. He unrolled a poster of a bullfight and another of Torremolinos. "It's the fun capital of the Costa del Sol. We have bars, beaches, restaurants, pubs, nightclubs, and discos." Juan was ok. He was from a well-to-do family and when Juan was a child, he told me that he had met Hemingway. I don't know how he got suckered into Ralph's mad scheme that made no sense and was "top secret." Ralph talked with anyone. He had me stop in a McDonald's where he chatted up a waitress. Then he called some woman in Dallas from his mobile phone, and had me speak with her to say that he's an honest and sincere and great guy. He had promised to marry her. I am shy and anxious by nature. It didn't take long before I saw this was madness. Ralph was divorced and had two kids who wanted nothing to do with him. Not unless he started taking his medication again. Ralph was bi-polar. One time when we were driving I owned up to my dreams. A writer. He started lambasting my father and how he must have fucked me up. Ralph said that he was a millionaire thrice over but money means nothing he said. Money is easy to make. Money is shit. He was a hustler, a con man, a perfect American. He showed me a small gun he carried. He said he didn't have a license. Why should he? It's protection. I was boiling inside and grabbed the gun and pointed it at him. I said apologize to my father you little piece of shit.

That was it. I never saw him again. Soon Saul and I were back on the road. But the best part of this story is that several years later I heard that he had killed himself. I guess he didn't take his medication. He had shot himself in the head and heart. How did he manage that! Did he shoot himself in the head or heart first? I could only hope that he shot himself with the gun that he pulled on me and I grabbed from him... maybe there is something to be said for a very dark irony after all.

Farmer Roberts

A Farmer Roberts lived down the road. Farmer Roberts drove his old blue Ford pick up truck down the dirt road and stopped by the rural mailbox. He picked up a tin can from under his seat and into the can he spat a long gooey brown wad of chewing tobacco. He cumbersomely got out of the truck and put his large hands into the pockets of his overalls. He slowly walked over to the garden where I was working. Farmer Roberts looked around disdainfully at the marigolds and other flowers. He sniggled with a snide know-how. "Shit, what the hell ya gone and put them flowers here for? They ain't nothin' but useless." He chomped on his toothless gums and spat on a flower. He looked at the pine trees. "Cut those pines down and raise ya sum pigs. Them pines ain't nuthin' but useless. Shit, I could et everthin' ya got growin' 'ere in a day! Git yaself sum pigs and chickens. Damn skeeters eat the head right off a chicken... man, I'm tellin' ya."

I showed him a snake that I had killed with a shovel. "Isn't it a copperhead?"

"Dat ain't no white oak snake, man... dat's a corn snake. Dem white oak's got a head just like my thumb... just like dis..." And he stuck his huge flat thumb up in my face. "Shit, ya got to clear out dem pines and raise ya sum pigs, man... when ya fatten' up and kill 'em, man, dere ain't nuttin' as pretty... ain't nuttin' else like it in the whole world, man, I'm tellin' ya now. It's the most beewdaful thin' in the world. Trim the hogs... C'mon wit me I gots to shows ya sumthin." I climbed into Farmer Robert's truck. A 38-carbine leaned uncomfortably on the front seat. He drove into the national forest. "What are you looking for?" I asked.

"Deer." Farmer Roberts drove slowly along the side of the sandy road looking for deer tracks. He found none. Robert's took a swig from a bottle and handed it to me. Bitter shit it was. Sassafras tea that he had made himself. I later read it was a carcinogen. Robert's pulled out from the forest and onto the paved road. Possum's Misery Road. At the edge of the road we came upon a group of pickup trucks and a row of hunters, shotguns perched. Roberts stopped to watch. Dogs were barking in the woods and chasing deer, trying to turn them toward the road. "Ain't fair," said Roberts.

Uncle Earl

Saul and I took a jeep borrowed from Stanley and went into the Croatan National Forest looking for the lake we had spotted on a map and that his tugboat friends told him about. Maybe it was Uncle Earl's lake. We ended up in a private area (there were signs indicating this but we disregarded them) with cabins and small fishing boats. As we were driving out from the campground, a pickup truck came roaring up behind us. We stared into the barrel of a shotgun and two rednecks. "What ya boys doin' out here? This is a right private place. Let me repeat myself: this here has been a right private place since before the war... that's the Civil War! As you folks call it... the War between the States, more accurately."

After this history lesson, Saul and I were graciously escorted off the private property and back out to the paved state road, the public road where possums were free to be crushed by convoys of military trucks headed to the port in Morehead City. A harrier thundered overhead. The sign outside the airfield at Bogue said: Pardon our noise; it's the sound of freedom. We rented a cabin at the edge of the Croatan National Forest. It was a place where Babe Ruth and Christy Mathewson used to go to hunt.

One day a car pulls in front of the cabin. A short heavy-set man with thick lensed glasses waved to me. I went over to talk with him. I thought maybe he needed directions. He spoke slowly with a slight southern drawl. He said he was a janitor in the local high school. He was interested in local history and discovering the truth about an old story he was investigating. He wanted to know if there was a graveyard around here. I told him we were only visitors and didn't know much of the local lore. He said that there's supposed to be an old black graveyard around here. He wants to find out if a certain person was buried there. The person's name was Robert Johnson. No, not that Robert Johnson. He said back in 1933 there was a small general store out on what is now Route 24, and that a young black man had robbed the store of a few dollars and shot the owner dead. The story goes that a vigilante mob found the black boy and lynched him. He is supposed to be buried in an old black graveyard in these parts. There are many old black graveyards and they are small and some are just buried in brush and in the woods, with only several headstones, if they even have a headstone. Then he started to talk about conspiracy theories. I asked him about Uncle Earl. He knew about him. But he said there ain't many Ku Klux Klan in this part of the state. But Earl might be some militia white Aryan type Nazi. He has a complex in a private part of the forest. Right in the middle of a national forest! I told him that we might have met some of Uncle Earl's disciples. And we were scared off with a shotgun. Yeah he said you boys better be careful. It's pretty safe around here for the most part but you never know. We got retired folk from the north and military personnel from all over the country, so there's a mix. He then started talking about the Kennedy assassination, and that Lyndon Johnson and the Council on Foreign Relations are the true killers of Kennedy, and then he started on evolution and the moon and on and on... I just wanted to get rid of him by that point. I mean he was a janitor, wasn't much educated, but he was curious and had a native intelligence, so he said. He finally left. We never saw him again. I hope he finds his graveyard.

Hobo Sackett

"Ooh dem bulls were mean," said Hobo Sacket, who lived down the red barn road. "I was a card carryin' member of the IWW, I Won't Work! Ain't no shame in being a hobo. I was no bum. I rode the rails fer ten years, from when I was fifteen, ooh dem bulls were mean. Then I changed, dabnabit. I got married and went to school to learn a trade. I had five daughters and moved from place to place. Minnesota, Illinois, Georgia, North Carolina... now I got twenty-four grandchildren and ten great grandchildren. Now I'm seddled fer good. They come and visit me if they wanna, I an't goin' there. One of um lives clear up in New York City. Hell ya couldn't pay me to go to that rat race. They want me to come, but I won't argi wit' 'em. No more moving around for me brother, that's fer the birds. I don't bother wit nuttin' no more. You read my sign: Every third person shot and two already been here. But I always wanned to go to Ireland when I was a youngin. The train took me everywhere but never there. It's somewhere near the ocean I think. I saw a picture of it once in a big book with lots of purty pictures. Color ones they were too. And little poems or somethin'. Damn purty. Real green grass, cows, horses, man, it was just booodaful. I'm not a book reading man like you, Stephen, but maybe they got some of those writer types in Ireland. If you don't like it here no more why not go to Ireland. You could send me a purty postcard. I ain't goin' no where no more, nonsiree, gee-willa-kers, papa's pants will soon fit willy... and this is it fer me, I'm old, an old man, years and years like great black oxen walked over me, broke me down, but real green grass, cows, horses, hills... booodaful, just booodaful..."

The Road to California. November 1980

Saul and I hit the road. This will be brief, because the road leads nowhere. Saul wanted to search for his father in San Francisco, his father who had abandoned him as a child... like Saul abandoned his child...

I dropped Saul off in Las Vegas, and we made plans to meet later in San Francisco. I didn't think I would ever see him again.

I found work at the San Fernando Electric Company, for the minimum wage, running some type of machinery that melted plastic to a transistor or conductor of some sort, while muzak was being piped into rooms filled with loud machines and the voices of chattering Mexican and Philippine women. I was the only white person, except the manager of course, among mainly Mexicans, blacks and Philippines, about 60% were women. It was here that I met Umberto (Robert). We became friends.

Roy Lee Dunn also worked in the building, as a janitor. I had picked him up hitching on route 40, just outside of Gallup, New Mexico. He helped with the driving, now that Saul was gone, the rest of the way to Los Angeles, stoned out of his brain. I wasn't sure where I was going or where I was going to stay when I got to California, so I took up his invitation to stay at his Aunt Edna's house in Sylmar. She was upset because a Republican, Ronald Reagan, had been elected president just yesterday, and she was a life-long Democrat from Texas. Her house was filled with cats and dogs and donkeys. The donkeys were a knick-knack menagerie of Democratic Party pride. A collection of donkeys of every shape and size and color: made of glass, made of paper, made of rubber, made of plastic, made of metals, made of wood, made of boredom, made of nonsense, made of loneliness, made in the USA (and in China). The cats and dogs were real enough though, and they looked it and smelled it, all strays. Edna was a nice woman, but she was scared of her nephew. He was a pure product of America: good chance he was psycho. Edna told me about her beloved dead husband and his concern for young drifters who made their way out to California to find a new way of life in the sixties but got involved in drugs (wasn't that part of the new life of the sixties?) and with the law… and my dear husband would take them in, all of them, he never refused no one who came looking for a place to sleep or a good meal. I must have cooked a thousand meals for those poor kids, and they all had motorcycles, they would repair them in the backyard, there are some out there now all rusted and stuck in the vines, and my husband would help fix them you know, that was his job, a mechanic; what a time it was, and Roy he would come and go, come and go, and the cops all the time, the cops, and my husband having to smooth things out. Some of them still come and visit me you know, they bring their kids and wives and girl friends with them. Skinny little kids. I don't think they eat too well. They always have dirty hair; don't they comb their kid's hair today. And always smoking that marijuana. My husband used to hate that man who became president.

You know he was governor once. My poor husband must be turning in his grave.

Edna also told me a little about her nephew. He had been in jail a couple of times for robbery, back in Texas. Had been a truck driver, and one time abandoned his truck out on the highway, just left it there and walked away. Roy Dunn himself told me that he at one time or another had been a truck driver, biker, drug dealer, writer, pot head, world's oldest hippie, gun expert, treasure hunter, runner with the rich, Hollywood stuntman, thief, inmate at San Quentin, and then he added almost redemptively, as if to be purified by omission, or was it just an oversight? "But I never did kill anyone, hoss."

Glad to hear it, I thought to myself. And I didn't want to hang around much longer and give Roy Dunn the opportunity to redress this momentary amnesia in his amoeboid mind of a prevalent American past time. After $150 went missing from my wallet and Roy Dunn disappeared for a week to buy dope, I decided I'd better get out before Dunn gets back. Damn thief. Should I confront him or not? Confront a real crazy American? I hung around for another week thinking that Roy Dunn might be gone for good. And then he was back. Poor Edna had hoped that he was gone for good too this time. But one day he showed up in the kitchen window and pretended to shoot at me with his fingers. "Bang, I'm back, hoss." I could sense that a shoot out at the Not OK Corral was inevitable unless I split fast. Roy Dunn sliced my tires and put salt in my bed. These are strange techniques unheard of in the Wild West. Edna had no say in the matter; she was powerless. If only my husband was alive, he'd get rid of him.

Maybe I was thinking Roy Dunn would be my Neil Cassady. Hell no! I could see through him and wasn't going to accept this Wild West frontier pioneer rustling hustling gun-toting lawless biker truck driving character from the annals of American Western lore. I'll go back to New York City because I do believe I've had enough. That's the scene I want… the village, or Paris, bohemia… fuck this myth of the west, of the continent's end, it's off the deep end, and all this rebel and beat and hippie shit… I need to hear the Ramones and see the Mets play again… and maybe get out of this country once and for all… become an exile, an expatriate… fuck the road and fuck the Wild West and fuck Main Street… sorry, Jack.

I said goodbye to Edna and wished her good luck. I moved in with Umberto and his friend Martino, who had three small children. His wife took off the previous summer and left the kids behind. On weekends, Martino dumps the kids with his sister and drinks tequila and spits at the women on the television. Monday morning finds him past out in his car in the front sandy yard with all the other broken down cars. Welcome to the San Fernando Valley.

It's New Year's Eve 1980. Umberto and I drove around all night in his old Audi. At a bar some asshole spilled some beer on me and Umberto decided that he had to beat the guy up to protect my honor. I felt kind of weird about that. Then the car broke down on a desolate road. Umberto says follow me. I don't know where he thinks we are going but we walk over a hill and up an incline toward a lone house in the distance. This worries me. I don't want to get shot looking for help. I say wait a minute Umberto, but he smiles and says come on. Before he even knocks on the door a small older man muttering something in Spanish approaches us. I look for a shotgun. But the man walks up to Umberto and embraces him in a mighty and manly hug. Stephen, this is my Uncle Raimundo. Umberto has relatives everywhere it would seem. We are given a bowl of soup to help with our hangovers. Raimundo and his wife looked at me strangely when I picked up the spoon. What? I looked at the reddish soup and said tomato? They told me it's called menudo soup. It's beef stomach. It's good. Eat.

The next morning when I am standing over the sink, ready to wash my face, waiting for the water to get hot, once again they are looking strangely at me. What? There is no hot water. Just cold.

I met Maria at a damn disco of all places. If I ever have to listen to Kool and the Gang's "Celebration" ever again I will shoot myself. But she had sad eyes and long strait black hair. Martino invited her to a party at his brother's house. The Oakland Raiders were in the Super Bowl. Everyone was saying to each other: Ya gotta be tough. Ya gotta be tough. The Raiders was their team. The party deteriorated rapidly. A little man went around with a vial of cocaine and a tiny spoon that he stuffed up noses of willing participants. Martino got upset when his married sister with two small kids told him that some big fat ugly white biker dude turned her on. So Martino challenged the big fat ugly white biker dude to a drinking contest. They stood and stared at each other. Martin and the biker each holding a full bottle, a fifth of Tequila. They lifted the bottles to their mouths and drank. And drank and gulped. They drank non-stop and emptied the bottles.

When I was leaving the party later that night I saw the biker passed out on the dirt in front of the house, next to his Harley motorcycle, in a pool of vomit. Martino was fine. He said, let's go, *vamos a casa*...

I drove north to San Francisco. Big Sur and Highway one... Henry Miller, Kerouac... Jeffers tower... we slept in the back of the car, and the fog rolled over us... *condenados al exilio*... in San Francisco she said that she had to return, that she missed her mother... she took the bus back... I stayed the night in a cheap roadside motel. A thin dirty couple with a thin dirty child, right out of a Steinbeck novel, came into my room, uninvited, and began helping themselves to the ash trays and glasses and what-not.

"You gonna be needin' these things?" asked the woman.

"Probably not," I said.

"Mind if we take them?"

"They're not mine."

"Well in that case you ain't gonna care one way or the other, are you?"

"Guess not." And I added, "Why don't you take the misery too."

"We got enuff of that. That's about all we got enuff of."

The next day I was on a Trailways bus back to New York. It's the end of the road, America.

Never Heard of Him

On Long Island I asked an old man, who was walking down the street, "Do you know where I can find Walt Whitman's house?" "Who? Lived here all my life. Never heard of him." In a museum in Bennington, Vermont, I asked an old man, a museum guide, "Do you know where I can find Robert Frost's grave?" "Who? Lived here all my life. Never heard of him." In Carmel, California, I asked an old man, a ticket collector at one of the local tourist sights, the nine-mile scenic highway, "Do you know where I can find Robinson Jeffer's tower?" "Who? Lived here all my life. Never heard of him." In Asheville, North Carolina, I asked an old man, who was sitting on a bench outside the General Store, "Do you know where I can find Thomas Wolfe's house?" "Who? Lived here all my life. Never heard of him." In Oklahoma, I asked an old Cherokee, who was sitting by the "Indian Souvenir Stand" on the shoulder of Interstate 40, "Do you know where I can find America?" "America? Lived here all my life. Never heard of it." The old Cherokee walked away in his faded jeans; a can of Coca-Cola in his hand; he got into his old blue Chevy and drove off into the burnt-out sunset. On Main Street, in front of the bar that my father used to run over twenty years ago, I asked an old bum heading into the bar, "Did you ever meet Jack Kerouac? Or have a drink with him in this bar?" He pointed toward the bar and said, "You buying?" "Sure." After several drinks he said drunkenly, "What was that name again?" "Jack Kerouac." "Hmmm. I lived here all my life. Never heard of him." He walked out the door and stumbled across Main Street.

Beyond Main Street

I was back in New York. I tried to find Tommy, searching in Brooklyn, but he didn't live at the old apartment on 5th Avenue anymore. I checked out the YMCA. Not there. So I looked around the Village. One day I was standing near the Circle in the Square theatre where Tommy and I saw *Hamlet* with Rip Torn a few years ago, for free, for four hours. I was walking around in a daze, looking in the old spots. I never saw Tommy again. Soon I would be in Europe and it would be goodbye to all that... but I remember the time we were standing here, on Houston Street, we had just walked over from Mercer Street... we had seen that Dylan film, *Renaldo and Clara*... another four hours... in a small Village movie house... and I told Tommy about my grandmother who was born and lived around here... Fiorenza Maggio was her maiden name. And that my father told me that he thinks his mother was born on Houston Street, and that they lived at Mercer Street at one time and Wooster Street too... he wasn't too sure. I remember my grandma so vividly; she died in 1969, that amazing year, I remember the dark circles under her eyes, and her long gray hair that she used to comb out. My Aunt Luisa took care of her. My grandmother was crippled by that time, bed-ridden, with diabetes, and nearly blind, she used to grab me with her long thin fingers and hand me a dollar that she retrieved from a small purse that she kept under her many pillows. She did it so my aunt wouldn't know. She always smiled when Jimmy Durante came on television. He was her favorite. She had met Theodore Roosevelt too, because my grandfather had a fruit and vegetable store in town, and Roosevelt would stop by. My grandfather had bought property right in the middle of Oyster Bay. I don't know how he had the money. But right there, on South Street, at the beginning of the century. He built these solid concrete buildings for his family and his fruit and vegetable store, and some other shops and apartments. Can you imagine some Italian immigrants among the Great Gatsbys of the Gold Coast, all those Anglo-Saxon and Dutch snobs? It was a strange place, Oyster Bay.

Demographically, it was a feudal village. In this mutilation of Demos, the vassals, the hybrid European descendants, occupied the hamlet and its (pre-scripted irony) Rockwellian Maple and Oak and Walnut and Main Streets. These were predominantly first and second generation Irish, Italian, German, Scandinavian, and Polish families, whose fathers were firemen, cops, post office workers, street-cleaners, janitors, bartenders, a few modest entrepreneurs, but generally civil servants of various sorts, whose mothers were housewives (maybe PTA but certainly not DAR) and whose sons would marry the girl next door, and whose daughters were the girl next door.

My rite of passage into the manifold hands of village life and lore and legality arose from the flames that I sparked off with a book of matches, during the Great Fire of 1962, by lighting a heap of garbage on fire. The garbage had been haphazardly piled against the front wall of Food Town supermarket, where it gave off a vile stench. I was six years old at the time and my "moll," my sister, who had egged me on to do it, was twelve, and in proverbial wisdom, should have known better. But the town folk did get a jolt. I got a jolt too, from my father's belt. My father used to take off his belt and fold it over and push it in and snap it out, but rarely did he use it. This time he did. After the smoke cleared, in which the front of the building was only charred, I became something of a local hero. The Town Fathers reprimanded Food Town for being so careless in the handling and discarding of its garbage, and ironically extolled little me for alerting them to the fact, though it be by rather uncivil and incinerary means. A little revolutionary was born. Who says there's no irony in American life? Food Town thereafter obtained large steel containers, which were conveniently hooked up, lifted up, and the garbage dumped into the belly of a garbage truck.

I was ready to take that big step, to find out if there was more to this life… it was time to go Beyond Main Street, that Main Street I remembered in Oyster Bay… and those who barely got beyond, who never left.

Beyond Main Street, a small community of blacks lived near the railroad tracks (the station is the end of the line in more than the literal sense for them), whose ancestors preceded the European mutts and many of the Anglo-Saxon and Dutch nobility and gentry.

Beyond Main Street, the village shopkeepers were mainly Jews. They owned the various stores (and there always seemed to be two stores of each kind): two hardware stores, two stationeries, two five & dimes, two pharmacies, two liquor stores. On weekdays they descended from their tribal heights, a new hill top development built in the fifties and sixties, of semi-large ranch houses with manicured lawns and sprinklers going all the time, and dispersed among the Gentiles, with whom they got along with aloof but cosmopolitan charm.

Beyond Main Street, the landowners, whose mansions and manor houses and horse stables spiraled around and down from the pinnacle of Theodore Roosevelt's Sagamore Hill and through the dense woods of the cove and on to the bay, who sequestered themselves within the green deciduous trees, but in winter, when the leaves fell, their consumption (and not the kind in Dostoyevsky) was make conspicuous, and then the village folk could take car rides and strolls along the public road up the cove to try to get a glimpse of that side of paradise.

Main Street. Beyond Main Street... but far beyond Main Street.

Norway 1984
A Lyrical Interlude

The Island

I arrived at the coastal town of Farsund on a bus from Kristiansand. Looking down out the large window of the bus I had seen nothing but the scant tops of spruce and birch trees dangling over water forty feet below, on the road from Lyngdal to Farsund, whose route was the hairpin curves of a road carved along the side of a mountain at the edge of a sheer drop to the Lyngdalsfjorden. The road, route 43, was constructed upon the old road, of which there were still some remnants of gutted wheel tracks fossilized and nestled within the niches of mountain rock with sharp trimmings of gouged marks where hand-held steel had struck stone. There was hardly space for one vehicle to pass through on the old road, around the curves where rocks plummeted into water or crashed upon the road. If a Norwegian had discovered gravity, it wouldn't have been an apple that fell upon his head.

It is written in an old tale that the rocks of Norway shall stand forever; it had been spoken through the ages before it was written; and before it was written or spoken, before man, the rocks stood. The rocks are standing now... standing? How odd a word... the rocks are standing now, now? How odd a word? The rocks are standing now, covered with birch trees and heather, long low sunsets and the winds that blow. Sunsets? What an odd word... there are no more sunsets. But to enter a lyrical mood of metaphor the words must hold their history.

My name is Stephen Knut Cazzaza and I am living on an island off the southern coast of Norway. Beyond Main Street.

A young boy climbed up the oak-branch rungs of an unsteady ladder and crawled into a tree house. He carried a soft moist piece of brown driftwood that he had taken from the cool water of a small inlet. The driftwood had been trapped and tangled within a green society, confined under the ocean's reaching paw with the jetsam and flotsam. The driftwood had been butting against the rock like a baby bull; had been scraping against the rock like a solitary mountain elk cleaning the husk from its antlers; had been banging against the rock like a mad philosopher banging his brains against the universe.

The tree, with its tree house like a cave in the clouds of a Chinese mountain, stood detached from the interglacial world-inheriting birches and the crowed coppice of beeches.

The tree house: just some wide and narrow irregular planks of old knotted spruce and pine that have been slapped upon the limbs diagonally and boxed-off asymmetrically, and fortified within the twig-twisted palm of the divided trunk of an ash tree. The late-leafing pinnate leaves whipped about and flipped about in the playful wind like the animated blinking eyelashes of a Parisian fashion model.

The boy lit a candle to quench the night's appetite. His breath wheezed through his nose and the candle's flame shimmered but survived. He placed the candle on the top of the driftwood in the center of the floor, and then he took an apple out of his pocket. It was the last apple from the gold-rim bowl on the sugar maple table in the kitchen. He hadn't wanted to share the apple with his sister, so he secretly stuffed it into his pocket along with the string, stones, and pocketknife. He ate the apple, cutting off sections with his knife, just the way he had seen his uncle do it so many times, and sliding the knife along his tongue.

The boy stepped outside on the slight, marginal, unsound deck of the tree house, and he climbed up to a higher platform, which afforded him a view in every direction, like a turret on a tower. He stood there like a lighthouse keeper, his eyes as bright as beacons in a fog.

He spiraled himself around a limb and swung down to another limb, which he slithered along and encircled like the Midgaard serpent curled around the sacred tree of life, Yggdrasil; and then without holding on to the security offering branches, he attempted to walk out on a horizontal limb, balancing himself with an inner and outer equilibrium. He feared the height but advanced one step farther each time. His legs wobbled; his heart beat rapidly; his head felt giddy. He stopped, and turned back to the center of the tree, carefully walking, and reached the trunk, embracing it with his arms. His heavy breathing expanded his chest against the tree's bark. He watched an ant crawl over his hand, carrying a tiny white object between its mandibles. The ant vanished behind a crevice in the bark, and the boy saw his hand suddenly impaled by a wayward trace of moonlight. He turned around; he saw the moonlight leaning over the ocean like a parabola of geometric luminescence.

The immense sea tried to exhume itself from its mirror of stars, shoveling insignificant drops of water on the shore, but reburied itself, rolling over the surface of its own massive modulating body like a delicate dragonfly skims over a pond when the hollow reeds of summer-memory bend toward the ears of nature's forgetfulness with cold whispers of the coming white sheet that shall tuck the earth into long sleep again.

The boy listened to the waves breaking upon the rocks, these lungs of matter. He imagined that the waves conspired with the wind to push this island across the ocean like a voyaging ship in a tumultuous storm. The island moved, floating toward some unknown place and destiny. The thought of an adventure excited the boy, stimulating his youthful energies, and he widened his eyes. He was also frightened that the island could be driven into one of those huge maelstroms that he had read about in a Jules Verne book. But he would be the lookout, on alert, he thought to himself, spying the seas for that hungry vortex that could suck the island down and strip it of its trees and inhabitants, its voices and identity, its ghosts, and cast up the smells of dead shadows, could even swallow the night and spew out the rocks gurgling in God's stomach like the sudden passage of being into consciousness, this nothing that leaves no fossil of its pain and despair, not a jot of evidence of its tears, like the broken bones encased in mud, encased in time, leave behind.

The boy located the Orion constellation in the sky. His father had taught him how to observe the stars. The boy saw the stranded hunter between the Tropic of Cancer and the Tropic of Capricorn, in the limbo region of the equatorial zone. With his naked eye he saw the quadrilateral of Betelgeuse, Rigel, Beallatrix, and Saiph. He saw the cluster of stars that comprised Orion's sword, which hung down from the three stars of Orion's belt. With his inner eye he saw the islands of exile, the states of exile, the seasons of exile, and all the places in between, and all the ships that sail at night, following the stars in their courses, going round and round like the old world went round and round...

The boy could see his father, mother and sister through the window of a small house, the room lighted by a kerosene lamp. They sat together and stared into the fire in the tall thin cylindrical wood-burning stove, the flames nibbling at their faces like little squirming red fishes.

Tomorrow the boy's father will go out fishing. He will go early and he will go alone. The boy can go fishing in the calm small inlet, but the father will go out where it is much deeper and more dangerous, far out in the rough edges of the North Sea, though it isn't necessary, because there is plenty of fish in the inlet to feed a family of four, who are staying on the island for only one month in summer, plenty of cod and whitting, plenty of mussels and crabs, and besides that, the mother is going with Mr. Håken in his boat to town early tomorrow morning to pick up some supplies. The boy's mother tried to dissuade her husband from going on a needless fishing trip, but he will go and that's that!

The boy sat down on the floor of the tree house, the shielding integument, and stared at the candle. He was like a random egg deposited into the dregs of a discarded ovipositor. The boy spun his web. He gathered pieces from numerous puzzles, which have been laid before him like stepping-stones across the pond near a Buddhist temple. He took one piece from each puzzle and tried to fit them together into some arrangement of support, some grounding of comfort. But his blank frame repelled each piece from its field. Blank! No connections. Failure. He would have to find pieces that would fit some undisclosed design and pattern; but where? How to begin? He felt an obscure frustration and punched his hand through the restricting cocoon, one more hole, and he blindly groped into the emptiness, his arm wriggling like a worm sticking out from a hole in an apple. He heard his mother's voice call him: "Come on, Johnny…" He was tired and hungry. He climbed down the ladder and fell softly into the brown soiled faces of the mythical Norns, and then he ran across the open area of tall grass and reached his mother's arms.

At one level of life he was a forest-dweller, in his hermit's cave, his mystic's tower, independent and aloof; a herbivore. At another level of life and death he was a hunter of the open spaces, a grass runner; a carnivore. At the level of culture he was a spinner of tales shared around the central hearth. A hunter whose weapon is words, whose target is control and power, whose arc of flight the visible circuit of the mind's mandala; a hunter who is omnivorous of language and time. At the level of civilization he was a grower, a planter, of our daily provincial bread, and a burner of the fields, but with a purpose in the thread of the year as it unwound its way through progress, that sprite trickster of the harvest, sowing seeds in the season of the crow… a reptile… a serpent… a bird… in hunger comes the hawk…

Twelve little monkeys came out of the trees in search of Plato, bearing the fruit of the forest and the fruit of their womb. They huddled in a circle. But one monkey kept coming and going, running back into the forest and returning again, as the trees of paradise diminished around him. He was as large and as long as the length of his breath, and terribly small under the stars. He had discovered that his breath touched the stars with the structure of symbols and a stone flung at death and brought down hard upon the hollow skull of time. Beech and hazel in the north. Stars on the inscribed ceiling of a cave. Hunting and weaning. The stone and the breast. Kinship and the horseshoe crab of nature, shelled and sunken in the sand of security beneath the restless waves. Driftwood floating above.

The symbols are no more the final ends in themselves than the borders of a tribal territory. But why aspire? Why go one step farther? The unreality of the symbol keeps us at bay and dies in the dogma and the agon of existence. At the edge of the knife the hunter met his brother's face; did he recognize him even as he cut his throat?

They huddled in a circle and the woods slowly grew up around them. The circle grew wider and the trees were felled. They chopped down the woods outwardly and the woods grew denser inwardly. Until all the circles came together in a desert of their own making. The topsoil had eroded, the grass had been burnt away, but the tangled vines hung from their ears and mouths, rooted in emptiness. The shaman of the tribe entered the symbolic forest and chopped his way to the center, to the mouth of the cone, and he traveled in the infinity of the core among a wilderness of shapes and numbers where the steps lead to doors and the doors lead to rooms where a boy sits and stares at a candle in a tree-house in an ash tree on an island off the coast of Norway… or a tree-house in an oak tree in a wood of one of the large estates on Long Island…

A poet leaves the desert in search of a new forest. He finds a lone apple tree in the desert. He picks an apple. The apple is filled with maggots. He eats it. The people come out of the desert in search of a new forest. They gather around the tree and climb upon each other's shoulders to reach an apple. The apple is filled with poisons and radiation.

The mutation of the angels. Eat this in remembrance of me, for this is our body and this is the earth of our inheritance.

When night comes nowadays her long black hair is turned to gray in the glimmering of the evening stars. Night has lost her wisdom and power. The moon has lost her glory and honor. But the days keep skipping along like the young girl who earlier in the day skipped rope, kicking up dust and counting 1 2 3, beneath the tree-house where her brother would later sit on smooth driftwood. But now they are fast asleep in their beds.

And in the other room their father splits the flesh of the moon and shoots liquid stars into her, and she bites deeply into the tip of his finger; and he is sinking in the white foam of the sea, squishing and gulping for air; she lies face down and will not turn over to face him, and he is drowning… but she will not breathe life into him.

A pale liquid moon, whether she appears as a majestic swan, or a fruit stealing magpie, or a ragged crow, or without the garments of light or dark, remains tucked away behind the silver cobwebs of the sky, which cloud-up the springs of inspiration, where she waits, deep in the black pools of a cold summer night. Beware her nakedness in a time of falling things, when the clock falls from the hands; for her strength is terrific, her energy boils furiously in the bloody cauldron she stirs frantically with her uneasy fingers. Today she reigns. She presides over a landscape drenched by a diffused and uncertain sun, weary and ready to set. She surreptitiously pours down her quietly conjured magic, casting shadows off the trees on the mountain: hazel and hawthorn, holly and elder, poplar and fir, ash and oak; mountains where no man go lest his heart jump in his breast like a wounded darting doe. This faded and haggard moon, so burdened by the long irreverent light of day that her pure, globed, fire-fly glow seems but a weakened and palsied thing, buried like a mouse in an owl's nest, reeking of a lingering pestilence, but come some chilled November night and her oval owl's face will fill the nest-hole in the side of the oak once again, where she will hoot like a rising wind, and hunt among the forest scrubs, frightening the little flittering wrens.

Moon of dazed owl-eyes closing shut under the tired lids of a fleecy, rose-petaled, midsummer night, the poet comes to kiss them open again, and touch your rip-red lips with his black-currant lips, and pass secret words of worship between the apple and the bite.

Langøy, the long island. The wind took nine giant steps upon the waves and crashed upon the rocks like knights in black armor falling from white horses. The wind blew through the neglected orchard, lifting leaves up like the skirts of maidens, and flustered the forming buds of fruit trees. The wind carried seeds of transformation, the wind impregnated the poet's mind; it recaptured life from the decaying air. The wind chased the hare that chased the mouse; the mouse became a serpent. The hare became an eagle that chased the serpent; the serpent became a seed. The eagle became the hen that swallowed the seed, and the hen laid an egg that became a woman, and that woman gave birth to a cauldron; the cauldron became the sea. And the sea brought forth an island.

She will come to the island again; she will be on the sea again; she will be waiting in the orchard for him again, by the apple trees, tomorrow night.

The season was summer and the month was June; the day was Thursday and the hour was dawn; the sun was hiding behind a cloud-laden sky; the place was an island... but we have not come to it yet. We will come to it by-and-by. We have not crossed the threshold, nor passed through the dolmen; nor entered the pathless woods; nor turned the wheel; nor pulled down the pillars; nor pushed the millstone around the post, nor ascended the spiral stairs; nor descended into the bottomless lake; nor climbed the peak; nor sailed through the maelstrom; nor found the source of the north wind; nor journeyed to the glass castle in a crowned constellation. We have not come to it yet. We may never come to it. The year has been dragged halfway around the earth like Hektor, poor tricked warrior, and the sun-god and thunder-god are pleased with the mighty performance of sky-chariots and arms. They have paid gold and received oil. Bold Alexander cut the knot; the Gaul threw down his sword; and the atom was split by the many-bladed mind of man.

Mass destroyers... the sword falls from above the door; it strikes once, and strikes no more. Thursday will pass and Friday will come. The fires will burn and a king will be hung. But we have not come to it yet.

John Durre carried his fishing gear down the path. Little Johnny watched his father from his bedroom window. Why can't I go too, he thought. His lips quivered and a tear rolled down his cheek.

A woman walked down a sea-bound path, guided by old Aanen Håken, the lighthouse keeper. They carried their supplies, going to his boat, which will take them back to the island.

The sounds of the earth were softly brooding, rising out of the grass on the precise flapping of moist butterfly wings. The sloping field was strewn with mossy stones, crabbed with wind-struck crooked trees, flushed with blushing wild flowers, and braided with buzzing bees. The last cricket sang with a dewdrop glittering on its antenna like a tiny jewel bestowed upon it by the night for its continuing song of praise, because the darkness comes late now and is not very deep; it lies down in the grass and then there is nothing as tall, leaving traces of dew in the morning like tears and tales of separation.

Beneath the cloud-low sky, colored like crushed bone in a mortar (is it the moon that wields such a heavy pestle and scatters this dust among the weeping eyes of morning?), the air is filled with a mist and sprinkling powder of placid rainfall, cool and bare as a baby's foot.

Down the path-saddled hill the young woman followed the lighthouse keeper, but like a cart follows a horse, for she holds the reins. With the first scent of the sea the old man's mind rattled with a thousand silent shells of memory; with the first sight of the sea the cracks in his face seemed to fill with salt water like twisted fjords, and the flesh turn hard as stone. They arrived at the path's end, reaching a small nook of the endless jagged coastline, where two more essential acts of the earth's elemental drama were being enacted for a redundant human audience of two. The land and sea were strangely hinged in the young woman's mind. If she could find the meaning of this secret where would this place be? Is this place an island where something important turned? A dolmen? A door? A wheel? A word? A stone? A spiraling stair? An arctic tern? She couldn't remember her origins... to find the beginning in the end, and the end in the beginning was the… doubt… but to stand in the springtime rain again, waiting for him, in the month of May, to make a garland for her hair.

She imagined that she saw the shape of two heads carved into rock, one faced north, one faced south; one fed upon lichen, consuming itself, and bled from the mouth.

The old man opened the small red door of the boathouse, holding it open for the woman to pass through; she crouched and entered, passing beneath the sagging lintel, and found the boat swaying in the water, the waves lapping their greedy tongues upon its bottom, and curiously, she thought about her husband who had gone out fishing early this morning, before the sun rolled up the hills like a burning wheel.

The boat clashed its old wooden hull against the waves, and they moved farther out into the fjord, leaving the damp creaking boards of the dock behind them. The old man stood sternly at stern, steering the rudder; the young woman sat at bow, steering her thoughts through ancient beliefs and desires. The rocks of Norway haughtily crowded down upon them; some rocks perched like dark, giant vultures; others jetted out like huge spears stuck in the mountainside.

"Mr. Håken, will there be fish today?"

"*Jeg tror det ikke… ja…* I do not think so, yes… you see the tide is wrong."

Cardea smiled, and said, "My son is fishing in the cove off the west side of the island; do you think he will catch any fish there today?"

"Oh *ja, det er sikkert… kanshje torsk,*" he answered. And then he inquired, "*Hva heter torsk på Englesk?*"

"Cod. It is called cod in English," answered Cardea.

"Oh *ja*… cod… cod… yes, I remember now… cod…"

Cardea stroked her hair away from her face. The old man said, "I will try to speak English… yes, it is good to me to… how you say, *å laere?*"

"Yes, to learn… it is good to learn."

"*Ja,* I remember now… learn… I have forgot so many tings; it was many years since I leave America to come home. But we talk and I remember, *ja.*"

There was something in Cardea that felt a thousand years old; something there that is there when she is not there; her legacy on earth forty thousand years old; some fraction of her consciousness a million years old. If it can be equated in time, if it could be equated at all. And these were her thoughts as she drifted on waves of... time?

The engine suddenly stalled. Aanen Håken removed the lid from the lacquered wood box that contained the engine, which was situated in the middle of the boat, and he tried to repair it.

"*Sånn... sånn... sånn...*" he repeated to himself as he worked on the engine.

The boat drifted on the waves, trough and crest, door and dorn, wheel and axle, passing through time into timelessness. Cardea saw in a kind of vision the boat rise and fall on the crest and trough, but as if it remained at one still point, fixed within a glass bottle on the shelf in the library of a 13th century theologian. At this level of contemplation the sun receded and was subsumed by a black flower of darkness that turned its face toward its own absence of light, engulfing itself like a fog-enveloped island. Out of the darkness one still point of flickering light sent forth a beam, a current, a thread, an eye, like the trail of a tern's flight nine times around the island, like a burning in the clearing of a night-hooded grove, like the burrows dug boustrophedon by the ox, dragging his plough through the barren field...

...All in a moment the fire-eye of Cardea's consciousness shines on the icy confines of her beauty, melting time away in three moon-flashing winks, and through the green veins of nature she graciously sinks with the midsummer moon hung like a bleeding bull's horns in the wavering purple-robed sky beneath the watchful eye of the planet Venus...

At this level of contemplation infinity passed helically through nature, which passed through mythical time, which passed through her consciousness, which passed through a dynamic anamnesis, and back again, back and forth, inward and outward, like a sea-shell with whorls aspiring to an apex and inverting itself through itself, incessantly and repeatedly, but seeming to remain at one still point, like a mollusk, a horseshoe crab, an island, a doorpost, the center of a wheel, an eye... or a stalled boat. It passed through Cardea's mind like a thread weaved around and through the center of a spiral staircase, the spiral staircase of a lighthouse, perhaps? Each iron step an echo left behind, each revolution the massing of time in death. To reach the top is to reach the bottom and start again; Sisyphus caught in an Escherian world, enlightened by itself to itself, a motionless center of no center, no fulcrum, a Mobius strip, no beginning, no end, time burying time, space burying space, the horse faltering and stumbling, the rider falls...

A mystic current shared Cardea's dream. Cardea would have called it mystical. Aanen Håken had oil on his hands. He was not privy to her fantasies. The current pulled and pushed the boat, back and forth. Cardea saw the current radiating out from the black, cavernous, spumescent vortex, developing its destiny in a serpentine flow, eating its tail, laying eggs in the sky, and wrapping itself around the tree of life. The current came and swept through her consciousness; it conveyed the blue-green bounty of life in the algae of her submerged psyche; a photosynthesis of civilization; a thread, a current, a colliding chlorophyllic process of discovery; a metaphorical equivalent of rebirth and renewed life. Her consciousness: a seer, a sage, a shaman, a poet; it drudged up poetic pearls from the inhuman depth. She would go down; she, not anyone else. She of mythical time; she of flesh and blood. She listened. Aaneen Håken was silent. Waves. Trough and crest. The processional waves, the thread to the beacon in the brume, all the ships that sail at night, the algae to the sun, the current to the moon, the ladder to the tree house...

The mechanical steel blast of the boat's engine suddenly shook Cardea from one trance to another. She heard the engine's power ripping through the current, slicing the water, in a valley of its own self-insulated, self-aggrandized, self-important, conscious trough, where rivers of blood converge, falling from cliffs, cluttered with naked, dead bodies. The arrogant, arbitrary will power of man-centered centrifugal force; propeller blades tearing apart the current as it passes through the poet's mind, through the child's mind. Something remains, heeded or unheeded... listen, a life-preserver splashes on the dark navel of the water; a sound like a prayer reflected off an icon on a rural road in peasant Europe... take aboard the fool, the obstinate fool. Collective ichor, stagnation of seaweed and sludge, inculcated barnacles on the hull; the back of the north wind, the island off the coast of Norway...

In the year 1984 the most extraordinary events took place in a small coastal village in Norway. That's a paraphrase of the opening line of the novel *Mysteries* by Knut Hamsun. It was a cool rainy day when I arrived in Farsund, a few days ago. The small, squarish plane landed at Kristiansand after an incredible flight over the mountains and fjords, from Bergen. I am staying in a summer cottage on a small island just off the coast, the island is called Langøy. The cottage was once the house of my great uncle's wife. Before the war the house was not a summer cottage, not a vacation rental; people eking out an existence from the sea occupied it the whole year round; that was before the war, before the oil. My great uncle's wife died young. He's lived in an apartment in Bay Ridge, Brooklyn for many years now. He comes back *hjem til Norge* nearly every summer. He also has a summer cottage on the Jersey shore.

My mother was born in Lunde, a rocky area across the fjord from Farsund. She was born in a little white house. Her grandparents raised her. Many of the houses were torn down after an aluminum company bought the land. The rock foundation of her house still stands for now and I will go see it one day. The aluminum company put many locals to work. There was little protest. The people who still lived in Lunde at the time were quite old, and were glad to move away to new, modern homes. They threw away most of the old stuff, unless a son or daughter or grandchild or nephew or niece came back to claim it, to put in their nice house or apartment in Oslo.

But on Langøy there are some people of advanced age that the modern world forgot. There is a house near the high ridge occupied by a mother and her daughter, Bible-bearing Pentecostal ravers. And an old lighthouse keeper who lives in the small house at the base of the lighthouse, and also an old woman named Amalia who once was a neighbor of my mother on Lunde but was removed to this island and now lives in the house where she was born. I don't know why they still live here. The lighthouse keeper brings them food and looks after them.

There are, additionally, several other houses that have been converted to summer cottages now occupied by tourists. A few Germans, and an English couple, with two children. Otherwise, that's it, and for the most part we don't see each other, and if we do it's just a brief exchange of pleasantries. Head nods.

Amalia, the old woman who knew my mother... my mother had visited her before she returned to America with my sister and me after her second trip back to Norway. The other children never went near Amalia's house because they believed she was some kind of witch, because their mothers had told them that. Little Torhild, my mother, was also warned by her grandparents to keep away from the old heathen woman. She never attended church or meetings. She must be in cahoots with the devil.

When my mother visited Norway in 1957 after an absence of six years, she brought my sister, who was five, and myself, who was nine months. My mother took us to see Amalia, and she bestowed chocolate candy upon me and her strange blessings. In later years my mother would tell me about this visit over and over again. It became just another tale, another one of those vague images that activated my imagination; and for many years I seemed to know everything about this area and the people who lived here; all from my mother's stories. And when I visited here again, when I was seventeen, it was as if I lived here all my life.

"…So you know, when I was a little girl in Norway, you know there was this old lady, she lived up in the mountain in a real old house, you came around the main road, the dirt road, and then you went up this big hill, I can still see it, the big hill, and you know right next to the hill was a was a whadda you call it, in Norway you call it a *fuss, a bekk,* you know when the water comes running in a stream out to the water, it was like you know, a creek, *ja* a creek, you know but it was a noisy one, a noisy creek, so you know you went up the hill, there it was so spooky you know because there was trees on both sides and there was this running water coming real fast, you seen the water you know, it goes real fast and makes noises you know, and then when you come up to the hill, you saw this little house, out in the woods there, and this house was right under the mountain, *ja* like built right into the mountain, big stone steps going up, old fashion door, knock on the door, little old lady, a witch who lived in that house opens the door, the door was squeaky, when I was a little girl I was always afraid to go to this house you know, but when I was older I came home to Norway, Sylvia was six years old and Stephen about a year and a half, he walked in Norway when he was ten months old, up over the hills, *ja* I took Stephen in the carriage and Sylvia by the hand, I said we are going to see the old lady, the witch in the woods, you know, so like I said we went up the hill there and we knock on the door, and she opened the door and it squeaked, and we came into that little tiny hallway, and another thing there was, and you had to know just the time of the month to go to this old lady because there was only one time of the month she was in a good mood, rest of the month real bad mood, so ask the neighbors, is she in good mood now? Always dressed in black, never married, never had children, she had sisters who lived further up in the woods, she was hunchback, *pukkel,* a hump, you know, so we went into the tiny kitchen, not really a kitchen but a room to keep wood and coal, one big room with a bed against the wall, a table, two chairs, a rocking chair and a fire place with a big kettle, like a cauldron, just like a witch has, and she gave chocolate to Stephen, I'll never forget it, but not to Sylvia because she was always hopping around, restless..."

And now over twenty-seven years later I stand on the grassy knoll where the house that my mother was born in once stood. Now only a rock foundation. It was on this hill that I first walked, like my mother always told me, my first steps and my first falls, and heard my great uncle's voice, the one whose summer cottage I'm staying in, call to me "Hoy! Hoy!" but I didn't heed him and kept walking down the slope until they fetched me back.

I returned to the island and the summer cottage. I was snooping around in the loft and in closets and in drawers. In the loft I found a trunk. It must have been moved here by one of the family members who didn't want to take it with after they sold their houses to the aluminum company in Lunde. It was old and tattered and frayed. It smelled musty and moldy. It had worn stickers plastered all over it, address labels; the top stickers overlay several others. One of the top stickers had our address in America, the address where we lived when I was born, Narcissus Drive, Hicksville, New York. This must have been a trunk that my mother used on her early trips to Norway in 1951 and 1957, on a transatlantic journey, with my sister and me, before she took an airplane. She must have left the trunk here. I noticed some of the other stickers. They had the name of my grandfather, smudged but legible, next to a sticker that said *SS FULDA*. Could this be the trunk that my grandfather brought to America from Italy in 1893? I opened it. It was empty, smelly, except for a few *National Geographic* magazines, a small oil pump and a small tobacco container. I kept them. I noticed a block of wood under a shelf. I busted it open, there were some wrinkled yellow papers. And there was a gun! It was a Berreta. I was astounded by this discovery. I knew right away that this was the gun that my father had brought back from Italy after the war, and that his nephew had got his hands on and had accidentally shot at a mirror in the bathroom of my grandmother's house and had almost hit her. They must have hidden the gun in this trunk and my father must have forgotten, and my mother was unaware that the gun was hidden in the trunk when she travelled to Norway in 1951. The gun had three bullets in it. After all these years would it fire? I took it outside and pulled the trigger. It fired a bullet into the air. I looked over the old yellow brown papers. Some were written in Italian. Some in English. Some in Norwegian. Why were they concealed in the hidden compartment?

I saw Amalia this morning; she must be close to ninety years old. She was standing in the doorway of her house, leaning on the frame, unencumbered by grace and solitude. I spoke with her but she remembers neither my mother nor me.

Most of them have long gone. Many to America, first to Bay Ridge, and then to New Jersey or Long Island. But some of the old ancestral houses are still there, and the rocks that form the foundations, rocks like pillows for old ghosts who lay their cold heads down to sleep and weep through the night, warming the invisible walls. In the beginning was the word. In the end there will be silence. That which passes through the middle, these words, this book, living, dying, we need not make any extra comments. That which came before the beginning and that which comes after the end, we cannot speak of... we cannot even be certain that it is the same place. I know that I am not on this island anymore, and yet this is the place where I have come searching for words... words touching silence and silence touching words... but where is the world? The speed of dark in the apprehensive spark of indeterminacy. The metaphysical waves waiting to fall on the ineluctable shores of constancy. The empirical drain of water over the white grains of the unwashed ground of imagery. Hunger with the hand of a soft hammer has cracked the scabbed seed in the chewed heart of my life. The approach of shadow in a structure of strife, uncertain surfaces, attraction, repulsion, gravity's cradle of soil in the rootless struggle of being. Strangled whispers of light. Abstract breath. Cosmic glass. Scavenger space. Negative time.

A poet senses vibrations rising in the air. A poet searches for a current, a tree house, a doorpost. I place my experience in a chair in a cabin on an island off the coast of Norway and paint her as she sits there. She is in a boat with an old man... and they are going to an island; but we have not come to it yet.

Cardea heard a gull's cry. Aanen Håken had the engine running again. Cardea saw the mountains and trees and water. She smiled with a tender feeling of recognition and compassion. But the engine throbbed on and troubled her. Sad thoughts pervaded a portion of her consciousness.

The engine's relentless power, followed by the skeleton ships carrying the defiled ghosts of Hiroshima. Hinges creaking beyond endurance, straining to hold him to the post. Bitter rust of neglect. Blazing sundown of extinction. The center, the post, steadfastly stands all storms, like an ancient herm in the earth, terrible and mysterious, approached by white-gloved hands in the misty darkness.

I explored the lower part of the island, the barren eastern ridge with its humps of rolling rock like beached whales. The fishing boats and cargo ships pass by here on their way in and out of port. Across the water, along the mainland, under the hills of Lunde, I saw the large aluminum plant with its high silo and conveyor belt ramp dipping into a docked ship. Twenty-five years ago the company bought out the locals, some of whose families had lived here for hundreds of years. The company put many to work, so there were few complaints, except for my mother's objections, who saw it as an ugly intrusion into her ideal childhood memories. During the war, the Germans had built a massive concrete mooring along the side of the fjord, and the aluminum company utilizes it for its own purposes, very convenient. On the small island of Faroy, where another of my mother's uncles lived, there is another concrete structure, a long sunken ditch, a former artillery outpost, built by imprisoned Russian soldiers and manned by Nazi soldiers. I sat down in the elaborate foxhole. Still here... concrete, bastard of matter... still here... I saw an aluminum can of Coca-Cola bobbing up and down in the water.

He lifted his rifle to his eye and took aim. *Eins... zwei... drei...* and then he put the barrel of the gun to his forehead and rested the butt on the concrete.

For some reason I thought about this man I had known briefly back in North Carolina when I stayed there with Saul. His name was Stronzo. Smart-ass businessman. He claimed that he had made a million dollars three times and lost it all each time. Sometime later I heard that he had shot himself. Supposedly he was a manic-depressive. He somehow managed to shoot himself in the head and the heart. I wondered how he ever managed to do it, in the head and heart. Head and heart. Happiness and doom.

I keep writing in this notebook... that was my intention before I came here... but oh my damn stomach is acting up again. I am sick and vomiting. I have diarrhea. My stomach is an avatar of the Holy Spirit. My stomach is releasing its bile and spleen and anger and hatred again. That rope that was tied in knots so many years ago. I am discharging my pent-up angels of the Milky Way into a black hole of despair. Praise God through whom all blessings flow. I should be in some miserable little garret in a ruined decadent city... the bombs falling... the children crying... the people marching... I would take her on the cold fallen gravestone. I would walk away like the plague. I would smoke my houkah with Baudelaire in the Café Sweet Melancholia. I would piss in the Seine with Henry Miller. I would hurl thunderbolts from my tower like Jeffers. I would parry with Hitler like Hamsun. I would scratch obscenities on the sidewalk like Rimbaud. I would drink my brains to mash like Kerouac, yeah heroes... we would discuss the flora and fauna of female genitalia, I'm being polite here, I scratched out the other word... words... I'm an adult, but we would be boys again, Huck Finns, walking the railroad tracks of the New World at night, the chinks, the niggers, the micks, the guineas, the squareheads, the exploited immigrants, anarchists, we would walk together. An outlaw band of saboteurs and renegades. In a symbolic gesture, because we are all artists, we would place pennies and dimes and nickels on the iron rails, and thereby flatten the faces, erase the dates, and topple the beginning of the American Empire. The buffalo would flee from the crushed nickel and roam the land again. Theodore Roosevelt is turning in his grave back in Oyster Bay... how could it come to this? How could America produce such a counter-productive creature as I?

Cardea saw the scattered islands in the beckoning distance, like shrouded semblances of hunchback prophets. The bulk and mass of great rocks rose to meet Håken's boat with harsh and stern grimaces; the rocks were like huge hairy fists punched through the North Sea by Titans. The boulders bellowed like gnarled, passive sea lions. The wine-gauzed stained patches bleached their sides like wounds; rambling cracks jaggedly gaped like crazed mouths. The rocks like folds of dough, baked in the sun. Gulls gathered on rocks, becoming one bird, one beak, one instinct. The rock was a life-starved, life-dreading thing, fused together by the delicate crystals of form in the scorching energies that liquidate, melt, thaw, and change at the caprice of a temperature's rise and fall over many millennia. Trees and rock: things so fervently in earnest. No fog-enshrouded, disoriented ship of a mind gliding into dark harbors; no perplexed, abstract ghost of a mind trying to escape from the weight of the universe like crushed Pascal, heavy Buddha, or hung Christ.

The island rocks blend into smooth, shifting contours; in round, running edges; into brash, hoodoo configurations; swollen up from the deepest reservoirs, vomited up from the seething vapors, from the ice-barren chines, from the flaming tides of the world's dawn. They are submissive victims of the element's endless, mighty and subtle thrusts; as staunch and immobile as colliding caribou. But there are soft scourings hidden in the wind under the hawk's wings. Air, rain, sea and wind are also stark predators.

The inexorable, regressive grasp of the sea tugs on the rocks like a young mother tugs on the shirt sleeves of her son, knowing that she will lose him, but that she will have him back in the end. In hunger comes the hawk to the house of the mother...

In hunger comes the hawk to the island where I walk along a ridge high over the sea and watch the birds in a mutual concord of suspended and tightening feathers, under the cover of a prodigious, guardian sky. Today was the Norwegian Independence Day. I went to Farsund to watch the parade. There are faint flickers... my impressions in the midnight sun. At midday a pink effusion of sunlight softens the exposed mountain rocks, a blush of prosperity and complacency. The blond suntan-smiling girl, holding a small Norwegian flag, stands on the small concrete car bridge. I walked pass her and entered the narrow, hilly streets of Farsund, searching for characters out of early Hamsun novels. My impression is that there are few to be found. Have North Sea oil, global markets, corporate capitalism, and the welfare state put an end to them? Their poverty, their sickness unto death, their mania, their depression, their fear and trembling, their angst, their destructive impulses. It's the good life now... at least in Norway.

Over fifty years ago my mother and her grandmother (all her sons gone away to sea) planted potatoes in the scarce soil between dark rocks, and then the Nazis stood on the hillside, and Hamsun shook hands with Hitler.

I walked down by the harbor and fishing boats, drunken bored teenagers also walking around after the parade, shouting... breaking a shop window with a rock and running away. Then break a stain glass window in the Lutheran church at the top of the hill near the graveyard where my ancestors lie. I walked back, crossing the bridge; the girl is still standing there. She appears happy healthy and patriotic. I turned one last time to look back; she stared at me, blank and empty. Beneath the suntan and smile I saw a ghostly existential expression... the Scream of Munch. And darkness finally settles on the canvas. Is it socialism that makes the young complacent drunks? No, think of the Vikings... they were always drunks, rape the women and pillage the village... and yet... she is a white raven; her tears wet the veil of Isis. She is an owl-eyed maiden, as ungainly as the long-billed ibis. I was the grey kingfisher, master of moonlight snatching up minnows. But I refused the Eastern covenant by fouling my flesh where the north wind blows back the cock's baleful crows. Now I streak across the silent seas like one-eyed Horus, falcon-bold. Too many years in the scorching sun have burnt my breast and turned my wings a blue-green sapphire. O halcyon! I am the kingfisher. The black raven unfurls his ravenous lust.

When Håken's boat cleared the ocean rim of the fjord, he and Cardea crossed the outer edge of a cove. From deep in the inlet one could imagine hearing the thunder of many oars pounding the sea in poetic saga rhythm, and the great canvas unfurling. A resounding, stentorian voice shattering and vibrating the still waters of the gullies, as big Harald Fairhair walks over the push-pulling oars, commanding the synchronized strokes.

Out past the cove the wind began to greet Cardea and Håken with more sovereign severity, with a little nip and bite. It stretched their cheeks back, wavered their clothes, and fluttered up Cardea's hair wildly. They squinted their faces against the moderate fury, and clamped their teeth tightly together; but the sea was only slightly agitated. She was not unleashing herself like Fenris the Wolf, not baring dagger-teeth beneath pulled-back lips, not raising hackles, nor snarling with rage; the sea just gently licked them with her tongue, yet the boat tumbled like a young wolf-pup at play.

Small islands darted the sea vista, where elegant seagulls stood and spread wings like sentinels to the gates of Valhalla; and arctic terns, black-helmeted, dazzled in the dim gray light of dawn. Fishing boats churned by, bringing their catch into Farsund, their horns hoarse from the dampness and fog. Cardea could see the island that is her destination. A gray mist rising from it, the island unveiling itself like a blood-splotched altar. Terrible revelations inviting her; brazen sword shearing the white bark of birch, the phallic penetration, the telescopically enhanced vision peering with big, baffled lemur eyes, peeling back the curtain of the sky, splitting the firmament of the mind into stellar coition, material cognition. Then come the mysterious plaintive sounds: beseeching, the paws, hands, reaching, touching, entering, smothering, lungs gurgling in hot blood, the brain reeling from the fires of discovery in a grid of possibility, the pallid artifice of representation cast against the sun's brilliance; and a murky silhouette of dark columns constantly crumbling upon the beguiled worshippers; atomic worms squirming through the microcosms of the bent mind devouring the light; deafening roar of thunder and skull-splitting lightening unbridled in the flooded valley; the sacrificed flesh revealed welted and scabbed over the dewy spider-silkened fields of nature, to catch with fangs consciousness fleeing the web in the corner of the barn's loft.

Life springs from the crevasses in the rocks, from the casual soil, where mosses cling and spread like designs on Persian carpets. Agape openings with fresh fibers of succulence. Rocks heave and breathe like giant hearts torn from the chests of strong warriors by terrible talons. Green life spumes like torrents of broken water down the coarse rocks. The rocks cry like a fetus aborted from its sea womb. They tremble as they break strong shoulders through the black surface of the sea, rising up to the clouds like a child raised to the sun in a Greek god's massive hand, his golden, muscled shoulders shining, his long wet hair undulating on the ocean.

Cardea leaned over the side of the boat and touched the cool water. A crescent-moon shaped pendant, sparkling and spinning like a birch leaf in the wind, dangled down from her neck. The reflected glare called forth the attention of Håken's eyes. He became transfixed for a moment, trapped by her wild beauty. Her fluffy, chestnut hair that flung about her face; her cheekbones like smooth, pink conches; her thin, delicately beaked nose... her lips... her...

The power of the boat separated from the focus of Håken's mind. Clouded human instinct without direction; drive stranded without need; lust stranded without love; a man stranded without a center, without control... but the cool and sensible wings of Apollo fluttered in Aanen Håken's mind, and he steadied the rudder, avoiding a collision with the sea-buried boulders. Intelligent man. Redemption in the dust and bones of civilization.

I stepped outdoors from the cottage early this morning and took a walk along the winding path down to the sea. I proceeded to follow the edge of the island around its entire circumference, a fairly treacherous journey over slippery rocks and along narrow edges of soft earth. I brought along my binoculars and a guidebook to native wildflowers, pausing occasionally to leaf through the pages and locate the name of a wildflower. Beneath a photograph of each species the book listed the local name and the scientific name, followed by a brief description of the plant and its characteristics. I looked up the entry for a small violet with the native name of *stemorblomst* (stepmother's flower), sometimes called *natt og dag* (day and night), because of its segmented petals of dark purple and white. The scientific name, Viola tricolor, seemed alien and aloof from the actual life in the field, as I stood there with a book in my hands. And then the book felt alien. It reminded me of the times I went with my father to the school where he worked as a janitor; I would go into the nurse's office and weigh myself and get this terrible feeling of antiseptic coldness and death... a monolithic swamping of expertise. The plant had had its wings pinned back and there was nothing more to be said on the subject. The organic spirit of place had been removed by white gloves and put in a test tube and brought to the laboratory for analysis. Speak the name of a god and the god no longer exists. Remove a wild animal from its native habitat and it is no longer the same animal; it has a scientific name; taken out of context, its meaning has been changed. It is the same with language. With the numinous power of naming things. So it was playfully that I exerted the verbal power to articulate the qualia of things and gave additional names to each plant. My private vocabulary. In a mock ceremony I recited a litany of names from literature: this flower I named a Cervantes, this one a Homer, this one a Dante. And then I unnamed them. No one else was there to hear my voice, or my mind's voice, the words stuck in my mind's ear. Un-named, and yet the flowers are still here. Do you accept your names, *natt og dag*, Viola tricolor, or can you reject them? Do you have a voice? The flowers are still here, the poetry prior to poetry, as they say about Zen Buddhism being the religion prior to religion. And then I named them again, according to my personal experience, names so private as to be unmentionable. Mere dust specks. The impossibility of ultimate aloneness. The native name represented a multiplicity of indigenous participatory consciousness; the scientific name represented the nominalist, post-Cartesian division of historical fact and imagination. My names from literature represented a tradition; Kant's "a priori forms of sensibility" translated to poetic terms; and the personal names represented the unfolding of Schopenhauer's "intelligible character." For a brief moment I felt some revelation of my being, some rooting in the earth, in place, in time... an at-homeness, some connection with the growth of civilization, with my feet on the ground of being... but, no, it was gone.

When I returned to the place where I had begun my dubious trek, I sat down on a rock and remembered the words of the Japanese Zen Poet, Ikkyu. "Having no destination, I am never lost." But I am lost, I feel lost... I have a destination; I just don't know what it is, or else this is it... this is it. It's the journey itself that is the destination. And yet...

My mother and father gave me the middle name of Knute, in honor of the Norwegian football head coach at Notre Dame, Knute Rockne, who died in an airplane crash in 1931. And because my father was a football fan and my mother was Norwegian, this pleased both of them. In later years I denied my namesake by claiming that I had been named after Knut Hamsun, the Norwegian writer, in an attempt to re-invent myself? This was a decisive moment in the evolution of my mythographic viewpoint. The re-invention of self. This was poetry challenging authority, orthodoxy, institutions, which strangled the poetic impulse. Renaming, un-naming, was a poetic act of investigating the self-conscious labyrinth in which one finds oneself... of retrieving words from the Minotaurs of the modern state: technological, corporate, military, who have gained control over the ways-of-thinking and ways-of-saying, through mass media, and have amputated us from direct observation and experience, from concrete thought and natural processes, and placed us in a sensory-deprived, mediated, environment, and focused our minds on the holy icons of the all-mighty dollar and the American Dream, to want more and more and more.

So here I am on an island off the coast of Norway, isolated, to study my consciousness? My self-consciousness? Do I not need the Other to expose myself to my self-consciousness? If all I wanted to do was investigate my "consciousness" then all I needed was my own consciousness, any old place. But this is not a scientific study, no empirical data... no theory...

just words like arrows flung at some unknown target, and when words fail, like Emerson suggests, I fling myself at the target. Wittgenstein isolated himself in a cabin in Norway... where he played with words... his words bounced back at him.

One morning I woke up to find myself in a place where I didn't belong. There was nobody there to show me the way out; there was nobody there to show me the way in. Show me the way to go home, Dad's Mitch Miller songs. I didn't know where I had to go; I just knew I had to go. I was left alone in the dark. Poets are born, not made. Do words make things? Or do things make words? Man makes things: makes war, makes money, makes a good marriage, and makes history. No ideology. No theology. I just want to dance on this island and see the moonlight in strumming streams of the sea. I shall watch the current flow to the far horizon, riding on the shoulders of the silver-backed gorilla of night as it climbs to the moon, and to all points beyond, for the key is waiting there, and the door of words that opens up on the far side of a rose-wreathed constellation, where the magic crown is drawn across the skies by white stallions, horses in armor, where no impurities intrude into the magic circle of poetry... poetry has its own way of seeing things. But so does science, philosophy, politics, that man on the street corner, and my folky vision, or else why is that moon so large on the horizon, when I *know* that it can't be... but what do I really know?

And yet... Georg Lukacs, a forgotten commie, writes that art always says "and yet!" to life. He has also written this: The language of the absolutely lonely man is lyrical. But of course, that explains everything. That explains these poems that I am writing against my reason, against my instinct as a post-modern writer, a novelist. Levi-Strauss writes that the man who steeps himself in the allegedly self-evident truths of introspection never emerges from them. Was he thinking of Kant, Sartre, Kierkegaard? but also the novelists and poets: the Rimbauds and Hamsuns, to all those writers for whom the world is only their existence in the world, the exegetical authority of one's despair as revelation? Their text of the world. And yet there is no authority in any text. When I go tomorrow with my nature book to identify wildflowers, do I go in the name of flowers? Are flowers then the world? Subjectivism finds its own exile in the self... the forms of *gestalt*... ever since my arrival on this island, a lyrical mood, a mythical mood, has descended upon me. It has put me in a mythological quagmire. I don't think that I like it. Myth tends to naturalize historical tendencies... so how can I read the writing on the wall? Can Apollo stand on the same podium as Caesar? It seems Apollo stands alone. But Caesar cannot speak without the spirit of Apollo, cannot condemn and be powerful without the hint of celebration. So where am I in time and space? An island off the coast of Norway... Novalis writes that philosophy is really homesickness, it is the urge to be at home everywhere. Is that true for science and art? But the key is everywhere. Not just this country or that, not heaven, hell, this house, city, but deserts, jungles, mountaintops? Where? And how do you get there? How do you get from a basketball court in a small town in America to an island off the coast of Norway? Why start there? Initial conditions, chaos... can I feel at home here, there, where? Why is this so important? The essence of Zen is the suppression of logical thought, of dualistic thinking, and verbal nomination. To un-name creation is to speak the void without a voice. I should be like Ivan Karamazov and refuse the ticket... the ticket home. Even if! And yet! No heaven, no paradise, no utopia, and I'm damn glad of it. Home. Place. A picture place or a story place. That was the question I asked myself: Is this a picture place or a story place? Bars, dives, cheap cafes, these are story places. Stories told, and bolstered by the authority of personal experience. Narratives. No use for linguistics after Saussure, or literary criticism after Coleridge. No theories. No critic could deconstruct their experience, their hopes. And then there are the avant-garde, parasites of the bourgeoisie who came from the bourgeoisie revolting against boredom. They stand against the Philistines. They have a gripe with aesthetics. Whiffs of Dada, and Duchamp... revolutionary?... political? Nevertheless... they belong in the picture place. The 20th century belongs in the picture place. Of course the camera helped... a photo opportunity. The story place is communal, the picture place is individual; the story place is civilization, the picture place is culture; the story place is a broadside and graffiti, the picture place a tabloid and fashion magazine; the story place is mutual aid, the picture place is competition; the story place is revolution, the picture place a political convention; the story place is Nestor Makhno's peasants and Spanish anarchists, the picture place is Bolsheviks, Trotsky, Lenin, Stalin, Hitler and the private tyranny of Corporate America; the story place is Rimbaud, the picture place is Warhol; the story place is waitresses, divorcees, whores, cocktail lounge clientele, people who ride public transportation, vagabonds, organ grinders, porters, janitors, tinkers, literati, the unclassifiable disintegrated mass, what the French call *la bohème*, the lumpenproletariat... according to Marx. I think he didn't like them. The picture place is four degrees of the bourgeoisie... the story place is *krumpe*, the picture place is fusion food... in the story place art is political, in the picture place the political is an art form...

Oh hell... I need to get back to the city...

Håken pointed to Cardea's pendant. "That is lovely," he said. Cardea's green eyes widened, and she quickly glanced down and coyly looked at the pedant, grasping it between her thumb and forefinger. "Oh yes, this... this belonged to my father." She was quiet for an lingering moment. Håken understood that he had awakened a memory by invoking the correspondence of a thing and words. Håken spoke again; he dug into her past with words like toy shovels.

"Could you tell me about him?"

"My father?"

Aanen Håken nodded.

Cardea turned her face askew of the old man, and then she solidly gazed into his waxed eyes, and spoke, "My father. Yes, of course." Her mind filled with a flurry of images. She drew her fingers across her lips as if to mould the words as they were spoken. The tone of her voice was soft and graceful as a swallow flying out of a barn door. "Well, let me see, my aunt, that would be my mother's sister, was awakened late one night by a knock on her door. And there I was, cradled in the arms of a priest. My aunt could not have imagined that I was her only sister's only child. You see, my father was an Italian soldier; he was a prisoner of war taken to Scotland to do field work. But he escaped and stole a boat. That's one story. My aunt was never entirely convinced. Because he may have left Italy before the war began. We know that he had been a fisherman in Genoa, and that he had had his own boat. So maybe he just sailed up the coast. Spain, France, England, Scotland... an adventurer, another Columbus! Of course, I think it's unlikely. Anyhow, in some way he came to Norway, to this very island. He probably escaped from Scotland, got on a boat, and here he met my mother. She was only seventeen. And soon she was pregnant and my father was accused of raping her. They escaped together, on a boat, and traveled up and down the coast, hiding in coves, and following the gypsies in their boats, and maybe they helped them and were protected by them. I was born at sea. My mother died giving birth to me. All this information is from my aunt. My middle name is Marina. I like that name. I like to think that my father gave me that name."

Cardea's words slowed in their nervous pace as she raked the fallen leaves of her memory into a pile, and the present moment returned by setting them on fire. "For some reason my father brought me to Scotland after my mother died. He brought me to a church and left me with a priest. All I had was this pendant and the name and address of my aunt who lived in England. The priest brought me to her. She had married a Scotsman and settled there. In Edinburgh. So she raised me. She's like my mother. I met my husband at university. He's an American. He studied botany and natural history... and I studied literature, that kind of thing, and now I am a professor at a university in America, where we live. I am working on a book about Knut Hamsun, the Norwegian writer, do you know him?"

"No... never heard of him," said Håken. "What happened to your father?"

"I don't know. My aunt doesn't know. We never heard from him."

I am sitting at my desk staring at the nameless "thing" that the blank paper signifies... until now... now that I have scribbled these words on it. The fire from the wood-burning stove scribbles red shadows across my hand resting on the paper like a large spider ready to strike. A man is a poet because he was left alone in the dark, because darkness is heavy, because words have some small power to lift darkness, because memory is a clouded gray island... I remember the safe deposit box that nobody in my family cared enough about to discover its contents, just as they hadn't cared about Teresa after she went mad and spent the rest of her life in a mental hospital, never once paying a single visit to her during the fifty years that she was institutionalized. Supposedly she had taken to burning money; and hiding it and burying it somewhere; she must have been mad. No doubt. She was committed. The safe deposit box was in her name at the bank. Maybe there was money in it. I was always curious about the story of the box. When they finally got around to opening it in 1947 they found some scraps of paper and fragments of old letters written in Italian. My father told me this. Could those scraps of paper be the same as the papers I found in the trunk? They were trying to hide them away, forever, like they hid Teresa away in Kings Park, forever? I have to look over these papers from the trunk. I have avoided them so far. I can read some of the English, much of it is scribbled and illegible; I can read some of the Norwegian, also scribbled and illegible; but the Italian I cannot read at all. I need someone to translate it.

I have identified these wildflowers so far:
Skrubbar- Cornus suecica- in US: Northern Dwarf Cornel-
   Dogwood family.
Strandvortemelk- Euphorbia palustris- Spurge family.
Vanlig gasemure- Potentillia anserine- Rose family.
Strandflatbelg- Lathyrus maritimus- Pea family.
Bitter Bergknapp- Sedum acre- Sedum family.
Strandsmelle- Selene maritima- Carnation family.
Smasyre- Rumex acetosella- in US: Sheep Sorrel- Buckwheat family.
Graslauk- Allium schoenoprasum- in US: Chives- Lily family.
Strandlovetann-Taraxacum suecicum-Sunflower
   family- type of dandelion.
Strandkjempe- Plantago maritima- Plantain family.
Rund Soldegg- Drosera rotundiflora- in US: Round-leaf Sundew
Stemorblomst- Viola tricolor- locally called Natt og Dag- Violet family.

The constant soothing murmur of falling rain. It fell on the trees; it fell on the stones; it fell on the yellow hair of a young girl. She was barefoot and slender-flanked, with eyes as big and bright and round as a fawn's. She was clad in a loose-hanging, cream-colored dress that swayed in the ubiquitous breeze. Fern Abby is her name; Cardea's daughter. She is tending to her wildflowers in a field east of the house; the forehead gabled house that rests on granite blocks, where she is staying with her mother, father and brother.

A face appeared in the window; it was Gulene, who is minding after Fern Abby while Cardea is in Farsund getting supplies with Aanen Håken.

Hanne sat on the steps of the house, watching Fern Abby's reverie of child's wonder and innocent delight in the smallest of things. Hanne is twenty-five years old, but her innocence had been violently arrested by a past act. In the end was the act. She had been a missionary in Africa, spreading the word of her God, in the beginning was the word, but what she had to give was cruelly wrested from her. In the sudden darkness they came, a tribal remnant, and performed their bestial frenzy in the flattened grass, leaving her flesh and soul bleeding among the whimpers of dispersal, and a bastard seed in her womb. In the beginning was the act... they are dispersing; the race vanishing, breaking into clusters of stars. The ape with the expanding brain dealing in bloody deeds, in the beginning was the deed. The ape moping along with the bone club smeared with a purplish discoloration, the proud smirk bending back the corners of the lips; the thrilled hunter with his tortured captive; this animal to be burnt and eaten as the glorious embers of dusk soar over the far hills, and gentle breezes flit the leaves of trees, and the sands lap up the leavings of hungry mouths. How many years and how many days on the path of angels ascending, but cruelty opened its wide insatiable jaws again? The soul of a woman crushed like ice and swallowed like impure water.

The constant soothing murmur of falling rain. Fern Abby danced about in the misty morning field... no, not danced, nothing artistic, just natural. She didn't dance... she jumped, hopped, ran, rolled, spun, tossed, turned, as natural as a butterfly. Several sheep followed her around. Fern Abby stopped to scratch under the neck of her favorite; the one her mother named Sigmund. When she walked away Sigmund came up behind her and nudged her in the back of her knee with his wooly head, so she scratched old Sigmund's head again.

I sat on a rock at the highest point of the island. The spruces reached up to me with their withered hands. I saw deer droppings around the junipers. A magpie snapped at berries. The magpie flew into a field, it squawked and squabbled and sardonically chuckled. And then it flew away. It had nothing more to say. The deer looked down from a ridge and saw 9th century men gathered around a fire together. The deer browsed on twigs and defecated the last seeds of spring on embedded rock and clumped heather.

That white withered old hag the moon dragging the night behind her like a long black broom; she sweeps the evening mist from the mountain's spruce grizzled spires, she flings her cape over the sun's desires, as all of a summer's day's many hues of green fade into the shade of whispering leaves strangely seen in the curling smoke of ancient baal fires... scarves of red smoke slink upwards... The deer looked down from a ridge and saw 20th century men gathered around a fire together. The deer browsed on twigs and defecated the first seeds of summer on embedded rock and clumped heather... stop... defecated... shit, shit, shit, they shit, and they shat the deer shit... stop this myth from perpetuating another illusion...

The constant soothing murmur of falling rain. Intertwining ripples spread out on the water. Little Johnny in a rowboat split a mussel with his knife and baited the hook of his drop line. He let the hook out and felt the liquid slimy smoothness and the soft burning of the tackle as it slid over the middle groove of his forefinger. Pieces of seaweed gathered in his hand. When the weight hit bottom, he pulled the line up several feet and quietly waited, holding delicately, watching his hand, and watching the line bend beneath the surface of the water, flickering with light. His finger twitched; he felt his heart pound and the slow rise and fall of the boat in the waves. The waves carried the boat toward the half-buried boulders on the shoreline. The boy unaware that the boat was floating toward the boulders, stared at the dark olive water and saw the jellyfish float by; he thought about the hidden cod fish that swan deep down. Suddenly, the boat scratched upon the boulders; it thud and thumped and scratched again. The boy pushed off with an oar, pulled in the fishing line, and rowed back to the center of the small inlet. His light brown hair waved over his forehead; his young arms drove the oars back and forth against the resisting and indifferent force of the water.

One more... just one more, he thought to himself. He let out the fishing line again, and wrapped it around an oarlock. He grabbed the pail and dumped the fish out, counting them, three cod, two whitting; dad will be pleased with me. I wonder how many he caught. His father had gone out for mackerel, a slow trolling with a long line with many hooks dragged near the surface of the water. Little Johnny picked up one of the codfish and snapped its head back, brown slime squirted into his hand. He cleaned the fish, cutting off the head and throwing the innards overboard; an easy feast for the gathering gulls. He started to row to shore, only stopping to scrape some mussels from a rock. He broke them off in chunks and filtered out the debris. He thought, oddly, I'll eat these; this is bait to catch myself.

He saw his sister, Fern Abby, on the shore. She had come down from the field to greet him. Gulene and Hanne stood back a ways, on the top of the slope, and mumbled to themselves, holding hands. The boy heard his sister's voice calling him. Come in now, Johnny, mom will return soon.

Johnny stood up in the rowboat, and he pretended to act like a caught fish, yanking at his cheek with his hooked finger, forming O shapes with his mouth. Look Fern, I'm caught. Help. He screamed out full from his lungs. Fern Abby reproached him. Stop it, Johnny... come in now, will you. Fern Abby got up on one of the large boulders in the water's edge. She made a lovely sight. Her shaggy wet mane of hair, prominently dwarfing her petite body. She was twelve years old, and Johnny was ten. She played the mature young lady, and Johnny the rascal. She called again. Come in now, or I'll tell mommy you were playing in the boat, and she won't let you go fishing anymore alone. He wisely heeded her admonition and sat down and rowed the boat to shore. But I don't want to go fishing by myself; anyway, I really wanted to go fishing with dad.

They started walking up the path together. Johnny stopped at the tree house. He climbed up and put his drop line into a wooden box. He noticed the brown core of the apple that he had eaten yesterday, and he picked it up and carried it outside. He threw it into the trees and climbed down and ran to catch up with the others. Johnny trudged up the path with his pail of fish, carefully avoiding tripping over the large rocks and exposed roots on the path, or stepping on the black slugs.

When I was a boy I was fascinated by old buildings, deserted and dilapidated. In Oyster Bay, when I was young, there was an old building that had been a bank; the floor had collapsed and the place smelled of rot. I can still picture the large iron safe which stood lopsided in the corner of a room, sunken through the broken floorboards, and upon which a black rat stood and stared at me. Above the safe hung a tilted portrait of Theodore Roosevelt, enshrined in cracked glass. And scattered all around the floor were papers and ledgers. Of course the money was all gone. Money is never deserted. Money is never lost. It just fades away, dissolves, like God, into air, into thin air.

There are several old deserted houses on this island. I entered through the window of one of them today. I thought I heard a woman's voice. The rain was softly falling. All day it's been raining. Rain falling on deserted buildings, deserted dreams, falling on passions that died many years ago... can passions survive? Can consciousness, outside its dull containment? Rain falling... falling on the bulrushes and buttercups; falling on the dandelions and curlydocks; falling on the catchflies and cattails; falling on the forget-me-nots and the wild violets... *forglemmegei, vergissmeinnicht, wasurena gusa... natt og dag,* night and day. The old house that I explored today. A woman lived there. Her name was Remina. There was much unhappiness. How do I know this? Her name is Remina.

Dawn will come and night be done, and you'll awake to the heather on the hill, and see the sun shining still, O my dear Erik Eriksson. Winter will come and autumn be done, summer will come and spring will be done, but with you my life is one long season of being happy and young, O my dear Erik Eriksson. And this sharp knife will cut fine fish that we shall eat when you come home with a handful of wildflowers; and in the early evening hours we'll lie by the fire and burn our desire through the cold cold winter night, O my dear Erik Eriksson, will you hold me, hold me tight.

Erik Eriksson, where have you been this cold, cold winter night? I had your dinner on the table, I had your slippers by the door, I've done all that I'm able, I just can't do no more. The fire is burning, the baby's been fed, the spinning wheel's been turning, and all you can say is that somethings are best left unsaid. And now you sleep beside me in the comfort of our bed, and touch my warm woman's body on white sheets where I have bled. Yes dawn will come and night be done, but this dulled knife is now my spear, and though the heather on the hill will still be there, you'll be asleep too deep for any more dawns my dear.

There it is. Rural life. Somethings are best left unsaid. Didn't Wittgenstein come to the same or similar conclusion while he was staying in a cabin in Norway? Perhaps not.

Cardea and Aanen Håken crept over the waves in the rising and falling boat. The morning clouds and drizzle were now departing. The sky slowly transformed into a cool immaculate azure, as if it were sifted through with diamonds. The day was displaying prospects of a dry bristling brilliance, sparkling like a radiant spectrum. A few clouds glowed, trimmed by a dark corona, dashing by in haste, coupling with the wind. The distant horizon glistened; the sea and sky squeezed it into a tenuous thread of hazy black and orange, like a drapery of tigers pawing the clouds down to their den. The dark green water shimmered with dabs of opulent flashes, like fallen bits of broken sun. The water was streaked with slender strips of silver on black background; then shifted to slender strips of black on silver background with every readjusted view of the eyes.

In their slothful flow, an armada of jellyfish portrayed the physical capabilities of the day as they floated by the small boat like marooned sacks of amorphous prehistoric wombs, when blood was slime. The green and brown seaweeds, like ostracized vegetation, searched for a tree's barren branches on which to hang and be nourished and held in Medusa-arms like the arabesques of green-gray lichens that twinkle in the play of the sunlight.

Cardea sat toward the bow of the boat, and with every chop of a wave the water sprayed on her face. She could taste the salt and feel the moist crispness of the falsetto air, invigoratingly swooning with the screaming gulls. The old man, his large rubbery hands affixed to the rudder, stood erect, slightly hunched, and surveyed, guiding the boat with half-conscious instinct, with his pale blue Nordic eyes... eyes bred in the soul of the sea, as if secreted pearls from unfathomable oysters. How many fishhooks have stuck in those hands? How many ropes and nets have blistered and bled them? Perhaps they are empty of blood, and cool seawater flows through his veins.

"The tide is wrong," he said. "There will be no fish today." Aanen Håken wore his tattered white captain's cap, with the black and gold ruffled fringe. He always wore it at sea; and wore it for his Sunday morning strolls through Farsund, when, to each passerby, he would tip his cap with his right hand, lifting it just inches off his head; but when a woman or respected gentleman would pass, he tipped his cap with a long graceful swoop of his right arm, and scooped it back up again as if he were ladling soup.

"Have you seen Amalia this morning?" Håken asked.

"I saw her yesterday; she didn't seem well."

"*Ja,* yes, soon they will come and take her away from the island. I hope they take the others too."

And Cardea: "She went on and on about some ghosts in a house... she kept repeating to herself: *Min stakkar Oscar, min stakkar Oscar...*"

Håken explained: "Oscar was her son. The house over by the old orchard where the *rips* still grow... do you know it?" Cardea nodded. Håken went on:

"You see after *krigen,* war, world war one, there was many German orphan babies that was sent *til Norge,* and grew up here to be took care of, *ja,* because Germany was smashed in the war, so poor… so, a young German boy, I think his name was Wilhelm, lived in that house, until he was eleven or twelve years old. And then the Germans want their children back, to be soldiers I think, for Hitler, so the boy was made to return. Then the Germans come again, Hitler and all that… the young boy is German soldier now; he come to Farsund; but when he see the town he live in as a boy it make him very sad to be enemy now… *ja,* I believe so. And one day he go out to the island where he was boy. Nobody lives there no more, the people who took care of him are gone, and he take gun out and shoot in his head. *Ja,* it was Amalia's son who find him dead. So the Germans say Oscar kill him. The Germans shoot Oscar right outside the house and bury him there. Amalia was there; she see it; she see them kill her son; and she believes both their ghosts, Oscar and Wilhelm, are still there, *ja…* I don't know; maybe so…"

A contemplative silence surrounded them. Then Cardea said, "To think that all that suffering happened here."

"It happened everywhere, the whole world. *Ja,* it will happen again."

"But I mean, when you look at the place and see how beautiful the country is, you think, how could they come here, how could it have happened here."

Forty years of headaches and nightmares remind Håken's mind that they were here. "And the ghosts," continued Cardea, "quiet possible. My children once told me that they saw our dog running along a path where they had always run together with her. They said that they saw her so clearly. But the dog had died a month earlier."

"Ja visst… there are many such stories here too," said Håken.

"Where will Amalia go?" Cardea asked.

Håken grinned cynically. "Yes, her family will take her away and put her in a *gammel hjem…*old people home, *ja…* this way they can rent the house in summer and make some money; they rent it to Germans!" He laughed bitterly. "*Ja,* they are all over the place in summer; they still want the country!" His face grew stern. "Once they come as soldiers with guns; now they come as tourists with money. Yes, prosperity. Once there was only potatoes and fish; now everything. But it is an empty everything; empty all over. *Ikke sant?"* Håken turned from Cardea and looked toward the coast; he whispered to himself: *"Ja, det er som om vi bo på et fremmed land nå."*

Today I went to Lunde, once again to walk around the place where my mother was born and grew up. I hopped the fence... maybe it's private property... belongs to aluminum company... I saw the crumbling foundation on the side on a dirt road overgrown with weeds. A small church had rested its wooden frame here. During the war the Germans had established their local headquarters here, and nearby erected a high barbed-wire fence compound in which to imprison Russian soldiers. My mother was fifteen years old at the time. She walked by the church and heard the screams of Russian soldiers being tortured. The Nazis had painted black the windows of all the houses on Lunde and imposed a curfew. But my mother would sneak out with bags of food, which she brought for the Russian prisoners, and toss the bags over the high fence. She thought one of the prisoners was rather handsome; and for a fifteen-year-old girl that was enough of a reason to risk being shot. The prisoner wrote his address on a torn envelope and gave it to her.

C. C. C. R.

Ukraina   Konolop

Deineka   A. M.

The A.M. was his initials. My mother kept it all her life and showed it to me when she told me the story, many times.

"You know a German officer took over my aunt's house; he was so ugly, the German, he had a bald head and a little hair he pulled over the top, and he was fat, he made my aunt live upstairs with her family and he took over the downstairs, the German officer then found a fifteen-year-old mistress, a Norwegian girl, and you know and you know she lived with him, and after the war we grabbed her and hold her down and cut off all her hair, I was in on a lot of those things, this Russian prisoner that I liked, he was so handsome, he was a cook for the German officer, in my aunt's house you know, and then at night he went back to jail, his name was Alexander, he was so good looking, well I used to put my bike outside the cellar window and go up and visit my aunt, for a while you know, so when I came down my bike was tied up to the window, I looked in the cellar window and he stand there and grin at me you know, oh he was so good looking, I have a picture of him, I couldn't date him of course, he always flatter me telling my aunt how beautiful I was, *hu er so skjonn pike*, he said, he learned to speak a little *Norsk*, Norwegian, yes, so when the war was over and all the Germans left Norway my grandfather and grandmother invited some of the Russians for dinner to our house, we invited Alexander and others for Sunday dinner you know, Alexander fell in love with my grandfather because he would always read the bible, grandfather good man Alexander would say, you know, one day we had a big dance in Farsund to celebrate, everybody went, my friends we all took a walk over the bridge, we all had a Russian friend, but they couldn't go to the dance, you know, they weren't allowed, there was English soldiers and Norwegians, I didn't like them English soldiers, they were so fresh, I was dancing with one, not for me, so I went home, an English soldier wanted to walk me home you know, Alexander followed us home to my house, to see if I was all right, you know, one day he was a little drunk, and came to the nursing home where I worked, Sister Lina was so mad, but she fixed dinner for him, he was so sloppy you know, but so nice and polite, you know why he was drunk because he was going back to Russia, that's why, so we put him to sleep on the couch, put his feet up, put a blanket over him, the next day he was going to his boat, he came to say goodbye, so I could get down to the boat and say goodbye, Alexander saw my grandfather on his way to the boat by accident, he got so excited, waving at him from the boat, he yelled Papa! Papa! And threw my grandfather a pack of cigarettes to him just to show him, you know, just to say thank you, my grandfather was hard man you know not soft, and he said that he saw Alexander by accident, but he really went to say goodbye, you know, we heard a few weeks later that the boat was torpedoed, you know, in the Baltic Sea, the Russians didn't want them back to the country, we don't know if the story is true, all I know is I wrote to Alexander and never got an answer, he was so sweet, all the Russians were good, they kept to themselves, so quiet, no trouble, never one Russian baby was born in Farsund, all German babies, the Russians were there two months after the war and could have got into lots of mischief, they were in jail most of the time, you know I went to school my grandfather packed my lunch, I never ate it, we used to go and stick the lunch between the fence, when they went to get water, when the Russian prisoners walked by to get water, all these prisoners were brought to work for the Germans, they were took as prisoners off ships, used to wait on them and cook for them, the Germans killed a lot of them, after the war when they dug up the buried bodies, you know, they could tell that they were buried alive, their feet and hands tied, and there were marks, struggle marks, many Norwegians were tortured so bad their wives couldn't recognize them, and there was many traitors too, Quislings…"

One day not long after the war had ended, my mother saw the severed head of a German soldier, sallow and emaciated, with blue bulging eyes, washed up on the shore of the fjord. The head was nestled between two rocks of the same proportions as the head. My mother screamed and ran. When she returned with her grandfather the head was gone. There was a head there, she insisted. Her grandfather believed her. An omen, he said, an omen of the end of the world. And when the thunder rumbled at night he told her that God was angry with his children. My mother would often hear her grandfather praying in the field among the cows and sheep, pray to protect little Tulle, the nickname he had given her. He kept his religion to himself, she would tell me. And the ghost of her grandfather followed her everywhere, and watched over her. She really believed this; followed her even to America…

To see the human in nature. Is it pathetic fallacy or poetic truth? Is it a disease or a balm? Consciousness… the rock that looked like a head looked at me: What do you want? I asked. I want to die, it answered. I want to die.

In the midsummer Norwegian night the black waters slap and hiss their silver serpent tongues upon the rocks, licking at the over-hanging leaves and shuddering sands like a famished child, darting out to frighten the ghosts of men long dead. But why should the dead fear life and want to die again?

Håken's boat approached the island called Langøy. To the northwest, across the harbor, the town of Farsund climbed the hillside; a town where the wind always blows. To the west, the North Sea lay stretched out in primeval limbo. They docked in the red boathouse, and Cardea gathered her supplies and jumped on a rock, and then stepped lightly upon the island. The boat moved off shore, sputtering and throbbing, and Aanen Håken waved his cap. He disappeared around the bend, on his way back to the lighthouse. Cardea walked up the path. We have come to the island.

On the island's east rim, a small square white house stood cowering beneath a little rock-vaulted dome of mountain, which, to an old woman's mind anyway, seemed to pace back and forth like Beowulf on the eve of battle. A large bent-over woman with gray hair sat in the parlor, sewing a sweater. Her lips imperceptibly moved, just tiny puffs of breath making a frail whisper; a child's lullaby emanated from her wrinkled pursed lips. She sang in her native tongue, a country dialect from the southwest tip of Norway. The melody was vaguely and strangely reminiscent of the andante second movement of Schubert's Quartet in A minor... loosely translated: Who'll tell my mother, who'll tell my father, who will tell them what I must do... O my darling girl, I'm off to see the world, but what I must do, I can't tell you...

The old woman lifted herself from the chair by lurching forward like a snorting boar grubbing at roots. She wobbled over to the window and stood there. She stared at the mountains. Her vacant eyes followed a bird's flight as it sailed into the trees of the mountain and disappeared. Then she saw a white butterfly land on a twig of a bush right outside her window. She smiled. The butterfly flew away; her hand reached up to grab it; she frowned. In her mind a recurring image flashed like water breaking on rocks. Amalia thought to herself: "Yes, the mountains will fall down. I am watching them carefully. Sometimes they move. They will fall and bury me and the ghosts and the entire evil world. The thunder will come crashing down from the north, dragging everything into the sea... into the sea..." She heard the certain silence of the womb. The loneliness. The silence like a scream of nothingness. A bird, *tårnseiler,* sleek and black, cutting a swift path through the air, high above, circled around the old woman's house, around the mountain, around the island...

...the bird's wings beat, beat, and beat rapidly in rhythm above the glittering sea. The glistening nuance of light and shadow shift and shimmer on wings that suddenly firm and stretch to full length. Then the bird glides, glides, and glides; it dips downward and slides along, slicing the air; it ascends upward, turning east to west; the wings flap again, again, and again. Soon it is gone into the distance, just gone, as if it flew out of this world.

Poor old Amalia stepped out doors, under the spruces' gray needles, by moss covered stones, and fern unfurling in the dampness of the sheltered air. She thought: Just a rock... that's all this land is; all the world is; all God is; all this country is... a rock... just a rock that fell down from the North Pole.

I stood on the shore in darkness and saw a star fall into the sea. Really, the sea? Of course not. My mind knows better... but my tale does not: Out of the sea a serpent came and curled up about my feet. I reached down to pick it up. I held a piece of driftwood in my hand. I knew the story. At the end of the seventh day of creation an exhausted God sat beneath the Alder trees of Saturn on a Saturday afternoon, chewing tobacco, spitting it out, and drinking whiskey. He propped his long legs upon the Oak trees of Jupiter, reaching all the way back to Thursday night. He caught meteorites in his right hand and flung them at the moon in Monday with his satirical left hand. If He hadn't been as tired as He was He would certainly have shattered the moon into a thousand tiny fragments. Tiny, that is, by God's standards. And if he had accomplished this unconscious wish of destruction there would never have been poets, and I would not be thinking of this. Unfortunately for me, and for you too, God failed.

But why did God try to destroy the Moon? Was it just a game? A display of power? Or was He trying to suppress some disturbing unsurfaced and repressed desire within himself by expressing aggression like a puerile child-king? Well, be that as it may, God was damned pleased and proud as He surveyed this little corner of the universe, with its suns and moons and planets; with its arrangement of years and months and weeks and days, measured according to natural, fixed, immutable laws in time and space.

Now let it be said that Adam was not the first fallen man; nor Lucifer the first fallen angel; the first to fall from God's grace was the fallen angel-man, and his name was Poet. And where did this Poet come from? It seems that God was so exhausted at the end of the seventh day of creation, that He not only rested, but He slept. And He had a dream.

He dreamed that He had created an eighth day; and on the eighth day God created the Poet. But God saw that it was not good; so God destroyed the eighth day and would have destroyed the Poet too, but God awoke from his dream; or was He awoken by some mysterious power? God did not realize that dreams are often projected upon the world of reality, or that because He had already created the world in fixed laws in space and time, that His dream of the eighth day coincided and overlapped with the cycling return of the first day, Sunday, day of the Birch tree, and it was into here, a natural, physical day, that the Poet ran away to, escaping from God's dream, and remaining to this day half in time and half in the timelessness of God's dream.

I create good and I create evil, thus saith the Lord.

So God chased the evil Poet across the starry wheel of the universe. Fiery breath poured from His nostrils, and at that very moment God dreamed of Hell, provoked by his wrath for the ever-fleeing Poet. And because of this, many Poets have had to spend their season in Hell.

The Poet ultimately deceived God by splitting Himself in two, and one of the Poets disguised Himself as a serpent and hid beneath the apple trees in a garden on Friday; and the other Poet disguised Himself as a star and hid behind the face of the Moon, on Monday. And though God and his retinue of saints and scholars and soldiers have raged against the Poet ever since his defection, the Poet remains faithful to Monday, day of the Moon, and Friday, day of Venus.

In the night sky the day's wounds are made visible; those cradled stars are the puncture-holes of Gaia's fangs. She is wrenching Apollo's hand of his dulled chisel; she is shaking the mountain from which the disposed god hangs. She is cooling the blown ash of a whirlwind...

Cardea saw her children stumbling up the path. Johnny raced twenty paces ahead of his sister. "Wait up, wait up, Johnny!" Fern Abby called out. Johnny shouted back, now that he had a substantial lead, "Last one home's a rotten egg!"

Cardea went to greet her children at the front door. The boy eagerly and breathlessly stammered his words, "Look at my fish... five... where's dad? I want to show him." "Not home yet" was all that she said. Cardea took the pail of fish from Johnny and waited for Fern Abby. When she arrived, Cardea kissed her children and said, "I'll get dinner ready; go wash up."

Cardea took the fish to the sink. She scaled and cleaned them, occasionally looking out the window, watching for the figure of a man to appear on the path. She looked over the gully-sunken treetops to the sea. Far out there was a speck, only an oil tanker, moving drearily, like a somnambulist in the dark. Cardea cooked the cod in boiling water for seven minutes, with plenty of salt, a tablespoon of vinegar, and a sprig of seaweed. She served the fish with boiled potatoes, carrots, peas and melted butter.

Today I walked along the path by the cliff's edge high over the sea. I felt lonely and separate. New experiences reveal old habits. New places reveal old anxieties. New fulfillment reveals new emptiness. I have found some consolation in books, the lives of writers and poets, in nature... some. Never enough. I sat down on a flat rock in the old orchard. The insects have been alerted and aroused by the clear mild summer air and many for the first time experienced their new world of light and scents. They applied their various dexterities to their appointed tasks at hand. Duty and loyalty called them back home; they never strayed from their limits. Travel and experience narrow the mind, they seemed to say; discipline and structure make life. A small spider stepped across the grass. I watched the spider long-legging it over the tips of grass blades... and... suddenly someone was standing there. I saw the large black working shoes. I looked up and was startled to see my father. He sat down. He looked much older. He put his arm around my shoulder. I knew then that it couldn't be my father.

"Do you wanna go fishing? Howabout a ball game? Hey, the Mets won yesterday. Seaver pitched a good game; beat the Dodgers 5-1."

"Why have you come here? Why don't you go away. You are twenty years too late. And anyway you are not my father. Who are you?"

The old man looked at me. He felt pity for me. The old man said, "I am searching for my son. His name is... I can't remember. He was a sport's hero back in high school. He was handsome and strong. And smart. All the girls had a crush on him. Have you seen my boy?"

"I don't understand. You desire my twin, my brother, my *doppelgänger*, do you understand, hypocrite father?"

"I see says the blind man. Listen, do you hear?"

"Only the birds, the wind..."

"There are no voices calling me. There are no voices in the village. There is babble and a discord. There are ranting hallucinated grins and grimaces. The stream went dry; we cut our feet on sharp stones when we gathered the last of the flapping fish from the beach. The well went dry; the source is in the mountain. But who will go into the mountain? The bones at the bottom of the well have come down from the mountain. We fear the mountain, we fear the forest, we fear the desert, we fear the sea, and we fear their grave and constant silences. Only a few have heard a voice there, somewhere, in the wilderness. We would prefer to remain in the village. I remember one of us, a hunched and foolish man, but he had magic in his words, and though strange, his words seemed true. True as when you put your hands in cold water and wash your face; true as the snowflake that melts on your lips. We lap at it like dogs. He may have spoken for us, but he has gone into the desert. His feet were bare and cracked; he was hungry. I offered him bread, but he refused by lifting his hand and slowly waving it across his eyes like a dark cloud passing before the sun. I offered him drink; he refused.

"What I hunger for is peace," he said. "What I thirst for is knowledge. You cannot feed my soul with bread and water. There is life: perception and action are one; there is no word. There is experience of life: memory, desire, belief, thoughts, and deeds mixed into the shadow; that is a word. And then there is the experience of life when the shadow steps into the light: that is The Word. It is better that we wait and sit still and not stir and not speak. Do not let anyone put on the tyrant's false mask. We have seen his face too clearly. His ambition, his power. The wayward agitating savior with high ideals. I said there are more questions than answers in freedom. He called me a liar. If they want to be free of the wheel, they must pull down the pillars; cut the knots; and tear the door from the hinges. Do you dare? I was driven from the village. I wandered the earth. Vaporous forebodings filled the air. Acrid smoke from burning oak. A sickness stuck in the stalk of our humanity. We chopped at the green shoots; we scattered the beasts. Bleed bleed poor country. We shared the guilt. The king was lusty and cruel and capricious. But were we innocent? When he thrust the hot iron rod up the supplanter's rectum, we watched. The blade assuaged our anxious and lonely fears, and thwarted our aggressive rage. We remembered our mother's weeping eyes and her pillowed breast where we lay our heads. She was so kind; as loving as the lamb's blood. She only has survived to tell... but the stone rolled over her mouth." The old man stood up, and walked down the path to the sea.

I have identified the following birds:
Aefugl- Somateria mollisima- in US Common Eider
Siland- Mergus serrator- Red-Breaster Merganser
Laksand- Mergus marganser- Common Merganser
Vipe- Vanellus vanellus- Northern Lapwing
Rodstik- Tringa totanus- Redshank
Strandsnipe- Actitis hypoleucos- a type of Sandpiper
Sildemåke- Larcus fuscus- Lesser Black-backed Gull
Svartbak- Larus marinus- Greater Black-backed Gull
Gråmåke- Larus argentatus- Herring Gull

Fiskemåke- Larus canus- Mew Gull

Makrellterne- Sterna hirundo- Common Gull

Skjaepiplerke- Anthus spinoletta- Water Pipit

Linerle- Motacilla alba- a type of Pipit

Hubro- Bubo bubo- a type of Owl

Svalene-   a type of Swallow

Kråke-   a type of crow

Skjaere-   Magpie

Dusk had settled into the weary eyes of the earth, and night slowly chewed its way downward like a black vulture descending in great soaring asymmetrical arcs of spiraling flight, spreading its piceous wings over the carcass of light to swallow the day. A sleepy indigo mist hung heavily in the air; soft rain gently plucked the trees, rocks, and grass. A sea breeze shook the leaves, and stubborn in the season of aspiration, held on. Somewhere in the moist meadow, a soliciting fragrance, drifted on the proffering hands of the wind. The wind thinly parted her inviting lips, and seduced a butterfly, emblazoned rogue, delicately pumping his orange and black duplicate flags against the ember and rose hue of a horizon-sinking sun, which burned like a battle-scourged tower disfigured with smoky cascading ashes, collapsing like a million particles of dust.

As if from out of the clouds the butterfly appeared, a speck of shimmering color in the luminescent sky, pirouetting and gyrating like a falling crimson leaf in autumn when he still seeks out deliverance, searching for the sweet scent of consummation, but falteringly, for both butterfly and leaf lie down together on the moldy matted mor among the many million hosts of decomposition to prickle with the heat of a new life hunger.

The slouched sun was blurred by the lackrymalic cloud-ducts that lingered listlessly with iridescent shoots of stiff straight sun beams, flickering with jewel-like particles, like shining bronze-bladed swords stabbing and slashing down through the fleshless, murderous air, and then disappearing like King Arthur's Excalibur.

Wildflowers stood like battalions on the hillsides, reeling to a flourishing peel of the trumpeting wind, displaying their banners and pageantry. The clouds passed over this June day to contemplate the running waters of ages ago that had lashed the salt of the lands into the sea. The billion-year rain that even now cries down upon the dominance, but only apparent steadfastness, of basalt and granite, and still evokes boneless memories of dark skies over oppressed lands for a thousand years after the burning vapors, like the breath of man, turned cold. The ocean canyons were filled, and the creeping primal fires scorched through, storming down and shuddering the rock fertile womb and nerve-budding awareness of the flower of the body of the world.

Even now you can hear the belly growling, the bones rubbing and shifting, the lichen and sulphur-colored pollen glowing triumphant on such wet days, gray and green, embracing the trees and rocks. Even now the fallings and the cyclic spinning of the chrysalis; even now the earth and sky are falling into the sea and filling the sedimentary beds with dust and limey shells, nickel and iron, pebbles and small boulders; sand from deserts, silt from rivers, warships and contaminations of nations; all man's foul leavings.

I took the boat into Farsund and docked in one of the red boathouses along the side of the island called Faroy. I walked down the road and passed the fishing boats and small fish factories. I crossed over the concrete bridge. A young woman stood on the bridge; she had long red hair and was looking out to sea. I didn't see her face, but I imagined she had the face of a woman in a Munch painting. She held a book. I saw the title. *Mysterien* by the Norwegian writer Knut Hamsun. Maybe it wasn't a book; it looked more like a script.

On the other side of the bridge I noticed some unusual commotion. Unusual for a small town. There were cameras and lights. They were making a movie. I asked. A new version of Hamsun's *Mysteries*.

I watched for a while and then went to buy some bread and cheese, and a local newspaper, *Farsunds Avis*.

A fishing boat dock and a small square fronted the town where a flock of old men gathered. They sat on benches underneath four linden trees. They seemed amused by the activities. I spoke with them. A few of them knew my mother.

A dwarf came walking down the street in ragged clothes. They were filming a scene. He was followed by a man dressed in a yellow suit.

I went up the hill to the *bokhandler*, bookstore, by the *radhus*, the town hall building. A small man, a dwarf, stood next to me. He was not the same dwarf who was in the movie. He said, in English, "I know your mother too. I mean I know about her." He must have been listening to the conversation that I was having with the old men around the linden trees. I didn't remember seeing him there though.

"My name is Johan. Johan Farli."

"*Gleddig meg,*" I said.

"Speak English, please. *Jeg kan snakker Engelsk.*"

We became friends. Johan and I would meet at night by the four linden trees. We met in the evening when the area was sparse of people. We sat on the bench under the linden trees and stared out to the dark harbor and the North Sea in the distance beyond the islands.

"You will notice, Stephen, that most people avoid me in this town. And it's not because of my deformity. I am the son of a Nazi officer and a fifteen-year-old Norwegian girl. They do not trust me. My mother left after the war. She could not stay here. They held her down and cut off her hair and bullied her. I was raised in an orphanage. I never saw my mother again."

We had many long conversations about numerous topics. Johan was very knowledgeable. He described himself as a self-taught working man. He worked for many years in the new aluminum factory at Lunde, the area where my mother was born and lived until she was nineteen and left for America. One day Johan had an accident and part of his foot was severed. He collects a disability pension and lives in a *rekkehus,* a type of modern row house. He walks with a limp and is slightly hunchbacked.

"You can call me Captain Pukkelsen," he said to me one evening. We were sitting on the benches under the four linden trees. "Do you know Captain Pukkelsen?"

"Sorry, but I never heard of him," I replied.

The Mystic Night

Cardea's children were in bed. They waited for their mother's reassuring voice to tell them a story, and her goodnight kiss. She sat down on the edge of Fern Abby's bed. She opened a book and read...

The peace of the apparent earth is heard in mystic slumbers; there are crickets between the protruding tongues of grass; their chirps roll and joggle in a continuous wave of soft purling. They are heralds of green tidings in a dark world. Little burnt shamans hidden in the leaves. The night swoons to their call. Lugubrious breezes fall still a moment; night has coiled the dusk within its serpent den of wormy concavities. In the animal womb of the unconscious a human baby turns and moves; fingers grasping; the dank forest stenches rising into pulsating nostrils. Cardea, mother of flesh, waking from a tribal sleep, joins the dead, tonight. She hears the echoes of sleep.

The children are sleeping. Cardea hears a bird's repetitive trill. She sees the moon through the stain-glass window. She moves nearer to the window, so close that the colorful landscape images in the glass fade into calligraphic smears, as if drawn over her like a tide. She comes so near to the window that she can press her face against the glass, looking through the white moon in the glass to the white moon in the sky. She places her fingers on the glass, thinks of her husband, and cries.

Outside the rain has stopped falling from clouds; it fell from trees. It clicked and clacked, dripping on brown matted leaves; it distinctly dropped here and there; it softly and sharply snapped, near and far, in the frithy depths, among the drooping branches of the trees, until every accumulated rain drop had flowed in tiny meandering capillaries off the blunted tips of green vegetation, and in the steady procession to silence, fell to thirsty earth.

Then came a surprising stillness like a damp tomb; but one more drop fell somewhere… it's so quiet you can hear the roots drinking. The rain abruptly fell from the sky again, fresh with finality, with a quick and sudden shove of the wind it swept through the woods like a million hummingbirds diving for the nectar of dissolution, sacrificed on the ambiguous stigma of words, like insects impaled on thorns to feed hungry poets.

Tonight is your chance, Cardea… go, escape… tomorrow night we contemplate the configuration of those spiraling stars in silence. Corona Borealis, abode of kings. Symmetrical stillness of the rose. Rose of atonement. Burning brazen jewel turning like a crown, like a wheel, like a door. Bound to the steadfast post where the king kneels, where he is flayed for his impudent assertion of arbitrary power. We shall watch the turning of the year hunted by the hunter and the bear. We shall watch from here, where fireflies frolic and bedazzle and brighten this field. The ladybug is like a spot of blood on my arm.

In the worm of the warm womb of evaporation and the rain of resurrection your husband shall rise again. Come with me by moonlight down to the sea. Expose yourself beneath the oak trees bent over with knotted prophecy and cast over embryonic rocks. The slow resurrection of mutilated remnants of corroded armor, never again putrescent with rotting flesh, abandoned by maggots, never to speak, bitter blood filling the rain-instilled pools carved in stone; and I shall wash my hands in this vile water. In the nakedness of night, fade within the whiteness of the moon. Stammering and straining voice reverberating back from the vast wharving light of the beacon stars. Your eyes stare wildly from the dark that crawls around like a stealthy beast, a black-flanked mare grunting inhumanly, hung with slit throat from the sturdiest branch; blood dripping like drops of flashing photons into illuminated eyes; her white mane shimmering like neural sparks, her red ears as bright as carcharodant flames, among the vestiges of the night with horned owls and eager bats.

In Cardea's mind the spidery stems of roots spread their little parasitic mouths and sucked for water; they connected the clinging nodules to the carbon and nitrogen energy heating the earth like one compost heap, surging like bacterial hunger, the energy surged into the golden branch of a tree, into a twig, into a leaf. The five-pronged leaf like a star high atop the lopped tree. Birds fly out of a gorge. A five-fingered leaf, hand... a woman's hand. Summer castration, the forming of the fist, the tiny decomposers and the weeping woman behind the door. The sea where many fishermen have drowned.

Cardea stood at the top of the stairs. In the room behind her the children slept. She reached back and carefully closed the bedroom door. On the wall at the bottom of the stairs she saw the reflection of candlelight battling with the shaft of darkness coming through the hallway; the shimmering red textures of lacerated light straddled the purgatorial shadows, like a small pit of lava seething and erupting, violently spewing silent images.

Cardea stared at the various and multiform display of interlacing, blood-weaved waves, an ocean of slithering earth worms with no soil to contain them. It were as if she penetrated directly into the deep strata of her own mind, as if she could not move because she couldn't step out of herself without losing her private center of identity.

Inside the room the children dreamed; outside the house the world dreamed; she descended the stairs and entered the dream. These are the shadows but where is the source? She carried the searching candle down the corridor. She scuttled sideways along the wall like a crab, just like the crabs that Johnny and his father had plucked out of the cold water at midnight, shining a flashlight from the rowboat through the dark film where below the green hem of the rock the crabs commingled like a colony of outcasts.

At the front door of the house she pushed against the doorposts as if they were pillars supporting a massive lintel inscribed with indecipherable script, a codex of facts and laws and information buried through many layers of thin paint. The words were sentenced to a senseless term of encased imprisonment, all that is the case, a logic of cruelty and control which barters for a savior's excrement; like flies we are attracted, like flies we are stuck, like flies we drop off.

Cardea blew out the candle's flame of white praying hands. She stepped outside on the grass and proceeded down the path. The words, the weight of time and space, the welter of history, the weariness of the world, and finally the everlasting words dropped like flies on the worn path.

Mermaid rising; find the human half of you again. The mucky salt-sling and the fishy slime smell of the sea scaled the cliffs and wafted along on continuous tides of air. Cardea inhaled deeply the fluent nativity. Unseen stars streaked the skies, bolts of lightning sprayed down like a skeleton's splayed white fingers; insects hunted for blood in their quest for fertility, and thunder shook the hearts of tiny creatures who perked up their ears and stood up frozen in open patches of the woods. Rain clashed down on stone, sobbed in grass, and fluttered through curtsying leaves. A wet fresh earth refreshed and revived Cardea's senses. The steady rain slowed to a trinkling in the trees; the moon began to glance from behind quickly pacing clouds, moving like veils across the face of a pale, wanton dancer. Cardea reached up and broke a small branch from an oak tree; the crack of the wood was heard like the crack of a bone or like the crack of an atom all over the arc-world of this unfloodable island.

At the end of the path the brush became denser. She shoved to the side the last shrubbery of the thickest part of the plexus of intertwined leaves and twigs that blocked her passage, and she stepped up on a platform of rock. She saw the moonlight drinking up the ocean. Cardea stood near the cliff's edge. Stunted birch trees bent upward toward the night sky, squeezing out from the cliffside cavities cut in the massive and sharply hewed and buttressed rock fortress.

An enormous disarray of talus seemingly poured into the ocean and formed a long triangular slope of accumulated stones of myriad shapes and sizes. The side of the cliff was glazed with a luminous gray sheen. Cardea peered downward; she saw the water crash into white flashes on the rocks below, as if each dying wave signaled the birth and death of impossible consciousness in inanimate objects, shattering like sparks on the rocks of nature's anvil, disintegrating like a mist over the coastline and creeping upwards into starlight, a thing as insubstantial as itself.

In the rock upon which Cardea stood, two long cracks were plugged with grass; they ran athwart each other, forming a diagram of a cross. Cardea stood where the lines intersected. Another crack, filled with pellucid stones, formed a jagged seam. She picked up one of the loose stones and flung it down over the cliff. She idly gathered stones and placed them in a small circle. To the east of her, no more than twenty feet in distance, the rock piled higher, topped by a miniature plateau where two junipers were snuggly situated amid a thatch of heather.

She is loathsome to herself; she has been an abomination to herself; she has been disgusted with the sight of her kindred. Vile, wretched waste. Libations of innocence are poured over her half-clad body. She shines redly in the silvers boughs of a buried dusk. The moonlight opens the night's eyes; shadows fly in the air. She has come to the cliff where the osprey dives into black water. She is at the mind's junction, the tortured crux of discovery. Something stirs in the decaying leaves… the wind.

She is fed by the eagle; the serpent bulges in her throat and hangs from blood-speckled lips; she has come where the wild waters gurgle in torrents of gnashing fissures, far beneath her, in the craggy, convoluted, rock-immured cove. She has fallen beneath the pines and spruces and oaks; prone in supplication. The tragic torch of life has burnt her preconceived self down to insignificance. She is strong; she can hold an inconceivable vastness of symbols.

To the west of her, the rock slanted downwards into a ravine filled with oaks, beeches and birches, the tops of which reached no higher than the surface of the rock upon which Cardea stood. She heard the ocean moaning like the voice of eternity. She felt the rhythm of the tides in the rushing pulse of her bloodstream. But who stands there with you? He began to walk the ring with horrible head and hands wagging in the smoky sky. What is it that makes you dance and utter bitter whimpers among the tattered grass? What is it that makes you carve images in caves the way an irrepressible light of consciousness carves shadows in your own skull-cave? Why do you stand alone with dazed and dreary eyes, gazing outward upon the landscape, and then turn a contorted face toward your naked feet, and with perplexed fingers touch and taste the trodden dirt? Are you frightened of the dark clouds that gather? Why do you bellow a muffled growl as the earth dies in its impotent season? Did something soar out of your brain? Did some bird of disgust take flight toward the sun?

A death bird of prophecy, with battered wings, lost in an incandescent cage; baffled bird crashing into iron bars; dumbfounded singer bringing howls of distinction into the vast teeth of time. Cardea saw a bird appear in the sky; it flew out of the moon and was caressed by the black swan of night.

The bird, an arctic tern, circled and circled across the scope of the sea, begging attention of Cardea's eyes; not out of animal hunger, nor out of animal fear, but as a call to some undisclosed longing. The bird was illuminated by its sculptured grace and poise, and by all the surrounding forms that collided in a dark purple-pink-gray enjoining mesh of suffused impressions. A condensed dripping screen of moonlight poured over the world, covering the needless eyes of night like a partly-crazed, nearly-blind, old man covers his face in his wrinkled cupped hands to live deep within his own occasions of meditation, his own territory, a landscape where instinct broods silently over bone-cradled snakes, because the world is near enough when you feed and perpetuate your kind, feeling outward and connecting the mind to the belly to the womb with vibrating wires of physical flight...

This bird of disgust, this self-consciousness, this little suffering, wingless and wounded bird. Invoke the bird of discovery, the bird of the imagination, the bird of the longest migration of the mind. Earth, prophet of beauty, burn for her tonight. And what if all matter and all energy were annihilated: every dream, desire, belief, deed, shadow, and word... something would be here? Something would still be here? Is there no place else to go? No place at least to hide? No escape? No separation? Does consciousness live in the smallest and meanest among us? Is it somehow "felt?" A buzzing, a chirping, a whining, a whistle, a vibration of leaves, the fall of a stone in a canyon, the flower nudging through the soil on the farthest mountain, the splitting of the atom, the child's voice at play, the boy calling his dog to watch the sunset...

The arctic tern flew toward Cardea. Was she a dark wriggling motion beneath the water? Was she a mussel to be dropped on rock, her skull split for a meal? The tern became whiter; the moonlight seemed to pour down into the bird in a steady stream of silver, filling it with strange effulgence. The bird became brighter and larger; Cardea couldn't see the ocean anymore for the shining of the bird; nor the trees, rocks and stars. She couldn't taste, hear, smell, touch...

She saw only the bird becoming larger and brighter as it drew nearer and nearer to her. She saw only the beak now, a curved red arrow of blood dripping in a white cellular, protoplasmic void. The tern saw peculiar prey but speedily advanced. Into her eyes.

The beak opened fully and now bright vessel, blinded inversion of consummate consciousness; winged agent of discovery; bird of the longest migration; longest migration of imagination. It struck her through the heart and found itself flustering in the chaotic winds of her demagnetized, disoriented mind. Cardea opened her eyes: the moon, the tides, the trees, the stars, all that she could see returned to her mind through her eyes. The whirling winds settled into spontaneous patterns of weather; the bird restabilized its winnowing flight; it spiraled within her mind in perfect equilibrium, widening outward. Cardea stood at this fixed point in time and space, on this cliff, on this island off the coast of Norway; the season was summer and the month was June... a phenomenological lyricism.

The arctic tern circled outward gradually wider and wider; it flew around the door, around the wheel, around the millstone; but was it chained to the post? If it could break away would it out distance the burning edge of the turning wheel? It flew from this earth, from this solar system, from this galaxy; as it flew it gathered all and encompassed all; it became all; it became a bird with spread wings nailed to a post by a peasant woman of a village in Europe long ago...

Cardea climbed off the rock-cliff and made her way along the shallow escarpment; where it beveled into a slightly sloping ramp she veered to her right and scampered down, her shuffling feet scattering small stones into the stream flowing through the sunken rut-groove of the ravine. She cupped her hands and drank from the cold running water; and then she ascended the other side, burying her fingers in the soft padded cushions of moss-capped stones. She pranced through the thick grass combed over by the rain and wind and came to a trembling grove. She entered the grove and walked beneath the vaulted dome. A tangible, sonorous, odorous essence of things mellifluously rose upward and filled the night air. It was as if all the trees and earth were cleft, releasing redolent pine resin; fragrances of oak and holly; dampness of roric undergrowth; stilted scent of birch; and the dank drenched foliage of summers come and gone, wearing their death colors of brown and gold and russet, lying within the rot of nature. All of her senses were heightened; she heard the rush of the waves on rocks, the cool water spraying, geysers stewing and shuddering, whelming with froth and ferment. She heard the balmy waves ebbing and the soft receding plashes leaving the rocks dribbling with little sudden and forgotten streams. The wind came full blasting from the sea, and shook the pleached and knarred canopy of wet dripping greenery; branches swaying and reaching. The gray fog moved in and in-clouded the branches; it hung among the dark poles of the trees like the breath of the soothsayer Cassandra. All was cool; cool and damp on the skin. Everything moved; moved to a cryptic, expansive music, its rhythm wild with mantic gesticulations. Moonlight flowed down like a cataract; Cardea moved into the argos falling flames, canescent in the febrile zone, stepping across the boundaries of night and reality.

Out of the room where her children lie sleeping; one doesn't gather figs from thistles; and the branch cannot bear fruit by itself, unless it abides with the vine. The stubborn tillers put hoes to weeds, pruners to dead limbs. Cardea has come, rite-of-way, out of the room where her children lay asleep. Within a walled delight of vegetation, spreading suffocating suckers around the necks of tormented neurons, no exit through a blackened window of soot, in smokestacks demons dwell, as she was walking among the fires of this hell; the silver staff of Hermes's moonlight beam, awe-humming, calling through a crack of mirrored nature, poured forth creation from the wounds of Anfortas. Turn away from, Cardea, the inverted passion of Medea, door of echoes, door of the source; the applied sciences of revenge in a criminal century, the law-giving tablets broken over the back of a faithful Jew in the surrogate days of blood, when the last syllable of his words was love of mankind, wordless whispers of Dante's *Paradiso*, hell on earth, night and more night.

Out of disorientations in dark corridors, descending stairs, missing a step, falling, dragging her Cretan axe through the charred labyrinth, mazes of paths all confusing, the snorting of the Minotaur in the distant room, unroll your ball of thread fair Ariadne, from that glass castle...

Who commands this fleet? Who navigates? Tern of the island, flying, shipwreck to shipwreck, the tides smile upon you lovely Nausicaa, but where is your father's ship? I am coming out of this deep-sea darkness. I am coming out of this sleep. I dreamed of the light flickering above me on the surface of the distorted sea.

Who journeys for a Golden Fleece, bought and sold, handled by grubby hands in the market place? Let's disembark! The Witch of Colchis reconciled with her father; the poop fell on Jason; he saw it falling. He did not move. He was weary of all his days, all spent, ennui. The shit fell on us.

Out of the door where words turn back, shaking their twisted bodies in the agony of recognition, the labeled and documented scars of time. Sad flesh. Lightning lifted the shadow of the bent cross from the slanting hill and etched it in the horizon in the west. The sun is at summer solstice and he has cried out from the stricken flesh to be released, no shadow, only extreme heat and pain of high sun, till the shadow falls again. And one could go on multiplying these shadows and fragments of the past, multiplying by two and three and four, and break the hinges from the door; hard wood to build cathedral ships like lungs of the sea, future dry-docked museums stocked A to Z... yet multiplying all contingencies by zero, opening the door of the future, equals zero, the hero who hung by the brick wall when Babel fell, above an earth dipped in hell...

Cardea has come out of the door of the dungeon house. She was alone, dragging history's chains behind her, breaking them on stone. The Gorgon tilts its head east and west, and spreads snakes in fields where tree-abandoning apes swing aggressive bone clubs and fling them at the tern's flight above; longest migration of the mind and imagination... green as *primavera*... you cannot drown in a sea of rising air bubbles, lifting you to the surface where your scallop ship awaits you, Cardea, myrtle and dove, *pulchritude, amor, voluptas*... the division in the unity of Venus in the Three Graces.

Out of the door, on the path, through a thick hedge, to the cliff's edge, through a pathless wood, Cardea has passed through the simple lintel and posts of a door, through Corinthian columns of trees, under the arched limbs of oak, under the groined vaults of birch, under the ribbed groined vaults of spruce, and she has entered under the dome of the grove.

The arctic tern swooped back into its cage, frightened, but certain that it was home again. It perched in the strangely lit chamber. Cardea has broken herself on the altar in the trembling grove, beneath a lofty cascade. She was a captive again. She ate the sacrament in the baptismal moonlight.

Cardea came to the shoreline. She lowered herself into the smooth bowl-rock pool. A tear of salt fell from her eye and dissolved in water. She submerged herself. She rose...

She saw an arctic tern fly out to sea, into the silver hanging coats of the moon. She saw the trees and the sky of a billion stars; she heard the baa of sheep on the other side of the hill; and the presence of the pungent sea's clammy grip on her face, and the bellying, bellowing waves, and the wind tossing stray leaves...

She felt the cool and damp. She picked up a five-armed sea star in her left hand. Cardea crawled out of the water like a worm. She curled up low to the grass, and she slept.

I walked for several hours today, felt restless, an *onrust*... an old Dutch boat thus named that came to Oyster Bay in 1653... and then, for no discernible reason, found myself in front of Amalia's door. I went over to the ivy-draped window and looked into the front room. I saw Amalia bending over a large basin that had been placed in the center of a round table... stirring the cauldron to stir the cauldron she has stirred all night and day... the voice of my mother cries in the wind, return, do not seek what lies that way. The private moonlight impaled upon my face betrayed my presence outside the ivy-clad window. If I hear her words and taste the potion and not these fragments of an echo, I must offer myself as a target and chance the poison arrow. Sweeping the floor to sweep the floor she has swept all reason out the door.

Twelve lynx-eared candles illuminated the room. I kept my eyes on Amalia as she reached into the basin and then slowly raised her hands to her face. Her hands were on fire in the photism of my eyes. Amalia opened her mouth and blew on the flames. The flames liquefied into blood. She froze; her hands before her face. Blood ran down her bovine arms and dripped from her elbows. She turned her face away from her mask-like hands and fixed her piercing eyes upon me, standing on the other side of the window. Her lips slowly separated with breaking bubbles of blood and saliva. She smiled fiendishly with her large crooked teeth. I felt mummified. I drew back a few steps and nearly fell down. I came forward again to look... but she was gone. The door was opening.

"Come in, come in, if you dare to know," said Amalia. "I have some chocolate for you little boy. Where's your mother?"

...the voice of my mother cries in the wind... return, do not seek what lies within...

I followed Amalia into the house. I turned to look into the old oak-framed hat rack mirror as I passed through the vestibule. I saw myself briefly. I saw myself for the last time. The mirror shattered. I was braking into pieces; puzzle pieces with jagged edges, disintegrating, and my purple lips trembled, my face twitched, my head shook, and I made infantile noises... I couldn't speak. I couldn't communicate rationally. A thousand venomous bees stung my flesh. I saw my father fall by the side of the pool. He shit his pants.

"Put your hands into the basin," Amalia said. "Do you hear me, Stephen? Put your hands into the basin before it is too late. Take hold... you must take hold of something! It's blood or water..."

I put my hands in the basin. Blood slowly began to seep up through my fingers and fill the basin. I heard the old woman's voice, barely audible, as if from a distance. "Take hold! Take hold!" But there was nothing to hold. I was falling... drowning... splitting apart... I was falling from the sky and I was crying as I was falling...

Suddenly another hand was in the basin, holding my hand. Where will this hand lead me? Can I trust it? The hand pulled me down... I was passing over a threshold... the mirror cracked... I am a ten-year-old boy standing on the shore...

I am a ten-month old baby taking my first steps on the hillside of Lundevågen... I am a fetus in a womb...

The boy put his ear to the mother's stomach. It was so quiet and peaceful. Why is the baby making blood on mommy? Please tell the baby to stop making blood on mommy. Where is the valve? I can't breathe, there is no air... Patent Ducus... the doctor said, You can't keep this baby. Needles in the arms and feet, take more blood... the baby kept her hands over her face, didn't want to see this horrible world... small bruised body... she was always crying... sorrowful life, only pain and tales of separation... I am dislodged, driftwood, why hast thou forsaken me? I am hung from a tree. Bound to the scaur. Fixed to the wheel. All is vanity... I am the passive victim. Via Crucis, Shiva the destroyer, Sodom and Gomorrah, New York City, London, Paris, Tokyo... bacchanalian orgies, her wild dogs tore me apart, a sacrifice, guilt, torture, sex, suicide, drugs, visions, violence, murder...

I took my hands out of the basin. It was filled with water. There was no blood on my hands. I am limping out of the limbo of my blood lineage, from the insane and the invalid, toward the cracks in the circle... a snake, a lizard, a bird, in hunger comes the hawk. I am limping out of the darkness where the blind, crippled, paralyzed, and outcast gather like damaged insects at the incestuous altar where the baby who died at birth is worshipped for refusing to live, too weak... we shall not live; we are doomed and damned like Electra and Oedipus in the house of mourning and fatalism. We shall remain in our sexless bodies, our lifelessness, our wretchedness, our apathy, our blindness, our broken candles burning time into lumps of wax, where the insects that we are are trapped and tortured, such is the nature of our life.

One day a baby shall be born and found on a river, and that baby shall go into many lands, like a piece of driftwood, and brought to an island, a hungry hawk tearing life to pieces, and break the chains of our captivity, and the family be redeemed through him... and from the hawk's imperious eye falls a drop of blood through the sky, it fell upon the warrior's land, and with blood the rivers ran... so go by moonlight to the hill, by the stone fence and the quietly flowing rill, where the hawk senses a patient kill. He cut off the head of the snake and hung it on a tree; before the night takes the day the hawk takes its prey. There was a severed hawk's head stuck on an oak branch. There were red bands and thin strips of animal fur and bird feathers hanging down from the hawk's head. I saw this totem in a museum. These dreams come again to seek amends without the consent of your will. The weird sisters grinned. I heard a cry in the night that gave me a chill. I dreamed I heard her voice scream, "The smell of the blood still!" I ran from the lone seagull on the rock to the broken ship's hull in the water of the cove.

I woke up in a bed crawling with long legged spiders. In a fit of panic I jumped up and violently sweeping with my hands brushed the spiders out of the bed. My heart pounded. I sweated. There were no spiders. I was having a bad dream. I am very sorry. Where does she rule? Come in, if you dare to know. A small wren flits on a bough. The root breaks beneath the blade of the plow. She stands in the doorway to lure you in. Thursday is her lover: Janus, Dianus, Jupiter and Thor. She dances on the moonlit moor. She piles apples in her cart. Small is her dominion, but within, all power is hers.

The Summer Solstice

…Cardea crawled out of the sea like a worm. She curled up low to the grass, and she slept…

In the morning two bodies lay on the shore. The seaweed draped, crumpled body of a drowned man, and Cardea.

She covered her husband's body with rocks, and she walked up the path. Friday has come. Tonight the baal fires will dab the islands and hillsides as if the portals of hell were opened.

Aanen Håken's uncle had been the lighthouse keeper at Lindesnes, the farthest point south in Norway, where he had built a fire every day in a flat, round, brick enclosure on the top of great bare mounds of rock, where heather sewed itself into the seams, high over the sea.

He had watched the bright lonely waves day after day take small bites out of the coastline; and he shot seagulls, his dog retrieving them, and together they ate them. One day he lit his last fire and calmly threw himself over the precipice, and the sea swallowed him, and the gulls swooped down from the cliff side, dropping mussels on flat rocks.

Aanen and his brother, Elias, had both gone to America in 1928. Aanen returned after a couple of years, but Elias, a rugged and determined individualist, stayed on for over thirty years, and then returned to Langøy, where he built a house on the foundation of his father's house, where he and Aanen had been born, with seven other children…

Aanen walked through the house, similar in structure to the other houses on the island: low ceilings and thick crossing beams, the off-balanced and tilted wide plank floors that always seem to squeak and sway upwards or downwards; and the unpretentious and un-ornate designs carved around the windows and doors. The entrance hall, like a main artery, went straight to the kitchen at the back of the house, the heart from where all the minor arteries began: the stairs going up to the two small bedrooms with narrow rectangular windows; the back door leading to the outhouse and small hill; and the two rooms in the front of the house, with two large windows, nine panels in each. Aanen stood in the west front room among the relics of his family and brother: the faded portraits and rickety furniture, the old *National Geographics* stacked high, the books on hunting, fishing, ships, natural history, and novels of Knut Hamsun, some in Norwegian and some in English. Aanen picked up from the desk an old photograph of his brother: Elias with the black patch over his right eye, Elias dressed in black, Elias with the New York Giant's baseball cap, circa 1933, Elias the tall, thin, angular figure seated in a chair, holding a model ship that he had made, his dog at his boot heals, as scraggy and unkempt as Elias.

Everyone used to gather here to listen to him tell his many tales of America and the sea. He would finish a tale, go silent, and spit wads of tobacco on the cast-iron stove, smiling with his black teeth at the hissing sound.

Aanen pulled out a drawer from the roll top desk and found a Cunard-Liner schedule dated 1911-1912; one of the ships on the cover was the *Lusitania*. On the wall over the desk hung two small framed portraits, one of George Washington, and the other of Abraham Lincoln. And in the bottom draw Aanen found an old baseball autographed by Mel Ott, Bill Terry and Carl Hubbel. The names meant nothing to Aanen; but he held the baseball in his hand like a precious reminder of his brother's eccentricities.

Elias Håken died at ninety-five years old. "You are sheep. You are all sheep," he would say to his fellow countrymen when he returned to Norway.

Aanen shut the door of the house. He didn't lock it. The sagging eyes of the house watched him disappear down the dark path. Sometimes Aanen imagined that he heard his brother's whistling behind him as he walked down the path.

It was a cool day in October, some years ago now, that Aanen heard his brother's whistling. He was in the lighthouse. It was unusual that his brother came to the lighthouse to see him. Aanen went outside on the high ledge and looked for his brother. He wasn't anywhere in sight. He went back inside. He heard the whistling again. He climbed down the spiral stairs and went up the path to the house. Inside he found his brother, reclining in his chair, dead, with a book opened in his lap, the *Adventures of Huckleberry Finn.*

Aanen continued down the path. He walked with his arms behind his back, the left hand grasping the wrist of the right hand, as was his wont. The wind whirled his snowy hair. His movements were virtually unnoticeable, yet he moved with the inevitable resolve of a glacier descending a mountain valley. He saw Cardea coming up the path. She moved with the stealth, strength, and speed of a lean and vigorous leopard. She was not vexed, not perplexed by the tightening vice of events that gripped her. If anything, she was transfixed.

Aanen called her name several times before the sound waves of his voice penetrated the halo of her hermetic mind and bombarded the nucleus with fictional echoes of reality. But it was the reflection of light from his white shirt that finally caught her eye. A non-verbal exchange of mutual recognition ensued. They came closer to each other; they stood face to face.

"Good morning, Mr. Håken," said Cardea.

"*Ja,* good morning. You are out very early."

"I like walking early in the morning. Things sound and look so different. Very peaceful."

"Maybe so… but with my headaches… *ja,* no peace. I do not sleep well… *ja,* you see, *under krigen var Jeg… ja,* during the war my ship was hit by torpedo… it sink… I was captain. I must go down with my ship. Many of my men die, jumping into hot burning oil… but I live… *ja, det var forferdelig…*"

Cardea said, "That's so terrible…" Then a pause, and she said, "Shall you join us tonight for the baal fire?"

"So, another year has passed… *ja,* I will come. We must travel or die or kill or go mad; the same words over and over. That is a song we used to sing at sea." Håken's gloomy utterance conveyed the extent to which experience will go to kill the spirit. "I should never went to sea. Better I stay home with my mother. But we must go… everyone go to sea… we come home and make our wives with baby and we go back to sea… *ja,* it's not the same now. Back then everyone go to sea, no other thing to do. I was fourteen years old. I went to seaman's school, and then I was on ship, my brother was the captain… he did not speak with me for a year, he did not want other men to see me as get favors because I am little brother. *Ja,* so many stories I can tell... so many places... so many... so many women, too."

He smiled. Very briefly. Then his face became stern and morose again; devoid of any solace, but his bearing was dignified and his manner was stoic. "*Ja*, I will see you tonight. We shall make *en stor*... big fire."

I lay in my bed with my eyes open. Outside the small window I saw the morning's light scattering off at tangents through the sparkling prism of the woods. No, not the woods, but through the dust and sand residues of the glass panes in the window. There was nothing outside the window, no trees, no sky, and no color; there was just an image in the refractive impulses that my retina sent through my nervous system. Everything in the room: the furniture, the walls, the ceiling, the floor, and the door, appeared sharp-edged, pixilated, convexed, linear and angular. My vision seemed bloatingly focused; objects imposed themselves upon me; they threatened and throbbed. A heap of rotten cabbage turned in my stomach. Anxiety attack, but why here? Nausea... but not Sartrean, not existential... I often felt this way... in my stomach, in my head, like my conscious mind is about to explode. I had to get outside and breathe the expansive air. I had to get outside to escape from the algebra of claustrophobia that muzzled me; from the spectral delineation of Cézanne-like triangular dimensions that cornered me. I had passed another dark night fighting with the shades of my mind. I've always hated dreams... in the brain's synapses where even the angels are asleep, thoughts are the tattered rags of words... sing, dance, a stone rolling from the sky... thoughts, concepts, shine like the moon lowered into a coffin lined with the black fabric of night, the stars are pallbearers, an American funeral... but I burn... take away the dance, take away the song, and remove the stone from my mouth. I squirm like a split worm in the midday sun of self-consciousness. A split worm, a split word, no bird can pluck me out of my muddy hole. Keep dancing or turn to stone. But the stone is the stone no angel rolls away. And the dance is the dance of destruction. Shiver. Shiva.

Hanne is cooking for her mother who is gathering red currants on top of the ridge. Gulene can see the roof of her house rise out of the gully like a ship's keel sinking into the sea. She can see Cardea's house to the north, high on the tor. The red currants grow along the fence of the orchard where trees put forth only small wrinkled fruit now; but the red and black currants, gooseberries, cowberries, and raspberries remain productive. The plums and apples make good puddings and pies. Gulene had helped to plant these trees; she had held the young saplings in her hands, and when the trees had grown to fruit-bearing maturity she watched little Hanne and her brother Erik chase each other and laugh and play, picking berries and tossing rotten fruit at each other, teasing each other with stories about hidden snakes and trolls and witches; that was before Hanne's mind was twisted like a dirty wet rag and the water of life wrung out; before Erik fled to the city, never to return, never heard from again, though the young boy had promised his mother that he would never leave here, for he was so happy here. Gulene sighed. She had gathered enough berries she thought.

Hanne sat at the kitchen table, reading her bible, the pot of potatoes boiling on the stove. She held her left hand over her pregnant belly; her right hand turned the pages.

"In begynnelsen var Ordet, og Ordet var hos Gud, and Ordet var Gud. Ha var I begynnelsen hos Gud…"

She flipped over the pages.

"…men ved Jesus kors stod hans mor og hans soster, Maria, Klopas' hustru, og Maria Magdalena. Da nu Jesus så sin mor, og ved siden av henne den disippel han elsket, sa han til sin mor: Kvinne! Se, det er din sonn…"

Hanne suddenly felt a spasm tear the fabric of her womb; she bent over and grabbed her stomach, the bible falling to the floor.

"O min kjare Jesus, O min Gud… min kjare Jesus…"

She struggled to get up and fell to her knees. A pool of purple clotted blood soaked the wooden chair. She crawled toward the front door, a heap of flesh, a chunk of meat, leaving a trail of blood. She rubbed her hand in her vagina and smeared the blood on her dress and face. When she got outside she felt strength enough to rise to her feet and make her way to the outhouse. She shut the door, hooking her fingers in the hollow of the crescent moon. It means, for ladies only.

Dark clouds docked around the sun in the harbor of the midday sky. Bursts of light shot through like swarms of yellow bees. Down along the ridge's path Gulene walked over smooth exposed roots like fossilized bones. She placed her hand on the rough gray rock to balance herself. *"Vaer forsiktig… vaer forsiktig,"* she muttered to herself. *"Ja, takk Jesus… takk Jesus…"*

She edged her way through the scratchings of long, thin stray branches bobbing like fishing poles; if her dress got caught she released the thorn-hook and proceeded defiantly, among the ferns, or snake-grass as the children call it, because their parents told them that snakes nestled beneath the ferns, waiting to bite little children who stray and don't obey; and such a tale Gulene had told Hanne, among other tales.

Amalia was hanging out clothes on the line when a vague sense of pain crawled out of her mind and down her spine, entering her belly like a spider descending upon a trapped insect. She felt as if blood were filling her eyes; a faintness made her sway; she touched her face, her fingers trickled down over her cheeks, lips, and chin. Her skin felt like stone. She drooled and sweated, clutching her breast. Somehow she realized what had happened to Hanne, and she had to go to her. Amalia crept over the small hill of rocks like a rabid wolf following a scent of blood; then, as if her bones unknitted from each other, she toppled down like a pagan icon slashed by a heavy Christian sword, and she rolled into the thick grass and shook...

She lay still; the sun burned her eyes. A white butterfly fluttered over her head; she reached up to grab it... but she pulled the mountains down into the sea. A calm beatitude of well-being enveloped her. The strange fit passed, and she got up and went to Hanne, poor midwife of the world's miscarriages. Only the dead come to this island, she thought, only the dead come here.

Hanne stumbled out of the outhouse; her dress was wrapped and enfolded around her waist. Through the bleary well of tears in her eyes she saw her mother coming toward her. Hanne sniffled, rubbing her nose, and coughed and gagged, swallowing wads of saliva.

Gulene came rushing over the rocks. She hugged her daughter, trying to comfort her in a fervent sanctuary of embrace. Hanne's feeble body shook in her mother's arms like a dry and empty gourd rattle. Her breathing heaved and she gulped, straining to speak. "A chunk... a chunk of meat came out of me... just a chunk of meat. Where's my baby, mommy? Where's my baby Jesus?" She broke away from her mother's grasp and re-entered the outhouse. Amalia came up the path and stood next to Gulene. They held each other, watching in anguish as Hanne knelt before the strange altar of her dreams. She was like a medieval alchemist reciting sacred formulas before the Vas Hermiticam, attempting to summons forth spirit from degenerate matter, blood, feces, and urine.

"O rise up my baby Jesus… rise up… oh poor little black baby, the flies are all over your face and eyes; let me brush them away…"

Then she spoke in a weird and harsh voice, cragged and old, not her own. "There is a beast in the manger at Bethlehem; there are beasts all around me." She turned around and looked at Amalia, and she lunged at her with a claw-like hand, straight for the eyes. Hanne fell down and looked up; her eyes wild and penetrating. Amalia felt a coldness creep through her skull, distending it like a bloated tick about to burst its bag of blood. She shivered. Hanne spoke again, "There is a creature on the hill at Golgotha. Oh take him down and let him fall into my arms and I will kiss him on his lips, on his breast, on his stomach, on his manhood… and he will enter me; we will be as one; my father and I… my father entered me once… he said never speak of this to anyone for the sake of Jesus… and he sent me away… to love them… the little black babies…." Tears fell from her eyes. Gulene went over and offered her hand to her daughter.

"Do not touch me!" Hanne said. "It is finished." She collapsed and crumbled to the earth.

Amalia and Gulene lifted her up, and Hanne walked with them. "He would have changed the world. He would have brought peace and joy to the world forever, but now we must walk in the wilderness again… until… until my baby is born… where is my husband, the carpenter? I must go to him. Where is my brother, who was dead but lives again… where is my son, little Odin? I mean Jesus… we must take him down from the tree… cross… Oh they have taken my Lord away; the angels told me… where are you, mommy?"

They escorted Hanne to the house, Amalia on her left, and Gulene on her right, with their arms linked. Hanne kept dropping to her knees, turning her head, and trying to return to the outhouse. Her mother kept imploring her to keep walking. "Please, please, please, please, please…"

"But I must go to my baby," said Hanne, "he is crying; he needs his mother. I can hear him. He is so hungry." She tore open her blouse and clutched her breast. "This is human milk. I know. I've seen the mothers in… some country far away… their babies suck here. I am no beast. This is not cow's milk, not goat milk. This is my goodness; my kindness. I am such a good mother."

They sat her down on the stoop to the front door of the small white house; the house crouched over them like a lepers' cave. Hanne stopped crying. Her head bent down and she stared blankly at her nakedness splotched with blood. "Let's go inside, Hanne," said her mother. They passed through the doorway as if they were entering the mouth of a white whale. Hanne turned around one last time. She choked to speak, and then finally she said: "The baby brings the father's death."

They went into the kitchen. Gulene and Amalia sat Hanne in a chair and they washed her body. "Once, I washed his feet and dried them with my hair," Hanne said. They brought her upstairs and put her to bed. She turned on her side and tucked her knees up to her chest.

"Sleep, Hanne," her mother said.

And Hanne: "Where will my baby sleep tonight? You must keep him warm. He is so little."

"Sleep" her mother said again, stroking her hair.

Hanne said, "Why is the baby making blood on me, mommy?"

Hanne closed her eyes, and she slept.

In the beginning was the Word... *En el principio era al Verbo... In den beginne was het word... No princípio era o Verbo... Im Anfang war Das Wort... Nel principio era la Parola... Au commencement etait la Parole... In begynnelsen var Ordet...* Whose word? Which word? Over the Babel of Europe the emperors and popes and reformers dragged their purple robes and heavy brass swords. Purple royalty and purple blood. Words... words sleep in my dark soiled mind like stunned beetles on the sacrificial altar of experience and desire. I am buried in the waste. I know the worms of creation; I am part and parcel of their conversion to black gold, polysemous bacteria... emotive forms... defining moments... if the Word was in the beginning and beetles were words words words, then God so loved the world that he gave his only begotten Word to engender beetles.

In the cave the Word is a diamond and the words are beetles. There are innumerable beetles... and in a thousand years the beetles shall begat a diamond. If there were but one language, even a *lingua franca,* a primal tongue, the beetles would lose their voice, become obscure and obsolete, does the tribe desire this? Cultivated silence? Stagnant as the horseshoe crab? A slight resemblance. The beetle and the horseshoe crab? The beetles are dropping from their circling of the mind to the dirt of the brain...

droppings... and undo excess and each man have enough said the old blind one before he went mad as bats in a belfry... but how had the king come to madness? In a dream he saw what gift cold perfection gave, like a shining mound of gold deep within a cave. So with rags of discovery torched with desire, he searched beneath the bats that hung above. But the mind is a brittle bone and it plays ghostly tricks. What nature has marked for its own, the serpent tongue licks. With his eyes gaping the king slowly approaches; but horrible and vile: a dung pile laced with spiders and roaches... enough of fable, parable... he turns the page. Can he discover new beetles? He will hold them in his hand, and if he discovers another new beetle he'll put the other in his mouth like that famous naturalist, because he needs them so badly... why? To preserve them for a stale collection? A book in an old bookstore... or for his recollection, of tranquility perhaps? No, music is closer to that ideal... so is there something more to say... turn the page... these books that he brought with him! Useless words! Footnotes... commentaries, theory. Is there an original power of speech? Can the emotions be rendered into concrete imagery? Have we followed Mallarmé's fading ideal too long? Have we cleaved poetry from nature and reason, moving closer to sound-effects? The amazing and the nonsensical? The fantastic and abstract? To preserve mystery? The sacred? Just silly diversions and amusements... no intensification, no incitement, nothing essential... deformed clowns who fancy themselves decadent... fashionable affectations... idle displays of imagination... specialized thought... loss of the primitive... abstract ideas... no figurative, no bodily senses, no aesthetic emotions... I'm sick of it... the ahistorical life of the mind: I read in a book that death died with Jesus Christ.... I read in a book that God died with Nietzsche... I read in a book that life died with Buddha... I read in a book that beauty died with Baudelaire... I read in a book that love died with Keats... I read in a book that poetry died with Rimbaud, so I became a novelist...

My life, my consciousness... did I read that in a book? I picked up a book, held it a moment, and put it back down on the desk. I walked over to the window. The dusk was creeping into the woods. Clouds crept by like Aztec ghosts carrying corn. Slash and burn. Sacrifice and supplication. And then move on. Does anyone believe anything anymore? I could smell the smoke. Already the fires have begun... I have already made up my mind... I must leave... as planned... I will leave for England... tomorrow...

They gathered for the midsummer's eve celebration, which is called St. John's day on the Christian calendar. Aanen Håken carried small logs of oak and birch and kindling wood. He built the baal fire on the massive boulder embedded next to Cardea's house. Upon the black wound of previous years' fires he piled dead branches and old boards from the broken down barn, its roof sunken in, covered with a green valley of grass and moss. Gulene threw garbage on the pile: cracked plastic cups, cardboard milk containers, cellophane wrappings, and old newspapers, which Håken lit with a match, re-opening the never healing wound.

The fire began to crackle; a small and contained fire, breathing upon the light breezes, biting into the rusted nails in the barn's old rotten wood. Aanen and Elias had driven those nails into the wood over fifty years ago. When the fire dies, only the bent nails will remain to be resurrected by Aanen's hammer, acute and constant reminders of time the crucifier.

Hanne sat upon the rock; blankets were draped over her shoulders and wrapped around her lap. Her mother threw some more garbage on the fire, and she went over and sat down by her daughter's side. Gulene held her Bible. Johnny came out from the side door of the house and stepped directly unto the boulder. He carried a plate of food: sardines, mackerel, herring, and flatbread, stuff that Cardea had brought back with Håken on his boat from Farsund. Amalia followed the boy from the house; she held a tray of glasses filled with black currant juice. Gulene saw the boy and impulsively responded, reciting from the Bible by memory. *"Her er en liten gutt som harr fem byggbrod og to små fisker; men hvad er det til så mange?"*

Gulene took the bread and the fish from the boy. *"Takk,"* she said, *"du er en fint gutt."*

She took the drink from Amalia; and Gulene said, *"Den som er av Gud, horer Gud's ord."* Gulene and Hanne kept their communion to themselves, a stale and flat ceremony, pathetic and graceless, colder than the rock upon which they sat, and spilled the dark red juice. Gulene read from the bible; but only she and her daughter were enrapt by the stark words. *"Den som eter mitt kjod og drikker mitt blod, har evig liv, og Jeg skal opreiser ham på den ytterste dag; for mitt kjod er i sanhett mat, og mitt blod er i sanhett drikke. Den som eter mitt kjod og drikker mitt blod, han blir i mig og Jeg I ham."*

Idiot incestuous flames; you drive dragon teeth into dry wood, but your teeth break upon the rock. Aanen Håken looked out toward the lighthouse netted within a thick mesh of fog, the beacon flashing like a jumping salmon struggling up river to spawn. Amalia stared through the fire and saw the hieroglyphic patterns of smoke reflected in Hanne's phantom eyes. Gulene stared through the smoke and saw the hieroglyphic patterns of fire in Hanne's wedged eyes. The wind blew the smoke against their ashen faces. They stood up like ancient, weathered slabs leaning upon each other in a lonely field. Lichen and moss filled the sword-slashed chinks in stone. Lichen and moss covered the tool-etched engravings in stone. Lichen and moss filled the world-wearied cracks in stone. The mice ran up and the mice ran down; the hooded crow's rasping call rioted the air... kaw... kaw... kaw... of the corbie over the bones where the "wind sall blaw for evermair."

Johnny and Fern Abby playfully roasted marshmallows. Gulene and Hanne sang a song about Noah's Ark. "And there will come rain, rain, rain, and there will come rain, rain, rain."

Amalia wrestled with some branches and fed the flame.

"Det er nok," said Aanen, "That is enough... no more."

Cardea sat upon a large tree stump. She seemed beyond their desire and fear of the fire. Petrified, preserved, entombed in ice. In the fire she saw a burning boat...

The human pantomime lasted past midnight while the long sunset's parade of colors followed the sun's booming fatal drum beat and dripped down into the horizon and spread among the palette of the sea: pink, purple, orange, and gray ran together and turned a deep blue, into which night dipped her brush and painted the soft evening upon the canvas of a summer sky.

Cardea called her children over to her side, hugged them, and said, "Come on, off to bed, tomorrow we head for home."

"But, daddy?"

She didn't know what to say. "He's all right... don't worry."

The children followed their mother into the house; they went up the narrow stairs to their bedroom. Johnny asked his mother to tell him a story. "No story tonight; it is too late," said Cardea. Fern Abby lay in the bed on the other side of the small room; she was propped up on her bent elbow, her head leaning in her hand, her hair hanging down. "You are getting too old for stories; grow up, Johnny," she said.

Johnny ignored her and said to his mother: "Open the window; it's warm in here." Cardea opened the window. The breeze blew in and poked through the window and stroked Cardea around the hips. She picked up the lamp from the night table, said goodnight, and abruptly went downstairs.

As Johnny lay in bed he stared out the window into the dark treetops patched against the slate sky. He saw animal shapes: a section of the oak tree was a lion's head; the spruce a lamb's; the beech a pig's. A slight exchange of quiet voices spoke of far away things, and of a father who hasn't returned. The soundless voice of sleep spoke the final word on the edge of the dreamed image, and soon they were sleeping. Johnny dreamed that he was helping his father build a small boat. His father couldn't pull a nail out from a plank, and when Johnny offered to try, his father shouted at him, "If I can't do it how the hell are you gonna do it!"

"I hope it sinks!" Johnny shouted. "I hope you drown in it... drown in it... drown in it..." Johnny woke up and called out, "Dad... dad... daddy..." But his father couldn't hear him.

The baal fire gasped against suffocation, slowly dying in the mouth of the rock. Cardea stood at the kitchen window and watched the four figures speak silently through a curtain of smoke. Small flames darted up from the black ashes and swallowed bits of darkness. Hanne took a few sluggish steps forward. The fire beat hotly on her brow like two white flower petals decomposing in her mind; and beads of sweat formed on her forehead.

"Not so close to the fire," said Gulene, sternly to her daughter.

"But I am so cold," said Hanne.

Hanne folded her arms and pumped herself up and down on the soles of her shoes. Her eyes were horribly fixated on the fire. Aanen inexplicably walked over and stood next to her, as if some shrapnel of thought had exploded in his mind but had been launched from Hanne's mind, cutting a fearful premonition through the waves of thought between them. Hanne spoke, "I and my father are one." She moved toward the fire. She put her hands out in front of her as if to warm them. She reached toward the fire and she kept walking. She was about to step into the flames when Aanen grabbed her and held her; she writhed back and forth; and then she didn't resist any more. Her mother squealed like a trapped rat.

Amalia moved forward and spoke: "I saw the handle of my door turn down three times by itself last night." She paused. Everyone looked at her. "I heard three knocks upon my door; but nobody was there. I saw three candles burning over the head of my baby; I saw the angels over his bed...

I took my baby in my arms, but he was dead... he didn't move... so still. His tiny hand didn't tightened around my finger. I was frightened. I dropped him. He started crying. Blood ran out of his nose and ears. He stopped crying... there was blood on his little hands... just like Jesus on the cross. My baby is dead and your baby is dead, Hanne, and we are all dead. My poor Oscar is dead. But he is here now; he wants to come home to me. I hear him crying... I heard the guns; I saw him falling. I ran to him and held him. The soldiers laughed at me and dragged me away. There was blood on my hands. Listen... do you hear him? He is calling me. A man visited me last night. He had blood on his hands too. He laid his head on my breast and he cried like a baby. I dreamt about babies; it means something bad will happen. I know; I can feel it."

Aanen Håken had heard enough. "*Hold kjeften*! Shut up old woman."

It was too late. Something rank and foul was growing in their minds; it bound them together; minds filled with thorns and thoughts dragged over flesh. Aanen thought to himself: Something must be done. They can't live here like this and I have to bring food to them like animals. It can't go on... they just can't live here like this in this day and age. Someone will provide for them. They are mad. Look at them. Stinking, filthy beasts... look at them.

But they were looking at Aanen, as if three wolves had trapped a caribou. They approached him with insane smiles. They surrounded him. They foamed at the mouth; strings of spittle hanging from their lips. They got down on their knees and hands; on all fours... Gulene knelt down behind Hanne and straddled her. They bayed like animals in heat. "I shall be a man," said Gulene, "and you shall be a virgin."

Hanne said, "You shall be black and powerful and violent. I shall bleed. The baby brings the father's death, and the father must die, or how shall the earth live again?"

Aanen fled down the path. He had seen enough.

Cardea returned to the children's room to see if they were sleeping. They were. She placed the lamp on the nightstand and turned down the wick. The room went dark and she stood without moving until her eyes readjusted to available light. She groped toward the door but turned around when she remembered that she had come to close the window also. She lost her sense of direction for a moment; blood drained from her brain. A dervish of vertigo whirled in her body, and drops of perspiration boiled out of her pores. Cardea felt a strange tension and tightening in the walls of the room. Air was sucked out the window and the walls collapsed inward. A cavernous darkness crept into the room on all fours. She backed up against the door to balance herself; then she slid down to the floor. She pulled her legs back, and each leg flopped to one side. Outside the window she saw a dim brush-dab of moonlight in the pubic treetops. She felt the rising and swelling of the sea, the unstoppable force of all the waters of the earth released from constraint of gravity; uterine contractions; the opening of the cervix; an unremitting and irreversible surge and drive and thrust forward; the door swung open, the wheel turned, a plant was torn from the soil, a worm squirmed in the warm mud... all motion and circular flow, a violent gush of a river breaking its banks asunder; interminable flux of turning seasons, stars, sun. Process of discovery, possibility of being, intense trauma, fear and pain and loss. Existential disgust, indiscriminate hunger, metaphysical torment, sorrowful life. The first experience, the first preparation for meaning, the first center, inclusive, the half of the hinge that holds the door, moths between the creviced bark of trees, the light of day comes and we fly away. The first ritual, the first claw, horn, tooth, shell, wing... there is nothing to fear is heard fading from behind, from the center, from the post. To return? Why do we ever come? The rapid flight of terror, propulsion through the birth canal. Cardea imagined that she saw her husband outside the window. His face was contorted and furiously enraged: the fierce countenance of a tyrant. Cardea's whole being seemed to cry out. "No! No! They are mine! You can't have them. No more. No more. I'll kill them before I gave them to you. I'd slit their throats. I would. You are dead. Drowned." She crawled over to the window and closed it.

Birth-pangs of the maiden-breath breached. Horse-hoofed thunder of the northern mountains galloping blind crushed the crescent vine. Dispensable man aped the beast between the mimicry of sexual howling and a basal vocal sign. Staunchly pouched mothers gave their alluring eyes to the mystery of the alabaster moon. The geometry of geography is mapped, the course is charted, the scrolls of blueprints are rolled out on the grass, and the scaffolding is erected around the brain's architecture. The king shall lead you out from this jungle of hidden serpents, scorpions, and bewitchments; he shall gather his twelve men in castle chambers and plot new invasions, new conquests, new inroads into the human mind. In the city a lone man cuts a dark figure through the streets. He sneaks away, pulling at his red beard and mumbling under his breath, *and yet...*

Contriver of riddles bespeaks the two-mouth conflicting river. The woodpecker's flickering tongue lashing at encrusted insects; the berry-eating birds drop seeds into a glass lake, smooth after storm. Fallen star of morning in the mist-shrouded days, hoarder of the jeweled tales, bestower of the cryptic veil, and thief of the sun's wings, garrisoned, chained, eroding and dropping scales. Banished from God; exiled from the land of the Nod. Whose dream do you keep now? The acceleration of terror, the slaughter of the innocents, the girl babies, and the revenge on life. Dragged out kicking and screaming.

Cardea opened the window and looked out into the pale darkness. She imagined that she saw a man's body hanging from a tree. She kissed her sleeping children. She cursed God. She cursed man. She cursed...

Cardea went outside, through the back door, avoiding the three women, and she looked up to the sky. The moon wore her crown of a billion stars. Cardea scrambled down the path and came to the cairn she had built on the shoreline. She removed the rocks and dragged her husband's body to the small rowboat. She piled on branches and doused it with gasoline. She untied the ropes and the boat stirred as if green sap had returned to its wood. She struck a match and tossed it on the boat, a lion's roar of red flame shot up. The purple claw of the tide dragged the boat out to the wine-dark sea. The stars reflected in the water. The burning boat was transported to its starry castle in the cold northern skies.

Cardea walked back up the path. She heard a moan coming from the bottom of a small ravine dropping down from a large boulder near her house. An owl? An animal? The wind? She followed and found Aanen Håken spread out upon the rocks and moss, his face spotted with mud, his clothes torn, and his arms and legs scratched and trickling with lines of blood. He was conscious, and Cardea helped him to walk to her house, where she cleaned his wounds. He lay on the couch covered by a quilt, and Cardea watched over him.

The faces of the three women stared in through the window. Their eyes followed Cardea as she came into the room and placed a cold towel on Håken's forehead. "Send him out to us, Cardea; we need him. He is too old for you. He isn't strong enough for you. You are young; you can find another man. Your husband has drowned. Your John, your Janus, your

Juan, your Giovanni... whatever you want to call him; he shall never return to you." The three women sinisterly shrieked like a concentration of helter-skeltering bats. They exposed their large sagging breasts. They pressed their thick lips against the window and steamed the glass with their fetid breath. Hanne said, "Come out old man. We can be made one. I and my father. Let us burn in the delight of my lovely young flesh."

The three women suddenly fled en masse like a school of fish. They danced around in a circle on the large rock where the baal fire smoldered and simpered. The ashes crackled in guttural horror as the three women spat upon the cracked coal-encrusted embers of hot wood; and then the rain came down, down, down; a searing sound jumped up from the ashes, and an explosion of smoke loomed up as if the earth had cleared its poisoned throat. Amalia held a large bread knife in her hand. "This nightmare will soon be over," she said. "Someone must suffer for the people. The hand knows what the mind has done in the plagued ruins of time." She began slashing at her wrist.

A weird ominous blankness filled the gruesome raven darkness of the window. Cardea watched the raindrops dribble over the glass. A furious wind wracked the island.

It was Saturday morning. Cardea opened the door and squinted her eyes at the brightness of the morning. The small white house was washed in the sunlight; and so were the figures of three passive and naked women on the large rock landing.

"Come and see," said Gulene, "come and see, a new baby was born unto me in the night... a boy... what shall we name him? The name is important." Gulene sat with her legs spread apart, leaning against the rock. "See my baby... I am the mother of a fine boy... a baby boy! He will do great things for the people." There was no baby; only poor Hanne sat rocking back and forth on her buttocks, her legs pulled back to her chin. Blue veins showed through her pale translucent skin. Her mother went over to her and crouched beside her, and held her, like some strange and beautiful Pièta.

By mid morning a boat drifted away from the island. It carried the three women, an old man, two children, and Cardea. The boat approached the gaping cavity of the boathouse. Aanen Håken cut off the boat's engine, and the sudden absence of its monotonously sputtering steel nostrils and clanging reverberations was like an avalanche of silence crashing down from the slopes of a distant peak. They shook the white mantle from their hair and heard the pristine sounds of lapping waves and pivoting gulls again. The wind ploughed a passage towards winter. The boat coasted over the shallow, lilting water. Aanen directed the boat with an oar, pushing off from a rock be-speckled by algae, and he maneuvered into the boathouse. A straight, unswerving line of shadow spread over the boat like a curtain dropped upon a stage. Aanen grabbed the hanging ropes and held fast, bringing the boat to rest. He stepped off the boat and opened the small door, and the sun flashed through. He offered his hand to Gulene, and then Hanne, and then Amalia. They bowed in turn passing through the exit door; the leaves clapping in the trees. The three women saw the faintly shadowed figure of a man standing at the top of the hill. He looked like an elk under the antlered spruces. The man waved his arms; Aanen gestured in reply. The man picked up a bucket of fish and started walking down the hill to the boat. The three women started trudging up the hill, following each other on the path, stooping over as if they carried an enormous weight on their backs. They passed the man as he made his way gingerly over the thick, wet grass. "Good day," the man said.

The three women slightly bowed their heads. The man proceeded down the hill. Hanne called out to him. "Where are you going?" But the man did not answer.

Then Hanne spoke: "We have come this way before; nothing has changed for us. When did it begin? For two thousand years I have been a sweet, benevolent virgin, and now the womb is too weak to bear. We have played out this farce for far too long, and not a witness remains... not a tree, not an animal, not a star, not even a man, what a fool, as dog is me witless."

Amalia turned to Gulene and Hanne. "I believe we three shall meet again when under a cold December sun we lift the baby from the basket in the river. Let us return now; our time has been and yet not come; the same path is here, look, follow until the eyes of the lynx mark you."

They looked at each other, silently, and then they looked out over the sea. The islands slid over the water like snails, the silver currents their slimy trails. A weird and wild bloody sunrise burned in their fogged eyes. Then the transformation began. "Listen, sisters, a new incantation. Eye of Newton, bone of Darwin, gracious lady give us pardon, give us leave, give us the desire and the wonder to conceive, give us a fire for midwinter's eve."

The man limped down the path and passed a split oak tree. He slithered through the door of the boathouse. The man appeared in the doorway, and Fern Abby looked up from the boat and saw the silhouetted face change from a formless, featureless blur to a familiar and distinct presence. She smiled. "Hello father," she said, "where have you been?"

"Between the devil and the deep blue sea," he said. "Look at all the fish I caught."

Aanen Håken returned to the lighthouse. Tonight he will dream his last dream, that the moon is a large white moth attracted to the beacon flame, and that she will descend upon the lighthouse and wrap her wings around it, and burn and endure, smothering Aanen in the ashes of peace.

The following morning Aanen Håken stood on the platform of the lighthouse. He saw the great ocean, the great mother of all living things. And he said, *"Jeg ville ikke være en ensom øy på et havet av menneske."* And he followed his uncle's footsteps to the edge of the cliff and to the rocks and waves below.

It's my last night in Norway. Tomorrow I take the bus to Kristiansand and from there the ferry to Denmark and England. I am feeling restless tonight. Anxious. Can't sleep. So I take a walk into Farsund. I walk along the harbor. The fishing boats are out to sea. They will return toward dawn. With their mackerel and cod. I am alone. There are no other night strollers. I go over and sit down on one of the benches by the four linden trees. It's a cool fresh evening. A soft breeze blows. Millions of stars are clustered overhead. I hear the water lapping. Dark mountains beyond. The air has a salty pungency. A light misty fog moving in. The streetlights throw angular shadows. A figure approaches from around the corner of the bakery. Small and hunched. It is Johan.

"God kveld, Herr Cazzaza..."

"Hello Johan. Very pleasant evening, yes?

"Ja vist... der er veldig stille. Overrasket deg?"

"You didn't startle me. You know it's my last night in Norway. Tomorrow I leave for London."

"Ja, ja... I will miss you. I have enjoyed our talks."

"I have enjoyed talking with you too. Perhaps you can visit me in London."

"Yes, I would like that. I will try. Keep in touch, as you say in English."

"Good."

"But I want to finish something I brought up the other day in our discussion. We were talking about writers and politics. And I asked you why from one side of your mouth you speak of justice... for the oppressed, this impossible idea... liberty, fraternity, and equality... what you speak of is what the French call libertarian-socialism... but who? What I have read of the current French writers, they are anti-humanist... anti-enlightenment... so you mean like Rocker? The Spanish anarchists? and yet out of the right side of your mouth you tell me of those writers you admire... but those writers, are they not associated with the right? Or neither perhaps? Those individualists! So why this ridiculous political nonsense... an oxymoron no doubt... liberty and socialism... we have that in Norway already!"

"And capitalism too... but it must be both... it is perhaps an aporia, like an X on an uncharted map, but... one without the other is truly oppression..."

"Not a treasure map then? Maybe Melville's map? A place for Bartleby and Pierre and Ishmael... not down on any map... a true place."

"You are well read Johan..."

"I suppose being an outcast, an outsider in this wonderful Norwegian paradise has turned me inward... but you must just step back from that world and write, Stephen... whatever happens happens... *Men Levet Lever....* life lives... life goes on... after all... the poor have their lives, don't they? True? *Ikke sant*, Hamsun? "

"Hamsun?"

"I have some friends that I want you to meet. You have met them before I am sure."

"I don't think so... I haven't met too many people here..."

Several dark figures came walking slowly from around the corner.

"Ja vel... nevertheless... I want to introduce you to *Herr* Hamsun."

"*God kveld*," said the voice coming from the white phantom, tall and thin, haughtily approaching, holding a cane...

"And our next visitor, *Monsieur* Céline..."

"*Bonsoir...*" said the ragged ghost, his dark sunken eyes focused on the cat he is carrying in his arms.

"And next is your fellow countryman, Mr. Kerouac."

"Good evening," said the figment, his eyes bent to the pavement.

"And from far away... Osamu Dazai-san."

"*Konbanwa*," said the shadow, wearing a black robe... "if you give your thoughts to things, you will give your thoughts to suicide..."

"And there are more phantoms waiting... shall I bring them forth?"

"Who?... my God, Johan... this is a dream, right? Or am I going mad?

"*Ja vel...* Mad? *Er du gal?* Schizophrenic? Modern or post-modern?... *ja,* shall I introduce you to the others?... "

"Others?"

"*Ja...ja...* Kierkegaard, Baudelaire, Dostoyevsky, Melville, Rimbaud, Henry Miller, Proust, Kafka, Jeffers, Camus... only the dead come here... they are waiting..."

Céline: everyone liked my journey book. The damn black feet and the pale feet... both wanted to claim me... but the snobs didn't... that prize... a scandal... I was a witness... that is all... a chronicler of the dark journey... of the Grand Guignol of life... of the end of the white race... the end of European civilization... the yellow hoards, the slavs... my style... I had to pay the rent... I wanted an apartment.... Oh King Hamsun... all modern European writing came from you... are you and me mad *Herr* Hamsun? They think that we are mad... "

Kerouac: you guys, Hamsun and Céline, you both came to America... that's where you got your style, right? The energy of the prose, the shorter sentences, the psychological... admit it..."

Hamsun: That damn Churchill... he wanted to provoke the Germans into Norway. He was mad to fight the Russians. Oh how I despised the English. That crazed imperial power... their sea power... Empire... Churchill wanted to invade Norway so his soldiers could march into Finland you see and ... there was a war between the Finns and the Russians... Churchill mined our waters... our water was our territory... the English infringed... provoking Hitler... Norway declared neutrality on September 1st... but ... yet if Churchill used Norway to fight Russia I think Norway would have had no choice but to side with Germany... you see... everything is not black and white... like your country thinks... I lived in America... I was there in Chicago when they killed those anarchists... a judicial lynching... no one stood up for them... I think only that William Dean Howells of all your writers and so-called intellectuals defended them... of course I was no anarchist... but I wore a black armband in support... and the Norwegian government called the King in the middle of the night and told him that Norway was at war! And do you know what the King said. He said, At war with whom? Ha Ha. With whom? With whom? At war with whom? But it is true Quisling did not have the support of the Norwegian people.

I said that my mother's uncle once told me that Quisling sent out a message to all the Norwegian ships at sea: Go to the nearest German port... and then the regular government sent out a message that said: Go to the nearest allied port... and no ships went to a German port... all went to Allied ports!

Bah! Cowards! *Ja ja* Céline... we are all cowards... and now the yellow hoards are coming and your white race will be no more...

Merde... did you think I really cared about that? Céline's cat jumped down from his arms in pursuit of the smell of fish wafting from the docks... *merde...Berbet?*

Hamsun: And who are you little man? I seem to remember you from somewhere.

Johan: I am a monster... an outcast... I was born of a Nazi officer and a fifteen-year-old Norwegian girl. Oh how brutal we were treated after the war when my Nazi father left and it was just my mother and I...

Hamsun: I wasn't treated too kindly either, little man...

London - Paris

I take a peek at the front page of the newspaper that the fat American Tourist is reading.

Document 86-7689

INTERNATIONAL
HERALD   TRIBUNE
Published with the New York Times and Washington Post

London, Wednesday, October 29, 1986

In a 4-point ruled box in columns 6-7 at the bottom half of the broad sheet there is a photograph of relief pitcher Jesse Orosco, arms extended upward and falling on his knees, celebrating after striking out Marty Barrett of the Boston Red Sox to end the final game of the World Series with an 8-5 Mets' victory. Page 21

I am sitting at a coffee shop in London. I am in Camden Town. It's a trendy area. I have been in London for over a year now, I think. I'm not sure. Johan is sitting across from me. His thick lips sipping a cappuccino. Up the street there is a blue plaque on the wall outside a flat where Dylan Thomas had lived. Dickens lived around here too, and Orwell, and Rimbaud and Verlaine. It's like I'm chasing phantoms... that's what she said about me, didn't like it that I wanted to know where a certain writer lived and all that. She's out of my life now. Johan's happy about that. He hated her.

Johan and I were walking in Hyde Park earlier today. Cold and gray and misty rain, and it was my kind of weather, chasing phantoms weather. We sat on a bench in front of the nearly hidden statue dedicated to the obscure writer W. H. Hudson. I told Johan about Hudson. About his wonderful autobiography, *Long Ago and Far Away*. I told him about Rima, the bird-girl of Hudson's novel *Green Mansions*, who is carved into the stone monument in front of us, who would not rise from her rock and let the birds alight on her fingers and shoulder. Some old English nature books brought him here, some dream of ancient weather, but not me... not Johan... what did we come for?

We walked along the canal and then through Primrose Hill where we passed the flat where Yeats had lived and Plath had killed herself. I told that to Johan but he was quiet and introspective and didn't have much to say on the subject. We crossed over the train trestle and down toward the tube station. Johan got on the tube at Chalk Farm, he's staying at some nasty bedsit by King's Cross Station. Chasing phantoms. I saw an old man walking on the pavement and wondered about him: where he was born, grew up, and most importantly, how did he get here... here. What's his story? Like a phantom out of Dickens.

Sometimes I go to a working class Greek café in Kentish Town, up the road from trendy Camden Town (I preferred Story Places to Picture Places). On some days I chat with the Irish street workers in their tweed jackets with patched elbows; or follow the different red flag processions up the hill from Archway to Marx's grave in Highgate Cemetery; or sit on the benches with the drunkards and their large bottles of hard cider outside Kentish Town Underground, as the wind blows people out from the station like swirling bits of newsprint; or some rainy day I'll just sit in the cafe and drink coffee... talk about the Proust novel and the light that follows through it from page to page... that's what some jerk said.

During my first year in London I lived in a bedsit in Muswell Hill, north London. It was the first place that I went to look for a room. When I entered the house on Church Crescent, I immediately noticed the sculptures and pottery and paintings that hung on the walls or lined the shelves and nooks and crannies of the stairwells. I met the landlady first. Her name was Magda. She and her husband were from Poland. She showed me the room. I asked her about the paintings and pottery. Just things that her husband had collected from his travels, some pre-Columbian pottery, and the sculptures and paintings were his work. His name was Stanislaw, and he was an artist.

The next day I met Stanislaw in his studio downstairs. He was working on a glass sculpture. The studio was very hot; a large kiln was blazing. I could see through the small door the blue glass sculpture being born.

Over time I had many conversations with Stanislaw, often in his studio or in his kitchen. The French singer, Georges Brassens, was singing from Stanislaw's cassette player. Stanislaw spoke about six languages: Polish, Russian, French, Spanish, Italian, and English. He told me that Brassens' French is very difficult, very idiomatic and colloquial. It was hard to translate, he said. I spoke of my desire to go to Paris after London.

I learned much about Stanislaw from our conversations, and he was never reluctant to talk about his life. He was seventy-one, almost bald with curling grey hair on the sides, and he was short. He came to London as an ex-service Polish artist. He has worked in woodcuts, sketches, collage, abstract painting, prints, clay and glass. He was a descendant of Swiss painters who could be traced back to the early 17th century. They were born in Basle and Berne, and were portrait painters of royals, Louis XIV in France, Emperor Leopold I in Vienna, Prussian King Fredrick in Berlin. His family migrated from Berne to Rome to Dresden to Paris to Gdansk to Warsaw. His father, also a painter, died in the war with the Bolsheviks. Stanislaw lived in Warsaw as a child, and when the war began, his family tried to escape the advancing Germans and the advancing Russians by getting to Switzerland. But just before they crossed the border the Russians picked them up and put them on a train. A long trek through Russia ensued. When Poland sided with the allies, Stanislaw and his mother and sister were released. He joined the Polish army in the Middle East, and lost touch with his mother and sister. In Palestine he offered his first works, sketches that he had made of his long journey from Warsaw and through Russia to the Middle East. He showed these sketches to me one day, and we talked about writing a text to accompany the sketches, but Stanislaw wasn't very motivated to conjure old demons. The sketches were not that good he said.

One day by chance he met his mother and sister on a street in a city in the Middle East. He was stunned. He wept. Later his sister moved to Canada to teach at a university. She was a poet. She died in Bergen, Norway, when a funicular collapsed. After the war he was accepted to Rome's Academy of Fine Art, and came to London when the Polish army was evacuated to Britain. He then studied at an art college in London. He illustrated books for Cape, and did many commissioned works in England. When I arrived there Stanislaw was in his glass sculpture period.

Nigel, a strange character who lived on the second floor, also does some glass sculpture, mostly plates and bowls. I never understood why Stanislaw and his wife were taken in by this prat, this toff. They had no children. They kind of adopted him. They also had a dog named Aga, a big black Labrador that I used to walk in Highgate Wood.

One time we sat in a café and Stanislaw talked about art and artists and Paris. I thought I had finally arrived… that's what I took from my relationship with them, a connection to the past, but his end was tragic. He had such enthusiasm for art; we went to museums together… he seemed childlike… he even looked like Picasso… his wife had been an alcoholic and was fifteen years younger than he. She had had affairs with tenants. This was a rumor. She liked vodka. That was not a rumor. Years later they sold the building in Muswell Hill and moved to Moorgate, on the coast. They moved into a big old Georgian building, located on a square. I visited them one time. But they were lonely there. A few years later Stanislaw had a stroke, and while he was in hospital, his wife hanged herself. The dog died, and Nigel, well, who knows what happened to Nigel.

I stood outside the closed doors of the 134 bus, which was parked under a span of concrete rooted by columns, in the dark cavernous passage-way behind the monstrous Center Point Building, in front of which an inappropriately located fountain sprayed mist of water on a concourse of crustaceously-clothed punksters who were sitting on the low gaudy blue-tiled wall which surrounded the pool of neon-lit water. A group of pedestrians were scattering through a barrage of shiny black cabs. The cabbies waiting at the traffic lights, ready to advance. Diesel engines harrumphing like blithering old diehards. I stood by the bus doors. The driver sat in his chair and looked at his watch. Not time yet. Do the drivers really pay attention to the time schedules? It was chilly out here but the driver wouldn't open the doors. "Open the fookin' door!" bellowed a crustacean from the pool, with his girl. He was wearing a tattered Ramones T-shirt.

The driver sat behind the wheel in a cramped compartment shielded by Plexiglas with an orb of small voice holes drilled through it. He was reading *The Sun*, which was spread across the flat steering wheel, kind of like the Page 3 girl is spread across the page. The driver took a drink from a steaming Styrofoam cup and then placed it back down in the circular indentation in the panel. I held a blue Dillon's bag, with an image of Virginia Woolf on it, which contained two paperbacks. The bus doors suddenly slooooshed opened. I boarded and placed 60p in the tray. A ticket machine stuck a ticket out like a tongue and I tore it off. I walked down the aisle and swung around on the pole, heading upper deck. The upper deck was empty (this was the starting point for the 134) and I sat down in the front seat on the left side. I wiped the gray smear of condensation from the window with my jacket sleeve. The engine suddenly stomped its pistons like grinding hooves and the bus bucked forward a space and then another space as it edged its way into the traffic and lights and commotion of St Giles Circus, where Oxford Street and Tottenham Court Road and Charing Cross Road converge. As the bus turned right onto Tottenham I glanced down Oxford Street where the Christmas lights were swaying in the wind and blinking and glaring from places where the wetness stuck like treacle.

There was a long queue waiting at the first stop. The bus filled up and the windows fogged up. Again I wiped the gray smear of nebulosity that barred my vision. At the next stop a tree branch whacked the front of the bus and I flinched. Voices cackled a cacophony of words that streamed forth on warm breath and separated: the breath steaming the windows and clinging like silence, the words arching across space and falling upon empty targets like unstuck arrows. The windows fogged up again. A winter night closed on London like a collapsed umbrella.

The bus proceeded up Tottenham and passed Warren Street Station. It continued north on Hampstead Road, pulling over to and pulling out of bus stops, moving in and out of traffic, seeming to swallow bicyclists and motorcyclists and anything else in its path; and then butting its front right up against the posterior of another bus (another 134 of course) and jerked to a halt, the people getting on and off. The young Ramones' couple were sitting across from me, be-slobbering each other with kisses. The girl seemed nervous about the onlookers; the young man looked back to meet their gazes, but they had already buried their eyes in their Christmas packages. "Ah fookin' now't."

The bus trudged up Archway hill. At the top of the hill the bus turned right and stopped by the gate of Highgate Wood, across the street from the ramp that leads down to Highgate Station. I decided to walk the rest of the way to my bed-sit. I got off and entered the gate to Highgate Wood. I walked along the path that ran adjacent to the road. W. H. Hudson, the writer and naturalist, used to walk in this wood. I have passed by the statue in Hyde Park dedicated to Hudson, and wondered about this man who was born in Argentina of American parents, and came to London to live in "poverty" for twenty years before gaining some recognition for his writings. He came from Patagonia, where snakes slept under his bed and large spiders ran up his whip as he rode his horse over the pampas, to the sleepy soft English countryside of bland birds and country vicars and village greens. From the frontier of green mansions to the front-pieces of London, a far transatlantic transition from the pampas and the famed gaucho with his big blade, to the cricket pitch and the lads in white with their flat bats and breaks for tea. I continued on through Highgate Wood, chasing phantoms...

If God, or some authority figure, smacked you across the face and then told you that that was for being too good, what moral lesson would you derive from that? The moment that he smacked me, when I was thirteen, and said that to me, I knew that it would be very difficult to make any sense of this world, and I knew that the memory of that smack would never fade, that a long rope tied in knots bound me to the past...

I walked up the stairs to my bed-sit. I met Nigel on the landing. As usual, Nigel looked distressed. Nigel does not like to meet people. Stanislaw said that Nigel was some kind of computer genius but wasn't able to get along with people, so he left his job. He's on the dole. We greeted each other abruptly and Nigel fled back to his room. His demeanor is aloof and standoffish. He speaks in mumbled, barking patterns. His eyes are deeply recessed, his lips thin and debauched. I entered my room and sat down at the white table. Three high rectangular windows stood side by side at attention in an alcove that beveled out forming a niche where one right angle of the table disjointedly misfitted. Each morning fallen chips of speckled paint were lying on the table. I swept them off with my hand; they accumulated on the floor like shattered fragments from the ceiling of a Tarkovsky nightmare.

The writer makes his appearance. A young man leaning over a table, with overbearing melancholy; this is the last attempt at life. In a fusty, dust-infested room; a thunder-decayed air; a dose of many rainbows... he slithers from his sluff. In this grave hour of solitude, a sound as feeble as a curtain rustling or a larva moving in carnage could stun him into madness. A silence vibrates above. Overcast sky. A baleful night like drizzling rain falling on a pile of oyster shells. He has read too much French literature in his youth. Too much French philosophy. He's sick, like the 20th century is sick. Sleep wafts like black ribbons through his mind. A horrible mesh of tangled ropes lurks beneath him like snakes. He is an animal pacing his desire and ideas around the confines of a mental cage. One rope, and all these knots tied to his past. In the middle of the night his belly comes alive with unconscious teeth sharpened on his nerves. The rope slinks into a knot and tightens. Where is the end of the rope? Who holds the end? This tug-of-war into the past. The crucible of his guts, weighing down the brown intestinal mush of experience. I get up from the bed and stumble to the sink. I sit on the sink and diarrhea, the endless difficult novel of life, spurts from my rectum and into the sink like industrial disease. I get down and turn around to vomit into my own shit. The muscles of my throat wrench in spasms. I fall naked on the bed; burning with fever, burning not with poetry, leave that to Nerval and Baudelaire and Rimbaud. Why do I get sick like this? O anywhere out of this world!

There is a young attractive Jewish couple who live upstairs. He had some strong hash and brought some to my room. O anywhere out of this world... but I got sick, took too deep drags and too much, I almost blacked out, I went blind, I couldn't hear, everything was far away, was I finally going out of this world? I crawled out onto the small roof over the back door and heard music coming from the outdoor concert on Hampstead Heath, by Kenwood House... is that you Ludwig? *Even the oysters down in Oyster Bay do it...* Oh God, giant oysters are coming to eat me!

The English shopkeeper, in a used book store on Charing Cross Road, said to me, "Why would you want to publish your poetry?… isn't that just a hobby?" O thank you, thank you, I am so glad to hear it said. At last, a smack in the face that had moral relevance, that meant something, that made sense. Damn shopkeepers!

I sat on a bench at an entrance to Highgate Wood, across the street from Highgate Underground Station. I had just stepped off the 134 bus and decided to walk through the wood to my bed-sit in Muswell Hill. I sat on the bench for a brief moment because I wanted to catch my breath, not the breath that feeds my lungs, not the breath of life, but the breath held in suspension by disbelief. A deep breath, a pre-hyperventilating breath. An easy, unconcerned, alert, and self-contained breath. At that moment I didn't want to be anywhere else in the world. It may have been the first time that I ever felt this way in my life. It was a strange sense of freedom, creative freedom, stemming from within, perhaps just a mood, a whim. No matter how solitary and isolated, I just didn't want to go back again. I didn't want to go "home." I didn't want to go back there, anywhere, and yet every word I write points back there, every sentence points back there… for every step forward on the real earth I take two steps back in my unreal mind in these unreal cities… and more unreal phantoms. I use the word phantom and not the word ghost because that is the word that she used. I find it strange about the English, that they don't really believe in God but they all believe in ghosts… except her of course, but she's not English, she's Jewish, and from Vienna, and she called them phantoms.

My first months in London were marked by an isolation that deepened to a solitude on the verge of despair. Most of my time was spent walking from my bed-sit in Muswell Hill to the West End and its cluttered bookstores. The rest of the time I was staying in my bed-sit, reading from books culled from the anemic library at East Finchley, or writing a long narrative poem about the inhabitants of an island off the southern coast of Norway.

I learned from my time in New York in the seventies that it's not prudent to make eye contact with strangers, with the Other, and that there are some truly demented people in this world who will never release you from their eye-stare, their ugly, mind-draining avarice. They may beat you up, mind you, but it's really not about violence, it's always about the power to possess, to humiliate, their Mario the Magician howls of derision. My old friend Tommy back in New York, he could play that game of confrontation so well, so madly, sitting on the subway and catching the eyes of a crazed-looking fuck across the way, staring him down, until the first one breaks, cracks, turns away. The big walk down, the show down, a mug's game, put on your game face. Now I... I can walk from my bed-sit all the way to the Thames without speaking or looking at another soul. When you feel trapped the best thing to do is walk. Drift.

I was happy when Johan arrived toward the end of my first year. He reminded me of my friend Tommy back in New York. I would decide to go here or go there and he would lead the way. All four feet of him, ploughing through the crowds. He was like a new person in London. But he still was unhappy.

I'm up for a walk now. Johan agreed to walk. It's quite long. I'm starting at the top. From Victorian heights. Ali Pali. I have a Dickensian perspective from here, a Matthew Arnold tide of cultural detritus drooled over the Pitch and Putt golf course at the bottom of the hill, a T. S. Eliot shore of ruins at the pointed tips of my James Bond shoes. We commence our walking excursion at Alexandra Palace, opened in 1873 as a Victorian "entertainment complex," as it might be described today. This palace for the people burned down just sixteen days after it opened. Yeah, well, that's what The People do, they burn down palaces. It was rebuilt and reopened two years later. Now it's mainly a convention center for trade and consumer shows. We walked pass a garden center and entered the Grove, where idle layabouts lay about in each other's arms. I thought of Anna. That was us once. They're all on the dole, you know, some elderly lady comments to her acquaintance. An underpass takes us out to a path that skirts along a high ridge fronted by an old wall overlooking the rooftops of London. The path is lined with bushes, lots of blackberries. This path was part of the Great Northern Railway that shuttled Victorians to Alexandra Palace. We go through another underpass and it's just a short walk down the sloping road to Highgate Wood. There's a used bookstore by the entrance. We walk along the path that runs parallel to Muswell Hill Road. Tired yet Johan?

We exit the park by the bench where I sat yesterday afternoon. Highgate Underground station is across the street. There's another bookstore, Ripping Yarns. We continued on our trek, over Southwood Lane, and arrived at Highgate Village. To my left there's an art gallery decked out in purple that my landlord told me about. Stanislaw said that I should mention his name; he knows the proprietor. The gallery is cluttered with artwork, sculptures and paintings, pursuing the "making use of everything" theory. I spoke with Stanislaw's friend, an old High European Modernist like Stanislaw. When he found out that I was a friend of Stanislaw, he bade me to follow him. We went through the back door and out into the secret garden. There was a shoddy building, an old carriage house, and inside were more paintings and sculptures. This was the "serious art," he informed me. Here art appreciation ran the gamut. A lesson in anatomy, twisted, distorted, raped and pillaged. I felt like I entered some smutty Victorian novel. Bad pornography. I had fallen asleep and woke up inside the knickers and crinoline hoop skirt of a Madame from a brothel on Grub Street. Impoverished hack that I am, only a servant, I wouldn't even gain back entrance no doubt, oh please let me back into my postmodern novel. It reeks of soot and spunk in here. Or at least cast me down on a street in Paris in 1933. Would I be able to look someone in the eye back then, in Paris, 1933? Could I make the connection, make the contact, through this magnetic field of resistance, my body language of repulsion?

We continued our walk down the hill and entered Waterlow Park, with a pleasant pond and quacking ducks surrounded by weeping willows. We left the path and cut over to the edge of the park and I grasped an iron bar of the gate, and saw old Karl high on this pedestal. What about that, Johan? You little Nazi. We exited the park and passed the gate to Highgate Cemetery, where Mr. Marx and Company greet other phantom chasing pilgrims.

Then down Swain's Lane where I passed the brick dollhouses where Anna brought me to visit some Israeli arms dealer and his family. The wife was a hoot. She had been in therapy with RD Laing. I argued with her husband and got the boot. Anna also introduce me to a well-known German poet, and the brother of the Israeli physicist who was imprisoned in Israel for telling the truth... and to some 1968 radical who still lived in 1968... he dropped me at Compendium and told me to buy his book about slogans painted on the walls of Paris in 1968.

We passed through the gate to Hampstead Heath, beneath Parliament Hill, and passed the bowling green, the tennis courts, the bandstand, athletic track and swimming pool. We exited the Heath over the railroad tracks and proceeded along Savernake Rd. and down Grafton, passed the City Farm, passed the market street of Queens Crescent, passed 21 Marsden Street, where I stayed with friends for a time, along Prince of Wales Road to Crogland Road, by the Italian Restaurant, the Round House, you know the Ramones, Johan? Up pass the Chalk Farm tube station, and over the bridge to Primrose Hill. We walked through the park along the slanting hill, crossed over the street to the London Zoo, saw the elephants, continued through Regents Park, down the Broad Walk, passed the Open Air Theatre, Shakespeare in the Park, then at Portland Place, entering the traffic of the city now, down Cleveland Street, Newman Street, across horrible Oxford Street, to Dean Street and Soho... then over to the book stores, Dillons, Foyles, Etc Etc... and maybe keep going, through Trafalgar Square, the Strand, Villiers Street, Charing Cross Station, or Embankment Station, and over the Hungerford Walk Bridge, to the South Bank, and all the book stalls in front of the National Theatre. Then back to Charing Cross Road and catch the 43 or 134 or 24 bus back north.

Watch out the *Nautilus* is destroyed and Mr. Aronnax ends up in a fisherman's hut on the Loffoden Islands, north of Norway, in a hut on an island off the coast of Norway, to find consciousness? Ned Land and Conseil holding hands. The Pequod is destroyed and Ishmael is afloat a coffin on the open sea; they have survived to tell the story. Isolatoes... Hamlet holds Horatio's hand in death, draw they breath to tell my story. A single consciousness... a story... *sui generis*. But he who makes a universe unto himself and places himself at the top, rids himself of humanity, begins not at the beginning but with "In the beginning," begins not with space and time, but with "Once upon a Time." The supreme speech act, the story of our forefathers, national identity, discovery, building of nations, myth, I and My Ship, the voyage of expropriation, the accumulation of resources, I and MY Ship are One... This book then, this book is a mutiny!

In 1960 MGM studios built a replica of the ship *HMS Bounty* for its movie *Mutiny on the Bounty* with Marlon Brando. A new *Bounty* built from scratch, seaworthy and constructed just the way it would have been 200 years before, and based on the original ship's drawings that were still on file in the British admiralty archives. After filming, the *Bounty* went on a promotional tour. It was berthed for a short while at Heemskirk's Shipyard in Oyster Bay. I stood on the shore and saw it high in its dock. Is this the same ship? It has the same name. Is this the beginning or another "In the beginning?" Can words ever *be* in the beginning? Can words ever *be* in time and space? Twenty years later I worked briefly as an outside mechanic in that shipyard, and met Saul...

Once upon a time there was an ark; a Viking ship; the *Nina, Pinta and Santa Maria*; the *Pequod*; the *Nautilus*, the *HMS Bounty*; the *Fulda*, the *SS Stavangerfjord*, the steamboat up the Congo River, and the rowboat that George Harbo and Frank Samuelsen rowed across the Atlantic Ocean in 1896. I discovered that during the war my mother took care of Frank in a nursing home in Farsund, Norway. The beginning and the end, space and time, these words: fiction or fact? Accumulation of resources. Is the novelist just a colonizer of the consciousness of another? A smug imperialist of another's story? The boy stood on the shore. The ships sailed into the small bay. Marlow on his steamship in search of Kurtz. Ghost ships. Chasing phantoms... Chasing phantoms... that is what she said. I'm still making sense of that one. A very stinging smack in the face. She who said it was a girlfriend at that time in London, a time when it rained. She was Jewish and from Vienna and her name was Anna. I see her standing in the dark green doorway of the house in Kentish Town, wearing her small round glasses and Isodora Duncan dress. Flowers in her hands, held at her waist. She obviously had stolen them from someone's garden! We had dinner. After dinner we discussed dinosaurs and extinction, the death wish and human mutation; after all, she was a dance-movement psychotherapist! O how romantic! O how structurally semantic! But from Freud and the Void we progressed to schmaltz and the Viennese waltz; like the rainbow over Bloomsbury, ceremonious steeping of Earl Grey tea, the smell of cut grass on Primrose Hill, cuttings of spider plants in jam jars on the windowsill. Finding a flat near Brick Lane Market, at 3am buying bagels of cream cheese and lox, hearing Bengali music and East End accents, buying 100 Jonquil plants in a box for a quid at Columbia Street Market, putting them everywhere in the flat, in the basin, sinks, glasses, cups, pots, and toilet. I got sick from the overpowering scent, but she just said that I didn't appreciate her spontaneous Zen act. Soon we were unable to pay the rent, and love was turning to resentment and hate... and walking aimlessly around Hampstead Heath in the rain, until... until... dancing through a broken circle, a return to the suicidal fin de siècle; the Rothko's at the Tate, the anarchist bookstore in Whitechapel, and art deco lamps, Jews and family and concentration camps. All this talk of this and that... the English language, German, Hebrew, Israel, Palestinians, poetry, Peace Now, Jews in Vienna, the horrors of ballet, her sister was a dancer with the Viennese Stat Ballet, married a Catholic... had good-standing in the society, dyed her hair blonde... and here you have the story of civilization... from the same home comes two very different people. Anna said that her family was like a concentration camp. When I met them they seemed perfectly normal to me... much more "normal" than my family.

Rain falling on scraps of bark in a London park on an autumn day. Stuck in the tube between Camden Town and Chalk Farm, or alone on the top of a double-decker bus, or talk of an IRA bomb, or loss of trust between us... but what has been lost? What has been gained? A few soggy blurred memories of a time when it rained.

Jewish and from Vienna. She used to cry on the underground for no reason. "I don't know why I'm crying... maybe it's my condition..."

"What condition? A postmodern condition?" I asked.

"My condition... Jewish and from Vienna."

"I don't understand," I'd reply. Is this another case of Jewish Metaphysics? Like the time we were fucking, just jabbing away at her and she says, "Where you going?"

"China, I'm fucking my way to China!"

Where are you going? What the hell was that? A smack of Jewish Metaphysics? Will I ever return to America? Will I ever return in body, in flesh, or only in mind, in memory... in memory? My ancestors chose America. Why do I choose exile?

Once Paumanok

Once Paumanok, where my father held my hand as I walked upon the short, squat stone wall, a purgatorial tight-rope strand determined by its slip-knots and root-rot to make me fall... which separates Roosevelt Memorial Public park from the placid bay of gypsy gull and circling shark... to fall into my father's arms, Methodist hymns, work-day psalms and Sunday's social tip-of-the-hat? Or into the hungry high tide, deep and dark, dragging me like an orphaned water rat from my nest in stones split-in-half to a quest on an oar-guided raft? And then I felt my fingers sliding from my father's feckless fish grip, unnerved by him unloosening his belt, though instinctively half-willfully diving, granting myself the privilege to slip over the edge into madness or rebirth, to let myself be healed or hurt.

And then I fell and saw my father's face bloated in whisky and wine, and heard the cord tug and snap from my mother's heart; I sank through the dark part of the dream in the Lotus Eaters' land, protected from the curse of the swine; and then I touched Circe's hand. I emerged; my head surged out of the sea with the sound of a whale's tail's slashing swish, I saw the floating head of John the Baptist; I saw Salome dancing in the island's gray mist, but was I a head without a body? Upon my legs I felt the nibbling fish. The name Ishmael was carved into the driftwood upon which I buoyed myself as best as I could.

I drifted on a timeless expanse of sea; I saw the raven canvas, the cutting prow, the gulls, and the chopping oars; beware, the raven comes! Whither goest thou, Leif Erickson of Norge? I saw the Nina, Pinta, and Santa Maria, the three little caravels of Christoferens, the faith of one faith in the gold of a western isle; whither goest thou, Christoforo Colombo of Italia? They came and they came... my mother was an immigrant. My father was an immigrant's son; what destined that they should re-discover America from the lands of the "discoverers?" And what have I discovered? That 95% of the population of Latin America had been butchered after Anno Domini 1492... that in the last 200 years the great benevolent state of the rule of law, reason, and religion, the most powerful country in the history of the world, has directly and indirectly slaughtered men, women, and children, burnt them, bashed in their skulls, lynched them, disemboweled them, maimed them, mutilated them, confined them, exiled them, shot them, bombed them, napalmed them, cut off their hands, heads, and genitals, raped them, peeled back their flesh, tortured them, destroyed their villages, poisoned their lakes, forests, jungles and fields, all this in the holy name of freedom, freedom of the market place, in the defense of life, liberty and the pursuit of happiness, all this against the "aggression" of the barbarian hordes of native Americans, Africans, Huns, Bolsheviks, Anarchists, Mexicans, Filipinos, Vietnamese, Timorese, Arabs, etc...

O Doom and Happiness! I have been through these United States: In the east, where I stood in the room where Melville wrote Moby-Dick, gazing over Mt. Greylock. In the South, where I stood on the porch of Thomas Wolfe's home, gazing over the far hills. In the West, where I stood on the top of Jeffer's tower, gazing over the Pacific. Gazing inward, gazing outward... chasing phantoms... where are you going, America? Whither goest thou, Poet? My mother was an immigrant from Norway; I can see her on the deck of the ocean liner, the *SS Stavangerfjord,* and I can hear the gull's cry over the North Sea. My father was the son of an immigrant from Italy; I can see my grandfather on the deck of the ship, the *SS Fulda,* and I can hear the gull's cry over the Golfo di Genova. They came and they came... whither goest thou, O immigrant?

Once Paumanok, where I was born in the fifth-month, when the lilac-scent was in the air, and the bright yellow forsythias ablaze, starting from Oyster Bay, where my father worked construction, was a bartender, a ticket collector at the movie theater, a shipyard worker, a bartender again, a furniture mover, a janitor, mopping up shit... and my mother a home-maker, and then a nurse's aide, wiping up shit.

Swinging from the A B and C of an unequilateral triangle, I was thrown from a pendulum onto a navel-island Atlantis, my discovery, where I am self-exiled, standing on the side of the river, gazing toward some far unknown home, like Odysseus on the Isle of Calypso; gazing into the offing at the end of the river, like Marlow going into the heart of darkness. The gulls crying over the Thames.

One day Anna and I were walking along the Thames. And the next day it was just my phantoms and I. We were done. All that and then all that gone. I was reading one of the letters that Anna wrote to me: I thought about your mother. Thank her very much for not minding that I'm Jewish and from Vienna. It never crossed my mind that it would be a problem. But you'll be happy to hear that I don't mind you being Italian Norwegian American. What a combination! One of my favorite plays in school was "Nathan the Wise" by Lessing. You remember the story of the rings? The authentic one has yet to be found. I thought about your Dad, too. And imagined that I could get on with him. He could not resist my charm. I'd talk to him about baseball. He'd have to explain the rules first. Is it similar to cricket? I remember some cartoons with Charlie Brown standing desperately alone on a hill, while Snoopy races around like a meshuggener, and Lucy smiles maliciously.

I sat on the train leaving Victoria Station and closed my eyes. The sun through the trees flared on my eyelids like an ariel bombardment at night. Red flashes over the smoky saintly dome of my vision to some other place. Goodbye London, goodbye to all that, is it any better with Balzac? Or where Beethoven hung his hat? We are crossing the channel, crossing the bar... give Tennyson's eyes a rub; he must have meant a pub. Loud are the football hooligans on the ferry, and their wives in tight jeans, see them pushing their prams, side by side, high heels clickity-clack, clickity-clack down in Bethnal Green. Oi look at the bum on that bird in black. Oh Tom O Bedlam, me lovely 'ooligan, return to me.

We lived for a while in a flat in Bethell Green, near Brick Lane, lived through so many disasters, both personal and social. She wanted to move there. She wanted to experience the place where many Jews had once lived. The area was just beginning to change. There were some renovations of older buildings. She found a flat that was near St. Matthews Church and a primary school. The area had an interesting history. I walked a lot, as usual. I walked down to White Chapel and over to Stepney Green. I went to the White Chapel Gallery and an anarchist bookstore down a nearby alley. Johan would come with me on some of my more radical walks. But Love and Revolution were not in the air. Unless you want to refer to Thatcher and Reagan's Love and Revolution.

It was a private disaster. Our love as tragedy and farce. And during our time together there were public disasters. There was the ferry that topsized, the *Herald of Free Enterprise,* what a name! There was the Hungerford Massacre. There was the Great Storm of 1987. There was the Kings Cross Station fire. I had passed through that station earlier on that day, on the Northern Line. And there was the Lockabee crash the following year.

There was the time that I went with Anna to Vienna. We took the ferry and then the train. All night the train rumbled on through Belgium and then Germany, we stopped at the big station in Düsseldorf, where trench-coated men, like in the movie *Von Ryan's Express,* you know where Sinatra is running out of the tunnel trying to reach the moving train, but the Nazis shoot him and he falls on the tracks. They knocked on our compartment door and asked... passport, *bitte, danke.* It reminded me of a story that some Jew in New York told me about his grandmother who lived in Germany during the war. She survived and moved to New York... but if anyone visited her she always left the door ajar; she just could not stand to hear someone knock loudly on the door because that would make her recall the chilling effect on her in her youth when they came and banged on the door.

It was Christmas, 1987. She was miserable most of the time. Of course she was, she was visiting her family. We were looking through each other's eyes, and neither of us could see anything fresh and new. She thought that I would bring the old city back to life for her. But why? She told me many times that she hated the place. She left it at age eighteen to go live in Israel. There she married a Jewish Prince. He entered the Army and was converted to a typical hard-line Israeli soldier, "completely changed," was how she put it, and the marriage disintegrated. Then she lived openly with a Palestinian in Haifa, who later accompanied her to London. That's where I came into her story. Or she into mine. Or us into nowhere.

There are many phantoms in Vienna, but the phantom of Beethoven is everywhere. The city, the woods, the Danube. One day I took a walk in a park near her parent's apartment. Beethoven's 7th Symphony echoing in my mind. That great First Movement like some great majestic sea shanty. It was a Sunday afternoon, a Sunday afternoon in the Augarten, a place where Ludwig Von Beethoven raised his baton and struck the notes of alarm: Bomb Bomb Bomb Bomb. A time when Napoleon grazed upon the rotten fields of Europe and stacked corpses of hay in preparation for the bloody summer of burning Dresden: Burn Burn Burn Burn. And destroyed life less than language (tortured but still more resilient) on the indigestible borders where oppressive worlds collide; for there is always time enough to die, time enough to lie, time enough to cut off the rhyme; but never language enough to listen to the music as when Mozart raised his baton to the sky and stabbed the Nazi heart as if they (could they really hear it!) heard the warped melody above the human agony... but did culture drown in a blood bath of senseless noise? The loudness of the sounds and the words was mobilized into a nationalist symphony in which Caesar and Hitler pounded the tympani; the Berlin music halls were filled with pale echoes and crass banalities; the curly girls and burly boys put their hands over their ears and goose-stepped to their mother's cheers. Beethoven went deaf. He heard the holy clef distort his fears into a twisting wild rhythm. Poetry went silent. My poetry went silent. *Warf ich mich Steinen zu.* Sound became violent. Morality and Beauty took separate baths, both filthy, with form and content evacuated from dark bowels, like a house without structure, a home without compassion. A mind without reason.

Vienna is a clean city; there are suds of soap in her shaved armpits. Whose soap? There are suds of soap where all the bombs hit. Soap pours over the walls of the German anti-aircraft bunkers in the Augarten. Vienna's genius was washed away with blood and exile and soap. My landlord Stanislaw, a Polish artist living in London, told me that somewhere in a field in Europe there were children swinging from a dead body hanging from a rope.

"In ze last hours of ze war zey killed," Anna's father told me. "In ze bunkers zey killed."

Somewhere in a field near Hiroshima there were children swinging from a rope hanging from a tree. In the first hours of an August morning a power is willed against reason to slaughter all hope and meaning.

Sunday afternoon in the Augarten, I walk and stare (is everyone else unaware?) at the terrible presence of these massive structures, the anti-aircraft bunkers. The old couples walk arm in arm through the garden, between the beds of marigolds, begonias, and fuchsias. The children fly kites, knock chestnuts from trees, happy dogs run, and old men play chess on cement benches covered with leaves. Could so much old world charm cause any harm? As much as an atomic bomb? Near the bunkers they play American basketball; ironic display of cultural power... and other kinds of power, as the pigeons flutter up to the concrete tower; from high above it must look just like a flower with its rounded platforms projecting like petals with no dream of earth upon which to settle. They (the local government) say that they (the bunkers) are indestructible and can never be demolished. The bunkers stand like a symbol of something intangible and unarrangeable: the darkness of the heart? Or maybe it's the government that should be abolished. But we believe that there is another side, like in that play of Sartre, wherein the people stumble against a wall with a window filled with an infinite blue; the people look; but never pass through.

Emperor Josef II opened the Augarten for the people of Vienna "as a place dedicated to the enjoyment of all men." Ah but some bones were only stones, some blood was only soap and mud, some humans were only biblical ruins, and some men, women and children were not human... they were only Jews.

One more thing. About Anna. About hands and nails. A Greco-Roman thought. A wrestle with the ragged one, the outcast, dark-diver. A Judeo-Christian thought. A crucifixion. A meditation at Christmas. A Christmas in Vienna. A week in December. Seven windy days and blue icy nights; not the heroic weather of the North where Odin hung from a tree, nailed through the palms, proving his vulnerability, proving that symmetry is predictability; nor the tempestuous weather of the South where Prometheus was bound to a rock, nailed through the palms, with the iron-age addition of chain and lock, and exposed for the new gods to mock. But I sense a strange weather in this city of beautiful gold and gray, where for seven windy days and blue icy nights a bright star has strayed from its majestic height and has fallen over a sunny African Bethlehem; has fallen into the small hand of a child who has never smiled but has continuously cried... then one day he died. If it's the hand of a child... nail it to a cross! Oh Christ in the cradle had such little hands, kissed by his mother and licked by the lambs.

There are impressions of human hands in the caves of southern France, made before the sandals of Christ were laced, made before the mythical moon was chased. What do they beseech? To what do they aspire? They appear to reach from out of a fire. They are like time-frozen hands nailed to the wall; they seem to say: We fell; and you too will fall. Or whoever made these marks in the deep of the dark, did he actually mean to say that he was against the powers that be, that there is something beyond all orthodoxy. O hands of Spinoza, hands of Bruno, hands of Copernicus, hands of Galileo. If it's the hand of a heretic... nail it to a cross! Oh Christ in the cradle had such little hands, kissed by his mother and licked by the lambs.

Vienna couldn't hold her in its arms, these arms that had embraced Hitler before she was born. Well... if not embraced, held out a hand. If it's the hand of a Jew... nail it to a cross! Oh Christ in the cradle had such little hands, kissed by his mother and licked by the lambs.

Putrid lingering smoke of corpses and bombs rings a spiral through skulls where history is traced by the chaotic pattern of swarming gulls over the rubbish dump of time where the flesh and the fossils of the future are left behind like bones fallen from a mind. How tedious is this rhyme. How can these things rhyme? The dogs of guilt and hate pick the bones of memory clean, but still the dogs growl and still the gulls scream. The guardians of society and state sweep the streets of rubble clear, they poke their brooms in the corner where a child cowers in fear. When the child became a woman she broke loose from their grip, and in her anger and rage she clenched her fist and left blood on her wrist. She would strip away both culture and language and wander into the welcoming hand of the Promised Land; O Israel! O Zion! If it's the hand of a Palestinian... nail it to a cross! Oh Christ in the cradle had such little hands, kissed by his mother and licked by the lambs.

The victim becomes the victimizer; rivers of blood flow on from the Danube to the Nile, and we are none the wiser when the flame sings *heilig and heil!* Then one day I met her by the Thames river; Boadicea had come down from the hills to stand by Cleopatra's obelisk among the sterility and infertility of the world's ills and pronounce disgust from cynical lips: all is *kitsch... fichs...*

The English reluctantly offer their hand to friend or foreigner; it wasn't always so in the days of imperial splendor. The deceitful hand went out first; it grabbed and squeezed with Empire hunger and material thirst. In the sweatshop slum of the East End of London, industrial and economic oppression splits the jewel into scattered remnants, who work their hands like their ghetto descendants. If it's the hand of an immigrant... nail it to a cross! Oh Christ in the cradle had such little hands, kissed by his mother and licked by the lambs.

They say that poets go about with an open mouth; that our hands are always sticking out. "You take and take and never give!" Oh what does it take just to live? I am in a cold sweat; my hands shake. O hands of Van Gogh, hands of Blake, hands of Rimbaud tied to a stake. If it's the hand of an artist... nail it to a cross! Oh Christ in the cradle had such little hands, kissed by his mother and licked by the lambs.

Though lovers still hold hands in this century of uncertainty and mass destruction and machine force, even lovers nail each other to a cross! Oh Christ in the cradle had such little hands, kissed by his mother and licked by the lambs.

Goodbye Anna. Goodbye Vienna. I have to move on. I board the bus in Bethnal Green, the number 8 bus to Oxford Street. Every day he travels to and fro, he's not lost, there's just no place to go, for Henry Jones. Oh Henry Jones. Goodbye 'enry. Your Yank mate is leaving. America? Nah, just up to Archway... North London. Henry thought that that sounded a thousand miles away. Henry was blind as a bat. Every day he rode the number 8 bus, and at every stop he loudly described the area, the buildings, the shops, the pubs, and no one had the heart to tell him that that building or that that shop or that that pub was no longer where it use to be.

The last time that I saw Anna was at the South Bank. I had got tickets for a production of Beckett's *Waiting for Godot*. We met at the National Theatre. We had already broken up. I had moved out of the flat in Bethnal Green, and left her to pay the rent and see her intrusive psychotherapy patients without my presence behind the bedroom door. I just couldn't write and listen to all that shit at the same time! All that psycho-Freudian angst and neuroticism... no, not for my novel!

Oh the unintentional genius of the absurd (or, waiting for the Northern Line). When the common icons lack eye contact and the familiar images, the buildings, the buses, the bridges, which I tended to believe were real, are revealed from the city like a pre-posted, post-posted bill, corners shredded in the marketing mill, stuck and suspended on the Underground wall, like a black abstract nude, waiting to be fashionably dressed, waiting to be sensorially caressed, posing for gawkers and gapers, and you're becoming unglued, aren't you? From so many post-modern signs, with nothing revealed between the lines, not a wit of a Wittgenstein, not the marks of a dialectic, just boldly stamped significantly on black paper, in mechanical stenciled white letters, saying, not-saying:

THIS SPACE RESERVED FOR SAMUEL BECKETT

Let us go... yes, let's go... *allons-y*...

One day I was in a bookstore on Charing Cross Road and bumped into an old acquaintance from New York. His name was John. I think the bookstore was Foyles. It was easy to steal books from Foyles. I think that's why we were both there at the time. There was a side door with nobody around and it was nothing to slip out if you had the nerve. John was a writer who has lived in Paris since 1979. I had met John in Bay Ridge because his older brother went to school with Tommy. They were good friends at Fort Hamilton High School and they both enlisted in the army when they got out of school. But John's older brother, James, didn't make it back. He was killed in Vietnam in 1969. I went to a park one day with Tommy, and John was there smoking grass. That's how I met him. Tommy and John didn't talk about James at all, but I talked with John and found out that he was a writer, and we hung out together for a while, going to concerts and stuff... John was writing poetry at the time. We both laughed when we acknowledged that it was difficult for working class kids brought up on rock music to try to write poetry, because every time we started writing words on the paper some damn rock tune came into our heads and we found the song was pushing the words. I think I wrote ten poems to the tune of Dylan's "Tangled Up in Blue," said John. Tommy and I saw John off at the airport when he left for Europe.

Johan didn't like Anna, the life-long student, avoiding real work, Johan prodded her. Then what was I? You are a writer, not a pretentious intellectual Jew and phony dance-movement psychotherapist! Nonsense! Nonsense! Johan got quite worked up about it. Well, his father was a Nazi officer. They almost came to blows one day when he called her "a typical intellectual Jew." This really upset her. Anna cried all day.

But then I met Isabelle. Johan approved of Isabelle and Isabelle liked Johan. I met her… she was studying English and was soon to return to France to study at the Sorbonne. She was going to study philosophy and sociology; she talked about Bourdieu, Derrida, Foucault.

We sat at a table in a high-ceilinged café near Piccadilly Circus. Isabelle sat on my right and Johan and John sat on my left. I introduced John to them… John spoke in French with Isabelle… and he told her that he lived in Paris and was a writer. Isabelle's friends, two of her students, sat across from us. She was teaching them French; it was part of the London café culture, hundreds of students teaching each other different languages for a few quid, mainly English, Japanese, Spanish, French, German, in varying directions of this to that. One of her students was an Italian, not an actual student, but a businessman of some sort who needed to learn French for some professional reason I assumed. He was dressed very Italian, very sharp, with a suit and tie and mauve scarf. He was very full of himself. I had the papers from the trunk with me. I got Isabelle to invite me along and meet up after her lesson was over so that the Italian whose name was Giorgio might try to translate the scrawl on the old yellow paper.

Johan had been very restless for a while and was drinking heavily. He had no desire to return to Norway. But he was going to have trouble staying in London. I had been staying on tourist visas that lasted six months and then I would leave the country and return. One time I was kept for six hours at Heathrow Airport as they ransacked my suitcase, and read all my papers and letters. They discovered my affair with Anna. They would let me in if I'd promise to leave the country together with Anna. She did not want to leave and that was the beginning of our problems. At one point during my time in London I got lucky when the passport amnesty was going on and tons of passports were being sent to the Home Office to be processed. I sent mine in, asking for an extension. It didn't come back for a year. I couldn't leave the country without my passport but at the time I didn't want to leave anyway. When my passport was returned I had been given a three-month extension and it declared quite politely that I had to leave at that point. I had managed to stay in England for nearly twenty-one months on a tourist visa, including the six months before I sent my passport in and the three months after it was returned. Isabelle and I decided that we would go to Paris then, something I had been hoping to do for a while. She had to return anyway to start school. I had taken a brief excursion to Paris with Isabelle but this would be something different, perhaps something permanent. Oui, we will live in a garret over a bookstore and bakery... oh what fools these mortals be...

The other student whom I met that day was an American, a real snot-faced American from one of the Ivy League schools, I think Yale, I don't remember, talking all kinds of academic rubbish, something about Lacan, and how he was reading Proust in French and had discovered that a pale light was leading him through the book, some abstract, Platonic notion of something or other. And Isabelle was helping him! He was a pedantic bore. I asked him when the light first appeared to him. Did it appear on page 7? Or did it appear on page 156? Did it appear in the first book? The third? He was visibly annoyed with my line of questioning, so I stopped.

Finally I got my chance to interrupt and presented the old yellow papers to Giorgio and asked if he would not mind trying to translate it. He looked them over and said that it was written in a very formal and old Italian, probably from around Genoa, the Liguria region. I told him that that was correct because my family had come from that area in Italy. He tried to translate it but some of it was faded and illegible.

Giorgio translated: I write the truth. My name is Maurizio Cazzaza.

That's my grandfather's brother, I interjected.

My name is Maurizio Cazzaza from Orero, Italy and now living in New York, America. He says that this is his confession, but that he is not guilty, not in the eyes of the God because God has no eyes and doesn't exist. I know that this will upset you... he says this to Teresa... the letter seems to be addressed to a Teresa.

Yes, that was my grandfather's wife's sister... it gets confusing...

I think that perhaps that they were in love.

My mother told me that there were rumors about that. But that it was my grandfather that Teresa was in love with and not Maurizio.

That may be true. See, he says, that he knew that she could never be his; he says that very properly, formally, in his Italian. It is a very humble form. So he says that he is guilty of many crimes against man. But that they were bad men. And not the Catholic Church or the American authorities would understand. They were corrupt and powerful. He is only guilty of bad faith, he says. Of not being true to his ideals. That he may have caused his brother's death and will she, Teresa, ever forgive him for that? She must forgive him or he cannot live anymore. Life is cruel. Fate is absurd. He sounds very modern. He says that he killed a bad man in Italy, with his comrades, using dynamite. He says that he is an anarchist but that his brother never knew about this, and his family never knew, and that you, Teresa, did not know, but now he must tell her. He says that he is ashamed that he hid his true self and beliefs out of a family love and loyalty to his brother who always helped him and believed in him. He was weak and preferred the security of his brother's home, and that he loves you, her, Teresa, and he says that after she reads this letter she should destroy it, burn it... for he will be in prison for the rest of his life or murdered just like Sacco and Vanzetti was murdered by the state...

I knew that there was some kind of incident in the family and that my grandfather had been shot by police at a picnic but I had no idea about any of this. Teresa must have put the letter in the safe deposit box. And somehow the letter got into the trunk. I had to explain to them about the safe deposit box that was opened years after Teresa was committed to Kings Park Mental Institution for the rest of her life. She was committed in 1927. She died in 1977, so she was in there for fifty years and my father said that no one talked about her or ever visited her. And I remember my father went to her funeral. The funeral parlor director said that she had all her teeth and that they were still white. Odd thing to say. After they opened the safety deposit box, you know they thought they were going to find money, because I always heard the rumor that she was burning money and that's why she was put away. There was no money. But somehow she must have put the letter into the hidden compartment in the trunk and then my mother took it with her to Norway. And with the gun in the secret compartment in the trunk also. And now the papers are here in London. It's quite a crazy story. It's like chaos theory, said the American student. But we cut him off. Giorgio said he was a *tuttologo*... I'm not sure what the word means, something like a know-it-all, but he said it with a disdainful bite of the lip.

All this talk was getting to Johan. He was acting restless and disturbed by something. He spurted out: weak... weak... and he pulled out a gun from his coat pocket. Everyone flinched. Don't worry I won't shoot you, said Johan. I immediately recognized that it was the Beretta, the gun from the trunk. See, not just the papers but also the gun is here in London too! Suddenly Johan got up and ran out of the café. Isabelle and I chased after him. He was running toward Trafalgar Square. We saw him in the crowd. He fired a shot at one of the large stone lions at the base of the monument. The shot had hit one of the lion's ears and broke it off. My God, the gun still worked! Yes, Isabelle, but I should have removed the bullets. People screamed and fled. Pigeons flew up in a noisy explosion of air and wings and pigeon shit and peanut shell dust. Then police sirens. Johan was gone. We couldn't find him. We looked all over for him. We didn't go inside St Martins, or the National Gallery, we didn't think he would hide inside. But where did he go? About an hour later Isabelle and I were walking up Tottenham Court Road; we had lost hope of finding him, when all of a sudden the back doors of a police van flew open and out shot Johan flying as fast as he could on his short legs and he ran down an alley with two bobbies in hot pursuit.

A few days later we were amazed to receive a phone call from Johan. He told us that he was in Paris, and that we should meet as we had planned. He wanted to meet by the Eiffel Tower for some reason.

After Isabelle and I got all our stuff in order and everything sorted out we left on a bus from Victoria Station that took us to Dover, where we boarded the hovercraft to Calais, and then we took the bus to Paris with a strange stop at a deserted Paris Disneyland for some reason.

Johan told us that he had tossed the gun down a drain in London. It reminded me of the gun that I had found years ago and threw down a drain. It made me wonder which gun, the Berreta or the gun from Oyster Bay, had caused more death and bloodshed over the years.

We were together on the second platform of the Eiffel Tower. Johan was looking over the railing to a platform below us. On the ledge beneath the railing he saw a few cigarette butts and some ashes and dust and dirt, and then he saw a faded empty box of Marlboro cigarettes, the red color on the box faded to pale yellow. How does it not blow away? asked Johan.

What? asked Isabelle

A box of cigarettes on the ledge, answered Johan.

Johan started to climb over the rail.

No, I shouted, just leave it there. I thought he was trying to grab the cigarette box. But he turned around and looked into my eyes. I am very unhappy, Stephen, very unhappy. Thank you for everything. But... *tusen takk skal du har...* he let go and jumped over the railing and tumbled and fell. His body drifted backward and he disappeared. Isabelle screamed. We ran up to the railing but could not see his small body smash against the steel girders of the lower pavilion. We heard shouts and screams from below. I grabbed Isabelle by the hand and said, Let's go... *allons-y...*

Johan's body landed by the edge of a small pond behind some trees.

I told Isabelle to leave. I didn't want her to appear involved. It may cause trouble with family and school. I will talk to the police and try to explain if I am approached, if anyone had noticed that we were with Johan. Otherwise, I will say nothing.

A few weeks later I was in a blue bed in a blue room on the rue Guisarde in Paris. When I awoke, Isabelle was gone. It was before dawn. Still dark. It was autumn. John Coltrane's *Love Supreme* was playing on the cassette player. Isabelle's navy blue corduroys were slung over the arm of a chair. I picked up the Kleenex stained with our mingled body fluids and dropped it in the trashcan. Where has she gone now? We had argued. I walked over to the window. Words steamed up from the streets. Outside the window were four grey cracked walls. Looking down where you would expect a courtyard there was only the roof of the ground floor café. Looking up toward the front of the building I saw in the blue sky the top of one of the round mismatched steeples of the church of Saint-Sulpice. The dim lights of the city glistened on the window. My breath fogged the windowpane. It was chilly out. I walked down the five flights of stairs. The walls were a makeshift of wood, tiles of various shapes, plaster, brick, stone, in a building from the late seventeenth century. I went out into the street at break of day. The air bites with sharp attention. I walked down rue Princesse to the English language bookstore, Village Voice Bookshop, but it wasn't open yet of course. I walked back toward the flat but decided to keep walking. Around a corner from our flat I saw Isabelle through the window of a café on the rue Bonaparte. She was sitting by herself in the corner, drinking coffee, smoking. I didn't bother to go in. I didn't want to bother her. Isabelle. That the trees were sad and bare I had no doubt. One look in her eyes told me it was so. In spring we felt the fisted-buds of trees punch their leaves into the sky and open small hands to catch the rain. The rain that sparkled on the streets of Paris. I spent the last day of my wisdom widening these skies with her eyes. My hand passed through the lost sight of Homer, in a majestic beat of night solemnities, a voyage veiled in secrecy, and she moved these words across the page, and when I read these words to her I saw in sadness all the roofs of Paris blinking at me. One look in her eyes told me it was so. Can you not love another instead? Solitude is for a sufferer. Has she not had enough of me? The melancholy of remembering the act of love's awakening, in the story of our senses, without verbs trapped behind tenses, without nouns trapped behind fences. *Au revoir.* I walked on with no destination in mind. I bought a baguette and a bottle of red wine. I crossed the bridge and walked along the Seine. Before I reached the Place de la Concorde I cut into the gardens of the Tuileries. I was tired and cold. I found a quiet niche between the legs of a female statue and waited for the blue dawn to appear over Paris like a silk negligee slips off her lightly and dreamily. How did Henry Miller stay merry and bright when I feel it's all been a big fucking mistake... a great big fucking mistake... this can't really be me... a working-class boy with a peasant pedigree, a father who was a bartender and a janitor, a mother who was a nurse's aide, and I am pretending to be a writer. I'm not the first, but I still can't get passed the idea. I am not in Paris... I must still be back in America... and everything is as it should have been...

...When I was ten years old and sitting in a tree house that my friends and I had discovered by sneaking into the woods around one of the large estates of Oyster Bay Cove, which we ventured onto despite the No Trespassing signs, the boy that I should have been was back home with my father, playing catch, the plastic baseball bouncing off my roly-poly tummy as I belatedly clapped my hands together in the air trying to catch the ball and then shouting: again, again. Fetching it and throwing it wildly backward and chasing it down once more, my father urging me on. It was the summer of 1964... and my father was inadvertently molding an ideal

American citizen, not an over-achiever, not a straight A student, not a valedictorian bidding farewell, but the heroic hometown boy, the one who stays put and keeps the lawn cut, gets a bank loan for a car and house, marries the blond cheerleader with the nice tits, has a few beers with the boys in the local bar after blue collar work, and keeps the barbecue burning and the flag flying on the Fourth of July. Or throws the ball over his father's head so he jumps up and cuts his back and curses and goes inside and never plays catch again... so to the tree house...

When I was standing before Judge Amberstein in Family Court, with tears streaming down my face and my stomach knotted, the Judge saying, "There won't be any free trips to the icebox anytime you want a glass of milk anymore," the boy that I should have been was saying to my father, "Can we go home now. I want to watch *Yankee Doodle Dandy* on channel 9..." but I was sent away to some private institution in upstate New York, The Cayuga Home for Boys and Girls. The boy that I should have been went home to watch James Cagney sing "Give My Regards to Broadway."

When I was in California, having crisscrossed the country in search of poet's homes and poetic places, the boy that I should have been was back home, reading the sports section of the *New York Daily News,* and discussing yesterday's game between the Mets and Cubs with my father.

When I was in Mexico with Umberto, searching for treasure along the Rio Grande, the boy that I should have been wrote a letter to himself as if it were to an imaginary older brother. In the letter my brother proclaimed his attainment of some beloved basic American freedoms. "Shit man, I smoked my first joint. It was killer, and guess what, I've been laid. Do you remember Cindy? Yeah, the cheerleader with the nice tits. I think we'll get married one day." But these were only minor preliminaries on the road to the American Dream. Not long afterward my brother wrote again: "I got my driver's license!" Now he was truly prepared to discover the New World, and to follow the dollar-logic of free enterprise: Step One: buy a Chevrolet. Step Two: Buy a Pontiac. Step Three: Buy a Buick. Step Four: Buy a Cadillac. Progress according to General Motors.

When I was living in the woods of North Carolina, the boy that I should have been was back home on Long Island scoring touchdowns and scoring with girls on cool autumn Saturday afternoons for my High School football team in the town where I grew up.

When I was staying on an island off the coast of Norway, the boy that I should have been was still back home, this time hitting home runs for the Old Homestead Bar and Grill softball team in Theodore Roosevelt Memorial Park; and across the railroad tracks and the parking lot, where the fire department held the New York State Tournament in the summer of 1966 (The boy that I should have been was a volunteer fireman), was the playing field where the previous summer I had been hitting home runs for the high school baseball team, watched by a small crowd of students and my girlfriend. And the brass eagle on top of the flag pole shined over the field where my father had many times marked the lines with a chalk machine and raised the flag in the morning in the same field where years before he had played for the high school football team, until he was kicked off for eating apples during a practice session. My father had been a construction worker, bartender, shipyard worker, furniture mover, movie theater usher, and for twenty years until he retired and collected his pension and Social Security, an elementary school custodian. He never saved a dime in his life. He collected plenty of mom-inspired debt. When the eagle shit he headed straight for the bar. He paid the bills (the main ones, sometimes not even those), bought food, and was broke again, a week or two short of the next payday. So he borrowed 20 bucks here and 20 bucks there. And every morning he diligently raised the flag to the eagle's ass; but not when he worked the night shift, when he had to clean the shit bowls, as he called them with no betrayal of shame. There was one redeeming feature to working the night shift: I had the run of the school. I went with my father every once in a while and while my father cleaned and mopped and swept and emptied and waxed and put away, I entered the class rooms, entered the private domain of the teacher's lounge, the principal's office, entered all those restricted places and snooped through desks and closets, and I collected paper clips and paper and No. 2 pencils. Oh how I loved the supply room! And then I'd shoot some baskets in the gym until my father was finished mopping the hall floors and then we'd play 21 together.

When I was living in London, the boy that I should have been was getting married to his high school sweetheart, and my uncle Frankie got me a "good job" working for the Town of Oyster Bay (provided that I register as a Republican). This is the town where Eisenhower was paraded through the streets in the fifties, and where Nixon came to visit Theodore

Roosevelt's home at Sagamore Hill, after his near impeachment, though with less fanfare than that accorded to General Eisenhower, the war hero, or to Theodore Roosevelt, the fat Dutch squire of that big creepy house on the hill, with bear skins and elephant tusks that have frightened hordes of school children over the years, including me, on pilgrimages to pay homage to the bogus hero of San Juan Hill.

When I was in Vienna, the boy that I should have been and my wife were having our first baby. We were so happy when we went to the supermarket together and we pushed little Joey up and down the aisles in the shopping cart and my wife plucked the cellophane wrapped bread and chop meat and ketchup from the shelves and don't forget the six pack of Bud, I'd say, and everyone smiled and said Oh what a lovely couple, have a nice day. Go home, sit on the couch, and watch the Met's game.

When I was in Paris the boy that I should have been was taking out a mortgage on my first home, with a white picket fence, and a flagpole, back home in the town where I was born...

I am in Paris today. I break off some bread and take a swig from the bottle of red wine. I am dead. I am alive. I drink from the bottle of red wine. I am dead. I break off some bread and eat it. I am dead. I drink from the bottle of red wine. I sit under the nakedness of this statue; I am wet and pink, a little squirming thing, falling asleep... I don't want to wake up... it's just a dream...

Today we are sitting at a café on Boulevard Saint-Germain, looking at this existential bricolage, reading all those French writers, and Isabelle is sitting next to me. And she invited John to join us. I already knew.

We spotted a red-haired man coming out of a café, going to the metro, thinking of rain; another man went, going back to a hotel in the rain. Nothing will be done. Something should be done? Yet if tomorrow comes... shall we say: Do you remember what we did? What could bewray the meaning of how we lived? The wisdom of our choosings. The foolishness of our ruserings. Nothing new under the sun, the wretchedness hath not been undone. Expose thyself! Though heaven must; then who shall be just? Is that Sartre I see? Is that de Beauvoir I see? Is that Camus I see? It's a little game we play to amuse ourselves. Isabelle says, Look, there is Mitterrand going into the Brasserie Lipp... it really was... what excess of pelf, O humanity? What excess of dearth do you crave? What excess of vanity? All is vanity... am I a slave to determinism? Shall I always be blind to your ways? Prison within prison. The dungeon of the self. This is surely the end of all my days. Self-violence? Let me put a riddle to you... this is the night. Sudden panic and fear. Is that Lautréamont that I see... perhaps he has in his mind a phenomenological description of the good... to counter the evil that he invoked... is that Jarry that I see? Merdre! A *New Directions* black and white book... Rimbaud up in flames... just words on the page... death after death in life. As we hie to our confinement... the pulp of this fruit is a bit stale. These formulas are bound to fail. We wait and we wait. Is that Beckett that I see? Still the innocent die. *Je ne veux pas.* Again and again we come... happy and sad places. Autumnal faces smile again. I rise to the wind. Return to the land. Is that Rimbaud and Verlaine that I see? Where? *Où?* Asks Isabelle. There! A seed drifting far. *Au sol. Aux barricades!* Faithless stars. Soft now. Do it. The leaves on the trees. The rose in the hair. It grew there. She threw it upon the sea. Is that James Joyce that I see? From an island. Falling. It still clings. A root. Yes. The lark at the gate sings. In her mouth an olive leaf. She came. Rain falling on her face. In Paris... so brief. Enjoy the fortuitous mixture of the atom's leisure. There will come no pain, nothingness, the highest pleasure. Greece. I think I'll go to Greece next, or Tangiers... death is nothing to us. We are. We are not. Miserable minds trembling in fear. Let it concern you not a jot. We wait and wait... we are free. From ills. Death is a vile burden. Live wisely, well. Behind the silence of these walls of stone. Soon we shall be like stone. A few measly bones. We shall be stone. She knows that I am leaving... to Greece? To Africa? To Asia? She says nothing. What is there to say? O little brother, are you asleep? O little angel, I am the wonder child, the great Rimbaud, magician of words, tramping the roads with rocks in my pockets and a stone in my slingshot to shoot all poets and angels dead. I have to leave... farewell to Isabelle. Take care of her, John. I need to get away... to part for a while... a tale of separation... O Paris... roll the stone away... and let me rise... Greece? Tangier? I am going away with the wind to where the hemispheres are hinged. I always wanted to go to Japan... I always liked the Japanese writers and French writers the best... did I ever mention that to you? I can chase more phantoms... do you like clichés? Maybe I'll open an American Café in Tokyo... you can visit... international intrigue... isn't it romantic? I hear the wind blowing the rain across the earth and against the window that frames her face. One look in her eyes told him it was so...

Japan

Call me a Dekunobo! The pig wins! Tasted delicious!

Kappa picked me up at Narita Airport in his yellow Volkswagen beetle and we went driving around Tokyo and then Yokohama and finally into Kawasaki... all this endless nondescript signage was like some crazy unlimited semiosis, reflecting back upon itself into millions of mirrors where neon bulbs flashed and momentarily blinded. This was an open city... a city that appeared limitless, but as I would eventually discover, there was just so much to be said about anything, and the inexhaustible ping-ponging of signs had to be abandoned at the point of exhaustion, paradoxically at the moment the structure is just complete enough to enter with careful steps, and exit out into the pale light of a Saturday afternoon, and take those final steps back out into the world, where something has changed... but what has changed? Only more signs pointing at other signs, targets for arrows, false blank space for words, so I'll just say as Bogart as Rick said, We'll always have Paris.... and now we have Tokyo...

Kappa and I met in London. He became one of Isabelle's students. We got along famously, as Kappa liked to say, and had much in common, not least of which was a morbid curiosity to visit old graveyards and chase the phantoms of writers long dead. London provided ample opportunity for phantom chasing, down its many narrow streets and lanes, blue plaques itemizing names and dates. Not as impressive as Paris, but enough. Our initial phantom chasing encounter was at Karl Marx's tomb in Highgate Cemetery, our chance meeting occurring after we just out of curiosity had followed a group of "revolutionaries," whose origins was perhaps a country in South America or Central America, so we assumed, from a pub in Archway up the hill to Waterlow Park and then down to Highgate Cemetery. The group carried a red flag and some pamphlets and books, and their leader made a flamboyant and fiery speech in front of old Karl's overbearing countenance, in English. I observed from a distance, and Kappa stepped out from behind a tombstone like a wood sprite and stood next to me. I was curious to find out about the group, but... were they members of the notorious Shining Path? Just bandits and drug smugglers, said Kappa. I discovered that Kappa was a discerning and critical anarchist. Let's not disturb them. Later we had coffee at a café on Delancey Street in Camden Town, across the street a blue plaque reminded us that Dylan Thomas had lived here. Kappa told me that his real name was Masahiro, and that Kappa was a cruel childhood nickname, from an old Japanese folk tale about a mythical turtle. His fellow school children thought he looked like a Kappa. Later that day at the British Museum, Kappa and I came upon the "revolutionaries" that we had seen at Marx's gravesite. Their leader was now speaking English with a pronounced East End accent. They were in fact a troupe of actors rousing themselves for an upcoming performance of Bertolt Brecht's play *Saint Joan of the Stockyards*.

It was early Saturday evening and Kappa and I were returning home from the supermarket with three bottles of sake, four six-packs of Asahi beer, dried salted squid, and a bag full of assorted rice crackers. A man selling fried eel on the street called out. Kappa waved (he never bowed his head for anyone) and continued walking down the middle of the narrow street. There were no sidewalks and only a few small cars drove passed us. Plastic flowers hung from concrete electrical poles and pinging-panging music blared from speakers placed high on these poles. At the only busy intersection in town, music emitted from tin speakers played "Coming Through the Rye" when pedestrians were notified that it was safe to cross the street. When a body meets a body, crossing the busy street. There was much mischief here.

There is a popular Buddhist temple, Heikenji, in this small town of Kawasaki Daishi; the town takes its name from the temple and its ancient monk, Priest Kukai, informally known as Kobo Daishi. The town lies on the outskirts of Kawasaki, the large sprawling industrial working-class city mislaid between the more fashionable cities of Tokyo and Yokohama, and one of the streets leading from the Kawasaki Daishi train station to Heikenji is lined with shops selling sweets and souvenirs. Such streets are common in towns with an ancient temple. Kappa and I were not walking down this street. We were walking down the other street that branched out from the train station, the street bounded by the insufferably noisy and brightly lighted pachinko parlor on the left and the pool hall on the right. Residents this way, tourists the other way. Most of the year the tourists were relatively few; mainly Japanese who attended the special ceremonies to "ward off evil" in Yakudoshi years (Yaku means misfortune of all kinds); those dangerous years are the ages of 25 and 42 for men, and 19 and 33 for women. These are culturally specific it must be assumed. I just happened to be 33 years old, and Kappa 42 years old. It's a sign? Other tourists arrived in cars and stopped at the drive-through Buddhist blessing temple in the parking lot, in front of the Prayer Hall for Safe Traffic. You can pull up your Toyota, rain or shine, and for 3000 yen receive a blessing, good for one year. The monks don't do car washes. Foreign tourists, mainly American military personnel, inundated the small town during a fertility festival, the Kanamara Matsuri, Festival of the Steel Phallus; or as the locals refer to it: the chin chin matsuri, or little weenie festival. Different groups, including transvestites, parade through the streets carrying mikoshi, or portable shrines, with large erect phalluses. The transvestites prefer a pink phallus. Elderly gentlemen can be seen smiling for photographs while they hug and kiss huge black phalluses, while grandma sucks on a multicolored phallic-shaped candy lollipop. Others prefer phalluses carved from daikon, white radish. All shapes and sizes of phalluses constructed of various materials can be purchased from the many souvenir vendors.

Kappa found all this pretty much contemptible. He didn't care much for this old-time exhibitionism for the delight of the patronizing foreigners, or the silly superstitions of the "driving out evil" ceremonies at the Buddhist temple; the buildings of the complex were rebuilt in the 20th century after being bombed by the Americans during the war. Kappa didn't like any of it. Kappa preferred world literature, philosophy, science, history and politics. He was also a stanch and committed member of an anarchist collective.

Every Saturday night the various members of the *Furui Yabuketa Jaketto no Dekunobo ga Atsumata Bungei Kurabu,* roughly translated as the Old Torn Jacket Good-for-Nothing Literary Club, gathered at Kappa's house. On alternate Saturdays the club met at the Muse Café in Yokodai on the outskirts of Yokohama, or at the Cinema Café in Kamakura, right next to the train station. Some of the members were affiliated with the Japan Communist Party. Other members would have disdained that association, like Kappa, but they all got along because they were all outsiders. They held conflicting views on innumerable subjects and were not reticent about articulating their opinions.

Kappa had spent several years in London studying English and French. His English was very good, with a pronounced American accent despite the years studying the Queen's English. The American accent was formed even before he traveled overseas. He had listened to the American Armed Forces Radio Network in Japan ever since he was young, mimicking the DJs and commentators that he heard, and singing along to the pop and rock music. Kappa even picked up the truncated intonations of one of the station's personalities, Paul Harvey. Sometimes after a long discourse on the history of anarchism in Japan, Kappa would ape the fervent Harvey's famous pause and say in English, *and now, the rest of the story...* followed by revelatory analysis that would cause most American minds to self-destruct in incongruity and paradox, the right-wing Harvey for sure. But I enjoyed the irony, and the impishness. I guess I didn't have a quite wholly American mind. My mind had never bloomed in the academia or the mainstream media of those florid American gardens.

Kappa placed the sake bottle and rice crackers on the low table in the middle of the room. Two paintings hung on the wall. When I first came to Kappa's place, I had asked Kappa about the paintings, one of Louis Armstrong and the other of Jesus Christ, wearing a flowery hat? That's not Jesus Christ said Kappa, that's Bob Dylan!

It was an old house. Kappa's parents had left him the house. He was their only child. He was able to rent out the upstairs and take in a little money. He also worked part-time at the hardware store and the pharmacy, cleaning up, stacking shelves, both places were operated and managed by his friends, Sato and Nomura, respectively, who were also members of the *Furui Yabuketa Jaketto no Dekunobo ga Atsumata Bungei Kurabu,* and would soon be arriving for the club's weekly meeting, or soirée, as Yamamoto prefers to call it; he's the expert on all things French.

The Old Torn Jacket Good-for-Nothing Literary Club consisted of the following members: the aforementioned Kappa, an autodidact, anarchist, who publishes a small political magazine on the old copy machine donated by Nomura; the magazine is called *Red and Black Jacket.* Nomura, a pharmacist; communist; sometimes anarchist, he's not sure. Sato, a hardware dealer, communist. Yamamoto, a writer, well versed in 19th century French poetry, Derrida and deconstruction, and who is an editor of his own literary magazine, *Grey Jacket.* Nishi, a published poet, eldest member, and editor of his own poetry magazine, *White Jacket.* Iwata, who runs a small *juko,* or private cram school attended by children. He is also an expert on the Pre-Raphaelites; Nico, the German chanteuse; Jean de Ville; and Led Zeppelin. Keida, a poet and Beat literature expert, translator of Kerouac's poems, editor of his own magazine, *Blue Jacket.* The pattern should be fairly clear by now; the Jacket magazines and hence the name of the Old Torn Jacket Good-for-Nothing Literary Club. There was also

Sanjo, and his wife Noriko. Sanjo is a journalist for the *Asahi Shimbun*, a major newspaper, and a liberal democrat; his wife, the only female member, is translating a musical play from English to Japanese. She had asked me to help her translate it. She told me about it a few weeks ago. "It's called *The Hired Man.*" "Oh, the poem by Frost," I said. "Who?" Noriko questioned. "No, this is a musical by Melvyn Bragg." "You mean the guy in England who does the South Bank Show? He writes musicals?" "Yes, it's about miners in the north of England about one hundred years ago." I nodded, and thought to myself: That should be a big hit in Japan.

Ogiwara, owner of the Muse Café in Yokodai, a jazz-crazed beatnik. Kawagata, owner of the Cinema Café in Kamakura, expert on Japanese films, especially Ozu and Mizuguchi, whose first words to me after seeing my shoes, Oh, James Bond shoes. He asked me to make a list of my top movies. He has his regular customers make lists of their favorite movies and then he hangs them on the walls of his café. So I made a list for him. Nakamura, a childhood friend of Kappa, he was a hairdresser who spent ten years in New York City during the late seventies and early eighties, and returned to Japan a complete wreck after years of cocaine abuse. Last week he was found dead. He was found hanged in his bathroom. Kappa found him. Just a week before he committed suicide he had given me a haircut. We talked about New York. His hands were shaking.

Sato, our hardware dealer and communist, cheered on by a few of his fellow communists, stood up to make a speech. Sato cleared his throat. "It was precisely sixty seven years ago in the middle of our wars of aggression, that our party was founded, in 1922. We had three principals: Replace the rule of the emperor with a democracy. Stop our wars of aggression in Asian countries. Defend working people and establish rights, the right to vote for women and men eighteen years and older. We were persecuted as a criminal organization. We were brutalized and murdered." Sato had another ten sheets of paper or so in his hands, and his friends were already bored. Sit down! Shut up! Have a drink! I am an anarchist! I am a surrealist! I am a deconstructionist! I am a situationist! I am a poet! Sato yelled back at them, all right, *urusai*, be quiet, then let's the sing *The Internationale*! So some of them sing it, in Japanese. *'Tate uetaru monoyo, imazo hiwa chikashi, sameyo waga harakara, akatsukiwa kinu…"*

On a Sunday morning in Japan I saw one of Henry Miller's ex-wives, Hoki Tokuda, on a television program. She was singing and there were huge portraits of Henry Miller hanging over the stage in the background. This seemed so wonderfully incongruous that I wanted to scream out that I was the happiest man alive; but I didn't do it; I let the moment wash over me in silent delight. It was a Sunday morning no less, when American television is filled with religious quackery and right-wing buffoonery and free market consumer dementia. It was hard to imagine that this could ever occur on American network television.

One of our club members, Iwata, an artist and mathematician, who has no pre-conditioned grounding in rudimentary Western academic categorization, speaks of Pre-Raphaelite art, Led Zeppelin, Nico, Platonic mathematics, Jean de Ville (Jean de Who?), Paul McCartney (not John, he doesn't like Yoko), H. P. Lovecraft, Jacques Brel, and all in one prolonged breath, and sees some kind of interesting connection amongst them. What am I missing? I used to say to him, that I thought that they don't really fit together, you see... it's an odd combination, but I learned my lesson and stopped trying to partition what was sensible to him. Was it some kind of naiveté, a reflection of cross-cultural misbirth, an uninformed judgment? I questioned myself about it. Why did I still look at certain arrangements of literature and art as connected and viable, and who had led me in that direction? I had never been a student in a literature or creative writing course at some prestigious college, so did I just assume that those writers that I liked were not associated with the gold standard, and therefore I could lump them together? Creative writing classes at a college! Are you shitting me? I learned to write at the Cayuga Home for Boys and Girls... at risk... like these words... or did something else account for my tastes in books? Iwata opened my eyes to a more than kitschy post-modern hodgepodge playful chatter. He challenged my preconceptions and caused a reassessment of the nature of art and creativity. My friend had his pet peeves also; he doesn't like Japanese enka music and karaoke. Enka is like Japan's version of country music, Iwata said. But it was his other enthusiasms that just didn't jibe. He had read enough occidental writers to know where this or that artist was placed in the canon, in the pantheon, but such absolutes didn't faze him. It was just a matter of personal aesthetics, a matter of personal taste. As for Henry Miller's huge portraits on a television screen in Japan on a Sunday morning... this was no sensitivity to the writer's plight, no knowing openness toward the value of free speech and expression. I suppose the only measure was fame. Miller was a famous man, a celebrity, in a way that he could never have been in America. The Japanese education system must be very inclusive. Everyone I met in Japan had heard of Rimbaud, Baudelaire, Kerouac... try that in America, you'll get blank stares. It may not have been an extensive knowledge, or anything of that nature, but that these names would pop up in ordinary conversations was so surprising to me. To be known, and like a Hollywood starlet, loved. That's what mattered. It was disappointing to realize this but not totally disillusioning. Little Hoki there was exploiting her relationship to Miller. Celebrity and fame is what America offered to the 20th century, defined in pop culture, kitsch, whatever. Hollywood fame. American fame. All those wonderful Hollywood stories, Hollywood movies. I always thought Hollywood movies generated a lot of collateral damage. At no cost. Everything smashed up. Bystanders left behind in the dust. I wondered what ever happened to that poor fake nobody who just had his life fucked-up forever... but nobody will ever know... it's not part of the script. Let's sing the sukiyaki song? The what? *Omoi dasu natsu no hi... hitori botchi no yoru...* oh we don't call it the sukiyaki song. Okay, let's sing that song that I hear on the radio all the time... *Tombo...* about a dragonfly? *Ah ah shiawase no tombo yo doko e...* we talked about the Maruki Hiroshima murals. Sato says the party didn't approve... but I wanted to see them... and the Berlin Wall... that was about to come falling down... and the night continued, and after midnight Iwata challenged us to translate a Japanese poem into English. It would be a group effort. What poem shall we translate? There were many suggestions, perhaps a haiku? You know it's three hundred years since Bashō travelled into the interior of the north... something more modern? They scoured through the books on the small shelf. The poem must be short. We must complete it or abandoned it by dawn, which amounts to the same thing. Yamamoto reminded us of the line by Mallarmé, or was it Valery? He couldn't remember. You never complete a poem; you just abandon it. Okay, very well then, we told Yamamoto to choose a poem. All right, then how about this one. It's by Nakahara Chuya. Yes. That's a good choice, said the others. I never heard of him of course but they explained to me that he was the "Japanese Rimbaud." Here is the result of our endeavor, abandoned and/or completed at 2:37 a.m. - Japan Time.

Nakahara Chuya was born in Yamaguchi Prefecture on April 29, 1907 and died in a hospital in Kamakura on October 22, 1937.

A Fairy Tale

On an autumn night
Somewhere far away
Surrounded by pebbles,
Light was falling
Very softly softly,
Purling like pearls,
Falling like sillica,
Like a fine powder.

A butterfly settled
On a stone
In the river,
Her shadow faint and clear
On the riverbed...

Unnoticed the butterfly
Has flown away,
And the river
Is running again.

And then I said let's translate a poem that I had written. It was very late. But we battled on until the break of day, until another false sunrise.

The Modern World is Loud

In America Poe sounds the alarum.
Loud loud louder the warning bells bells bells
In France Baudelaire dodges the poor in the boulevard
Loud loud louder the old buildings pulled down down down
In England Marx grinds the bourgeois in Blake's satanic mills
Loud loud louder the churning wheel turns turns turns
The modern world is loud
The clangor of iron is loud
Traffic is loud
Machines are loud
War is loud
Loud loud louder the bombs bombs bombs
Not even nature's warning bells are as loud
As the modern world;
Fire, wind, rain, flood, and earthquake.
Not since the Big Bang.
This morning the monk rang the bell at Shoun-ji

現代世界の音は大きい

アメリカで、エドガー　アラン　ポーが警鐘を鳴らす
恐ろしい鐘　鐘　鐘の音
高く大きく大きく

フランスで、ボードレールが貧困者に溢れた大通りを潜り抜く
古い建物を倒す　壊す　壊す音
高く大きく大きく

イギリスで、マルクスがブルジョワを挽き
ブレイクが闇のサタン製粉小屋の粉砕器を廻す　廻す　廻す音
高く大きく大きく
現代世界の音は大きい
カチンカチン響く鉄
交通渋滞
いろいろな機械

戦争の音
高く大きく大きく
爆弾　爆弾　爆弾

自然さえも
近代世界と同様には大きな音で警鐘を鳴らさず
火災　風　雨　洪水　地震
ビッグバン理論以来

今朝早く　祥雲寺の和尚が鐘を鳴らす

They insisted on writing the Japanese translation across the page from left to right, and not downward and right to left. Now a funny thing about translation. There is a joke that Kappa told us that night that got a reluctant laugh. It was a riddle that went like this: *buta to ushi ga kenka shitara dochira ga katsu ka...? tonkatsu...* ha ha ha. Here is a literal translation: If a pig and a cow have a fight, who wins? The pig wins... ha ha ha... then I came up with a similar riddle: *uma to ushi ga kenka shitara dochira ga katsu ka...? umakatta...* ha ha ha. Here is a literal translation: If a horse and a cow have a fight, who wins? Tasted delicious! Are you bent over in convulsions of laughter? I have no time to explain now. Maybe later. There's that French proverb: Translation is like a woman, if she is beautiful, she will not be faithful, and if she is faithful she will not be beautiful. *Les belles infidèles.* But language holds cultural nuances that can only be understood within the language itself. She is not beautiful or faithful. It is incomprehensible that the pig wins and it tasted delicious. But the pig always wins.

Kappa said, "Did you know that when the Japanese transplanted the Chinese logographic writing into Japanese, there was no idea of translation. The Chinese was just transposed, the word order changed, like a mirror image. We thought we were reading Japanese. It wasn't until centuries later that this mirror was smashed and broken. There is no word to word."

Our philosophy member, Yamamoto, spent an hour one day trying to explain to me the meaning of *Dasein*. At least I thought that's what he was trying to explain. In fact half way through his talk I realized that he was not taking about *Dasein* at all but the Japanese writer Dazai. And yet what he said made sense either way. I guess the pig wins again.

And as the evening winds down, and the morning light fills the shoji, and the talk about poetry and politics acquires an incoherent babble, swells into mangled Japanese and English, suddenly the discussion turns to the Hanshin Tigers and the New York Mets... then early in the morning Nishii leads in rousing renditions of his favorite American tunes: the songs of Stephen Foster, doo dah, doo dah and everyone falls asleep lying down right where we sat on the tatami mats. But we did manage to make plans to take a bike trip to the north country and follow Bashō's path... rather, take the train there and then rent bicycles.

Kappa suggested to me one day that I should try to teach English and make a little money. I didn't realize that this was such a big deal in Tokyo. He said that there are thousands of people in Tokyo teaching English, and that half of them can barely speak English. This was 1989 and the Japanese economy had boomed and was about to go bust, but there were still enough Japanese who wanted to learn English and who were more than willing to throw lots of money at you for some pretty much useless lessons. It won't last, said Kappa, it's just a fad and soon the money will dry up, but for now you should try and do it. I found this advice very pragmatic coming from my anarchist friend. I discovered an English language school in Meguro, in Tokyo. It was hard to find the place. It was as nondescript and as unremarkable as most addresses in Tokyo. Even Japanese mailmen have a hard time finding places, so I was told. It was on the sixth floor of a building whose front was plastered with signage, both large and tiny, neon and dull. A man introduced himself and we went into a room with several desks. I was just one of five people that day who were looking for a job. The man told us a brief story about how he came to Japan and started this school. The man was from Austria. He sounded just like Arnold Schwarzenegger. He had a strong accent. He was very arrogant. He said that this was a group interview.

I told him that I didn't have any qualifications. No problem, he said. I filled out the application. I was not hired. Arnold hired a girl from some eastern European country. She spoke English like Bela Lugosi. She was pretty. I'm sure that's why she was given the job by Arnold, and I am certain that she will give Arnold a job in return. It didn't take me long to realize that this English teaching business was just a scam. Foreigners were here to bilk money and bamboozle some especially naïve Japanese people. Kappa laughed at me when I told him the story. He knew that such "schools" existed and that their main purpose was duping Japanese people to cough up money for phony English lessons and for procuring some willing and otherwise sex partners. Kappa said that I had to find my own students and give private lessons. He and his friends at the Old Torn Jacket Good-for-Nothing Literary Club can help me find students. He also told me that students find English teachers who leave their names and telephone numbers on bulletin boards at coffee shops all over Tokyo. I ended up giving English lessons at cafés, at places of business, on park benches, at train stations, and at apartments. I had to travel all around Tokyo and to some far-flung areas on the outskirts and transportation was expensive. My friends taught me how to take the cheaper trains and to avoid taking the more expensive JR trains. The JR trains were more serviceable, convenient and took much shorter times to get around. Kappa said that I should include a transportation fee for some of my students. I was able to use Nomura's old photocopy machine to make hundreds of copies of lessons from the *English for Busy Japanese People* book that I bought at the bookstore near the Yurakucho JR Station. The only indication that there was a bookstore located there was the neon *Hon* 本 sign that protruded out from the building. English books were on the fifth floor. Kappa also knew someone who ran a kind of knitting and baking club for women. I taught there two days a week. And then they started bringing their children along and I had to teach English to five and six year olds. The *ichimans* (about a hundred dollars) were piling up.

Kappa told me that most Japanese were well aware of the swindles and cons of the Japanese language schools and that most Japanese preferred private lessons, as long as it was with native speakers. American or English. But they never seemed to be too concerned or inquisitive about the varieties of English spoken by native speakers, whether they were from Alabama or Brooklyn, White Chapel or Hull, Edinburgh or Dublin, as long as you told them that you were a native speaker, born and raised and educated in England or America. I told them I was from New York. This bit of information seemed to hold a certain cachet with the students. Oh Woody Allen, Andy Warhol, Martin Scorsese, Times Square. And of course there were the more discriminating students. These were typically girls who wanted to learn the "Queen's English" or the English spoken by Margaret Thatcher because she spoke so clearly and was so much easier to understand. I didn't reply to these comments. I didn't think they would have understood my scorn cloaked in sarcasm. There was a set of even more discerning students, the snobs, the social-climbers, again generally girls, who didn't want to learn English at all but wanted to learn French or German. English was too common for them. Everybody was learning English. They also wanted to study the precise manner to hold an English teacup or the proper way to eat spaghetti with a fork and not slurp, God forbid. But most commonly the Japanese students wanted to learn basic conversational English either for business purposes or for tourism or because it was just the thing to do. So I was able to make a little money to travel. I had to leave Japan every three months because I was staying on a tourist visa. If I had been able to get a job at one of the established and licensed English language schools, and not one of the many assorted rip-off schools, *botteru, botteru*, said Kappa, it means rip-off, then the school would have tried to help me obtained a part-time work visa. But I didn't care for the likes of all the Arnolds in Tokyo and I was trying to avoid foreigners anyway.

Korea

There's a young Seoul soldier with a rifle in his hand, and he's smoking a cigarette, an American brand; and he's holding a green shield, wearing a green helmet; I think he'd rather be at Disneyland; he'd rather be driving a Corvette. But he's doing what his government commands. He sits, squats, and stands in the hot summer sun, lounging around a street corner, daydreaming of some blond girl in California, of drinking Coca-Cola and eating popcorn with her. The young Seoul soldier hears a man preaching from a bible, and the young Seoul soldier sees posters of a Japanese pop idol. But the young Seoul soldier dreams an American dream of fun fun fun, maybe meet Michael Jackson and Madonna, maybe make a million dollars, maybe buy a big house for his father, the fisherman, and sometimes rice farmer, from Pusan. Maybe buy his father a Cadillac, or, at least, a Nissan. Young Seoul soldier, what enemy are you protecting your people against? All the tea in China? All the rice fields in Vietnam? All the Toyotas in Japan? All the hard-liners north of the border with Kalashnikovs in their hands? Young Seoul soldier, what enemy are you defending your people against? Your own father who plants rice beyond the fence of Kooni Range? Where the American Air Force drops its bombs and fires its mortars, to make strange the sound of your ancient forests and waters. Somewhere car horns are ranting, somewhere students are chanting, sitting like Buddhas, wearing yellow visors, rows upon rows, in front of a military-truck's tires, in front of a fire hose. In front of young Seoul soldiers who climb into an army bus with a cage, soldiers the same age as the young Seoul students who climb out of their books and into the streets to vent their rage. There might be unrest in the streets of Seoul. If the student protest can't be controlled. But by sunset the streets are quiet, there'll be no riot; so go home all you G.I. Joes. Young Seoul soldier with a rifle in your arms, now that your off duty you can meet your Korean cutie, maybe see an American movie. Young Seoul soldier with a rifle in your arms, you've got to hold her, or has somebody already sold her, to an American soldier with bigger and better bombs? Better grab a hamburger before its murder;

better grab your U.S. aid gun from the land of Ronald Reagan; and take some sound advice of Ronald's, maintain the arm's race and the magic of the market place. After a dog day afternoon in the middle of June, take your girl by the hand and lead her to the Promised Land, you deserve a break today, so get up and get away... to McDonalds.

In Spring in Kyoto

At Kinkaku-ji, Temple of the Golden Pavilion, the thin guide-leaflet provided a short poem: Mountain is sharply etched; woods are colorful, Valleys deep and rapid streams with spray. Moonlight is clear in softly breathing wind. Man reads in the quietness "Scripture without words."

I stood at the bamboo fence overlooking the pond of small islands and gnarled pine, like a player on a Noh stage. Light rain falling on my head and feet. The golden phoenix lifted the temple skyward, shimmering, like a spaceship traveling beyond time and space. Oddly, I was at the time reading a sci-fi book by Roger Bethell that included a character named Aliaspun, captain of a space ship called *No Rule II.*

The present temple was built in 1955, a replica of the much-valued Golden Pavilion that was burned down in 1950. In 1956 Mishima Yukio published his novel, Kinkaku-ji, in which he grafts his imagination to historical limbs, searching for root events and motivations in the life of the young Buddhist acolyte who set the Golden Pavilion on fire. The young Mizoguchi has a stutter; he lacks a deft command of words. Words are the key that opens the door to the inner and outer world. Burning without words. Words are made of air and must pass freely. Mizoguchi chokes on the smoke before the Golden Pavilion is even set ablaze. There is no water in his mouth to douse the burning of solitude. A Buddhist trapped in words because he cannot blow sweet air through their crooked pipes. The Golden Temple becomes an erotic fixation. His love and hate must burn. Solitude without words. Paradox of scripture without words. Nature and beauty the object of rape. The sadistic prolixity of words tied in bondage to human events. The Chinese sages say that happy was the time when trees were many and men were few... fewer words were spoken. Time and language, a conjunction of past, present, and future. Europe, Asia, and America had blown all the air out of language. And re-breathed with fire. They heard the breath in Hiroshima; the stutter of fire in death. The sound of lungs popping... like at an Hindu funeral pyre. Mishima committed *seppuku.* Ritual disembowlment. *Harakiri* has the same meaning, stomach cutting. But the Kanji are reversed. One is read through Chinese, the other is read through native Japanese. But Aktugawa overdosed, Dazai drowned himself, Kawabata inhaled gas, Arishima hung himself. The general word for suicide is *jisatsu*... Kappa had explained all this to me... he said only ancient Samurai and a modern Fascist like Mishima commit *seppuku,* and mentioned his friend, Nakamura, the hairdresser, who hung himself. It's all right. *Daijobu desu.*

At Ryoanji, I sat on the wood platform overlooking the famous rock garden. Fifteen rocks in white gravel. Islands in undulating water. From whichever perspective you take of the 30-meter rectangular garden from the platform, one rock will always be hidden from view. The hidden-ness. Descartes' motto: To be hidden is to live well. Is it imperfection or perfection? The walls that surround the back of the garden are made of clay boiled in oil. Over the years the wall's face has taken on different designs and patterns because of the oil seeping out. The garden is said to be, thought to be, (saying and thinking are misnomers in this context) the essence of Zen art. The paradox of being in hidden-ness. And if you master the art of Zen, you will artlessly hear the sound of the roaring waves. Here is another secret, another paradox, that I heard. The old Japanese man sitting behind me on the wooden platform said to his companion: When I was a young boy I used to come here and play in the garden, climb over the rocks, because there was no wall then. Can this be true? Isn't this wall very old? Isn't this a sacred garden? Or has it been this way only in recent years since the West has taken an interest? Just another tourist attraction? Is the old man telling the truth? Is his memory tricking him? I felt as if I had been instructed to unravel a difficult Zen koan. What was the answer? Who was telling the truth? Did truth matter? I certainly like to imagine the old man as a boy playing in the rock garden and climbing over the rocks.

At Ginkakugi the moon garden and a stone mound mouthing the moon's echo. I am not really here. I pass like moonlight. Where was I yesterday? But here is my ticket stub. Here is my guide leaflet. Thoughts falling like a leaf... unguided.

I have just finished reading a novel by the Japanese writer Kafu Nagai. It is a novel in which there is no strong concrete sense of physical dirt: Squalor, filth, pollution, poverty, misery, and wretchedness. They do not exist. There is also no strong abstract sense of metaphysical dirt: Sinfulness, evil, depravity, disgrace, vileness, and wickedness. There is a smudge on a kimono or a tear in the shoji. There is a smear on a geisha's face or a tear on her cheek. It is permissible to get Western clothes dirty. It is unpardonable to get a kimono stained. She slaps a mosquito on the forehead of a man and there is blood on her hand. Is the mosquito her excuse? Is there blood on my hand? Human power, over the dominion of earth and all its creatures, well, perhaps not all, bacteria and cockroaches may one day eat the paper of this book. Human power... and the worst kind is the kind that doesn't get its own hands dirty, kills thousands of mosquitoes with one slap... at a distance... and later calls them children...

Summer rain in London. Autumn moon in Paris. Winter snow in Vienna. Having no destination, I am never lost, wrote Ikkyu. And now it is spring in Kyoto, and the Path of Philosophy drops its cherry blossoms on my head and feet.

Hong Kong

With the money I made from teaching I was able to travel to Seoul, Taipei, Bangkok, Guam and Hong Kong. These were brief three day excursions. I found a travel office in Takadanobaba that sold inexpensive tickets and had staff who spoke English. There were also several cafés that I liked in the area where I met my students. It was my next to last trip from Japan when I encountered some problems. I flew to Hong Kong. There was a bad storm and as the plane was landing it was tipping right and left, thunder and lighting flashing all around the airplane. The airplane descended right between skyscrapers on both sides of the plane and I could almost see inside the windows of the rooms in the buildings. Surviving that, I then had to survive Hong Kong. For some reason I wanted to be more careful this time and acquire a visa to return to Japan. I may not have needed it anyway. But I had already left and returned to Japan several times and though I was grateful that immigration kept giving me an extra three months every time, I thought my luck might just run out. I had booked a room in a small hotel. I had my ticket to return the next day. But when I applied for the visa I was told to come back Thursday. It was Tuesday. They wanted to hold my passport. Now I was in a pickle. If I waited to Thursday I would have to buy a new ticket and would have no money left over for a hotel. I told them I'd be back Thursday. I went and tried to exchange my ticket but they wouldn't do it. I had to buy a one-way ticket back to Japan. Now I had just a few dollars left. I got into a conversation with a friendly old security guard at the Japanese consulate office. He was sitting in a chair in the hallway, half asleep. I told him about my predicament. He said that he knew of rooms where I could stay very cheap. So I went with him. We went to the subway station and we ended up in Kowloon. I had no idea where I was. We walked under buildings, through buildings, alleys, walkways, boxes of fruits and vegetables and all manner of clutter, everywhere, until we came to a narrow shabby elevator that barely held three people. We went up to the seventh floor. He took a few dollars from me and showed me the room. I never met the proprietor and I didn't think the security guard was the manager. I never asked. Maybe it was some kind of youth hostel. It was a small room with a cot and no windows. There was a vent in the wall that must have reached down into a bar or something because all night I heard some type of music and loud talking. There was a cot with a dirty sheet. A lightbulb with a string to pull. The bathroom was down the hall. I heard voices behind the other doors as I walked down the hallway to the bathroom to wash up. The voices were in different languages. I heard Italian and French. The walls of my room were covered in graffiti, scrawls and scribbles. People had written their names and sayings and dates on the wall. *I was here* type of jottings. They were written in different languages. I recognized Norwegian, German, Japanese, Italian, and French but there were others.

On Thursday I got my passport and visa. I went there with the security guard and waited around all day to return with him to Kowloon. I didn't think I could find my way back by myself. It had already crossed my mind that I was staying in a tiny room on the seventh floor of a building that most certainly was a fire hazard and if I died here in a fire nobody would have ever found out what had happened to me. My flight was scheduled for early the next morning. I went down the elevator and tried to find my way out to a street. It was still dark. I had only enough money to get a taxi. I walked through the maze of buildings, not sure which way to go, just trying to find a street with cars. I came to a street at the end of a tunnel and luckily waiting right in front of me was a taxi, as if sent from above. I got my ride to the airport. Then at the airport I met Saul. Here's a cliché: small world. He had returned to the place that held many memories of Ko. We talked for an hour before I had to catch my flight. I said, Good luck.

Hiroshima

I am riding the Shinkansen to Hiroshima. I will be there for August 6, 1989. *Ano Hi.* That Day… I am reading Kenzuburo Oe's book *Hiroshima Notes*… in the beginning was the word… has the word survived? Of course there are no more beginnings; we cannot start over again. Hot weather. The cicadas are ripping the air wide open. There are many people walking around. Buddhists are chanting in front of the A-bomb Dome. Rows of chairs are set up in front of the flame of the Cenotaph. Television cameras. Trucks with imperial flags, the right-wing blaring words from megaphones. Thousands upon thousands of paper cranes in bright colors hanging from monuments. The Peace Memorial Park and the Peace Memorial Museum. The wax model of the dying figure, walking with arms stretched out, flesh melting, *mizu kudasai,* the first thing that I see upon entering the museum. I am walking. Looking. Walking. Seeing. Walking. Like a Naruse movie: just wandering, walking, walking into oblivion. Baudelaire described it thus: To be away from home and yet to feel oneself everywhere at home; to see the world, to be at the center of the world, and yet to remain hidden from the world. Heidegger's *die Unheimliche,* the uncanny, not-at-home, not down on any map, the ambiguity, *angst,* the anxiety, the nothing that is there, the something that is not there, the transcendental homelessness, *das Nicht, le néant.* Kenzuburo Oe writes that the Americans trusted too much in "humanism," in human strength. As if evil creates good. People will overcome. Endure. Struggle towards a miserable death. Most people will survive. With humiliation, shame, and dignity. A humane hell. But they have their lives, don't they? Doubtless, Truman, and others, slept well, ever after.

One in every crowd. Probably more than one. Started with one. Now many. But it only takes one to make a bad system worse. Adam was the first man and therefore the first man to mess up a bad system.

After I returned to Tokyo a few of us from the Torn Jacket Literary Club went to the cinema. We saw *Black Rain… Kuroi Ame,* the Japanese movie about the results of the atomic bombs dropped on Hiroshima and its aftermath. It was in black and white. The attempt to depict the magnitude of the collective pain of that day was unbearable. The raw wounds of skin peeled off, the flayed flesh, the women and children marching toward the river, with their arms held up and out with their skin dripping like wax… how can you speak about these things? Everyone was quiet after we left the theater. Then Kappa said, Where's the Hollywood movie? There won't be any because... did you know that there were laws of censorship imposed by the US government during the occupation? The truth of Hiroshima was discovered later... but this was worse than Auschwitz. Yes, I will say that. It is a mad and absurd comparison that I am forced to say. Yes, I know, the gas chambers, the death marches... but there was nothing like Hiroshima in the history of the world. There are movies about surviving a future nuclear war, that's entertaining... the gaze is directed to the future... and hundreds of movies about the Holocaust... but Hiroshima was worse... Hiroshima, Hiroshima, Hiroshima... never again... that's what they write in the greeting book at the Hiroshima Peace Memorial... never again... but... did you write something in that book Stephen? Yes, I told him. But I told him that I wrote something other than what I actually had written. Everyone had written *never again*. So I just scribbled that. I couldn't think of anything. But I told Kappa that I wrote: Humans beings never learn. It was what the old man said in the movie. Toward the end of *Black Rain*. He is listening to the radio, reports of new threats of the A-bomb. He says, *ningen yuyatsu wa shōkori mo nai monjya*. Human beings never learn anything.

Kappa asked me if I had heard of the Maruki Hiroshima panels. They are in a museum in Tokyo. Kappa said that they are as great as *Guernica*. We shall go, he said.

Yokohama

On the last day of the year we went to a park in Yokohama. We went to the Kanagawa Museum of Modern Literature. It had manuscripts and letters from Tanizaki and Akutagawa. We stayed in the park all night... waiting for sunrise. When I went to Hong Kong I took two books with me. One book was called *Real Presences* by George Steiner. The other book was *The Name of the Rose* by Umberto Eco. The Steiner book begins by saying that our language is trapped in outworn phrases, like sunrise... because we now know, us moderns, that the sun does not rise or set. Galileo, Copernicus, mathematics, physics, theory, but also meta-theory, extra-territoriality, structuralism, deconstruction are the new cultural battlefields. God, spirit, logos, will, presence, original creation, self, subject, author, enlightenment, emancipation, and dignity, all lie cold and dead beneath the reductionist sword. The book is a discreet *l'action d'arrière-garde*, an eloquent and flawed and fatal attempt to build an Hellenic-Hebraic barricade of Western Babel and hope on too wide a boulevard, and in the dust of the Library of Alexandria, where the Muses wept. Marx, Darwin, Freud, Nietzsche, and their progeny live on that fashionable boulevard. Nietzsche said it first: I believe we are not getting rid of God because we still believe in grammar. Anna, the girl from Vienna, had to leave Austria to get rid of God and family and language so that she might find her "native tongue" in the "promised land." A deeper home, a deeper language. Some notion of origins and language. She had to learn Hebrew, but she really hated language. She couldn't express herself with words without becoming silent and frustrated. She couldn't say what she thought she wanted to say. German, Hebrew, English. I told her that Hebrew was not the language before Babel, but that Norwegian was the original language; in fact the form that my mother spoke, a dialect from the south-west part of Norway, that was corrupted by a little New York American-English. Anna wasn't really amused. But that was my world, false or not. I remember watching a show on television in London. It was an interview with George Steiner. Anna said that he couldn't be trusted. Look at his eyes darting here and there. This never even occurred to me. Steiner spoke contra Freud, sublimation, psychoanalysis, endless enunciations of repressed sexuality. Body movements reveal more than words, Anna said. Non-verbal communication. Dance movement and psychotherapy. Words are polluted bits of society, class, gender, roles, family, politics, oppressive power structures... and yet she and her client sat and stared at each other, and talked and talked and talked... and maybe even discovered a very few personal insights, and stared at each other... until that stare becomes the gaze into the abyss... speak truth to power, they ain't listening. Is there a divide? Knowledge and truism and facts on this side, power on the other side? Or is knowledge insinuated into power, step by bloody step. And this is so crazy that trying not to be crazy is crazy...

Ever since the pursuit of happiness (classical capitalist liberalism) unseated the pursuit of wisdom (classical philosophical naturalism) within the loomings of scientific advancement and technological application, can we say that we are *happier* because we *know* that the earth revolves around the sun, and that we no longer speak of a "sunrise" with its relational meanings lost forever, only a type of primitive and childish folk knowledge. Yet we still *perceive* the sunset... as if the Ptolemaic system was not false.

But you are never happy with death looming, only heroic, and the worm is in the apple still; yes sit up high on your throne with your well seated ass, as Montaigne clearly saw, but what he did not see is that the heroic king of man, with power and knowledge, claims and reclaims, the infinite use of his crown, projects his glorified name into the future, refuses to be unseated, and sits like a child until he sits on his own shit. Something is there... or nothing. Nothing is a human concept. There really *is* nothing before or after man, because there is the word *is*, *being*, before or after a word, a name. Oh but the scientists have appropriated the poet's nomenclature. Yeah, they talk about the beautiful cosmos, elegant string theory, gorgeous enumerations, awesomeness... and what do the artists do now? They drop turds from the leaning tower of Pisa and say they are rediscovering a new kind of gravity! Anna hated her family... or rather, the concept of the family as "concentration camp." I could not understand this hyperbole. Her family just seemed "normal" to me.

I was reading *The Name of the Rose* in the small claustrophobic room in Kowloon. The scribbling in different languages all over the walls. What do these words mean? I thought of Sancho Panza. The promise of the island. But poor illiterate Sancho did not know the meaning of the word *Insulo*, island.... there are many islands in this book by Umberto Eco. I was stranded on an island. I will have to visit many islands before I know the name of the rose, but first I must discover the meaning of the name of the island.

So, before we come to the end of this, I ask this question, once again: Why bother to write? Why use the name of the writer? Because we are all going to die, said Jack, in *Visions of Cody*. Did Jack have a greater empathy for mankind than other men, for our suffering, for his own suffering, in the face of all our deaths, our mortality, our extinction? Is that a reason to write? Just death? Wouldn't everyone write, in the face of death, or do most of us just turn away... and say, it's a sad story?

"Do you know Roy Lee," I heard the presence of a voice address me.

"No," I answered.

"He's in this book."

"Are you in this book?" I queried the voice.

"I am now," said the insolent bastard. "Anyway," the voice continued, "Roy Lee is on death row. Roy Lee was asked this question: Why do you kill? And you know what he said? Roy Lee answered me, because I was the one who asked him the question. Roy Lee said: Because we are all gonna die anyway. Just like that. He said the same thing as your writer said. Do you think Roy Lee has any empathy? He's a psychopath. He's mad."

"But he added the word, anyway... there's a difference. Just that small word made a big difference. It stands at the edge, at the border of madness and sanity, just a thin line."

"Difference? You mean like an empty sign? Deferred meaning?"

"Are you a journalist?" I asked the presence of the voice.

"You know what else I asked him? I asked him: Roy Lee, the young girl you murdered, what was her name? He answered: She sure had a pretty name. Her name was Rose. Well that just made my blood run cold. My body shivered when he said that."

"Are you comparing a writer with a cold blooded killer?"

"No," said the presence of the voice, "of course not. But... unless one kills oneself. Or kills the writer in oneself..."

"What self?"

"Why did you stop writing, Stephen? Don't you feel lost? Unanchored? Adrift? As if everything is blank and empty now? A tale of separation? Don't you feel as if you have lost everything?"

"I have my life, don't I?"

"But is that enough? It's not enough!" The presence of the voice shouted.

"It's enough," I whispered.

Lack, empathy, instinctual awareness of life-death. Consciousness, a conceptual awareness of being-nothingness... always within thought inside itself. Not outside itself. Self is an object? A fiction? Fiction is an object but not real. Not parts only, as in Hume and Buddhism. Rousseau wasn't transparent to Hume. Yet the fictional self must insinuate self? Fear of death? Get rid of the fear... die... suicide... close forever the gap from subject to object or self from other, be objectified under the gaze and be subjected to history by the forms of experience. Remove self from society, creates loss. Refuse the oath, creates disloyalty. Care of self, creates separation. When I say that I have to shit is it the I that has to shit or the body? Death is that which you seek and that which you fear. That which you seek and that which you fear are the same. How and why do I write what I write where and when I write it? Modern money and the modern novel. Two fictions that grew up together and will disappear together. But is the self a fiction? Is there something real behind the presentation of fiction? Is there something real behind the presentation of money? Both fiction and money can resolve into an ungraspable mist or a new object, the object of nothing. A book. Money, the "visible God..." The holy loot... Money is God. The pursuit of happiness, the money abstraction. Self-Transcendence is lost. The bank is our house of worship. Easier to believe in this God because in the end you have something to show for your faith... material stuff and inheritance... but maybe it is more than a belief-system, maybe it is ultimate knowledge. Power is knowledge. You can buy the truth. No escape from the power that shapes a subject after birth, cast into society. This clinging to identity. This internal discourse maneuvering through the labyrinth of self. Beware, ladies, this dark stranger in the night. He looks in your window. He sees you undress. But he stands behind shattered glass. He is no more in focus than the tangle of scars on his face. He turns away. He runs along the border with the flow of blood. He is naked. Great theorists of the unconscious, specters of society, have chased him. You have entered the kingdom and found the palace empty. Only a few old servants remain. Bounded by their boundaries. Servants of the human spirit? And therefore you have slaughtered them too, just to prove your pointlessness. Why don't you finish the job, finish them all off. Burn down the village. Is your degradation of the servant your final victory? Against belief and imagination and hope, you cannot do it. You can kill your philosophical idols. They were your secret accomplices anyway. You cannot kill my sunrise, my sunset, as long as I can write these words. The creation of the subject is repression? Not liberation? The answering subject affirms his subjection to power. Is silence possible? A slap in the face is the answer. Wake up! Once you "know" something are you socially compel to accept it? Or is knowing independent of the compulsion to accept it? You can argue that human nature is a blank slate or not, but the powerful few have always manipulated the means and the ends of the many, blank or not, and there is only experience and history, that's where the lessons are learned, because when the day comes that genetic engineering can change "human nature" at will, then where is nature? Where is freedom? Where is dignity? If not in experience and history, and if not now... when?

Harbor View Park
New Year's Day 1990

Lovers and young girls and three old men gather in *Minato no mieru oka koen*. They are here to see the apparent ascension of the sun; but who will heed the angel's declension into madness and dung and dun. The city moth strikes a stylish match that flashes a moment on the casement and sash in the bedroom window of his fashionable mistress, beneath whose satin sheets the bankers wank their business.

The night butterfly opens one eye and winks, her face painted in neon, her neck wrapped in minks; she lay down in the harbor, spent and breathless, the Yokohama Bay Bridge her bracelet and necklace. Red taillights, white headlights blink round her ankles and waist, her pert pink nipples protrude through gray fumes of lace; her scarves of silk the ripples of oily perfumed water, commerce and industry the creatures that bore her. The city moth sucks his steel cigarette and blows a long curliform of surly smoke across the gross billboards advertising Toyota and Coca-Cola, blows through a fish baited plastic net where the stars are caught and the moon and anything is sold and bought.

The sun shall not rise but the earth shall set, and civilization lean over the horizon as if to let its swill and spleen and rubbish slide with the vomit of its newspaper tide into a corporate furnace where words turn to dust and Copernicus burns and green thoughts rust. The alchemist walks his apocalyptic worms through Harbor View Park; he is waiting for the dark mystic to lift and then he will bring his belated offering and his savior's gift: the alliance of applied science and numismaticentric man, mixing the final solution in his Vatick Hermiticashcan. A delightful dilution of physics and jam, a sacrificed lamb, water and wine, three and nine, tea and burnt toast, and the Holy Ghost.

There suddenly appears the blue veil of Aurora; the smokestack whips her with his scaly tail and claws at her. There suddenly arises an iconic morning of blue and gold; but Giotto's tales have all been told. There suddenly shines the first light of the New Year; but where is de La Tour? And where is Vermeer? Has the sacred child with the halogos of flame been killed? Can we bow our heads and be re-enkindled? Render unto to Caesar a solar disk; and unto to God a word put at risk. Break of day... Scaling streaks of sienna; acolytes of embers solemnize the scarlet ardors of sunrise; austere amber magnifies the Ave Maria in our blinded eyes.

O Holy O Hosanna O break of day O...

O westernization of the eastern sun... lovers and young girls and three old men ooh and ahh and like childbirth push push push finally to witness the Fiat Lux as the ancient artisan's cragged hand shucks the husk from kernels of corn that burst into a glorious dawn. Lovers and young girls walk away; three old men stay to pray. They clap hands and bow... the earth reaches across the wounded beast, and black candles lower their heads to the East.

Bike Tour of The Old Torn Jacket Good-for-Nothing Literary Club
North Country of Japan- Spring & Autumn

I am still chasing phantoms. Here we go. Let's go. The Old Torn Jacket Good-for-Nothing Literary Club takes a bike tour of the north, like Bashō, like Miller in Paris. This is our bicycle trip to Genbi. At 7 am, we hear the sound of the Buddhist bells from Shoun-ji. We rise and dress and leave the ryokan. We start out on our bicycle trip. We are in the city of Ichinoseki. At the beginning of our trip to Genbi gorge we stop for a while on Kaminohashi Bridge, and lean against the railing, balancing ourselves on our bicycles; the cars rushing by... at one end of the bridge, at the end of the railing, there is a statue of a white swan; at the other end of the bridge, there is a statue of a drum. The Iwaigawa River flows beneath us. Tsuriyama Mountain stands in front of us. We pause on this spring day in April and remember last September when we paused somewhere to remember that Bashō had paused here to remember... whatever it is that poets remember and some men forget. Time keeps beating the drum, the swan flutters its wings, the snow thaws, and seasons change.

Swan of mountain snows, the constant drum of the heart, Iwaigawa flows. Last September... Kaminohashi is beneath the small mountain, Tsuriyama, where the dragonfly spirals around the misty paths where Bashō once past like a mist, where his haiku are carved in wooden posts; and where electric lanterns light the way into dark low clouds. In the distance, but not visible, is a mountain, 1627 meters high, called Sukawa if you view it from Iwate prefecture, but if seen from Miyagi prefecture to the west, it's called Kurikoma. Kaminohashi is above Iwaigawa River, where the waters have risen from heavy rain, threatening its banks. On the bank of the river the Lady Buddha protects against floods. A flood forty years ago devastated the town of Ichinoseki. Today, the river forcefully flows breaking white splashes against rocks like fists jabbed through shoji. Kaminohashi leading to the streets, lined with salvia and marigolds; leading to shops and houses of Ichinoseki. The river runs through the heart of the town, leading to the surrounding areas... to the west Genbi gorge and the mountains, to the east the low flat valley, where tall thick concrete pylons hold the span of cement and steel that supports the Shinkansen, the bullet train, speeding along, zooming... shattering the air, shaking the houses, rumbling the earth like the dreaded earthquake. The Shinkansen, speeding along, zooming... high above the plotted green fields below, where an old woman harvests her garden; the new and the old, the fast and the slow, like oil and water, resisting each other, yet part of each other, like the red leaves and the first cold winds of winter that was last autumn...

Now April, Kaminohashi is still beneath Tsuriyama, where the cherry trees have blossomed pink and white and shine on the side of the mountain like paper lanterns; where daffodils and paper lanterns line Bashō's path and young school children dressed in navy blue uniforms stumble along the paths. It is also the place where teenagers kill themselves. But that's not a topic that the locals care to talk about.

In the distance, Sukawa is visible and snow-capped; is it still 1627 meters high? The cherry blossoms fall like tears on a brightly-cladded kimono. Kaminohashi is still above Iwaigawa, where the river is low and the banks are plotted with blue plastic canvas to mark places to sit and drink sake and celebrate Ohanami, where a cable of koi, carp kites, are strung across the river for the annual Children's Day holiday. The bridge leading to the streets of Ichinoseki, the shops, the houses, the rice fields, where the Shinkansen speeds along, zooming... high above the plotted green fields below, where an old woman plants the rice, the new and the old, the fast and the slow, like oil and water, like the cherry blossoms and the first warm winds of spring.

We continue our bicycle trip, crossing the Kaminohashi and going straight on passed the farmer's high school, after which we make a left and go down a hill, then we come to another bridge that once again crosses the winding Iwaigawa. We pedal pass farmhouses and barking dogs. We take a narrow road along the side of the mountain. A green snake appears in the road and we hear bird song. We pause to watch the snake slither into the grass at the side of the road. Then, coming around a corner, once again we see the snow-capped peak of Sukawa mountain. Cedar and cherry trees line the road to Genbi gorge. We cross the bridge leading to this local tourist site. The tourist buses cross with us. We get off our bikes and walk down to the gorge; the water is rushing and smashing and echoing... everyone is crowded around a weaved basket on a cable, held by a looped rope attached at several places to the cable, and pulled by someone across the gorge. He stands on the platform to a small restaurant; he wears white gloves while dexterously pulling the rope and the basket upward towards him. He fills the basket with dango and tea and lets it fly down to the other side where it softly alights. The tourists take their food and the next person puts his money in the basket and then strikes a wooden board with a wooden mallet, signaling for the puller to pull. The sound of the wooden mallet hitting the wooden board echoes through the gorge. Kakko Dango, the rice balls covered with either sesame paste, or adzuki bean paste, or a soy paste, were named after Grandfather Kakko, who wore a red vest and red hat and who sang while he made and sold dango, and whose singing sounded like the "kakko" bird, the Japanese cuckoo. In the restaurant the members of the Old Torn Jacket Good-for-Nothing Literary Club sit out on a tatami veranda overlooking a small garden. There is a water wheel turning and bamboo and sunlight snipping the edges of leaves; we listen to the rushing water... it is almost too peaceful and perfect to be real...

We are in Iwate Prefecture. Our next stop is the famous Hikarido Temple. The Golden Hall at Chuson Temple. When Bashō passed through Haraizumi on his journey through the interior of the remote North Country, he wrote a famous haiku: Stands Hikarido/ Untouched by endless May rain/ Shining beautiful. Was it the walls and roof enclosing the walls and roof of Hikarido that fended off rain and time and erosion? Or was it the shining beauty of Hikarido? Hikarido was already five hundred years old when Bashō came here, that was 300 years ago... and I can announce that Hikarido is still untouched by rain; it is also untouched by wind, snow, hottest summer sun, and human hands, the modern ferro concrete building housing it sees to that; shining under electric lights, shining behind a glass partition through which tourists peer with dazzled eyes. The sign NO PHOTOGRAPHY ALLOWED, but a camera flash penetrates the glass; does a Buddhist prayer penetrate the glass? After the tape plays its explanation in Japanese, the tourists walk through a briefly sunlit exit door. Modern pilgrims traveling comfortably, the sunlight glaring off their Nikons. I listen to the English version tape that I had requested. Hikarido is covered with gold leaf, mother of pearl, and lacquer; inside the tomb of the temple are the literal heads of the figureheads of the Fujiwara clan, ancient samurai warriors. Battles, fires, and more battles brought their dynasty to an end. Bashō wrote: Of old soldier's dreams/ Nothing but summer grass is/ Left to fade away.

And several dreamless heads! When I walk outside a brief September rain is falling... touching the earth, but not, of course, Hikarido. In my mind I see the rain plopping into Oizumi Pond at Motsu Temple, not far away, which we had visited earlier in the day. The rain touching the bush clover, the maple trees, cherry trees, azaleas and lotus on the grounds at Motsu Temple... the rain touching the rocks, the stone boats in the pond, and the stone monuments of Bashō... the rain touching the world, the galaxy, the universe, everything, but not, of course, Hikarido. We leave the Golden Hall and walk up the path, where, at the side of the path, we meet the stone statue of Bashō, wearing a monk's hat and holding a walking stick. We stand before him; the rain runs down our faces like a poet's tears. Poets... Not beaten back by the rain, not beaten back by the wind, not beaten back by the snow, not beaten back by the hottest sun, so wrote Kenji Miyazawa, Poet of the North Country.

North of Haraizumi is the village of Hanamaki, where Kenji Miyazawa lived and died, and where a museum now stands halfway up Mt. Koshio. A modern building houses the Kenji Miyazawa Museum. Near the museum is a garden that Kenji had designed, but which was not laid out until after his death, as a poet's reputation is not laid out until after his death. The garden is on the slope of the mountain where descending meandering paths lead down past flowers and sculptures of vegetation and tile paintings and symbols taken from his stories and poems.

Sato wrote: Owl sitting on branch. Silhouetted by the moon; Pines, meadow, shadow.

Kenji Miyazawa was a multi-dimensional man, a poet, Buddhist, scientist, who created a four-dimensional dreamland that he named Ihatobu, his imaginary name for Iwate Prefecture. But his real life was no dreamland where rain never fell; life was hard and he was sickly and poor and died at the age of 37 in 1933. He wrote moving poetry about his dying sister Toshiko, wrote children stories, metaphysical poetry and tanka. His advice to himself was to eat four cups of brown rice a day, miso soup and some vegetables. When he could not be found writing it usually meant that he was in the garden. He made a sign for visitors: I am in the garden. Call me a good-for-nothing, he wrote. *Dekunobo.* His garden was his galaxy and the galaxy was within him; we must find the galaxy within each of us, he wrote. Does it rain there? He placed the Lotus Sutra at the center of his galaxy and at the center of his meditations. Does it rain on the jewels that strike heaven like spears of ice? Will it all end in ice or fire, will it all end in a whimper or a bang? The poets of the West ask that question. The Buddhist replies: will what end?. Will it rain at the end? Let us seek happiness for the world, Kenji Miyazawa wrote. Does it rain on happiness? Does it rain on Hikarido? It may not rain on Hikarido, or on Dreamland, or on the Jewels in the Lotus... but it rains where Kenji stands in his garden, it rains where Bashō stands on the narrow path, it rains where we stand... us ragged wayfaring poets. The rain wets the daikon leaves and the rice fields, but... not beaten back by rain... and in the morning after long rain the sun comes out again and together all the rice stalks stand up straight as if utterly alive.

Ichinoseki. We have returned to the ryokan. I write: The early morning Buddhist bell from Shoun-ji. Lying on futon and sliding open the *shoji*; incense remembering the dead. Young monk's *shuji,* new spring growth on tall *sugi,* fresh rain rippling the pond at Motsu-ji, yet so old, so old.

The temple of Chuson-ji is located in the village of Haraizami. Little stone Bashō on the hill above Hikarido with your hat and walking stick; who is the big *gaijin* who walks beside you? Old monk's shuji, cool crisp smell of tatami, high thatched-roof of Shobo-ji, yet so green, so green.

Hanamaki... at museum of Miyazawa Kenji. Your poetry. Your poverty. Your simple soul. Is that what museums are made of?

Return to Ichinoseki. September evening. Sweet potato man calls from his cart in the street, *"Ishi yaki imo... Ishi yaki imo..."*

It was a warm and dry spring day in Tokyo. I was sitting on tatami. I heard the voices of children, mingling and chattering, indecipherable, a wave of sound that I imagined were myriad languages blended into a hum; I've often heard this sound in many places around the world, in cities, towns. It is pleasant, for a while, till a sense of banality sets in, a sense of no sense. This time, it's the voices of Japanese school children from the playground across the street. Occasionally, surprisingly, a word that sounds like English rises out of the air like a bubble to my ear and goes pop! Not an English word, of course, just a trick of the mind. Bow-wow, Pooh-

pooh, Ding-dong, Yo-he-ho, La-la... the naming of creation by Adam, the Egyptian god Thoth, the Hindu Brahma, the Nordic Odin, the Chinese water-turtle with marks on its back... divine beings who brought speech and writing as a gift to man. O this gift... can I return it?

At the last gathering with the Old Torn Jacket Literary Club.... a farewell party for me... always they want to hear about America and New York City, as if two different countries. I leave picture postcards for my friends, speaking different languages, in a small room, surrounded by infinity, supported by columns of books; poets, drinking sake, with Kerouac! Rimbaud! Chasing the phantoms of names down dark memory; poets, singing Stephen Foster songs, late into the night, "Gonna run all night..." what else could we say but "Do-Dah Do-Dah?" say, *au revoir* and send some belated postcards. Here are mine: New York 1977, New York is in America, New York is not America, New York is a toilet bowl on a ceiling of a Greenwich Village dive; two huge paintings of Homeric battles on a SoHo gallery wall; 4 am, in a bar listening to Patti Smith, Television and The Ramones, popping pills, taking drugs, hallucinations of American battles; the Vietnam War is over... Paris time tonight... "Gonna run all night... Do-Dah Do-Dah." Driving through the Mohave Desert, midnight, 1980, the radio says, Ronald Reagan is the new president; shall I search out the lizard? Live in a cave? Survive on cactus? I drive on to Los Angeles; I give a ride to an outlaw truck driver from Texas; I meet a Mexican factory worker at our factory job; the former robbed me; the latter befriended me. The Mexican and I had planned an expedition to find treasure buried somewhere along the Rio Grande; the Mexican and I had planned an expedition to explore the jungles of Mexico; hallucination of American dreams; but my 1972 red Torino Dodge station wagon broke down in Pacoima. I abandoned it and caught the Greyhound back to New York. "Gonna run all night... Do-Dah Do-Dah." I sit on the curb in front of the City Lights Bookstore; I sit in the Chinese restaurant, eating Lo Mein... I look out the window, it's raining, lightly, my chopsticks are like two antennae, I hear the Buddha call my name, I have no name, I hallucinate a religious paradox: there is every reason to praise God, for God exists; there is no reason to curse God, for God does not exist. "Gonna run all night... Do-Dah Do-Dah." On an island off the coast of Norway 1984, Hamsun's wilderness, a can of Coca-Cola in the water; I take aim and pee. London 1987, Bethnal Green, Brick Lane Market, Bengali music, and bagels (24 hours a day)... through a warehouse loft window an American flag on the wall, James Dean poster, Elvis-look-alike working on his motorcycle, Jack Daniels on the table; I awake from a nightmare at 3 am, I go out and get a bagel. Anna. Vienna 1987. Kafka's cockroach in the skull of the middle-class; Cold War secrets, kisses of betrayal on the Riesenrad. Paris 1988. Henry Miller's crab scuttling in the gutter; I capture it with my teeth... "Gonna run all night... Do-Dah Do-Dah." Tokyo 1989, in Shinjuku, red light district, a stripper inserts an American eggplant into her cunt and squeezes it out... swish, and the American soldier from Idaho is amazed and disgusted; he wonders if she could do that with an Idaho potato; the Japanese professor is amused and studious and reverential; it's an aesthetic experience. The stripper hands him some polyester gloves to wear so he can feel her up. He inspects her vagina, close up, very scientific... I ride home on the blue train, filled with sake, and vomit on the floor of the Muse Café. These are the postcard memories I bequeath to my Japanese friends, the members of the Old Torn Jacket Good-for-Nothing Literary Club. They can't believe or understand my restlessness, my wanderlust. For the past ten years I have kept two literary dreams in mind: Henry Miller, almost forty, a healthy, unsuccessful writer, travels to Paris with ten bucks in his pocket, lives off his wits, and writes a book. Bashō, in his mid-forties, an unhealthy, successful poet, journeys into the deep, remote north of Japan, survives with a few necessities, and writes a book. And now, almost forty, these literary dreams persist despite having merged my footsteps with Miller and Bashō in pee-stained alleys, on smooth tatami, on the Rue Delambre, on Tsuriyama, by the side of the Seine, by Kitakami, on the sidewalks of Clichy, the paths of Chusonji... I have fried my soles with luminous holes, walked on words like stepping stones across the pure and polluted ponds of the world. And now what?

I say goodbye to my friends. The last thing that I say to them, that I shout to them is: The pig wins! Tasted delicious! Call me a *Dekunobo!* A good-for-nothing. They laugh, bow and watch me walk away until I disappear around the corner. I took an Aeroflot flight to Moscow and transferred to London. The plane drew some turbulence not long after takeoff and some people screamed. The airport in Moscow was dark. A large woman was pointing for us to go this way or that way and shouting: Berlin! London! Berlin! London!

The pig wins! Call me a *Dekunobo!*

Do It like Elgin Do It

...but listen Isabelle, I want to read you something... no because you never did write anything like this before, Stephen, and I don't want to listen to it now, said Isabelle... well, I'm back in Paris... well, what year is it? It really doesn't matter... 12 July 1992. Or a Sunday in Paris... should I write it that way? The date? Can I read it? Go on, let's just get it over with. Gee, thanks dad... what? And did you know Isabelle that today in Manhattan the sunrise and sunset can be seen as a full disk rising and setting right up and down between the buildings, east to west? Don't you want to see the sunset in Manhattan...? and here are my last and late night thoughts on being an American writer... an expatriate... no no no says Isabelle... just this once, a last time, and the captive listener, Isabelle, is right here with me. Go ahead and read, Stephen, she says, restlessly. Elgin? The Elgin Marbles? No. That's not it at all. Here it goes: This is my favorite view of America: from the *terrasse* of a café on the Boulevard du Montparnasse in Paris. It's not only a postcard view; it's a post-view view. It's not the Grand Canyon, not Niagara Falls, not the mighty Mississippi, not the Manhattan Skyline, but from here I see all that I want to remember and all that I don't need to remember, and all that I need to remember and don't want to remember, and that which I don't need to remember is made less memorable and less disagreeable and to a certain extent made tolerable and endurable by virtue of the fact, or the fiction, that I am here, with you, by the way, that's important, and not there. Did you write that? No, I just said that to keep your attention. I'm listening, Stephen. Needless to say, I also see what is actually here and not ontologically and abstractly "there," most importantly, that I am here and not there. That's as plain as day; this day, July 12, 1992, almost *quatorze juillet,* and this condition of post-being is adduced from a set of observations predicated on a certain pre-being that lives in my memory, which are personal examples beyond the scope of this presently belated writing, and because at the moment of this post-writing my post-being is surrounded by, nominally, an Anarchist, a Poet, a Fashion-Model, a Physicist, an Artist, a Philosopher of Post-Modernism, a few self-styled Writers, my Girl Friend, and a fat American Tourist reading the Herald-Tribune. Perhaps later there will be names. Though one of the writers is Charles Mouche, the famous French writer. *Qui?* Who? Oh, shut up Stephen. You make me laugh, this French intellectual nonsense... wait Isabelle, I'm not finished. It could be somewhere else; it has, in fact, been somewhere else, London, Vienna, the southern coast of Norway, Japan, and a lot of little places in between. I haven't a romantic postcard notion of place; rather, an alienated notion of drifting combined with either a primordial sense of place or a pilgrimal sense of place. But the former offers too little in the way of self-definition and the latter offers too much. In the end I adopt a practical sense of place; I adapt with my wits and remain intact. You, practical? With your beautiful soul? Don't start with that, Isabelle. Drifting randomly and stopping somewhere because something or someone has come in between two points on a slack, non-linear line that has a million possible interfacial lapses, is so compellingly indeterminate that one's jaw drops in a speechless pantomime of the absurd condition of being in a particular place and time. From here I see all that I need to forget, and all that I need to imagine about America. What to include and what not to include, that is the question. Most words are caked in mud, and most memory too. The angel of flight illuminates her transparent molecular structure. Night fades in her arms. Memory is all the presence that man has ever divined anyway. It's not just what you remember, it's also how you remember and why you remember and where you remember. It's also a matter of when to stop. How about stopping now? Damn, Isabelle, do you really mean it? The problem... the problem is that there are certain things that I can't forget. Some trivial things; for instance, a good portion of the baseball statistics compiled by the 1969 New York Mets. You're not gonna get any of this stuff, Isabelle, I'll explain it later, let me keep reading. Don't bother to explain... I don't need to know. Cleon's .340 batting average. Agee's 26 home runs. Seaver's 25 wins. Or glimpses into my childhood in the town where I grew up. For example, I see myself playing basketball with my friend on the playground of Theodore Roosevelt Elementary School. Roosevelt, now there's a name from American history. Not so trivial, rather pivotal, historically speaking; but ulterior to my living memory. Nevertheless, a cultural presence, part of the bedrock of history over which the critical lens moves in search of nuances of meaning. Theodore Roosevelt was the 26th President of the United States of America. That's an historical fact. You can look it up in a big book. The New York Mets won the World Series in 1969 and Tom Seaver won 25 games, lost 7. That's not only history, that's a statistic! You can look it up in a very big book. I think your book is too big, Stephen. That we were playing basketball on the playground on a Sunday morning at

Oyster Bay on a cool October day in 1969 in a small town in America is not so easily proved. Ronny always had the big dream about getting to Las Vegas and singing a duet with Elvis Presley. Keith always dreamed about getting to Madison Square Garden and playing basketball like Elgin Baylor. That's the Elgin, not the marbles. Richie never knew where he wanted to get to, so he never got out of small town America. But then again, neither did Ronny nor Keith. I always wanted to get to Shea Stadium and play baseball for the New York Mets. The four of us were playing basketball in a schoolyard in a small town. It was October 1969... It was. It was the month and year that the New York Mets won the World Series and Jack Kerouac died. It was the year man landed on the moon. We were American kids playing an American game and we were thinking about the World Series and our heroes: Elvis Presley, Elgin Baylor, Tom Seaver... none of us had ever heard of Jack Kerouac, though he was as American as the World Series. America, America, America, I really don't want to hear anymore about America. Neither do I... but for some reason I keep writing this shit... Ronny, Keith and Richie never did hear about Jack Kerouac. But I did. I discovered his books the usual way for someone who had moved outside the parameters of the status quo high school curriculum. I searched books out, on my own, and then books searched me out, you might say. How did it begin? Every book begat a new writer. Rimbaud begat Baudelaire, not vice versa. What is begat? It's a biblical term. Give birth to... historical and biological chronology was irrelevant. I moved through books like that crab in T.S. Eliot's poem, "claws scuttling across the floors of silent seas," devouring Literature. But I felt more like the crab in Henry Miller's *Tropic of Cancer,* a symbol of doom, death and despair, but without Miller's incredible pronouncement of being the happiness man alive; and then in the next few lines he proceeds to make that strangest of proclamations in an unpublished work (unpublished at the moment the ink was drawn from the pen): I am an artist, he writes. Miller had found himself as a writer. I don't care for Miller. I know, Isabelle, you have mentioned that before... can I continue? Okay, but hurry up please it's almost time. He doesn't think about being an artist; he just is. I am that I am. To hell with Literature. There are no more "books" to be written. Miller is singing (according to Miller, and perhaps Whitman); though sometimes it just sounds like a lot of talking. Miller defies classification. An enigma, like his idol Hamsun. Everything that was Literature had fallen from him, he claims. This was a pre-mature boast coming as it does at the very beginning of a book strewn with the corpses of "Literature." This was something new. It is difficult to classify someone whose work reveals so many contradictions and ambiguities. He can't be pinned down. That's Miller and Kerouac, and they both have figured prominently in this story, as representations of an idea, and also as characters (who are, come to think of it, *cerebis paribus*, also just representations). What? Latin? Take that out! Take that out, now! Too academic. You are not an academic, Stephen. They have been chosen not necessarily because they are "great" writers, in a great tradition, or in a great breaking-with tradition, but because they are thematically suitable. I am more interested in their lives as writers. This vulgarly intrusive word happiness keeps gnawing. Why did Miller say it? Anyone who would write in WORDS that he was HAPPY can have no sense of FORM. Democracy without style is repressive. I think I heard that one already. Well, Isabelle, you just heard it again. A momentary sentiment like that sucks the marrow out of the bones. It leaves a glob of flesh on the page that no formal apparatus can reconstruct. No money, no resources, no hope. I am the happiest man alive. An innocent abroad. A hungry animal never bites the hand that feeds him; not while he's being fed. Remembering is a kind of regurgitation. A catharsis. A biting back at all the hands that were empty or full. Every crack, crevice, wart, blister, callus, broken nail, bent finger, stains and scents, fists, slaps, punches, whacks, grips, touches, pokes and prods, mutilations, pencils, pens, pointing fingers, fork, knife, spoon, chopsticks, cuts and bruises, baseballs, basketballs, penises and testicles, tits and rims... Ah! Youth! Somehow it didn't always add up to ten. Here we go with the words again and the lists, too much... counting every detail, remembering every detail. It just added up... then escape, the innocent in flight, with his only baggage his memories and his only passport his wits. No wonder Miller wrote it. He meant it, for whatever it was worth. Two cents worth. It was just another way of saying fuck you, ya miserable world. He knew that his life and his work was a blending of body and spirit, of fact and fiction, and that someone one day just might hear him speak. He wanted to scream out that he was happy and fuck the world. And the barbaric yawp shatters the still air of the Paris streets and penetrates the walls of Proust's bedroom. Mother, bring me my happiness pills, please. Now you are just being silly. Where did you learn your English, Isabelle? Silly? Miller associated happiness with life, and by extension, experience; not with private ownership like a Jefferson, not with reason, as with Arthur Rimbaud, *enfin, bonheur, raison*; and French again... where did you learn your French, Stephen? Maybe that's why Miller survived, intact, and Rimbaud did not, quite literally, though he wrote that he had. Americans don't care much for Miller's amoral, hedonist, pagan happiness. Americans like to hear a pure hero like Lou Gehrig in the face of certain personal death proclaim himself the luckiest man on the face of the earth. Who is that? Baseball? Not again. I know. It's physiological. My heart races. My nerves are on edge. It's a cliché buried deep in the psyche. Can I go on? If you must. Henry Miller wasn't facing certain personal death, he was facing up to the prevailing winds of death that were in the air; and in the miasmic midst of it all he was Mr. Happy-go-Lucky, with a hungry belly and a "personal hard-on" no less. So if Miller did choose to go gallivanting off in foreign countries, starving, not doing a proper job... well fuck him. America had more marketable heroes who could say what the American public was told they wanted to hear, and with the conciseness of a male predator's incisors biting deeply into young female flesh, the pure and virtuous maidens of Hollywood movies, the strong handsome leading men shooting their wads into their pants and crawling off into the sunset sand to weep on the shores of the Pacific, empty, empty, empty and aching in their bowels. How many Faulkners, Fitzgeralds, Brechts and Odets gazed down at them from the cliff, thinking death is not that far away for any of us? But there was Henry, still in Paris, the smell of a whore's stale perfume more real in his brazen nostrils than all the painted unreal faces wrapped around a real steel reel and twisted and tied up in celluloid like the girl next door in bondage. Ha! Is that your fantasy, Stephen? Hardly... Henry Miller in the guise of Henry Miller did write that he was the happiest man alive before Gary Cooper in the guise of Lou Gehrig said that he was the luckiest, though neither was the first to discover that he or she had been lucky or happy. Americans have been pursuing this policy ever since Thomas Jefferson first declared it in the guise of Thomas Jefferson. Americans are always talking about the most this and the most that, the best this and the best that, the -est of it all. Allen Ginsberg saw the best minds of his generation destroyed... the best and the brightest men were gathered around John F. Kennedy. Sports statistics offer the most, the fewest, the highest, the lowest, and everyone has his or her opinion about the greatest this and the greatest that. Top Ten Lists...

do you want to hear my Top Ten Movie list, Isabelle? No, not really. Henry Miller was no exception; he had more opinions than a Lonely Heart's columnist, and sometimes just as rosy-colored romantic, especially in the later books written in sunny California. But in the *Tropic of Cancer* every idea, opinion, sentiment that came into Miller's head like a tulip pushing up from the dirty soil of cerebral gray matter was quickly snipped off in the bud of self-mockery. He's not much of a thinker, is he? No, Isabelle, he's not. Not a Parisian intellectual. A saving grace, as far as the book is concerned. And youth, another saving grace for Miller; *Ah! cette vie de mon enfance,* that life of my childhood, wrote Rimbaud, and then grew up and wrote no more poetry, but engaged in the business of making money and private ownership. *La raison m'est nee.* Reason is born to me. And then later: *Mes deux sous de raison sont finis.* Pronounce that for me, Isabelle. Oh please stop with the French. I want to hear you say it. No? He had spent his two cents worth of reason to buy his way out of poetry, but neither poetry nor reason would save him; the wild spirit took over; and then duty. Rimbaud never understood, like I will never come to understand, that poetry, fiction, literature, *inter alia,* yes, I know, Latin, has an ultimate value of about two cents worth of reason. That is, a brief but enduring spectral look-see at truth, beauty, free will, consciousness and human nature. The endurance part is truly inspiring. To the point that it's not *what* but *that,* that anyone bothers to keep creating Art at all. Long live Copernicus, Galileo, Darwin, and Einstein. So for what it is worth I will continue with my two cents worth of reason. Add my two cents and get out of the game. The rest is lost. Past, Present and Future lost. You should write unreason, Stephen, that's the latest French word of the Parisian smarties. I'll think about it, Isabelle. With Miller the body took over. Rimbaud did not add to his account of his expenditures his imagination, creativity, desires, dreams, and hopes... or the debts he had accumulated in his fall from grace. Everything had been wasted in the confusions and rebellions of youth and the hell of women... but from now on... *et il me sera loisible de posse der la...* free to possess the truth in one soul and one body. It is heartbreaking. Hell of women? Did you write that? No, Rimbaud did... can you put that cigarette out, please... or open the damn window... of course no heart will "break" literally. I locate pain or pleasure in life; locate "tragedy" and "triumph" in "history." My flesh crawls with words like spiders that must be brushed away in a nightmare. The "soul" of the numerical does not possess the same "truth" as the enunciated. And beyond that un-moveable barrier words cannot reach, into the realm of higher mathematics. Poets posit the Word, are possessed by the Word, and wait for The Fall. There is no redemption or salvation in playing games designed to self-destruct in their own axiomatic finalities. Ah you have been reading the Parisian intellectuals! Rimbaud's words are written originally in French, the heart that bared them had nothing to conceal but the naked translation of life into language, of language into life, possibly the very structure of the "mind," when that uncertain organization of cognition turns inward its outward impetus of the "other" and turns outward its inward impetus of the "divine." Oh my, I'm wrong, you've not been reading the latest trends in philosophy. You know, Stephen, there is philosophy after existentialism. And why do I do that, hmm, Isabelle? Because I question my privilege to write? Or I doubt my ability to write? The words Free and Truth and Body and Soul and One are not the last words from Rimbaud's season in hell. Each word is The Word. Each Word is a theologically underwritten assurance of authentic at-presentness. So the poet would have us believe. But he wagers in the dark because the reader might not be "there." The "other" is the poet's God. The "other" is discovered in one's own cogito, as Jean-Paul Sartre remarks in his lecture on existentialism. And the Self is shredded like a cabbage. On the other hand, and he has many hands, the writer of fictive and imaginary discourse does not depend on The Word; but words, words, words. Nor does the writer have to bring the same conceptual framework to the word *mind* as it appears in Shakespeare, Tolstoy, Proust, as a philosopher or scientist or psychologist does to the word "mind," as it appears in Plato, Einstein, and Freud. The approach of the writer of fictive and imaginary discourse is idiosyncratic, anarchic, recursive, and, paradoxically, formal. God is one word. Robinson Jeffers said, "For those for whom the Word is God, their God is a word." And so on. The old poets and classic philosophers walk out the door. The scientist remains by virtue of the "fact," or the "fiction," that the Number is greater than the Word and all that remains is words words words... the text that goes all the way down, according to Derrida, like Ed Norton down into the sewer hole. Ed Norton down the sewer hole? What the hell is that? And you have read Derrida? I prefer Foucault. Yes, me too... that's just another reference to American popular culture... television... or any other direction, for that matter. And all will be well as long as you heed the consensual strains of belief playing MUZAK of relative DNA in the corporate endplay of cultural chit-chat, as long as the words don't break loose beyond un-vaultable fences unseen in the mist by young rebel poets running through pastures of public manure because by their own private admission are unable to write the word SHIT on sidewalks in front of churches, libraries and other institutions anymore. *Merde!* Is that any better for you? More physiological? The writer is irresponsible. A lazy sod. Huh, don't I know... don't make this personal, Isabelle... this is not an ethical question; it is a technical one. Shakespeare, Tolstoy, Proust, Henry Miller, Jack Kerouac, Rimbaud, etc., weigh upon a writer in a way that Newton, Einstein, etc. do not weigh upon a scientist. At least not until the so-called paradigm shift takes place, and then anxiety and alienation sets in for the scientists too. So welcome to the world of literature. The two cultures are one after all. For a moment, anyway. Listen, Stephen, I don't think this should be in your book. Why? Because I didn't attend a great university? Like you. *Oui, exactement.* The writer struggles to break free from that burdensome word influence. Am I a burden to you, Stephen? *C'est mon Parisienne à moi...* so what if she is better than me... but of course this is just illusion, like free will, so they say. Is that Brel? Sort of. The scientist knows it. The scientist fills up the dark spaces as he takes things apart. The writer reveals the dark spaces as he puts things together. And we are all working in the dark. But we know that someone was there before us. The writer hurls words at the empty page, sprinting to the edge and back to the center, playing King of the Hill with his idols of youth, trying to push them off the edge of the page and into the abyss of a jumble of words words words. But the writer is ever the deceitful one. The concealer. The outright fabricator. At dusk we find him fishing in that abyss, not with a single golden hook to catch that one mystical fish, but with a net to catch all the variables and contingencies and verbalizations of human experience grafted to an inconceivable and ill-conceived "human nature" that may be fathomless but for the very structure of the mind, that word that the writer can use this way in a way that the philosopher can't. If you want rigor, read rigor mortis. We can get away with so much. Poetic license. As for Rimbaud's season in hell, the 20th century can claim no greater autumnal prologue to our winter epilogue. Everything in between, content, context and form, you can erase or put in doubt. Freedom, Truth, Body, Soul, One... cross it out or put the word in dubious marks. Here they are: "..."

With an ellipsis thrown in just for the hell of it. Or so the story goes... as for the story, let's get back to this story, if there is one in here. If only I could escape from this book, this postmodern rigmarole. This is the best cup of coffee I have ever had, said the fat American Tourist reading the Herald-Tribune, sitting at the other table at this cafe, being observed by the writer. Tomorrow's cup of coffee will also be the best. It's why Americans are so good at marketing their products, at advertising themselves as Americans. We know what's best, so why can't the rest of the world see it that way? In America there is monetary greed of all or nothing and there is metaphysical greed of all or nothing. There is the pursuit of happiness. The pursuit of doom. The pursuit of knowledge. Measured against the land, the unreal land, the American can DO anything. Measured against the sea, the elemental abstract sea, the American can KNOW everything. Turn toward the absolute and strike through the mask like Captain Ahab. Or turn to Europe and Faust and decay. Or turn to the free market place, not gothic madness. O Jerusalem Athens Alexandria Vienna London Paris. Where gravestones are monuments; a mosaic of the old. The dream of renegade Americans, to kiss the old bones of Europe, to stand in the Cimetiere du Montparnasse and hold the skull in one's hand and say: Alas poor Whore, I screw her Fallatio. That's as far as we go, word games, crossword games and no Word on the cross to bear. See I do read some new philosophy. Where are we? It is not down on any map, true places never are, wrote Melville in *Moby-Dick*. And that is true, if we take it to mean that each of us must discover LIFE for himself or herself anew, for the first time, whenever we must escape to wherever that true place may be. Why did the 19th and 20th century see such an outburst of Self, of "I" novels. Think how many books written in these centuries begin with the word "I" or that contain the word "I" in the opening sentence. Proust regretted that he began his great novel with the "I" word. Was it a cry against too much revealed death? A cry to let language live? And yet language was degraded on all sides, and was that not the Orwell take on things? Before the 20th century the poets possessed the "I" as if it were part of their writing hand. And 20th century novels (why even talk of novelists), like Miller's and Kerouac's, writers of prose, took their lead from two poets, Whitman, whose poetry is so prose-like and whose book *Leaves of Grass* begins poundingly and resoundingly with the I-word, and singing of One's Self, to boot; and Rimbaud, who wrote prose-poetry, and begins his *"Une Saison en*

Enfer" with a litany of je-words, every one of them aimed at denial, every one of them linked to the past by memory, every one of them linked to nostalgia…... but, miraculously, *je suis intact.* Until they chopped off his leg. When was the writer born in me? How was the writer born in me? To answer how, would require descending into my unknown past and into my unknowable psyche, in a manner inappropriate. There are no tools to find my way in or out. I am neither psychologist nor philosopher nor scientist nor literary theorist nor statistician nor polltaker of my impulses and ideas, and I haven't their specialized vocabularies. Rimbaud used poetry to delineate the burnt skins of hell. He opened the door, entered, and poetry lit up the dark places that few dare focus their eyes upon without inducing madness. So he says; so he would have us believe. Do we? Do we need to believe that some truth lies beyond his posturing proofs of poetic diction; merely that. Did he need poetry to find his way out? Or did he just take a side step and was on the outside of the door once again. The house called society then put him in order, under the obligation of life, and life put him to death. Same old story. A cliché. Pain was his ultimate fiction, too painful to be a fact. The fiction, the myth, the legend, that we make of a fictive self, is sometimes far greater an organism than our corporeal being because it is so much less complex; like any flattened myth elongated over time. So when did it begin? It began in October 1969; that will do. Soren Kierkegaard, the Danish philosopher, wrote that man is unwilling to begin at the beginning, and therefore he begins with "In the Beginning." In other words, a man prefers to create a myth of himself, or of the gods, or the world for that matter. The beginning that is lost is rejected in favor of a beginning that is found, as if a psychological Big Bang lay dormant deep in our soul waiting to be discovered. The real and true self. The authentic self. But a real and true self moving, shifting shape, and throwing patterns against the wall. In the beginning we find those shapes in the books that we are reading at the time. Those books that begat books. I didn't read them. Too depressing. I discovered Henry Miller's and Jack Kerouac's books at a time when I was deeply entrenched in the mortified blood-sapped flesh of 19th century literature. How did the I get in here, Stephen? You just slipped yourself into the text. I know. The Symbolists, Decadents, Romantics, Baudelaire, Rimbaud, Lautreamont, Nietzsche, Hamsun, Dostoyevsky, Blake, Holderlin, Heine, Rilke, Rousseau, Cowper, Shelley, Coleridge, Byron, Keats, Hugo, Kierkegaard, Huysmans, Jarry, Verlaine, Mallarmé…

and the moderns of the 20th century, Joyce, Céline, Beckett, Camus, Sartre, Kafka, the Surrealists, the Beats, Dada. From Knut Hamsun in a hut in the cold exposures of the Norwegian North to Nietzsche in a villa in the warm exposures of the Italian South, the hot and cold climates of the European Mind. From the Maelstrom to the Volcano. That house that housed the Word in every room except for a bit of mystical light in the attic and a dark unknown in the basement. But when the 19th century dragged its body to the door of the 20th century, it was nothing but a corpse and the house had become, as Henry Miller said, "a charnel house." Miller too was steeped in it. The world was dying all around him. Death was in the air. Yet he writes that he was the happiest man alive. Go figure. It doesn't add up. I was stuck in the 19th century reading Dostoyevsky's *Notes from the Underground* whose first line is, "I am a sick man..." All the *poseurs* left in the hot August of 1929... you want to be an American *poseur*, Stephen, in Paris, in the twenties? Oh Isabelle... *Quand Isabelle rit...* when she laughs... *Quand Isabelle dort...* when she sleeps... *Quand Isabelle chante...* when Isabelle sings... *Belle Isabelle...* beautiful Isabelle... Oh please stop, Stephen. I know the songs of Brel. Where was I? Hemingway to the south of Spain and F. Scott Fitzgerald to the south of France... and the American contingent of hangers on slithered from their café terrases into the gutter that flushed them back to America. I like that phrase, flushed them back to America. *Merci*, Isabelle. Then the crash. But Miller washed up on these shores after that... it is now July 1992 and I am in Paris, sitting at the table of the cafe. A rather famous cafe. There is something about it in the tourist guidebook. The names Hemingway and Fitzgerald are mentioned, sounds like a brand of whisky, or a law firm, pro bono work only. The tourist guidebook is on the table, and next to the tourist guidebook are two other books. Two old, torn, worn, beat up paperback books. One book is *On the Road* by Jack Kerouac; the other book is *Tropic of Cancer* by Henry Miller. And two more, *The Sun Also Rises* and *The Great Gatsby*. Why Stephen are you so steeped in American themes, this absurd *nostalgie*... though a thousand miles away, said Isabelle. No, it's over three thousand miles away! *Pédantesque!* And you used the word absurd! Kerouac had lived in a town on Long Island with his mother, and had frequented several bars on Main Street in this town. The town is named Northport. I did not live in this town but my father traveled every day to go to work in Northport. I read a biography of Kerouac and it mentioned bars in Northport. One of the bars must have been my father and uncle's bar. They ran the bar from 1950-1962. Kerouac had lived in Northport from about 1958-1962. The author of the biography calls this bar by a different name, though, in fact, from 1950 until 1962, it was called Joe & Frank's Commercial Restaurant; I can show you the swizzle stick with the imprint; and not until 1962, when my father and uncle sold the bar to their part-time cook, and her son, did it become a different bar. I just want to get the facts straight, you see. Why is it so important to get this one fact right? How come my father can't get his name in a book? Why should it be so different from all the other real life experiences that have been transformed into "fiction?" We know that Sal Paradise is Jack Kerouac. We know that Eugene Gant is Thomas Wolfe. We even know that Walt Whitman is Walt Whitman! Imagine that! We know that Henry Miller is Henry Miller. We know that Isabelle is Isabelle! Don't be so sure! We know that they wrote about their lives, that they turned their experiences into fiction, or something like it, choosing, as Emerson foretold that we would, among what we call our experience and how to record truth truly. We know that this bar is a certain bar, but not until 1962 goddammit! But could I be wrong? Could my father have remembered wrongly. It doesn't matter. How did I get from a cracked blacktop basketball court in a schoolyard in a small town in America on a Sunday morning in October 1969, to a cafe on a street in Paris in July 1992, sitting here thinking that old cliché about being thirty years too late for the Paris of the 1950s or sixty years too late for the Paris of the 1920s, so why not eight-hundred years too late? I could've been chasing Héloise around the muddy streets of Paris while her uncle the canon could've been chasing me with a carving knife aimed at my balls, yipes! So much for going back there. There weren't any expatriate American writers hanging around the cafés either so it wouldn't have mattered much. No big American Experience. No Great American Scene. No dreams of the Great American Novel. Isabelle laughs. Finally. So you enjoy cynicism? *Mais oui.* And have things changed that much? Miller wrote that a kind of symbolic cancer and syphilis were everywhere and eating into our souls. Today the transcription of time writes AIDS on the cold shithouse wall. The spirit is dead and the past a muddy ditch. Miller found a golden peace in this vision. And toward the end of his book his thoughts drift back to America, "Do you want to go back?" There came no answer. One doesn't dare answer a drifting thought. And then in one of the most touching moments in all of literature, Miller writes, "I wondered in a vague way what had happened to my wife." Throughout the book we have had brief encounters with Miller's wife (he calls her Mona), unlike the later volumes that are saturated with Mona-rabillia. Miller transfixes the international cunts, Danish cunts, Georgia cunts, French cunts, rich cunts to the page like butterflies with their wings pinned back, scattered in a scrapbook amongst the Jews, Hindus, whores, bums, lesbians, and French phrases, and all the "friends" who it seems are only good for a meal. It is not until Miller travels to Greece, and writes a book about it, that he uses the word friend with anything that remotely resembles the warmth of the climate in which he immersed himself, experiencing a kind of human rebirth. The word "friend" hardly appears in the insouciant devil-take-all chill of *Tropic of Cancer*. But Mona he cannot transfix to the page. Not in this book. She first appears as an apparition in Miller's mind when he is sitting with a bottle of wine between his legs reflecting on the misery and splendor of his first days in Paris, and then after a strange mixture of a Zola-list and Baudelaire-litany of first impressions, everything from fat cockroaches and getting erections looking at statues, and lice and beggars and old hags and the strange people and the poverty, and gathering butts and squeezing his guts out to stop the gnawing rats of hunger, and mad with the beauty of the Seine at night, and after all this we meet Mona, walking with Henry down the Rue Bonaparte, both of them sick and tired and fed up with the faces and cathedrals and the squares of Paris. Then with a characteristic gesture Miller proclaims that this was his golden period in Paris, when he had not a single friend. Are we to believe him? It was 1928, one of the few times that Miller pins time to the page along with the butterflies, but we are not with the butterflies, this is his time with Mona, and it's not quite the same thing. On the night before he is set to sail back to America, he spends his time dancing with every "slut" in the place, we are not told what kind of place, we know by now; are we to trust him? He's with some cunt in the toilet, fiddling with his erection in a cabinet and he can't get it into her, this way, that way, it just won't work, and she's clutching his prick and won't let go as if her life depended on it, then Miller comes all over her gown and now she's sore as hell and though Miller's waiting for Mona to come and fetch him, he doesn't care. He finds Mona waiting at a table with her disapproving eye and that night Miller goes back to the hotel and vomits all over the bed and notebooks and his manuscripts cold and dead. The next day they are off to

Brussels... then suddenly we are back in Paris. Brought up to date. Miller is waiting at the Gare St. Lazare to meet Mona, but she's not there. Then the first chapter closes in a dream-like state of memories about a Mona who is there and not there. How do you fill in the blanks of time and experience over a plethora of memories impacted in a life's obsession? You just go on living and writing, another balancing act, like Nietzsche's tight-rope walker at twilight, but you're walking the streets of Paris, and the ground is moving beneath you. Miller returns to Paris without Mona. It is without Mona's presence that Miller writes *Tropic of Cancer*. Yet without Mona, no *Tropic of Cancer*. Without Dean Moriarty, no *On the Road*. Sal Paradise calls Moriarty the sad and fabled tinsmith of his mind. Mona was the creatrix of Miller's imagination. Am I your Mona? Your Dean? Don't bet on it, baby. Ouch, an American tough guy, you sounded like a gangster. Yeah, like Belmondo in *Breathless*? *Ch'uis vraiment dégueulasse*. Shall we go out to the street and have a death scene? Or should I keep reading? Which do you prefer? And if you say death I will understand. Without Mona, Paris opens up to him festering and festive arms, and he sees her reflection in every detail of every nook and cranny of every cathedral and tombstone and morsel of food and written word. He's searching for her on every street and on every page, and in the end it amounts to the same thing. In the end he finds something else altogether, he finds "Henry Miller, Artist." Or does cities like Paris find the artist within? Stephen, have you read Blaise Cendrars? Yes, Miller met him. I've read... what's the name? *Mora.. vagina?* Almost... *Moravagine*... death to the vagina! Is that so? Yes, that is so... and also about the double... killing the evil double with words... death by literature, you see... I see... and have you read Jean-Paul Clébert's *Paris insolite*? I never heard of that. Well, it's right up the alley, as you say. Up my alley. Right up your alley. Kerouac writes about finding someone who looks like your father in places like Montana, or you look for a friend's father where he is no more. Where he is no more. Where she is no more. Mona wasn't in the place where Miller was looking for her. Never was. The passionate idealist becomes the poet of the body when he finds the person sitting next to him to be the person he had been searching for all along. She may be a whore without teeth. Don't smile! You're beautiful. He may be your best buddy in the whole world forever. It was as if Mona embodied life itself, the principle of life itself, the generation and transformation of time released in a Big Bang of words, with gaping abysmal black holes sprawled beneath him, not to mention a void of dark cunts. How about not mention it, Stephen. Without her, no action, no movement, no deed, no body, no senses, no desire, nothing but stasis and stagnation and death. The cancer of time is to live always in a world of words, a world of mind, a world of spirit, a monastic shithouse with golden turds. We get a glimpse of the new Miller who will write *Tropic of Cancer* even as we are reading the book. It is on that illuminating night, Miller's last in Paris, when he vomits all over his notebooks and manuscripts; it was a shout of prophecy and liberation. Miller returns to Paris alone, without Mona, and his new life begins. The second chapter commences: A new life opening up for me at the Villa Borghese. We will not hear about Mona very much anymore. Several chapters later Miller is once again waiting for her; this time at the pier, but no Mona. Are we in Paris or back in New York, Henry? He considers pawning his wedding ring, a ring that he had purchased after he had left her. He is hungry. *Sult.* What's that? Norwegian for hunger, like Hamsun's book. Miller's mind often turns to food after thinking about Mona and America; but there's more here than meets the stomach. When he thinks about America he cannot separate America from the idea of Mona being there; at this point Mona has become nothing more than an idea. Midway through the book Miller virtually explodes in sentiment, pristine notions about this woman, this goddess, this Her, this idea, whom he can hardly think about without being tossed back into the wretched refuse of his past, his New York City past, and yet he tells us that he went about for seven years with only one thing on his mind... Her. She is gone forever. Later he will be told word-of-mouth that she is sick and starving in New York. He reels in a void of loneliness. Finally he realizes that he has created a Paris that exists solely because he has hungered for her. Her absence. It is her absence as he walks the streets of Paris in tears that brings about the flaming image of bright venomous crabs heralding the approach of cancer. Shout it from the belfries, declare it in the cafes, announce it in the squares, and stammer it in the streets, if Mona did not exist it would be necessary to invent a "literature" that would invent her. It is in the absence of God, Beauty, Man, Time, Destiny, Love, such Words as Miller kicks in the pants at the beginning of the book, that Miller conjures up his happiness. But he says that what he is about to "write" is not a "book." What is it then he asks? And she asks? Yes, Isabelle wants to know? His answer is not worth the spit it invokes. That I believe. He calls it libel and slander. Yet he wants to tell the truth truly. He wants to be honest about HIS life. Not God or Beauty or the gold standard of Literature. To hell with all that. In the absence of all that, what else can one do? After all that, all that is left is man's cruelty, a lesson from his God, as Albert Camus had testified on behalf of the Absurd. What was that? I'm not repeating it just so you can mock me? Are we almost done here? It's getting dark out. It's getting dark in here too. So how do you get from that basketball court on a playground in a small town in America to Paris twenty years later? You walk across the muddy 20th century like a clown on stilts. It was found necessary to write, it was found necessary to travel to Paris, to get to Paris, to get to here from there; flickers faintly like a corona encircling the fleshless ribs of civilization, and out of the muddy-dud-dud of literary theory and the Great Tradition I saw a man with lightness in his shoes, holes in his soles from too much traveling, too much experience, too much rejection, turn it all upside down, reverse the formula, accept the contradictions, and on that day life overcame art, out ran it, out walked it on the streets of Paris, and that was one of the books that pointed the way, from that basketball court in that small town to a cafe on a street in Paris. The Norwegian writer Knut Hamsun, whom Miller admired, named one of his early novels *Sult*, meaning hunger, about a writer who hungers not only for food, but also for life and the words to convey that life. Miller lived by his wits; he was omnivorous and insatiable. An encyclopedic community of insiders who know the score, and the score is a bunch of garbled voices singing, a little off key, as Miller says, but the essential thing is to want to sing. Sing the body electric! Yet the book is not a paean to life (death, doom and despair are everywhere) but a paean to living, living a life where death, doom and despair are everywhere. The very first words proclaim it: I am living... where are you living, Henry? At the Villa Borghese... alone? No, with Boris, who talks about death and despair and the cancer of time... is it all too much, Henry, all this talk of being alone and dead? Not too much at all, I am the happiest man alive, I am in Paris... so am I Henry, sitting at this cafe, with a beat-up paperback copy of your book. You began your book in the fall of your second year in Paris, is that right? You were sent to Paris for a reason that you have not been able to fathom... what did you do that first night in Paris, that second night, and so on... when did you become the happiest man alive? I want to know, Henry. I don't know why I want to know. I don't know why I have been "sent here." Isabelle is laughing again. I am not really at a café as I write, with those types. I am in a small room on the Rue Guisarde in the 6th arrondissement. It's Isabelle's flat. If I look out the window and upward to the sky above the brown cracked walls I can see the top of one of the towers of St. Sulpice. It's 5 p.m. and its bells are tolling. You know me Isabelle... I'm not into gender victim politics... I have a fetish you know... I think it's inbred... an enlightenment fetish... you give me these books, Derrida, Foucault... but it doesn't seem to catch... I've tried... believe me, I want to believe... I do, some of Foucault I get... Miller says that everything that was literature has fallen from him. I carry Miller's book around with me, English and French versions, does that have anything to do with literature? But the names, Henry, the names in your book, where did they come from if not from literature? Conrad, Maugham, Moore, Strindberg, Hugo, Rimbaud, Baudelaire, Emerson, Villon, Rabelais, Goethe, Poe, Homer, Cervantes, Nietzsche, Schopenhauer, Dostoevski, Hamsun, Byron, Gautama, Jesus, Dante, Whitman... good old Walt, contradictions... acceptance... on the last page of your book you say that man needs to be surrounded by space, space more than time... is there not more space in America? More time in Europe? Think of Proust and Balzac, but never mind, no sweeping statements. Or do you mean inner space; is there more inner space in Paris? A Paris of the mind, Miller's mind. I have looked at the river, the Seine; Miller says that its course is fixed; am I fixed in its course? Is Isabelle? Has the river been flowing through Miller and me from the beginning of time? Sufficient space, more than time. Did the river flow through me that day on that basketball court in America? Did it flow through the others? Experience, Henry, what a fall! But that's what he meant, right? He was going to sing and dance and live, even as the world was falling to pieces at his feet... Paris before my eyes... I'll take to the streets... but let me reflect a moment... a moment... shall we take a walk, Isabelle? After this. What of the others? Who? Oh, the others. Where did they get? asks Isabelle. There were four of us. Four of us playing a two-on-two pick-up game that day. Question, America: How do you get from that basketball court to a mental institution eight years later? Or how do you get precisely nowhere, because you're now a thirty-three-year-old town mainstay (mainstreetstay) still playing basketball on that same court, with a paunch of a belly and thinning hair? Or how do you get a bullet in your head ten years later? Did they lack that native strange saintliness to save them from iron fate, as Sal Paradise described his buddy Dean Moriarty in *On the Road?* Two books, one pointing its light toward Paris, Europe; the other book pointing toward the American West, Mexico, the great American Night. And either way iron fate clamps us in its inevitable jaws, clamps us in a mental institution, clamps us in a small town, clamps us to an iron rail, clamps us in an electric chair, clamps us to a toilet vomiting the blood out of our boozed brains, clamps us with a bullet in the head... but in Paris? Can one be clamped to an iron chair in a café on a street in Paris? Paris before my eyes! And the problem of living. Food, money, a place to lay my head. But why go in to all that, all that down and out stuff. I am sitting at the aforementioned café... in Paris... thinking, God knows why, of the four of us on that basketball court twenty years ago. There was Richie, who was my friend. We were both thirteen years old. Richie was a superb burgeoning athlete, with a natural flare for the game. Even at that age he could dunk, jam the ball, well just about, his hands weren't quite big enough to palm the ball, grip the ball with one hand, but we conceded that it qualified as a dunk because he was able to "touch the rim." Ah the magic of those words: Touch the rim. That's all we dreamt about back then, to be able to touch the rim. The magic touch, that was before we had dreams about being able to touch other things, that other magic touch of discovery, but we didn't care then about touching female body parts and whatnot, only that rim! I never did make it. I never did touch the rim that is, couldn't get off the ground. In compensation we turned to other things, like making it with girls, touching that stuff, and put away childish things. And what did you do, Henry, in those days before Post World War Two A-Bomb Cold War Pop Culture Music & Sports? You ran the streets of Brooklyn with your true heroes, those boys on the block, when experience was real and unfiltered through the glaze of Hollywood and Disney and Television, that early 20th century dream-land, that naked-land, that 1910 that Old Bull Lee recalls with criminal affection in *On the Road.* The good old days when bars were bars, where men gathered during and after work, there was a player piano instead of a jukebox, brass rails instead of chromium, spittoons instead of worrying about offending drunken women, barrels of whiskey and beer instead of shiny taps with golden emblems, good old Joe bartenders instead of hostile bartenders, in other words a pre-mass media pop culture America, a country that was wild and brawling and free, with abundance and any kind of freedom for everyone. Sal goes out walking the American Night in New Orleans, hoping to sit by the muddy banks of the Mississippi River, but there's a wire fence between him and Huck Finn America. "When you start separating the people from their rivers what have you got?" "Bureaucracy," says Old Bull Lee. Good old Anglo-Saxon freedom! But Miller will have none of it. There's no nostalgia for anything American in Miller's book, only deep contempt. At the turn of the century there wasn't anything but the boys he ran with on the streets. A face-to-face community. We were shooting baskets when Keith arrived on the scene. We saw him coming, bouncing his basketball along the sidewalk behind the chain-link fence. Richie and I looked at each other excitedly and apprehensively; should we ask him to play with us? Keith went immediately to the other end of the basketball court and started shooting baskets. We watched him out of the corners of our eyes. He moved like silk, jumping, soaring, driving to the basket and dunking the ball. Whew! Keith was five years older than Richie and me. He played for the high school varsity basketball team. He was the star of the team. We were both in awe of him. What a crazy privilege it would be to play with him. We just had to approach him. Richie said that I should ask; I said that Richie should do it. Neither of us had the nerve to ask. Then Ronny showed up. He didn't have a basketball with him. He was just looking for... well, trouble. He was a classic greaser, blue jeans and a white T-shirt, black pointed shoes with taps on the heels and soles, clicking along the blacktop, a pack of cigarettes rolled up in his sleeve and bundled up at the point of the shoulder, a cigarette hanging from his lower lip, a tattoo on his arm that read Love Me Tender. He was singing. The words seemed to be these: Bright light city gonna set my soul, gonna set my soul on fire... Viva Las Vegas, Viva Las Vegas. A song from an Elvis Presley movie. Elvis was his hero. Ronny walked onto the court and just took our ball and started shooting baskets. Richie and I were afraid of him. He was much older, in his twenties, probably, and his reputation as a crazy bastard preceded him. Fortunately Ronny was afraid of Keith, and when Keith, to Richie's and my relief and exaltation, dribbled up to half-court and asked us if we wanted to get a two-on-two game going, Richie and I said gloriously and shyly that yes we would like that. Ronny was a bit reluctant to play, seeing that he was completely incompetent at sports, like many a bully of his ilk. Keith and Ronny weren't our friends. They weren't each other's friends either, not by a long shot. They weren't quite enemies either. Though Ronny thought that everyone was his enemy. He's the guy who ended up in the mental institution, needless to say. I saw him there years later when I was visiting my sister who was there because she suffered from something what's called in the trade "schizophrenia-depression." Ronny hadn't changed much in eight years, same outfit, jeans and T-shirt, singing "Viva Las Vegas." When he heard the news of Elvis' death, Ronny put on his Superman costume, which he had first worn for Halloween when he was thirteen years old, he hadn't grown much in size since then, and went around town capturing stray cats that he then hung up by their tails on clotheslines in the backyards of the suburban homes of horrified families. As for Keith, he's the guy who was shot in the head ten years later... but... back then... there were dreams in our heads, not bullets or Lithium, there were dreams in all our heads back then, though there were probably nightmares in Ronny's head. Ronnie the Vietnam veteran. So how do you get from a blacktop basketball court in a schoolyard in a small town in the USA in October 1969 to Madison Square Garden in Manhattan playing basketball for the New York Knicks, a teammate of Walt "Clyde" Frazier, Dick Barnett, "Dollar" Bill Bradley, Dave Debusshere, and Willis Reed? You do it like Elgin do it... that's what Keith said. He said it to himself, dribbling the ball, standing at the top of the key, about to make a silky smooth move to the hoop in a two-on-two half-court pick-up game; he's whispering to himself: Do it like Elgin do it. Do it like Elgin do it. And he did. He faked left and drove right, down the lane, the ball sheltered on his right hip as he ascended the airy stairs of the basketball ether, all and only 5'10" of him, thin as the pole that held the backboard, a piece of gray galvanized sheet metal with drilled round holes and attached to a wooden frame, it's been here as long as any of us can remember, only the net has changed, if there is a net... and Keith is still rising through the brief American decades, rising and gliding, and I've already returned to earth. I tried to hack the ball away, but Keith's dipping the ball underhandedly to his left and around his back, bringing the ball back around and up to the right, sweeping, looping the ball around, over, under, twisting and floating, ever upward, suspended in the sky, hanging, and then releasing the ball, a cool finger-tip roll, the ball falling through the rim and slightly nudging the net... do it like Elgin do it. And he did. Elgin Baylor had been a prolific scorer who had had his best years playing for the Los Angeles Lakers, his career now coming to an end. Keith never did make it to Madison Square Garden. But he did become an all-league guard in high school. On another drive to the basket Keith's steel Afro-comb in his pocket came down and jabbed into the flesh just above my knee. I felt a sharp pang and the blood rolling down my shin, but I wasn't about to stop playing. See, Isabelle, I still have the scar above my knee. I hadn't noticed. Richie and I did manage to score a few baskets, but only because we insisted on playing "losers take out," so that every time that Keith and Ronny scored (and they scored every time that they had possession of the ball, which meant that Keith scored every time) Richie and I got to take the ball out, otherwise, if we had been playing "winners take out," Keith would have scored continuously, he was simply unstoppable, not even a bullet could've stopped him then, he was faster than a speeding bullet, could leap tall buildings in a single bound, just like Superman, but Ronny thought that he was Superman... America is filled with Supermen. Anyway, Keith and Ronny won 20-6. Rather, Keith won; he never passed the ball to Ronny, who just bounded around with a cigarette hanging from his mouth, bumping and elbowing and shoving, and if he was shoved back he would look me in the eye, trying to instigate a stare down match, which could have led to some kind of confrontation, no one knew for sure what Ronny was capable of; he could've been all bark and no bite for all we knew. Richie and I just avoided him and concentrated on guarding Keith, but it was hopeless; we were in over our heads. Ronny kept saying to Keith, "Pass me the fuckin' ball, man, shit." But Keith paid him no mind and just went on whispering to himself: "Do it like Elgin do it, gonna do it like Elgin do it." There was a mounting tension between Ronny and Keith; it became a real grudge game, and grudges die-hard. It was Elvis versus Elgin. It was the pride of Keith's and Ronny's self-image as seen in the image of another more potent popular image that was being called into question. When the game was over, Keith joined some of his friends who had arrived and were shooting baskets at the other end of the court. They were going to get into some serious hoops that Richie and I were exempt from participating in by the mere fact that we couldn't hang out with these guys, not unless they were short a player, and Richie or I could be the odd one out to make it all even. Ronny decided that he didn't want to hang around with eight big black guys each of whom could've beaten the shit out of him no sweat. Being the sissy-bully that he was, Ronny followed Richie and me into town, trying to bum a dime from us. We gave him the dime just to get rid of him. Finally he left, walking down Main Street, singing bright light city gonna set my soul, gonna set my soul on fire... Viva Las Vegas, Viva Las Vegas... So how do you get from that basketball court in Oyster Bay to Las Vegas singing a duet with the King of Rock and Roll? How do you become famous? Popular? Hip? Cool? A swaggering icon of ambivalent sex? And filthy rich? You do it like Elvis do it. You could almost hear him whispering to himself as he walked down Main Street: Do it like Elvis do it. Do it like Elvis do it. None of them got out of small town America. What they got was death and madness and deterioration. Did Sal Paradise ever get out of small town America? Out of America itself? Sal hopes that someday he and Dean will be able to live on the same tree-shady street together with their families, and leave behind the shady streets of American cities, leave behind all that awful continent, all that road-going, and become a couple of old-timers together, Patriarchs of middle-America, Gentile paterfamilias. A couple of white guys sitting on the front porch drinking beer. At the beginning of part four in *On the Road*, we get a glimpse of that which binds Sal and Dean together in a way that the intellectual Carlo Marx or old-world-dandy-aristocrat Old Bull Lee can never quite grasp. The simple pleasures of two working-class white boys. Dean is listening to a basketball game on the radio. Dean really digs the way that Marty Glickman announces basketball games, "Swish! Two points!" ("Swish! Yes!" says Marv Albert announcing New York Knick games twenty years later from a radio on a blacktop basketball court where Keith and Ronny and Richie are I are playing...). Things haven't changed all that much. Simple pleasures. One early Sunday afternoon, the American working-class man's day of simple pleasures, Sal and Dean are watching a baseball game on television, and listening to another game on the radio on which they switch back and forth to listen to a third game. Gil Hodges of the Brooklyn Dodgers is on second base; Joe DiMaggio of the New York Yankees is at the plate with a three balls count; Bobby Thompson of the New York Giants is at bat with a man on third... Heroes. Idols of Middle America. Media icons. Later we find Sal and Dean playing baseball with some kids in a sooty field by the Long Island rail yard. Then they play basketball like maniacs with the same kids who easily out jump them and out-shoot them, stealing the ball away and dribbling, pulling up for jump shots, while Sal and Dean, two old-timers, huff and puff and collapse on the concrete court. The kids thought that they were crazy, "mad of American back-alley go-music trying to play basketball against Stan Getz and Cool Charlie." There is that beautifully revealing moment early on in the book, just after Dean meets Carlo Marx and they go off together on a sojourn, a "tremendous season" of self-discovery and exploration, and Sal is left behind; after which Carlo reports back to Sal what had transpired between him and Dean, their attempt to communicate with absolute honesty and absolute completeness everything on their minds, but... that beautifully rendered truth about Dean, that beautifully funny moment that captures the essence of Dean Moriarty and Sal Paradise's friendship, and it is Carlo who discovers it, but he just doesn't't get it; he tells Sal that he finally taught Dean that he can do anything, become mayor of Denver, marry a rich women, or become the greatest poet since Rimbaud. But Dean keeps rushing out to see the midget auto races. Carlo goes with him. They jump and yell, excited. And then Carlo reveals the beauty of it all: You know, Sal, Dean is really hung-up on things like that. Poor Carlo, the Jewish intellectual from back East; he just does not get it. He just does not get what a couple of working-class gentile white boys get up to on a Saturday night or Sunday afternoon in post-war, atomic bomb, Jazz America, American Night, kicks, joys, darkness, ecstasy, girls, T-shirts and sneakers and blue jeans, Rock and Roll, Coca-Cola, basketball and baseball and Elvis and Elgin, the 1950's pop culture taking over the world with dollar certainty. They make it to Mexico but Dean has to get back to his wife and abandons Sal on his fevered sickbed. They make plans to go to Italy together, Rome and Paris, but Dean looks at Sal with tearful eyes contemplating Sal's concern and care and, when all is said and done, Sal's naiveté and innocence, because, believe it or not, Dean has his obligations, just like Rimbaud, and must return to the soil, the American soil, to his wives and families and simple pleasures. Later, Sal will abandon Dean on the streets of New York, to attend a Duke Ellington concert. There is no nostalgia for America in Henry Miller's book. America only has meaning for Miller because Mona is there. Miller's youth was spent on the streets of Brooklyn, and, this is the essential thing, in books, 19th Century European books. American pop culture had not spread across the world. No Rock and Roll, no Disney, no Elvis, no Joe DiMaggio, no Humphrey Bogart, no James Dean, no Jack Kerouac, no Henry Miller. If fiction is fiction, if Sal Paradise is Sal Paradise and not Jack Kerouac; if Henry Miller is Henry Miller and not Henry Miller, then Henry Miller never returned to America, to that California coast, and wrote all those boring books there;

instead he kept going, Paris, Greece, India, China, Japan, where he died, a writer of haiku, living in a mountain hut; and then Sal and Dean finally made it to the tree-shady street together, and both of them are playing basketball in the driveway with a basketball rim nailed over the garage door, two old timers, the radio playing, the October leaves falling to the grass, in ideal small town America. But things aren't quite like that in the real world. Kerouac often waxed eulogistic about the black experience in America, about being a white man disillusioned, wishing that he were a Negro because the best the white world had offered was not enough, not enough ecstasy, life, joy, kicks, darkness, music, night. American Night. In Henry Miller we also get moments of "praising God" for "the great Negro race which alone keeps America from falling apart..." This is from Miller's book on Greece, *The Colossus of Maroussi*. He praises Greece: I love the sun! The nudity! The light! This is no longer the world of Miller's Paris, where Miller was predatory and lived in dreadful night. This is a Rosseauian Miller. He then praises not Anglo-Saxon America but the America of Louis the Armstrong, son of the Boogie-Woogie man himself, Agamemnon. Louis was for peace and joy. Louis wanted to make everything golden. Louis made a few friends, the Duke and the Count, the last direct lineal descendants of the great and only Rimbaud. And together they blew the world away with hot sweet sounds, blew the world away. What a wonderful world. What a wonderful country America is. It has produced Louis Armstong and Herman Melville and the 1969 New York Mets. But things aren't quite like that... are they? What's this Mets? asks Isabelle, once again. It was in 1979, ten years after that day on the basketball court, on a hot summer day, another Sunday morning, when Ronny, out of the mental institution, where he had become an outpatient and committed himself at his own discretion, my sister was there too... I told you that, didn't I? *Oui,* you told me. Ronny showed up at the basketball court, singing an Elvis song. But it wasn't "Via Las Vegas." Not this time. Elvis was dead. Ronny was singing, shouting: I'd rather see you dead little girl, than to be with another man... and then he would stop singing, stand still, and stare into nothing. And then he was singing, shouting again: you may have a pink Cadillac, but don't ya be nobody's fool. It wasn't 1979; it was 1959 all over again and Ronny was cool and hip and dangerous. He walked onto the basketball court and began ranting and raving, screaming at the top of his lungs: "That nigger fucked my girl!" This was directed at Keith, who had put on a few pounds in ten years but could still dunk the ball. "What the fuck you talking about man. Get atta here," said Keith. That Ronny even had a girlfriend was doubtful. But Ronny kept screaming, sweating, jumping, "I'd rather see you dead little girl, than to be with another man..." But there was no girl in Ronny's life. Everyone playing basketball knew that Ronny was some kind of Vietnam war screw-up, so he was tolerated to a certain extent, but this was just too much. Keith and a few of his friends approached Ronny, "I'm gonna kick your fuckin' ass, man." "C'mon man, I'm ready for ya. Try it." Ronny pulled a gun out of his jacket and fired one time into Keith's head. And he ran. He tossed the gun in some bushes that lined the wire fence on the side of the courts. Do it like Elvis do it. Ronny heard the story about Elvis shooting the television with a shotgun. Son of Sam. Viva Las Vegas... do it like America do it... we have all we need, guns and a bibel... guns and a bibel... guns and a bibel... guns and a bibel... Ah holy holy holy Sunday mornings at Oyster Bay... pika pika boom boom beep beep... we are a million miles from a Proustian Sunday morning. Isn't that right, Isabelle? After Ronny threw the gun away, I picked up the gun from the bushes, and on a Friday night, yeah I remember it was a Friday night, I almost shot myself in the corner of the dark alley by the side entrance to the bar, and then I went after him... but why bother, he's just another bastard... so in the end I tossed the gun down a drain. Oh my poor Stephen. What, Isabelle? Anyway, I told the cops, "It's down the drain, in front of Food Town..." and then I added, "Oh, and if you find a baseball down there can you get it for me? I lost it down there about ten years ago." The cops looked at me kind of funny.

Isabelle has a sad look on her face. I'm done reading. Am I done writing? Isabelle looks at me kind of funny. Anyway, I met someone in London. No, not English, not American... so, I'm returning tomorrow.

She married John in 1993. I was invited to their wedding. I did not attend. I had responsibilities to attend to at home. I never heard from either of them again... until... well... no, not until this year, almost twenty-five years later, when I met John at a quiet café in New York City, but that's another story. I returned to London. Then I returned to America. The writer lived on in the night when the work of day was done. This is the work of those nights. Oh say hey ho America... *skal vi, andemo via, ikimasho, allons-y...* let's go...

Finis

Afterword?

My mother used to tell me about this man that she took care of in a nursing home in Farsund, Norway, when she was about sixteen years old. His name was Frank Samuelsen and he told my mother that he was the first man to row across the Atlantic Ocean in a small rowboat.

My mother told me that Frank said that the king of Norway, King Håkon, called him a fool. Another time my mother told me that King Håkon awarded Frank a medal.

My father used to tell me about the time that he went to the Polo Grounds in 1933 when he was a boy and saw the New York Giants play the St Louis Cardinals. The Giants won 1-0 in 18 innings and Carl Hubbel beat Dizzy Dean and they both pitched complete games. It was a double-header but he couldn't remember what happened in the second game.

Document 43-5847

King Oscar II of Sweden and Norway visited the exhibition hall in Christiania where the rowboat that Frank Samuelsen and George Harbo had rowed across the Atlantic Ocean was on display. The King gave Frank and George each a ten-kroner bill. Frank died in the nursing home in Farsund in 1946. A year later my mother left Norway for America.

Document 33-4756

The Polo Grounds were filled with over 50,000 fans. It was a Sunday, July 2, 1933. In the first game of the double-header, Carl Hubbell pitched 18-innings and didn't give up a run. The Giants defeated the Cardinals and their starting pitcher Tex Carlton, 1-0. The Giants won the second game by the same score, 1-0, and Roy Parmalee was the winning pitcher against Dizzy Dean.

The answer to the answers to the Japanese riddles: *Tonkatsu* is a popular dish of pork cutlets; it can also mean the *pig wins*. *Buta* and *ton* are two readings for pig. *Umakatta* means that the meal *tasted delicious*; it can also mean the *horse won*.

Top Movie List for Cinema Café in Kamakura as of 1989

1.	*Tokyo Monogatari -Tokyo Story/Banshun*	Ozu
2.	*Ikiru/Rashomon*	Kurosawa
3.	*Ugetsu Monogatari/Sansho the Bailiff*	Mizoguchi
4.	*Wings of Desire*	Wenders
5.	*Nostalghia/Mirror*	Tarkovsky
6.	*À bout de souffle/Bande à part*	Godard
7.	*Citizen Kane*	Wells
8.	*Down by Law*	Jarmusch
9.	*Les Enfants du Paradis*	Carné
10.	*La Règle du jeu*	Renoir
11.	*The Third Man*	Reed
12.	*Eros + Massacre*	Yoshida
13.	*Smultronstället/Persona*	Bergman
14.	*Mouchette/Au hasard Balthazar*	Bresson
15.	*City Lights/Modern Times*	Chaplin
16.	*Ladri di biciclette*	*De Sica*
17.	*Roma città aperta*	*Rossellini*
18.	*Floating Clouds*	*Naruse*
19.	*Les Quatre Cents Coups*	*Truffaut*
20.	*8 1/2*	*Fellini*
21.	*Kuroi Ame – Black Rain*	*Inamura*

Favorite Baseball Players as of 1979

1B Willie McCovey
2B Ken Boswell – "Baaarz-Well"
3B Brooks Robinson
SS Bobby Wine
LF Henry Aaron
CF Willie Mays
RF Roberto Clemente
C Johnny Bench
P Tom Seaver

Orders and Conditions of Probation 1969

(6) *the rest of the list... avoid any undesirable persons, places, habits or activities... driving without a license, poetic license, disorderly conduct, reading books by degenerates, perverts, sex fiends, drug addicts, anarchists, communists, Buddhists, and listening to rock and roll, the Ramones, and here they come, my themes: hey ho, the white man landing, *les blancs débarquant,* Baudelaire, Rimbaud, Kierkegaard, Dostoyevsky, Melville, Whitman, Hamsun, Crane, Proust, Céline, Jeffers, Joyce, Camus, Miller, Kerouac... weapons, bibles, get dressed, go to work! We have all we need!

Author Shot at Award Ceremony - 2029
By Sigmund Simon Argilla

The author Stephen Cazzaza is in critical condition at New York Hospital after being shot twice by an unknown assailant at the Albert Hotel last Friday evening as he was leaving the stage during a literary award ceremony. The shooter is in police custody. His identity has not been released... stay tuned... more to come...

The shooter has now been identified as Stephen Cazzaza. He was shot by his own *doppelgänger*... of course, who else? If only I were someone else... if only I were born somewhere else... if only I were born some other time... the I is self, subject, persona... but who is this I that was unborn...? The author remains in critical condition.

Coda

Sunrise, like *God,* like *self,* like *I* is just a phantom of language... after Copernicus, after Nietzsche... and yet pre-conceptually in sensation we perceive the "sunrise" and every word, in any language, from sun up, dawn, break of day, rosy-fingered dawn, aurora, aubade, the words carry the keys... and it is the work of the janitors and porters to open the door at midnight, clean the filth of the floor and carry out the objects of history...

Kappa-San said that only a fascist like Mishima and ancient Samurai commit *seppuku,* ritual disembowelment, but there was an old man, an A-bomb survivor, a *hikubusha,* who, in his own words, printed in the "Testimonies of Hiroshima," speaks of his attempt to perform a ritual suicide in front of the Cenotaph in Hiroshima Memorial Peace Park, to sacrifice himself to prevent the ongoing nuclear testing by the Soviets and

Americans. He had written letters of protest to the embassies of the Soviet Union and the United States of America, and of course had never received an answer. There are no answers. Where are the words after Hiroshima? He was so old and sick from radiation poisoning that the small knife that he drew across his abdomen could not even break his skin, and then he tried to cut his throat, but failed to kill himself. Sacrifice himself to whom? For whom? For what? Who listens? Who answers?

In an attempt to protest the proliferation of the technological means that caused the most horrendous experience of miserable suffering and death in the history of the human race to nowhere, he believed that he had shamed himself, he had humiliated himself. Could he find dignity in himself after all? Could he find his self in himself? He found shame outside of himself, then why could he not find dignity in himself, for himself?

Even if... and yet... both-and... no resolution. No conclusions. Paradox and ambiguity till the end... *du couchant...va et vient...* come and goes... *mono no aware... les nuages qui passent...* the long march to rid ourselves of the self, the subject... to become the subject of... the subject in... the subject for... the armies of philosophers, structuralists, marxists, post-modernists, sociologists, anthropologists, psychologists, scientists, have reduced the subject to an object of real but secondary discourse... a fiction, like the bourgeois novel and capitalist money... of course, we educated moderns, we postmoderns, know for certain that there are no gods, spirit, logos, hope, presence, original creation, will, chance, fate, substance, self, subject, object, persona, author, enlightenment, emancipation, dignity, or sunrises, and that there is only this something at the bottom, the fact of matter, what we call physics, atoms, and that there is only this nothing at the top, what we call fiction, words, and that in-between there are perceptions, sensations, and then just a long stretch of horizon where death looms... a distortion... a celestial crown, an illusion of the shining city on a hill, an ideal, an object that seemingly rises from below and then falls and retreats, recedes, retires, withdraws... into blinding light... pika-pika-boom-boom-beep-beep, of an unknown origin, a weapon, a word, a hammer, a tool, a sign...

The First Monday after Modernity #22

Sunday Mornings at Oyster Bay is over. Sunday as such, is over. Look! Look up there! We are not in paradise, utopia, heaven, and so on. Here we are. We have arrived at the first Monday after Modernity, in Capitalism. If on Friday we witnessed the agony, the conflicted cross of time and space, the terror, horror, tension, anxiety, suffering, A-bombs, and death... or the delusion of the end of work that hides the pain in immediate gratification, and if those who did not die or who survived with minor injury, and if we did survive it's not that we survived for the goodness only, it's also the Saturnalia, it's Saturday, debauchery, endless night... when all else fails, there's decadence, like the disciples of Sade; or a momentary reprieve from nightmare, like Scrooge, a drunken orgy or redemption, or the quiet café... and when we wake, if we awake, on the shore of Sunday again, as a child, a primitive, naïve, innocent, there will be no paradise waiting, no utopia, no heaven, no new age, no new world, no new tomorrow, no new dawn, no happiness, no immortality... just money and glorified man projected into the future... and no turning back... and so when Sunday fails, again, as it will... here we are again... it's called history. Monday again... and here we come. We... the races are landing, with our modern weapons, our holy books, our books of knowledge, our tools of shaping, our words of wisdom. We get dressed and go to work, knowing full well that which lies ahead is Friday again, in the distance... so steal immediate time from the universal oppressors, because on Friday it collapses in horror and pain, and Saturday you revel, rejoice and forget, and Sunday you wake and mourn and cry... and Monday you start over... all over again... and I'm a fraud, a joke, because in truth, I have been attempting to escape from this book for forty years, because this book *is not* life, *is not* death. It's just a creative way to approach life. A creative way to approach death.

Sunday, June 28, 2015, early evening, in Paris, visiting, revisiting, walking, facing west to see the faces of my wife and daughter by the *Pont Neuf*, alight with gold, calling to me, and I looking to the west, the sunset, the passing clouds, look up, stranger, foreigner, author, up there, the passing clouds... and we walk across the bridge into another sacrament and grace of a beautiful mistaken sunset...

where this book was written

Oyster Bay

New York City

Norway

North Carolina

California

London

Vienna

Paris

Japan

Chicago

1975-2015